THE SEAFORT SAGA

"A ripping good read – the sort of thing that attracted us all to SF in the first place"
S. M. Stirling

"Something special indeed . . . Feintuch has at last captured for the science fiction community the quintessential spirits of greats such as C. S. Forester and F. Van Wyck Mason" *Bill Baldwin*

"An excellent entertainment" *Analog*

"Feintuch has constructed a fascinating story . . . You'll find his adventures highly entertaining"
Science Fiction Chronicle

"An excellent job of transferring Hornblower to interstellar space. A thoroughly enjoyable read"
David Drake

The Seafort Saga

MIDSHIPMAN'S HOPE
CHALLENGER'S HOPE
PRISONER'S HOPE
FISHERMAN'S HOPE

Fisherman's
HOPE

DAVID FEINTUCH

ORBIT

An *Orbit* Book

First published in Great Britain by Orbit 1997
Reprinted 1997

Copyright © 1996 by David Feintuch

The moral right of the author has been asserted.

This edition published in arrangement with
Warner Books, Inc., New York

A CIP catalogue record for this book
is available from the British Library.

ISBN 1 85723 440 5

Printed and bound in Great Britain by Clays Ltd, St Ives plc

UK companies, institutions and other organisations wishing
to make bulk purchases of this or any other book
published by Little, Brown should contact their local
bookshop or the special sales department at the address below.
Tel 0171 911 8000.   Fax 0171 911 8100.

Orbit
A Division of
Little, Brown and Company (UK)
Brettenham House
Lancaster Place
London WC2E 7EN

DEDICATION

To Nicholas Ewing Seafort, Philip Tyre, and
Derek Anthony Carr, good men all, who taught
me much about the struggle of life.

FISHERMAN'S HOPE

Being the fourth voyage of
Nicholas Seafort, U.N.N.S.,
in the year of our Lord 2201

PART 1

August 4, in the Year of our Lord 2201

Chapter 1

"But Vasily's a Russian, and we're short on Eurasians." Lieutenant Darwin Sleak flipped through the stack of folders on the polished conference table, each an application to the United Nations Naval Academy. Sleak glanced at Commandant Kearsey for approval, squinting in the bright summer Devon sun.

The Commandant tapped his folder. "Born September 2187. Grades put him in the eleventh percentile among applicants, admission tests put him eighteenth. Low, but someone has to be near the bottom." He shrugged his unconcern. "Put him on the list, I suppose." He turned to me. "Any comment, Captain Seafort?"

I blurted, "I thought the Selection Board didn't consider nationality." Damn Final Cull, anyway. My aide Edgar Tolliver carefully studied his fingernails, accustomed to my outbursts.

Commandant Kearsey said, "Officially, we don't. And we wouldn't take some unqualified joey simply to gain another Russian. But with a war on, we need public support from every continent. A balanced cadet class doesn't hurt."

I knew he was right. The Navy's appalling losses to the fish-like aliens that had attacked our Hope Nation and Vegan colonies had to be made up, and the cost of rebuilding the fleet would be enormous. The deadly assaults had destroyed fourteen ships of the line and killed untold hundreds of crewmen, some my friends. And then we'd lost Orbit Station, where Vax Holser had died hoping to save me.

I forced my thoughts into a new channel. "What if we just took the top three hundred eighty?"

"We'd lose all geographical balance."

My tone was acid. "So? Balance wasn't a consideration when you took Senator Boland's son." I shouldn't have said it, but my new shoes hurt and so did my chest; I'd grown accustomed to one-sixth gravity during my recent stay on Lunapolis.

I braced myself for the Commandant's withering glare that

had transfixed me as a raw cadet only fourteen years ago. Certainly my manner warranted it. But I was no longer a frightened thirteen-year-old reporting for induction; now I was the notorious Nicholas Ewing Seafort, "hero" of Hope Nation. My face scowled from a recruiting poster, and in two short weeks I was to replace Kearsey as Commandant of both U.N.N.S. Academy bases, here at Devon and at Farside, on Luna. I alone knew of the perversions on which the public's adulation was based. I, and Lord God. Someday I must face His reckoning.

Commandant Kearsey concealed whatever annoyance he felt. "We can't very well turn down a U.N. Senator's son, Captain. Especially when Boland's on the Security Council's Naval Affairs Committee. Anyway, the boy's grades are acceptable."

"Lower than the Russian's, I think. Who are we bumping for the Boland boy?"

His staff aide, Sergeant Kinders, handed him a folder. "A Parisian. Jacques Theroux." The Commandant frowned. "It's not as if the boy will know why he's off the final list. What's more important: putting another cadet in Boland's place, or having powerful friends at appropriation time? Do you want the new ships built or not?"

I stared at the door, knowing I had no answer. The Navy must be restored, to guard our far-flung colonies, and to protect home system if the fish attacked. I muttered, "I'd still pick the first three hundred eighty."

Even Tolliver and Sleak looked at me strangely. It was a moment before Commandant Kearsey answered. "Then we'd lose Final Cull. We'd be stuck with the candidates the Selection Board sent."

"Yes."

Lieutenant Sleak cleared his throat, waited for the Commandant's nod. "Final Cull is Academy's hard-won prerogative, and our only input into the Selection process. Would you have us give it up?" His tone was cold, despite the fact that I'd soon be his commander.

Final Cull was a traditional privilege, and the Navy shouldn't surrender its traditions easily.

Yet, still . . .

"Father, can Jason stay for dinner?" At thirteen I knew better than to ask in front of the prospective guest. I hoped I could get away with it, as I'd just thrown Father's cherished obligations of hostship into the balance against his stern disapproval of my friend.

Father's eyebrow raised. "He could abide our prayers?"

Jason flushed, his eye on the orchestron we were updating on the creaky kitchen table. He paused, chip in hand. "I may be a freethinker, sir, but I respect the customs of your house." Quickly, as if he'd gone too far, he bent over the orchestron motherboard.

Father grunted. "Respect for Lord God isn't a custom. It is life itself." Still, I knew Jason's forthrightness had gained him favor in Father's eyes. "Perhaps you too will find Him, before you consign yourself to damnation." Oh, please, not a sermon. Not in front of Jason.

Father gave the gleaming teapot one last swipe with the soft cloth. "I can't imagine why Nicholas thinks asking permission in your presence will sway me. He knows better manners than he practices." I swallowed. More verses at bedside, or worse; Father always remembered the day's sins. Still, the corners of his mouth turned up grudgingly. "Pea soup, the fresh bread, and tomatoes from the garden. Can you tolerate it?"

"That's fine, sir," Jason said quickly. I flashed him a grin across the table; he surreptitiously kicked my shin.

Later, washing for dinner, Jason asked softly, "Heard anything yet?"

I shook my head. One way or another, word had to come soon. Time was running out.

"He's said you can go for sure?"

"Aye." Perhaps my imploring and tears had nothing to do with Father's consent. I suspected they'd helped, despite the switching he'd given me when I persisted.

"Well, you reached the second interview, and didn't get a washout letter. You made it to Final Cull." Like any teener, he was familiar with Academy admission procedures. If I passed Final Cull I'd be admitted to Terrestrial Academy at Devon, where they'd subject me to basic training before shipping me to Farside for my real education.

"Aye." I wished Jason wouldn't talk about it; I'd persuaded myself that not discussing my chances somehow improved them. At dinner Father drew himself from his customary meditative silence, for Jason's sake. For the moment, Jase was Father's guest as well as mine. "Your, ah, plaything is fixed?"

"The orchestron? Aye, sir. But it's an instrument, not a toy."

"An instrument of . . . electronics." He and I both knew his unspoken thought. An instrument of Satan, as all idle amusements.

"And of music, Mr. Seafort. There isn't much the Welsh Philharmonic can play that we couldn't re-create on it."

"By pushing buttons." But Father's tone was agreeable, as he mopped at his soup with the hot bread he'd pulled from the oven an hour before.

Jason's lean face lit with the grin I cherished. "It's all in knowing what buttons to push, sir."

Father looked to me, shaking his head as if in exasperation. Recklessly, I grinned back; Jason had that effect on me. He was courteous to Father, even respected him in a way, without taking Father's manner seriously. At first I'd been scandalized, then put off, but now I knew it was part of Jason's singular view of the world.

Father asked, "You'll be in Third?" Two conversational gambits in an evening. He was treating Jason as an adult, and I was grateful.

"Yes, sir. This year I'm taking Engineering for electives."

"Why?"

"I like to build things, or fix them."

"A city and a tower, whose top may reach unto heaven."

Jason looked confused. I explained, "He means the tower of Babel. Genesis Nine."

Father swung to me in rebuke. "Genesis Eleven. Don't pretend to learning you lack, Nicholas."

"I'm sorry, sir."

"Nicky could sign up for half days, Mr. Seafort. We could work on projects together."

Father raised an eyebrow. "Nicholas learns best at home, where his idleness is held in check." That was like Father, to discuss my faults in front of anyone, as if I had no feelings. But to my surprise he added, "Anyway, Nicholas won't be at your school next year. I imagine he'll be at Academy." I was astonished. Father had never once hinted he thought I had a chance of being accepted.

"Of course," Jason said quickly. "I just meant if he didn't — I mean, I forgot."

Two days later I was on my knees pulling the stubborn weeds from our garden, knowing Father's vigilant eye would judge my work, and that my chance of parole on Saturday depended on his approval. Jason had bought us tickets to the football game with the Irish, though I hadn't told Father yet.

A shadow fell across the black dirt. I looked up, a bead of sweat trickling. "I'm not done yet, sir. I'll catch the rest of that row, after."

He waved it away. "The post is here."

"The post?" Why would he interrupt my chores for— "It came?" I was on my feet. "What does it say?"

"I don't know. It's yours to open."

I reached out, but he shook his head. "On the kitchen table." I dashed to the door. "Mind you wash your hands!"

I took enough time to rinse so I'd leave no grime on the towel. That would infuriate Father, and I wouldn't enjoy the consequences. I rushed back to the kitchen, tore open the embossed envelope. Father waited, leaning against the sink, his face grave.

"The Selection Board of the U.N.N.S. Naval Academy always has more qualified candidates than places. We regret to inform you that after careful consideration we are unable . . ."

I dropped the letter on the table, blinking away a blur. Unbelieving, I snatched it up again. ". . . you are to be congratulated that you were one of the final candidates in this year's selection process. If you wish to apply again next year we would be happy to consider . . ."

My eyes stinging, I ran into my room, slammed the door, threw myself on my bed. Footsteps. The door opened almost instantly. "Stand up!"

"Let me be alone for—"

"Up!" Father's tone brooked no argument. I stumbled to my feet. He stepped back into the hall. "Close your door properly."

I gaped. "You care more about—" His eyes narrowed and I stopped just in time. "Aye, sir." I turned the knob, closed the door quietly. Through the door Father said, "I won't have you slamming doors in my house."

"No, sir. I'm sorry." I crept back to my bed, kicked off my

shoes. I buried my head in the pillow, determined to smother my sobs.

He gave me about an hour before he came back into the room. "May I read your letter?"

My voice was muffled. "You know what it says."

"From your reaction, yes." He paused. "They rejected you." His phrasing reduced me to helpless tears. For a moment his hand lay on my shoulder, then it was gone, as if it had fallen by accident. "Nicholas, turn so I can see you."

"I want to be alone."

His tone was sharp. "Yes, to feel sorry for yourself."

"Why shouldn't I?" My voice was muffled.

"So you set yourself against the Lord?"

"I—what?"

Father pulled at my arm until I turned onto my back. Reluctantly, I looked to him, eyes red.

"If Lord God wanted you to attend Naval Academy, do you think they'd not have admitted you?"

I was outraged. "You're saying He didn't want me to go?" Father was silent. "Why should He care one way or the other? It was the stupid Selection Board, not Him."

Father shook his head. "He cares. About you, as about all of us."

My tone risked a strapping, but I didn't care. "Then why did He have me waste my time applying?"

Father's eyes bored into mine. "Perhaps to teach you to accept failure like a man, rather than as a whining child."

I closed my burning eyes. Father would never understand. "Nicholas, this is hard for you. But you must accept His will. I'll pray with you later. Perhaps we can find His consolation." It meant I would spend hours on the hard bedroom floor, knees aching, while I sought the relief Father himself could give, but would not.

I looked up at the Commandant. "Give up Final Cull? Is that so awful?"

Kearsey's fingers drummed the conference table. "The Selection Board . . . you know who's on it?"

I said, "Admiralty appoints two members, the Secretary General appoints two, and three come from the Senate."

"Did you know the Navy used to select its own applicants?"

"Of course, all the services did, until the scandals." Seventy-five years later, the Navy hadn't forgotten its humiliation.

The Commandant smiled grimly. "There was a battle royal when the changes were proposed. We lost; the Navy would no longer be allowed to choose its own candidates. Elitism, they called it, though why the Navy officers' corps shouldn't be elite, only Lord God knows. As a sop, they left us Final Cull. The politicians send us their selections, but at least we can weed through them."

I stabbed at my folder. "Is that what we're doing by making sure we have proportionate Russians and Equadorians and Yanks? By making a place for the Boland boy?"

He flushed. "We do the best we can. Next year you'll get to decide alone. But even though it's my responsibility, you're the one who has to take the class through Academy. Do you object to Vasily Karnyenkov? Would you rather have Jacques what's-his-name?"

I'd rather not have to cull at all. "No," I said wearily. "Let it be." Under the table, my nails left marks in my creased trouser leg.

Tolliver and I walked slowly across the immaculate lawn to Officers' Quarters. "Even if you did alienate him, sir, what difference does it make? Another few days and he'll be gone."

"He's been the Commandant for, what, eighteen years? They'll still look to him for advice. I don't need another enemy."

"You didn't make an enemy," Tolliver soothed. "He was only defending Final Cull."

"It's not as if we can predict what kind of middies they'll turn into." I brooded. Test scores and grades couldn't reveal which of our green cadets would mature into outstanding officers after two years or more of our instruction.

I parted with Tolliver at my door. As a full Captain and the Commandant-elect, I rated an apartment that was large and luxurious by Naval standards. I'd be spending much of my time here, as Commandant. I stripped off my jacket, loosened my tie, and sat on the edge of the bed with caller in hand. Two days had passed since I'd last visited the clinic. Perhaps Annie was better.

I waited for the connection to New York. "Dr. O'Neill's office, please." Another wait. I drummed my fingers on the bedside table. The marvels of technology. Finally he came on the line.

"I'm glad you called." He sounded harried.

"How is my wife?"

"She's, ah, progressing as expected."

I waited, but he didn't continue. "You had something to tell me, Doctor?"

"Not particularly. Why?"

"You said you were glad I called."

"We're always glad when relatives take an interest, Captain. In general the patient's progress is more rapid—"

"How is Annie, Dr. O'Neill? Do you know?"

He lapsed into incomprehensible medical jargon, analyzing Annie's blood tests for each of the seventeen hormones known to be responsible for mood and behavior.

I listened, trying to filter truth through his statistics. At length I could stand it no longer. "But how is she?"

"She continues to stabilize. Right now she's responding to changes in her secondary meds. Taking more interest in surroundings, but her mood swings are greater."

I closed my eyes. Annie, I wish I knew how to help you. If only I hadn't let you meet me at that gutted church, in the stricken Hope Nation city of Centraltown. But for my folly, you'd be whole, rather than languishing in a clinic undergoing hormone rebalance, to our mutual humiliation. I wondered if any of the Academy staff knew the nature of her illness. Rebalancing was seen as shameful, and discharged patients were patronized if not ostracized. I myself struggled with those very feelings.

Tired, helpless, I grunted vague responses to Dr. O'Neill's prattle until I could ring off. Though I hated the embattled city of New York, I yearned to chuck everything and jump on the next suborbital. Instead, I had to endure two more days of Final Cull. I supposed I could find some excuse for not attending, or tell Commandant Kearsey I didn't care whom he selected, but such an attitude approached heresy. Better to delay my visit another few days, until after Handover.

Still an hour to dinner, and the silent apartment was oppressive. I thrust on my jacket, left my quarters. The Admin Building's brass door handles were polished and gleaming, the compound's walkway meticulously edged. With a start I realized it was the same path on which I'd labored for hours with hand clippers and spade, while my bunkmates were enjoying their Sunday afternoon freedom. Well, I wasn't the only one, and I hadn't earned punishment detail often.

I wandered past Officers' Quarters to the wide parade ground. I kicked at the gravel track that surrounded the field where even now cadets exercised under the vigilant eye of their drill sergeants.

Avoiding the squads of perspiring cadets I crossed to the classroom complex beyond. It was the first time I'd seen the classrooms since I'd returned. On impulse I entered a building, automatically smoothing my hair and tucking at my jacket. Old habits die hard.

The walls held the same pictures of squads in immaculate uniforms standing at ease with their sergeant, looking directly into the camera. All so young, so innocent. As I'd been, once. All cadets were recruited young as a matter of necessity. The N-waves our Fusion drives produced could trigger melanoma-T, a deadly cancer, but exposure within five years of puberty lessened the risk.

I perused the hopeful faces. Where had I turned wrong, from the eager lad in a picture lining the classroom halls?

Footsteps. Two cadets turned the corner, talking softly. When they saw me their eyes widened and they snapped to rigid attention against the corridor wall. Had I been a sergeant they'd have saluted and gone about their business, though with brisker step. But an officer—not just an officer, but a full Captain—was something else again.

I could have returned their salutes, growled, "As you were," and gone on my way. Instead, embarrassed at having been discovered mooning over old pictures, I made a show of inspecting them. Even as I did so, I knew it was a mistake. By tradition, a Captain barely noticed a midshipman, to say nothing of a cadet.

Like all our charges, these two were in their middle teens. The boy was taller, with short, curly black hair. The girl's locks were somewhat longer, almost to her collar, as the regs permitted for females. Their gray uniforms were neat and clean, their shoes spit-polished to perfection. Their belt buckles shined, though the boy's tie was slightly off-center. I scowled as I adjusted it. He bit his lip before remembering he was at attention.

"Name and year?"

"Omar Benghadi, sir. I'm second." His voice came too loud; he flushed with embarrassment.

"And you?"

"Alicia Johns, sir. First." Had it been earlier in the term I wouldn't have had to ask; a plebe was easy to spot. But later, one couldn't always tell by appearance or demeanor. Not if the drill sergeants were doing their job.

"Very wel—"

"May I help you, Lieutenant?" The voice was cool; not impolite, but with perhaps a touch of impatience.

I turned.

His eyes flickered to my insignia. "Oh, please excuse me, sir. Staff Sergeant Ramon Ibarez." He came to attention.

"As you were," I said immediately. One didn't harass the Marine staff in front of their Naval charges.

"Sorry, Captain Seafort. I didn't recognize you." He hesitated. "Is there a problem with these two?" His tone implied that if there were he'd eliminate it, perhaps along with the cadets. His manner wasn't lost on the blond boy, who gulped. The girl waited impassively.

"No, Sarge. I was just, ah . . ." I found myself searching for an excuse to explain my presence. I managed to avoid licking my lips in nervous tension. He was only a sergeant, for heaven's sake. I was long since graduated, and far outranked him. "Just an inspection," I said more firmly. "Carry on, you two."

"Aye aye, sir." The cadets scurried off.

The sergeant repeated, "May I help you, sir?" His manner seemed to enquire, what were you doing in my building?

So barracks scuttlebutt had it right: drill sergeants were afraid of nothing, even the prospective Commandant. No wonder we'd feared them. "No thanks, Sarge." It seemed too bald a dismissal, so I added lamely, "Getting them ready for exams?"

"No, sir. Not really. Just makework, mostly, and giving the plebes a head start on next semester's work, though they don't know that." He smiled; the grin went to his eyes and transformed them. "I missed you by a couple of years, sir. I got here in '94."

"I left in '92."

"I know."

I blurted, "You do?"

"Of course. You berthed in Valdez Hall, in bunk three, when

you came down from Farside your second year. We give that bed as a reward to joeys who've done well."

"Good Lord!" Was he pulling my leg? Not even a drill sergeant would try that on a full Captain. Would he?

"Everyone who was here claims to remember you. Even if they can't, they say they do."

It was absurd. I cast about to change the subject. "You're a classroom instructor?"

"Yes, sir, but my kids are dispersed to Training Station and the Fusers, so I'm taking a shift at gunnery and physical defense while waiting for my incoming plebes. I was just conferring with Sergeant Vost about one of my kids. We're trying to pull him through Elementary Nav."

Suddenly I liked him. "Join me for a cup of coffee, Sarge?"

"I, uh . . ." His composure was momentarily gone. "If you're sure you don't mind, sir."

"Not at all." I hesitated. When last I'd bustled through these halls, an afternoon cup was the farthest thing from my mind. "Where can we go?"

"Staff lounge is at the end of the corridor, sir."

I took a seat in a comfortable battered leather chair and let him pour me a cup.

"Twelve days to go."

I looked up. "Pardon?"

"To Handover. Then the place is yours." He paused, said cautiously, "Excuse me if I'm out of line."

He was, but we weren't shipboard, and his forthrightness came as a relief. "No, not at all." I gestured at the coffee table. "Will they mind our making ourselves at home?"

"Mind?" He gaped. "Mind that Captain Nicholas Seafort relaxed in their lounge?"

I felt a fool. "I suppose not."

He studied me, started to say something, looked away. The silence stretched. I fidgeted, anxious to finish my coffee and be gone. Sergeant Ibarez blurted, "You're not comfortable with fame."

How dare he? My jaw dropped. "I beg your pardon?"

He flushed. "I suppose I've just thrown away my career. I apologize, sir."

I began indignantly, "Certain matters are—" I ground to a halt. I'd sought companionship with the man and I was about to blast him for offering it. Swallowing my wrath, I stood, walked to the window, watched the perspiring cadets exercising on the parade ground. "No, Sarge, I'm not. In fact I hate it."

This time our silence had a different flavor. At length he said, "Odd, isn't it? Most of us would give anything to be like you."

"You don't want to be like me," I said with finality.

"Everyone thought you'd take another ship. Until the announcement, no one believed the rumor you'd be assigned here." In the corridor, a bell rang. In a few minutes cadet classes would be dismissed. None of the youngsters would close their books or snap off their puters until the instructors gave them leave. Doing so was an invitation to demerits.

"I didn't want a ship." I didn't want to be Commandant either, but I'd finally let them persuade me.

"You're needed, sir."

He sounded like Senator Boland, and my resentment was kindled. "Not really." I braced myself for another lecture about the Navy's need for heroes now that we were at war.

"The place has . . . stagnated."

I turned; his eyes were on the carpet. I asked quietly, "How do you mean?" It was somewhere between an invitation and a command.

"Just . . ." Sergeant Ibarez looked up, paused. "I don't mean to talk out of school, sir." He put down his cup. "I believe in tradition. It's a glue that binds together the elements of the Service." He crossed to the window, looked out at the field and the helipad. "And I also believe the Commandant should be a remote figure of authority. But sometimes tradition can be carried too far. The Commandant can be too remote." He studied the transplex. "Commandant Kearsey believes strongly in tradition, sir."

I knew better than to press. "I'll keep it in mind." I looked at the clock. "Time to get ready for dinner." I offered my hand, and we shook.

Four hundred twenty folders still littered the conference table. Perhaps that was what Sergeant Ibarez meant by tradition. It would be far easier to sort personnel files on puter, but the Navy had always handled admissions with hardcopy files.

"Any other changes?" The Commandant looked around the table.

"We have a pretty fair balance," said Lieutenant Sleak, his tone diffident. "Both ethnic and regional." Beside me, Edgar Tolliver doodled on a pad. "The age mix is about right, though we're leaning a bit heavily toward fourteens this year."

"Mr. Seafort?" The Commandant glanced my way.

I shook my head in frustration. How could I guess which youngsters to admit? Beside me Lieutenant Tolliver played with his pad, refusing to meet my eye. Why hadn't I rid myself of him when I had the chance? Even when we'd been cadets at Academy, I'd abhorred him.

"I don't—" I paused as Tolliver slid his pad to his right. I pushed it away, but not before noticing the sentence underlined twice. "What about Theroux?" I realized I'd spoken it aloud.

Kearsey wrinkled his brow. "Who's that? The Parisian?"

"Yes, sir." Tolliver's voice startled me.

"I suppose we could revise once more," the Commandant said. I looked up; this time Kearsey's eye held the stern disapproval I'd feared as a cadet.

All I wanted was to be gone from here, but Kearsey's annoyance triggered something in me. "I'd like to see Theroux on the list."

Kearsey shrugged. "Very well. I won't deny you your selections. You'll have to live with them. Darwin, put the Theroux boy back, and drop the three hundred eightieth name."

"Aye aye, sir." Sleak made a note.

After the meeting broke up I strode briskly back to my apartment; I'd be leaving within the hour for New York and Annie. Tolliver hurried alongside. He'd see me to my suborbital, and then he'd be on his own for a week. "Why Theroux?" I demanded. Absentmindedly I returned the salutes of passing cadets.

Tolliver panted, "Why not, sir? It makes as much sense as any other name." We turned into the Officers' Quadrangle.

I stopped; he continued a couple of paces before he realized I wasn't following. He turned and waited.

"Tell me the truth."

He shrugged. "I don't know why. Because he was on the list originally, and got bumped for someone else. Because his test scores and grades were fifteenth percentile, and the Russian boy's were lower."

I raised my eyebrow. "You, an idealist?"

Tolliver stood his ground. "Call it what you want, sir. I thought it wasn't fair. If you disagreed, why did you go along?"

I had no response to that. "Mind your manners," I growled.

"Aye aye, sir. As always." Damn it, the man was hopeless.

A few minutes later he watched my heli lift off for London Shuttleport.

Chapter 2

The clinic had been built atop the abandoned Yankee Stadium parking lot, after New York Military Command had decreed that public team sports were ipso-facto incitements to riot. It stood by itself on a huge lot long gone to weeds, not far from the crumbling stadium walls that were New York's answer to Rome's Coliseum.

Incongruously, the clinic was bordered by a pleasant, manicured lawn. The only concession to its hostile environment was the high barbed-wire fence surrounding the complex. Outside the fence, squatter shacks had sprung up on all sides, but for whatever reason none stood within a stone's throw of the clinic grounds.

The clinic's security arrangements were low-key but omnipresent. Closed gates, cameras, doorways with bomb sniffers concealed behind their painted trim. The usual adjuncts of urban life, not only in New York, but in all sophisticated cities. In London, just a year before, Lord Mayor Rajnee Sivat had barely escaped assassination, thanks to the bomb sniffers.

My appointment with Dr. O'Neill was for two P.M., but he wasn't yet on the hospital grounds. They told me he'd be "indefinitely detained." I conferred instead with Mrs. Talbot, his nurse, who made a show of having all calls held while she escorted me to a private office. I noticed that our indirect route managed to take us past many of her co-workers. For Annie's sake I held my peace.

"Of course you may see her, Captain Seafort. Doctor says visits will do her good as long as you both want them."

"Tell me again about the mood swings."

She waved away my concern. "They're to be expected at this stage. Your wife is undergoing a complicated course of hormone rebalancing." I tried not to flinch at the bald phrase; the fact of Annie's treatment was something we would have to live

17

with. "She's settling into new glandular patterns, and Doctor is constantly fine-tuning, as it were, based on her blood tests."

I twisted my cap in my hands. Oh, Annie.

Mrs. Talbot lowered her voice. "And of course your wife had some terribly traumatic experiences, quite apart from the rebalancing."

I looked up. Was there a hint of reproach? I couldn't be sure. Well, I had no right to object. Before the rape that had devastated her, Annie had endured the bombing of Centraltown and its accompanying chaos. To say nothing of abandonment and starvation on *Challenger*.

Mrs. Talbot's tone was gentler. "She's among strangers, too. That doesn't help, especially with her background."

I searched her eyes for the slur that must be there, found none.

For many decades Lower New York had been abandoned to bands of ruthless transpops who roamed its broken streets. Savage gangs comprised the city's transient population, many of Asian, Hispanic, or black origins. They preyed ruthlessly on each other and on the homeless. Above, in luxurious aeries, the civilized, cultured denizens of Upper New York shielded themselves from the harsh reality below with well-armed guards and their heavily fortified buildings. The Uppies referred to the transpops below as "trannies," an insult that could cost a life, if overheard.

Annie had come from those brutal streets. So had Seaman Eddie Boss, whom I'd inducted into the Navy. I'd banished him to U.N.S. *Waterloo,* the first ship sailing out-system, after I'd found him lying with Annie one awful Hope Nation afternoon.

"You've been through terrible times, both of you. It must have been ghastly, Captain."

I stiffened, brought myself under control only with effort. "It's past."

"You look ever so much better without—now that you've recovered."

Without my scar, she'd meant. Unnoticed, my hand crept to my cheek, where the plastic surgeons had done their work. I shifted uncomfortably. "I'd like to see my wife, if I may."

"Of course." She stood, and we went out to the corridor. "Doctor says Mrs. Seafort may go anywhere on the grounds. Shall I take you to her room?"

"I know the way," I said hastily. Mrs. Talbot's disappointment was obvious. "Thank you. Oh, and, uh . . ." I forced down my revulsion, groped for a way. "Do you perchance have any children?"

"Yes, two. Kathy and Jon."

"You have their pictures?"

"On my desk. Would you like to see?"

"Very much." I followed her back to her tiny office outside Dr. O'Neill's larger one. They were antique-style photos, not ordinary holos. I took out a pen. "May I?"

Her eyes widened in pleasure. "Oh, yes. Of course."

I wrote, "To Kathy and Jon, with gratitude for all the help their mother has provided. Nicholas E. Seafort, Captain, U.N.N.S."

Mrs. Talbot was breathless. She clutched the photo to her bosom. "Thank you, Captain. Thanks ever so much."

I took my leave, trying to force a calm while my stomach churned with disgust. People like Mrs. Talbot would bend backward for someone whose face was blazoned across the holos. But any humiliation was to be borne, if Annie received better care.

I sat with her in a sunny lounge, one hand thrown casually across the back of the sofa, the other in my jacket pocket, knuckles white, fist bunched. Annie stared sullenly at the wall. "I wonder why you bother coming, Nick."

"I want to see you. I'd be here every day if I could." I debated moving closer, decided not to risk it. "I'm sorry you're angry."

"I ain't angry!" She crossed her arms, turned away.

I said gently, "Annie, I love you." I held my breath.

When she turned, her eyes were scornful. "That ain't enough, Nicky."

My hand ached. I forced my fist to relax. "What would be enough?"

"Nothin'. You put me in dis—this place."

"Do you want to leave?"

"Yes! No! Damnit, I don't know what I want no more. You and your medicines done this to me!" I reached to her but she spun out of her seat and retreated. I watched, helpless. After a time she said quietly, "Come on, let's walk."

We strolled along the footpath. Eventually she took my arm. "Nicky, I'm all mixed up. I din' mean shout at you."

"I know, hon."

She kicked at a small stone. "Dr. O'Neill says I be gettin' better. He's prolly right. C'n you wait it out with me?"

My throat ached. "Of course. As long as it takes."

"Good. 'Cause dere's somethin' I wan'."

I tensed. Only at moments of stress did Annie revert to her transpop dialect.

"Nicky, I be gettin' mad every time I see you. Dr. O'Neill, he say it don' have nothin' to do with you, that I'm angry at Hope Nation and the fish and all. He keeps sayin' talk about it, and I keep tellin' him dat jus' make me madder, I should shut up 'til it go away."

"He's right, hon." Though the Freudian cult had long been discredited and repressed, even the Reunification Church approved of confessing sin and facing one's fear.

"It don' matter if he be right or wrong, the thing is, every time I be seein' you I get all mad again. What I wan' . . ." She faltered.

I steeled myself against a growing unease. "Yes?"

Her tone was determined. "I wan' you not to come see me fo' a while, 'til I be feelin' okay. It just get me all confused." Despite her words she clutched my arm tighter.

"Oh, Annie."

She turned toward me. "I mean it, Nicky. It ain't just what I'm feelin' dis moment."

"I know."

"I wanna keep lovin' you. Jus' lemme be, fo' now."

"All right."

Softly she wiped my cheek, and her hand came away wet. "Bes' you go now, 'fore I change my mind again."

"Yes." My tone was dull. I enfolded her in my arms, kissed the top of her head. "I love you. Remember that." I hurried off.

An armored cab took me to the nearest heliport. I'd planned to spend several days with my wife, but found myself cast adrift. I could go downtown to the towers of Upper New York, and look down from my hotel room to the ugly streets. That held no appeal; I'd toured New York twice and hated it. I had five days leave, and nothing to do. If I returned to Academy at

Devon I'd just seem to be interfering with Captain Kearsey's final days as Commandant. Better to stay out of the way, in London. I booked myself onto a suborbital. When we landed, I arranged a room in the old and decaying West End, where were located many of the hotels that had survived the Fire of 2070.

By mid-evening I'd settled into my room. Almost at once the hotel made me uneasy; wherever I went the eyes of the staff followed. Chambermaids and bellmen who never spoke to guests found occasion to talk with to me. Even the chef had come to my table, ostensibly to inquire if I liked the food.

I tried going out for a walk, but was soon recognized, and had no peace thereafter. People stared. Some even pointed. Perhaps I might have avoided the worst of it by donning civilian garb, but I'd be damned if I'd skulk about as if ashamed of the Navy. I frowned at the unfortunate phrase. I *was* damned; Lord God would have no forgiveness for what I'd done.

I paced my room, restless. I could run up to Farside, but I'd already scheduled a trip aloft a few days after Handover. No point in visiting Lunapolis, either. I'd just seen my old friend Alexi Tamarov settled in to his new post there, as assistant to the Chief of Naval Operations; after that hitch he'd surely be rotated back onto a ship. Good officers were scarcer than ever these days.

Nowhere held any appeal. For years I'd lived aboard ship, occasionally taking brief jaunts ashore. It was what I knew.

A vacation, then? There was nothing I wanted to see. I couldn't abide an hotel. I wanted to go . . .

Home.

I jumped off the bed. A heli, or a plane, first thing in the morning; nothing would be leaving at this hour. Or I could drive, though even today the roads through the hills to Cardiff were difficult. The only other way was . . . I snatched the caller. Moments later I thrust gear into my duffel. The desk would have a rooftop helicab waiting; if I raced, I could just make it. I signed for the unused room, let the bellhop carry my bag up to the cab. "Paddington Station, and hurry!"

The driver smiled sourly. "Sure, and I'll hurry. One of these days some bloke will get in and say, 'Take your time, lad. I checked out early.'" He turned the ignition and the blades whirred. We lifted off.

Half an hour later I settled into my railway compartment. I

hauled down the bed while we rumbled through the endless sub-
urbs of Extended London. We would pull into Cardiff in time
for breakfast. I took off my shirt and pants, stretched out on the
tiny bunk, relaxed at last.

Father. Home.

I slept.

I took breakfast in the ancient railway station before ringing
for a cab. I didn't bother bargaining the fare though I knew Father wouldn't approve of extravagance. I could afford it, and the
cabby deserved a living.

I stared out the window at the remains of the ancient
foundries. Jason and I had played in these eerie vacant buildings, a lifetime ago. The cab climbed deeper into the hills, on
the twisting Bridgend road.

The cabby was content to follow my directions. When finally
he pulled to a stop I got out, thrust bills at him, and waited until
he'd disappeared before I faced the familiar cottage down the
hill from the road. I hadn't called ahead, knowing with absolute
certainty that there was no need. If Father had gone to market,
his door would be open, and if he were at home I was welcome.
Except on Sunday, he would be nowhere else. It was as it would
always be.

Still, I knocked, rather than entering. I was thirteen when I'd
left this place, and as many years had passed.

The door swung open. Father seemed older, worn. He'd been
washing breakfast dishes, and still wore his apron. His eyes
flickered to my uniform, to my duffel. "You'll be staying,
then?"

"Aye, for a while."

He turned away and I followed him into the kitchen. "The tea
is hot."

"Thank you." I took a cup, poured the boiling water, set the
ball of tea leaves in it. I held the chain and swished it in the darkening water.

"I'd heard you were back. The grocer told me it was in the
holozines. He wanted to give me one."

I sipped at the tea. "Father, do you mind if I stay the week?"

"You are home, Nicholas."

"Thank you."

"You can help with the fence. Garth's cows want my grass and my garden, as always."

"All right."

He gestured to my jacket, my crisp blue slacks. "Work will ruin them."

"I have old pants. The shirt won't matter."

"You'll do your old chores."

I nodded. Nothing had changed, or could. I'd once pleaded: Do you love me? He hadn't answered, of course. Perhaps he didn't know himself.

I took my duffel into my old room, almost unchanged after a decade of absence. I sat down on the bed. The springs still creaked. They had caused me difficulty, trying to conceal my youthful passion from Father's notice.

My clothes changed, I worked at repairing the fence until Father set out a simple lunch of soup and vegetables. After, I returned to work; he rinsed the dishes before rejoining me. Later, when the gloomy sky darkened to dusk he surveyed the stretch of ragged fence we'd restored. "It's a beginning, anyway. We could have done more."

"I'm sorry, Father."

"Sorry builds no fences." Still, his hand brushed my side as we walked to the house. "I'll be making dinner."

"I could help."

"You'll have to wash first."

"Aye, sir." A smile twitched the corners of my mouth. He saw it, and frowned.

After grace, we ate our cold chicken, with cucumber salad. I helped Father with the washing up, and in the quiet of the evening I sat in the kitchen to read books I'd brought, in my hand-held holovid.

Father appeared in the doorway. "Will you join me for prayers?"

"I'd like that." I snapped off the holo, followed him into his bedroom. We knelt, and I closed my eyes. He spoke the Bible, rather than reading it. He had no doubt of the words.

Somehow, the ritual brought me a modicum of comfort, though my knees ached abominably by the time we finished. Afterward, when we'd gotten to our feet, I gave him an awkward hug before going to my room. Surprised, he neither thrust me away nor responded.

I undressed slowly, opened the window to the cool night air, and crept into bed. I lay on my back, arms behind my head, examining by moonlight the once-familiar icons of my childhood that Father had left in their place. A model of U.N.S. *Repulse* I'd built from balsa. My abandoned clothes, still hanging on the closet door. A souvenir banner for the Welsh national football team. I stared at the faded felt emblem. So long ago, and just yesterday.

The game was always on Saturday.

"Is he always like that?"

I pedaled hard to keep up. "It's Father's way."

"How can you stand it? 'Are your chores finished? Have you read your verses?' Jeez."

I changed gears, came abreast of him, wind whistling in my hair. "I'm used to it."

He grimaced. Jason didn't understand that none of it mattered. Whatever work I was given—studies, memorizing verses, chores, weeding—I could still sometimes ride with Jason. Father always acknowledged that I was free to choose my friends.

I suspected Father disapproved of Jason not because he was a freethinker, though that was bad enough, but because we chattered like magpies and giggled over whispered secrets. Father's house was normally silent.

Jason and I locked our bikes to a rack in the parking lot and joined the crowd moving to the stadium entrance.

He ventured, "We could try for beer."

"No," I snapped. Some of Jason's notions were outlandish. "You know what happened to Andrew and Llewelyn."

"It was their second offense."

"I'm not going to prison for a tube of beer." Didn't he know the Rebellious Ages were long since past? Society didn't approve of wild children, and to tell the truth, neither did I. Sneaking out at night to meet Jason was one thing; at worst that meant chastisement from Father. Breaking public decency laws was quite another.

We sat on the hard benches waiting for the game to begin. "Nicky, you gonna reapply next year?"

"I don't know." I stared down at the chalk lines on the field.

"You should."

I couldn't keep the bitterness from my tone. "So they can turn me down again?"

"You almost made it. So much work; all the forms we filled out, and then the interviews, the recommendations we got from everyone. Don't throw it away."

I kicked the bench below me. "I'd have to start all over. Who cares about being a frazzin' cadet?"

He studied me. By swearing I'd revealed more than I intended. "You care. And so do I."

"Sure, it means a lot to you," I jeered. "You're the one who'd go to Devon, not me."

"Nicky, sometimes you're an arse." He took a stereoplug from his shirt pocket, set it in his ear.

I turned away, furious. The teams went to their benches. A moment later a hand came around my waist and squeezed my side. "Sorry."

I said nothing.

"I'm sorry, Nicky."

I pried his fingers loose. "You know I don't like that."

"Don't be pissed at me, Nicky. Please?"

I glared at him, but my frown quickly faded; I couldn't stay mad at Jason for long. "Okay."

Jason giggled. "Maybe your father will let you go to Third with me, and we end up in Engineering together."

"I doubt he will." School was voluntary. It had been so for nearly a century. Unfortunately the choice was Father's, not mine. If I had my way, I'd have gone. I knew that by studying at home over the rickety kitchen table I learned more than other joeys, but it was lonely, sometimes, with no one but Father. And after satisfying him, a public school would be a breeze.

After a time I said, "Farside would have been nice."

"I know." Jason had helped me prep for the exams, and had shared my fantasies of leaving Cardiff as a local hero. He didn't know how I'd cried myself to sleep when the letter came, and again during the week that followed. I'd been so sure, after getting to Second Interview.

The crowd came to its feet with a roar when Archie Connelly took the field against the Dubliners. I cheered as hard as any. Maybe this time, with luck, I could get an autograph.

Once I'd been the next joey in line when Archie had turned away for the bus.

By now the first group of cadets would be reporting to Devon. Rather than cope with hordes of confused plebes, the authorities had recruits show up on staggered dates. Or, as scornful middies were said to remark, the plebes came staggering in. Like most Navy-struck boys I pored over the frequent articles in the holozines.

We lost, five goals to two. Archie had been shaken up in a collision that earned Riltz a yellow card, and gave no autographs after the game. Disconsolate, we trudged back to our bikes. Jason already had our tickets for next week's big game, against the Italians. The one we'd been waiting for.

We stopped at McCardle's for shakes and synthos. In a glum mood, I swirled the glass back and forth, while the holovid blared overhead and Jason chattered about our side's missed goals. If only Reggie hadn't missed the easy block, if the Micks had just—

Jason's fingers tightened on my arm. Annoyed, I twisted loose. We had an understanding about his affections, yet twice today he'd—

"Listen!"

I gaped at the holovid. ". . . when the suborbital went down. Airport officials say the craft had lost an engine but the pilot was expected to land safely with the remaining two. Debris is scattered across several runways, and Heathrow traffic has been diverted. Among the passengers was Dr. Raphael Tendez, inventer of the Hodgkins vaccine. Also aboard were twenty-eight cadets reporting for admission to the U.N.N.S. Naval Academy at Devon—"

"Lord God!" I was on my feet.

Jason stared at me white-faced. "It would have been you, Nicky." His eyes glistened.

"Come on!" I grabbed my jacket.

"What's the—"

"I want to go home!"

"But—"

"Now!" I ran outside, unchained my bike. Jason fumbled for a coin, inserted it in the holovid, waited impatiently for the chip to pop out below.

I was already pumping up the hill, all my effort in the strain of the pedals, grateful for the opportunity not to think.

It was several minutes until Jason, panting, began to catch up. "Wait!"

Head down, I pumped madly, eyes fixed on the mottled pavement streaking below.

"Nicky, slow a bit!"

Reluctantly I coasted until he pulled alongside. He gasped, "What in hell is the matter with you?"

"Shut up."

"Nicky? Are you crying?"

Deliberately, I swerved, knocking Jason onto the grassy shoulder. As he tried to right himself I smashed into him again, throwing both of us onto the soft grass. I untangled myself from the bicycle and swarmed over him, pummeling him with blows to the shoulders and sides.

He threw me aside, his temper well and truly ignited. "Get off me, you frazzing arsehole!" I wrestled him down again, climbed onto his chest. He bucked and kicked. Finally he yanked free an arm and caught me a staggering blow on the side of the head. "Ow! Jesus!" He nursed his hand. "Christ, you've broken it!"

"Good!"

"I mean it, you stupid grode!"

I loosened my grip. "Let me see."

"Get off first!"

I rolled aside. He kicked me in the stomach, for evenses, as he called it. I doubled over, but he made no attempt to follow up his advantage. He buried his knuckles under his arm. "Damn!"

When I could breathe properly I said, "Let me look." Reluctantly he extended his wrist. "Can you move it?"

He wiggled his fingers gingerly. "I think so."

"Then it's probably not broken. Can you ride?"

"If my bike's okay." He wiped his face. "Jesus, why'd you do that?"

"I don't know."

"You don't—Nicky!"

Ashamed, I looked down. "I'm sorry, Jase."

"Sorry? You drive me into the ditch, beat me up, break my arm, and all you can say is you're sorry?"

"I'm sor—" What was wrong with me? How could I have done such a thing, and to my best friend? My only friend. "I mean it, Jason." I looked up, but already he was laughing, in that way he had of changing like a summer storm.

"Give me a hug, then."

"I'm not a gay, Jase. You know that."

"But you owe me." He held up his swelling hand.

"Arghhhh!" I pulled him to his feet. Shyly, making sure no one was driving by, I embraced him. He let his head rest against my shoulder. "There, you satisfied?" I drew back.

"It'll do, 'til another time."

I righted his bicycle. It seemed undamaged. "Let's go home and soak it in ice."

"Soak my bike?" His tone was incredulous.

"Your hand, you twit." Then I saw his face. "I could kill you, sometimes."

"Yeah. You try, sometimes." He walked his bike to the road and hopped on.

Father read the newschip gravely while Jason sat at the table, his hand in a bucket of icy water. Father raised his head and his eyes found mine. "So, Nicholas."

I studied the table.

"Is that why you fought?"

"Yes. No. I don't know."

"I would be disturbed too, at such proof of my folly."

"Folly? What did I do?"

"You questioned your Lord's will. Didn't I tell you, if He'd wanted you summoned to Academy you'd have been admitted? He spared you the horror of that inferno."

My voice dripped scorn. "He killed those cadets just to teach me humility?"

Father slapped me, hard. "Alone with your friends you may mock Him. Not in my house."

Jason drew in a sharp breath, but was silent. My hand crept to my reddened cheek. I muttered, "Aye, sir."

"If it's His purpose to teach you humility, He still has work to do."

I nodded. It wasn't safe to say anything else.

"We'll pray for them tonight."

My voice was barely audible. "I'd like that."

Much later, after dinner, after chores, after my evening verses, in the solitude of my darkened room, I knelt at my bed and closed my eyes in the customary manner. I'm sorry, Lord, for having doubted You. I didn't understand. I still don't know why they had to die, but thank You for sparing me. Yet, I wanted so much to go to Academy. Do You understand that? Can You find me something else to want as much? Could I ask that of You?

Please?

My eyes roved the room, to the Captain's insignia on my jacket that hung on the chair, to the scarred desk, to the window out of which a boy had occasionally climbed, his heart pounding, knowing disobedience was sin but anticipating the glory of a night ride in the moonlight through caressing wind, tires whispering on the dark asphalt.

I left my creaking bed, walked to the window. Lord God knew where my old bike might be now. And if I wanted to ride, I had but to walk out the door; I was too old to be climbing through windows. I wandered the room. My fingers stroked the desktop. No dust; Father had kept my room clean. I sat at the chair. Had everything shrunk? I felt almost a Gulliver.

I opened the drawer. Pencils, lined neatly in a row. Old scraps of paper, a teen's doodles. A folder, neatly labeled by hand in block letters. "ACADEMY APPLICATION." The letters "U.N.N.S." had been carefully added before "ACADEMY," as if in clarification. I opened the aging file.

The letter had come four days after.

September 1, 2190.
Circumstances have required the Selection Board to reopen admissions for the U.N.N.S. Naval Academy's entering class. This is to inform you that your application has been reviewed and that you are accepted for admission as a cadet in the United Nations Naval Service. You are to acknowledge by return mail, and to report on September 10, 2190, to Academy in Devon.

Lauron E. Kearsey, Commandant.

I closed the file, turned from the desk. I knelt at the bed.
Lord, help me find that boy, the one who'd reread that letter

until each word was burned into his memory. The innocent lad who'd vowed to do his best, to struggle through cadethood to the exalted rank of midshipman. You see, he's been extinguished, somehow. He left behind a vindictive, deceitful man who's broken every rule he cherishes, who disobeys orders, lies to his superiors.

May I pray to You? Will You be offended, even if You don't listen? I know I've forfeited Your grace, and that You will punish me. What I don't know, Lord, is why. Why did I do those awful things?

Is that what You had in mind for me when You sent me to Academy?

Chapter 3

The cab waited in the lane. In the doorway Father stood gray and worn. I paused, laid my duffel at my feet. "It's been good to see you."

"Aye." His blue eyes met mine. "And the fence is fixed."

"That too." I shifted uncomfortably. "I'll be closer to home now, when I'm not at Farside. I could help keep it mended."

"There's always work to be done." It could have been a re-proof.

"I could come at Easter, if you like."

"If it be His will." I knew that passed for assent. I made no effort to hug him; it wasn't his way and he'd be as embarrassed as I. I turned to go.

He spoke suddenly. "Pray to Him." He raised a hand, as if to forestall my objection. "He may turn His head, but pray nonetheless. It is right, and it does you good."

"Aye, sir." How could he know? I hadn't spoken the words aloud. "Good-bye, then." He nodded, and I hurried to the waiting cab.

Struggling for an expression of polite interest, I looked down on rows of shining young faces, gleaming buckles, immaculate gray uniforms, while Commandant Kearsey continued his interminable address. Every cadet in Academy had been brought groundside for Handover. A waste of resources in wartime, but it was an odd war. Only one fish had ever been seen in home system, and we had no idea where the aliens bred, or where they might next appear.

A few seats from me, Lieutenant Tolliver's eyes glinted with amusement; he knew how I hated the necessary ritual.

Kearsey said, "Just twelve years ago Mr. Seafort was a cadet like you. Who'd have thought that quiet youngster of thirteen would soon astound the world?"

Not I, certainly. More to the point, who'd have thought that eager youngster would commit treason and damn himself?

"As a midshipman, Mr. Seafort was posted to U.N.S. *Helsinki.*" A green young middy, reporting to the bridge of a U.N. warship, trying to control the trembling of his limbs.

"Mr. Seafort's next posting was to *Hibernia.*" A starship on the Hope Nation run, sixty-nine light-years from home. We'd Fused for seventeen months, Defusing only for nav checks.

"Most of *Hibernia*'s officers were killed in an explosion of the ship's launch." It had left my friend Lieutenant Malstrom the sole commissioned line officer, until his death soon after from cancer.

Kearsey said heavily, "Now Captain, Mr. Seafort brought *Hibernia* to Hope Nation, but was unable to find new officers."

Lord God, would he never end?

"He sailed on, but on his return from Detour he encountered the wreck of *Telstar* and, in it, the first alien creatures ever seen by a human being."

I recalled the alien form that had quivered inches from my face. Moments later there had emerged from behind *Telstar* the bizarre fish that was home to the outrider I'd found.

"Captain Seafort sailed home with his momentous discovery. Admiralty confirmed him as Commander and gave him U.N.S. *Portia,* part of Admiral Tremaine's relief squadron to Hope Nation. En route, Mr. Seafort's son was killed by fish and his wife died soon after. Then the Admiral's flagship *Challenger* was disabled."

How would Kearsey phrase the events that followed?

The Commandant said firmly, "The Admiral transferred his flag to *Portia,* and decided unwisely to off-load those he disapproved of to the disabled *Challenger.* Mr. Seafort agreed to stay with *Challenger.*" Mr. Seafort chose to die with *Challenger,* but Lord God did not allow him his wish.

"Despite starvation and rebellion, Mr. Seafort impressed a new crew, trained them, and fought off the aliens. In his final battle he rammed a fish just as it Fused, and by the grace of Lord God the fish Defused in our home system."

I'd brought *Challenger* home, but at the cost of my soul. I'd sworn not to harm a rebellious sailor, then I'd killed her at the first opportunity. For that, I am damned.

The Commandant paused, examining the young faces of his

audience. "Even you plebes know that Captain Seafort sailed yet again to Hope Nation, and was groundside when the fish devastated Centraltown. Mr. Seafort was left in charge of the few shoreside Naval officers.

"Hope Nation was again attacked, and the fleet sailed for home. Ailing and alone, Mr. Seafort managed to lure the aliens into attacking Orbit Station, where he destroyed them by detonating the Station's atomic self-destruct device."

Until a few weeks before I'd planned my sabotage, even a proposal to use atomic weapons had carried a mandatory death penalty. When I'd nuked the Station, I'd thought it treason.

"Captain Seafort's courage and resourcefulness need no further detail. On my retirement, I can leave the training of our cadets in no better hands. Ladies and gentlemen, I present your new Commandant, Captain Nicholas Ewing Seafort."

I stood, to the sustained roar of applause. Commandant Kearsey, smiling, joined the acclamation.

"Thank you." I waited for the din to cease. It did not. I raised my hand for silence, but they applauded with undiminished enthusiasm. The young fools. "Thank you. Enough."

They began to rise, in a standing ovation. I couldn't allow it. If only they knew the truth . . .

"Be silent!" I bellowed into the mike, fists knotted at my side.

The applause stopped as if turned off by a switch. I paced the stage, my crafted address scattered to the winds of rage. "When I was last here," I grated, "cadets obeyed their officers." No one moved. "As you will again, I promise you!"

What was I doing? I lurched back toward my planned speech. "Commandant Kearsey, I thank you for your most generous remarks. Your tenure here has been unblemished." Unblemished mediocrity, I thought bitterly. Test scores falling, morale low . . . I'd been shocked at the reports they'd given me. But the man meant well. "I hope I may accomplish as much."

I nodded briefly to the outgoing Commandant, took a deep breath, turned back to the stunned cadets. "By order of the Board of Admiralty of the Government of the United Nations, I assume command of Terrestrial and Farside Academies. Dismissed."

*   *   *

I slouched behind the desk in the luxurious office Commandant Kearsey had vacated only that morning. "I made a mess of it."

Tolliver shrugged. "If you say so."

I wished he'd show the respect due my rank, if not my person. But I'd done him too much harm, and he knew me too well to retain any respect for me. He was a penance I bore with as good grace as I could manage.

"I made a fool of myself," I muttered.

"Oh, you weren't that bad. They might as well find out you have a temper."

I growled, "Don't go too far, Tolliver."

He showed surprise. "No sarcasm intended, if you can believe it. You're not one to be crossed, and the cadets are better off knowing it from the start."

From the start. I grunted. As of this day, Terrestrial Academy, Farside Base, and the Naval Training Station high in Lunar orbit were all under my jurisdiction.

Not for the first time, I wondered how I'd let myself be talked into my new post. After I brought *Victoria* home from Hope Nation I'd asked to resign my commission, but Admiral Duhaney and his colleague Senator Boland prevailed on me to stay. I should have declined, but at least I'd had the sense to refuse a ship. I'd already killed innocents enough.

"He should be gone by now."

Tolliver checked his watch. "Anytime now, sir. His aide told me they'd be out of the apartment by three."

"Edgar, I hope I've made it clear . . ." I fumbled for words. "Your, uh, special dispensation. I won't have an outsider overhearing you. Be warned."

He smiled grimly. "I'll take great care, sir."

"Good." Uncomfortable, I stood to pace, changing the subject. "Two days, then up to Farside."

"Yes, sir. Farside's personnel files are in the puter, if you want a look. Are you aware there's no console in your apartment?"

"You're joking. Have one installed."

"Already ordered, sir. I assumed you'd want access."

"Don't assume," I said, petulant.

"I can cancel it if—"

"I want the console. Just don't assume you know what I want." As always, Tolliver brought out the worst in me.

He raised an eyebrow. "Aye aye, sir. Shall I cancel the order, and reinstate it now that you've told me you want it?"

Damn the man. I leaned back, recalled the conversation we'd had in my Lunapolis quarters, after I'd agreed to take him as my aide.

"Do I have a choice?" His tone was bleak.

I gaped. "It was as a favor to you."

"Of course, sir. Serving with you is a great privilege."

"How dare you!" His insolence was astounding.

He shrugged. "I wonder that myself, at times. I guess I've learned from you."

"What do you mean?"

"I just don't care anymore." He thrust his hands in his pockets. "Captain Higbee at BuPers mentioned that I was lucky to get a posting at all, after my misdeeds."

I closed my eyes. I'd done that by demoting him, after he'd seized control of my heli in an effort to save our lives. "He was right. If I hadn't taken you . . ."

"Should I resign, then?" His tone was bitter.

"That's your decision." I hesitated. "Mr. Tolliver, it's hard for me to be fair to you; my memories of Academy are too strong. I put you back to Lieutenant. What more do you want?"

"Nothing in your power to give." He turned away. Then, "I'm sorry. I mean that. What I want is to go back and undo the past."

"The heli?"

"Among other things." He turned back with a wry smile. "We're stuck with each other. Your conscience won't let you abandon me, and if I want a career it must be with you."

"I allow you to goad me, but nonetheless, I'm your superior officer and you owe me courtesy. You seem to forget."

"Not for a minute!" His eyes burned into mine. "If I'm, um, difficult with you, it's my resentment. Never negligence."

"Do you imagine I find that reassuring?"

He smiled, but his eyes were pained. "When you can't endure it, cashier me. I may hate you, but I'll understand."

Why did his hurt matter to me, after all we'd been through? My voice was gruff. "No, I'll tolerate you. You can't help being who you are, and you remind me of what I've done."

"If that's pity, I don't want it!"

"Not pity, Edgar. Perhaps . . . understanding."

He'd let it pass.

Now, in my new Academy office, I was restless. "I'm going to my apartment."

He checked his watch. "Kearsey may still be there."

"I don't care." But I fell back in the chair. "Tell me the schedule again."

Tolliver's look was of resignation. "We start shipping most of our joeys back to Farside, some today. Those we graduated will stay groundside until their postings come through. We'll keep a few midshipmen, of course, for the scutwork."

I gestured impatiently. "Get on with it."

"The new class staggers in. They all begin training down here at Devon."

I growled. "I *was* a cadet, Tolliver."

"Right. I must remember that. The first batch of sixty will be here in a week, and about sixty more every five days until they're all aboard."

"What am I supposed to do before they get here?"

"What will you do *after* they get here, sir?" He shrugged. "Answer questions, I suppose. If it's anything like shipboard, they always have questions."

I smiled at that. Most inquiries were trivial, and could be answered at random. "How many cadets on base this week?"

"I don't know, sir; some of the upperclassmen had leave. Just a minute." He went to the caller, spoke into it, waited. "We have thirty-two graduates without families to visit, and about sixty of our plebes slated for Farside. Then there's about four hundred they brought down from Farside for the ceremony, who'll be going back."

I swore under my breath. Our cadets were being moved like chess pieces, and to no real purpose. I got up, restless again. "I'm going for a walk. See you at three."

"Yes, sir."

"And set up a meeting after dinner with the middies who'll be staying."

"Aye aye, sir."

I nodded to Sergeant Kinders in the outer office, left the Admin Building, picked a direction and set off briskly. In a few minutes I found myself at the main gate. Many of the upperclassmen had been selected for graduation this day, and it was odd to see visitors strolling inside the gate, each with a cadet in crisp gray. Other than on ceremonial occasions, no civilian visitors were permitted on the grounds. Shortly, our graduates would change to their midshipman's blues, which they would wear with inordinate pride until they learned that even middies were insignificant creatures in the eyes of working Naval officers.

I thrust my hands in my pockets, walked with head down. Our real task would start when our new class arrived.

Shipboard, most Naval personnel served belowdecks. They were recruited in their thousands by any means available, including the enlistment bonuses that attracted so many undesirables. But officers were another matter. The Navy selected only the best, carefully evaluating test scores, school grades, interviews and recommendations. Only a fortunate few were allowed to take the oath as cadets.

I reached the heavy iron gate, absently returned the salutes of the guards, and turned onto the perimeter path. Here I was virtually alone.

Unlike midshipmen, deemed by act of the General Assembly to have reached majority, our cadets were minors, by law and regulation the wards of their commanding officer. As Commandant I was their legal guardian, with all the prerogatives their parents had hitherto possessed. I could punish them in any fashion I saw fit; they had virtually no rights. They were the lowest of the low, until they were appointed midshipmen. Then, as Naval officers, they'd begin the slow climb to the exalted rank of Lieutenant, and perhaps thereafter to Captain.

While in an emergency it was possible to enlist a cadet aboard ship—I had done so myself—ordinarily cadets were sent to Academy for their training. As plebes, they were taught the basics of navigation, physics, radionics, electronics, gunnery, and the like.

As soon as cadets could be trusted not to wander in front of the firing grid of a laser cannon or unscrew their suit helmets Outside, they were sent for a long term to Farside, the "real" Academy. There, freed from distractions and distanced from visiting busybodies, their advanced training commenced: simulated docking maneuvers, airlock security, Orbiting Station procedures, and the other skills they'd need to be set loose in the corridors of a U.N.N.S. starship. Often, they were then returned to Devon for further training.

The term of enlistment was five years, and theoretically a youngster could serve the entire term as a cadet and never make middy. In practice, most were graduated after two years or so, some after only one year. Graduation was at the discretion of the Commandant.

This practice was a radical departure from the military institutions of previous generations, and I was somewhat apprehensive of the responsibility it thrust upon me, but overall, the idea made sense. Though a cadet might not be ready to serve as a midshipman, that didn't necessarily mean he was failing his coursework. Further, under the Naval system, holding back a cadet for a few extra months bore little of the stigma that would attach if he failed to graduate with a scheduled class.

In any event, a cadet might be pulled from classes in the middle of a term and sent to the fleet as a middy, or might be held on all or part of another year for further training.

One never knew, and the eagerness to prove themselves ready for graduation spurred cadets to greater efforts.

I struck across the large expanse of front lawn, toward the barracks and classrooms on the far side of the parade ground. Here, tall oaks gave welcome shade from the heat of the spacious front grounds.

I followed a path worn in the grass. A pair of gray-clad legs protruded from beyond a tree trunk. As I passed, the youth jumped to his feet, stiffened to attention. I saluted, moved on, stopped.

"Jerence?"

"Yes, sir." His belly was sucked in tight, spine stiff.

Aboard *Victoria* on my flight home, I'd enlisted Jerence Branstead, of the Hope Nation Bransteads, as a cadet. Once home, he'd been transferred to Academy for proper training.

I strolled back, pursed my lips, examined him. Though the seat of his pants was dusty from where he'd been sitting, his shoes were polished, his uniform crisp, his hair combed neatly. A far cry from the miserable boy locked in a sweaty cabin, desperate for the vial of goofjuice that lay unopened on his bed.

I smiled but immediately converted it to a frown. After all, he was but a cadet, and I shouldn't deign even to speak to him. "Stand easy."

"Aye aye, sir!" His shoulders relaxed; he spread his feet, clasped his hands behind him in the at-ease position.

"Hasn't your leave begun?"

"Yes, sir. I—" He gulped, stopped. Quite right. A cadet answered questions, but otherwise spoke only when spoken to.

"Well?"

"I'm being sent to Farside, but I have no place to go for leave, sir. I'm staying on grounds." He swallowed, essayed a small tremulous smile.

I reddened. "Of course." Harmon and Sarah Branstead were on Hope Nation, lacking even the knowledge that their son had survived. "No Terran relatives?"

"No, sir. I'm fourth generation."

"Very well. Carry on." I resumed my stroll. He'd made his bed; now he could lie in it. It was he who'd begged for the opportunity to enlist, and loneliness was part of the cost. Giving him special treatment would do neither of us any good; I had to treat him like any other cadet.

I crossed the parade ground, wandered toward the barracks. Yeltsin Hall was silent and empty. Beyond it was Valdez Hall. No reason to go farther. But still, Valdez . . . I sauntered closer. No harm in going inside, just to look around. It had been so long.

I took the steps two at a time. The door was ajar; the sergeant wouldn't have liked that. Inside, I heard voices, a gleeful shout. I swung the door wide and strode in.

A pillow hurtled past my head. The girl prancing on the bunk ducked, snatched it out of the air. "You missed! Can't you even—oh, God!" She leaped off the bed, stiffened to attention, as did five other youths. A young voice shouted, "Attention!"

I stared unbelieving at the disorder. Valdez, like all the barracks, held two rows of single bunks in meticulous order, one on each side of the narrow corridor, some thirty beds in all. Now, mattresses were overturned, pillows scattered everywhere. Dust motes danced in the sunshine streaming through the windows. The contents of two duffels had been dumped unceremoniously on the beds.

"What is this?" No one answered. I wheeled to the closest boy. "You! Report!"

He was in trousers and shirtsleeves. Perhaps it was his jacket that lay crumpled in the corridor. "Cadet Rafe Slater reporting, sir! We were, ah . . . uh—"

I snorted. "You sure were. Who's in charge here?"

A small voice answered, "I guess I am, sir."

I wheeled. "You guess?"

"Cadet—oh, I—Midshipman Anton Thayer, sir." A slim youngster, red curly hair.

I looked at his cadet grays and raised an eyebrow.

"I was just promoted, sir. Today."

"Ah." The place was a shambles. How many demerits to give? Two each? Four? A middy was an officer, not a child. How could he allow—

Just promoted, the traditional fierce hazing of Last Night finally past. The rest of the barracks on leave. I cleared my throat, glad I'd come to my senses in time. "I see. Carry on."

"Sir?" He gaped. "I mean, aye aye, sir!"

I made sure to maintain my scowl until I was well outside the door. Then my grin broke loose. Children. I shook my head. They'd get enough discipline during the term. Today, graduation day, it didn't matter. Anyway, it was the sergeant's worry; I was supposed to be a remote figure, aloof from day-to-day concerns.

Most of the middies had taken chairs at the burnished conference table. The others were seated uncomfortably on an overstuffed couch, trying to appear businesslike. Seven boys, four girls.

I gazed around the crowded room, saying nothing. How could midshipmen be so young? I doubted some of the boys had ever seen a razor. Surely it hadn't been so in my day.

In my day! I snorted. I was but twenty-five, though I felt eons older. Several of these youngsters were from the class that had just graduated; a few had been midshipmen for more than a year. One old-timer had three years experience under her belt.

I perched on the edge of my desk, letting the silence stretch. A couple of the middies shifted nervously. None dared say a word. I looked down at the curly redhead sitting in the closest chair; Midshipman Anton Thayer flushed, studied the carpet. He was in his blues now, far more presentable than when I'd surprised him in barracks.

"I've already been introduced to most of the staff, and I

wanted to meet the rest of my officers." Midshipman Guthrie Smith's mouth turned up in a shy smile. Officers. I knew how hard he'd labored to achieve that acknowledgment, at seventeen. "You, the lieutenants and I will be working together from now on."

They sat straighter. "You're no longer cadets, and you wear officers' blue. By Act of the General Assembly, you are deemed adults. On leave you may go into town and carouse, or do whatever else strikes your fancy." Some had a faraway look; I suspected they would lose little time.

Time to bring them back to earth. "I want to make clear my expectations. You're here for two purposes: to help where you're needed, and to set an example for the cadets. If I find that your conduct on base is less than exemplary, you will answer to me." That got their attention, all right. Though my powers weren't as absolute as those of a Captain under weigh, my displeasure was a calamity no midshipman would enjoy. A word from me would have them over the barrel.

"As you know, Academy drill sergeants are noncom Marines. When you were cadets you were required to obey them. Now you're their superior officers." I waited until the sudden grins had faded, before shattering their illusions. "In name only. The sergeants will treat you with due courtesy; if one does not, you are to report him to me at once. Nonetheless, you will treat requests from the drill sergeants as if they are orders from me. Is that clear?"

They all responded, "Aye aye, sir," their voices subdued.

I stood to pace, found I had no room. I eased my way around to the back of the desk. "As to the cadets." I glared at them. "Technically you can order a cadet to do anything you wish. I suggest strongly—" I paused for effect. "I suggest strongly that you refrain. Occasional hazing is acceptable; they have to learn to cope with it. But keep it within bounds."

Some of them looked crestfallen. I didn't care. A cadet's life could be hell, and I didn't need these unseasoned youngsters making it worse. Not too much worse, anyway.

"As to striking them, you have every legal right to do it." After all, I had the right, and the middies acted in my behalf. "However, I forbid it. You'll be put over the barrel at the first violation, and the second will result in dismissal." During my second year on Farside there had been an incident, a nasty one. I wanted no repetitions.

Time to lighten a little, perhaps. "Who's senior at the moment?" I asked. It would change, as middies were transferred from here to Farside. Academy hierarchy was less rigid than aboard ship.

They didn't need to look at one another's insignia. They knew. Middies always do. "I am, sir."

"Sandra Ekrit?"

"Yes, sir."

"Very well." The other middies would call her by her last name, as a mark of respect. Until someone with more seniority showed up, she was in charge of keeping the middies under control and out of my hair.

It also meant the others could challenge her, as was Naval tradition. I wondered if the lanky young woman could hold her own against some of the burlier middies. We'd see. Like anyone else, she would sink or swim on her own.

"Any questions?"

A dark-haired boy raised his hand. "Midshipman Eduard Diego, sir. Will we have specific assignments?"

Sandra Ekrit scowled, knowing it was better for him not to bother me with trivia. Still, I'd invited him to ask.

"I don't know. I'm as new at this as you are." That brought a few startled grins. I rebuked myself silently. A fine start as their Commandant, confessing I knew nothing about the job. "We'll see. Anything else?" I waited. "Dismissed."

Chapter 4

Striding with Tolliver through the concourse of Earthport Station, I tried to ignore the ache in my chest, a legacy of my recent lung replacement.

I peered at the flashing signs. "Terminal 4. G Concourse straight ahead. Shuttle to Lunapolis, turn right." After a moment I gave up. Earthport was the largest orbiting station we'd ever built, and invariably I lost myself in it.

I waited patiently at a counter for the red-jacketed civilian to look up from his puter. When he did his eyes widened in recognition. "Aren't you—can I help you?"

"The shuttle to Farside?"

He pointed. "It leaves from the Naval wing. They can tell you the gate."

"Thank you." I should have known better. Naturally the shuttle would leave from the Naval bays; no civilians could visit Farside. I hoisted my duffel, strode past the guard. "Come along, Mr. Tolliver."

"Aye aye, sir." My aide was unusually silent, perhaps as a consequence of my earlier rebuffs. My mind was on our forthcoming visit. I'd never been to Farside as an officer; three days after I'd made midshipman I'd been sent onward to U.N.S. *Helsinki*.

The Station corridor took an abrupt right angle. As I reached the turn, a midshipman tore around the bend and cannoned into me. We went down in a tangle. Tolliver thrust him aside, helped me to my feet.

I bellowed, "Watch where you're going, you young pup! Haven't they taught you a thing? What's your rush?"

The boy saluted, stammering. "Sorry, sir. I was trying to make it to the shuttle to meet—to meet—" He ground to a halt, paling as he realized to whom he spoke.

"Yes?" I barked.

His voice faltered. "You, sir. Midshipman Adam Tenere reporting, sir." He came to attention. Tolliver's expression was carefully solemn, though I detected a glint of amusement.

My shoulder throbbed, and I wondered if I'd twisted my ankle. "You're from Farside?"

"Yes, sir. My lieutenant sent me to escort you to base."

"He told you to race through the Station as if a squadron of fish were after you?"

"No, sir!"

"He told you to knock me down when you found me?"

"No, sir." The mortified middy could guess what was coming.

"Four demerits, Mr. Tenere. Consider yourself lucky." Each demerit meant two hours of hard calisthenics. I could as easily have had him caned, and most Captains would.

"Aye aye, sir. Thank you, sir. I'm sorry."

I snorted, stooped to pick up my duffel. "Which way?"

It was a foolish question. He pointed back the direction he'd come. "Down there, sir."

"Very well." I limped off.

"May I carry your duffel, sir?"

"No." Inconsiderate children, racing like mindless idiots . . . I took a cautious breath, half expecting something to grate. My chest seemed all right. "Yes. Here." Let him lug the damned thing. It was heavy.

"I already offered to carry that, sir."

"Shut up, Tolliver." We walked the length of the corridor in silence.

In the shuttle I strapped myself in, took a deep breath, strove for calm. "Tenere, you said?"

"Yes, sir. Adam Tenere."

"Any relation to . . . ?"

"Captain Tenere? He's my father, sir. He has *Freiheit.* He should be home in a couple of months with the fleet."

Because I'd Fused home in the fastship *Victoria,* I'd completed the trip in nine months, while the rest of the fleet was still in Fusion. They'd be home shortly. Though I'd brought news of the fleet's terrible losses, the details were still not general knowledge.

I made up my mind. It was his father; the boy should know. "*Freiheit* was lost. Mr. Tenere was fortunate; they found him in a lifepod."

"I didn't know that. Did his men survive?"

Immediately I regretted the demerits. "Not that I know of."

He bowed his head. "I'm sorry. All they told me was that he was coming home."

"You're assigned to Farside?"

"Yes, sir. Posted two months ago."

"I'll see to it you get leave when he's here."

The midshipman turned to me, his demerits forgotten. "Thank you, sir." His face lit with gratitude. "We'd both appreciate that."

I flirted with canceling the demerits, but decided not to. The boy had run over me like a tank.

The trip from Earthport Station to Farside took five hours. The few other passengers aboard our shuttle were techs returning from leave. When the Pilot began surfacing maneuvers I shut off my holo and watched through the porthole. The round domes of Farside stood out clearly against the ragged terrain. Of course they would, with no hazy atmosphere to impede vision. I squinted, trying to spot the Hull.

Settling the shuttle onto the Lunar surface wasn't as effortless as docking at Station, but it was far less an ordeal than diving into Earth's gravity well. I waited to unstrap until the lights blinked. Young Mr. Tenere had his belts loose the moment our jets stopped squirting.

The Pilot came back into the cabin as I stood carefully in the one-sixth gravity. "Welcome to Farside, sir."

"Welcome back, you mean." I smiled. "I've been here before."

"Oh, yes. Though it's hard to imagine you a cadet."

I could find no reply, so I waited, watching the airlock lights.

When docking at an orbiting Station, it was the vessel's responsibility to meet the Station's lock. At a groundside installation, the lock came to the ship. Ponderously, the thick plastic and alloy tube rolled across the landing grid toward our hatch. A pause while Farside's puter negotiated its mating with the shuttle's lock. A gentle bump, another, a click. The red light flashed. The tube stiffened slightly as it pressurized.

In a few moments the green airlock light flashed; the shuttle was mated. We crowded into the tiny lock while it cycled. Though shuttle and lock tube were both pressurized, as was Farside Base itself, as a matter of course the hatches were never opened simultaneously. Doing so would court disaster.

In the tube two rigid portholes, one on each side, offered a view of the unforgiving Lunar surface. It was a far cry from the manner I'd come to the base as a cadet. Fully suited, checked and rechecked by our instructors, we'd been released a few at a time from the shuttle locks and shepherded across the Lunar surface to one of the wide dome locks.

I noticed my weight increasing as I neared the inner lock. It took a lot of power to maintain near-Earth gravity in a Lunar installation, but that's what our atomic generators were for. Lightlife would hinder the cadets' training to an unacceptable degree; therefore the expensive, fusion-powered gravitrons buried below the base.

At Farside's inner lock Adam Tenere touched the pad; the hatch slid open. We gathered into the tiny chamber in silence, the few techs pressed against the bulkhead, the middy careful not to brush against me. The outer hatch closed. Because we were fully pressurized the inner hatch opened immediately.

I stepped forward while the others held back. Quite right. The Captain was always first to enter.

Several officers awaited us in the corridor. They saluted and came to attention; I released them. I said formally, "By order of the Board of Admiralty of the Government of the United Nations, I assume command of Farside Academy Base." There; that was out of the way.

"Aye aye, sir. Welcome aboard." An elegant, slim figure, graying. "First Lieutenant Jent Paulson reporting, sir."

Rightly, he didn't offer his hand, but I extended mine.

"You're senior?"

"Yes, sir, at the moment." That could change, but it was unlikely to. Admiralty tended to be sensitive to the niceties of hierarchy, where possible.

My gaze traveled to the next officer. "Lieutenant Darwin Sleak reporting, sir."

"Of course. Everything under control?"

Sleak was our systems officer, and I'd met him at Devon. He'd gone aloft two days earlier, to make sure all was ready for the returning cadets. Here on Farside, he was responsible for our life-support systems: recycling, gravitrons, air purification. Groundside, he did little more than supervise Quartermaster Serenco.

At Paulson's gesture a thin young woman stepped forward,

smiled pleasantly. "Lieutenant Ngu Bien, sir. Classroom programs and training."

"Very well."

Paulson beckoned to one of the remaining two figures, who stepped forward. "Lieutenant Ardwell Crossburn, sir. Maintenance and control systems."

I fought to keep the venom from my tone. "What are you doing here?"

The short, paunchy man in his early forties drew himself up. "I've been here some years, sir. Since our cruise in *Hibernia*, in fact."

I grunted, too disgusted to speak. Toward the end of my first fateful cruise, Ardwell Crossburn had been assigned to me as a replacement officer, by some Captain no doubt delighted to be rid of him. Crossburn had a conspiratorial turn of mind, and a habit of asking seemingly innocent questions that suggested he would in time uncover whatever misdeeds were being concealed. Worse, he claimed to have the ear of his uncle, Director of Fleet Ops Admiral Brentley.

"I trust you are well, sir?"

My glare caused him to drop back a pace. Paulson and Sleak exchanged glances, but of course said nothing. They couldn't know of the endless trouble Crossburn had caused on our long return voyage on *Hibernia*, until I'd cast all caution to the winds in dealing with him.

Lieutenant Paulson hesitated, cleared his throat, moved on to the last of the group. "First Midshipman Thomas Keene, sir."

"Very well." I nodded curtly, which was all the middy deserved or expected.

"Our other middies are with the cadets, except for Mr. Tenere, here. Obviously he was able to locate you."

"Yes. He ran into me in the Station corridor." Adam smiled weakly.

"Good. Normally we don't send a middy unescorted to Earthport Station, but Mr. Crossburn suggested it. Will there be anything else, sir?"

"Yes. Come to my office. You too, Mr. Sleak. Midshipman Keene, take my duffel to my cabin. The rest of you are dismissed." I turned on my heel.

It took me a moment to orient myself and set out for the Commandant's wing. My usual haunts had been far from the warren that held the Commandant's offices and apartment, though I'd been sent there on one memorable occasion. While Sleak trailed behind, Paulson matched my pace, wise enough to keep silent. Half the trick to being a good lieutenant was knowing when to leave the Captain alone. I wished Tolliver would take note.

Still seething, I stalked into my new office. The sergeant at the outer desk rose. A dark-skinned woman, somewhere around forty. She saluted. "Sergeant Kina Obutu reporting, sir."

"You're my staff?"

"Staff sergeant first, sir. I run your office during nominal day. At night we leave a middy in charge."

"Very well." Chairs lined the outer cabin, occasionally occupied by unfortunate cadets. I crossed to my new office, took a deep breath, flung open the hatch. Rather, I tried to. It was locked.

I spun around, feeling a fool. "What the devil?"

"He didn't leave it open?" Sergeant Obutu raised her eyebrow.

I shook my head. "Why would it be—where's the code?"

"The Commandant has it, sir." Paulson.

"I'm the Command—"

He said quickly, "I meant Commandant Kearsey. Sorry, sir."

Obutu asked, "Is there a copy in the safe?"

Mr. Sleak seemed embarrassed. "I'll check right away, sir. Excuse me."

"I'll look too, sir." Paulson hurried after him.

I nodded, too furious for words. I paced the outer office, ignoring the sergeant, who stood alongside her desk with a placid expression. I was working myself up to withering sarcasm when a thought intervened.

"Sarge, why is the hatch locked in the first place?"

"The Comm—Captain Kearsey always locked it at night, sir."

"Wrong question. Why does his hatch have a lock?"

"All our offices have them, sir." Her expression was carefully neutral.

I couldn't hide my amazement. "How long has this been going on?"

The outer hatch swung open. Lieutenant Sleak, followed by Paulson. He shook his head. "No code in the security safe, sir."

Obutu answered, "Since I came here, sir. Five years that I know of."

I glared at them both. "What else is locked around here?"

Sleak said, "The mess hall, I think. That's about—and the officers' apartments, of course."

"Of course?" No one responded. I snarled, "OF COURSE?"

The outer hatch opened. Tolliver saw the others, saluted. "Good aftern—"

"Tolliver, they lock the hatches here!"

He said only, "Good heavens."

Sergeant Obutu said helplessly, "Sorry, sir. I don't know what you're talking about."

Sleak ventured, "I'm class of '72, sir. I remember."

"We're trying to teach them to be officers! If we expect thieves in the night, that's what we'll get. These joeys are officer candidates, not transpop crewmen! What idiot ordered the locks put on?"

Sleak said evenly, "Commandant Kearsey, sir."

"Yes. Um." I rubbed my eyes. "It must have been the first day they told us. 'Nothing is locked at Academy. You will conduct yourselves as gentlemen. A gentleman doesn't take things from another's home, or sneak into places where he's not welcome.'"

"Second day," Tolliver said. "The first was haircuts and clothes and making beds, about twenty times."

"Whatever." I prodded the hatch. "Get this bloody lock off. Torch it if you must. Take the locks off Admin and the mess hall and wherever else you find them. Do the same groundside."

Sleak said, "Aye aye, sir." It was his responsibility, as systems officer. "Does that include the safes?"

"Not if there are weapons or cash or confidential papers. That's going too far."

"Yes, sir. I'll get right on it."

"My hatch first, damn it! I'll be in my cabin!" I stormed out.

I'd barely unpacked my duffel before Sergeant Obutu buzzed me on the caller. "Your office is, ah, accessible, sir."

"Is Paulson still there?"

"Waiting, sir."

"Very well, I'll be up."

Moments later I was back in the anteroom, restraining an urge to slick my hair and check the shine on my shoes. I took a deep breath, stepped through the threshold into my new office.

I crossed the room crowded with furniture, eased myself into the Commandant's leather seat, behind the Commandant's desk. No lightning bolt struck me. I willed myself to relax. "Shut the hatch. Sit." I pointed to a chair.

"Aye aye, sir." Lieutenant Paulson took a place near my desk.

"Why is that man Crossburn here?"

"I have no idea, sir. I presume he was assigned by BuPers." That meant nothing. Everyone's assignment came through BuPers.

"How much trouble has he made?"

"Trouble?" Paulson studied me curiously. "None that I know of, sir. He's a trifle odd in some respects, but he carries out his duties. He spends his spare time in his cabin, writing."

On *Hibernia* the lunatic had nearly caused a mutiny, interrogating officers and crew about the tragedies we'd suffered, writing his secret conclusions in a little black diary to show his uncle upon our return. When his inquiries had begun to imply I was an accomplice in the death of Captain Haag, I'd put a stop to it, consigning him to busywork in the ship's launch for the remainder of our cruise.

I drummed my fingers on the gleaming desktop. "Does he ask questions?"

"Pardon?" Paulson leaned forward. "Questions?"

"About the base. About incidents that have taken place."

He shrugged. "At times. He was most interested in the shuttle crash, two years ago. I believe he fancies himself something of a historian."

I snorted. "I can imagine. I want him out of here."

"Yes, sir. I believe you'd have to take that up with BuPers. I have no authority."

I growled, "I'm no cadet. Don't lecture me on procedures."

"No, sir. I'm sorry."

"That's all."

He rose, saluted, left me.

I sat, head in hands. This wouldn't do. I'd been on base a mere half an hour and already I'd alienated my first lieutenant. I stood to pace, thrusting aside a chair that blocked my path. I strode the few steps to the bulkhead, turned back, passed the desk, squeezed past the table. Finally I returned to my seat, took up the caller.

"Sarge, call BuPers at Lunapolis. Get me whoever's in charge of our staffing." Waiting, I turned to the console alongside my desk. I called up a menu, explored idly. Personnel records, paymaster reports, supply logs. I'd have to learn the system, but I knew virtually all our data would be accessible from this console.

I switched to cadet records, examined one at random. Everything was there, from original applications through ID photos, to the latest grades.

The speaker buzzed. "Seafort."

"Captain Higbee, BuPers. What can I do for you?"

"I have a lieutenant I want replaced, sir." Like most Captains on the Naval list, Higbee was my senior.

"For what reason?"

Wasn't a Captain free to choose his staff? I tried not to let my annoyance show. "We've, ah, had problems. His name is Crossburn."

"What has he done wrong?"

"Nothing at present," I said lamely.

"I see." A long pause. "Captain, perhaps you're unaware of the staffing problems we've—"

"The man is a time bomb. I want him off my base!"

"Yes, you've made that clear. I'm afraid I can't help you. All current assignments are frozen. Though I suppose if he'll volunteer for the fleet he'll be snapped up."

"Lord God, no. Keep him off a ship!" I pounded my forehead. What was I doing? I'd just muffed a chance to get rid of him. Still, I couldn't inflict Crossburn on a ship of the line. He could destroy morale in no time, and if his ship encountered the aliens . . .

"If he's so much trouble, court-martial him," said Higbee. "I'm afraid we can't help; we're not swapping officers until the emergency is over. Better at present to keep men in jobs they know. The order comes directly from Fleet Ops. Is there anything else?"

"I— No, sir."

"Very well, then."

"With your permission, I'd like to speak to Admiral Duhaney." It was insolent, but not as insolent as going behind his back.

A pause. When he responded his tone was cool. "As you wish, Commandant."

"Thank you." I rang off, stood to pace. Was I making too big an issue of Crossburn? Surely I could manage to live with him. I wondered if Farside Base had a ship's launch. Well, I could always have him polish the Hull, half buried in the Lunar dust Outside.

I blundered into a coffee table, barked my shin. Cursing, I retreated to the desk. "Sergeant Oba—Ob—Sarge!"

A moment later she was in the hatchway. "Obutu," she said calmly.

I nursed my leg. "See if we can reach Admiral Duhaney in Fleet Ops."

"Aye aye, sir." She turned to go.

"And have someone get this bloody furniture out of here!"

Her face was expressionless. "I beg your pardon, sir?"

"Out. The furniture. Have them take it." Now I sounded a complete idiot. I took a deep breath. "Leave my desk and chair. The console, of course. That leather chair near the desk can stay, and the couch against the bulkhead. I want everything else gone."

"Aye aye, sir. May I ask why?"

"So I can walk." A Captain needed to pace. Hadn't Commandant Kearsey ever trod a bridge? Good Lord.

"Very well, sir."

Normally the mess hall would be full of cadets at their long plank tables, poised to leap to their feet when the officers filed in. Now, during term break, fewer than two hundred were seated, and the meal was more informal.

The officers' table was round, like those in a ship's dining hall. It was the only round table in the room, perhaps to emphasize the difference between officers and cadets. Though we ate the same food as cadets, the officers' meals were served by stewards, whereas at each cadet table a designated server brought trays full of serving dishes from the line to their comrades.

Our steward passed salad and bread. When he left, Lieutenant Ngu Bien nudged Paulson. "There's the Chambers boy. Looks like they let him back in."

Paulson said, "I'm surprised he can walk so soon."

I raised an eyebrow.

"A fracas with two of his tablemates, sir. Just pushing and

shoving, until Cadet Chambers lost his head and poured a pitcher of milk over them."

"I see."

"Caned, of course. By the Commandant himself. He's been fed on the corridor deck outside mess hall for the last two weeks."

Appropriate. Cadets had to learn to conduct themselves like officers. Only in the privacy of the wardroom could middies release their natural tensions in horseplay. Certainly not in front of their betters. Though once, when Cadet Corporal Tolliver had pushed me too far . . . I pushed away the thought.

"You've kept our troublemakers aloft, then?"

"Leave was denied for the problem joeys, and the few others with no good place to go, sir."

"How are we keeping them busy?" Until the new term, classes wouldn't be in session.

Ms. Bien. "Bill Radz and I are taking them Outside this afternoon."

"The whole lot of them?" She nodded. Well, the discipline and exercise would do them good. I remembered my own tremulous first steps with magneboots, on the Hull.

"Would you like to come along, sir? We're giving some of them thrustersuits, and they've all heard about your jet into *Hibernia*'s lock."

I gagged on my coffee. The huge alien form had emerged from behind *Telstar*. Our sailors were helpless in the gig. The acid. *Fuse, Vax. Fuse the ship.*

"Are you all right, sir?"

In desperation I'd jetted my thrustersuit full bore toward *Hibernia*'s lock, tried to do a fliparound as Sarge had once shown us, waited a bit too long and crashed into the airlock with bone-jarring force. Still, I'd gotten there, and Vax Holser had instantly Fused.

"Of course I'm all right." I wiped coffee from my chin. Despite the later incident, the freedom of a T-suit was one of the few joys I remembered from cadet days.

I looked up. "Yes, I'd like to go along."

Two hours later, at the training lock, I was perspiring in my thrustersuit, trying to conceal my impatience. Suiting nearly a hundred frisky teens called for the patience of Job. The two officers assigned to the task were coping as well as could be expected. Even with the full cooperation of the eager cadets, it took time to recheck every clasp, every helmet seal.

"Stand still, Johns! Is there a spider in your suit?" Sergeant Radz gave her helmet a final twist.

Behind me, a youngster giggled. I snapped, "Be silent!"

"Aye aye, sir." A chastened tone.

"Cadet Drew always laughs, sir." Radz favored him with a withering frown. "I'm sure he and I will find something funny in barracks tonight."

The boy gulped. "I'm sorry, sir." He was almost as tall as Sarge, but his voice was barely broken.

I grunted, turned to the training lock. Though it was far larger than the VIP lock we'd used from the shuttle, the cadets' suits were bulky, and it had to cycle three times before we were all Outside.

The officers broadcast to the cadets on one frequency, using a second to communicate among themselves. Now, as an adult, I could appreciate the logistics necessary to maintain order.

While waiting for the last cadets to emerge from the lock I kicked at the Lunar dust. It spurted lazily and fell in slow motion, a foot away. I looked around with a twinge of guilt. When I was a cadet it would have brought me a rebuke, though I was never sure why. Lord God knew there was plenty of dust to kick.

"By twos, now." I jumped as my radio blared. "To the Hull. Maintain your distance." I hung back with Lieutenant Bien as the troop dutifully started forward. North of the lock stretched the familiar pockmarked terrain, unchanged since Farside Base was built and for eons before.

To the south sat the Hull, a life-size replica of a ship of the line, half buried in the Lunar surface, so that from stern to prow only the upper half of its length protruded.

A U.N.N.S. starship was shaped like a pencil with two or three foam rubber disks slid down to its midpoint and pressed together. Forward of the disks were cargo holds; aft were the lower engine room and fusion motors, tapering to the fusion drive shaft at the very stern. The disks held cabins, crew quarters, exercise rooms, and the hydroponics and recycling that sustained our lives.

Generations of cadets had clambered over the Hull, learning first the mere trick of walking, and later, how to carry tools and power packs they might need if sent Outside for repairs. At the end came the T-suit training.

All of today's group had mastered at least the art of walking, though many had an ungainly lope, and a few still carefully regulated the size and timing of their steps. But none crashed into the cadet ahead, or sprawled facedown in the dust.

At last the youngsters were assembled alongside the Hull. Lieutenant Bien organized most of them into squads, set them walking along the top of the Hull from one end to another. From time to time she varied the drill, sending one group into the drive shaft, another to the prow. The Hull had no jagged edges to rip their suits, but moving from one section to another, and over the disks, was tricky. Just edging past each other could be a problem for inexperienced cadets.

At the stern, Sergeant Radz had a few cadets making practice hops in jumpsuits. All in all, I appreciated the training more now than I had as a participant.

Radz keyed to my frequency. "Sir, would you be willing to demonstrate a jump?"

"Me?" I turned in astonishment. I was hardly an expert.

Like all sergeants everywhere, he was unafraid of rank. "Yes, sir, if you wouldn't mind. They'd listen far more closely than if I were demonstrating."

"No, I don't—" Wasn't that what I was here for, to train cadets? True, I hadn't anticipated doing it in such hands-on fashion. I sighed. "Where would you have me jump?"

"From the prow to the drive shaft, if you'd like?"

"Thanks a lot," I muttered. If I missed, I'd sail past the stern of the ship and look a complete fool. "I may not be good enough, Sarge." I tried a little jump, spread my legs as I settled down.

"Sure you are, sir. You passed training, didn't you?"

"Barely." He took my resigned nod for approval, and keyed his mike to gather the cadets. While they assembled alongside the stern I nervously gauged my distances.

Managing a thrustersuit on Luna wasn't quite so easy as on the Training Station aloft, or outside one of the eleven Training Fusers moored at its docks. Here at Farside, you had gravity to contend with. Not all that much, but enough. You had to use more propellant, and you couldn't merely aim for the point you wanted to reach. You had to aim beyond it, allow gravity to hold you back. And though gravity was far lower than on Earth, inertia was just as great. When I'd crashed into *Hibernia*'s lock I could have broken my legs, despite the zero gravity.

". . . in one hop, as the Commandant will now show you. Pay attention to his angle of ascent, and the point at which he squirts his thrusters to change course. You at the end, step back another ten meters." He waited until they'd complied. "When you're ready, sir."

"Very well." I keyed my mike to the general frequency. "Watch carefully. I only intend to do this once." If I could do it at all. I loped alongside the Hull in the peculiar floating gait appropriate to the Lunar surface until at last I was at the stern. Clutching my straps, I keyed the jets, felt the lift, and quickly switched them off. I sailed up onto the prow, almost overshooting it to fall down the port side. I snapped on my magnetronics, allowed my boots to grasp the Hull, stiffened my knees. I peered down the length of the Hull to the drive shaft, more than a hundred meters away.

What had I gotten myself into? I groaned, then realized with dismay that my radio was on the cadets' frequency. Cursing under my breath I switched channels.

Now or never. I estimated distance one last time, grasped the straps, keyed my jets.

I had no intention of going ballistic; what I wanted was to maintain a relatively steady height over the Hull. That meant varying the power in minute increments. I lifted, bent forward to angle the jets, tried to maintain the ideal balance between upward and forward motion. Below, the Hull drifted past.

More power, else I wouldn't have enough inertia to straighten myself and prepare for landing. Too much, damn it! Now I'd shot way above the Hull. I'd have to fire the head jets and I always hated burying my chin in my chest and firing blind. I was veering to starboard. Careful, you idiot. Keep your mind on your work.

"A touch to port, I think." A quiet voice in my ear. "Straighten your legs, sir. Tuck your chin in. Fire about . . . now. Good. Let go, orient yourself to land."

I had it under control. I twisted my body over, fired my backjets to slow myself, dropped slowly toward the Hull. Time to flip forward, fire a couple of squirts so I didn't land too hard. My feet touched. Done. I flicked off the jets.

They shouted their approval, until the outraged sergeant regained charge with a few crackling words. Nonchalantly I stepped off the Hull, relied on the jets to bring me down, and almost fell flat on my face. No one seemed to notice.

Legs trembling with delayed reaction, I watched Lieutenant Bien help Radz get the youngsters in thrustersuits ready for practice. First she lined them up on the Lunar surface parallel to the Hull. Sergeant Radz walked behind, showing the joeys how to bend to achieve forward motion.

"Now, it's just a simple hop onto the Hull. You've practiced forward motion before. The only difference is that when you come down you'll be a dozen meters higher than you started. Bronski, you're first."

A nervous young voice. "Yes, sir."

"Jump when you're ready."

The boy took a deep breath, launched himself. He didn't do badly, though he stumbled when he landed.

"Move aside a bit, and wait for Salette." He adjusted the next youngster's harness and stepped aside. I took the opportunity to touch helmets, my mike keyed off. "Thanks, Sarge."

"For the backseat driving? Sorry if I interfered, sir." He winked, turned back to his charges. "Edwards, are you ready?"

The boy's tone was tremulous. "I think so, sir."

"Up and away, then."

The cadet miscalculated his bend, launched himself straight up. A yelp of surprise.

"Easy, lad. Come down and try again. Taper off your jet."

"Yes, sir." Edwards turned his jet off entirely, drifted down slowly at first, then ever faster.

"Squirt! A short one!"

The boy complied, slowing his descent in the nick of time. He reached the ground, flipped off his jet. "I'm sorry, sir! I don't know how—"

A voice whispered, "You can do it, Dustin. Hang in there."

Sergeant Radz spun around, raising a tiny cloud of dust. "Who was that?"

Sheepishly, a boy stepped forward. "Me, sir. Kevin Arnweil."

"Two demerits, Arnweil! Maintain radio silence until you're spoken to!"

"Aye aye, sir!"

Radz shook his head. "Your buddy is right, Edwards. You can do it. Go join Bronski and Salette on the Hull."

"Aye aye, sir." The boy tensed, bent his knees. "I think—" Convulsively, he fired his jets. The propellant spewed; slowly he lifted, legs kicking wildly. He took too much height, but was smart enough to cut the jets and wait until gravity reclaimed him. He landed on the Hull, caught his balance. "I did it!"

"Of course you did." Radz adjusted the next cadet's harness. Cadet Arnweil grinned, waved approval to Edwards, but was careful to say nothing.

I smiled to myself. Only a twenty-foot leap, and both boys were exultant. Wait until we took them outside the Training Station.

"Very good, Edwards. You four, move astern a bit to make room. Drew, you're next. Then you, Arnweil." He adjusted Cadet Drew's harness.

"Sir, I don't think I'm ready—"

"Of course you are. You've jumped up and you've jumped forward. Now you're combining the two. Bend before you jet."

"I—aye aye, sir." The boy leaned forward, lost his balance.

"For God's sake, Drew! One demerit!"

"I'm sorry, sir!" The youngster stumbled to his feet. "I don't think I can—"

"Orient yourself first. You don't—"

The anxious boy clutched his harness, keyed his jets to full. He lifted off, legs kicking.

"Throttle down!"

The cadet bent forward toward the Hull, jets still set at full. He hurtled across the gap.

I shouted, "Cut your—"

"Look out!" Sarge waved violently at the boys on the Hull. One cadet ducked more slowly than the rest. Drew sailed into him at full power. Their helmets collided. A puff of vapor.

"DUSTIN!" A shriek of dismay, from below.

I launched, bent forward, sailed onto the Hull. I pulled Drew off Dustin Edwards's kicking form, scooped the downed cadet under my arm, snapped my jets to full and launched. Endless seconds passed while I jetted toward the distant airlock. Below me, a cadet loped toward the waiting lock in a stride that took him meters off the ground.

The form in my arms had gone still.

No time to land and walk into the lock. I sailed straight in, tucked my head down, fired retros, spun about, kicked the approaching bulkhead. In slow motion I fell to the ground. I staggered to my feet, slapped shut the hatch just as Sergeant Radz sailed past to join me.

As the hatch closed the boy who'd run to the lock dived through. Radz swore a blue streak without pausing for breath. The cadet who'd followed us pounded the bulkhead, shouting incoherently. I glanced at his helmet. Kevin Arnweil, who'd been demerited for calling encouragement to Edwards.

What in hell was the matter with the lock? Surely recycling couldn't take forever. I keyed my radio, yelled, "Emergency medical to the Training Lock, flank! Decompression!" I should have thought of it sooner.

Endless moments later the inner hatch opened. Arnweil tore off his helmet. Short-cropped black hair, the faint hint of a mustache, his eyes frantic.

No med techs. I gasped, "Sickbay?"

Radz grabbed Dustin Edwards's slack legs in one arm, pointed. Awkward in our suits, we dashed through the suiting room to the corridor beyond. Arnweil had the presence of mind to hold the hatches open.

The med techs met us halfway along the corridor, their crash cart skidding to a halt. Radz yanked Edwards off my shoulder, laid him flat, twisted off his helmet.

Blood oozed from the boy's mouth. His eyes—

Arnweil moaned.

The eyes would give me nightmares. A tech slapped an oxygen mask over the cadet's face, mercifully concealing them. The techs stripped off his suit, cut his shirt. The moment the paddles were secure, the techs fired. The boy's chest muscles convulsed. There was no other response. A tech straddled the inert cadet for CPR. Another whipped off the oxygen mask, fed a breathing tube down the boy's throat, switched on the respirator.

Arnweil whimpered incessantly. Radz, kneeling alongside Edwards, hissed, "Stop that noise!"

I stepped between the cadet and the still form on the deck. The boy darted around me, knelt at the body. "Dustin!" His voice was agonized.

Sergeant Radz watched the struggling techs, saw he could do

little to help, got to his feet. "Step away, Arnweil! Get hold of yourself."

"Let me stay with him!" Kevin clutched Dustin's inert hand.

Radz shook his head. "You're in the way."

"But—"

The Sergeant's voice hardened. "Obey orders, Cadet! Be a man! Stop that sniveling! Stand against the—"

"BELAY THAT!" Something in my voice gave him pause, as well it might. I cleared my aching throat.

"Sir, he—"

"Be silent!" Had I no sense? I was putting myself between a cadet and his Sergeant.

Kevin Arnweil, on his knees, leaned forward until his forehead touched his companion's still hand. He moaned. The sound pierced my suit, my soul.

He wailed again.

I knelt, threw my arm across his shoulder.

I closed my eyes. Not this, Lord.

It was the biggest game of the year, and tickets had been sold out for weeks. Lord God knew how Jason had gotten ours. For a time I'd been afraid Father would forbid my going, on account of some unfinished lesson, some chore not to his satisfaction. But at last, weak with relief, I found myself peddling down the road behind Jason's green jacket, lunch in my backpack, coins in my pocket.

We would see the Italians play the Welsh home team in the big game of 2190.

At the Cardiff stadium we locked our bikes, joined the crowds streaming toward the entrance. Lines of buses unloaded at the curb; men descended jabbering in fluid Italian. Other buses bore the logos of Manchester, East End London, Liverpool. Tough-looking joeys, who lived for football.

Jason stopped short with a look of alarm, patted his jacket pockets. "Christ, Nicky, I left the tickets home!"

"Don't blaspheme. I saw you tuck them in your shirt pocket."

His face lit in a grin. "Worth a try." His golden hair threw off sunshine. We passed through the turnstiles, found our seats in the upper bleachers.

"You got coin for drinks?"

I fished in my jacket. "Two bucks." I hauled out the crumpled unidollars.

"Now or later?"

"I don't care."

Jason shrugged, clasped his arms behind his head. "Let's wait." He studied the empty field. "New lines. Are you glad?"

"What do I care about lines?"

"No, you feeble snark. Glad that you're going."

I hesitated. "I guess. I'd feel better if they hadn't sent the first letter."

He peered across the field. "They need new benches."

"What about you? Are you glad?"

He lowered his hands to his lap, kicked at the bench ahead. A burly man tossed back an annoyed glance.

"What do you want me to say, Nicky?"

"The truth."

"Am I glad you're getting what you've always wanted? That you'll finally get to see the stars? Am I glad my best friend is about to leave while I get to take Engineering in Third?" His eyes flashed my way, spun back to the field.

"Oh, Jase. I wish you could come."

After a moment he shrugged. "That's life." His hand dropped for a moment to my leg. I tried not to stiffen. I reached to pry off his hand, instead clasped it for a moment in mine. It cost little to give him that.

"They're coming on!" I jumped to my feet as Archie Connelly lumbered out. Not the fastest man on the team, but it took a tank to stop him.

I waited impatiently through the anthems, and joined the roar of approval as the teams lined up for the kickoff.

"Nick? I'm glad for you. Really."

Reggie booted the ball past Connelly, shouldered aside an Italian guard. I reluctantly tore my gaze from the field. Jason's eyes glistened. "Thanks, Jase. I'll miss you."

"Four days."

"Aye." My bag was already packed; no change of clothes, we'd been told, no need even for a toothbrush. Just my favorite holochips, paper for writing to Father and Jason in case I couldn't get to a fax console. A few pictures.

Ten minutes into the game, the Italians scored. Reggie and

Archie seemed disconcerted by their opponents' sudden shifts. They played on, ignoring howls of glee from the Italian fans.

"How are you getting there?"

"To Academy? Father says by train."

"It's only an hour by plane."

"That's what I told him. He said there's no need to race through the air."

We surged to our feet as our right back intercepted the ball. He booted it to Couran in center after a lovely bit of footplay. I wasn't looking forward to a long subdued train ride with Father, who would discourage any excitement I displayed.

The period ended with the Italians ahead, 2 to 0. Jason slipped on his green jacket, ran up to the stand for our drinks. The crowd was so thick that halftime was nearly over when he returned. I unwrapped my sandwich, sipping at the softie Jason had brought.

He nudged me. "Try some of mine."

"I have plenty."

He thrust his cup at me. I took a sip, and gagged. "Jesus, where'd you get this?" I shoved it back into his hand.

"Don't blaspheme," he mimicked.

"Tell me!"

"Angus Terrie was up there."

I drank from my own cup. "You'll get us arrested!"

"Don't be such a droob." He took another swig of beer. "Have a little fun, Nicky. What's life for?" He waved the cup.

I hissed, "Put it down!" If he spilled it, some busybody might smell alcohol and call the jerries. I could get booted out of Academy before even reporting there. Sometimes Jason had no sense.

People brushed past to their seats. The players were taking the field. I finished my lunch, sipped nervously at my softie.

"I talked to Ma. She'd loan me coin for a ticket if I wanted to go."

I stared at him. "You mean, to Devon? With Father and me?"

"Would he let me come?" No need to ask whether I'd want him along.

The second half began. Could I convince Father? Though he didn't care for Jason, he knew I did. I'd have to pick my time, ask in just the right way. What a different trip it would be. I couldn't wait until the last minute to ask, though. I'd have to plant the idea ahead of time.

"Oh, no!"

The Italians had stolen the ball again, and were working it downfield. Reggie closed in on his man, who had the ball.

In a daring move Archie Connelly abandoned his own man and double-teamed the Italian. Their left forward raced over to help. In the confusion Archie and the Italian ball carrier bumped together. The Italian went down.

Whistles shrilled and the play stopped. On the field men were gesturing. The ref flashed a yellow card, indicated Archie.

"Violent charge?" Jason was indignant. "The Dago ran into him!"

The crowd didn't like it, either. Boos erupted through the stands, except in the Italian sections. The Eyties took a free kick, ran the ball to our back line, lost it. We blitzed through their defense, scored. Jeers and catcalls pelted the Italian team.

"Just twenty minutes left." Jason bit his lip. The Welsh had to come out on top to make the finals. A tie wouldn't do.

Ten minutes passed in inconclusive play. The crowd grew more fervent. Jason, thank heaven, had finished his beer. I stashed the incriminating cup between seats, where it could have been anyone's.

A hoarse yell from behind us. "Go on, Archie! Get the frazzin' Wops!" I frowned, but somehow Archie heard the call, and waved. Our bleachers responded with a mighty roar.

With a few minutes to go, Cardiff got the ball downfield. De Ville passed to Reggie, who lumbered in to kick a goal from twenty feet. We were tied.

They faced off for the throw. "I'll ask Father tonight, Jase."

"What if I just showed up on the train?"

I considered it. "I don't know." Father would know Jason's appearance was no accident, but what could he do? I could wander the train with Jason even without Father's permission. Rebellion surged in my breast. I didn't *always* have to do as Father said.

Four minutes. The roar was deafening. The Italians lost the

ball. They surged to the defense, but Archie Connelly shouldered aside all opposition. My throat was hoarse from yelling.

Abruptly Archie passed to Reggie, who just as quickly
passed it back. His path momentarily clear, Archie slammed
down a defenseman and aimed a great kick. The ball sailed
majestically into the corner of the goal. We'd won, with less
than a minute to go.

Jason and I danced on the benches, mad with excitement.
The burly man in front of us spun round and snarled, "Snuff it,
you twits! They disallowed the goal!"

"What?" But it was true. They'd not only voided the goal,
but red-carded Archie. On the field the Cardiff team surrounded the referee. He stood with arms crossed, shaking his
head.

"Fraz the Dagoes!" Across the field, joeys were chanting.
Others took it up.

"Kill the ref! Kill the ref!"

"Wow, gonna be a donny." Jason grinned with excitement.
"If Reggie doesn't watch it he'll get tossed too!"

"He'd better not." But matters were already past that. An
Eytie player took a swing at De Ville, who lashed back.

Roars of rage from the benches opposite. Italian spectators
swarmed across the field. They joined battle with Cardiff joes
from the lower bleachers, well below us. Jerries waded in
with their riot sticks, asserting control.

"Look!" Jason pointed to the next section of bleachers.

High in the next section, across the aisle, a couple of joey-
boys had pried loose one end of their bench and were rocking the other end to break it free. Spectators, half amused,
stood back to give them room. For a moment the bench held.
Abruptly it broke loose. One of the joes took up the bench,
swung it over his head as a shot-putter his shot. He spun
three times until, dizzy, he let go and fell back.

The bench hurtled down the stands, bowling over spectators like tenpins.

Enraged bystanders leaped over benches and bodies,
clawing their way upward to their attacker. Some fell or were
pulled down.

I grabbed Jason's wrist. "Let's get out of here!"

"The closest stairs are up top!"

"But—all right!" We pushed to the aisle, threaded our way

up toward the exit. Abruptly the riot leaped across the aisle like a blaze across a fire lane. Our section was full of shoving, screaming fans.

"Move, Nicky!" Jason pushed me.

Something lurched. Above us ten rows of seats suddenly disappeared.

As one, the crowd turned to the safety of the ground below. Men jumped down from bench to bench, heedless where they landed. The aisle was jammed to immobility.

Jason twisted to face downward, trying to squeeze through the mob. I hung on to his arm. The press lifted me off the ground, carried me ahead still clinging to Jason.

Our aisle ended at a rail separating the upper and lower stands. Squeezed against the rail, a woman fought with savage intensity to free herself. At her side a man braced himself against the throng. A moment later he went down. Then the woman. The crowd drove toward the safety of the field crushing those on the bottom into the rail or down to the concrete deck.

Jason's hand tightened. "Hang on, Nicky!"

I gripped his wrist. The crowd surged. An elbow jabbed at my side; my hand tore loose from Jason's. We parted. I clawed at the bodies between us. A man lashed out, caught me in the stomach. I doubled over, fell into a row of benches.

"JASON!!" A glimpse of golden ringlets. I clawed my way back to the aisle. Below us something gave way. The crowd lurched, arms and legs flailing. I slipped on something wet, managed to right myself.

"Jason, answer me!" The crowd swept me past the broken rail, catapulted me into the stands below. I landed on heads and arms, the breath knocked out of me. The joes I'd fallen onto threw me aside, cursing. I thumped onto concrete.

Someone stomped on my hand. I screamed, rolled under a bench. Shouts of anger and pain. A crash, and the crack of splintering wood.

Eons later, it began to subside. I lay half crushed by the broken bench. Voices. The pressure lifted. Light.

A jerry. "This one's alive. You all right, laddie?"

I began to cry.

They hauled me out. "Anything broken?" Below, jerries carried bodies on stretchers to the grassy field.

I fell onto a nearby bench. "I don't think so." I looked

around. "Where is he?" Most of the crowd had disappeared. Injured huddled together as if seeking solace. Some were bandaged, others were bleeding, many in shock.

"Who, lad?" A jerry, riotstick tucked in his belt.

"Jason."

He shrugged. "He's probably out by now. If you want, look on the field. The ambulances are outside, hauling the wounded to hospital." He patted my shoulder. "Can't stay, boy. There are others." He turned away.

My ribs ached. I gritted my teeth, made my way to the aisle, shut my eyes. If Jason was here, I didn't want to see him. I steeled myself, opened my eyes a crack. Nothing. Reddish brown stains on the cement steps, trampled coats and shoes strewn about. Not, praise God, a green jacket.

I made my way out of the stadium. Hundreds of injured sat or lay on the curbs. An ambulance landed; techs jumped out with stretchers. I walked down the line of wounded, searching. Jason wasn't there. He'd be waiting with the bikes. I trudged across the concrete lot. Our bicycles sat locked, untended.

No point in going back to the grisly field. I thrust my hands in my pockets, lowered my head, stared at nothing.

Reluctant steps pulled me back to the stadium entrance. Just so I'd know he was in hospital. Nurses could be so severe, and if there was a mixup they'd argue with me. Better to say I knew that's where he had to be waiting. I followed the signs to the lower boxes, walked unhindered across the new-chalked playing field. A jerry intercepted me. "What are you doing, lad?"

"I'm—" My tongue was thick. "I'm looking for someone."

"Don't touch anything." I nodded, and he let me be. I hugged myself as I reached the first row. They'd left most of the faces uncovered. A woman stared up at me, eyes bulging, one side of her head crushed. I turned, took two steps, vomited my lunch onto the field, wiped my mouth, stomach still churning.

Jason, you won't believe what I went through today. Searching through all those bodies, afraid you'd be among them. What is it, your leg? You'll be walking in a week, don't give me that. Lord Christ, you gave me a scare.

Some bodies were covered entirely. I knew from the size that Jason couldn't be under the blanket. A baby, a small child. I fought not to retch again. Another body, covered with a carelessly thrown blanket. I hurried past, stopped.

No, it was someone else. The sleeve sticking out from the blanket was mostly brown. Only parts of it were green. That's not you. With baby steps I inched toward the blanket. Tentatively I reached to the top, pulled it down. It wasn't Jason's face. I sobbed with relief.

It wasn't anyone's face. Just a mass of congealed blood, above a green and brown collar. I pulled the blanket away, exposing the rest of the body.

Any boy could have been wearing brown slacks, those jumpboots.

Any boy could have had golden curls. Any boy could have been wearing that green jacket, mottled with blood from the mangled chest.

Any boy.

I bent almost double, took the hand, pressed it to my side. From deep inside, I made a sound.

They found me there, hours later, in the dark.

The med techs exchanged glances. One shook his head. Kevin Arnweil's fingers brushed the tunic of his still friend. I caught him as he sagged, pressed his locks against my chest. He wept in silence. Sergeant Radz looked on with disapproval.

The corridor was filling with subdued cadets, restrained by the quiet commands of Lieutenant Bien. Kyle Drew, whose jump had caused the accident, was white with shock.

I said, "Send them to barracks, Lieutenant."

"Aye aye, sir. Arnweil also?"

"Let him stay."

A young middy hurried down the corridor, reached me and stopped. "Midshipman Keene reporting, sir. Sarge says to tell you Admiral Duhaney is returning your call."

"Who? Oh. Very well, I'll—" Arnweil sobbed. I took a deep breath. "Tell him I'm busy. I'll call later."

The midshipman stared in amazement, caught himself. "Aye aye, sir." He scurried off.

Chapter 5

I paced my office, cursing my imprudence. One didn't spurn the Admiral in charge of Fleet Ops, if one ever again wanted his favor. Cadet Arnweil could have waited. Besides, it was Sergeant Radz's role to console him, not mine.

My caller buzzed. Ms. Obutu. "Do you have time for Mr. Radz, sir?"

"Very well. Send him in."

He saluted, came to attention. I nodded to release him, bade him sit.

"Sir, I'd like a transfer groundside. Out of Academy."

"Because I overruled you in the corridor? Don't be silly."

"No, sir." His eyes were pained. "I failed Cadet Edwards. And Kyle Drew will go through life remembering he killed a boy because I didn't do my job."

"It was an accident."

"Yes, sir. My job is to prevent accidents, especially stupid ones."

"It wasn't your fault, Sarge. It was a fluke."

He shook his head stubbornly. "You can say that about any accident. Drew wasn't ready; he even told me so. He made one clumsy jump, and I forced him into another."

I stood to pace. "What do you want me to do?"

"Send me somewhere else, sir. Get a competent instructor."

"No." I held his eye until he turned away, defeated. "That's all."

He had no choice. "Aye aye, sir." He stood to go.

The man needed absolution. I thought quickly. "I want a report on all training accidents in the past five years, and your recommendations on improving safety. No deadline, take a couple of weeks if you need to. And one other thing."

"Yes, sir?"

"It's too late for the Edwards boy. But you have two walking wounded on your hands. Kyle Drew, and Arnweil. Nurse them back to health."

His brow wrinkled. "How, sir?"

"I don't know; that's what you're here for. Drew must be sick with guilt, and Arnweil is crushed. They need you." My tone sharpened. "You weren't responsible for the boy's death, but your conduct after was a disgrace. Arnweil and Edwards must have been close."

"They enlisted together. Kevin has to learn that soldiers die, sometimes to no purpose." Unbidden, he sat again, rubbed his hands over his face. "But he's still a child, you're right about that. I expected too much of him."

I was silent. Eventually he looked up. "We don't want to be nursemaids either."

I said, "Find a balance."

"Aye aye, sir. I'll try." He left.

Late in the evening I sighed, flipped off the console. Farside statistics swam in my head. Cadet days in residence. Number of beds. Consumables per cadet. Instructor-student ratios. Charts they'd sent me before I'd assumed my post, and as meaningless now as before.

I stretched, turned down the lights, shut the hatch behind me. In the outer office the midshipman came to his feet. Small, narrow-boned, a serious face. "You're here all night, Middy?"

"Mr. Tenere relieves me at twelve, sir."

"Very well." I peered past him to the console. "What's that?"

He blushed. "Advanced Nav, sir. It's easier to read here than in my holovid."

Aboard ship a middy never stood watch alone, and on the bridge he wouldn't dare study anything but his instruments. But the caller was the only instrument this lad had to watch. "Very well—who are you?"

He snapped to attention. "Midshipman Tommy Tsai reporting, sir!" A glint of worry, lest I be annoyed he hadn't identified himself.

"Very well, Mr. Tsai. I'll be walking about. Call on the general circuit if you need me." I left.

As on any Lunar installation, the domes and warrens of Farside were connected by a maze of corridors. All had safety hatches that would slam shut in case of decompression. The larger compartments, such as mess hall and the physical training rooms, were in the domes above, at surface level.

My office was near the end of the north warren, connected by corridor to the VIP lock and the classroom chambers to the south. Other passageways branched to the dorm warrens. Below us, on Level 2, were our atomics, gravitrons, recycling, and the other machinery that allowed the base to function. And, of course, housing for the techs who serviced it all.

Hands clasped behind my back, I wandered through the maze of corridors to the classrooms I remembered from my youth. Naturally, they'd be empty at this hour; the cadets would be back in their dorms, enjoying what little free time they were given before Lights Out.

". . . wonder why they wouldn't give him a ship."

I stopped. Low voices, inside a hatchway, chatting amiably. "Maybe he didn't want one."

"Adam, who'd pass up a ship of his own?"

I poked my head into the classroom. A gaggle of middies. Two lounged against a bulkhead. The third was perched on a desk, legs dangling. Seeing me, they jumped to attention.

"As you were," I said quickly. "What's going on?"

One of them spoke. "Nothing, sir. Just talking."

I gestured to the empty classroom. "Why here?"

The oldest middy shrugged. "Why not, sir? It's just where we happened to stop."

My fist tightened. When I'd been a cadet, we weren't allowed to wander the base at will, unsupervised. What was the place coming to?

"Does your Serg—" I swallowed my angry reply. These were middies, not cadets, and off-duty. As aboard ship, they were free to go where they chose. "Sorry. Quite right. You're, ah, Keene?"

"Yes, sir. First Midshipman Thomas Keene, sir. I'm sorry if we disturbed—"

"No, I forgot. You see, I never served as a middy at Academy." Few cadets were chosen to stay on as midshipmen. I'd been posted to U.N.S. *Helsinki,* where—I bit off the thought.

Keene seemed uncomfortable. I wondered if he'd ever heard a Captain apologize. Unlikely. I turned to the other middies. "Mr. Tenere I remember. And you?"

"Midshipman Guthrie Smith, sir." Lean, ears that stuck out, a tentative manner.

"Oh, yes. Very well, carry on."

Adam Tenere blurted, "Is there something we can help you with, sir?"

I turned. "What?"

"I'm sorry, I didn't mean that the way it—are you looking for something, sir?" I stared. He reddened. "Pardon me, it's none of my business. I'm sorry if I—"

"That's enough, Adam." Keene's voice was civil but urgent.

"I mean—aye aye, Mr. Keene." Like any middy, he called his senior by his last name.

I raised my eyebrow, annoyed at the youngster's effrontery. "Do continue, Mr. Tenere."

"Yes, sir. I mean, aye aye. No offense, please, sir. I just thought, if there was someplace you were trying to find—I thought perhaps we could . . ." Flustered, he took a deep breath. "Please excuse me, Captain Seafort." I said nothing. He squirmed, added desperately, "It being your first day here, was all I meant. I didn't know if you remembered . . . Of course you would, though. I wasn't thinking, I meant no dis . . ."

I turned to Keene. "Is he always like this?"

The first midshipman's tone was icy. "No, sir. Only when it's important he not be." Now Tenere was in for trouble. A middy was supposed to be seen and not heard, and it was the first midshipman's job to keep his juniors in line. Once, on *Hibernia,* a lieutenant had caught the younger middies frolicking in the corridor, and it was I, the senior, who'd paid the price.

Perhaps Keene had similar thoughts. "I apologize, sir. He won't trouble you further."

Adam studied the deck, miserable. Well, a couple of extra demerits wouldn't hurt him, though he'd already earned four when he'd cannoned into me in Earthport Station. Ten uncancelled demerits meant the First Lieutenant's barrel.

"Very well." One way or another, Tenere would learn to be less clumsy, both physically and verbally. Yet, the boy had meant only to offer help. I sighed, relenting. How to divert Keene without interfering with his prerogatives?

"Actually, Mr. Keene, I was looking for someone to walk with. It's been years since I've been on Farside. Would you gentlemen care to accompany me?" It would cost me my privacy, but I could think of no better way.

"Of course, sir." There was nothing else to say. An invitation from a Captain was as a command.

"This is the simulator room, sir." Guthrie Smith.

"Ah, yes." The equipment was brand-new. There hadn't even been such an installation when I was a cadet; I remembered the compartment as just another study room. Now it was used to simulate battle with the fish, using puter re-creations from *Hibernia* and other vessels lucky enough to have encountered the aliens and survived. I moved on.

"The nav room, sir."

In this classroom I'd been introduced to Lambert and Greeley's *Elements of Astronavigation*. At the time I'd thought that with hard work I could master Nav. Now I knew better.

I asked, "What was your best subject, Mr. Keene?"

"Engineering, sir. This year I asked Mr. Vriese to tutor me on the new fastship drive."

"Is he still here?" He'd seemed ancient twelve years ago. He must have been at least fifty. I smiled at my innocence. "And you, Mr. Tenere?"

Wisely, the boy had said as little as possible during our stroll. Faced with a direct question, he had no choice but to respond.

"Nav and pilotage, sir."

I had to draw him out, to show there were no hard feelings. "Were you good at it?"

He looked down. "First in my class, sir."

"You were?" I couldn't keep the surprise from my voice.

"Yes, sir." His tone was bitter. "I'm not always incompetent, sir. Though you'd have no way of knowing that."

"That's quite enough, Mr. Ten—"

"No, Mr. Keene. He's feeling badly. We had, um, a run-in yesterday." My shoulder was still sore from it.

We left the classroom warrens. "What's down there?"

"The ladder to belowdecks, sir. The gravitrons, and engineering. Off-limits to us." Adam looked hopeful.

I saw no reason to take them below. I'd only been there once myself, on a failed mission with Midshipman Jeffrey Thorne. "And that way?"

"The service corridor, sir. It goes to mess hall." They led me down the deserted corridor, used by sailors to wheel cleaning machines and other heavy equipment to the domes.

"This way's longer, but it's faster if you're late to class," Adam Tenere confided. "No cadets allowed." I imagined an anxious midshipman sprinting to class along the service corridor to avoid the displeasure of his instructor. Running in the main corridors, on the other hand, was strictly prohibited.

"Here's the mess hall, sir. The cadets enter from the far side."

"Yes, I remember." We continued toward the barracks, passing an emergency hatch, open now, but ready to slam shut at decompression. "The barracks are to the right, I recall."

"Yes, sir." In a few moments the warren widened.

I chose a dorm at random. "Let's look in."

As the hatch slid open Keene bellowed "Attention!" Cadets leaped from their bunks to form a straight line along the aisle.

I'd thought the barracks would be unoccupied, during term break. "As you were. Carry on." I smiled. "This isn't an inspection." Keene shot me a dubious look, said nothing. I understood his confusion; a Commandant was explaining himself to mere cadets. I knew I'd appear even more ridiculous poking my head in and disappearing immediately. I strode down the rows of beds. I paused.

A duffel lay atop an empty bunk. The bed had been stripped and remade without sheets. I asked the girl in the next bunk, "Edwards?"

"Yessir."

The duffel would remain overnight. In the morning the cadets would gather round, open the duffel, go through the meager belongings. Close friends would help themselves to mementos, and the duffel would be repacked for shipment home. It was the Navy way.

I looked around. "Where's Mr. Arnweil?"

Another boy spoke up. "With Sergeant Radz, sir."

"Very well. Come along, gentlemen." We left.

Keene said, "Edwards seemed a decent joey."

I was brusque. "I didn't know him."

"Would you like to stop at Krane Barracks?"

"Why?" One barracks was like another.

"You stayed there, sir."

I raised an eyebrow. "Is there a bronze plaque on the head I used?"

"I beg your pardon?"

"Nothing." I shook my head, disgusted. Somehow I'd have to put a stop to it. "We have, let's see, sixteen barracks?"

"Twenty now," Tenere blurted.

Of course. I'd read that, somewhere. "Not all in use."

"Not until the plebes come aloft, sir."

Thirty cadets to a dorm. Housing for six hundred cadets at a time. The Training Station could take another fifty. Terrestrial Academy at Devon had barracks for another three hundred eighty. Some overcapacity was necessary; otherwise no cadet could be transferred without another cadet being shipped out. I shook my head. Logistics.

I let them tour me through the exercise dome, then down the ladder to the service level. I stopped. Enough for one day. "Thank you, gentlemen. That will be all."

"Aye aye, sir."

I hesitated. "Mr. Tenere, I'll have a word with Mr. Keene."

"Yes, sir? I mean, aye aye, sir."

"Alone," I prompted.

"Aye aye, sir!" Red-faced, he saluted and hurried away.

"Sir, I'm sorry about—"

"I was first middy, once. On *Hibernia*."

"Yes, sir." Keene waited, puzzled.

"It isn't an easy job. You might think, for example, that I'd want you to go hard on Tenere."

"He's—Of course I'd—I'll do whatever you want, sir."

"Will you? Good, then. Do as you'd have done if we'd never met this evening." I smiled pleasantly. "Sometimes, Mr. Keene, problems work themselves out on their own."

"Aye aye, sir." He smiled back quizzically.

"That's all."

I found my way back to my apartment. I was undressing when the caller buzzed. "Sorry, sir." Tolliver. "Just a reminder. Senator Boland's boy will be reporting to Devon in two days."

"What of it?"

"Don't you want to be there, just in case?"

"In case what, Edgar?" I tossed my shirt on the chair.

"His father will most likely drop him off. He's on the Naval Affairs Committee, you know." Of course I knew. If Boland hadn't talked me out of it I'd have carried through with my resignation, after *Victoria* brought me home.

"Tolliver, the Boland boy's a cadet like any other. Anyway, we're going groundside tomorrow night, after I talk over the budget with Admiralty."

"Very well, sir. Sorry if I woke you."

I growled a reply, rang off. If Tolliver thought I could be a politician, he was mistaken. I drifted to sleep.

Once again, I waited in the crowded anteroom of Admiral Duhaney's Lunapolis office. The last time I'd been there, months before, I'd been ragged from the long hostile voyage in *Victoria,* and barely recovered from my lung implant. I'd stalked out of the Admiral's office in a rage, expecting court-martial and not giving a damn. Instead, they'd chosen to reward me with Academy.

When the bored lieutenant called my name I passed through the hatch, saluted, came to attention with the same discipline I'd require of my cadets.

"Hello, Seafort." Duhaney came to me, hand extended. I took it as permission to stand easy. He beckoned to a chair. "Sorry my call missed you yesterday." Was it a reproach? It didn't seem so.

"I apologize, sir. We had an accident. A cadet died."

He pursed his lips, shook his head. Still, I knew he'd received too many reports of death to be shocked by one more. As Sergeant Radz had said, soldiers die, especially in wartime. "Why did you want to see me, Commandant?"

I couldn't bring up the issue of Lieutenant Crossburn; Dustin Edwards's death made that issue seem too trivial. I would cope. "I had some questions about the budget."

"I can't get you any more money, Seafort. Don't even ask. We're strained tight."

"No, sir, I understand that. I wasn't asking."

He stared at me suspiciously. "I've heard that before. I tell you, no special appropriations!"

Despite myself, I smiled. "Orders acknowledged and understood, sir. If I'd wanted more money I'd say so."

"Well, then?"

I fished in my pocket for a chipcase, opened it. "May I?" I slipped the chip into his holovid. "These expense columns, sir. Why do they say 'guidelines'?"

He frowned. "Didn't Kearsey go over any of this with you?"

"He gave me the budget to study. That's all."

"Don't worry about it. The number that counts is that bottom line." He stabbed at the expense totals.

"But this column, sir, that details the food expense per cadet, the uniform cost—"

He waved them away. "They don't mean anything, Seafort. How often do I have to tell you?"

I spoke coolly. "That depends, sir."

"On what?"

"On whether you want me as Commandant."

He glared at me. "Don't start that again. I have too many prima donnas as it is." I held his eye; he sighed. "Very well, what don't you understand?"

"How do I find out how much we're spending on food per cadet? I won't know until we exceed our budget."

"You have a quartermaster to keep it straight, Seafort. Let him do his job. All you need be concerned with is that you have two point six million unidollars to spend. How you allocate them is your own business."

I shook my head. "But the uniforms per cadet, training allocation per cadet—"

"You have some seven hundred sixty joeys, right? We try to break costs down per cadet, because the Senate committee likes it that way. That's the only reason the columns are there."

"But—" My head spun. "When we go to the Naval Affairs Committee, don't we have to assure them—"

"Yes, we tell them how much we intend to spend, and on what. But the Security Council knows better than to tie us to our line estimates. Spend your allocation for the good of your cadets. Don't forget to reserve for structural repairs. Look, Seafort, it all comes down to seven hundred sixty cadets. For years we've run the number through a simple formula to pull out the guidelines. You don't have to follow them. In theory, you don't even have to account for the number of cadets."

"Huh? What about Final Cull?"

"Oh, the Selection Board presents your candidates, you have no choice about that. But they only go by—" The caller buzzed; he picked it up. "Duhaney. He what? Are you sure?" He listened. "The son of a bitch! Yes, I'll be down. This afternoon. Potomac Shuttleport. Set up a meeting." He keyed the caller.

"Bill, cancel this afternoon. Get me a seat on the Potomac. Bump someone if you have to."

He slammed down the caller. "We had a deal with Naval Affairs, and Senator Wyvern is jumping ship. Now he wants our promise the hull components will come from North American foundries. We've already promised them to—look, Seafort, I've got to clear my calendar and be out of here in less than an hour. Let me know if you run into a problem." He popped my chip from the holovid, handed it to me.

"But—"

"Thanks for coming. Get out of my hair, will you? If we lose the replacement fleet, we won't need your cadets."

He had a point. "Yes, sir." I paused at the hatch. "That memo I wrote about the caterwauling bomb, sir. Are you going—"

"We have a team studying it. It's more complex than you think." He opened his drawer, fished for a chipcase, thrust it in his pocket.

"Sir, it's too important to—"

"Damn it, man, you want us to take a puter-operated drone, send it somewhere and let it generate skewed N-waves, or caterwaul, as you call it. Not too close to home, because it will call every fish within hearing. But we've never sent a successful drone out before, not one with a fusion drive. Anyway, the drive is inherently inaccurate by one percent, so we won't even be quite sure where we're sending it."

He took a leather case, stuffed papers within. "Say it caterwauls until it attracts fish. How many fish is enough? How close would they come?"

I said, "It doesn't matter if a bomb doesn't get every last—"

"Let me finish, I have to catch the shuttle. At some point the bomb goes off, unless the fish destroy it first. Well, when it goes boom, how can we be sure it got all the fish? Could any surviving fish follow its trail back to us? And most important, if this caterwauling calls fish, how can we send a ship into a sector swarming with fish to find out if the bloody thing works, without risking the ship? If the fish didn't get our ship the bomb would."

He paused, waved me to the hatch. "The idea has merit, Seafort, but we need to iron out the bugs." He snatched up the caller. "Karl? Make sure Boland is told about this afternoon's meeting."

I retrieved my duffel from the anteroom, trudged along the busy corridor toward Old Lunapolis, absentmindedly returning salutes while I pondered Duhaney's comments about my budget. Running Academy wasn't quite like commanding a ship; I couldn't execute a felon, for example. But in other respects the Navy allowed me to act as autocratically as any shipboard Captain. Here are your tools: accomplish the job. Don't bother us with details.

I checked in with Naval Transport, learned the next shuttle was full. Three hours to kill, until I could connect through Earthport Station to London. I should have hitched a ride with Duhaney. Well, he'd left me ample time for a meal here in the Lunapolis warrens, where I had a better choice of restaurants and the prices were lower than on the Station.

I dined alone, unaccustomed to the solitude. Though several of my officers had gone groundside for start of term, none of them had detoured with me to Lunapolis.

After dinner I boarded the London shuttle. Most of the other passengers were civilians, a few Navy. There were also U.N.A.F. personnel, but we pointedly ignored each other. The Armed Forces were another service, and we had little in common.

To my discomfort, the Pilot unstrapped and came back into the cabin, stopping at my seat. "Captain Seafort? My name is Stanner. I'll be flying you down tonight." He offered his hand. Resignedly, I took it, muttered some polite phrase.

"It's an honor to meet you." He hesitated, turned back to the cockpit. "If there's anything we can do for you . . ."

Just take me home. "No thank you, Mr. Stanner."

"Very well, then." Again he hesitated. "The copilot's seat is empty tonight. Would you care to ride up front?"

What I wanted was to be left alone. On the other hand, I'd had one experience piloting a shuttle, a wild ride with Lieutenant Tolliver across Hope Nation's Farreach Ocean. It might be interesting to watch an expert handle the craft.

Ignoring the envy of the U.N.A.F. officers, I got to my feet. "Well, if you don't mind . . ."

"Of course not." He ushered me to the cockpit. I suspected it wasn't really me he wanted sitting alongside him, but my damned notoriety. Now he'd be able to say he'd flown with

Nicholas Seafort as his copilot. I couldn't avoid that sort of thing unless I chose to become a hermit.

I strapped in. Once the cockpit hatch slid shut the Pilot gave the checklist his full attention. I wondered if my presence had anything to do with that; flying the shuttle must be second nature to him.

"Steward, confirm shuttle hatch closed, please." He wouldn't rely on the blinking light on his console. Quite right. Consoles and puters could be wrong.

"Shuttle hatch is secured, Mr. Stanner."

"Departure Control, London Shuttle Victor three four oh ready for breakaway, requesting clearance."

The speaker crackled. "Just a moment, Pilot." Several minutes passed before flight control came back on the line. "London Shuttle Victor three four oh, you're cleared for breakaway. Have a pleasant flight."

"Thank you." Stanner's hand settled over the thrusters. The shuttle's maneuvering engines, like most craft, used hydrozine as propellant.

With a deft hand the Pilot squirted first his forward thrusters, then the thrusters abaft, rocking us ever so gently until the airlock seals parted. Once we drifted free of the Station he maneuvered us to a safe distance, ignited the main engines. The hull throbbed with muted power.

I tore my eye from the receding Station to focus on Earth, looming in the starboard viewscreens. We didn't appear to be heading toward Terra, but of course we were. If the shuttle dived headfirst into the atmosphere we'd go incandescent. Instead, we'd enter at an angle, almost parallel with the planet's surface.

The Pilot flipped switches on his console, watching his display closely. As the readout counted to zero he cut the power. The engines went silent.

His work done for the moment, Stanner relaxed. "You're headed to groundside Academy, Captain?"

"Yes." It seemed too bald a statement. "My new cadets report tomorrow."

"A busy time for you, then."

"I suppose." I had no idea what was expected of me. Perhaps the sergeants knew.

He punched in numbers, erased the screen, ran more calculations. "Twenty-five minutes. If you'd like coffee we can—"

"London Shuttle, respond to Departure Control."

The pilot keyed his mike. "London Shuttle."

"This is a scramble. Repeat, a scramble." The voice was edged with tension. "Steepen your glide path for immediate entry. You'll be out of position for London; divert to New York Von Walthers, or Potomac Shuttleport."

The Pilot swallowed once, but his voice was calm. "London Shuttle commencing dive." He flipped switches, reignited our engines. He glanced to me, back to the console. "Something's up."

"Obviously." I reached for the caller, remembered that this was his craft. "Can you get Naval frequencies?"

"General comm, but not the restricted channels. Go ahead."

I keyed the caller. Voices flooded the speaker.

"—have a visual on him at four thousand kilometers. We're on him."

"Understood, *Charleston*. You and *Tripoli* are the closest."

"Tell the Admiral we have radio contact with *Tripoli*."

A crisp voice. "This is Admiral Le Tour, acting as ComCinc-Luna. I'm on the circuit, Captain Briggs. Are you absolutely sure?"

"The puter's on full magnification, sir. He's just sitting there, plain as life. A fish, just like the training holos."

My grip tightened on the console. Lord God, no.

"Just one?"

Briggs' laugh was harsh. "At the moment, sir."

Stanner said, "Stay strapped in tight, Captain. We'll get some buffeting."

I checked my belts. They couldn't go any tighter. "Just drive us home, Pilot."

"We'll probably lose radio contact for a few minutes. That's natural when we're diving into the atmosphere."

"I'm not a groundsider." My tone was sharp.

"I know, sir."

"Sorry. Nerves." Fish, in home system? Queasy, I swallowed several times.

"ComCincLuna to all ships. Execute Maneuver C. *Argentine* and *Brunswick*, hold your current positions. I'll join you with the squadron covering Earthport Station. If I'm disabled, Captain Lusanski in *Waterloo* is senior."

A whispering, outside the hull.

"Report all sightings directly to—" Static. *"Confirm your positions every five minutes."*

"Aye aye, si—" Static. A muted roar, transmitted through the hull.

"Attention all ships, *Tripoli* reports a second sighting, coordi—" The shuttle bucked. Stanner kept our nose down, used the jets to position us.

"Until we have confi—" The speaker cut out.

Stanner's voice was taut. "We've lost them for a while. Hang on."

"Can we make it?"

His jaws tightened. "Oh, we'll make it, one way or the other. I forgot to buy insurance." He took quick breaths. "Another ten thousand feet and I'll spread the wings. That'll help some."

"Whatever you say." My one attempt at the controls of a shuttle had been suborbital.

"Potomac Shuttleport, do you read London Shuttle Victor three four oh?" No answer. He shook his head.

"Are they hit?" My voice was unsteady.

"Hit? It's the static buildup. We'll have to wait to get through."

I felt a complete idiot. "Yes. Of course."

"Try every minute or so. My attention's on the readouts."

"Right." It would give me something to do.

To my infinite relief they answered my fourth call. "London Shuttle, this is Potomac Shuttleport, we read you."

Stanner keyed his caller. "We've had a scramble, Potomac. I will be approaching from the Southwest at forty thousand feet. Can you take us?"

I held my breath, but the answer was nonchalant. "No problem, London Shuttle. Earthport alerted us an hour ago. All outgoing traffic has been grounded. Come on in."

Had it been that long? I gripped the dash while Stanner took his approach coordinates, then cursed under my breath. If we could hear Approach Control, we could hear Admiralty as well. I switched from speaker to earphones, keyed the caller.

"— no, sir. I'm sure. So's the puter. No encroachments except *Tripoli*."

"Where the hell did he go, *Charleston*?"

A pause from *Charleston*. "I couldn't say, sir."

"Right. Um, sorry."

Another pause. "ComcincLuna to all ships. Current status: one sighting confirmed, coordinates thirty-four, one eighty-seven, two hundred. The alien apparently Fused to safety. Current whereabouts unknown. Second sighting is unconfirmed, may be an anomaly."

I snorted. The "anomaly" was probably an overexcited young officer, now shriveling under his Captain's extreme disfavor.

A scream of protesting air, as Stanner eased the wings back into flight mode. The buffeting slackened. He asked, "What's it all mean, Captain?"

I waved him silent, strained to hear voices through the static. Every ship of the squadron had gone to Battle Stations, waiting for further sightings. None came. At last I sighed, keyed off the caller.

Stanner began a long, slow swing to port. He said nothing.

Coloring, I realized I'd snubbed the man in his own cockpit. "Sorry, Mr. Stanner, I was listening. It seems there was just the one fish; the second was a false sighting."

"Are they planning an attack? This is the first time they've shown up in Home System."

The second. The one I'd speared with *Challenger* was the first. "Too early to tell. It could be a fluke, or some kind of scout. In Hope Nation . . ."

"Yes?"

At Hope Nation the fleet had stood by for days, sometimes weeks, between sightings. "There's no way to tell."

For a moment Stanner's attention was on the shuttle's long turn. Then, "Captain, I have a wife and kids. Are they safer in Lunapolis or at home?"

"I haven't the faintest idea." After a moment I tried to make amends for my tone. "No one knows, Pilot. On the one hand, Lunapolis is a smaller target. But Terra has an atmosphere, and is less fragile. If I had a choice, that's where I'd want my family."

He muttered, "Christ protect us."

"Amen."

Half an hour later we pulled up to the terminal. The engines sank into a whine. I unbuckled, made as if to stand, hesitated. I offered my hand. "Godspeed, Mr. Stanner."

"And you, sir."

"Thank you." I ducked through the hatchway into the cabin.

He called after me, "We need you on a ship." I pretended not to hear.

The steward had my duffel ready. He'd held back other passengers so I could go first. Well meant, I suppose, but I'd have preferred him to ignore me entirely.

I strode along the moveway, hoping I'd find the right counter.

"Captain Seafort! Wait, sir!" I turned, saw a florid lieutenant running after me. I waited. "Lieutenant Greaves, sir. Mr. Duhaney is in the Naval Liaison Office and sent me to get you."

"The what? And how did he know I'm here?"

"Naval Liaison Office, sir. It's really just a conference room reserved for Naval officers. Lunapolis Base reached him there while he was in a meeting. When he heard the London shuttle diverted, he knew you'd be on it."

"Very well." I slung my duffel over my shoulder, followed him through the corridors.

He held open the door. "Go right in, sir."

Admiral Duhaney looked over his shoulder, straightened, rubbed his back. "Ah, there you are, Seafort." With him was Senator Boland and another man I didn't know. They hovered over a caller. "Have you met Senator Wyvern?" We shook hands and sat.

"What's the latest, sir?"

"Nothing since the son of a bitch Fused. We'll hold Battle Stations for a few hours, then stand down unless he shows again."

I nodded. There was little else we could do.

Richard Boland let out his breath in a long sigh. "It's one thing hearing about these adventures on the holos, Seafort. It's another to have a fish overhead."

"I know."

He leaned forward in his chair. "What do you think they're up to?"

"Me? How should I know?" Perhaps it was the adrenaline surge. I felt a bit shaky.

"You've been there, and we haven't."

Duhaney and Wyvern watched me intently.

"I've no idea." I stood to pace. "My guess is you won't see any more of them for a while."

"Why not?"

"Just a hunch. In Hope Nation we never could anticipate their patterns. And it was years between the loss of *Telstar* and their next attack." But once that attack started, it nearly obliterated Hope Nation and our defensive fleet.

Senator Wyvern cleared his throat, as if before a speech on the General Assembly floor. "This makes it all the more important we settle where the new hulls originate."

Boland said sharply, "Not now, Brett."

I wasn't interested in politics. "Can you get them to speed up the caterwauling bomb, Admiral?" I sat.

"This gives me an excuse to knock some heads together." Duhaney paused. "On the other hand . . . Seafort, don't make any public comments on this affair, understand?"

My annoyance showed. "I've never given interviews, sir." Didn't he know even that?

"Say nothing. That's an order." He hesitated. "I might as well tell you; we've already agreed. Unless the fish show up before tomorrow, we're treating this as a false sighting."

"You're what?" I came to my feet.

"As far as the public is concerned, that is. Of course, we'll increase our vigilance."

"But why?"

Senator Boland's voice was soothing. "No point in causing alarm, Captain. Or panic."

"You'll lie about an enemy in home waters?"

"Think, Seafort. What good would the truth accomplish?"

"What good—" He had a point. As long as our Home Fleet maintained its watch, publicizing dangers that were unavoidable might cause panic. Worse, it might evoke demands that our Navy stop serving the colonies, so as not to attract the fish. "It's not my decision to make, Senator." And thank Lord God of it.

Duhaney cut in, "Let him be, Richard. He's as fatigued as we are. Seafort, I'll arrange a suborbital to London for you. One flight won't disrupt our ground defense."

"I can wai—very well, whatever you wish." Let the Academy gates swing shut behind me, shield me from politicians and armchair Admirals.

Boland got to his feet. "Mr. Duhaney, if you'll ring Naval

Transport, I'll walk Mr. Seafort to Departures." Smoothly done. I barely felt the dismissal. Moments later I was striding with Boland through corridors packed with frustrated travelers waiting out their delays.

"We're doing the best we can, Seafort. I'll use the sighting as a club to get Brett back in line, and we'll have your new ships built. Alarming the public would only interfere with that."

I grunted. For all I knew, he was right. U.N.S. *Wellington* was almost ready for launch, and we needed many more like her.

The Senator's tone was casual. "I'm bringing Robert to Devon tomorrow."

"Robert?"

He frowned. "My son."

"Oh, yes. Pardon me. I'm sure he'll do well."

"I'm most interested in seeing that he does. Any way I can possibly help, please let me know." I waited for more, but he left it at that.

It was late evening before a helicab finally deposited me on the Academy tarmac. The guard saluted, waved me through without showing my ID. I thought to make an issue of it, decided not to. My face was too well known to question, even without my scar. I called Admiralty in Lunapolis, checked with a staff lieutenant I knew. All was quiet in the Home Fleet.

The compound was a madhouse, callers ringing off the pad. Arrival day, as if by magic, caused parents in each of the subsequent groups to verify dates, reconfirm what their cadets were allowed to bring along, and query each of the admonitions spelled out in the acceptance letter and pamphlet.

Lieutenant Paulson and the sergeants had been through it before, and weren't fazed. Two middies waited in my outer office to run any needed errands, and Tolliver was out on the grounds, keeping an eye. Still, I sat in my office, expecting at least an occasional call to slip past their vigilance. After a time I conceded none might come.

Restless, I paced my way past coffee tables and chairs, made a note to have the furniture thinned as I had in my Farside office.

It was past lunchtime before I'd had enough. The only call I'd fielded had been from Quartermaster Serenco, asking approval for a special order of milk to replace some that had spoiled. I ran my hands through my hair, adjusted my tie, and closed the door behind me. "I'll be on the grounds."

"Yes, sir."

As on board ship, I didn't carry a caller. On a vessel I could be reached through any of the corridor speakers; here I could not. But on ship I might be needed instantly for an emergency, and that was not the case at Academy. In any event, I'd be damned if I'd have a caller squawking under my jacket, or be seen with a mini plugged in my ear. I might as well be a teener with a stereochip.

I headed toward the barracks, hesitated, reversed my course, and strode the trimmed pathway back to Officers' Quarters and beyond to the shaded expanse of front lawn.

The recruits were instructed to arrive between ten and two. Parents drove their nervous offspring to the curved drive in front of the imposing iron gates, or walked across the commons from the heliport or the train station several blocks away.

Inside the gates, middies on special duty corraled the cadets-to-be, and every few minutes took a group of them to the Admin Building, where their Naval careers would commence. Once inside the Academy compound, cadets would be allowed no contact with their families, other than by letter, until their first furlough far in the future.

From a safe distance I watched the tearful good-byes. One recruit spotted me among the trees and pointed excitedly. Quickly I turned away and struck out for the mess hall, between barracks and classrooms.

Though formal lunch was over, I wandered into the galley. I ignored the startled cook's mates, peered into the coolers. Surely there must be something.

"Would you like a sandwich, sir?"

I grunted. "Whatever's easiest."

"Why don't you sit down in the hall? The mess steward will bring it out."

"Very well." I chose the closest cadet table, cupped my head in my hands, and brooded.

The start of a year. Some of my charges were halfway through training, others about to begin. How could I help the new recruits understand what they'd embarked on? An officer did not work for the Navy, he *was* the Navy. Now, with the fish devastating our colonies, we needed responsible officers more than ever.

My hand caressed the table's rough plank. The joeys who'd be eating their next meal here were yet children. How could they be expected—what? Initials? I rubbed at the faded marks, noticed others. I wondered which sergeant wasn't doing his job. When I'd been a cadet . . . Could we identify the malefactors by the letters? No, the carvers had wisely left but one initial each.

"Your lunch, sir."

I jumped at the unexpected voice. "Very well." The steward set down the tray. They'd gone to the trouble to heat a full meal: meat, vegetables, mashed potato. A heaping salad, steaming coffee. I sighed. I'd have made do with anything.

The door flew open and a middy rushed in. He hurried to my table and came smartly to attention.

"Midshipman Anton Thayer reporting, sir." His carrot-red hair was neatly brushed, his uniform in order. "Lieutenant Sleak's compliments, and Senator Boland is asking for you at the gate."

"Tell him—No, wait." I got up, crossed to the caller on the wall by the doorway, keyed my office. "Seafort."

"Sleak here, sir. Shall I have the Senator escorted to your office?"

"What does he want?"

"He's brought his son."

"Yes, send him—" I hesitated. An important politician shouldn't be alienated; what did tradition matter when a member of the Naval Affairs Committee was— No. "Keep him at the gate. I'll be along."

"Are you sur—aye aye, sir."

I rung off. Anton waited for dismissal. I growled, "Have you no work to do?"

"Yes, sir." He ran off.

I hurried to the door, slowed my pace. The Commandant was no Senator's lackey to come scurrying at his call. Still, as I skirted the edge of the parade ground, my stride lengthened. Perhaps it would have been better to offer him the hospitality of my office.

I crossed the front lawn to the gate. A middy, shepherding an awkward group of recruits, saluted as he passed. At the curb two cars were parked. Alongside one of them a slim youth was enduring an older woman's embrace. Senator Boland waited patiently near the guardhouse.

I stepped outside the gate, tugged at my jacket. "Good to see you again, Senator."

"And you, Commandant. May I present my son Robert? Robert, Commandant Seafort." The lanky fourteen-year-old smiled shyly, unsure whether to offer his hand.

I clasped my hands behind my back as casually as possible, nodded politely. "I'm sure he'll make a good cadet, Mr. Boland."

The byplay hadn't gone unnoticed; something in the Senator's eyes changed. Still, he said affably, "I was hoping to see Robert's barracks."

"I wasn't told which one he'll be assigned. Sorry." The information could be read from the guardhouse console, a few steps away. "I'll have someone phone your office this afternoon." Surely that wasn't too great a concession to his rank.

"I won't be able to place the barracks by name alone."

I smiled. "They're all alike."

"Yes. Well . . ." His eyes locked on mine. "My wife and I are most anxious that Robert justify the honor of his admission."

"That's commendable." I tired of the sparring, turned to the boy. "When you're done with your good-byes, one of the middies will take you in."

"Thank you." Robert's tone betrayed his uncertainty.

"Is there anything else, Senator?"

"Admiral Duhaney mentioned your questions about the budget. I'd be happy to go over them with you."

"I suppose I—um, well, perhaps—" I broke off, knowing I sounded a dolt. I took a deep breath, spoke more firmly. "Robert, I'll speak with your father alone for a moment."

"Yes, sir." He retreated toward the car.

My heart pounded. "Senator, I know what you want. It isn't possible. The Naval Affairs Committee's visit is months away. You're here privately, and parents aren't allowed to enter Academy. I won't make an exception. We'll take care of your son, as we do them all."

Senator Boland's eyes were pained. "Including the boy whose helmet was smashed a few days ago? Oh, yes, I know about that." He paused. "Can you imagine how dear Robbie is to me? I'm proud, but frightened at the same time."

"Yes, I think I can understand that."

"He's leaving home, leaving my custody for yours. See how eager he looks? Inside he must be terrified." His voice turned bitter. "Of course, you wouldn't know about that."

My eyes turned back to his. "You can't possibly . . ." My voice faded away. He couldn't know. I'd never spoken of it.

I sat hugging myself, oblivious of passing fields as the train labored through the rolling English countryside. In the seat across, Father read from his Bible.

Four days earlier, the jerries had brought me home from the stadium in a police wagon, a blanket thrown across my shoulders for the shock, an untouched cocoa cooling on the bench at my side. Father had come outdoors at the light flashing in the night. We had no caller; he hadn't known.

When Father summoned me from the back of the wagon I dutifully followed him into the house. Mechanically I sat at the kitchen table, staring at the faded wall until the teapot screamed its readiness.

"Drink."

"I can't."

"Of course you can." He rested his hands on the back of my chair, turned back to the stove, made sure the burner was off. "Then you'll go to bed."

I sat motionless. They hadn't let me follow Jason to the mortuary. I'd given them his mother's name; Jason had never known his host father. His tired-eyed mother would be at the mortuary, confronting the ghastly remains of her son. Would my own host mother grieve me, if she were told of my death? She'd never known me, nor I her. Still, in some sense at least, I had two parents. Clone offspring had not even that.

"Leave your shirt out to be cleaned."

I looked down, saw the blood on my sleeve. "Damn my shirt."

He raised his hand to strike me, lowered it. "Not tonight. I understand." He sat across from me. "Though I don't approve." He searched my face. "There are times His will is hard to fathom."

Damn His will, I thought to say, but knew better; there were limits to Father's tolerance. I hunched over, resolved not to speak, but in a moment sobs broke through my determination.

After a time Father's gnarled hand slid across the table, gripped my wrist. He waited. When still I didn't respond, he shook my arm insistently until I looked up. "Your friend didn't live in His ways. You know I didn't esteem him."

"Aye." I tried to free my hand.

"He wanted to lead you into . . . vile practices. I hope you resisted. If not, your conscience will suffer." I twisted away but Father's grip was like iron. "Yet he was your friend, and I respect your grief. He was young enough to have changed his ways, had Lord God given him time."

I looked up. "That's why you tolerated him? Because he might have changed?"

"No, Nicholas. Because he was your friend." He released my arm. "I will pray for him, now and after. Perhaps you will join me."

I said in a small voice, "Yes, please."

"You'll go to the funeral?"

I recoiled. "The what?" They couldn't put Jason into the stony ground. That would be too cruel. I tried to swallow; my throat was full of ache. Father, hold me. Embrace me, tell me I'll want to live again.

"I imagine they'll bury him before you go."

I shivered. "Go? Where would I go?"

Father stood, poured himself more tea. Mine sat cooling, untouched. "Nicholas, have you forgotten Academy?"

"I don't want—there's no reason to go."

"There's no reason to stay."

I looked up, startled.

"It was your dream. Jason's death is no reason to abandon it."

I cried, "How could I leave him?" If there was a grave, it would need tending. Flowers. Weeding.

"He's left you already, Nicholas. The flesh is nothing."

The funeral was two days later.

Dressed in my ill-fitting suit, I stood between Father and Jason's dazed mother, torn between calm and fits of grief. I even bent to scoop a spadeful of dirt on the inexpensive alumalloy coffin. His mother smiled at me, squeezed my hand. I was grateful she'd allowed me to give him the balsa model of *Trafalgar* he'd admired, to take into the dark.

When it was done we'd gone back to our silent, dreary home, where I sipped steaming tea while Father opened the Book. We read from the Psalms, and in Proverbs. Perhaps because I wasn't comforted, he turned to Luke 18. I whispered with him the memorized words. *"Suffer little children to come unto me, and forbid them not: for of such is the kingdom of God."*

Two days later I'd closed my bag, followed Father to the cab, climbed onto the train.

I sat listlessly, feet kicking under the bench, my scrubbed ears protruding from my close new haircut.

Academy. The sum of all my dreams.

When finally the train had stopped I clutched my bag, stepped down into the depot, waited while Father asked directions of the agent at the window.

"It's near enough to walk. No need to waste coin on a bus."

"Aye." I followed Father out of the station. He paused, took his bearings, struck off down the road. I clutched my bag, heavy with my uneaten lunch, the large Bible, the printed books I'd thrust in at the last moment. I gaped at the unfamiliar shops.

We walked in silence. Occasionally Father's hand touched my shoulder to guide me. At a busy corner I shifted the duffel to my right hand so I could clasp his with my left, but the light changed and he strode on. We crossed the slope of the commons. I shifted the duffel to my left, reached for his hand, but Father moved to my left side.

Is this good-bye, then? What will I be when next we meet? Father, what advice do you have, what comfort?

Do you love me?

You left your cherished Cardiff to bring me to this place; I know that is proof enough.

I want to tell you I'll make you proud. I'll try hard, Father, truly I will.

The great iron gate loomed. I shifted the duffel again, reached for Father's hand. It was thrust firmly in his jacket.

We approached the gates, where the impassive sentries stood stiffly at their guardhouse. I turned to Father, my throat tight. He pointed to the guardhouse, put his hands on my shoulders and turned me to the waiting gates. Gently but firmly, he propelled me toward them. In a daze I passed through the gates, clutching my duffel.

After a few unwilling steps I turned. Father strode toward the station. Willing him to glance my way, I waved to his back. He didn't pause, didn't once look over his shoulder before he disappeared from view. An iron ring closed itself around my neck.

I blinked back the sting, and walked alone into Academy.

Senator Boland gripped my arm. "Are you all right, Mr. Seafort? You've gone pale."

I shook off his hand. "I'm quite well." After a moment I added, "Thank you."

I beckoned to his son. "Robert, once we're within the gates I won't speak to you, or take special notice of you. You understand?" He nodded. "When you've said good-bye to your father, come inside. Remember he loves you, or he wouldn't be here." I cleared my throat. "You have nothing to fear." I nodded to the Senator, strode quickly into the compound.

Chapter 6

Tolliver knocked on my door, stuck in his head. "They're ready for the oath, sir."

"Very well." I stood, switched off my holo. "Care to come along?"

"I wouldn't miss it for the world." His eyes danced despite my disapproving frown. As if he hadn't already gone too far he added, "I have the words on a card, sir, if you'd care to read them."

"Tolliver!"

"I gather you wouldn't." He fell into step beside me. As we strode down the steps he asked, "Remember your own oath, sir?"

I stopped. "As if it were this morning." Something in my tone dampened his smile. "And you?"

"I could show you the spot I was standing." Somber now, we walked in silence to the Admin building. I climbed the steps, turned to the meeting hall.

"Attention!" The sergeant nearest the door stiffened as he barked the command. The other drill sergeants did likewise, along with Lieutenant Sleak and the middies. Several of the recruits made a halfhearted attempt to comply, which I ignored.

"As you were." I marched to the front of the hall, wondering what to say. "Sergeant Radz, line them up in two rows."

"Aye aye, sir! You, two steps forward! You, next to him. Get in line. Not so close!" In a moment, forty-seven boys and thirteen girls were in two ragged lines, arms at their sides.

My words rang out. "I am Nicholas Ewing Seafort, Captain, U.N.N.S., and Commandant of the United Nations Naval Academy. The oath you are about to give is no mere promise, no formality. It is a commitment given freely to Lord God Himself, binding you to the U.N. Navy for five years, as my wards until such time as I may see fit to graduate you. The United Nations

Naval Service is the finest military force ever to be assembled at any time, anywhere.

"Those of you who wish to take the oath of enlistment, raise your right hands." All complied at once. I cleared my throat. "I—your name—"

A murmur of voices.

"Louder, please. This is not a thing you do in shame. I do swear upon my immortal soul . . ."

"Do swear upon my immortal soul . . ." The voices strengthened.

"To serve and protect the Charter of the General Assembly of the United Nations . . ."

"To serve and protect the Charter of the . . ." One boy was trembling, perhaps in fear. Another lad's eyes glistened.

"To give loyalty and obedience for the term of my enlistment to the Naval Service of the United Nations . . ."

"To give loyalty and obedience for the term of my enlistment to the Naval Service of the United Nations . . ." Their voices, firmer now, echoed mine.

"And to obey all its lawful orders and regulations, so help me Lord God Almighty."

"And to obey all its lawful orders and regulations, so help me Lord God Almighty."

A moment of silence. "You are now cadets in the United Nations Naval Service." I came to attention, snapped a parade ground salute, spun on my heel and marched out.

Halfway to the office Tolliver caught up with me. "Jesus, son of God."

"Um?" The blood coursed through my veins; my stride was swift.

"Nothing I ever heard . . ." He swallowed. "I've never heard the like."

"Don't mock me."

A moment's hesitation, then his voice came quieter. "I didn't, sir."

"Hmpff. Come along, we have business to discuss."

In the privacy of my office I pulled off my coat, tossed it over a coffee table. I put a chip in the holovid, spun it so we could both see. "Our budget."

"Yes, sir."

I indicated the expense columns. "First, keep an eye on expenses, make sure we're staying within the guidelines."

"Aye aye, sir. But doesn't the quartermaster—"

"You do it. Second, I want you to spot-check that we actually receive items we're paying for."

He looked at me with surprise, grinned abruptly. "A sort of inspector-general, as it were?"

"That's not funny, Edgar." On Hope Nation I'd been appointed inspector-general, an escapade that ended with my relieving the commander of the Venturas Base, to my Admiral's spectacular wrath.

"No, sir, of course not."

I gritted my teeth, determined not to be bated. "Third, examine last year's accounts. Skip the items for which we indent, that are delivered from Naval stores. Look to all cash purchases. Verify what you can, and report any anomalies."

He watched me closely. "You suspect something?"

"Admiral Duhaney said we have sole discretion as to how our funds are spent. Our accounting system is bizarre. It's come about because of the Navy's cherished independence, but whoever dreamed up—" I bit off the rest, realizing I'd been about to criticize my superiors in front of a subordinate. "Just check what you can."

"Lieutenant Sleak is systems officer, and he's also my senior. He won't like my stepping on his toes."

"Try not to be obvious. If he objects, refer him to me."

"Aye aye, sir." Tolliver frowned, perusing the figures. "Does it matter whether we exceed the guidelines for each column, as long as—"

"The Admiral said . . ." I tried to recall his words. "He was anxious to catch a shuttle. We don't have to follow the spending guidelines. And something else: theoretically we don't have to account for the number of cadets. I had no idea what he meant, and I didn't get a chance to ask. Follow up on it. Look at the regs, ask someone in Accounting."

"Aye aye, sir. Anything else?"

"Not at the moment. Dismissed."

By now the plebes would be lined up in front of the supply lockers, to be handed armfuls of gear in the age-old ritual of inductees everywhere. I leaned back, clasped my arms behind my head, rocked in the comfortable leather chair. First they'd be given gray slacks, then white shirts, then their gray jackets. Shoes and underwear on top of the pile.

They would split into separate groups for each barracks, line up in single file, awkwardly carrying their loads.

Surprisingly few officers were to be found in the groundside compound. Plebes were taken in hand by their drill sergeants, whom they would learn to obey without reservation. Officers, whom even the sergeants stiffened to salute, would be exalted beyond all understanding.

Or so it had seemed at thirteen.

"Fall in! Did I say to face left? If you dropped it, pick it up, you twit!"

He was six feet, two inches. He was burly; his voice had the menace of a wounded tiger. He was Marine Sergeant Darwin P. Swopes.

He was God.

We marched in a ragged line to Valdez Hall, a one-level alumalloy building clustered among many similar structures. Windows punctuated its clean white siding; three steps led to a wide doorway. I clutched my bundle of clothing in one arm, my bag from home in the other.

"Single file. The first fifteen of you, stand at the foot of the beds to the right." He waited. "The rest of you, to the left."

I stood in front of my new bed, exchanging glances with the tousled boy to my right. His grin vanished as the sergeant entered the room.

"Turn around, dump your gear on the foot of your bed, and turn back. Stand with your hands at your sides." He waited for us to comply.

"You already heard my name, but some of you will be too dimwitted to remember. I am Sergeant Swopes. I will tell you how to address me. It is 'Sergeant Swopes,' or 'Sarge.' "

"As you know, a sergeant is not normally called 'sir.' However, you are—" he spat the word—"children, not officers or troops. Therefore you will call me 'sir,' as in 'Yes, sir' or 'Aye aye, sir.' In fact, you will call anything that moves 'sir' unless it is wearing gray like yourselves, or unless it is female, in which case you call it 'ma'am.' Do I make myself clear?"

There was a ragged chorus of "Yes, sir." I began to sweat in my heavy flannel shirt.

"The correct response is 'Aye aye, sir.' If you're asked a question, the answer might be 'Yes, sir.' When you're given an instruction, the answer is 'Aye aye, sir.' "

Across the aisle a hand wavered. Sergeant Swopes glared. "Well?"

A tall, gawky boy whose ears stuck out at angles. "You asked if you made yourself clear. That was a question, wasn't it? So shouldn't we say 'Yes, sir'?"

Sarge smiled. He sauntered to the ungainly boy. "Name?"

"Von Halstein. Erich Von Halstein."

"Erich Von Halstein, run around the outside of the barracks seven times. I want you back in two minutes. Move!"

The boy gulped, "Yes, sir!" He scrambled to the door.

Sarge roared, "Come back here!" The cadet skidded to a stop, ran back. "Was that a question or an order, boy?"

"Uh, an order, sir."

" 'Sarge' will do. As you so wisely pointed out, you respond to an order with . . .?"

"Aye aye, sir!"

"Good. Since you already knew, three demerits for disobedience. You'll work off each demerit by two hours of calisthenics. Meanwhile, around the barracks! Get moving!"

"Yes—aye aye, sir!" He ran out the door.

As the door swung closed Sarge muttered, "I *hate* sea lawyers." He turned to the rest of us. "Any more questions?"

After the perspiring and frantic Von Halstein had returned—and received another demerit for tardiness—Sarge had us move the items we'd brought from home to our pillows, leaving the gear the Navy had issued us at the foot of the bed. "You will now, each of you, strip off everything you are wearing, put it on your pillow, and head for the showers. Towels are on a rack in the head."

I blanched. Everything, in public? Amid girls? Impossible; I couldn't do it.

"After you shower I will choose two cadets at random for close physical inspection. Lord God help you if I'm not satisfied with your cleanliness. Move!"

I hesitated just long enough for Sarge's eye to stray in my direction. Mortified, I began to strip. The room was absolutely silent except for the scrape of shoes and the rustle of cloth.

Covering myself as best I could, I stumbled to the shower

room with the rest of my squad. Most of the boys were too embarrassed to steal looks at the girls among us. I scrubbed with diligence, praying fervently that Sarge not choose me for inspection.

By the time we returned to our bunks, towels tied securely around us, Sergeant was almost done with our gear. A few items remained on my pillow: my books, my chips, the paper. The clothing I'd worn was on the floor, along with my bag.

"You will dress in your cadet clothing. Then you will pack the bags you brought from home with everything I put on the floor. Those items go into storage. Anything left on your pillow you will put in your duffel, which you will stow under your bed. Return the towels to the head, and when you're done, fall in outside and I'll take you for haircuts. Oh, yes. You . . . and you. Come here."

He hadn't chosen me. I was dizzy with relief.

Numbed and docile with shock, we followed Sarge from barber to mess hall, and back to barracks. We spent the entire evening stripping and remaking our bunks, until every bed was made to his satisfaction.

"Lights Out will be in half an hour. You will be in your shorts, ready for bed. Anyone wanting to use the head must do so before then." I closed my eyes, sick with dread. The toilets were set in a row opposite the sinks, with no fronts to the stalls. I knew I'd be unable to relieve myself, perhaps for days. "I'll be back just before Lights Out."

When Sarge returned, boys and girls were talking quietly across their beds. I sat alone, yearning for solitude, for my creaking bed in Father's familiar home.

Sarge's voice was surprisingly gentle as he turned the lights down. "You, sit on that bed. You too. I want both of you over there." In moments he had us sitting three to a bed, apparently at random. I sat stiffly, trying not to rub shoulders with the shy girl whose arms were crossed over her short white T-shirt.

"Some of you joeys were from North America. A few were from Germany, two from Lunapolis. From across the globe, and beyond. That's where you *were* from." He slowly walked the aisle. "But that's over and done. Now you're from Valdez. This is your home, and these are your mates."

He stopped in front of our bed. "Seafort, touch her face.

Both hands, she won't bite. Sanders, put your hand on his shoulder. I want all of you touching each other." Embarrassed beyond words, I raised tentative fingers to Cadet Sanders's face, while the third boy's clammy hand rested on my knee.

Sarge's voice was hushed. "You are now members of the finest military force known to man. These are your brothers, your comrades. You need not be embarrassed at their touch, at their view of your bodies. Their accomplishments are your own. Your honor is theirs, and their honor yours. If you lie, you shame them. If you betray them, you betray yourself, your Navy, and Lord God.

"Years from now, when you sail the void between the stars, you will know that every officer in the U.N.N.S. shares your bond. For now, strive to be the best you can, for your mates' sake. From time to time you will fail, and you will be punished. Eventually, you will succeed.

"This morning, you were strangers. Now you are bunkmates, embarked on a mission to prove yourselves worthy of the Navy and of each other. Return to your beds."

I crept back to my bunk. "Good night." He strode to the door, left.

Within the barracks, all was still.

Our cadets settled in to the whirlwind of their new lives. Five days later, I gave the oath to our second group, and, from a distance, watched the rituals repeat themselves.

During the week Senator Boland called three times to inquire about his son Robert; I managed to duck all his calls. The desk sergeant offered him the same rote reassurances that any other parent would receive.

Furlough ended for the second-year cadets; soon every barracks space would be taken, until we began shipping youngsters back to Farside. I debated going there myself, but didn't. Here in Devon, I could be in New York within hours, should Annie call.

Aloft, the Home Fleet patrolled in vain. No fish were sighted anywhere.

Days passed; our third and fourth groups of cadets arrived and we processed them as we had the others. Increasingly restless, I stalked the Academy compound while exasperated sergeants taught their cadets the rudiments of calisthenics, military posture, obedience. I marveled at their patience.

One evening I strolled through the barracks area, avoiding dorms I knew to be occupied. My drill sergeants had enough on their shoulders without surprise inspections by the Commandant. Musing, I stopped in front of an empty building.

Our next to last group of recruits would arrive in two days. Within a week our roster would be complete. Which among the anxious youths we took into our company would become another Hugo Von Walthers, which a dismal failure? If only we knew. It all began here, in aging barracks like the one I faced. Idly, I stepped through the door, switched on the light.

Thirty bare mattresses, thirty empty bunks. I wandered past the steel bed frames, ran my fingers over the dusty windows. In days this dorm would be throbbing with activity and anticipation, with fears and suffering as boys groped to become men.

"Can I help—oh, pardon me, sir."

I turned; Sergeant Olvira flipped an easy salute, came to attention.

"As you were." Embarrassed, I thrust my hand in my pocket. "I was just—wandering."

He nodded, as if encountering the Commandant in a deserted barracks were a common occurrence. "Yes, sir."

"And what are you doing here, Sarge?" It wasn't much, but I had to say something.

"Valdez will be my barracks, sir. I heard the door open." Sergeants were housed in apartments adjacent to their barracks, sharing a wall. They had privacy, but were on hand should need arise. Though it was questionable how much privacy they enjoyed, if Sergeant Olvira could hear my quiet step.

"Sorry, Sarge. I didn't mean to intrude."

"No problem, sir. I was looking over my paperwork, before the joeys get here." He hesitated. "I have fresh coffee, if you'd like."

"No, thanks." My tone was cool. Bad enough I'd spent an hour with him in the staff lounge. It wasn't appropriate for a commander to socialize with subordinates, and worse, some would see it as favoritism.

"Sorry to have disturbed you, sir. I'll leave you be." He waited for dismissal; I nodded. Alone, I sat on a bed, tried to quell my annoyance. He had to have noticed my abruptness. What had been his sin: to offer me a cup of coffee?

I stood, wandered to the end of the room. Whatever enjoyment I might have had in my visit was gone. I snapped off the light, left the building. I started back to Officers' Quarters, but my pace slowed. It was only coffee. I'd been too brusque. I returned to the barracks, found the outside entrance to his apartment.

"May I take you up on the drink?"

Sergeant Olvira concealed any surprise at my abrupt appearance. "Of course, sir. Come in." He stood aside.

I sat at his table, waited while he fetched sugar, cream. He poured my cup, warmed his own and sat. "It'll be good to get back to work again."

I smiled politely. "You didn't fancy your leave?"

"I'm not much for time off. I only took a week."

"In a couple of days you'll have your hands full." I sipped at the steaming brew.

He pushed aside the pile of folders to hunch forward, elbows on the table. One file slid down; I grabbed at it. The cover flipped open to a half-page photo of an earnest youngster. I closed the folder, tossed it back on the stack. "What are you working at?"

"Putting names to faces. A head start really helps. And I like to know about the joeys when I see them."

I hadn't known sergeants did that. I'd never known much about how they worked. "Find anything interesting?"

"No, not really." he sighed. "This one, for example. French. Theroux. Fourteen, mother a Dosman in Paris. Father deceased. In his admissions essay he said he'd dreamed of joining in the Navy ever since he saw *Celestina Voyage*. Awful bilge, that holo, but I can see it inspiring a young joe. Maybe it will never help me to know that. Perhaps it may come in handy."

"Theroux."

"Jacques Theroux. He's just one of—"

"Let me see the folder."

"Aye aye, sir." Social visit or no, he immediately obeyed an order.

The boy looked solemnly past me to the holocamera and beyond. But for Tolliver's intervention, he'd be languishing over a rejection letter rather than rechecking his traveling bag, counting anxious hours. Which youth had been left off the list, so Theroux could attend Academy? I hadn't even bothered to ask. I snapped shut the file.

"Is something wrong, sir?"

I shook myself back to reality. "No, nothing." I made small talk until I was free to escape into the night.

I paused at the mess hall door, tugged at my jacket. "All right, I'm ready." Tolliver held open the door.

"Attention!" The bellow rang through the room. Two hundred forty cadets stood instantly, came to attention. Most of them got it right. Hair neatly brushed, ties straight, trousers creased; their sergeants wouldn't have permitted otherwise. I strode past their benches to the circular table at the front of the hall. My officers saluted as I approached.

I raised my voice. "As you were." More quietly, to my own table, "Be seated, gentlemen." Lieutenant Sleak, Edgar Tolliver, Sergeant Obutu, and several instructors without barracks took their seats. Until now, I'd had little contact with them. Perhaps I should drop in on the classrooms from time to time, though that wouldn't make the instructors' tasks any easier.

"That tryout of the new gunnery simulator was great," Sergeant Olvira remarked, helping himself to soup.

Sleak passed the bowl along. "How's it look, Gunnie?"

Olvira grinned. "You should have seen Ramon's face when he came out. He can't wait 'til it gets here."

I asked, "Ramon?"

"Ramon Ibarez, sir. He's assistant gunnie."

"Oh, yes." I colored, chagrined that I hadn't remembered. "He was that impressed?"

"It's overpowering, sir. When we get it installed you could give it a try. You're in a cabin just like laser fire control on a ship of the line. When the fish appear you practice with the usual firing screens, but there's also a huge puter-driven simulscreen, and you actually see the fish you hit. It's more like the real thing than . . . the real thing!"

I tried to warm to his enthusiasm, though the idea of facing fish once again, even in simulation, was repugnant. "I'll give it a test. Though gunnery was never my best—Yes? What?"

"Midshipman Sandra Ekrit reporting, sir." She paused to

catch her breath. "Mr. Diego says, a call from Admiral Duhaney, and do you want to take it in your office?"

I don't want it at all. "No, I'll get it by the door." I stood, waving my fellow officers back to their seats. Across the hall I took up the caller. "Seafort."

"Just a moment for Admiral Duhaney."

I waited. Several minutes passed. I shifted uncomfortably from foot to foot, aware of curious glances from the cadets. It wasn't good form to let them see their Commandant holding the line like an errand boy waiting for instructions.

Finally the receiver crackled. "Seafort?"

"Yes, sir."

"Glad I reached you. Give Senator Boland a ring, would you? He's worried about his boy."

"Are you serious?" The words slipped out before I could stop them.

A pause I thought would never end. "Yes, I'm serious, Captain Seafort. He had trouble getting through to you, and I promised to look into it. Talk to the barracks sergeant, make sure everything's all right, and give the man a call. I'll check later to make sure he's satisfied."

"I don't—aye aye, sir." There was nothing else I could say. It was an order.

"You might let the boy talk to his father now and then."

I stared at the caller; surely he couldn't mean it. I swallowed an unwise reply. "I'll consider it."

He snapped, "Don't get on your high horse, Seafort. Boland's committee controls our purse strings."

"I know that." My voice was cold.

"Oh, by the way, that new puter program you brought back on *Victoria*. The Dosmen have gone wild over it. We're going to reprogram most of the fleet."

"Is Billy all right?" I felt a fool for asking.

"Billy is what you call it? *Victoria*'s puter hasn't been powered down, if that's what you mean. It warned us that data would be irretrievably lost. The program's too complicated to unravel quickly, so we're taking no chances."

I smiled. William, Orbit Station's late puter, had even thought to safeguard his son's life. Or maybe Billy had thought of it on his own.

"Keep Boland happy, Seafort. One hand washes the other."

"Very well, sir."

He rung off. Brooding, I walked slowly to my seat. What he'd asked of me was wrong, and I'd agreed to it without protest.

Tolliver looked up. "Everything all right?"

"Fine." I stared at my cold meal, beckoned the steward. "Take this away." Subdued conversation resumed while I stared at the starched white cloth.

After dinner I went back to my office, closed the door, slumped in my leather chair while behind me the day turned to dusk. Just a call, a quick reassurance. No need to make so much of it. The boy needn't even know. But it was hardly customary for the Commandant to ask after the health of a cadet; the moment I spoke to Ibarez, he'd know Robert Boland was under special scrutiny. Inevitably, the boy's treatment would subtly change, and just as inevitably, it would poison the boy's relations with his fellow cadets.

Yet I had no choice. I'd been given an order, and I'd assented.

The caller buzzed. Tolliver. "About those figures you asked me to look into, I have some interesting—"

"Not now!" I slammed down the caller. What was the point of a receptionist, if any officer on the base could harass me when—Well, Tolliver was my aide, and could bypass the middy in the outer office. Still, his calls were an annoyance; I should have them blocked. But then, what was the point of having an aide? Muttering under my breath, I stood, paced the room until my ire cooled.

The caller buzzed again. I snatched it up. "No more calls!"

"Aye aye, sir. Sorry." Midshipman Guthrie Smith. "I just thought, it being your wife—"

Cursing, I keyed the caller, dropped back in my chair. "Annie?"

"Hullo, Nicky." Her voice seemed eons away. "I talked to Dr. O'Neill and he—I wanted to call."

"I'm glad. I've missed you."

"How are things? You gettin' the cadets in line?" She giggled, sounding her old self.

"I'm trying." I withheld my questions, determined not to press.

"Nicky, I ain't felt too good, these days. Sometimes I think, if you just came, took me someplace, it'd be all right. I lie down in bed wid . . . with you, you hold me tight."

I took a slow breath, controlled my tone. "I could come anytime. Tonight, if you like." Even if I had to steal a training heli.

"No, I don't want that." She sounded firm. "Sometimes I feel that way, like I said. But other times I don't. I wan' wait 'til it's right, alla time."

I ventured, "Maybe that won't happen until we're together, all the time."

"Yeah. I don't know. Thas' what I wanted ta say, I don't know. And I wanted ta hear your voice."

"God, I love you, Annie."

Tears were in her tone. "I love you too, Nicky. Can you understand that, and still I wanta be alone?"

I hesitated, chose honesty. "No, hon. I can't. Maybe it's because I want to be with you so much."

"Oh, Nicky." She sounded sad, and I felt twinges of guilt.

"It's all ri—"

"Lemme think about it some. I call you, maybe a few days. Maybe tomorrow."

"All right, love."

"Bye, now." She rang off, and I sat, desolate.

After a few minutes I stood heavily, determined to get my unpleasant chore done with.

Outside, the evening air was braced with the crisp tang of early fall. As I strode the white walkway a lone cadet looked up, quickly returned to his clippers. I wondered what had been his sin.

I crossed the compound to barracks, found Valdez Hall. Lights Out would sound in fifteen minutes. I would wait to see Sergeant Ibarez after he came out; better that than making my mission known to his cadets. Meanwhile, I didn't want to skulk around as if spying on the barracks. I moved off, wandered in the dark past other dorms.

Wright Hall; the front door swung open, a gray-clad youth dashed down the steps, ran to the corner of the building, faced the wall, assumed the at-ease position. I sauntered over. "What are you doing?"

"Sir, I—"

The door opened. "Go on, tell him! Good evening, sir." Sergeant Radz.

Jerence Branstead said loudly, "I'm learning not to be insolent to my betters, sir."

The sergeant gave no quarter. "And how long will that take, cadet?"

"I—as long as you say, Sarge."

"I'd guess about half the night, if you start now."

"Yessir!"

I'd had no business interfering, but it was too late. Well, in for a penny . . . "Why are you letting him off, Sarge? We have ways of dealing with troublemakers."

"Yes, sir. I'd hoped—"

"Send him to my office in the morning." Jerence blanched. "If I decide he's going to be a problem I'll have a middy pick up his gear in barracks. We've plenty of candidates who'll appreciate their training."

"Aye aye, sir."

I would let Jerence off with a couple hours of running around the compound on errands, but the boy needn't know that yet. Let him spend the night in anticipation of a Commandant's caning; he wouldn't be so quick to irritate his sergeant in future.

"Very well." The sergeant saluted; as I turned to go, he winked.

Reluctantly I retraced my steps to Valdez. Lights were out, and the door shut. Swallowing my distaste I went around the side to Sergeant Ibarez's door, knocked.

"I thought I told you— Oh, good evening, sir." he waited. "Is there . . . did you want to come in?"

"I—no." I yearned to turn on my heel, go to my apartment. But I couldn't ignore Admiral Duhaney's order. On the other hand, how would he know I hadn't really checked with Ibarez? I could tell Senator Boland all was well with Robert, as surely it was.

No, I couldn't require my cadets to obey orders if I myself refused. And the Admiral had been quite specific: ask the barracks sergeant how Robert was doing, and tell his father. "Sarge, I—"

Was that how Duhaney had put it? I strove to recall his words. "Talk to the barracks sergeant, make sure everything's all right and give Boland a call."

Did I dare? Was it outright disobedience? I knew what the Admiral had meant. Was I turning into a sea lawyer, at this late date? On the other hand, for the boy's sake . . .

I smiled. "Is everything all right, Sarge?"

Ibarez stammered, "I, um, I don't . . . Yes, sir."

"Very well, then. Carry on." I walked with jaunty step to my office, looked up Senator Boland's number.

Walking back to my apartment, I grimaced. My fatuous reassurances still rang in my ears. I'd pointedly ignored the Senator's hints about speaking directly with his son. He hadn't been satisfied, but had chosen not to press me.

I buzzed Tolliver. "Are you awake?"

"Yes, sir. The Navy never sleeps."

"Belay that. You wanted to discuss your report?"

His tone became businesslike. "Are you in your apartment? I can be right over."

"I didn't mean to—"

"Quite all right, sir. By morning you might be in a mood to hang up again. I'll be right there."

I growled a rebuke, rang off. The man could be impossible. Still, he was conscientious, and knew me as few others.

Fifteen minutes later he sat on my couch, legs crossed, scanning his notes. "I'll tell you right off I haven't found anything specific, sir. But in many cases there's nothing to find."

"How do you mean?"

"Fuel deliveries, for example. There's nothing in the files to show whether we've actually received them. No invoices to check, no receipts."

"How does the quartermaster explain that?"

"I haven't asked Sergeant Serenco, sir. You told me not to be obvious. And it's not just fuel. The uniform allowances—"

I felt uneasy. "Perhaps we ought to get Sleak in on this."

"Perhaps we shouldn't, sir." His eyes met mine.

I grimaced. If my systems lieutenant was engaged in accounting fraud . . . "Keep searching. See what else you find."

"Aye aye, sir." He closed his file. "By the way, I checked with Lunapolis on that other matter. It seems—"

"Other matter?"

"The way expenses are broken down per cadet. It seems your expense guidelines are rather pointless. They're only valid if you assume the same number of cadets each year. But—"

I was nettled. "What else can we assume? We take three hundred eighty."

"Yes, sir, but apparently that's just tradition. The number of cadets is a function of the budget, not the other way around. If—"

"What's that supposed to mean?"

"Perhaps you might occasionally let me finish a sentence. It means that historically the number of cadets we enrolled depended on how much money they gave us. But Naval staffing, like all tradition, hardens to stone, so when we achieved three hundred eighty cadets all future budgets were based on the assumption we'd admit that number the next year. If you want to spend more on each cadet, you can reduce enrollment. There are no orders or regulations to stop you."

"Good Lord."

"Fascinating institution, the Navy."

"Well, it's of no consequence. We're not about to cut back when a third of the fleet needs replacement. Keep tracking those expenses."

"Aye aye, sir." After he left, I turned out the lights and went to bed.

Chapter 7

Midafternoon. I left my office, crossed the compound to the meeting hall.

"ATTENTION!" The clump of recruits tried unsuccessfully to imitate the stiff demeanor of their sergeant.

"As you were. Line them up, Sarge." Boys and girls settled into two ragged lines. "I'm Nicholas Seafort, Commandant of U.N.N.S. Naval Academy. I am about to give you the oath of enlistment into the Naval Service." I paused, trying to recall the speech I'd made to the first group, some weeks before.

"By this oath you will be bound to the U.N.N.S. Navy for five years. You will be my wards until I deem you ready for graduation." One older boy sniffled, wiped his eyes. I looked away. A sergeant would have his hands full with that one.

"The U.N. Navy is the finest fighting force in the world. You will be privileged to join it. Those of you who wish to take the oath of enlistment, raise your hands." I waited a solemn moment. Sixty youngsters stood with right arms raised.

"I—your name—"

Someone cleared his throat, loudly. I whirled, furious at the interruption. Tolliver pointed urgently to the front row. No, not sixty arms raised. Fifty-nine.

I glared at a tall, ungainly joey of fifteen. "Raise your hand for the oath!"

Hugging himself, he mumbled, "I changed my mind." He shuffled his feet. "I want to go home." Other youngsters stared.

"I—but—" I stumbled to a halt. "Good Lord."

A red-faced drill sergeant moved toward the recruit, murder in his eye. I waved him back, looked helplessly to Tolliver, who shrugged. "I don't know, sir. Has it ever happened before?"

"Sarge?"

Sergeant Olvira said, "Not since I've been here. Eleven years." Someone snickered.

The ceremony tottered on the verge of chaos. "Take him out,"

I snapped. "Flank!" Two instructors converged on the miserable boy, hustled him out the door. Should I talk to him? No. A cadet had to aspire to Academy. The Navy wouldn't beg for recruits.

"Raise your right hands." The gap-toothed row complied immediately, as did the row behind. Our recruits were volunteers, not draftees. We'd send the unworthy child back to his family in disgrace. "Now. I—" Damn. I ground to a halt. "Keep them in place!" I strode to the door.

A drill sergeant had the boy by the collar, as if to prevent his escape. I planted myself in front of the abashed youngster. "Name!"

"Loren Reitzman."

"Age!"

He gulped. "Fifteen, last March."

"Inside, I have thirteen-year-olds who know what they want. Why don't you, Reitzman?"

"I'm sorry. I didn't mean—"

"Answer my question!"

"I don't know, sir. I wanted to be a cadet. But the soldiers, the yelling . . ." He wiped his eyes. "If I go back now, Dad will . . ." He hugged himself tighter. "I can't ever show my face at school. But if I stay—"

"Yes?"

He whispered, "It's just . . . The other joeys are all smarter than me; I couldn't even understand their jokes today. I don't want to be with people like that. I get scared."

I said softly, "You'd rather go home, remember all your life you gave up without trying?"

He shook his head. "What if . . . I can't make it?"

"Then you'll have failed. But you'll have tried first."

He bit back a sob. "I'm afraid."

"Very well. Sarge, take—"

"Wait! I'll take the oath. Give me another chance."

I turned his face to meet mine. "You're sure?"

He swallowed. "Yes, sir."

Was I doing the right thing? I couldn't know. "Sarge, take Mr. Reitzman back inside."

Moments later I was intoning the familiar ritual. "To give loyalty and obedience . . . to obey all its lawful orders and regulations, so help me Lord God Almighty." I waited until the last murmurs had subsided. "You are now U.N.N.S. cadets." I saluted, turned to the sergeant. "Get them out of here," I growled. I pointed at Loren Reitzman. "Except him. He's to be caned for bringing dishonor to the ceremony of enlistment."

I ignored Cadet Reitzman's anguished look of betrayal. Harsh, perhaps, but necessary. He'd get over it, and he'd serve as an example to his mates that Naval traditions were not to be trifled with.

After dinner I went to my apartment, loosened my tie. I sat at my newly-installed console, idly flipping through cadet files.

The caller buzzed. "Yes?"

"Lieutenant Sleak." His voice was tense. "I'd like to meet with you as soon as possible."

"Come now, then." I rang off, perused my folders until his knock.

He saluted, followed me into my living room.

"Well?"

"You have my resignation if you'd like, sir. Or if you prefer I'll request a transfer."

I blinked. "The boy was way out of line, refusing the oath in front of all the others. If I'd known you felt that strongly about—"

"What on earth are you talking about?"

I ignored his acid tone. "Loren Reitzman. The cadet. I know it was his first day but—"

"This isn't about a bloody cadet!"

"What, then?"

He faced me, hands on hips. "Your clumsy undercover examination of my accounts. Your man Tolliver sneaking about, checking serial numbers on laser rifles. His innocent questions to my quartermaster."

"He's doing that at my—"

"Whatever you'd like to know, ask me outright. Or, if you don't trust me, cashier me! I swore an oath just as those cadets today, and I'm not about to betray it for a few bloody unibucks!"

"It's not that—"

"Commandant Kearsey would *never* have—"

"How dare you interrupt a Captain!" My voice rose. "HOW DARE YOU?"

His tirade ground to a halt. "I'm sorry."

"I'm sorry, *sir*!"

"I'm sorry, sir. I apologize for interrupting. But that doesn't negate my point."

My tone was icy. "Stand at attention, First Lieutenant Sleak." He complied immediately. "You'll pardon my confusion. I've spent my career on ships of the line, where a lieutenant couldn't imagine dressing down his Captain." He flushed. "So, not knowing the proper shoreside protocol, I'll respond as if we're in the real Navy. Will you go along with the pretense?"

"I—yes, sir. Aye aye, sir."

"Very well. Three weeks pay for insubordination, and a reprimand in your file. One more incident and I'll write you up for court-martial. Is that understood?"

His look was wary, his voice under control. "Yes, sir."

"Stand easy. As to my investigation, I see fit to audit the Academy accounts. They are my accounts, not yours, even though you're handling them. Since you're aware of the inquiry, you will give whatever assistance Lieutenant Tolliver may ask. Acknowledge."

"Orders received and understood, sir." A surface calm, flickering anger beneath.

"Is there anything else?"

"I request a transfer, sir." The man had backbone.

"Under advisement. Dismissed." I waited until he'd gone, sat staring at my list of new cadets. The nerve! Even groundside, nothing could justify Sleak's conduct. What kind of commander had Captain Kearsey been, to tolerate such an attitude?

Yet how was Sleak's outrage different from mine, when I'd heard of Lieutenant Crossburn's insinuating questions on *Hibernia*? I flushed. At least our audit was out in the open. Tolliver would accomplish more, and faster.

A knock at my door. Was there to be no peace? I flung it open.

"Lieutenant Paulson reporting, sir." A sheen of perspiration on his forehead. "I, um, have a message."

"Well?"

"Admiral Duhaney called, and the middy transferred it to me. He—"

"You should have put him through."

"He asked for the duty officer. I was to give you the message, sir. He—" Paulson paused.

"Get on with it!"

"Aye aye, sir." Paulson seemed relieved by my order. "Mr. Duhaney said to tell you he was fed up with your prevarications."

"What?"

"That's the word he said to use, sir. You're to give Mr. Boland every cooperation, and stop wasting his time and the Admiral's. He said he recognizes that you are in charge of Academy, that you are free to act within your authority and carry out regulations as you see fit, but that Naval policy is set from above and you will comply with it."

My ears burned. I closed my eyes, forced myself to respond past the humiliation. "Is there anything else, Lieutenant?"

"No, sir. He ordered me to give you the message word for word, and to log it."

"Very we—"

He blurted, "I wish I hadn't been there. He shouldn't have—I'm sorry."

"Thank you." I shut the door, paced the silent, accusing room. I'd resign, of course. Admiral Duhaney had delivered his rebuke publicly, before my subordinates. The approach conveyed the clear message I no longer held his confidence. He'd chewed me out like a rank cadet, like—

The corners of my mouth twitched. Like I'd just done to Lieutenant Sleak. I'd gotten as I'd given. Still, at least I'd had the decency to censure the man in private. Well, no. By taking Sleak's pay and logging a reprimand, I'd made the matter public for the world to see. I sighed. Perhaps I could withdraw—

The caller buzzed. I whirled, snatched it from the console. "Now what?"

"I—Sergeant Olvira reporting, sir. I hope I'm not intru—"

"Yes, you're intruding, but that's why I'm here. What is it?"

His tone stiffened. "Aye aye, sir. I apologize; perhaps I shouldn't have called. About that cadet, Reitzman, the one who refused—"

"Yes?"

"He's in my flat, crying and carrying on like a baby, sir. Lieutenant Sleak went hard on him, he's got a few welts on his rump, can't sit down. I can deal with it, but I thought, given he didn't even want to take the oath . . ."

"Yes?"

"Should we cut our losses, sir? Send him home after all?"

I controlled my ire, considered his suggestion. We had no room for weaklings in the wardroom. Middies had to—no, Reitzman wasn't a middy, not yet. He was a cadet until I decided he was qualified.

"He made his bed, Sarge. Now let him sleep in it. Give him a little comfort, he needs that, but put him back in barracks. If he won't settle down, warn him if you send him to me in the morning, I'll have him begging to report back to Mr. Sleak."

A pause. "Aye aye, sir."

I shook my head with impatience. The man didn't understand. "And, Sarge, see to it that he doesn't need to be sent to me."

His tone warmed noticeably. "Aye aye, sir. I'll handle it."

I replaced the caller, paced anew. What was happening to the Navy? First Sleak's tantrum, then the Admiral's appalling message to my duty lieutenant, then Sarge . . . I shook my head. It was all my doing. If I hadn't gone behind Sleak's back, if I'd trusted him as a conscientious officer, he wouldn't have taken offense and wouldn't have been penalized. If I'd obeyed my own orders from Duhaney, the Admiral wouldn't be incensed.

And if I had trusted my instincts and sent Reitzman home when he'd refused the oath, the boy wouldn't have been brutalized and I wouldn't be dealing with a miserable, frightened youngster, when other, more willing joeys had been denied the chance.

To top it off, I now had to call Senator Boland and eat humble pie before that situation worsened.

I stalked the room, whirling to pace the opposite direction. "Policy is set from above and you're to comply with it." Damn his policy. Now I was to be a lackey, supervised in every detail. I should have asked for ship duty. Was it too late? Probably, for now. The Commandant couldn't resign during his first month, it suggested scandal.

None of this would have happened if Admiral Brentley still had Fleet Ops. Well, Duhaney had admitted he was more politician than Admiral. But how could I command Academy, subject to his every whim? Comply with policy, Seafort. Toady to the Senator.

I flung myself into my chair. Be fair. That's not all he'd said. "You're free to act within your authority and carry out regulations as you see fit." But what did that signify, if he decided that special treatment for Senator Boland was a matter of policy?

I was but a cog in the machine. Take three hundred eighty cadets chosen by others, run them through the process, spit them out the other end. Other than Final Cull, I had no say in which cadets we took, or how many, no way to . . .

I stared at my console. "You're free to act within your authority . . ."

Was there a way?

I chewed on my finger, mesmerized by the console screen. A long time later I roused myself, keyed my caller, spoke to the middy on watch. "Seafort. My compliments to Lieutenants Tolliver and Sleak, and would they meet me in my office in five—what time is it?—ten minutes." I rang off. It took only a moment to straighten my tie, thrust on my jacket. I crossed the compound, ran up the Admin Building steps, hurried into my outer office.

Midshipman Thayer came to attention. "They're not here yet, sir."

"What's keep—very well. Is there coffee?"

"It's old, sir."

"That'll do." I sipped at a cup of warm sludge, grimaced. Tolliver was the first to arrive; like me, he'd recently served on ship and was used to being called at odd hours. A few moments later Sleak followed; the look he gave Tolliver was within the bounds of civility, but barely so.

"Edgar, you said if I wanted to spend more on each cadet, I could reduce enrollment. Is that true?"

"Yes. Are you aware what hour it is?"

"Belay that." I looked to Sleak. "Are you familiar with those regs?"

His tone was aloof. "I understand their import."

"Does Tolliver have it right?"

"Technically speaking. But—"

"Very well. What if I want to spend less on each cadet?"

Tolliver said, "Sir, is now the right time to cut back on training just to save money?"

"Not to save it. To spend it." Like a child at Christmas I savored the moment before turning to the console. I tapped the keys, working through the menus to the screen I wanted. "Here. The list of admissions."

"Yes, sir."

"And this list of candidates before Final Cull. A difference of forty names."

"Yes, sir?"

"Send a letter, immediate delivery. 'We regret that an inadvertent miscalculation of the number of spaces available caused you to receive a notice rejecting your application. You are hereby granted admission to the United Nations Na—"

"What?" Tolliver was on his feet.

" '—Naval Academy. You are to confirm by return mail and report, et cetera. Signed Nicholas E. Seafort, Commandant.' You know the form."

Sleak said, "But we don't have spaces for—"

"We have empty beds aplenty, now that all second year cadets have been shipped aloft."

"Supplies? Food?"

"There's slack in the budget. Use the money set aside to entertain. Cancel staff travel perks. Cancel my liquor ration, I don't use it."

Tolliver. "We'd have to open up another dorm. Who'd take it?"

"Use one of the classroom instructors, or take it yourself."

"Me?"

"What's the matter, can't handle a few starstruck cadets?"

"No, sir, I'm not—but why?"

My fist struck the table. "Because I think it right." And to get even with Admiral Duhaney. I banished the unworthy thought.

As if reading my mind Sleak said, "Perhaps you should check with Admiralty, sir?"

"No. I had a message from Fleet Ops tonight." Sleak wiped off a look of satisfaction, but not before I'd seen it. So he'd already heard. Even here, scuttlebutt flew faster than a ship in Fusion. I said firmly, "Admiral Duhaney made clear that I'm free to act within my authority and carry out regulations as I see fit." That hadn't been the gist of his message, but the words had been included. They'd be in the Log, if I cared to look.

Sleak said, "You're sure that's what you want to do, sir?"

"Yes. Any objections?"

He shook his head as if I hadn't spoken with sarcasm. "No, sir. We'll have to recalculate all our . . . The letter is first, of course. It has to go out right away."

"Yes."

"Mr. Tolliver, you'll help me draft it? You'll want to sign it tonight, Captain, so it will make the morning faxes. If you want to go to bed, I can have the middy knock when it's ready. Then Tolliver and I can set up staff meetings for tomorrow. Even if we open another barracks we'll have to squeeze a couple of extra cadets into each of the other dorms."

I watched, amazed. Sleak was deep in logistics, as if my savage reprimand were forgotten. Perhaps for the moment, it was.

I left him to his work.

At breakfast Tolliver looked bleary. I said nothing, knowing he could catch up on his sleep when opportunity arose. Any middy knew how to do that. After, on the way back to my office, I crossed the parade ground, stopped to watch a squad of shirtless cadets sweating at jumping jacks, sit-ups, and push-ups under the tutelage of Sergeant Ibarez.

In the front row, Robert Boland struggled diligently at sit-ups while another youngster held his ankles. I quickly looked away. He'd get no special attention. Still, on the way back to my office I braced myself for the call to his father.

I perched on my desk, scanned the morning's memos. For the new dorm, Sleak had drafted a classroom instructor who'd had a barracks before; Tolliver wouldn't have to undergo the ordeal.

I dawdled at my console, scrutinizing figures, approving indents, rechecking the arrival dates of our last, largest batch of cadets until at last I could leave for lunch.

In the crowded mess hall I passed Cadet Reitzman's table, realized he hadn't been sent to my office. Well, I hadn't expected he would. For all their toughness, our drill sergeants usually knew when a gentle word would help. After all, their job was to help the joeys succeed, not destroy them. I looked again, noticed that the boy was absent from the hall. I assumed he'd remain so for a couple of days, until he could sit on a pillowed chair.

Already I could observe improvements in the cadets' demeanor, their dress and grooming. In a few weeks they would come to look like officer trainees, instead of spoiled civilian children. I spooned my soup. The discipline, the physical exertion, the sense of brotherhood of those early days of Academy were almost too much to grasp. I stared into the bowl. Almost too much to grasp . . .

*   *   *

A hand closed around my upper arm, hurled me from the bed to the cold hard floor. "One demerit, Seafort. You too, Sanders. Reveille sounded three minutes ago!"

I groaned, stumbled to my feet. Arlene Sanders glanced to my shorts, grinned. Scarlet, I spun around, clawed for my pants. I couldn't help the bulge. It wasn't fair that she laugh.

In ten minutes we'd be marched to breakfast. I had to hurry. I dashed into the head, waited in line for a stall. After, I grabbed a towel, ran to a sink, scrubbed myself. A few days earlier Sarge had decided Von Halstein wasn't clean enough, had hauled him back into the head, made us all watch while . . .

I soaped my chest, under my arms. There were limits. I'd die if he did that to me. I ignored the razors sitting on the sill; I didn't need one yet. Soon, I hoped. Some boys used them every day.

After breakfast, the calisthenics. I didn't mind them so much, other than push-ups. Sergeant Swopes had a way of flicking his baton if you faltered. It stung. When we were ready to drop from exhaustion he gave us two minutes rest before leading us to the track at the edge of the field. We mingled with Sergeant Tallor's squad from Renault Hall.

Tallor smiled. "My turn, Darwin. Okay, joeys. Four laps today." We groaned. "Tolliver, you take the lead."

A tall, slim second-year cadet ran forward. "Aye aye, sir!"

"I'll bring up the rear," said Sergeant Tallor. I made a face. If he came close enough to touch you with his baton, you were caned after the run. It hadn't happened often, and they said Lieutenant Zorn went easy, but I didn't want to find out.

Afterward, we ran back to the showers. Soaping up, I looked over my shoulder, found myself next to Arlene Sanders. Her hair smelled clean.

She giggled, and after a moment I smiled weakly. I remained facing the wall, though, until at last I screwed up my courage, turned casually. But she was gone, thrusting her way through the steamy shower room to the door and the towels beyond.

A dark-skinned Indian boy groaned theatrically. "Oh, if she were only a civilian." We laughed.

After lunch and classes Sarge ran us to the training grounds, where our instructor threw suits at us from the rack.

We had to stand holding them while they ran a training holo on the large screen overhead. "Okay, lads. Help each other put them on. Make sure your air is turned on before you attach your helmets. Then, one at a time, walk through the room to the left, meet me outside."

"Aye aye, sir!" Our response was still ragged, but improving. Back in barracks, where we'd grown used to Sergeant Swopes's cadence, we spoke almost as one.

I fumbled with the helmet clamps. No, the air tank first. I waited for the hiss. Now the helmet. The holo had said something about . . . clamp and turn. I twisted dutifully. The helmet seemed secure.

I took my place in line. One at a time, Sergeant Swopes thrust us into the mysterious room to the left, closed the door again. When it was my turn I stumbled in, propelled by his shove. The room seemed unusally foggy. I walked to the door at the far side, my breath loud in my suit. The door was locked. I twisted at the handle, to no effect. After a long moment the door opened. I plodded out to the lawn, where several cadets were peeling off their suits.

Sarge tapped at the helmet. "Off!" I fumbled for the clamps, twisted it loose. I breathed in the cool welcome air, turned to Robbie Rovere, grinned. "If that's all it takes, I'm ready for Farside!"

He smiled weakly, but suddenly his eyes bulged wide. He doubled over, vomited urgently onto the grass. "Jesus, what—" Another spasm caught him.

The instructor came running over. "Get away from that suit! Around the side of the building with the other grodes!" He spun Robbie around, gave him a kick. Moaning, the boy stumbled off.

He put hands on hips. "What about you, joey? You going to give back your lunch?"

"I don't—" I swallowed, but I seemed okay. "No, sir. What's wrong with Robbie, Sarge?"

The instructor stalked to the door, pulled out another cadet. The boy turned green, clawed at his helmet. Sarge made no move to help. Suddenly the front of the helmet was splattered; the cadet sank to his knees. "They're learning how to listen," Sarge growled.

Half an hour later we were lined up alongside the building,

some of us still wan and shaky. The instructor's tone was drenched with disgust. "You're the saddest, stupidest bunch of joeys Academy's ever had! In a week or two you're going to be sent aloft; didn't anyone tell you there's no air Outside the locks? This time we were watching over you, so we gave you nothing but a tummy ache. Next time you might die!"

Chastened, we shuffled our feet, but he wasn't done with us. "Each of you who threw up, two demerits." Two hours per demerit, and the strenuous calisthenics made our morning exercises seem easy. I'd done them until my muscles screamed, for infractions I couldn't avoid no matter how hard I tried. This time, though, I was safe.

"And the rest of you, three demerits!" I looked up, outraged. It wasn't fair.

"You all watched the holo, didn't you? Your mates were going where they needed suits. Did any of you check your mates' clamps?" His voice rose. "Did you? Rovere could be dead now. So could Sanders, or any of you! And you didn't help!" His look was one of loathing; his voice soared to a scream. "Next time it will be vacuum! You ever see anyone breathe space? You disgust me, all of you! Get out of my sight!"

Later that night, we lay, numbed and exhausted, in our bunks. Across the aisle someone sobbed. I buried my head in the pillow. A voice whispered, "It's all right, Robbie."

If Sarge heard us . . . I lay quiet.

"I've got to get out of here!"

Someone laughed, a harsh sound.

"Crybaby!"

"Mama's boy!" A loud whisper.

"He cries over a little puke, like a—"

It was Robbie who'd covered for me when I forgot to toss my towel in the bin. When Sarge had come into the head, the towel lay abandoned next to Robbie's sink. For some reason Robbie had said it was his own. Only one demerit, but . . . My hand tightened to a fist. Leave him alone.

Silence, then another strangled sob.

At the end of the barracks a joker imitated the sound. Someone else laughed.

I threw off the cover, leaped out of my bunk. "Shut up, all of you!" My voice hissed.

Von Halstein sneered, "Gonna make us, pretty boy?"

"If I have to." My voice trembled. I shivered in my shorts. "Leave him alone. Pick on me!"

"That's too easy." Someone giggled.

"Keep it down, you joes. Sarge'll hear." Arlene Sanders.

"Get in bed, Seafort, before we all get it." Voices murmured assent.

I crossed the aisle, found Robbie's bunk. Awkwardly I pulled his blanket tight about him. "You're all right, joey." For a second my hand touched his shoulder. I thought to pull away, remembered Jason. I let my hand remain a second longer. "You're okay."

I turned for my bunk, almost made it to the safety of my mattress when the voice came from the door. "What's going on here?"

Silence, everywhere. My heart pounding, I forced myself back to my feet. "Cadet Seafort reporting, Sarge. I was out of my bunk."

"Why?"

I paused. It had to be the truth, but . . . "I thought I heard a noise."

"Then you'd better guard us. Bring your mattress."

"Aye aye, sir. Where?"

"Outside."

All was still while I dragged my heavy mattress across the barracks floor.

"Are you finished, sir?"

I looked up from my cold soup. "Yes." The bowl disappeared, a salad was put in its place.

Squads of cadets came to their feet, their meal done. At each table the cadet on cleanup duty filed past the counter, depositing trays piled high with dishes. I'd dropped mine once, and was banished from mess hall for a week.

I stood, stretched, walked to the door. Cadets respectfully stood aside. Among them I saw Robert Boland, cheeks flushed, his gray uniform crisp, shoes gleaming. I pretended to ignore him, as a Captain would any cadet.

On the way back to my office I sighed, knowing I couldn't avoid the call any longer.

I closed my door, sat at my desk, bracing myself, knowing I

was about to throw away everything, for pride. I picked up the caller. "Ring Senator Boland, please." I waited, musing. Perhaps if Duhaney hadn't called me out so publicly . . .

It was early morning in Washington, but he was in. "Seafort? Good to hear from you." Boland could afford to be genial.

My muscles tensed. "I apologize for avoiding your calls."

"You don't have to—"

"Oh, but I do, sir. I failed to appreciate the extent of your influence."

"Thank you, Captain. I've been worried—"

"Please let me finish. Admiral Duhaney ordered me to give you every cooperation, and of course I will. I checked on your son. He's quite well. If you want further information, contact me."

"I'm most grateful—"

My heart pounded. "Senator Boland, I underestimated you."

He paused. "You what?"

"Not just your committee's power, your own. You hold my career in your hands."

He was wary now. "I don't understand."

"It's simple. If you want information about your son, call. If you ask to speak to him, I'll put you through. Feel free to drop in anytime for a visit. I will obey Admiral Duhaney to the letter. But after your first call or visit, or if I hear you've complained again to the Admiral, I will immediately resign as Commandant, and from the Naval Service. I so swear before Lord God Himself."

The speaker was silent. I added, "My future is in your hands. Forgive me for having underestimated you. You have but to reach for your caller, and my career is ended."

"Jesus, Seafort."

"Sir, you have a son to be proud of. Let him go, and let us do our job."

"I—"

"I won't have it any other way." I listened, heard no answer, gently hung up the line.

PART 2

October, in the year of our Lord 2201

Chapter 8

To my annoyance, a midshipman again met me at Earthport Station; this time they'd sent First Middy Thomas Keene. I growled at him as if it had been his fault.

Henceforth I'd have to travel unannounced, or better, leave orders not to send a shepherd. I wasn't some airsick cadet who needed a chaperon, and I could carry my own duffel.

Hours later, still cross, I cycled through the Farside lock to scowl at the duty officer waiting to greet me: Lieutenant Ardwell Crossburn. I returned his salute in silence, wishing I'd taken the effort to get rid of him.

"Have a good trip, sir?" His tone was civil.

"Yes."

"If there's anything I can do—"

"Dismissed." He turned to go. "Wait. Come to my office."

"Very well, sir."

During our long walk through the warren the stocky lieutenant was mercifully silent. In my office I set down my duffel, tossed my cap on the desk. "Do you still write your diary?"

His brow wrinkled. "Yes, sir, but just for my own—"

"You write about current events, as you used to?"

"It's my way of analyzing, sir. I think about things and—"

"Do you talk with other officers about your writings?"

"Well, I suppose—yes, sir. Idle conversation, at mealtimes."

As I feared. "Lieutenant, I order you to desist from writing in your diary any matters that do not directly concern you. I specifically forbid you to discuss anything you write with any of my officers. No, make that any officer, crewman or cadet." No telling what the man was capable of.

He shook his head stubbornly. "Sir, with all due respect, that's an infringement on my personal freedom that has nothing to do with—"

"Be silent!" I waved my finger under his nose. "Complain to Admiralty if you don't like it. You have my leave." I doubted they'd give him a hearing. "In the meantime, obey orders, or I'll —I'll—" I groped for a threat.

"Yes, sir?" He seemed unafraid.

I growled, "We have no ship's launch, but if I hear you've asked a single question about how things are run here, I'll make you supervisory officer of the Training Station."

His chest swelled. "That would be an honor, sir. I'd be pleas—"

"In permanent residence!" That brought him up short. Several months of the year the Training Station was entirely unoccupied. He could walk its lonely corridors, writing to his heart's content. I felt a pang of regret at my warning; now I couldn't banish him until I actually caught him at it.

When he was gone, I paced until my anger abated. Finally I keyed the caller. "Where's Mr. Paulson?"

"In his cabin, sir."

"Get him."

I met Paulson at the hatch, waved at a chair. "Have a good trip aloft? Everything under control, Jent?" Of course it was, or I'd have been told.

"Cadets are all settled in, no problems." He hesitated. "We were a bit surprised when you shipped sixty of them early, sir."

"We needed the space." Lieutenant Sleak had recommended it, and I'd agreed. Better to reward our achievers with Farside than crowd the Devon barracks unnecessarily.

"Yes, I—we've heard something about that." His expression was carefully neutral. "What was Admiralty's reaction?"

I leaned back. "I haven't heard from them." Not about anything. Perhaps they were debating what to do with me.

In the two weeks since my spectacular display of insolence, Senator Boland had not called once. Taking pity, I considered sending a brief note, but came to my senses in time. A battle once won ought not be refought.

"How long will you stay with us, sir?"

"A week or so." Time to wander the base, making a nuisance of myself. Time also to revisit the Training Station, where our more advanced cadets were introduced to shipboard life. "Schedule a formal inspection later this week, Jent. Tell the sergeants, but not the joeys." The anxiety and excitement would be good for the cadets, but no need to harass the drill sergeants as well. "Anything else I should know?"

"I sent you the forms on the Edwards boy."

"I know." I'd sent on the reports to his mother, with an inadequate note of my own. "How's the other joe, Arnweil?" I'd had no contact with the dark-haired youngster since I'd guided him to his feet, led him to the comfort of his barracks.

"You'd have to ask Sergeant Radz, sir. I haven't really had contact." He grimaced. "The only ones I see much of are the troublemakers, across the barrel."

"Have you used it much?"

"Three times since term started. Twice for cadets who didn't work off demerits fast enough, and once last week . . ." He shook his head. "I can't imagine what gets into them. A cadet and a middy, fighting."

Could he be serious? "Who was in charge?"

"The cadet, Johan Stritz, was in Krane Barracks, with Sergeant Tripole. The middy . . . well, I'm first lieutenant. It's my fault."

I snorted. When the day came a lieutenant could keep track of what middies were up to . . . Midshipmen had a natural knack for trouble, as I could testify. Once, on *Helsinki*, I'd— "Which middy?"

"Guthrie Smith, sir. He's seventeen, old enough to know better."

I remembered a shy boy, sitting stiffly at my midshipman's meeting, cap in hand. "What happened?"

"He was hazing, of course. What else?" Cadets were fair game for hazing, by middies as well as anyone else. After all, they had to learn to take it. A Captain aboard ship was an absolute dictator, and some of them were tyrants. A middy who couldn't handle unpleasantness wouldn't survive.

"Go on."

"There isn't much to tell. Mr. Smith had a squad emptying the dining hall for a thorough cleaning. He decided Stritz was doing a sloppy job, made him crawl to the hatch and back, pushing a chair."

"Doesn't sound so bad."

"Then he made him do it again. The cadet had enough, and refused. So Smith took him out to the corridor, where Bill Radz found them going at each other. He called me at once, since a middy was involved."

"Good Lord."

Lieutenant Paulson shook his head. "I gave Stritz a dozen, sent him crying back to his dorm. He has to learn to hold his temper."

I nodded. I would have gone easy too. It sounded like the boy had spunk, if not judgment.

"The truth is, I felt like giving Keene half a dozen for not knocking more sense into Guthrie Smith's head. What's a first middy for?"

"Did you?"

"No, but I set him against the bulkhead and reamed him so he'll remember. And four demerits. When Midshipman Smith came in, I let him have it. He ate lying on his bunk in the wardroom for a while. Damn it, he should know better."

A midshipman—any officer—couldn't maintain his authority by brute force, even with a cadet. Else a crewman physically stronger than his officer would have his own way. True, we caned middies as required, but they were considered young gentlemen and ladies, adults by law, but capable of youthful indiscretions that should be chastised. Belowdecks, sailors weren't beaten.

I mused, "Sometimes I wonder . . ."

"Yes, sir?"

"Whether we rely too heavily on the cane." I realized I spoke near-heresy. "I mean, a few strokes for a really serious offense is one thing, but is anything gained by making the barrel our first resort?"

"Our first resort is demerits, not the barrel, but, yes, something's gained." Paulson's reply was without hesitation. "Cadets, and middies, for that matter, have to learn to obey their betters. Life on a starship is no zark."

That was true. Disobedience or inattention could be fatal, and not only for the midshipman. I shrugged. I was no wild-eyed idealist. Society had finally recovered from a century or more of coddling rebellious children, and we were all the better for it.

"Is there anything else, sir?"

"No. See you at dinner."

After Paulson left I turned to my console to review a stack of reports that had accumulated since my last visit. Then, restless, I got up to walk, glad I now had room to pace without cracking my shins on low-slung coffee tables.

I sat back at my desk, flicked on the console. The trouble, I realized, was that I had no conception of what to do, either on this particular trip to Farside, or more generally as Commandant of Academy. When I'd become *Hibernia*'s Captain, my goal was obvious: guide the ship safely to Hope Nation and off-load the cargo and passengers. When I'd taken charge of Academy, I had no such aim. I had only to pass time until the cadets were ready to be graduated, until another group took their place. And, even more than as Captain, I was expected to govern as a remote, unapproachable figure.

I was the wrong man for the job. Too restless to immerse myself in minutiae better left to experienced drill sergeants, I had little to do but wander the halls, an awesome figure because of my reputation, but essentially useless.

Well, so be it. If I was to be a wanderer, I might as well begin. Perhaps in the process I'd learn something. I left my office.

I trudged through a deserted corridor to the classroom wing, beyond it to the barracks. Now, in nominal day, cadets were in class or in training. I stopped at Krane Hall, glanced about, saw no one. Sheepishly, I went in.

Rows of empty beds, blankets taut, the deck spotless. Sergeant Tripole seemed to have his joes well in hand, despite the altercation between his Cadet Stritz and the middy. I closed my eyes, oriented myself, crossed to the port side, walked along the row of bunks. There. That one had been mine. It seemed smaller, somehow, as did the whole barracks.

Had I been happy here? I reached over, ran my fingers along the bed frame. Innocent of treason to come, of betrayal of my oath, I'd striven to please my masters, while my body and mind altered. Less and less often did my voice break unexpectedly into the higher registers; daily I ran my fingers over my upper lip, waiting for the magic moment when I could justify a shave.

I sat slowly on the edge of the bed. Had I been happy? Well, innocent, perhaps. Was it not the same?

I jumped out of bed, kicked at Robbie Rovere's bunk. "Get up, Sarge'll be here any second."

Robbie groaned, but sat, rubbing his eyes. "Yeah, thanks." He sat for a moment, heard the soft hiss of the hatch and had leaped to his feet before it had fully opened.

Sarge snapped, "All right, you louts, listen up!" I grinned.

Sergeant Trammel could call us what he wanted—and he did—but I suspected he felt something other than the professional disgust he communicated to us. There was an aspect to his look when you succeeded in a particularly difficult task; the apparently casual touch of his hand if you were on the verge of losing your temper, and your self respect . . .

"Aye aye, Sarge," I echoed dutifully, along with the rest.

"Tomorrow we're off to the Training Station, so today you get special instruction. After classes, go with Corporal Tolliver to assembly dome. I have some holos to show you"—subdued groans: Naval holos could be excruciatingly boring—"and then a quiz or two to see if you've paid attention." He smiled grimly. "I hope some of you don't listen, like last time. That was fun." He left, shutting the hatch.

Robbie lowered his voice in a rough imitation of Sarge, "Go with Corporal Tolliver to the head. I have some turds to show you—"

Several bunks away Tolliver buttoned his jacket, favoring Robbie with a cold look. "Keep that up, Rovere. You make friends wherever you go."

"I try to, Mr. Tolliver." Robbie subsided, knowing when to lay off. As a cadet corporal, Edgar Tolliver had considerable power to annoy us, if not make us miserable.

Every barracks had a corporal, a cadet entrusted by the sergeant to make sure we got to the dome on time, or that the barracks was clean for weekly inspection. A corporal was still a cadet; he didn't rate a "sir," but like a middy was addressed by his last name only.

His only recourse if we disobeyed was to report us, but a diligent corporal could exact fairly strict obedience as an alternative to a tongue lashing or worse from Sarge. Corporal Van Fleet had been nicer than Tolliver, but he'd made middy and been sent on to *Prince of Wales*.

Robbie combed his hair meticulously, hoping to garner a few more few days before Sarge sent him back to the barber. "What will the holo be this time?"

I shrugged. We'd find out soon enough. I brushed my teeth, spat into the basin. Tolliver squeezed past to the next sink.

As a rule, middies were nicer than corporals, perhaps because they had less to prove. Still, you didn't want to get on the middies' bad side, as their hazing could be severe. Once they'd even made me stand regs.

Stripped to my shorts, I'd stood sweating on the wardroom chair groping for half-memorized passages from Naval Regulations, while below me they'd interjected scathing remarks about my physique and behavior. Rumor had it that if the middies were sufficiently irked, even the shorts were dispensed with. I hoped devoutly not to find out. Midshipman Jeff Thorne had said nothing, but he hadn't shared the amusement of my other tormentors. As second middy, he could do nothing until his senior had had enough.

After making our beds we marched to breakfast. Tolliver took his place in line with the rest of us; a corporal's only authority was in the sergeant's absence. Too bad Tolliver wasn't at one of the other tables. Even at mealtime, I had to watch every word I said, so as not to attract his attention.

"Hey, Nicky, why so quiet today?" Though Robbie woke slowly, once alert, he was depressingly cheerful.

"Maybe because he's learning some sense?" Tolliver's tone was acid. "Then he could stop polishing lockers."

I flushed. That whole incident would have gone unnoticed if it hadn't been for Tolliver. My suit had flopped over the edge of the locker so my door wouldn't close. I'd have noticed if I hadn't been in a hurry to get to Nav class. And Sarge probably wouldn't have known at all if Tolliver hadn't kept staring at my locker until Sarge turned to see what was the matter. Four hours polishing alumalloy lockers had left blisters on my hands and savage hate in my heart.

My emotions made me reckless. "I'm good at polishing, Mr. Tolliver," I said. "I could spit-polish your shoes, if you like."

Now it was Tolliver's turn to redden. He'd had Arlene Sanders polish his shoes as penalty for some imagined slight, and had discovered too late that Sanders had deposited far more spit inside the shoes than she'd brushed off the tips.

Tolliver seemed in good humor, though his eyes were sharp. "No thanks, Seafort. Where I really could use your help is getting ready for inspection tonight."

I grimaced. Well, I'd brought it on myself. Now Tolliver would have me tag along as he sauntered through the barracks, and every speck of dust, every imagined blemish, would be mine to correct. I knew he'd pay particular attention to the stalls in the head, and I could do nothing about it.

For much of the day I labored at Nav, listened dutifully to a lecture on the mysteries of the fusion drive, and managed in Colonial History to show Mr. Peretz I'd read at least part of the chapter. Then lunch, Off Hour, and the rigorous daily calisthenics a cadet never escaped.

Later, we convened at barracks, marched to assembly dome, and settled in for holovid instruction. The first holo might have been entitled "Ten Obvious Ways to Avoid Getting Killed on a Station," and the second, "In Case You Weren't Listening to the First."

Admonishments ringing in my ears, resolved never to exit a Station lock without a clamped helmet or to stroll in front of a laser during fire practice, I changed for dinner. At table I kept a low profile, hoping Corporal Tolliver had forgotten my impertinence at lunch.

He hadn't.

After dinner I followed him through barracks, broom and dustpan in one hand, mop and bucket in the other, damp rag draped over my arm. How dirty can a barracks get that is cleaned almost every day? One might be surprised, unless one knew Edgar Tolliver. I wiped imaginary dust, swept the aisles, pretended not to know he was going to call me next into the head.

"Is the shower a tad moldy? What do you think, Seafort?" There was no right answer, and we both knew it. But there were tricks to dealing with a cadet corporal, and I used one of them. I peered at the spotless bulkheads. "I think you're right, Mr. Tolliver," I said with enthusiasm. "They ought to be scrubbed down. Do you want me to get started?"

He frowned, but played out the game. "Yes, I think so. Let's check the stalls first."

The toilets were cleaned twice daily by those cadets who had earned Sarge's disfavor, so I knew they wouldn't be offensive. I also knew their condition wouldn't affect Tolliver's decision in the slightest.

"Look at this, Seafort. Can't let Sarge see that or we'll all lose an Off Hour. Scrub them out, will you?"

"Yes, Mr. Toll—"

He tore off a small piece of rag. "By hand."

"Of course, Mr. Tolliver." Damn him. Humiliating, and my knees and back would ache after. I smiled.

The next trick was harder. It was all in the tone; the words had to be absolutely guileless, if repeated to Sarge. I said brightly, "I'm glad you point these things out, Mr. Tolliver. Not many barracks have a corporal who knows as much about dirty toilet stalls as you do." He eyed me, but I beamed pleasantly. I beamed like a cheerful imbecile.

Still, he was the one about to stroll out of the head, and I was the one who'd get to scrub the barracks stalls for an hour or two. "I'll check back, Seafort," he said. "In case there's something we missed."

I bent to my work, slapping at his face with every swipe of the rag.

Half an hour later, he was back. "Enjoying yourself, Seafort? It's nice you've found work you're suited for. I'll try to give—"

"Attention." The voice was quiet, the tone agreeable, but Tolliver leaped to attention, his back ramrod stiff. I scrambled to my feet and dropped the rag, pressing my arms to my sides.

"What's up?"

Tolliver said, "Nothing, Mr. Thorne. We were cleaning the head for inspection, sir."

Midshipman Jeffrey Thorne clasped his hands behind his back, peered into the stall. "Very presentable. Mr. Seafort does a good job."

"I was just telling him that, sir."

"Yes, I heard." Thorne prodded the bucket of soapy water. "We're all proud of you, Tolliver."

Something in his tone made Tolliver's lips press tighter. "Yes, sir." Imprisoned at attention, he could do nothing.

"I'd like your friend Seafort to read us some regs again. Mind if I take him from you?"

Tolliver's look held pure malice. "No, sir, not at all."

"Good." Midshipman Thorne glared at me. "Leave the bucket, Cadet. Left face. Forward march. Left face. Halt." I did as I was told, and ended up facing the entry to the head.

Thorne strolled over to Tolliver, fingered the corporal's crisp gray jacket. "I'll see you again, Cadet Tolliver. You may put away the supplies. Or, if you like, finish the job yourself."

He patted Tolliver's shoulder. "All right, Seafort, forward march." He marched me through the dorm to the outer hatch. The other cadets watched with sympathy. No one wanted to be singled out for a middy's hazing.

The hatch closed behind us. At his orders I strode down the corridor to the first turn. "That's far enough, Seafort. As you were."

"Thank you, sir." I eyed him, smiling tentatively.

"I should have made him scrub the toilet, but I couldn't undercut him in front of you." Thorne grimaced, then brightened. "Did you see the look on his face?"

"Yes, sir, in the mirror."

"Belay that bit about standing regs. I'm putting together another mission. You care to volunteer?"

He was my senior; he had no need to ask me, but I wouldn't have passed it up for the world. "Yes, sir!"

I don't know how I'd been lucky enough to be chosen for Jeff Thorne's fabled "missions." Until the night the middies made me stand regs he'd taken no notice of me. After they'd let me go, Thorne had seen me back to barracks.

In a service corridor, he'd taken me aside, said a few kind words. Wary of all midshipmen, I made no reply. As if he hadn't noticed, he strolled, hands in pockets, chatting about the Navy, his experiences as a cadet, his own hopes, until at last he'd drawn me out. I told him something of Cardiff, and Father. I'd even casually mentioned Jason.

The first mission had come a week later. Others had followed.

Thorne glanced both ways, whispered, "I've got Bailey from Reardon Hall and Justin Ravitz waiting by the wardroom. You know them?"

"I know Justin, sir." I trotted along, trying to keep up with Jeff Thorne's long stride. "What's our mission?" Last time it had been to spy, belowdecks, on the techs manning the gravitrons. I'd learned it was the perennial goal of the wardroom to reach the control room unseen, bring the gravitrons slowly off-line, and enjoy the resulting havoc. They'd never succeeded.

Thorne made sure the corridor was empty, lowered his voice. "Mess hall." He clapped me on the shoulder. "I don't know why we only got one slice of apple pie for dessert, when so much was left over. And there should be ice cream in the cooler."

His smile was infectious; I found myself grinning like an idiot as I did my best to keep up with his stride. Mr. Thorne could be firm if we didn't listen at training, but at heart he was one of us.

Half an hour later Bailey, Ravitz and I girded ourselves at the cutoff for the corridor to the mess hall dome. Thorne peeked around the corner. "Go!"

We sprinted down the long corridor. As an officer, Mr. Thorne could go where he wished, but we cadets were a different matter. Though, if we were seen, he'd cover for us, wouldn't he? Better not to find out.

At mealtimes the mess hall hatch was left open, but this late in the evening it was shut. "Is it coded, sir?"

"The mess hall? Don't be silly." He touched the pad, hesitated. "Let me look in first." As the hatch slid open he cautiously peered in.

"All clear!" It was a whisper. We slipped inside the darkened hall. I looked up. Farside was halfway through the long Lunar night; the open filters revealed the bright cold gleam of a billion stars.

We huddled at a familiar table. Thorne beckoned us close. "If we're found here by the tables, I can claim I was hazing you, though I really shouldn't be in here at this hour. But if we're caught in the galley, we've all had it." He eyed his fellow conspirators. "Bailey, guard the hatch. If anyone approaches, snap your fingers loudly. Can you do that?" The boy nodded. "Then duck under a table over there where it's darker, and hope no one sees you. If things go wrong, try to get back to barracks."

"Aye aye, sir." Bailey grinned with excitement.

"Inside the galley we won't be able to hear Bailey, so, Ravitz, you stand just behind the serving rail and relay the signal. Anyone comes, snap your fingers at us and duck down. I'll snap back to tell you we've heard."

"Yes, sir."

Thorne punched the cadet's shoulder. "Aye aye, sir, you meant. Don't forget your training just because you're so nervous you're wetting your pants."

Ravitz said indignantly, "I'm not wet—"

"Shhh. Seafort, you and I will breach the enemy's hull. I'll get plates and find the ice cream, you look in the coolers for the pie. Can you find it in the dark?"

"It's not that dark, sir. The safety lights are on."

"Okay, let's go."

While Justin Ravitz crouched behind the rail we slipped through one of the two entryways between galley and mess hall. Thorne grinned. "Scared?"

"No, sir." My pulse throbbed.

"Liar. So am I. You think I want to be knocking at Mr. Zorn's hatch?" First Lieutenant Zorn was custodian of the barrel. Thorne squeezed my arm, whispered, "Hey, that's what makes it fun. I'll get the plates."

I pawed through an unlocked cooler, found only vegetables from the hydroponics chambers below. I closed the cooler door harder than I'd thought; the resounding clunk brought Thorne racing over. He hissed, "Keep it down, you idiot!" I nodded, trying to apologize with a placating smile. I'd never heard that tone from Thorne; his nerves must be taut.

The pies were in the third cooler. I took two, put them on a tray while across the galley Thorne fished in the freezer for ice cream.

A sound. I looked to Thorne; he hadn't heard. I slid the tray onto the counter.

The sound came again; fingers snapping. Thorne was just turning from the freezer. The snap of fingers, one more time, lower. Ravitz must be beside himself. Thorne was still unaware; I raised my hand, snapped my fingers once.

Thorne looked up. I pointed desperately at the rail and beyond. His eyes widened; he nodded, beckoned. I scuttled across the deck while Thorne made for the other doorway.

A voice, outside in the mess hall. "Who's under there? What are you—hey!" Running feet. "Come back here!"

Thorne disappeared into the far doorway. I ducked behind the mess-hall counter.

"Anyone in here? What's going—"

A crunch, as if someone had caromed off a piece of furniture just outside the galley. A yelp, a crash, a cry of pain. Racing steps. Thorne, making a bid for safety. Steps fading into the distance.

The lights snapped on. I huddled behind the counter. Footsteps, approaching the cooler. Could I crawl out unnoticed? I huddled low, padded forward. The intruder muttered, "God damn frazzin' cadets, I'll have their balls in a—you!"

I scrambled for safety. The voice roared, "You, Cadet!"

I dashed for the hatch.

"Freeze! Stand to attention!"

Perhaps he hadn't seen my face, and all cadet uniforms were alike. But I couldn't help it; he'd given a direct order and I couldn't disobey. I stumbled to a halt, froze to attention, a few steps from the unattainable hatch.

"Don't you move!" He came closer. My back twitched. Who had been my undoing, my ruination? They'd cashier me, surely, if not worse. Theft of Naval stores? Breaking and entering? Could they shoot me?

At last he came into my field of vision. A rating, a mere seaman. Were I a middy I could disobey him with impunity, but as a cadet, every adult in my universe was my superior. My eyes flicked to the hatch. A puddle of water, an overturned mop bucket. Was that what Thorne had encountered?

His fists bunched, he stepped back. For a moment I thought he was going to strike me. "Name!"

"Cadet Nicholas Seafort reporting, sir!" My voice wavered.

"Stay right here, joey. Understand?" He walked to the caller. I could dash for the hatch, but to what point? He'd seen my face, knew my name. I stood rock solid at attention, awaiting my fate.

A few moments later the rating pulled up a chair, sat, leaned forward, grinning. "You'll get it now, boy. Maybe they'll let me watch."

I said nothing. It hadn't required a response, and I knew if I spoke my voice would break. The sailor smiled, showing gap teeth. "Anytime, now. You just wait there at attention."

"Aye aye, sir."

"Hungry, were you?"

"I—no, sir."

"God, I hate you snotty little grodes. Well, this time you uppies'll get what's coming to you!"

Sweat trickled down my sides. I was saved from a reply by steps at the hatch. I looked up. Oh, no. Oh, God, no.

Sergeant Trammel growled, "What's going on here?"

The seaman came to his feet. "Look at this mess! I found this boy in—"

"I asked the cadet." Sarge hadn't bothered to raise his voice, but the seaman's whine halted instantly. A sergeant could do that.

Lamely, I said, "Cadet Seafort reporting, sir!"

"I know who you are; tell me why you're in mess hall!"

Still held to attention, eyes on the bulkhead across the hall, I groped for an answer. On a mission? Being hazed by Midshipman Thorne? Sleepwalking? I took a deep breath. "I was getting pie, sir."

"In the name of Lord Christ!" Sergeant Trammel's voice held such loathing that I flinched. "I thought you'd learned something by now, Seafort. Back to barracks."

"Aye aye, si—"

"He weren't the only one, Sarge. There were three, maybe four others. It was a regular raid. They kicked over my bucket and everything!"

Sarge wheeled on me. "Is that true?"

"I—yes, sir."

"What were you up to?"

"Stealing pie and ice cream, sir."

"I din' get a look at the others, Sarge. It was dark, and they were under tables and things. But this joey knows who—"

Sergeant Trammel wheeled. "Your name?"

"Lewis, sir. Elton Lewis."

"Go about your business, Lewis. I'll handle this."

"Yes, sir." The rating's voice held unmistakable malice. "My business is to clean up in here. Now I gotta clean up the mess they made too. The chief petty officer oughta know—"

"Yes, he should, and I'll tell him. If I hear anything more from you, there's some other things I'll mention as well. Get moving!"

Grumbling, the man picked up his bucket, swabbed at the mess. Sarge glowered. The rating finally dropped his eyes.

"As you were, Seafort! Into the corridor! Move!" Sarge propelled me forward, slapped the hatch closed behind us. The moment it shut he grabbed my lapels, thrust me against the bulkhead. "You useless excuse for a plebe! Thanks to you, I have to toady to the damned CPO!" I'd never seen him so angry.

"I'm sorry, Sarge. I didn't mean—"

"Bah! Special duties, the rest of the term. Six demerits! And that's just the start. When I—" He broke off. "Who was with you?"

"What? A couple of other cadets, and—"

"Names, Seafort!" He cuffed me. It didn't hurt, but I wanted to cry. "Who was responsible for this?"

I bit my lip. Please, God. Could you transport me home to Cardiff? Give me a miracle, just a small one.

"Please, sir!" How could I tell him—

"Their names!" He cuffed me again.

I screamed, "I'm thinking!"

Shock registered in his eyes, but he gave me a moment. "Well?"

I took a deep breath. It didn't seem enough. I took another. "Orders received and understood, Sarge. I—I won't tell you!"

The enormity of what I'd done took a moment to sink in. I flinched, expecting a devastating blow. Instead, Sarge released my jacket. "Very well, you've made your bed; now you sleep in it. Return to barracks, joey. I'm writing you up."

"Aye aye, sir." I saluted. He gave no response. I fled down the corridor.

In the morning I was forbidden to join the others for breakfast. Instead, Robbie Rovere brought a tray to barracks. He lowered his voice. "I'm not supposed to talk to you. What happened?"

I swallowed. "I'm in bad trouble. Do what Sarge said."

"You didn't come back 'til way after Lights Out. They say you wouldn't tell him what you did."

I nodded. "We were—just go back to mess hall, Robbie."

He nodded. "Yeah, I got to." Seeing no one, he pulled me into a quick embrace. "Tell them what they want, Nick. I want you next to me reading the graduation list." Embarrassed, he hurried out.

Two hours later Corporal Tolliver came in. By that time, I'd worked myself into such a state that even he was welcome. "Straighten your tie, Seafort. I'm taking you to the Commandant's office."

"What for?"

"So he can stuff you out the airlock? How would I know, you twit?"

I sank back onto my bunk, legs trembling. I'd never seen Commandant Kearsey's office, and I had no desire to. My heart pounded.

"Move, Seafort. I'm not getting in trouble over you."

I closed my eyes, reached for an elusive calm. "Yes, Mr. Tolliver."

I followed Tolliver to the Administrative warren, damp with fear. He stopped at the Commandant's outer hatch, knocked politely, brought himself to attention. "Cadet Corporal Edgar Tolliver reporting, Ma'am. I've brought Cadet Seafort as ordered."

The dark-skinned woman tapped at her console. "Send him in. Dismissed."

"Aye aye, ma'am!" Tolliver saluted, spun on his heel, marched out the corridor. He pointed me toward the hatch. "Hey, Seafort . . ."

I paused. "What?"

Tolliver scrutinized the bulkhead. "Good luck," he said at last. Then he was gone.

"Sit there." She indicated a row of stiff-backed chairs. I chose the farthest seat from her desk. It was against the bulkhead of the Commandant's inner office.

Hands on my knees, I sat stiffly, waiting for my execution. The duty sergeant checked her watch, buzzed the caller. "I'm going below for a moment, sir. The cadet is here."

"Very well."

Without a further glance she was gone. The console hummed in the sudden hush of the outer office. I shifted, rested my head against the bulkhead.

Voices. Ashamed, I sat forward, but after a moment leaned back again, pressed my head to the partition.

". . . could have handled it in barracks, but twice he refused to answer me. A direct order!"

Commandant Kearsey's voice was acid. "Well, Sergeant, what did you expect?"

A pause. "I don't understand, sir."

"Don't you see what you've done?" His voice faded. I strained to listen. " . . . teach these youngsters to hang together, to look after each other! That's what the Navy's about, isn't it? We're shipmates. We handle . . . problems, first within the barracks, then within the Base, ultimately within the Navy. We don't go running to outsiders for help."

"It all starts . . . obeying orders, sir." Sarge's voice was stubborn. "That's what I was taught."

"Of course it does, Trammel, that's why you've fouled up so badly."

"Begging your pardon, I don't see where—"

"What did you expect from the lad, ordering him to inform on his mates? Of course you wanted to find out who was behind it. You had every right to. But the last thing to do was ask him outright! How do you think he'd feel if he'd obeyed your order? What would his bunkmates think of him?"

I wiped at my eyes, overcome by feelings I hadn't known I had. I wasn't sure why I'd refused. I just knew . . . it was as if Father had been watching, through the hatch.

"How else could I find the other culprits, sir? I'm not Lord God, you know!"

"Careful there, that's close to blasphemy. You could have asked the others to step forward and admit their guilt."

"And if they hadn't? We'd be worse off than ever."

"Yes. So you could have forgotten about his cohorts, dealt with the miscreant you had collared. But asking him to commit treason—"

"Good Lord. Treason, you call it?"

"Yes, Sergeant, or something damn close. By asking him to betray his bunkmates for your sake, you gave him an impossible choice."

"But we're all the Navy, together, sir. Even you and I!"

Commandant Kearsey said quietly, "How would he know that yet? We're so far above them, we're on another plane. For now, the Navy is his bunkmates. Later, he'll understand the rest."

"I—It's just that . . . I was angry, sir, or I'd never have asked. The overturned bucket, that loutish sailor sitting there grinning. I knew he'd spread it all over, belowdecks."

"And you wanted the boy to act nobly in front of the swabbie. Well, in his way, he did."

A long pause. "So you're going to let him off, sir?"

"Eh? No, of course not. I can't, now that you've made an issue of it. I have to back you up."

"You won't expel him, will you?"

"Don't be silly. I don't mind cadets thinking me an ogre, but you should know better."

Sarge's tone was more reflective. "Seafort's not a natural leader, sir. It couldn't have been his idea. I'd really like to get my hands on the ringleader, but now we'll never find him."

"It was Thorne, if you must know."

"But, how—"

"He turned himself in this morning, when he heard Seafort had been caught. He said he'd ordered the cadet to take part. I didn't believe him for a minute."

"I'll never trust that little bugger again."

"Oh, don't go that far. He'll straighten out, most likely. I sent him to Zorn." A chair scraped. "Next time, use your common sense."

"Aye aye, sir. Is that all?"

"Send him in."

The hatch opened. Sergeant Trammel came out, saw me sitting bolt upright, hands pressed to my knees. "The Commandant will see you now."

"Yes, sir." I stood, adjusted my cap, marched in. Commandant Kearsey, seated behind his desk, fixed me with a steely eye.

"Cadet Nicholas Seafort reporting, sir." I saluted, came to attention.

"So. You're the insolent pup who refused a direct order from your sergeant."

My sides were clammy. "Yes, sir."

"I'm always disappointed when a cadet is brought into this cabin. It means we haven't done our job, that we've failed to communicate the basics. Or that the cadet is a failure who never should have been admitted."

Some response seemed to be called for. "Yes, sir."

"I won't belabor the point. Instead, I'll endeavor to teach you that orders are to be obeyed, without exception. If you graduate, you'll be in a position to give orders to sailors. You must first know how to obey them."

"Yes, sir."

"Take off your jacket and cap, and place them on the chair." I complied. "Bend over my desk. Put your hands on the desk, under your chin. Lean forward."

"Aye aye, sir." He hadn't touched me, but already the humiliation was excruciating.

Commandant Kearsey rolled back his chair and stood. Taking his time, he walked to the corner, picked up the wooden cane leaning there. "Have you ever been sent to the barrel?"

"No, sir."

"A caning isn't pleasant. However, as only a noteworthy offense causes you to be sent here, my punishment must be more persuasive than the first lieutenant's. Cadet, remain still until you're given permission to move."

"Aye aye, si—" The cane landed with the crack of a shot. I shrieked. My head jerked upward.

"You were told to be still."

"Yes, sir!" I thrust my head onto my hands, hoping to pin them in place. The cane came down again, and again.

When finally it was over I lay against the desk, exhausted from the effort to hold my position, wracked with sobs. Commandant Kearsey replaced the cane, picked up my jacket. "Stand."

I straightened carefully. He helped me slip into the jacket, turned me to the hatch. "Every act has a price, Mr. Seafort. You've just paid yours. The debt is extinguished." Gently, he propelled me forward. "Continue to do your best."

"Aye aye, sir." Like a toy soldier I lurched out of his office, scarlet with mortification, my buttocks on fire. The young woman at the outer console paid no heed. I tottered through the outer hatch, closed it behind me. In the corridor, I sagged against the bulkhead and wept.

In my Captain's blues, I gently stroked the bed on which I sat. It had been a bitter lesson. Sarge himself had brought my meals to the barracks, until I was able to march to mess hall without pain.

A sound.

I looked up, startled. "Who are you?"

The gray-clad boy jumped to attention. "Cadet Johan Stritz reporting, sir!" Wiry, muscular, a young face, worried eyes.

I snapped, "How long have you been watching me?"

"I'm sorry, I—I came in, sir, and you were sitting there. I didn't know what to—I'm sorry!"

"You come to attention, whether I see you or not!"

"Yes, sir. Aye aye, sir."

"Stritz, you say? You're the young fool who raised his hand against an officer?"

He gulped. "Yessir."

"If I hadn't been groundside I'd have . . . I'd—as you were!" I stalked out.

The steward poured our coffee and left the conference room. I eyed each of my officers gathered around the table. "How do we start?" It was my first staff meeting at Farside.

For a moment no one spoke. Then Sergeant Obutu said with diffidence, "In the past, we've just gone around the table, sir. Usually starting with Maintenance."

"Very well. Proceed."

Lieutenant Crossburn switched on his holo, skimmed his notes. When at last he looked up, he addressed the others rather than me. "For some reason supply deliveries are slow, despite my repeated calls to Lunapolis. We're supposed to get fresh vegetables every couple of weeks, to augment the yield from hydroponics. Nothing's come in for two months now." He waited for a response.

"Well?" My tone was short.

"What do you want to do about it?" It could have been a challenge.

"Are we low on stores?"

"No, between frozen foods and hydro—"

"Call again. Anything else?"

His look was sullen. "Complaints from belowdecks about middies in the service corridors. Sometimes they leave softies—"

"Mr. Paulson, have a word with Keene for the middies to pick up after themselves." I wasn't about to prohibit midshipmen from standing around the corridors; Lord God knows where else they'd congregate.

"Aye aye, sir." My graying first lieutenant made a note.

Crossburn shrugged helplessly. "I never heard back from Commandant Kearsey on the maintenance review plan I submitted, sir. I refiled a copy with you two weeks ago."

I grunted. "Very well, I'll look at it." I suspected a glance would be all I'd need. "Systems?"

Lieutenant Paulson shifted in his chair, as if weary. "Nothing new, sir. All base systems are working properly, and the Training Station is closed down at the moment."

"Until when?"

"Hillman's cadets are scheduled to go in three weeks."

"Very well."

Crossburn looked up importantly. "When do you intend to inspect the Station, sir?"

"In a day or two. Why?"

"If you won't wait for Sergeant Hillman, I'll have to make everything ready." Well, I couldn't fault his preparation, but the self-satisfied tone left me itching to . . . I didn't know what.

"Next?"

Lieutenant Ngu Bien oversaw classroom training. "Test scores slightly above median for the month, sir. On the whole, no problems."

"That's it?"

"Yes, sir."

"Well, that was fast. Mr. Pau—" Sergeant Obutu cleared her throat. "Yes, Sarge?"

"Pardon me for interrupting, sir. Perhaps you might look at the individual highs and lows in each class."

Lieutenant Bien rewarded her with a frosty look. "Does that concern your administrative duties, Sergeant?"

Ms. Obutu showed hardly any reaction. Only I could see her clenched fist under the rim of the table. "No, ma'am, it doesn't."

"Well, then—"

I overrode her. "A good point, Ms. Bien. Sarge is only a glorified secretary and has no business interfering." Sergeant Obutu's mouth tightened. I kept my voice casual, "By the way, Ms. Bien, would you mind telling *me* the individual highs and lows in each class?"

She colored at the rebuke. "Yes, sir, of course."

While she ran through her notes Sergeant Obutu's eyes met mine. My gaze was impassive, but just before turning away my eyelid twitched.

"In Nav Two, sir, Cadet Alicia Johns has the highest scores; she usually does. Jerence Branstead was second. Two failing grades this time, um, Arnweil and Stritz."

Lieutenant Paulson said, "That's under control, I believe. Their barracks sergeants have set up special tutoring."

"Along with the usual loss of privileges. Now, in History, we have Benghadi, Guevire, and Boland at the top. The low grades are Kyle Drew and Kevin Arnweil."

"Drew?" I puzzled. "Where do I know that name?"

Paulson said, "He was involved in the fatality, sir."

"No, that was Arnweil. He ran to the lock while—" I snapped my fingers. "The other one." The boy whose overeager launch had caused Edwards's death.

"Yes, sir."

I drummed the tabletop. "Let's see grades for Arnweil, Drew and Stritz for the last three months."

He punched in figures; a moment later the screen flashed. Scores for all three cadets had plummeted.

"It happens that way, sir. They'll pull up, sooner or later, or—"

"Yes?"

"Or wash out."

Jent Paulson started to speak, but I shook my head. After a moment I said, "Conference over. We'll resume this afternoon. Mr. Paulson, I'd like a report on all cadets in trouble. Talk to the instructors yourself, interrupt classes if you must. Also the dorm sergeants. Some problems may not show up in grades."

"Aye aye, sir. Are you— I mean, are we cleaning house, sir?"

"In a fashion." I left them, returned to my office. After brooding for half an hour, I roused myself and called in Sergeant Obutu.

"Sarge, about the conference. Why your question?"

"I'm sorry if I intru—"

"Belay that. What was on your mind?"

She leaned back, clasped her hands around her knee. "She irked me, sir, with that talk of medians. We don't teach medians here, we train cadets."

"Go on."

"It's none of my business, but the joeys, uh, talk to me sometimes. Perhaps because I'm a woman." She flushed, as if maternal traits ran against the grain of her duty. Perhaps they did. "I came across Kyle Drew scrubbing corridors, two days after the—the accident." She smiled apologetically. "He went on with his work, but I watched for a while, and chatted with him. He was Edwards's bunkie, you know."

"He has a heavy load."

Her tone was forceful. "You can't imagine how heavy. Kyle

insisted he knew it wasn't his fault, yet a moment after, he began to weep and couldn't stop."

I sighed. "How did you leave it?"

"I patted his shoulder, went on my way, and saw to it that I ran across him later in the evening. I've talked to him twice since."

"You should be a psych."

"Lord God forbid. The point is, he's not the only one, sir. You act, I mean, we act—the Navy—as if we're dealing with adults. They're just children, trying to learn about adulthood."

"I know." My words were barely audible.

"Sometimes, sitting in that outer room, when they leave the Commandant's office, your office now, I see the look in their eyes, the remorse, the shame . . . Sometimes I think you don't know how hard they try to please you."

"Oh, I do. Believe me."

"I remember one such cadet many years ago, a brave one. He cried in the outer corridor, when he thought no one could hear."

After a moment I met her gaze. "That was you?"

She looked to the deck, as if shy. "I was younger then. I don't mean to drag up old—"

"I was so terrified, I barely knew where I was." I reflected. "You're a good woman, Ms. Obutu."

"Thank you."

A moment passed. I said, "She's an ass, isn't she?"

Sergeant Obutu looked shocked. "Ms. Bien? Well, it would be impolite to disagree with you." But then she shook her head. "No, that was wrong. I do disagree. She sounds foolish, yes, but maybe she just can't see past the paperwork. Perhaps, confronted with a real cadet, a real problem, she'd react differently."

I was ashamed, both of my indiscretion and my lack of charity. "Yes. Very well. Dismissed."

Again, we were in the conference room. I snapped off the holo; the dry statistics disappeared. "Makeup work, extra duties to occupy Drew's mind. What else can we do for him?"

Paulson shrugged. "What else is there, sir?" Good point. Academy had its routines, and we shouldn't disrupt them. Still, something nagged at me, and I wasn't sure what.

"Let's see if his sergeant has an answer."

"I beg your pardon, sir?"

"Radz. Call him in."

Crossburn blurted, "Into staff conference? That's not how we—"

"He's staff, isn't he?" I waved the objection aside. "Ms. Obutu, page him, please."

A few minutes later Sergeant Radz took the seat I indicated. I summarized. "What's your opinion, Sarge?"

"He's moody, yes. But they all are, at that age. Who can say why?"

"You think he'll come out of it himself?"

Radz's mouth turned grim. "If he's to be a midshipman, he has to."

I stood, paced a few steps, studied the seams of the bulkhead. "But don't you think . . ."

Paulson cleared his throat. "It's a question of approach, and the Navy's philosophy is clear. They sink or swim on their own. Edwards's death was a tragedy, but Drew has to learn to cope."

Radz said, "When it comes down to it, sir, we're teachers, not nursemaids. We can encourage, but we can't hold their hands throughout their careers. The sooner they understand that, the better. If Kyle Drew buckles down to his work, he can still graduate with his mates. Otherwise you hold him back, or wash him out."

"Just like that?"

"No, sir, not just like that. I've taken him for long walks through the warrens, like I have Arnweil. He shrugs and closes tighter, until I want to shake him. If anything, the Arnweil boy has it harder than Drew; he was closer to Edwards. They both knew the Navy was serious business when they signed on."

Lieutenant Crossburn stirred. "If I may say so, sir—"

"You may not. I have no interest in what you have to say."

"I—aye aye, sir." He made his injury evident.

I sighed. "Your joint advice is not to interfere further. You're probably right." More than probably. A hundred seventy years of Naval tradition supported their position. "Very well. Keep me informed."

Chapter 9

The next morning I suited, went Outside with Lieutenant Bien and two sergeants to observe another training exercise. I said little, watching every cadet's unsure step like a mother hen, ready for a second dreadful incident. By the time we recycled through the lock, I was worn and irritable.

I unbuckled my suit and hung it in a locker, vaguely aware that the cadets, whom I'd expected to be chattering from accumulated tension, were unusually quiet. One boy dropped his helmet; it clattered loudly on the deck. He wilted at my glance. What was the matter with them? Were they all cowed by Edwards's death? As soon as we were alone I asked Lieutenant Bien as much.

Her face lit in a wry grin. "Yes, they're cowed, sir. But they'll be all right next time."

"How can you be so sure?"

"Because you won't be along." Her smile broadened. "Couldn't you see how they tiptoed around? How they watched you Outside? They're terrified of you."

I grunted. It was understandable, perhaps even appropriate. But still, I found it disturbing. The elusive thought led me nowhere.

That evening I had Sergeant Obutu set up my visit to the Training Station. We needn't seek Admiralty's approval; the Station was under my authority and we had a minishuttle of our own. I could stay as long as I wished, recall the shuttle to ferry me back to base.

Ms. Obutu rang back just as I settled into bed. "Tomorrow, right after breakfast. Mr. Trayn will pilot."

"Very well."

I lay in bed thinking of Annie. Was it too late to call? Should I contact her at all, or was it best to wait? Would I ever again be truly married? I drifted into restless sleep.

In the morning I dressed, went to mess hall, strode to my

149

place. "Gentlemen, be seated!" Four hundred eighty cadets sat, almost as one. "Good morning." I reached for coffee.

"Morning, sir." Jent Paulson poured for both of us.

"Where are the others? Ms. Bien? Mr. Crossburn?" I chewed on a breakfast roll.

"Ms. Bien is rotated to Devon, sir. She's probably at Earthport Station waiting for her flight. I believe Mr. Crossburn is checking your shuttle." He hesitated. "Have you reviewed the Log this morning, sir?"

"I haven't been in to the office yet."

"Tenere was sent up again. Ten demerits. I made him wait outside so I wouldn't be late for breakfast."

"Adam?" I felt a twinge of guilt. Some of his demerits had come from me. "Mr. Paulson, could you go easy on him?" What was I doing? The boy had earned what demerits he'd been given.

"Aye aye, sir, if you wish." He said no more. Perhaps I was intruding on his prerogative, but a Captain, any Captain, was allowed to have his way.

"Why?" I asked abruptly.

"Hm? The demerits? Ms. Bien gave him the last ones before she caught the shuttle. Something to do with Johan Stritz; he made the cadet late to class. I don't know the details."

I grunted. How was Stritz involved with Adam Tenere? It was bad discipline for middies to consort with cadets. I thought of Jeff Thorne, and shook my head. Still, Ms. Bien had probably overreacted. By asking Paulson to go easy I'd negate most of the damage, but I felt a continuing disquiet.

"What about the Stritz boy?"

"I have no idea. Ngu sent him to his sergeant, I imagine."

I sipped at my coffee. Stritz had enough troubles, and if Sergeant Tripole was as unforgiving as Radz, the boy was in for more misery. I made a note to look into it, when I got back from the Station.

After breakfast, I took my duffel to the lock, vaguely depressed that I couldn't get a handle on our personnel problems.

The shuttle was mated and ready. First Midshipman Thomas Keene waited to secure after we left. With him was Ardwell Crossburn.

"Ready, sir?" The pudgy lieutenant smiled politely.

I turned. "Yes, Mr. Crossburn. Good-bye."

"Good-bye? I'm going with you, sir."

"The hell you—That won't be necessary."

Crossburn looked aghast, while Midshipman Keene watched the byplay with interest. "You can't go alone, sir. The Station is shut down. Someone has to start up the machinery, get things— who'd prepare your meals?"

"Not you, Mr. Crossburn." I'd cancel my trip first.

"Whatever you say, sir. Let me point out that as maintenance officer I know where Station supplies are kept. Shall I call Mr. Paulson instead?"

"No, he has work to do." I was brusque. Why hadn't anyone mentioned that Crossburn would go along? Why hadn't I asked? "I can manage alone, I think."

"Sir, be reasonable! What if something went wrong?"

He was right, but the thought of his company brought an edge to my voice. "Very well, then. Get your gear—" I stopped short.

My idea was unorthodox, perhaps, but it would solve another problem as well. I took the caller from the hatchway, keyed it to the first lieutenant's cabin. No answer. Good; I wasn't too late.

I turned to the waiting middy. "Mr. Keene, run down to Lieutenant Paulson's cabin; Adam is waiting outside. He's to get his duffel and report to me here. If you see Mr. Paulson, tell him I said Mr. Tenere's chastisement can wait."

The startled midshipman knew better than to question me. "Aye aye, sir." He started off.

I called, "For Adam's sake, you'd better hurry." Paulson would be returning any minute. The middy raced down the corridor, prohibitions against running voided by my august authority.

Ardwell Crossburn cleared his throat. "Surely you don't intend to take a middy as your only—"

I rested my hand on the hatch and sighed. "Ardwell, be quiet. So help me, I'll—just shut up."

"Aye aye, sir. I must advise you I will file a written protest with Admiralty over—"

"Fine. Do it." If Admiral Duhaney relieved me, so much the better. Several minutes passed in uneasy silence before the two breathless middies returned.

"Midshipman Tenere repor—"

"You have your gear? Good. Get in the shuttle, we're going to Training Station."

"Aye aye, sir." Adam was less surprised than I'd expected; apparently Keene had forewarned him. Good. It was his job to look after his middies.

We boarded and took our seats. The minishuttle was just large enough to ferry a squad of cadets between Station and Farside Base. For larger groups, we'd go through U.N.A.F. Transport at Earthport Station.

The Pilot busied himself calculating weights and trajectories. Adam buckled himself in. "May I speak, sir?"

Midshipmen were expected to be seen and not heard. On the other hand, I'd summoned Tenere to special duty with me. Why seek his company if I intended to ignore him in the traditional manner? "Go ahead."

"May I ask, I mean—" He smiled weakly. "What are we—why am I here, sir?" I raised an eyebrow. "That is, I know you ordered me, but . . ." He tried again. "Excuse me, sir, I didn't mean that the way it sounded. I just—"

I said nothing until he trailed off in confusion. No wonder Ms. Bien had sent the boy to be caned; any more blathering and I'd cane him myself. Even Ardwell Crossburn would be better company.

The Pilot called, "Ready for liftoff, sir. Stand by." I waved, gripping my seat, though I knew acceleration from Luna hardly compared to the breath-wrenching gees needed to claw our way from Earth's possessive grasp.

I leaned back, closed my eyes, felt rather than watched our ascent. After several minutes the hull became silent. I sat forward, loosened the straps. In the next seat, Adam Tenere carefully did nothing to incur my notice.

I sighed. He had to be dealt with, for my sake more than his. "Mr. Tenere, that performance was disgraceful."

"I—yes, sir. I'm sorry. I won't speak again." His hands crossed tightly in his lap.

"Unsatisfactory."

"Yes, sir!" Tiny beads of sweat shone on his forehead. "What do you want of me, sir?"

"Ask what you intended to before we lifted."

"I wanted to know why we were going aloft. I didn't mean to step out of line, sir!"

"Look at me, boy!" His head jerked around. I grabbed his wrist, pulled his hand to touch my chest. He yanked it back as if burned, while his eyes remained locked to mine. "I'm your Commandant, not Lord God. They've given me the power to cane you, even to have you dismissed. But that's no reason to gibber like an idiot!"

"I'm sor—" He gulped. "Please!" An anguished cry.

"If you say sorry—" No, that wasn't the way. I forced calm into my tone. "Adam . . ." I wished I'd let well enough alone. Now I'd have to discuss matters I loathed.

"How did you feel when you heard I was to be Commandant?" I swiveled to study his face.

He muttered, "I was—proud, sir. We all were. I couldn't believe I'd actually get to serve under you."

"Why?"

"You know why! You're a hero!"

"So they say. Why?"

"How brave you are. The things you've done."

I snorted. "I was so scared I wet my pants."

"But that didn't stop you."

"When I called you to the shuttle bay, where were you?"

"At Lieutenant Paulson's cabin, sir."

"Waiting to be caned." He nodded. "Were you afraid?"

"It hurts!" He twisted away, stared through the porthole. "Of course I was."

"But you've been caned before. You know you can stand it."

His voice was small. "Yes, sir."

"When I've had enough of your idiocy and dismiss you, what then? Will you kill yourself?"

"What?" His jaw dropped.

"Will your father ever speak to you again? Will your life be over?"

Adam's tone was tight. "Yes, sir, he'll speak to me again. He'll love me as he does now. And my life won't be over."

"So. You know the worst I can do, and you can stand it. Now you too can be a hero."

The boy's anger dissolved into bewilderment. "I don't understand, sir."

"That famous incident in *Challenger*, when I rammed the fish. All I did was decide to act, and the rest followed. It was a throw of the dice, do you see? Or when I nuked Orbit Station. Was that heroism? I didn't dither, that's all. I made up my mind to commit treason to get rid of those damned fish, and I did it." I looked away, too ashamed to meet his eye.

After a moment, I forced myself to continue. "It's ridiculous that you'd need heroism to speak to me without babbling, but here's how you do it. Open your mouth, say what you intended, and shut it. From the moment you asked if you could speak, you were committed."

"I wasn't sure if . . . I mean, I thought you might be angry."

"Then keep your mouth closed in the first place. But you can't speak, apologize, and be silent all at the same time."

"Yes, sir. Thank you, sir."

I wanted to slap him. "You still don't get it? To have any respect at all, either from me or yourself, you had to finish asking your question. If you can't understand that, the Naval Service has no place for you."

He twisted at the flaps of his jacket, whispered, "You don't understand. I—I was afraid."

"Adam, we're all afraid! Fear has nothing to do with how you act!" I turned away. I'd failed, and in the process revealed more of myself than I could abide.

Let him stew in his juices, then. When we got back I would send him groundside, with unsatisfactory ratings. I fished in my duffel, took out my holovid.

Adam Tenere slumped in misery against the porthole. When he thought my attention was elsewhere, he wiped away a tear.

I tried to spot the Training Station against the points of light blazing like pinpricks in a black cloth. Of course I couldn't find it. I had no idea even where to look. "How long now, Pilot?"

"Nineteen minutes, sir." He pointed to starboard. "It's in view."

I grunted.

"Wait, I'll light it up." He keyed the caller, tapped in a code. A moment passed, and lights sprang to life in the distance.

The Academy Training Station bore hardly any resemblance to Earthport, the colossal terminus that served as our gateway to the stars. Earthport's warehouses bulged with the ores and foodstuffs from our colonies that fueled the Terran economy, and from her bays colonists and administrators even now poured outward to the settled worlds, despite the recent menace of the fish.

Our Training Station was but a single disk, and a small one at that. Though eleven Fusers were moored alongside, the Station's two bays could dock only two boats at a time.

Designed for simplicity, the Station carried no hydroponics and had only primitive mess facilities. Its few cabins were crowded with bunks, where cadets slept as tightly packed as in a ship's wardroom. The Station was powered only by solar cells.

I'd been here just once in my life, for eleven days, along with my squad and two vigilant instructors. It was an odd feeling to return on my own, but I was unlikely to run into trouble. The Station was conceived for just one purpose; to accommodate squads of cadets while they trained on the Fusers, and then to shut down again.

Pilot Trayn maneuvered us closer. For a moment I watched, then went back to my seat, waited for us to come to rest relative to the Station. At last the outer locks kissed; the seals pressed tightly against their Station counterparts.

I stood again. "Suit up, Mr. Tenere." I climbed awkwardly into my gear, while the boy slid into his with a lithe grace. Though the Station would be pressurized, I checked my helmet clamps with care and made sure my oximeter dial was in the green.

The Pilot, already suited, cycled the lock shut. Expecting full pressurization on the Station side, he didn't bother to pump to vacuum, but grasped the safety grip firmly just in case. Our outer hatch slid open, as did the Station's. He fastened our steel safety line.

Just short of the hatch I turned the middy by the shoulders, checking all his clamps. As I expected, they were secure. It was an officer's responsibility to look after his own safety, yet I felt better for the precaution.

We cycled through the lock into the Station. The Pilot keyed his radio. "Shall I wait while you check things out, sir?"

If the Commandant couldn't figure how to power up the Station, who could? "No, return to base. We'll call when we're ready for you."

"Aye aye, sir. I'll cast off in a few moments, then."

"Very well." The Station lock cycled shut. I warned Adam, "Stay on suit air until we've checked every cabin."

Power-up first; lights and heat would follow. We'd find

plenty of Q-rations in the coolers. I could bunk in the instructors' cabin and let Adam sleep where he wanted.

The boy cleared his throat. "Sir?"

"Not now, Mr. Tenere." According to the holo I'd reviewed back at Farside, I'd find the command console in the stationmaster's cabin near the instructors' quarters. "Come along."

I passed vaguely familiar cabins, then the aft lock. It wasn't until we'd nearly circled to our starting point that I came upon the stationmaster's cabin.

The console had an oversize keyboard, to accommodate suited fingers; they'd thought of everything. I tapped in my ID code, waited until my clearance flashed. While Adam Tenere watched over my shoulder I typed, "Oral communication, please," and waited for my suit radio to crackle.

Nothing. I tapped, "Command response."

"READY FOR RESPONSE."

"Terminate alphanumeric only."

"ALPHANUMERIC ONLY NOT IN EFFECT."

"Puter, respond, please." I swore under my breath. "Why can't I hear you?" Communications were glitched, and I'd let the shuttle leave us. Unless I could power the Station, we might have no way to call it back.

Adam Tenere coughed. "Sir, pardon me, but—"

"Quiet, I'm busy." If only I hadn't been so impetuous as to send the shuttle away. I tried to think through the puzzle. My radio worked; Adam could hear me. Again, I tapped, "Command response."

"READY FOR RESPONSE."

Well, at least I could communicate alphanumerically, and that wouldn't be so bad, once we checked atmosphere and desuited. But somewhere in the puter's—

"Sir, you're on—"

I spun round. "Two demerits! Make that fou—"

"—shuttle approach frequency! Switch your radio!"

The room was silent a long moment. I keyed my suit's caller, said tentatively, "Hello?"

"Puter D 1004 responding, Commandant." A firm tenor voice.

"Yes. Well. Commence power-up." I was careful not to look at Midshipman Tenere.

Console lights flashed. The standby bulbs brightened.

"Atmosphere check."

"Breathable air in all compartments."

I had to get rid of the middy. "Mr. Tenere, check all cabin air gauges on the double."

"Aye aye, sir." He left me to my mortification.

By the time he was back, power-up was completed; corridor and cabin lights transformed the Station to welcome familiarity. "All gauges at normal, sir."

"Desuit." I undid my clamps, glad to be free of my own nervous sweat. I hung my suit on a rack. "Put your gear in a cabin."

"Which—"

"Any of them. Now!" I rested my head in my hands. God, what a mistake, bringing a midshipman to witness my debacle. The tale would be all over Farside. I'd be a laughingstock thanks to a blunder even a cadet would know to avoid.

"Reporting for orders, sir."

I searched for a way to keep him out of my presence, to lessen my humiliation. I could have him check stores, establish radio contact with Farside . . .

With effort, I raised my head. Whatever the embarrassment, I'd earned it. "Mr. Tenere, thank you for correcting me. Ignore what I said about demerits."

"I'm sorry if I—" He broke off short. Then, with resolve, "You're welcome, sir."

"I'll put my gear in the instructors' cabin. Call Farside, tell them we're here safely." I stood to make my escape.

"Aye aye, sir. Pardon me, may I speak?"

"Yes."

He hesitated but a second. "Would you tell me why we're here, please, and what duties I'll have?" He waited only a second before blurting, "I mean, if you don't mi—I'm—Lord God damn it!" He rushed on, red-faced. "You don't know how I rehearsed that, sir! I was determined not to run my mouth!"

My voice was cold. "Two demerits are reinstated, Mr. Tenere, for taking His name in vain." That I wouldn't have.

"Yes, sir." He sagged. "Am I dismissed?"

"No. Try your question again."

"Aye aye, sir." He licked his lips. "Pardon me, but why are we here? What do you want me to do?"

"Very good, Mr. Tenere. I'm here to familiarize myself with the Station after twelve years absence. You're here to make yourself useful. One way is to run a comm check with Farside every few hours."

"Aye aye, sir."

"That's all. You've been accumulating demerits at an alarming rate. Start working them off; I'll log them for you."

"Aye aye, sir. I'll set up a relay with Farside and do a demerit before we eat."

"Very well." I carried my gear to my cabin.

After a Q-ration dinner I went back to my cabin and pored through chips of reports and memos I'd brought along, while young Tenere tackled another demerit. Though his subsequent appearance left no doubt that he'd been exercising, I'd of course have taken his word. A midshipman, like any officer, was a gentleman whose pledge was to be trusted. Were he to be caught lying about a demerit, he'd be cashiered on the spot.

I decided I should visit the Training Station more often; it was an excellent place to work without interruption.

The next morning, after breakfast, I lounged on my bunk trying to memorize cadets' faces as I'd seen Sergeant Ibarez do. Adam knocked politely to report he'd worked off another demerit. I ordered him to desist for a few hours. Demerits were intended to punish, not to abuse.

In the mess cabin at lunchtime, I made the coffee while the middy popped the tabs on two Q-rations and set them out to heat. When the chemical reaction between the inner and outer skins was complete, he brought them to the table and sat carefully, with a sigh.

I tore open my lid and fell to. To break the quiet I asked, "What are your plans for this afternoon, Mr. Tenere?"

He grimaced. "I'll run a comm check with Farside again, on schedule. Then another demerit. Maybe two."

"No, you're overdoing it."

He shrugged bitterly. "It's the only way I have to keep up, sir."

"Was that a complaint?"

He looked up, astonished. "No, sir. I know it's my own fault."

"They say humility is the first step to improvement." For a moment I debated. "Instead of demerits, help me check out the Fusers." It would give us both something to do. Though I was hardly finished with my self-imposed deskwork, I was thoroughly tired of cadet dossiers.

He perked up noticeably. "Aye aye, sir."

After the meal we suited, trudged to the empty forward lock. I made sure the hatches were set to standard codes, then cycled us through. Moments later, we stood on the outer rim of the disk.

"Fuser One is closest," I said.

We clambered with our magnetic boots across the hull. The Fuser floated meters from the Station rim, moored by a line from its lock. Without a line, even the inertia of an instructor kicking off from the hull would send the boat on a slow unpowered journey that would end only when she settled into a new elliptical orbit, or drifted off into the void.

"You jump first, Adam. Be careful."

"Aye aye, sir." He reached down, turned off his boots. If he'd been a cadet, he'd be tethered to a lifeline, but any middy knew how to launch himself properly.

Adam took care not to kick off with too much force. He floated slowly across to the trainer, switching his boots back on in midflight. His landing was awkward, but his boot made good contact with the hull.

I decided I'd made a fool of myself often enough for one expedition. Before jumping, I switched on my hand magnets. A smart precaution. I landed on all fours and would have bounced back into space had my glove magnets not gripped the hull. I brought my knees down, made boot contact, switched off my gloves. "Open the lock."

Moments later we were inside the tiny vessel. I walked to the cramped bridge, looked back to the main cabin and the two cramped wardrooms that would house cadets during their training. It all seemed laughably small. "Ever been on a ship of the line, Mr. Tenere?"

"My father showed me through *Freiheit*, sir, just after I graduated. I know she was just a sloop, but compared to this . . ."

"Yes." I sat in the Pilot's seat, gestured for the boy to take his place alongside. I stroked the silent console. Much could happen, even in a Training Fuser . . .

"Listen up, you cretins!" Sergeant Garver floated in the center corridor, hands on her hips. "You've watched the holos, so you know a Fuser is a hybrid, built especially for the Naval

Service, useful for nothing but training dimwitted cadets. It has no galley, no hydroponics, no recycling, no cargo hold, no disk. No main engine either, just thrusters so we can maneuver to and from our mooring. That's why we call her a boat, not a ship."

I watched Sarge dutifully, making sure I seemed to be paying rapt attention. Even if I could parrot back what she'd just said, roving eyes or fidgets were good for extra duties if not a demerit. Excited beyond words at finally boarding a real vessel, I didn't want the burden of her displeasure.

"And of course, she has a fusion drive, which is the main reason you're here."

The Trainers' fusion drives operated just like those of a ship of the line, with two important differences. First, puters could carry out many Fusion calculations performed by crew on a larger vessel, so a day's training could be concentrated in one aspect of the Fusion process.

The other difference was our size.

Many lives were lost before it was fully understood that fusion drives didn't work properly near a gravitational mass. The larger the vessel, the farther it had to be from a source of gravity to Fuse. A U.N. starship could Fuse from within a couple of hours thrust of Earthport, but a loaded ore barge, whose mass was colossal, would have to journey much farther to reach Fusion clearance.

On the other hand, our Training Fusers were so small their drives could be ignited safely almost anywhere in the Solar System. Except, of course, within the B'n Auba Zone, so close to the sun that regardless of mass, Fusion was impossible. At times, in our training, I cursed the Saudi astronomer and his demanding formulas over which we struggled.

Sarge waited for our attention. "Fusion is nothing to be afraid of, despite the nonsense you see on the holos. There's no sensation of blacking out, no eerie tingling in your spine, no crackling ions. In fact, you won't feel a thing, you won't even know we've Fused unless you look out the porthole and see—Seafort?"

"Yes, ma'am, I—" I struggled to recall what she'd been saying. "See nothing, ma'am. No stars, no light."

"All right, but if you poke Cadet Sanders once more you'll spend the cruise as chief officer of the head. I don't care whether she started it." Ms. Garver looked away, at last. "By now you joeys should be interchangeable parts, but I won't tax your resources. Three of you will go to the engine room, three to the nav room, and two to the bridge."

She nodded to her fellow instructor. "Mr. Reese and the cadets on the bridge will maneuver the vessel clear of the Station, and the nav room will calculate a Fuse."

Please, Lord, let it be the bridge. I hated Lambert and Greeley's Elements of Astronavigation with a passion. The nav room would mean endless hours of calculations under Sergeant Reese's unflagging supervision. The engine room was even worse. Fusion was a dimly comprehended principle, good for hours of sweat, agony, and fear.

"We'll make several jumps, and I'll probably shift some of you twits to different positions, but don't get your hopes up." Over the next week, the Fuser would flicker from one lonely spot to another. In the process, we'd get infinite and nerve-wracking practice, both at Fusion calculations and at Nav. Each time the boat Defused, perspiring cadets would have to identify our positions with painstaking accuracy.

I knew the trickiest calculation would be the one that brought us back home to Station. On a long cruise, a ship merely Defused several times for nav checks. On quick trips like ours, that wasn't an option.

Nonetheless, we'd have to emerge near the Station when we Defused. Even though Fusers were equipped with over-size propellant tanks, unskilled cadets would be at the controls during docking, and prodigious quantities of propellant would be wasted.

Arlene Sanders caught me a good one in the ribs. I flinched, but kept my eyes glued to Sarge. Later, there would be time for retribution.

Naturally, I got the nav room.

Our first goal was an uninhabited spot between the orbits of Jupiter and Saturn, thirty-eight degrees above the elliptical. We labored at our calculations until they all agreed. That took an amazingly long time, because Van Roef kept dividing mass instead of multiplying. Finally, when even Sergeant Reese had developed an edge to his tone, we all got it right, and we passed our calculations on to the bridge. Then another endless wait, while the bridge crew completed their own chores.

At last Mr. Reese snapped, "For God's sake, get up and stretch; this fidgeting drives me crazy."

"A short drive," muttered Robbie Rovere, a tad too loudly. Mr. Reese glared, but decided not to hear.

If the object was to teach us the tedium of Fusion, the exercises succeeded admirably. Between jumps, the instructors divided us into squads, had us suit up, and took us a few at a time out onto the hull for exercise and training.

I was in the second group, with Van Roef and Sanders. This time it was Sergeant Garver who went Outside with us. I'd trained on the Hull, and I'd been taken Outside at the Training Station, but clambering on the hull of a tiny boat under cold unforgiving stars was a different matter altogether.

My breath rasping in my helmet, I made my way back and forth between the drive shaft and the prow. Though for once Sarge had no objection, there was no small talk among us; we were all concentrating on keeping contact with the hull, and on ignoring the terrifying vastness of space.

Before going in, we practiced airlock maneuvers. It was harder than one might think for several people in zero grav to enter an airlock, and remain oriented toward the same plane. But if we didn't, someone's stray kick could smash a helmet. Sarge demonstrated twice for us, and watched from inside the lock as we struggled to release ourselves from the hull, grab hold of the handrings, and pull ourselves in at a ninety-degree angle.

Our first try was clumsy, our second better, and our third a fiasco. Van Roef managed to let go of the ring too early and set himself adrift in the middle of the airlock, feet kicking helplessly in all directions until he floated near a bulkhead and grabbed a handring.

I climbed in with less difficulty, but Sanders, watching Van Roef's antics from the hull, doubled over with laughter and forgot to turn on her boots. She let go of the handhold, and, by some quirk, found herself floating inches from the hull, with virtually no discernible motion relative to the ship.

We all knew Sarge had a thrustersuit, but nothing was more frightening than being unattached and unable to reach safe haven. Without rescue, you could spend eternity in the coffin of your suit. It would be particularly maddening to be so close to the ship, yet unable to touch it. Without a T-suit, Arlene was helpless.

She let out a scream that rang distorted in my eardrums. Van Roef kicked convulsively, bounced off a bulkhead.

Sarge had seen it all before. "All right, Seafort, haul her in."

I grasped the inside ring, leaned out as far as I could, reached for Sanders's frantic fingers, just as Van Roef's boot slammed into the airlock control.

The hatch slid shut. A shriek. A moment before I realized it had been my own. I twisted. A wave of agony radiated up my arm. I was caught in the hatch seals, more of me Outside than in. Arlene Sanders's hand was inches from mine. My left arm was almost certainly broken. Desperate, I tried to free myself.

"*DON'T MOVE, SEAFORT!*" Sergeant Garver's urgency penetrated my panic.

"Ma'am, my arm's—"

"Don't wiggle! Your suit could rip!"

Oh, Lord God. *We are heartily sorry for having offended thee.* I was utterly still.

Van Roef whimpered. "I'm sorry, I didn't mean to—"

"Shut up. Against the bulkhead." Sarge slapped the hatch control. No response. After a moment she cursed, tried again. "Seafort, I'll have to reset the controls. Just a moment while I power down."

"Nicky!" It was an urgent whisper. "Reach out."

"Belay that, Sanders, he's not to move. You're in no danger, I'll come for you as soon as I can." Sarge dialed the code, waited for the light to blink.

"Nicky, I can't wait. Get me back now or I'll . . . lose it."

Tentatively, I stretched. Pain washed through my forearm. "I can't."

"I've got a red light, Sarge! My air!" Van Roef sounded near panic.

Ms. Garver slapped the hatch release over and again. "Calm down, Van Roef, you still have half an hour. Seafort, the hatch is jammed." She pounded the lock panel. "I'm going to wind it open manually. It'll take a few minutes."

"Yes, ma'am." I rested my head against the hull. God, it hurt.

"A few minutes?" Van Roef's voice came in a squeal. "My air is going bad!"

"Steady, boy." Sarge opened the emergency panel, fitted the lever to the gear.

"Nick! Now!" Sanders bit back a sob.

I stretched as far from the lock as I dared. "Open your fingers." We could almost touch.

"Seafort, she'll be all right. Don't stress your suit!"

"Yes, ma'am. She can't wait much—" I closed my eyes to the pain, stretched my broken arm. A moan. I pressed my lips tight, willed myself silent. Just another inch . . .

"The God damned winder is jammed!" Sarge's blasphemy echoed through our silence.

"I need air!" Van Roef dived past Sarge, slapped the inner control. The red safety light flashed. The hatch stayed closed.

Sarge flung him back across the lock. "Moron, the lock panel is defective! If the hatch opened you'd have killed everyone inside!" She keyed her caller. "Reese, get everyone suited, flank. We'll have to pump out; I need a winch here and we can't open or shut the outer lock. You have five minutes. And have a tank ready for Van Roef, he's running low." Only by pumping out the Fuser could her inner and outer locks be opened at the same time.

I stole a glance at my air gauge. Nearing empty, but still on green. I had time.

"Nicky!" Sanders's eyes held something I didn't want to see. I strained against the pinion of the hatch. If my suit ripped, I'd die instantly. Or perhaps not instantly; I thrust down that horrid thought. Sanders was my bunkmate, and she needed help. I had no choice.

I thrust my arm toward her, battling torment. It wasn't enough. I recoiled, gritted my teeth, lurched from the hull. Something slipped, and I nearly passed out.

Our fingers touched. I stretched the last iota, curled my finger around hers. Stretched as if on a rack, I fought dizziness, willing her closer.

Van Roef wailed, "Never mind them, I need air! I'm on red! I can't breathe!"

"Come near the panel again and you won't need to breathe. I'll kill you myself." I think Sergeant Garver meant it.

Our fingers locked. Sanders plucked greedily at my hand,

my wrist. After an endless moment, her other hand made contact. She hauled herself up my arm toward the hull. Even after she reached it, for a moment she clung to me as to a liferaft. Releasing the tension on my imprisoned, throbbing arm, I sagged against the lock. "You're all right, Arlene. Just hold on."

She was crying. "Thank you. Oh, Lord God, thank you."

"You're all right." I repeated my inadequate comfort.

Helmets touching, we waited together for the lock to open. "Do you have air, Nicky?"

"Enough. You?"

"I think so. I've just gone red."

"Sarge?"

"We're almost pumped out. Once I have the winch it won't take a minute."

"What if . . . the winch doesn't work either?"

Her voice was grim. "I'll torch through the lock, if I have to. I'll try the winch for five minutes, then get the torch. We still have more than enough time. I'm with you, Seafort. Just hold still, don't tear the suit. How's Sanders?"

"I'm—"

"She's fine, sir. I've got her now."

Reese's voice cut in. "We're pumped, Sarge. Opening up."

True to her word, Sarge had the outer hatch cranked open within a minute. I yelped as the pressure against my arm was released, but held still.

"All right, there's no break in the suit skin. I've turned on your boots; can you walk?" She slipped a steadying arm around my waist. Inside, we waited while air hissed back into the ship.

They helped me strip off my suit, gently supporting my injured arm. In the corner Van Roef whimpered, unnoticed. Mr. Reese plotted a course for the Station and we Fused at once. The portholes faded to black.

"I'll try to set it, but I'm no med tech." Sarge took my wrist, put her hand on my upper arm. I braced myself, cried out only once. While setting the splint she paused, reached to my face, gently brushed hair away from my eyes. Did her hand linger an extra second? "Good job, joey." She turned back to her work.

After, I sat on my bunk in the tiny wardroom crowded with

subdued cadets, sipping hot cocoa. Arlene Sanders came close. "Thanks for helping."

I rested the cocoa on my knee. "No problem. I was just standing around with nothing to do." I stumbled to a halt, realizing my humor was out of place. She helped me to my feet, embraced me. I hugged her awkwardly with my one good arm. For a moment her head rested on my chest. We separated. I sat quickly, odd and unexpected feelings rising.

We Defused, and Mr. Reese began maneuvering us to our bay. Sarge loomed in the wardroom hatch. "Mr. Seafort, in the airlock I ordered you to hold still so you wouldn't tear your suit. You didn't. What do you have to say for yourself?"

I stood. "No excuse, Sarge."

"Two demerits, when you're healed. Sanders, you were never in trouble. I would have retrieved you the moment the lock was open. You risked Seafort's life for nothing. Come with me."

Her face set, Arlene followed into the other cabin. After a few moments we heard her yelp as the strokes fell.

The day after we returned to base, Cadet Van Roef was shipped groundside. We never saw him again.

"Is your arm all right, sir?" Adam Tenere sounded anxious.

I realized I'd been rubbing my forearm. "Of course."

The boy looked wistfully at the thruster controls.

I needn't be a mind reader to guess his thoughts. Every middy yearned for that rare opportunity to pilot a craft. It was as close to making Captain as most of them would ever get. "Not a chance, Mr. Tenere."

"I didn't say anything, sir."

I snorted. "You didn't need to." I punched in the startup codes, waited for the boat to come up to full power. I checked the screens. I wouldn't care to be adrift in an undersupplied, underpowered Trainer. I touched the silent speaker. Even a Fuser's communications were disabled; her caller had but one frequency.

It had been so for some seventy years, ever since the Screaming Boy affair. Five cadets had stranded themselves too close to Mercury to Fuse; their N-waves were distorted by the nearby gravitational mass. The cadets' desperate cries for help across every band had utterly unnerved the cadets in the other Fusers, and made the matter a sensation for the holozines even though a rescue ship was speeding to the scene.

The embarrassing incident had enraged the Commandant, who ordered the radionics on every training vessel set to its own single classified frequency, decodable only by the Station and the command ship.

Despite the wrath of their Commandant, the boys were fortunate they hadn't Defused so close to the Sun that their heat shields couldn't cope. Such a potential disaster was one reason we always checked and rechecked Fusion coordinates with meticulous care.

I ran systems checks, powered down. "Let's go."

We resealed the hatch. Outside, the midshipman asked, "Where to, sir?"

"Mother. The Fifth one down the line." On occasions when several squads of cadets practiced at once, they were accompanied by *Trafalgar*, a fully powered command vessel, generally nicknamed Mothership. More than once, she had towed home a Fuser that had squandered its propellant before reaching the docking bays. It was not a distinction to be sought.

We negotiated our way across the flat of the Station disk, past the obstacles of our radionics and sensors. Finally, we clambered into *Trafalgar*'s lock.

The Mothership was substantially larger than the trainers, but though she had gravitrons and fusion drives, she wasn't designed for interstellar travel. No hydros, minimal stores. She took a crew of seven. Instead of the usual circumference corridor, her lock opened into a cabin that stretched from starboard to port, at the forward end of which was the bridge.

At the console I checked atmosphere, unclamped my helmet and stripped off my suit. I stretched luxuriously. Adam took his place at the second officer's chair, automatically straightening his tie. I smiled; *Trafalgar*'s was hardly a real bridge, and the middy wasn't reporting for watch.

I leaned back. "Power up."

"Aye aye, sir." The boy studied the console for a long anxious moment.

"Go ahead," I said. "If you blow us up I won't be around to complain."

His smile was strained. "Aye aye, sir." My remark had a purpose, however unpleasant. A middy had to learn to cope with pressure. If he was on the bridge when a fish loomed . . . my hand tightened on the armrest.

Tentatively he tapped a sequence of commands. Figures flashed across the console. After a moment the lights brightened. So did Adam. "Power-up achieved, sir."

I wouldn't let him cast off, but no harm in continuing the exercise. "Bring the thrusters on-line."

"Aye aye, sir."

I watched from my own console. "Check airlock seals."

"Airlocks sealed, sir."

"Fusion readiness, please."

"Aye ay—but, sir, we're still moored to the Station." If we tried to Fuse now, we'd destroy our ship, and the Station as well.

"I know, we're not going anywhere."

"Readying for Fusion, sir." He slid his finger across the screen; the green line followed.

Normally, at this point, the engine room staff would be monitoring N-wave generation, making sure we were within tolerances. Unstaffed, we'd have to rely on the puter, and that simply wasn't done. "Shut down, Adam."

He sighed. "Aye aye, sir."

As the fusion motors dimmed, the green console light faded. No, I wouldn't take him Fusing, but there was no reason the two of us couldn't make a short run on auxiliary engines. The middy would be in seventh heaven, and the practice would benefit him when—

The speaker crackled. "Station Puter D 1004 to *Trafalgar*, respond please."

I snatched up the caller. *"Trafalgar."*

"Farside Base on-line, for the Commandant."

I looked to the middy. "Your comm check, most likely. Don't forget to call them back when we reboard."

Adam shook his head. "It's early yet, sir, and they wouldn't ask for you on a comm check."

"True." I hesitated. I could give the youngster his chance at the controls, return the call later. Farside could handle things without me for another hour. "Tell them—" No, better to get it over with. "Relay to *Trafalgar*, please."

Moments passed. Sergeant Obutu. "Sir, your Mr. Tolliver, groundside. Shall I patch him through?"

"What does he want?"

"He wouldn't say."

"Very well, put—" I stopped. Not, "He didn't say," but, "He wouldn't say." She'd asked and Tolliver wouldn't tell her. Odd, even for my eccentric aide.

"Seafort here."

Seconds hesitation, while the voice was relayed from Devon. "Lieutenant Tolliver reporting, sir. I need you groundside."

I stared unbelieving at the speaker. A most peculiar summons indeed, from a subordinate to his Captain. "You what?"

Adam gave his rapt attention.

Tolliver's voice was taut. "We need you here ASAP, sir. Please come directly."

Had he lost his mind? "Full report, Lieutenant! What's going on?"

"Aye aye, sir. This, uh, isn't a secure line."

"Of course it is."

"Remember your report from *Challenger,* sir? The holozines had it as soon as Admiralty." Tolliver was right; with modern technology our news media could intercept and decode most interplanetary transmissions.

"I'm at the Training Station." My tone was petulant. "Can't you tell me now?"

"Yes, if you insist." Tolliver's voice had an edge. "On the other hand, you could trust my judgment."

On the other hand, I could cashier him. This was rank insolence. "Does First Lieutenant Sleak know about this rigmarole?"

A long pause. "No, sir. And there's no point in telling him."

I muttered, "Tolliver's gone round the bend." Adam Tenere studied his nails. "Very well, Edgar, I'll be down shortly. By Lord God, this had better be worth it!"

"Arrange a special shuttle with Lunapolis Transport, sir. Don't wait for the nightliner."

Enough was enough. "Don't give *me* orders, Tolliver." I rang off, seething. "What are you staring at, Middy? Call up Farside, we need the shuttle!"

"Aye aye, sir. You were just talking to Far—" Adam saw my expression, subsided just in time. Moments later, he had Sergeant Obutu back on the line. She told me Mr. Trayn's shuttle would need to refuel before returning.

"Wonderful." Three hours, at minimum, probably more. "Suit up, Mr. Tenere. It's back to the Station."

"Aye aye, sir." Tenere grabbed his suit, politely handed me my own. One leg in, he stopped short. "Sir, if time is important . . ."

"Yes?"

"Why don't we take *Trafalgar*, meet the shuttle over Farside?"

"That's ridicu—" I pondered. If we left immediately, we could be above Farside by the time the shuttle lifted off. "No, there'd be no one to return *Trafalgar* to the Station."

"I could, sir." He scanned my face, saw the refusal, fell back to a second position. "Lieutenant Paulson or one of the sergeants could come on the shuttle, change places with you. He and I could sail back here and wait for the shuttle to pick us up."

A waste of propellant, but the Navy was well stocked. Were a few saved hours worth the trouble? Probably not, but in that case, why was I rushing home in the first place? Either I believed Tolliver, or I didn't.

"We'll need our gear from inside." I ignored the delight in Adam's eyes. "Suit up, run back for our duffels. Do I need to go with you, or will you be careful?"

"I've been Outside on my own, sir. Many times." As an officer on Farside, he'd had ample opportunity.

While he was gone I called the Station yet again, made arrangements for the shuttle to meet us.

When he returned, we cast off. I gently fired our thrusters, rocking the ship to break us free. Watching me, Adam's face fell. I said nothing, rocked harder. The seals parted.

We drifted slowly away from the Station. I'd have to turn the ship so the auxiliary engines would bear. The boy watched, yearning.

I sighed. "All right, take over. Head us home."

His manner was almost reverent. "Aye aye, sir. Thank you, sir." He eased his hands onto the controls. Two squirts with the port thrusters, after a moment another with the starboard. He tapped the keys, calling up preprogrammed coordinates.

I watched from the first officer's seat. At the conn, all the middy's gawky hesitation had disappeared. His eye flickered from console to viewport and back, accomplishing both the navigation and the positioning of the ship with graceful competence.

"Ready to fire main thrusters, sir."

"Proceed."

His hand tightened on the throttle, but his eye never left the positioning grid on the console. At exactly the right moment he brought up the power. Slowly at first, but steadily faster, the Station receded.

"With your permission, fifty minutes burn, sixty-seven minutes cruise, fifty minutes retro, sir."

I tapped at my console, repeating his calculations. They seemed right, but then, Nav had never been my best subject. "Very well."

Adam set the alarm, leaned back, one hand ready to pull back the throttle if an engine shuddered. "I had another idea, sir. I could take you directly to Earthport Station, have the shuttle meet me there." His eyes were on the console. A vein in his temple throbbed.

"No." Docking at the shuttle was one thing, approaching the Earth's busy commercial hub was quite another. Even if we avoided disaster, a clumsy mating would reflect badly on the Navy.

"But we—I just meant— Aye aye, sir. I didn't mean any—" His mouth tightened.

I snapped, "Show that sullen face again and it's two more demerits."

He whirled. "Sullen? Sir, I—" He bit off his words, was silent a long moment. Finally he spoke with resolve. "Sir, excuse me, but you misunderstood. I was disgusted with myself because I can't get out even a simple sentence without stammering."

My anger melted. "Why, Adam?"

He studied the console. "I wish I knew. I can talk to Mr. Keene or Guthrie Smith, or the cadets. Maybe it's . . ." He trailed off. I waited. "I want so much to impress you," he muttered.

"Because I'm Commandant?"

"No, sir. Because you're Captain Seafort." He reddened. "I wanted to be able to tell my father I'd served under the great Mr. Seafort. Now I can tell him I knocked you down, babbled every time I saw you, and earned more demerits in two weeks than I did in a year as a cadet."

"No, you haven't." I cleared my throat, spoke gruffly. "All remaining demerits are canceled, including the ten for which you were sent to Mr. Paulson." It was bad for discipline, but the boy's pilotage deserved reward, and his idea had saved me several anxious hours.

"You mean that? Really?" His eyes held wonder. Then, realizing what he'd said, he blushed. "I'm sorry, that sounded, of course you—" He shook his head. "See? I meant, thank you very much, Captain."

"Very well." I closed my eyes, pondering. After a time, I said, "Mr. Tenere, for the next month, when I or any of the lieutenants speak to you, do not answer for at least five seconds. Every time you fail to do so, report yourself to the duty officer to be logged a demerit. I'll log this order so they won't accuse you of insolence. Is that clear?"

"Aye aye, sir."

"One demerit."

A long pause. "Aye aye, sir."

I leaned back, wondering if it would help.

While waiting for the shuttle to mate with us I had Sergeant Obutu put through a call to Devon.

In a few moments she came back on the line. "Sir, I can't get through. All incoming lines go to a recording. 'Circuits in use for training exercise.'"

My hackles began to rise. I said slowly, "Sarge, I think Tolliver may have lost his mind. Arrange for a squad of Marines to meet me at London Shuttleport, just in case."

"Aye aye, sir. Are you sure that's necessary?"

"Better safe than sorry."

"Do you intend to shoot your way in?"

I grinned mirthlessly. "With that joey, there's no telling." If Tolliver had indeed gone glitched, only Lieutenant Bien, Sleak and the drill sergeants were around to stop him.

I passed through the Earthport Station lock.

"Captain Seafort? Please follow me, sir." A tech, from Naval Transport. We strode through the busy corridor to the shuttle departure bays.

Though I normally disregarded the perks of rank, this time I was glad my standing allowed me a special shuttle. I could imagine explaining to some lieutenant at Transport that I needed to rush groundside to see if my staff lieutenant had carried out a coup on the Academy grounds. Would I care for a few tanks while I was at it? A couple of laser cannon, perhaps?

When we finally set down at London Shuttleport, my nerves were raw with worry. If Tolliver were no longer firing on all jets, he might kidnap or even kill me when I appeared. On the other hand, if I stormed Academy gates with an armed force when he had a valid reason for what he'd done, it would be all over the holos. I'd no doubt end up in a rebalancing ward next to Annie.

As dusk fell I met with the lieutenant of Marines, still undecided. In the end, I compromised: if I didn't call within two hours, the Marines were to enter the compound and sort things out. I boarded the waiting heli. Minutes later we put down on the Academy pad.

While the guards approached I jumped out, ducked under the moving blades. "Stand to! Where's Tolliver?" The guard aimed his light at my face.

"Aye aye, sir." He switched off his flashlight. "Just making sure it was you." He came to attention.

"What in blazes is going on?"

"Mr. Tolliver's on his way, sir. I rang Admin when your Pilot called for clearance." So much for surprise.

"Very well." I stood fuming until three figures hurried toward the pad. Tolliver, Sergeant Ibarez, First Midshipman Sandra Ekrit.

Tolliver snapped a brisk salute. "Lieutenant Edgar Tol—"

"Belay that! What's this about?"

"Lieutenant Sleak is dead."

"He's what?" I felt shock, instinctive fear, but it wasn't followed by a sense of personal loss. I hadn't known the man well. I took a slow breath, relaxed my taut muscles. No coup, no crazed Tolliver. "Damn it, why couldn't you have told me over the—"

"He shot himself."

I gaped.

"In his quarters. The Branstead boy found him after morning run."

I stood stunned. "But . . .why? It makes no sense."

"I agree."

My relief turned to anger. "Why did you seal the base? I thought you'd gone out of your mind!"

"Yes, sir. That's always a risk."

Sergeant Ibarez and the middy watched the byplay with fascination. I snarled, "Damn you, Toll—"

"I did it to give you time. To keep your options open."

"Time? Options?"

His tone was patient. "I didn't know how you wanted to handle this, sir. Once the zines get hold of it—"

"They don't care about a poor lieutenant on a shoreside—"

Sergeant Ibarez cleared his throat. "Begging your pardon, sir. It's you, not Mr. Sleak." He smiled apologetically.

"Have you two lost your minds?"

Tolliver. "If you blow your nose it's news, sir. Oh, I know you don't like it, but glaring at me won't change a thing. Once they hear that your second in command killed himself without motive, they'll camp outside our gates snapping at anything that moves."

Damn his insolence. The fact that he was probably right did nothing to lessen my annoyance. My mind spun. "Did Sleak talk to anyone? Who found him?"

"Jerence Branstead, sir. The cadet."

"What was *he* doing there?" I sounded petulant.

Sergeant Ibarez. "I batonned him on morning run."

I swung to Sandra Ekrit. "Why are you here, Middy?"

She replied with dignity, "Because Lieutenant Tolliver ordered me here, sir."

Her manner brought me back to my senses. We were all four of us standing under the heli blades, arguing within sight of the guards. It wouldn't do. "Very well, to my office." I stalked down the path.

Tolliver matched my pace, ahead of the rest. "You're right, it was probably the middy's fault, or Cadet Branstead's. I'm glad you're taking charge."

"Shut your mouth."

"Aye aye, sir."

I increased my stride, ablaze with fury. Not only had I lost a good lieutenant, I had to rely on an erratic, insolent dolt like Tolliver. Anything I said, he twisted with sardonic humor. Nonetheless, I needed to know more. "Even if Sleak killed himself, why seal the base? What am I supposed to do about it, bury him at midnight under the mess hall?"

"The flower beds would be a better—sorry, sir. Look!" I took another pace before I realized he'd stopped abruptly, waiting for my attention. He thrust hands on hips. "I can't second guess you, Captain. Would you prefer I'd radioed a message on open circuit? Very well, next time that's what I'll do. At least this way you can release the news yourself, the way you want to. Excuse me for trying to cover your arse!"

I swallowed as his rage dissolved my own. "You've had time to think about it. What should I do?"

We resumed our walk. "It probably depends on why Sleak killed himself. If it was for personal reasons, perhaps a brief, dignified announcement. If it was connected to Academy, I have no idea how to handle it."

"Connected? How?"

"How the devil should I know! Maybe he was buggering a plebe, or fixing admission tests. All I intended was to give you time to find out!"

Presently I said, "Sorry." We walked in silence to the steps. "Where is his body?"

"I had him moved to the sickbay. It seemed . . . indecent to leave him where he was."

"You're sure he killed himself?" A murder would be . . . unthinkable. And catastrophic for morale.

"Quite sure." He held the door. "You'll see."

In my office, I waved to chairs for the sergeant and Midshipman Ekrit. "Why you three? Are you acting as a committee?"

Sergeant Ibarez shook his head. "Not really. After Branstead found the body he ran and got me. I took a look, sealed the door, and called Mr. Tolliver. I put Branstead on special duty, away from the other cadets, and I've been acting as a sort of liaison with the other staff. They know something's up, but not the details."

Tolliver said, "I had Ms. Ekrit post a middy guard at Mr. Sleak's door. Middies outrank the sergeants and anyone belowdecks. Technically, that is."

Sandra Ekrit smiled resignedly at the reminder of her status. "Yes, sir, technically. I've set boys in shifts to guard the door. Thayer and Tsai brought the body to sickbay."

I turned to Tolliver. "You said you're sure he committed suicide."

"Yes." Tolliver inserted a chip in my holovid. "Let me warn you, sir, this is not—"

I flicked it on. Darwin Sleak's gaunt features stared into the lens. His hands reached forward, became distorted, picked up the holorecorder. The walls floated past, as he scanned the empty room, circling back to his starting point. With a lurch, the recorder settled back on his desk. He sat in front of it, reached into the drawer, his eyes still riveted on the camera.

His hand came up with a gun, an ancient one with lead shells. He checked the clip, paused, put the gun to his temple.

"This is suicide," Lieutenant Darwin Sleak said to the holo. "I'm alone, and no one else is involved. Commandant, I'm sorry. I was wrong. I never imagined—" He closed his eyes. "Trusting in the love and mercy of Thy Spirit . . ." He pulled the trigger.

I jerked back in my chair, the shot ringing. His head . . . "Jesus, Lord Christ!"

"Amen. I warned you."

My stomach heaved. I tried not to retch. The holovid remained focused on what was left of Sleak's head. With unsteady hand, I reached to turn it off, took a deep breath. "Very well, it's suicide. What did he mean, he was sorry?"

"I don't know."

I drummed my fingers on the desktop. "How long do we have?"

"To do what, sir? His body is in the cooler, that's no immediate problem."

"Before word gets out."

"The ones who know he's dead are Branstead, those of us in this room, the middies and the med tech. Sarge says the tech can be trusted."

Ms. Ekrit said, "The whole wardroom knows, of course. We can't keep that kind of secret from each other. No one will say a word, sir. I'll vouch for that."

I smiled. A first middy could be very persuasive, if occasion arose. "Very well. We have until tomorrow, at least. Edgar, does Ms. Bien know?"

"No, sir. I'm senior, and I pulled rank on her. I don't think she's speaking to me."

"Tell her. I want the two of you to go through Mr. Sleak's

cabin tonight. Sarge, you help them. We can have a middy cover your barracks."

"I already have one, sir. Mr. Thayer." The redheaded child I'd found tossing pillows in glee, only months before. I stood. "Report to me when you're done, regardless of the hour. I'll be in my quarters, after I have a bite. I haven't eaten since—I don't know when." I paused at the door. "Have Mr. Branstead report to me at mess hall."

I was wolfing down a home-made sandwich when Midshipman Diego marched young Jerence into the empty hall. I took their salutes, dismissed the middy. "As you were, Mr. Branstead."

"Aye aye, sir." Not knowing what to do with himself, he assumed the at-ease position. After a moment he blurted, "I'm—I'm sorry, sir. For whatever I did."

He'd been a cadet long enough to know he should speak only when spoken to, but I let it pass. "Sit down."

His eyes widened at the unexpected familiarity. "Aye aye, sir."

I studied his reddened eyes, his huddled and sunken posture. "You must have had a fright."

"I'm all right, sir." His reply was immediate.

"I know that. Still, I saw the . . . He wasn't something to come upon, unexpected."

Jerence shivered. "I knocked, like we're supposed to. The door swung open, and I thought he'd meant for me to come in. He was slumped behind—behind the . . ." He spun away.

I cleared my throat. "I'm sorry." I couldn't touch him, or even offer words of consolation. He was as any other cadet, and I was his commanding officer.

"I'm all right." His tone would have been persuasive but for his eyes.

"Yes, well." Many months past, I'd promised Harmon Branstead to keep his son safe. If that were not enough, he was my legal ward. Still, I hesitated.

My baby Nathan might have been a boy like this, given a chance to survive.

"Come with me." The boy followed me to the serving rail. I opened the gate, went into the darkened galley, put my hand on his shoulder to guide him. "Don't tell anyone, Jerence. We're not supposed to be here."

"No, sir."

"They gave you dinner?"

"Yes, sir. Mr. Tsai brought a tray to the suiting room."

"What were you doing?"

"Inventorying, sir. Checking off serial numbers."

I sighed. Ibarez could have found something more credible for makework. I opened the cooler, peered in. A large sheet of chocolate cake; that would do. I brought it out, found plates, dished out two portions. "Carry these, please."

I went to the freezers, hunted for ice cream. I gave him a generous dollop, took a smaller one for myself. I hoisted myself onto the gleaming steel counter, motioned for the boy to do likewise. "Go ahead, Mr. Branstead. Your dinner tray couldn't have held all that much."

"Thank you, sir." He made no move to eat. "Mr. Seafort, I mean, Commandant, sir, what did I do wrong? Should I have stayed outside? Why can't I go back to barracks tonight?"

"You did nothing wrong. The rest is none of your concern." My tone was harsh, and Jerence looked to his shoes. "Eat your ice cream."

Dutifully, he took a spoonful. "I'm sorry, sir. Forgive me."

I sighed; I knew better. We'd been shipmates, he and I. "Jerence." He looked up. "We don't know why Lieutenant Sleak killed himself. If word leaks before we find out, it will be a great embarrassment."

"That's why Sarge is making me sleep in the closed barracks? So I won't talk to the others?"

"Yes." The melting ice cream held no appeal. I put down my plate. "He thought you wouldn't be able to keep the secret." I hesitated, threw caution to the winds. "But I know better. When you've finished eating, I'll take you back to Valdez. You'll help us keep things quiet until we learn what happened."

"Of course, sir." His shoulders straightened. "I won't tell anyone, even my bunkies. I promise."

"Eat up, before the cook's mates find us."

"Yes, sir." He smiled, tentatively at first.

"It must have been awful, finding Mr. Sleak."

"It was, sir." He took a bite of cake. His head lifted. "But I'm over it now."

Chapter 10

Jerence safely back in barracks, I returned to my apartment, exhausted. The search of Lieutenant Sleak's quarters would take hours; in the meantime I needed sleep. I settled into bed with the visage of Mr. Sleak's head, after he'd pulled the trigger. I put it aside, but other images plagued me, among them Cadet Dustin Edwards, huddled lifeless in the Farside corridor.

I snapped awake to urgent pounding on my door, a voice shouting. I lurched to the door in my shorts, hurled it open. "Belay that nons—"

"Hands up!" The Marine's laser rifle brooked no argument. I flung my hands over my head, retreated several steps.

"Easy, Jodson, he's the Commandant. You all right, sir?" The burly lieutenant of Marines.

"Of course I'm all right! Why in God's own hell are you bursting in—Oh, my Lord." I flamed crimson. "Call them off, Lieutenant. I . . . forgot to call you."

His expression reduced me to a charred spot on the rug. "Forgot. I see. Very well, Commandant." He raised his caller. "Corporal Manners, sheath weapons, release the guards. This is a no go!"

I lowered my arms. "How did you get past the sentries? Was there damage?"

"Not much, sir. We took out the front guardhouse, where your man was half asleep. Then we secured the helipad in case the enemy tried to bolt. Next we surrounded Officers' Quarters. In the next corridor we have three Naval officers under guard."

"Let them go," I said quickly. "It was a false alarm. Just a training exercise."

"Right." He saluted, but allowed himself one last dig. "If you'd ever like readiness training for your guards, let us know."

I slipped into my pants and shirt, hurried outside to Lieutenant Sleak's flat. Tolliver stood in the doorway, arms folded, arguing with a Marine guard. He raised an eyebrow.

"Not a word, do you hear me?" I tried to turn embarrassment into fury. "Just get back to work!"

The Marine lieutenant followed me, to call off his guard. His young Marine said urgently, "Sir, there's blood in there. Someone's been—"

I snarled, "Lieutenant, get your man out of here, flank!" To my relief, the Marines complied. I followed them back to the helipad, waited for their transport to arrive while my own sheepish guards did their best to avoid my eye. While their heli settled, I warned the Marine lieutenant of consequences should word of this fiasco leak.

I doubt I overawed him, but perhaps taking pity on me, he agreed. When they were finally gone I turned on my heel and hurried back to Officers' Quarters. The door to Sleak's cabin was ajar.

Seated at Sleak's console, Tolliver said only, "Nothing yet, sir. Thank you for arranging a stimulating work break. We were just admiring—"

I growled, "I don't want to hear it." I shut the door, returned to my cabin. I tossed and turned for hours before drifting off at dawn.

"He must have left a clue somewhere." Tousled and bleary, I glowered at Ibarez and Tolliver.

"I went through everything, even his sister's letters." Tolliver seemed weary, too. "Ms. Bien is checking his puter files one more time."

"Don't you—" I forced down an unreasoning anger. "Did you find any notes, anything at all?"

"Of course, like anyone would leave. Lunch appointments, figures jotted. Nothing special."

"What kind of figures?"

His voice grew testy. "One note looked like logistics for transporting plebes up to Station next term. The others, I have no idea. Would you like to see them?"

I checked my watch. "Let it wait 'til after breakfast."

Darwin Sleak's death made no sense. He'd been angry with me, had asked for a transfer because I'd set Tolliver to investigate his accounts. But Edgar had found nothing to incriminate Sleak, and the man wouldn't destroy himself out of pique.

Tolliver had frightened me by sealing the base, but I had to admit his actions made some sense. The Navy mustn't wash its dirty laundry in public. Because my name was involved, the mediamen would look for a scandal connected to the suicide, or even invent one.

I sighed. My lieutenant's body was in the cooler, and must be dealt with. In addition, I didn't look forward to breaking in his replacement when I myself was still a novice. Beyond that, I was tired, I had rocket-lag, and I missed Annie. At least now that I was groundside I could visit her, as soon as matters were under control.

At breakfast assembly I sipped moodily at my coffee, watching the scrubbed and shining cadets. No one at my table commented on Lieutenant Sleak's empty place.

On the way out, Lieutenant Bien caught me alone. "The quartermaster has indent requests, and there are daily systems reports for Mr. Sleak."

"What do you want me to do about it?" Her look of resignation infuriated me. With an effort I contained myself. "Sorry, Ms. Bien. Pass the word Mr. Sleak is on special detail. All reports and requests go to you."

"Aye aye, sir. And the barrel?"

That was the first lieutenant's chore. I hesitated. "Take it to Tolliver, he's senior."

I walked through the compound to my office, shut the door. I paced, gnawing at the mystery of Sleak's death. We'd found no clues in his apartment. Perhaps there were none to find, and the man had simply succumbed to depression. If so, a simple announcement would suffice. I sat at my desk, played at drafting a statement. Deep in my stomach a knot began to form.

At length I erased my scribblings, buzzed the outer desk. "Tell Ms. Bien I want her." I waited impatiently until she knocked. "You stayed late in Mr. Sleak's cabin. What did you find on his puter?"

"Nothing much, sir. Notes, letters, reports. About what I expected to find."

"No hint of a problem?"

"No, sir. Check for yourself. I locked his files under your personal security code."

Two hours later, we'd found nothing out of the ordinary. Finally I gave it up. I dismissed Ms. Bien to her other duties, sat back to brood.

By lunchtime I decided I wanted the incident done with, mediamen or no. I snapped on my holo to draft a statement.

Sergeant Kinders knocked. "Weekly reports are ready to be sent to Admiralty, sir. Shall I—"

"Send them." The damned reports didn't matter, no one read them. As far as Admiralty was concerned, I was on my own, as Commandant Kearsey had been. I was free to spend or misspend my budget, cashier errant cadets, train them as I saw fit. Unless, of course, I failed to coddle Senator Boland. Then, Admiral Duhaney called me to account. Admiralty would do better giving me some reasonable guidelines rather than letting politics—

Guidelines. Very well. If Duhaney wanted to meddle in Academy I'd give him something to meddle with. "Mr. Kinders!"

The door opened. "Yes?"

"Put in a call to Admiral Duhaney. It's urgent."

"Aye aye, sir." He disappeared. I paced my office in relief. I'd tell Duhaney the truth. Let him figure out what to make of the problem. And let the announcement come from his office, not mine. The mediamen would withhold—

I cursed, flung open the door. "Cancel that call, Sarge."

Sergeant Kinders looked up, his face noncommittal. "Aye aye, sir."

"I can't tell him over the air, for the same reason Tolliver couldn't report—" I stopped short, studied his face. "How much do you know?"

"Officially? Nothing. But something's happened to Mr. Sleak, that's obvious."

I had to trust my own staff. "He killed himself in his cabin. I have to go see the Admiral." Another bout with the harsh acceleration, and I would miss seeing Annie. But there was no other way, unless . . . "On second thought, I'll draft a message. Call in a middy." I fumbled for a name, any name. "Mr., uh, Thayer."

An hour later I put the chip in a pocket case, gave it to the red-haired youngster waiting at-ease in front of my desk. "See Sarge for your travel orders. Go to Lunapolis Admiralty, announce yourself at Admiral Duhaney's office. You're not to surrender this chip except personally to him." Without that precaution, my notice might get lost in the stacks of reports Admiralty received daily. "These orders may not be countermanded. You understand?"

The boy's eyes sparkled with excitement. "Aye aye, sir!"

"Dismissed." I watched him stride out. His eagerness was understandable; it was his first trip aloft without supervision. And when his errand was done, he'd have some hours in Lunapolis, perhaps even overnight. An inquisitive young middy could augment his education, in its seedier warrens.

I leaned back. One way or another, Sleak's death would be handled. That aside, the man had to be replaced; Terrestrial Academy was understaffed with three lieutenants, to say nothing of only two. Aboard ship, on a long, dreary interstellar cruise, I would make do, or promote a midshipman. In home system I had only to call BuPers. Even with a staffing freeze, they'd give me whoever I wanted.

Who, then? I thought briefly of Alexi Tamarov, decided that even if his mind had cleared, I'd interfered enough in his life and brought him only harm.

We wanted someone with a special understanding, a special affinity for Naval traditions. A disciplinarian, who might transmit his high standards to future generations. No one I knew fitted the bill. I would have to leave it to BuPers. If I tolerated Ardwell Crossburn, I could work with anyone.

That afternoon I called the clinic, asked for Annie. She was out on the grounds. Tired and irritable, I waited in my office for Admiral Duhaney's call until I was nearly late to dinner.

The cadets stood smartly for my entrance. I strode past the tables, noticed Jerence Branstead with his bunkmates. I sang out, "Gentlemen, be seated." Chairs scraped, and conversation resumed.

Edgar Tolliver seemed to have caught up on his sleep; his wit was in full flower. I ignored a sly reference to the visit of the marines, but when he made another I leaned close. "No more, Mr. Tolliver. Granted, I made a fool of myself. But you're done rubbing it in."

His eyebrow raised. "Rubbing it in? Not at all, sir. If I, ah, dwell on the incident, it's because I enjoyed the relief from our dull Academy life." He managed to keep his face straight.

"Dull, is it?" He'd pushed me over the brink. "Very well, I'll give you some diversions. Finish your report on the indents, the one that irritated Mr. Sleak so. I want it on my desk within a week. And for amusement, you can supervise the morning runs for a month or so." That would roust him out of bed at least an hour early, every day. He wasn't a middy, subject to demerits, but he'd learn it was risky to goad a Captain, even shoreside. He ought to have known that by now.

"Aye aye, sir." He seemed unperturbed. Perhaps Tolliver was an early riser; I realized that after a year of close contact with the man, I didn't know.

"A call for you, sir." The mess steward, at my shoulder.

"Yes?" I leaned against the entranceway, blocking the room's muted roar with my free hand.

"Duhaney, here. Your chip arrived an hour ago."

"Yes, sir."

"You were right, it would make an unfortunate incident, especially after the death of that boy on Farside. We don't want any problem with enlistments just now. I'll arrange matters from here. Say nothing. I'll send some people down for the, ah, package."

"The what?"

"The package!" His voice sharpened. "The one you wrote about. I'll have it dealt with up here. We'll reassign some personnel and handle it in a routine manner."

Unbelieving, I blurted, "You want to ferry the—the . . ." I couldn't refer to the late Lieutenant Sleak as a "package." It was an obscenity. "You want to transfer the entire problem to Lunapolis, as a personnel assignment?"

"Damn it, Seafort, isn't that what you wanted? Why else did you dump it in my lap?"

"I—yes, sir."

"Give me a day or two. I'll send a heli to take the package to London Shuttleport. The paperwork will be backdated."

Suddenly it seemed all wrong. "Sir, if there's an inquiry, won't it look, I mean, I—" I was as tongue-tied as young Adam Tenere.

"Not to worry, Seafort. Security is tight. Remember, um, last month's false alarm over the mistaken fish sighting. We have these matters well in hand." He rang off.

Well, he was right; they'd managed to cover up the sighting. There had been only minor interest from the zines, whose commentators asked why our radionics were so inaccurate. I trudged back to my table.

"Good news, I trust?" Tolliver was at his most suave.

"Actually, yes." I tore viciously at a roll.

Behind me, a crash of dishes; a clumsy cadet had dropped his tray. Demerits, unless his sergeant was in a forgiving mood. Catcalls and whistles erupted from nearby. I jumped to my feet, stalked to the table whose cadets had jeered. "Sergeant Olvira! Put them all on report!" Conversation hushed throughout the mess hall. "How long ago did they take the oath, Sarge? If you can't straighten them out, I'll find an instructor who can!"

The Marine stood, assumed the at-ease position. "I'm sorry, Commandant. I'll see that they don't trouble you further."

"You'd damn well better. This is a disgrace! I want these hoodlums in my office first thing tom—"

"Excuse me, sir." Tolliver's voice was urgent.

I wheeled. "Get back to your table, Lieutenant. If these—"

"It can't wait." He interposed his shoulder between me and Sergeant Olvira. "Please. Right now."

Astounded, I followed him a few steps toward our table. "What's so damned important it—"

"Get hold of yourself!" Tolliver's mouth was set. His tone was so low I had to strain to hear.

"No more insolence, or I'll have you cashiered!"

"That's your decision, sir. But while I'm your aide, I'll protect you even from yourself. The business with the Marines was nothing. Right now you're making a total fool of yourself in public!"

Slowly I became aware of the overwhelming silence. I took a deep breath, and then another. With shaky legs I turned again to Sergeant Olvira. I strove to make my tone casual. "Sarge, it's not decent for them to laugh when a cadet drops a tray. Every mate's misfortune is their own. Speak to them about it, please." I turned back to my own table.

Lieutenant Bien eyed me, turned away. Lord God, what was wrong with me? I'd thrown a tantrum worse than any I'd ever seen from a plebe. Missing a night's sleep was no excuse; I'd learned to manage without. I muttered to Tolliver, "Thanks."

His tone was still low. "There's Sergeant Olvira too. I'll have a word with him after dinner, if you like."

"Yes." I closed my eyes, feeling my ears burn. If proof was needed that I was unfit for my duties, I'd just provided it.

"Pardon me, sir. Another call."

I whirled. "Now who?"

The steward smiled apologetically. "I have no idea, sir."

I might as well carry a stereochip caller, like a civilian. "Very well." I stalked to the doorway, took the caller. I snapped, "Seafort!"

"Nicky? I told dem not to be bothering you."

"Annie."

"They said you called."

"Yes, hon. How are you?"

A pause. "I don . . . don't know, Nicky. Times I feel good, other times I'm all confused. I think about . . ." Her voice trailed off.

"I understand."

"About what they did to me, in Centraltown." Her tone was determined.

I closed my eyes, leaned against the wall, my relief almost too much to bear. It was the first time Annie had ever spoken of her brutal rape.

"Are you okay, Nicky?"

"Yes, except I miss you."

She giggled. "Good, I want you to be missin' me. Day you don't, I be in trouble."

"Wait 'til you see our apartment, Annie. It's huge. And there are all sorts of shops across the Commons, in Devon."

She snickered. "Bet I know something else that's huge."

"Annie!" Despite myself, I blushed.

"Nicky? . . ."

"Yes, hon."

A sob. "I love you." The line went dead.

With heavy step, I returned to my place. I waited for dessert, aching for the solitude of my apartment. I topped off my coffee, relishing its warmth. The bowl of pudding came.

"Sir, excuse me." The mess steward.

"Now what?"

He said warily, "Another call."

I stared at my pudding. "Almighty Lord God in His heaven."

"I'm sorry. I didn't mean to—"

"And His angels! Amen." I stalked to the caller. "Seafort!" My tone was savage.

"Sergeant Obutu reporting, sir." She seemed distant, as she was. "I hope I haven't disturbed you."

"You have, and it had better be important!"

"That's for you to judge, sir. Cadet Arnweil was sent to Lieutenant Paulson this evening. To the barrel."

Too bad, but I couldn't do anything about it. "I'll read the Log later. Why bother me about—"

"Sergeant Radz sent him. And Kyle Drew just pulled his tenth demerit. He's to report to Mr. Paulson in the morning." Drew? He had enough misery, after his accident.

I paused. "Sergeant, who issued the demerits?"

Her formality matched my own. "I believe most of them came from Sergeant Radz, sir."

I let the silence stretch.

"The Stritz boy too, sir. The one with the low grades, in Kuhn's barracks. He's on punishment detail for a month."

"Why?"

"To improve his grades."

Something was going wrong. Sergeant Radz had felt remorse over Edwards's death, but couldn't accept his responsibility for the cadets' plummeting morale. He saw his role as toughening his youngsters into proper Naval officers. Apparently, so did Stritz's drillmaster, Sergeant Kuhn.

"Very well, I'll deal with it as soon as I get back."

A pause. "Aye aye, sir. I'll log off Cadet Drew's demerits when he reports back from Mr. Paulson."

Deftly done, without a hint of criticism. I sighed. "Tell Sergeant Radz he's to cancel Drew's demerits and see that no one else reaches ten before—"

"Aye aye, sir. Are you quite sure that's what you want?"

I gripped the caller tightly, forced myself to relax. This woman knew what she was about. "What would you suggest, Sarge?"

"I don't know, sir. But I wouldn't think undercutting Sergeant Radz in front if his barracks is the answer."

Damn it, she was right. Well, the alternative was letting Kyle Drew be caned. So be it, unless—

"Send the cadets groundside. All three of them."

"Surely there's a better way than washing them out."

I growled, "I didn't say I'd wash them out; just transfer them here. Do it before Mr. Drew has to report to the barrel." That would get the boy off the hook, without undercutting Radz too obviously. I hung up the caller, trudged one more time to my table, where all waited for me to dismiss the assembly.

Tolliver saw me to the door. "I'll be along after a word with Sergeant Olvira."

"No. Come with me." We walked in silence to my apartment. Safely inside, I flung off my jacket, threw myself on my couch. "Tolliver, should I resign?"

"I beg your pardon?" His eyebrow lifted.

"I'm out of control. Look at me."

Unbidden, he sat. "You're tired. We're not as young as we used to be."

"Goofjuice. Tantrums aside, I don't know what I'm doing. I veer between harsh discipline and coddling them."

"So, you're erratic. You're a Captain."

I snarled, "None of your middy humor, Edgar. Not now."

Tolliver shrugged. "You're having a bad day. Don't make too much of it." He stood. "If that's all, I'll smooth Sergeant Olvira's feathers. I'm sure he didn't enjoy being chewed out in front of his cadets."

"Sit. I haven't dismissed you." It sounded more petulant than I'd intended. "Sorry. Problems on Farside; a couple of the barracks sergeants are riding roughshod over their joeys. It's gotten out of hand."

"What will you do about it?"

"I don't know. That's why I'm the wrong man for the job." I brooded. "How soon can you finish your expense and deliveries report?"

"The audit? You gave me a week. I could do it faster, if I didn't have to supervise morning runs." His expression was bland.

"Drop everything else, finish the report. As soon as you're done I'm sending you aloft. The staff is—I need a moderating influence."

"I'm hardly the one for that."

I said gruffly, "You did well enough in *Victoria*'s wardroom." Tolliver, as Midshipman, had soothed the burgeoning hostilities among my junior officers. I realized, with a pang, that my long-nursed resentment of his hazing might be somewhat unreasonable as well. "That's all, Edgar. Get some sleep."

"Right. Aye aye, sir. I'll see Olvira first."

"I'll deal with him. No, don't argue about it!" After he was gone, I sat on the couch, head in my hands, trying not to think of the ordeal ahead. Finally, after an hour, I stood slowly, reached for my jacket.

I strode from Officers' Quarters across the compound to the cadet dorms, taking salutes from passing middies. The night air was chill; I increased my pace.

Sergeant Olvira ran Wilhaven Barracks, the third along the neatly bordered walk. I heard laughter from inside as I bounded up the steps.

A cadet saw me, shouted, "Attention!" They rushed into a line, stood with spines stiffened. Some wore jackets, other were in shirts and ties. A few were in undershorts only. Bunks were rumpled, holovids spread out and opened. A typical barracks evening, the relaxed cadets finishing their work before Lights Out.

"At ease." I looked around. "Where's your sergeant?"

A boy with a corporal's stripe said tentatively, "I think he's in his quarters, sir."

"My compliments, and would he please join us."

"Aye aye, sir." The cadet slipped on his boots, hurried out.

We waited in silence. After a moment, footsteps returned. "Sergeant Olvira reporting as—"

"As you were, Sarge." I took a position in the center of the aisle, addressed the cadets. "Someday you will command sailors, who have a right to expect your best. Let this be a lesson to you." I turned to Olvira, spoke for all to hear. "Sergeant, I tender my apology for the rude and unwarranted remarks I made in dining hall tonight. They show I am unable to control my temper, which I will endeavor to correct in future. I am sorry."

Every eye was fastened on me. I swallowed bile, turned to the line of cadets. "The only thing worse than misbehavior to a fellow officer is failure to acknowledge it. My discourtesy to your sergeant is not excused by your laughing at a fellow cadet, whose embarrassment at dropping a tray in the Commandant's presence can only be imagined. I rebuke you, as I rebuke myself for my response. That is all." With what dignity I could muster, I strode out.

That night I slept, free of dreams, a deep refreshing slumber. In the morning I hauled myself out of bed, showered, went to breakfast, settled in my office. I buzzed Sergeant Kinder. "Any word from Admiral Duhaney?"

"Not since last night, sir."

Well, he had said it would take a day or two. I thought of Lieutenant Sleak, in the sickbay cooler awaiting transshipment. His life, taken in despair, would end in travesty.

"I'm sorry," he had said. Would that he had waited long enough to add a few words of explanation.

I tapped my desk. Not only had we lost Sleak, I intended to reassign Tolliver to Farside. We needed a new lieutenant, and flank. I took up the caller. "Get me BuPers."

After a short wait I found myself speaking to Captain Higbee, the same official who'd refused to reassign Ardwell Crossburn. Lamely, I explained that Lieutenant Sleak was to be transferred aloft at Admiral Duhaney's orders, and I needed another officer. It was almost true.

"Do you have anyone in mind?" Higbee sounded preoccupied.

"No."

"Very well, I'll find you someone. You'll hear from me." He rang off.

I spent the morning skimming through reports. Shortly before lunch the caller buzzed.

Sergeant Kinders. "Midshipman Keene is down from Farside. He's escorting three cadets."

"Very well." In my pique of the night before, I'd failed to make arrangements for them. Just as I'd failed to call off the invasion of the Marines. Early senility, perhaps. "Send them in."

They came stiffly to attention before my desk, Thomas Keene proud with responsibility, the three young cadets subdued and wary.

"Did they give you any trouble on the way down, Mr. Keene?"

"No, sir."

"Very well." I thought for a moment. "Thank you. I suppose you're anxious to get back?"

"Not rea—yes, sir."

I felt magnanimous. "I suppose not. The acceleration must be terrible for a man of your advanced age." Keene was barely eighteen. "Well, take two days leave, if you'd like. You could see London."

His eyes lit up. "Thank you, sir!"

"Dismissed." When he'd left I turned to the waiting cadets. "At ease. You must be Stritz."

"Yes, sir. Johan Stritz. You met me in my barracks." I concentrated, recalled the wiry, muscular boy who'd slipped into the dorm during my reverie. The cadet's forehead gleamed; he was frightened.

"I won't bite, Mr. Stritz." I turned to Arnweil, my voice gruff. "How do you feel?"

"I'm all right, sir."

"Can you sit at mess?"

Kevin's face went red. "Yes, sir. I guess Mr. Paulson went easy on me."

I turned to Kyle Drew. As often as the name had been in our deliberations, I'd seen him only once, on the Hull. His face was sallow, his cheeks sunken. Puberty was barely upon him. At fifteen, a hard burden to bear.

"So you're Drew." Inane, but I could think of nothing else to say.

"Yes, sir." He shifted nervously.

I studied the three of them. I hadn't thought the matter through beyond calling them down to Devon, out of harm's way. I'd have to assign them to barracks. "Do you know why you're here?"

Kyle Drew. "Because we can't hold our own. We foul up." His tone was bitter.

Arnweil added, "To see if you'll give us another chance before washing us out."

"Who told you that?"

"Sergeant Radz, sir."

Damn the man. I blurted, "No, you're here to—" I hesitated. By bringing them back to Devon I'd consigned them to classes they'd already passed, to plebe dorms. They would assume I judged them failures, and they'd act the part. But what else was I to do?

I improvised, "You're here as—as part of an experimental program. Some cadets seem to do better with individualized instruction, and I want to see why." Johan Stritz gawked. "I'll bunk you in one of the dorms. You'll exercise with your bunkmates. Your academic work at Farside will be converted to individual study projects."

Kyle Drew said hesitantly, "Pardon, sir, but I don't understand. What do we . . . do? I mean, during the day?"

A good question, to which I had no answer. But of course they mustn't know that. Decisively I said, "That's the whole point. You're assigned to me. You'll accompany me back and forth to Farside and work at—at duties I assign from time to time. In my office." I was perspiring. "That's enough for now. Report to Sergeant Kinders. He's to assign you a barracks. To Sergeant Ibarez," I added. Ramon Ibarez would provide the nurturing Radz could not.

As the door closed behind them I sat, stunned. What in heaven's name had I done? I'd babbled as if demented about programs that didn't exist, independent studies that had never been authorized, duties I would have to invent before I could assign. And under my personal supervision, no less.

Effectively, I'd taken three troubled youngsters out of Academy and made them my personal responsibility. Worse, I'd shattered the tradition that cadets were so insignificant as to be beneath an officer's notice. How could these joeys respect me if they knew me so well?

Chapter 11

By evening, I'd gotten Arnweil, Drew and Stritz settled into barracks. The next day I arranged for Sergeant Kinders to assign them tasks to keep them occupied. As it happened, they were rather useful now, as we were short an officer. The middies, whom we otherwise used to run errands or help with chores, were helping fill in with Lieutenant Sleak's responsibilities.

The following morning a heli landed on the pad, and Darwin Sleak's remains were quietly hustled out of Academy. I accompanied the sad bundle strapped to the dolly, offering a silent prayer as I walked. Whatever the cost of announcing his death, I knew we had done wrong to conceal it, and the fact that the Admiral had decided on the course did not excuse my part in it. After, I returned to my office.

My three cadets took meals with their plebe barracks; I was relieved not to have them underfoot. I was uncomfortably aware that for all my words of reassurance, I'd shunted them aside the moment our interview was done.

The following day I managed not to see them at breakfast and lunch, but by dinner I could stand it no longer. I signaled the mess steward. "Three more places, if you please." With Sleak gone and Tolliver absent, we were hardly crowded.

The places set, I had the steward fetch my three cadets from Sergeant Ibarez's table. They approached with embarrassment, Kevin Arnweil in the lead. Lieutenant Bien made as if to speak, looked away. In living memory, no cadet had ever been summoned to the Commandant's table, not even for a rebuke. Tradition.

"Sit, gentlemen. From now on you'll take dinner with us." Arnweil sat shyly alongside Sandra Ekrit, the two other boys found a place nearby. The three huddled together as if for warmth in the disapproving chill.

I spooned my soup, waiting for someone to break the ice. At first, no one spoke. Then Midshipman Ekrit deliberately turned her face from the cadets, resumed her conversation with Lieutenant Bien. Arnweil went red, concentrated on his bowl. Johan Stritz whispered something to Kyle Drew, who played with his fork. Drew, after a moment, glanced sheepishly at Sergeant Olvira. "Good evening, sir. I mean, Sarge."

"Good evening." The sergeant's tone was wintry. He swivelled to Midshipman Thayer. "Was Lunapolis all you expected?"

Anton Thayer grinned. "Yes, I—"

No. It wouldn't do. I looked across to Stritz. "How old are you, Johan?"

"Fifteen, sir."

"You were having trouble with Nav, as I recollect. How are you doing now?"

"A little better, sir."

"Good." My tone sharpened. "I believe Midshipman Ekrit did well at Nav." I turned to the first middy. "Isn't that so?"

"Yes, sir." Warily, she studied my expression.

"Then you won't mind giving Mr. Stritz a hand in his studies."

Her distaste was apparent. "Of course not, sir."

"And since you won't know when Johan needs help, you're confined to base until his grades improve."

"I—"

"And your manners."

The midshipman looked down to her plate. "Pardon me for offending you, sir."

I smiled coldly. "You didn't offend me, Midshipman, though I'm sure Mr. Stritz feels affront. Of course, as a cadet he can't express it."

She said in a small voice, "I apologize, sir. And to you, Cadet."

I'd accomplished my purpose; time to let up. I smiled at Anton Thayer, gestured to Arnweil. "Tell Kevin about your trip to Lunapolis, Mr. Thayer. Did you go Outside for the light show?"

Lieutenant Bien probed my face as halting conversation resumed. I looked back, impassive. If necessary, I would make an example of her as well. Perhaps she understood; eventually, she turned to Kyle Drew and began to chat.

After dinner I returned to my office, fuming at the callousness of my staff. I'd invited the cadets to break bread with us, and my officers owed them the same courtesy as any guest, tradition or no.

The caller buzzed. "BuPers, sir."

A click. "Please hold for Captain Higbee, sir." The line went silent. Waiting, I tapped knuckles against my teeth. True, lieutenants and midshipmen alike assumed cadets were less than nothing. But even as a cadet I'd known officers who saw the person inside the creased gray uniform. Midshipman Jeffrey Thorne, for example. He'd shown me kindness, had taken me into his world of risk and adventure, had been my mentor and friend.

"Seafort? I have a lieutenant for you. Brann, age fifty. He's recovering from a fall; light duties would suit him perfectly."

"Very well."

"He was on the Vega run for several years, and isn't very happy about going shoreside. But that's his worry. When he's well, we'll see about transferring him out."

Brann wouldn't fit in at Academy, supervising frisky, healthy youths, resenting his own disability. What I really needed was a younger man, one with enthusiasm.

Higbee's tone became more guarded. "Your Mr. Sleak is on Lunapolis, by the way. Assigned to the Admiral's staff." I grimaced, but said nothing. "I'll transfer Brann's file to your puter and send him his travel orders."

"No."

"You can expect him—what?"

"I don't want him."

"I asked if you had someone in mind, and you didn't. We've been through this before, Seafort. Unless he has unsatisfactory ratings, you're stuck—"

I took a deep breath. "Don't bother sending him, I'll just ship him back."

"I'm senior to you, Mr. Seafort, please keep that in mind. And I'm acting with the authority of Admiral Duhaney."

I snarled, "Very well, in that case, reassign me Lieutenant Sleak!" There was silence. "In fact, I have a mind to give him a commendation. It would make a nice press release. The Admiral loves press releases, they stimulate enrollment."

Higbee's tone was cautious. "What do you want, Captain?"

"I don't know. I want someone—someone who . . ." Someone

like Jeff. "Tell me, whatever happened to a Thorne, Jeffrey? Graduated in '88."

"I haven't the faintest idea, and in any event we can't pull someone off—"

"Very well, I'll make do with Sleak."

A long pause. "I'll get back to you."

I put my head in my hands. Higbee would ring through to Admiral Duhaney, whose patience with me was exhausted. Perhaps he'd relieve me. It was just as well. The Commandancy called for tact and political skills I could never master.

I brooded. Men like Sergeant Radz strove to do their duty, and were excellent officers in their own fashion. But competence had to be tempered with kindness. I myself was incapable of it; I lashed out indiscriminately, regretting my impetuosity only when it was too late. The cadets didn't need coddling, they needed . . . a hand. Sometimes, all one could give them was understanding. I sat in the dusk, remembering.

Jeffrey Thorne looked away, his expression pained. "I'm sorry, Nick. I didn't mean for it to end this way."

I ignored his apology, echoed the word of greatest import. "End, sir?"

The midshipman scuffed the deck. "I have to watch myself for a while; any more trouble and they'll throw me ashore. Mr. Zorn warned me." His foot scuffed at the deck. "Even talking to you like this, I can't risk it anymore."

I felt the girders of my world snatched away. "Yes, sir."

"Seafort, you're second year now; soon you'll make middy. You don't need me."

I flared, "You don't know what I need!" Immediately I added, "I'm sorry, Mr. Thorne. Please excuse me." Friend or not, he was an officer and I was but a cadet.

"Oh, Nicky." He waved it away. For a moment he flashed the captivating smile that had brought about my humiliation and disgrace. "Anyway, no more missions. I told them it was all my fault."

"I know, sir." My eyes stung. "But it wasn't. I didn't have to go with you."

"Sure you did." He rested his hand on my shoulder. "I'm sorry, Seafort. I let you down. You weren't supposed to get a caning."

"I'm all right."

"Yes, you are. Do you understand that?"

"Of course. It hurts, but—"

"No, listen to me. You're all right, Seafort. Inside."

For some reason, I felt a desolation. "What do you mean?"

Thorne thrust his hands in his pockets, looked away. "It's just . . . you don't have many friends, do you?"

"There's Robbie, and Arlene, lots of —"

"Joeys you really talk to?"

I swallowed. "What is there to talk about?"

He came close, looked directly into my eyes. "You tell me, Nick."

I shrugged. "Father and I—we didn't speak a lot."

"But you feel the need, at times."

I looked to the deck.

"You're lonely, Nick. I am too, sometimes, but you seem to have an inner strength. You'll get through."

"Will I?" The cry sprang from me.

"Yes. It would be easier if you could . . . share, I suppose. Don't look at me like that. You give, when your friends need it. I saw you once, when Rovere was upset about Sarge chewing him out. The way you diverted him, until he got over his sulk. But I'm not talking about giving . . ." Again he trailed off.

"Say it, sir." My plea sounded almost a command. I held my breath until I saw he took no offense.

Thorne fidgeted. "Opening up. Sharing yourself. People can't help you unless you let them in." He looked away. "I wouldn't press, but I don't know if we'll get another chance."

"I'm all right, I—"

His look was one of sadness.

"I don't know how," I blurted. "I never have. Once I had a friend, Jason—" The memories flared, and I thrust them down. "I'm all right, sir. Really."

The young middy smiled. "Well, we had some good missions."

My return smile was tremulous. "Yes, sir."

"Hang on, Cadet. You'll get through." A quick squeeze, and he was gone.

I watched him stride down the corridor, never looking back. I thought of Father, and felt a chill.

* * *

After breakfast I left my apartment and wandered the compound. On the gunnery range, cadets practiced with their ancient laser simulator, while a few were allowed to focus an actual laser cannon locked to low intensity. Later, outside the suiting room, I watched cadets stumble through their suiting drills. Today, none turned green from the gas and clawed at his helmet.

I wandered toward my office, brooding. Perhaps I should schedule a surprise inspection. Tolliver or Bien could help make the rounds. Was I considering it merely to alleviate my own boredom? Well, even so, the cadets could use—

"Cadet Arnweil reporting, sir!"

I whirled. "Don't sneak up behind me, you young—what do you want?"

The boy snapped a salute, tugged his gray jacket into place. "Sergeant Kinders's compliments, sir, and there's a visitor at the gate asking—"

"Parents aren't allowed entry. Have the guards send him away."

"—asking for you personally, sir." He stopped to catch his breath.

"Who is it?"

"A Mr. . . ." He fished for the name. "Mr. O'Neill, sir."

Did we have a cadet by that name? I wasn't sure. "Tell the guard whoever it is should call for an appointment." I strode back to my office.

Sergeant Kinders looked up from his caller. "Oh, there you are, sir. Captain Higbee from BuPers on the line."

"Very well, I'll take it." I went into my private office, sat at the desk.

A click. "Seafort? I have a Thorne, Jeffrey R., lieutenant, four years seniority. A year on U.N.S. *Targon*, staff at Lunapolis Admiralty, now at Callisto Base."

"I want him."

"His enlistment is up in six months. Policy is not to transfer—"

"He'll reenlist, he's career Navy." Why hadn't I thought of Thorne before? His good humor, his occasional irreverence to tradition would be ideal. "He's the one."

Animosity leaked through Higbee's polite veneer. "I may not be able to get him for you."

If I'd stroked him, I wouldn't be in my predicament. Even knowing that, I couldn't contain myself. "Mr. Higbee, I don't know how to play this game. I'm no politician. But there's two or three people I could ring who do. One by himself might not have enough influence, but I'll bet that all of them together could clip your wings. Shall we see who has more pull, you or I?" I was astounded at my insolence. It verged on mutiny.

A pause. I wondered who I could call, other than the Admiral. The only person of influence I knew was Senator Boland, and he would merely laugh and hang up.

"Very well, you'll have Thorne in a few days. It's of no consequence." Higbee made no attempt to conceal his anger. "I'll look forward to assisting you again." He rang off abruptly.

Another enemy. I was so good at making them. Now I'd have to watch every new appointment like a hawk. I sighed, then relaxed. It didn't matter. I was getting Jeff Thorne.

Again the caller buzzed. "Yes?" I bit back anger. "The guardhouse, sir. A visitor is insisting—"

"A Mr. O'Neill? We don't take unannounced—"

"Dr. O'Neill, not Mister."

Lord God. The clinic. "Send him to my office immediately. Do you have a middy to escort him?"

"I'll use one of your special cadets."

I grunted. My special cadets. Well, I'd created that problem for myself.

I waited with an attempt at patience, but gave up after only a few minutes. I hurried out to the corridor, met O'Neill and Drew at the main door. "I'm terribly sorry. I didn't recognize your name."

"No matter." Well dressed, receding hairline, thin-faced. He shook hands, shot me a probing glance. "I thought it best to see you in person. Have you somewhere to talk?"

"My office."

He waited until we were seated with the door closed. "Mr. Seafort, this is an unfortunate situa—"

"What happened?"

"I don't know how to tell you." He hesitated. "You have to understand, the practice of medicine is not an exact—"

I came to my feet, gripped the back of my chair. "For God's sake, man, spit it out!"

He said warily, "She's gone."

"Annie's dead?" My stomach went hollow.

"No, gone from the clinic." He saw my face, hurried on. "I mean, procedures normally ensure . . . it's not as if we run a prison, you understand. I want to assure you that normally—"

"I don't care about normal. What about my wife?"

His forehead shone with perspiration. "Yesterday afternoon she left the grounds and never came back."

"You let her walk out, in her condition?"

"Almost all our patients are voluntary. Mrs. Seafort has free use of the grounds."

"But she's not on your grounds."

"One of our patients had his family visit. Afterward your wife walked them to the gate, strolled out when they did. We didn't even know how she'd left until we replayed the tapes."

"What was she wearing?"

"A light jumpsuit."

"Money?"

"As far as we know she had none. All her expenses were billed to your account."

My fists bunched.

"The police are looking. We called them within hours."

"Did you check the squatters' shacks outside the clinic?"

"When the police came. We couldn't go out alone."

"Of course not. You might have found her."

"I understand your anger, Mr. Seafort. That's why I came in person."

I ignored that. "Was she upset?"

"Her chart shows that she's been moody, of late. But that's natural, at her stage. Eventually her mood swings will lessen, and she may be quite placid as long as she takes her meds. But for now—"

"She's gone. Without money or proper clothing."

"Yes." He hesitated, blurted, "It may not be as bad as all that. Your wife's, er, background . . . she may be more skilled than most at coping with—"

I stood, my voice odd. "Background?"

"Well, after all, she is a trannie. They can handle the most appalling—"

I was on my feet. "Lord God damn you!" I could strangle him. I was young enough, strong enough. He was within reach.

"Captain, many papers have been written about the peculiar transpop subculture. It's not—"

I roared, "KINDERS! GET IN HERE!"

Within seconds the door popped open, and the Sergeant dashed in, eyes wide with alarm.

"It's not insult, only fact that she could well survive situations that—"

With effort, I made my voice steady. "Dr. Richard O'Neill, before witness I do call challenge on you to defend your honor! Let me know the name of your second. Choice of—"

O'Neill didn't move, and his voice was precise. "Though our clinic is private, we receive funds from the municipal government. As it happens, I am classified as a civil servant and therefore exempt from the dueling statutes."

I leaned across my desk, beside myself. "You pompous fool, find my wife, however you have to do it! If she dies, I'll kill you myself, if I end up in a penal colony."

Dr. O'Neill was pale. "As I said, I understand your anger. Even though your threats are actionable, I won't file a complaint unless—"

"Kinders, show him off the base, and that means NOW!"

The sergeant didn't bat an eye. "Aye aye, sir." He crossed the room, bent over O'Neill, took his arm. "Come this way, sir. Right away, please."

I paced the office in mounting fury, until finally I flung open the door. "Call Tolliver!"

I waited until my aide cautiously peered in. "I hear you're on the warpath."

"Annie's missing. She walked out of the clinic."

His manner changed in an instant. "My God. I'm sorry." He pulled up a chair, sat without my bidding. "What do you want me to do?"

"She sneaked out yesterday, and there's no trace of her." I faced the window, grappled with a sudden difficulty in speaking.

"They'll find her, sir. It's just a matter of time." He pursed his lips, thought. "You could help."

"Go look for her, you mean?"

"No, of course not. Where would you search that they haven't tried? But you could take advantage of your popularity for once. Light a fire under the jerries."

"I could do that." I turned. "Get the number of the local station."

His sardonic smile returned. "That wouldn't be your style, sir. Try the Commissioner of Police. The Mayor. Hell, call the Secretary-General; he'd take a call from you. Anyone would."

"Except Admiral Duhaney."

"Well, he knows you." When he saw my eyes his smile vanished. "Sorry, I'm out of line. How high do you want to start?"

"The Police Commissioner, if I can get through."

Tolliver rose. "Give me a few minutes."

Half an hour later, I hung up, the Commissioner's assurances ringing in my ears. They would make every effort, highest priority, etc. I sat, biting my knuckles. Somehow, it sounded like a brush-off.

I passed the rest of the day in an agony of anticipation. I snatched up the caller every time it buzzed, dreading a catastrophe, praying that Annie had been found.

No word.

At dinner I was silent. No one at my table had been told about Annie, but they knew my moods enough not to bother me. Subdued conversation detoured around me while I played with my food.

Two days passed in endless agony. I signed reports, caned a hapless cadet who'd been caught outside the fence, ordered a cabin made ready for Lieutenant Thorne. Admiralty called, requesting me to attend the commissioning of U.N.S. *Wellington*, two weeks hence. I agreed. By then Annie would be found. She had to be.

By midafternoon of the third day I was nearly beside myself. Several times I called the clinic, to see if Annie had returned on her own. I plodded mechanically through my duties.

"Captain?"

I swung round so fast I almost fell out of my chair. "What, Edgar?"

"I think I found something."

After a moment I realized that Tolliver wasn't speaking of Annie. I forced myself to concentrate. "Go on."

"Remember when Sergeant Ibarez was keeping Jerence

Branstead away from his mates? He had him recheck serial numbers in the suiting room. I looked them over."

"So?" At the moment I didn't give a damn about suits, or the cadets who wore them.

"Branstead's tallies match the suiting room manifest, but they don't check against the invoices in the puter. It may mean something."

"Is the number of suits correct?"

"Seems to be. It's an odd discrepancy, though."

"It happens all the time. An order is diverted from one ship to another. Forget about it."

"Aye aye, sir. Why don't I just forget about the whole audit, while I'm at it?"

"Tolliver!" My voice was dangerous.

Eyes blazing, he stood his ground. "You told me the bloody audit was important. I've gone without sleep, worked until the room spun to get out this damned report. The first time I have something that doesn't check out, you tell me to forget it. Make up your bloody mind!"

I retreated before his fury. "I'm sorry. I'm thinking of Annie. Do whatever you want."

"Aye aye, sir," he said, barely mollified. "Any word yet?"

"Nothing." I hesitated. "Edgar, what should I do?"

"What can you do? Wait it out."

"She's alone out there."

"You don't know that."

"What do you mean?"

His tone was gentle. "Sir, she's home."

My fists tightened. "That's not her home anymore. It can't be."

"That's how you and I see it." He left the rest unsaid.

"Those damned drugs . . ."

He shook his head. "Perhaps it was better in the old days, when they left people unbalanced. Even if they were schizo and glitched."

I waved it aside. "I want my wife, not your theories."

"Yes, sir, I'm with you on that. Wait it out. It's not as if you could go looking for her."

My head came up.

After a moment I said, "Why not?"

Chapter 12

Tolliver objected vigorously to my leaving, and was apoplectic when I suggested going alone. To placate him, I agreed to take a middy. He picked Adam Tenere, who was groundside with dispatches. Well, the boy was well intentioned; I'd just have to be cautious in spaceport corridors.

To the annoyance of the steward, I was on my feet the moment the suborbital landed. Adam at my side, I fumed while the ramp swung ponderously from the gate. Outside, New York was already darkening.

Was there any point going to the clinic at this hour? Better to check into our hotel, start fresh in the morning. My Academy schedule was no immediate concern; I'd canceled all appointments, leaving Tolliver to greet Jeffrey Thorne and look after the paperwork at Devon.

No, a hotel would drive me cabin-crazy. I needed to see the clinic, put myself in Annie's place.

After losing several helicabs I gave up waiting my turn and shoved like everyone else, only to end up with a cabby who argued for five minutes before consenting to fly to the Bronx.

I settled back in my seat and glowered at Adam's attempts at conversation. At last, we set down on the visitor's lot, as far from the fenced perimeter as the cabby could manage.

"Sign us in at the Sheraton, Adam. I'll meet you later."

"Aye aye, sir. Can't I come—"

"No."

The clinic door opened at my first knock; I'd been on camera from the moment the heli had landed. At night, security would be especially tight.

The orderly at the desk looked up with scant effort to conceal his boredom. "Captain Seafort? I'm Jose Gierra. Dr. O'Neill was waiting, but he left for home an hour ago."

"My flight was delayed." I set down my duffel. "Show me Annie's room, please."

"Sorry. The rules say only the supervising physician can approve a visit. Come back tomorr—"

I was already striding to the ward door. "I'm not visiting, I'm inspecting."

"You need an escort in the ward."

"Fine! Escort me!" I opened the door as he dived, too late, for the automatic lock.

The orderly panted as he caught up with me. "Easy, joey. This job ain't no zark."

We strode along the corridor past silent darkened rooms.

Annie's cubicle was as I'd remembered: spartan, tidy, white. Her few clothes were stored neatly in the tiny closet. The sheets were tucked under the mattress with hospital precision.

I opened the bedside drawer; a brush, a comb, a chipcase. Annie's holovid lay on the chair. I inserted a chip. A romance holodrama, of the type she loved. I looked for a chip on which she might have left a note.

"There's nothing to find. The jerries looked four days ago."

I yearned to knock out his teeth. Instead, I asked politely, "Are you married, Mr. Gierra?"

"Sure."

I sat on the bed. "What's her name?"

"Connie."

"Would you care if she were killed?"

His fists bunched. "Of course."

"What if Connie were wandering out there, where the gangs could jump her?"

"Yeah, but she's no trannie."

My face showed no expression.

After a moment his sullenness faded. Slowly he lowered himself into the guest chair. "I'm sorry, Captain. You got every right to worry."

"Sorry I snarled at you."

"No matter." He gestured to the closet. "We looked for clues, but found nothing. The jerries came, asked a few questions. Truth is they wouldn't bother if you weren't famous. Another lost trann—lost patient is the least of their troubles."

"If you had to find Connie in a hurry, what would you do?"

"I'd want to search, same as you. But not at night."

"You people come in to work, don't you?"

"By heli, during the day. That's why Dr. O'Neill couldn't

wait. Another few minutes and he'd have been stuck here for the night."

"We once took the Gray Line tour through Manhattan." A lifetime ago, Amanda and I. "It wasn't that bad."

He snorted. "Manhattan, on an armored bus, in daylight. The Crypsnbloods on the streets 'll eat them downtown grodes, they ever stray this far."

"I have to find my wife, Mr. Gierra."

"You Navy types go armed?"

"Not groundside."

"Well, there you are. You might try in the morning."

I stood. "If a cab won't come for me, where can I get one?"

"Across the river. Or maybe they'd land at the jerryhouse on One seventy-fifth; the block around it is cleared."

"Could I walk?"

"Ever try walking in the Bronx? You have no idea what it's like. They'd leave your carcass to rot."

"I've got to find my wife."

"Maybe in daylight, if you're lucky. Believe me, Mr. Seafort. Don't even think of going out tonight."

I sank back on the bed, shook my head. "Why build a clinic in an armed camp?"

"We been on this site for years. It wasn't so bad 'til the city abandoned the housing projects. When they went trannie, that was the end."

Annie was out there, somewhere.

"Captain, stay in your wife's room 'til morning. I'm sure O'Neill won't flare jets over it, after he let her walk out."

"All right." I had little choice. "Thanks, Mr. Gierra."

"Joe. I'm sorry I gave you face." He stood. "I'm on all night. Tomorrow I'll show you the neighborhood."

"I'd appreciate that."

I undressed for bed, eyes on Annie's few clothes in the closet. I yearned to press her head to my chest. When I lay down in the dark, her pillow proved a poor substitute.

I slept like the dead. In the morning I woke to an insistent hand on my shoulder.

"Captain? Care for breakfast?"

I groaned, opening an eye. "Give me a couple of minutes." I

ducked into the head. Joe Gierra was waiting in the corridor when I came out knotting my tie. "Where can I make a call?"

"In the cafeteria." He steered me along the corridor.

I rang the Sheraton, waited several rings.

Adam sounded sleepy. "You never showed up, sir. The clinic operator said you were staying in Mrs.—"

"I'll be out for a while. I'll call around noon."

"Aye aye, sir. May I come wi—"

"No." I rang off.

I chewed on a roll. "How do you get home, Joe?"

"Helicab, usually. There's a few armored ground taxis left, but they usually work the Holdouts."

"The what?"

"The families who lived here originally. The Bronx was part of civilization, once. When the last subways stopped most everybody left, but a few diehards bricked up their windows and carried on. Their children still live here. They aren't Uppies, but they have their own shops, their own way of life." He tore a piece of syntho bacon, dabbed it in egg yoke.

"But . . . what do they do?"

"Same as anyone, I guess. Try to survive. They go out in groups, armed to the teeth, and only in the daytime. Their convoys bring in supplies every week or so. They use ground cabs when they can get them."

"What a life."

"Me, I'll take helicabs, even if they cost a few unibucks more. I don't want to get caught in a tin can if the Crypsnbloods come out."

I finished my third cup of coffee. Each moment it became less difficult to keep my eyes open.

"Come on, Captain. I'll show you the gate."

Someone had alerted Dr. O'Neill to my presence. When we dropped off my duffel at the desk he popped out of his office. "Captain, I called the stationhouse just a few minutes ago. Still no word of Mrs. Seafort. I don't recommend you go out alone."

"I'll keep it in mind." It was all I could do to maintain a pretense of civility. "Mr. Gierra?"

A few moments later we were at the gate. He pointed. "These shacks run all around the old stadium walls. Maybe a squatter saw her leave. You can ask."

"Right."

"When you get past the shacks, One sixty-first runs that way, east and west." He pointed. "Best to stay off it."

"Thanks, Joe." As the guard clicked open the gate, Gierra hesitated, thrust out his hand. I shook it.

I strode toward the nearest shacks a half block away, stumbling over broken asphalt barely discernible under waving weeds.

"Hey!"

I turned. Joe Gierra trotted after. He stopped, shrugged as if embarrassed. "I just thought . . . Hell. I might as well go with you. Two's safer."

"It's not neces—"

"She was a good joe, your lady. One of the nicer ones." He buttoned his jacket. "C'mon, before I change my mind."

I smiled, feeling as if the sun had broken through the morning haze.

We trudged toward a ragged line of huts built from the scrap of a crumbling civilization: broken alumalloy panels, crumbling brick mortared with mud. Not a soul could be seen, even in midmorning.

At the first hovel, I tapped on the dented door. Silence. "Are they abandoned?"

Joe snorted. "Are you kidding? When we put out the garbage . . ."

I moved to the next shack, knocked again. "Please talk to us. We won't hurt you."

The door flew open. A haggard crone in a filthy jumpsuit. In her hand, a knife glinted.

"I'm looking for—"

"Get away!" Her voice was like a nail on slate.

"My name is Captain Seafort. My—"

She lunged. As I reeled back she darted into the hut and slammed the door.

"Jesus, Lord Christ!" I didn't know I'd spoken aloud until I saw Gierra's face.

We crossed the haphazard lane and knocked at another shack. The door opened at once, as if the occupants had been waiting. Perhaps they had. Two husky youths, in their early twenties. One leaned on a club. "Whatcha wan'?"

"My wife was in the clinic. I'm trying to find her. I have a pic—"

"Ain' seen her, and wouldn' tell ya if I did. Prong yaself!" The door slammed shut.

I said with feeling, "Bastards."

"You'll get the same from all of them, Captain."

"They're all this bad?"

"No. These are the civilized ones." He spun, yelled, "We got blades, joey! Don't even think about it!" A sullen urchin hefted his rock, spat, ducked out of sight.

I whispered, "Did you really bring a knife?"

"No, I didn't plan on coming with you."

I tried another door. A woman with ragged children clinging to her knees peered at my holo, shook her head. "Ain' seen her. If she been, she gone. No point lookin'."

"Did someone get her?" I felt a chill.

"Must of. No one comes out here. Even us isn't safe." She picked up the smallest child, bared her breast, pleaded, "Go 'way, mister."

"Thank you, ma'am." She'd been the most civil of the lot.

I pointed past the end of the lane. "What's that way?"

"The real street. Abandoned stores, old apartments."

"Let's try it."

"Too far. Let's look around the other end of the fence."

"All right." I'd walk the street by myself, after.

We retraced our steps. Joe stopped. "This is too risky. I'll go back for a club or a blade. It'll just take a minute."

Reluctantly, I walked him back to the gate. I checked my watch, anxious not to waste precious daylight. I said, "Meet me on the south side of the compound. I'll start at the shacks nearest the fence."

He strode off, and I made my way to the ragged huts. A whiff of something foul; I wrinkled my nose. Perhaps Tolliver had been right; best to go back to London and let the jerries do their work. These people—

"Whatchew wan'?"

I whirled. Three men, two of them bearded. The third was flushed as if from exercise or fever. He held one hand behind his back.

"I'm looking for someone."

"Girl?"

"You know about her?" My voice was eager.

Their leader looked me over, rubbed his scraggly beard. "How much ya got?"

I hardened my tone. "Enough. Where is she?"

He pointed to the side lane. "Dat way."

The path was deserted. "Wait until my friend gets back." I peered, hoping to see Joe.

"Prong yo' frien'." Fever Face leered through broken teeth.

"Bugger off!" My snarl surprised even me. I thrust my hand in a pocket. "Mess with me, you be dead!" They hesitated. "G'wan!"

Scraggly Beard flashed a hand signal. I turned to Fever Face. Smiling, I took a casual step forward and kicked him in the groin.

He squalled, fell to this knees, revealing the laser pistol he'd hidden behind his back. As the third joey lunged for it I stomped on his hand. He howled, scrambled to his feet nursing his hand as I snatched up the gun.

I jammed the pistol in my pocket. Lord God knew if it had a charge.

Scraggly Beard hurled a rock. I gasped as it slammed into my side. He hauled Fever Face to his feet. I braced for a new attack, but they disappeared around the corner.

Joe Gierra was right; I couldn't search alone. I would need Adam Tenere, or a police escort. A Naval gunship might come in handy.

A sound, as feral shapes emerged from a nearby shack. Teens. One twisted a rusty chain; another beckoned with a huge and filthy knife. The third dangled a splintered club. I turned to run, stumbled as the club caught me behind the leg. I needed a rock, a pipe, anything. I clawed in my pocket, pulled out the pistol.

"Get away! I'll use it!" The charge was so far down the low battery light didn't even blink.

"Ain't no good, sailorboy! Empty!" The boy's shirt was no more than rags.

"Leave me alone, damn you!"

The chain boy howled as he leaped. I hurled the pistol at his face. A spurt of blood. He dropped, clawing at his eyes.

His companion charged. His club caught me on the side of the head. Blinking away stars, I clung to his neck. He reeked.

"Leggo me, gayfag!" The boy tried to pull away, but my legs were unsteady. I hung on, weaponless.

The last attacker circled, his knife twitching. He lunged. I whirled the joey I held so he was between me and the blade.

With a shriek, the boy I clutched dropped his club, stood trembling. As if unutterably weary, he rested his head on my shoulder. His legs buckled and he slid slowly to the ground. The third attacker backed away, eyes wide. Blood dripped from the knife in his mate's side. I gagged on the stench, rubbed my aching head.

"Frazzing sailboy!" The remaining youth snatched a fallen club, charged. I caught the blow on my arm. A white blaze of pain.

I dug in, slammed my shoulder into his chest. He went down, rolled clear, sprang to his feet. I fled.

He was scant feet behind me. I dodged aside, crashed through the door of an abandoned hovel. I needed a club, a brick, anything. I stumbled over a broken table, smashed it into the wall. It disintegrated. I snatched a table leg.

The maddened youth charged through the doorway. As he raised his club I reared back, swung at his face with all my might. A crunch. His body flipped backward. His legs flew up and caught me in the gut. I lost my balance, slammed my head against the wall.

Chapter 13

My skull ached abominably. I pried open my eyes, saw only black. Was I blind? I groaned, probed the painful lump on the side of my head. I lay against a wall. I'd been in a fight. Running. Chains. Clubs.

Crawling on hands and knees, I groped for the door. Fabric, on a stiff cold form. Something jagged and bony. And sticky. With a cry I pulled my hands free, rubbed them frantically on my jacket, the floor, anything I could find.

I knew what I'd touched.

Blind or no, I had to get out. I clawed to my feet, stretched out my hands, stumbled over debris. Where was the bloody door? If I had to touch that . . . that thing again . . .

A breath of cool air thrust through the fetid stench. Shakily, I stood and sniffed, trying to sense its direction.

Where in God's own hell was the door? Hands outstretched, I lurched like an automaton. I collided with something hard that smashed my lip and nose. Cursing, I nursed my throbbing face. The edge of the damned door had passed between my outstretched hands. Dabbing at a trickle of blood, I tottered into the welcome air.

Why hadn't Joe Gierra returned? If I called aloud, he might hear and help. But others might also hear. Perhaps they watched me even now. Help me, Lord God. Not for my sake, but Annie's. She has no one else.

A dim glow, as if in the distance.

I rubbed my eyes.

Lights.

With a rush of orientation I realized I'd lain unconscious until night. The distant lights must be Manhattan's Uppie towers.

If so, the clinic should be . . . that way. No, I couldn't remember which direction I'd taken. I could think it through, if I didn't panic.

A dog howled. My skin prickled.

Voices, quite close. I stiffened to immobility. Shapes passed.

Without warning, I sneezed. Someone screamed. The thud of pounding feet. Silence. My teeth bared in a feral grin. The squatters were as fearful of me as I of them.

As my eyes became accustomed to the night I saw lights flickering through imperfect walls. The shacks were occupied. I squinted, decided I could detect the end of the lane. I trotted toward it, fell flat on my face. Cursing, I scrambled to my feet. Why had I been so stupid as to go out alone, without lights or a caller?

A heli droned far overhead. Its searchlight played on the broken asphalt. Jerries? How could I attract their attention? Not by noise; they'd never hear. Did they have heat seekers? No use, every living body would set them off. I needed a light. Break into a squatter's shack, find something for a torch. My lips curled in a savage smile.

The blow smashed me in the back, hurled me to the ground. Paralyzed, I gasped for air. Hands pawed at me. My breath returned in a convulsive sob.

Someone pulled my jacket loose, flipped me over. Hands tugged at my boot, opening the snaps.

I yanked back my free leg, kicked at a shadowy face. The form toppled. I heaved myself to my knees. A whistling sound; I ducked. The club missed by an inch.

I ran as if from Satan himself. I caromed off a wall, found the lane again, turned a corner. A stone twisted under my loose boot; I hopped a few steps, ran again, my ankle sending warning stabs of pain. The voices faded.

I blundered into a pile of garbage. A cat shrieked; so did I. Jesus, Lord God. Reeling, I fetched up against an abandoned electricar, realized I was in a regular city street.

"Annie!" My shout rent the air. "I'm here for you. Come out, for God's sake!"

Running steps. I came to my senses, ducked behind the car, scuttled away low to the ground.

Where in God's name was I headed? The lights to my right must be Manhattan. Was that west? No, south. I was running . . . east. Into darkness.

I stopped, leaned against a building, tried again to catch my breath.

The clinic was on One sixty-first. I strained to see its lights;

without them I'd never find my way. Hide until morning, then. In daylight I'd have a better chance; these savages knew their streets as I could not. I peered down the block, searching for shelter.

Ahead, a flickering light. Civilization? Behind me, a can clattered. I bolted toward the sanctuary of the light.

Some instinct made me slow as I neared. Stooped figures cavorted around a fire, in a vision reminiscent of Hieronymus Bosch. One toted a chair, another a bottle. A third held a bugle high over his head, cackling and cawing. A few of the dancers were naked.

A spit was propped across the blaze. On the spit, a dog. A bald creature in women's clothes capered in a dizzy circle, shrieking unintelligibly.

Pace by pace, I retreated, my heart hammering. Behind me, a growl. I spun on my heel. Two red eyes, over a toothy mouth. I screamed. The creature backed away. So did I, toward the fire, where the dangers were human.

The beast snarled again. Perhaps it was only a dog, but I didn't stay to find out. I sprinted toward the flame and the gamboling tribe. The wild dance wavered. Someone seized a brand, another a knife. I bolted past them into the campsite, sent the bald woman sprawling, leaped over a seated figure, and was gone into the night.

Favoring my aching ankle I galloped down the center of the road. I glanced over my shoulder. Naked revelers, a maddened hound, and the demons of hell pursued me. I was outdistancing all but the dog. A sprawl of gutted cars; I swerved left.

The shouts behind me redoubled. I risked another look. The beast loped ahead of the rest, determined, tongue hanging. I stopped to seize a brick. As the animal lunged I hurled my missile. The dog yelped, skittered away. Again I turned and ran, breath sobbing in my throat. The dog limped after me. Behind him came the calls of the humans.

I cantered on in darkness, my boot loose and flapping, a persistent hound and cavorting dancers in tow. Where were the jerries when you needed them? The nearest station was . . .

One seventy-fifth, Joe Gierra had said. I turned a corner, swerved left, charged on.

Rocks bounced at my feet; the campfire lads had reached the

corner too. Soon I'd be too weary to run, too tired to care. I had to save at least some strength for when they cornered me.

In the black of the night a bugle sounded a charge. Its notes echoed along down the broad, silent avenue, over and again.

Doors opened. Boys and young men poured into the road. Two more dogs joined the chase as the bugle sounded anew. I'd blundered into a fox hunt, and I was the fox.

Hands clawed; I tore through them and staggered on.

One sixty-fifth. Ten more blocks, but I wouldn't make it. My breath came ragged. Onward I ran, closing my eyes to maintain the rhythm . . .

"Move it, Seafort!" Sergeant Tallor reached forward with his baton.

"Aye aye, sir." I lurched along the Farside track until I'd gained several steps. Sarge could easily have caught me, but I knew he wouldn't increase his pace just to touch me. He was always fair. Still, I had to maintain my distance; one tap with his baton and I'd be sent for a caning. It befell one or another of us, not every day, but often enough. I wasn't sure, but I suspected they'd been slowly increasing the pace.

Two laps to go. Robbie Rovere was half a length ahead, alongside Corporal Tolliver.

Could I hold out? In the months I'd been at Farside I'd felt my stamina increase, and I'd already been made to turn in my slacks and jacket for the next larger size. I wasn't sure, but I thought my voice had deepened another notch too. Perhaps it was the food.

Sergeant Tallor was gaining again. I could sprint, probably even catch the stragglers a dozen meters ahead of me, but if I used my little reserve of energy I'd collapse before the last lap.

I stumbled, lost my pace. Tallor's steps neared. Damn! No choice now. I dashed ahead, stopped only when I had left him a quarter turn behind. Now, I had only to hang on.

I turned into the last lap. Behind me, Sarge's inexorable footsteps. My lungs heaved. It wasn't fair. I'd been caned only last week. Lightly, it was true. Track canings were always light. But the humiliation was unbearable.

I staggered on. His step came closer. "Move on, boy."

I nodded, too bereft of breath to acknowledge the warning.

The distance between us closed. He reached with the baton. I lurched forward, avoided it by inches.

Again he neared. If only I hadn't stumbled, the lap before. Now I couldn't last even the remaining quarter lap.

The baton reached out—

And I went down. "Ow!" I rolled in the gravel. "My foot!" I clutched my leg. "Oh, God, my ankle!"

Sarge knelt by my side. "Don't blaspheme." He pushed my hands away, felt the joint. "Can you move it? How about this way?"

I sobbed, "It hurts. I think I twisted it."

"That happens. You'll be all right." He blew his whistle to attract the attention of Sergeant Swopes.

I lay on the gravel track while the two conferred over my sweaty form. "Nothing's broken, Nick. We'll have the med tech check you just to be sure."

"Okay, Sarge."

Swopes reached down, offered a hand. "I don't think you need the stretcher, do you?" I came tremulously to my feet. "Lean on me." I did so. Hobbling and hopping, I made my way to the infirmary.

Bone diagnostics found no damage; the tech wrapped my foot in icy towels for an hour, then sent me back to my dorm. I showered and changed. By the time I caught up to my mates at lunch I was hardly limping.

During afternoon classes I managed to avoid the instructors' disapproval, though my mind wandered. Sergeant Swopes let me off tray duty for the night. I ate listlessly. After dinner we trudged back to barracks for Free Hour before Lights Out. I lay on my bed.

"You all right?"

I looked up, smiled. "Sure, Arlene."

She sat alongside me, whispered, "See Peterson? He pulled a fast one tonight."

"What do you mean?" I leaned close.

"Were you in his Nav class? He got caught passing a note, and Vasquez gave him a demerit."

"So?"

She looked disgusted. "That made ten, dummy. He had to see Zorn."

"Yeah, he got caned. That's why he's lying on his stomach."

"And after, he went to the Commandant's office."

I nodded. The unfortunate cadet would knock on the Commandant's hatch, say the ritual words to the duty officer. "Cadet Peterson reporting, sir. Lieutenant Zorn's compliments, and would you please cancel ten demerits."

Sanders slipped off the bed, sat on the floor, her mouth close to my ear. "I saw him in the shower tonight. He wasn't caned. No marks, not even red."

I whispered, "Maybe Zorn let him off."

She snorted. "Do they ever let a cadet off?"

I shook my head, puzzled. "How did he get out of it?"

"Don't you see? He never reported to Zorn. He just waited and went to the Commandant to have his demerits canceled."

I whistled softly at Peterson's audacity. If they caught him . . . "What'll you do about it?"

Her look was scornful. "Me? It's his affair, not mine. And pardon the pun, but it's *his* arse if they catch him."

"Geez."

After she wandered off I stared at Peterson, looked away, disappointed. I'd liked him.

The chime sounded, warning the end of Free Hour. We made ready for bed.

As the bulbs dimmed for Lights Out, the hatch opened. Sergeant Swopes surveyed us in our beds. When he spoke his voice was somber. "Cadet Peterson, out of your bunk."

The boy complied at once. He wore only his shorts. "Yes, Sarge?"

"Put on your pants and shirt."

"Aye aye, sir." He grabbed his clothes. I noticed he was careful not to turn his back to Sarge.

"And your shoes."

Half dressed, Peterson waited by his bunk. Sarge walked up and down the aisle, looking at each of us in turn before he turned back to Peterson. "Report to the Commandant's office at once."

"Aye aye, sir." He started toward the hatch.

"With your duffel."

"Aye—what?"

"You heard me. Move."

Cadet Peterson thrust his remaining clothes in the duffel, scurried out the hatch.

Sergeant Swopes walked down the aisle to Peterson's bed, sat on the end rail, a shadowy figure in the dim light. After a moment, he spoke to the opposite bulkhead.

"Your lives are committed to the United Nations Naval Service. The Service is worthy of you. It is our hope that you will be worthy of it. To that end we exercise you, train you, teach you the skills and crafts you must know."

He paused. The barracks was utterly silent.

"None of you would tolerate a cadet cheating his bunkmates. You know you must stand together, rely on each other without reserve, to survive the rigors of space. Likewise, your mates must be able to depend on your courage, your intelligence, your honesty."

He stood. "You must also learn that not only your bunkmates rely on your integrity. The entire Naval Service is as one with you. Captains, admirals, lieutenants, and middies. Officers and men. Cooks and engineers. Your word is your bond, to each of them. It must always be so."

He paused, until the tension was agony, sat again on the bed.

"You must not tolerate deceit. Not in me, not in yourselves. What is deceit? If I pull surprise inspection and you kick a loose sock under your bunk, that's fair. It's your responsibility to appear ready, mine to find the sock. But, if I ask, 'Cadet, is there a sock underneath your bunk?' you must respond with the truth. Dishonesty violates your oath of enlistment, but worse, it violates your integrity, and you will have become something you cannot long endure."

Somewhere, a sob caught in a throat.

"What Cadet Peterson did today was despicable, but the cancer has been excised. Whether it will reoccur is up to you. You are teens, and I am adult, but together we are the Navy. You, by your acts, will decide what kind of Navy that shall be."

He stood once more. "Does anyone have anything to say?" The room was silent. "Anyone?" He walked to the hatch, slid it open.

A voice wavered. "Yes, sir. I do."

He didn't turn. Still facing the hatch he said, "Yes, Seafort?"

"I lied today, when I said I hurt my ankle. I fell on purpose."

A long silence. "Come with me." He passed through the hatch.

In nothing but my shorts, trembling, I faced him in his cabin.

"Why, Seafort?"

"Sergeant Tallor was about to baton me."

He nodded. "You were that afraid of the barrel?"

My eyes stung. "Not afraid, exactly. I just—no excuse, Sarge."

"Belay that. The truth."

"I couldn't run any faster. I was looking for a way out, and I couldn't think of anything else. I panicked." My ears flamed.

"You threw away your integrity to avoid a few strokes from Mr. Zorn."

"I—yes, sir." If only I could crawl under the hatch. If he would just look away.

"I see." He went to his file, pulled out a folder. "Read it."

I opened the file. On the left, my picture. On the right various reports, exam grades. On top, a note, dated today. "Cadet Seafort pretended injury today to avoid the baton. Action withheld for the moment."

I closed the folder. "You knew." I forced myself to meet his eye. "Then why didn't you send me with Peterson, sir?"

"There was hope you'd redeem yourself."

I swallowed, too miserable to speak. "What are you going to do to me, Sarge?"

"Me? Nothing. It's up to Tallor." He gestured to the hatch. "Get dressed and report to him."

"Right now?"

"That's what I said."

Fifteen minutes later I was knocking on Sergeant Tallor's hatch, barely in control of my dread. "Cadet Seafort reporting, Sarge."

"It took you long enough."

I blushed scarlet. "You know?"

"Yes."

"I'm—" It seemed so inadequate. "I'm sorry."

"But the damage is done. Do I need to lecture you?"

I looked up. "No, sir. I understand what I've done."

"Is it any different from what Peterson did?"

Of course it was. Peterson had actually lied, pretended to have been caned. I'd just . . . I looked at the bulkhead, past it to Father and home. Maybe, after they expelled me, I could learn courage in those rocky Welsh pastures. Perhaps even honesty, someday.

"No, sir. It's the same. I deserve the same punishment."

His tone was sharp. "That's for me to decide."

"Yes, sir."

He sat on his bunk, shaking his head. "Would a caning do you any good?"

I blurted, "Maybe nothing would." At his surprised look I rushed on, "I shouldn't even be here, at Academy. I missed Final Cull. They knew I wasn't qualified. Cane me, or get rid of me, Sarge. Do something, so I won't hurt the others."

"Easy, Seafort."

I bit back tears. "It's true."

"Very well." He thought for endless moments. "No caning."

Relief and despair battled within me. "Why not?"

"You understand what you've done, and either you'll do it again or you'll mature. You won't learn anything from the barrel."

"You'll punish me, though?" My tone was hopeful.

"Four demerits. And pot detail, every night for a month. It's hard work, but it won't occupy your mind. You'll have time to think."

"Thank you, sir."

"That's all."

When I was halfway through the hatch he stopped me. "I wouldn't have batonned you, Nicky."

"I couldn't run a whit faster, and you kept getting closer!"

"But I hadn't touched you, and I wasn't going to. You were giving your best."

I cried, "How was I to know that?"

"You were to trust me, and the Service. As I want to trust you."

I wiped my eyes. "Why did you come so close, then?"

"I was trying for your Yall."

I understood at last. Since we'd arrived at Academy they'd exhorted us to "give your all" at one thing or another. It was an Academy catchphrase, giving the "Academy All," or Yall.

"I picked up the pace but you hung on. I picked it up again

and still you managed. When you're running, focus on each step, one at a time, as if it's the only one. Don't worry about the others to come. You have more endurance than you think. That's what I wanted you to learn."

"Sarge, I'm sorry. Please, I mean it!"

"I believe you, Cadet. Dismissed."

I slunk back to my dorm.

"Git 'im! He goin' for the jerries!"

My breath rasped. One sixty-ninth; six blocks more. I risked another glance back. One joey pedaled a rusty bicycle, a few others had rollerboards.

The boy on the bicycle pedaled furiously, swinging a heavy chain. He yowled, "Meat t'night! You be dinnah!"

I veered onto the sidewalk, but it was littered with broken furniture and debris. I yelped as my foot twisted again and I nearly lost my loose boot. I swerved back to the street. The rider came at me, chain whistling.

I stopped short, sprang under the blur of the chain. The rider crashed to the pavement. I ran on, mist seeping across my vision. I couldn't keep going.

"Yes you can, Seafort."

Not five more blocks, Sarge. Honest.

"Another few steps, boy."

Dutifully, I did as I was bidden. He'd take care of me. They always would.

One seventy-second street. Eons later, One seventy-third. Most of the mob had given up. A few grinning youths loped along, waiting for me to falter.

Surely the station would be floodlit. Ahead all was dark, but to the east, a glow. Please, Lord God. Joe told me 175th. Don't make me run crosstown. I can't, even for Annie.

Somehow, I reached the corner. Where's the frazzing jerry-house?

There. The next block east, lit against the night. Encircled by a high chain-link fence, the station seemed a fortress. Surrounding buildings had been cleared away so it stood in a great open square.

Gasping, I staggered to the fence. Two youths closed in on me, taunting. "He wanna fin' jerries!" A hand snatched at my shirt.

The snap of a laser. My attacker dropped. I flinched, realized the shot had come from the station. The other youths dodged across the street into the dark.

No gate. Exhausted, I grasped the fence to hold myself upright. A sizzle.

I shrieked with pain, nursed my scorched hand. Across the street, jeers of laughter. Weeping, I lurched along the sidewalk. A high gate. Thank Lord God.

I flicked a finger at the bar. No charge. I rattled it with my good hand, looking for a buzzer, a camera. "Help me!" I'd intended a shout, barely managed a croak.

A speaker I hadn't noticed, on the top of the gatepost. "Off the gate, trannie! We're closed until morning."

A rock crashed into the fence. The hunters, behind me.

"They're after me!"

"We'll cover you to the corner, then you're on your own."

"I'm Nicholas Seafort! *OPEN THE FRAZZING GATE!*"

"Dey no help!" A youth more daring than the rest scuttled to the center of the street, hefting a brick. "I eat you!"

A new voice, tinny in the speaker. "It's him, the one Commander Chai said to watch for! Open the gate!"

"Comeon, sailaboy!" A brick spun toward me, struck a glancing blow on my forehead.

I stumbled, and the world spun.

"You be dinnah!"

Black.

"Are you all right, sir?"

I lay on my back, cold cloth on my forehead. A bright lit room. I focused on the young face looming over me, the blue uniform. "You're a jerry?"

A momentary frown. "I'm a police officer, yes, sir. Patrolman Wesley De Broek."

"I'm in the stationhouse?"

"Fifth Consolidated Precinct, One seventy-fifth Street Station."

I lay gathering my wits. "Help me sit."

The young patrolman put one arm behind my neck. "Easy, Captain. You've had a rough time."

"I'm all right." I think.

"I'll tell Commander Chai you're awake."

"Wait a minute." I took stock. My hand was swathed in gauze. Shirt ripped across the front. No jacket.

Across the room was a wall mirror. I peered at it. Good Lord. On my forehead, a blue lump. My nose was bloodied, my lip swollen. I giggled. "Just like the cover of *Holoworld*."

"They made a mess of you, sir. You're lucky, though. Some of the Holdouts, after the trannies are done with them . . . "

"I see why you don't open the gate."

"Yes. Well." He looked embarrassed. "No one imagined you'd stroll to the stationhouse in the middle of the night. Jensik figured the word was out, and the trannies were playing with us."

"I see."

"We knew you were out there somewhere. Some Brit lieutenant's called half a dozen times. He's been raising hell."

Ah, Tolliver. I didn't know you cared.

I limped to a chair. "Mr. De Broek, this place . . . " My gesture took in the whole district. "The government's lost control. Why don't they abandon the area or send in the military?"

Patrolman De Broek stuck his hands in his pockets, stared out the reinforced window. "I have no say in that, sir. In my opinion, we should shut down the stationhouse. Give the Bronx to the trannies, fall back to Manhattan. If we consolidate our strength, we can hold some of downtown. Under the towers, at least."

"Why don't they?"

"The Holdouts still have their voting cards, as long as they scrape up the taxes. With land values fallen to nothing, they can afford to hang on to their cards. It's their only hope of even minimal police protection."

"Can you do anything for them?"

"During the day we fly patrols over their stores. We even hold most of the roads. At night, you see how it is."

"Surely you have enough firepower to—"

"Our heat seekers and smart bombs could kill anything that moves. But unless we're prepared to blast our way out, we'll lose a heli, like last November. Three officers killed." De Broek rubbed his face. "Some of what we see is . . . beyond belief. Even for me, and I've been a jerry six years." He went silent.

"My wife is out there." She had to be. The alternative was unbearable.

"I'd better get the Commander."

I lay back, weary and aching.

The Precinct Commander hurried in. "Thank heaven you're well." He held out his hand in a politician's handshake. "Stay with us until morning if you like, or we can escort you out now. What would you like?"

"Find my wife."

"We'll try. As you know, this isn't the Garden of Eden." He waited a moment. "As for tonight . . . ?"

I sighed. Until I knew Annie's fate I would have no peace, but I couldn't find her trail. The transpops wouldn't help; they banded together against all outsiders.

There was nothing I could do for her; I saw that now. And my cadets awaited. When all was said and done, I had duty.

Hon, I loved you. I'm sorry I was so weak.

I'd hoped Annie's picture, her shy smile, might pierce their sullen hostility. But she was nothing to them, or to the police. No one cherished her but I.

I, and—

I looked up, lips dry. "Take me to the Midtown Sheraton."

The Precinct Commander turned to De Broek. "Call up a heli. Drop him at his hotel."

I got to my feet, carefully. "My duffel's still at the clinic. We'll stop to get it."

We landed inside the clinic fence. De Broek jumped out to fetch my gear.

A figure ran toward us from the gate. "Is that you, sir?" Adam Tenere swung up on the step, hair disheveled. "Thank Lord God! I didn't know what to do, I called Mr. Tolliver and—" He ground to a halt, saluted. "Midshipman Tenere reporting!"

His eyes widened as he took in my bloody shirt, my bandaged hand. "Sir, are you—I know you told me to stay at the hotel but I was so . . ."

I snarled, "Finish a bloody sentence!"

"I was so worried for you," he said in a small voice.

I looked away, cleared my throat. "Forgive me. It's been a . . . trying night."

De Broek loped back to the heli, my duffel slung over his shoulder. Adam gave way.

De Broek climbed in. "Is this joey coming along?"

"It seems so." I slid over. "Let's go."

While we flew over the darkened city, I let Adam help me change into a clean shirt. Nonetheless, my appearance tested the urbanity of the jaded skytel clerks. Jacketless, bandaged, I limped through the penthouse lobby. Well, it couldn't be helped. I settled into my tub for a long soak.

With fresh gauze on my abrasions I emerged feeling almost myself, though desperately tired. "Hand me the caller, Adam." I eased myself into a chair.

I waited for my connection. "This is Captain Seafort. Get Admiral Duhaney, flank."

"Captain Helgar has the watch, sir. The Admiral's in his apartment, asleep."

"Wake him."

I wasn't sure if the gasp came from Adam or the lieutenant.

"I can't, except for impending fleet action. I'll give you Captain Helgar."

Helgar was senior to me and would bottle my call until morning. Precious hours wasted. I snarled, "I said Duhaney, not Helgar! Get him on the line or I'll have your job, if not your skin! *NOW!*"

The line clicked. I gripped the caller, wondering if I'd just thrown away what was left of my career. Duhaney had reason enough to cashier me even without this latest provocation. Restlessly, I tapped the chair arm.

Half a minute. Then, "Duhaney." His voice was groggy.

"Nick Seafort."

"I know. Lieutenant Sprey nearly wet his pants. This had better be important."

I blurted, "Sir, I'm in trouble and need help."

His tone changed immediately. "What is it, Seafort?"

"My wife." Quickly I explained about Annie. "I walked off my job without authorization, to try to find her. Lieutenant Tolliver's covering the base."

"What can we do to help?"

"First, authorize my absence. I'm AWOL, and I don't want it in the holos. I can't expect my cadets to toe the line if I don't."

"Done. Christ, Seafort, she's your wife. Of course you went after her." He paused for thought. "Why not tell the holozines?

With her picture on the public news screens, someone might spot her."

"Sir, it's worse out there than you think. A newsflash would set off a manhunt. Someone might hold her for ransom, or kill her." If she weren't already dead.

"Very well, it's your choice. What else?"

"I need help finding her. I have someone in mind, but staff transfers are frozen. Will you—"

"Anyone you want. Tell BuPers."

I gulped. "Sir, I don't know how to thank you."

"Stroke Senator Boland, once in a while. Is that too much, Captain?"

A silence. "I'm sorry, sir."

He snorted. "Whatever you did, he hasn't mentioned his son again. You pulled a fast one, I'm sure of it. Someday I'll find out how."

"I'll tell you now, if you ask."

A chuckle. "No, I'm sure you followed orders, in your own style. I prefer not to know the details. Can I go back to sleep now, Nick?"

"Yes, sir, of course."

His voice softened. "About your wife, you have my best wishes. And my prayers."

"Thank you, sir." I forced out the words.

"Good ni—"

"Admiral!"

His tone was startled. "Yes?"

I gripped the caller, took a long breath. "Something you should know, before you leave me in charge of Academy." Sergeant Darwin T. Swopes stood in the aisle, his eyes somber. I raised my eyes to his.

"Get on with it."

I said, "Captain Higbee, in BuPers. I didn't like the replacement he chose for Lieutenant Sleak, so I told him I had influence, that I would destroy him if he didn't cooperate." I held the caller to my cheek, waited for the explosion.

He sighed. "They trained you too well, Nick Seafort."

"I don't understand, sir."

He hesitated, as if groping for words. "Try to see it as two Navies, son. The one they told you about, the Navy you're in. It protects the star lanes and mobilizes its resources to fight fish.

The other one, that I'm a part of, fights for appropriations and commissions new warships. What they told you about honor, and truth, and integrity, that's valid for your Navy. It's never applied to mine. We're political, lad. Always have been, always will be. We admit Senators' sons, keep the bureaucrats content, requisition the supplies and arm the warships so you and your heroes can do the fighting."

"Sir, I—"

"Let me finish. That's the way it is in Washington, in London, in the corridors of the U.N. If you want equipment, you fight for it, or pay what has to be paid. If you want someone on staff, you pull him in with whatever it takes. Higbee complained to me three days ago. I told him to stay out of my hair. I figured if you had the balls to browbeat him, you'd get your staff. If you didn't, you shouldn't have been put in charge of Academy in the first place."

The silence stretched. He added, "Nick, you don't need to join my Navy, I just want you to know about it. Do what you have to, and don't punish yourself with guilt. It's how the system works."

"Aye aye, sir." It was all I could say.

"Good night." He rang off.

"Satisfactory, Cadet."

My head snapped up. "What, Sarge?"

Adam gaped. "I didn't say anything, sir."

"Not you. Mr.—" I bit off the rest. I'd made fool enough of myself for one day. "Adam, before you go to bed, call Naval Liaison. I want a groundcar and a heli standing by. And another jacket; I only brought one. Have them see to it."

"Aye aye, sir. It's four in the morning, sir, I don't know if they'll—"

"Someone will answer. The Navy never sleeps."

Alone, I undressed, lay on the bed, turned down the lights, dreading my next task. After a moment I took the caller once more, rang through to Admiralty. "BuPers, please." I waited while the connection was made. My heart beat faster.

"BuPers. Lieutenant Dervis, duty officer."

My voice rang with confidence. "This is Captain Nicholas E. Seafort, calling at the order of Fleet Admiral Duhaney. Triple A Priority, Immediate Action. I need a man transferred groundside from U.N.S. *Waterloo*; she's in home system. Start a shuttle out to him within the hour. I want him at Von Walthers by tomorrow afternoon."

"Who's your man?"

My heart was pounding. Through unwilling lips I said, "His name is Eddie Boss. Seaman first class."

Chapter 14

I stirred restlessly in the shuttleport caller booth. "I know what I'm doing, Edgar."

"He has no reason to trust you, sir, or want to help."

"I'll handle it. Meanwhile, you're in charge. I've got the Admiral's stamp on that."

"No matter to me, sir. I already had your okay."

Tolliver was right. Acting under orders, he was relieved of responsibility.

"The special cadets. Arnweil, Kyle Drew, and Stritz."

"Yes, sir?"

"You may be aware . . ." I sighed. No reason not to admit it, especially to Tolliver. "I have no idea what to do with them."

"I'll keep them busy running errands, but the plan was for them to be with you."

"Not where I'm going."

"You're due at the *Wellington* ceremonies next week. Why not take them along? Give them something to look forward to."

"Are you out of your mind? Raw cadets with the Navy brass, at a commissioning?"

"Why not?"

"Because . . . because—"

"You said that."

"I'll think about it." A woman approached the booth, stared meaningfully at the caller. I waved her away.

"Yes, sir. Pity I can't tell them now, so they'll know they're not just your errand boys."

"*All* cadets are errand boys." I paused. "Very well, tell them."

"As you wish, sir. I trust you'll go armed this time?"

"Yes." With a pistol, perhaps. No more. The object was to seek help, not fight a war with the transpops. "Is your report done?"

"I'm waiting for an answer from United Suit and Tank."

"Has Jeff Thorne come down?"

"Due this afternoon. I'm sending a middy to meet him in London."

"Very well. Give him my best. I'll see him when—when this is over."

"Godspeed, sir." We rang off.

I replaced the caller, limped to the counter. Adam jumped up from his seat to join me.

"Gate twelve is this way, sir."

"I can read," I growled.

"Yes, sir. If your foot's bothering you I can fetch him."

"I'm no invalid." Everyone had treated me as one, from the moment I'd taken command. Sending Adam to meet me at Earthport Station, as if I couldn't find my own way. He'd nearly made me an invalid himself.

I limped another few steps, past an empty waiting area. I sighed. "Very well, I'll wait here. You'll have no trouble recognizing him. He's no taller than you, but twice your bulk. If you have any doubt, just call out his name." I took a seat in the passenger lounge.

"Aye aye, sir. Shall I get you a holozine?"

"Go!" I didn't need a blanket or a pillow, either. Certainly not a bloody nursemaid.

I brooded. In a few minutes I'd have to look again on Eddie Boss. The young seaman's sneering face rose before my eyes. Arms that could snap a spine. His scornful gap-toothed smile. His—

I sighed again. Eddie had done wrong, but he was no monster. Plucked from the streets of Lower New York as part of an ill-advised transpop resettlement project, he'd been abandoned on *Challenger* with Annie and me. If I closed my eyes I could recall his huge hand reaching out to touch mine with awe, after I'd sworn to teach him to read.

I conjured Eddie at my polished conference table, laboring to form the difficult words. And I thought of how, moments after he'd taken the oath as a seaman, he'd slammed Chris Dakko to the deck when the Uppie lad had refused his own oath. I could see him—

Enough. I wanted to see him no more.

— in *Challenger*'s mess, hesitant, squirming with embarrassment. Would I teach him Uppie speech, Uppie manners, so he wouldn't have to die a scorned trannie?

We'd worked for weeks. Slowly, he'd mastered civilized diction, struggled to refine his unsophisticated ways. At last, he succeeded.

And then he'd brought me Annie, to do the same for her.

"Midshipman Tenere reporting, sir."

I wrenched myself back to the shuttleport lounge. "Very well, Mr. Ten—"

The sailor came to attention, his seaman's whites stiff and starched. His face was expressionless. "Seaman Boss reporting, sir."

"As you were, both of you." The midshipman relaxed; Eddie Boss did not.

"The shuttle was early, sir. It came in at—"

"Be silent, Middy. Hello, Mr. Boss."

The muscular young sailor grunted. He maintained eyes front.

I temporized. "Mr. Boss, did they tell you why you were brought down?"

"No." The response required a "sir," but I wouldn't make an issue of it.

"I asked for you. I need help."

His face twisted. "Do I have a choice, Captain?"

Good question. I could order him to comply, but what use would his enforced assistance be? Anyway, could I order him to risk his life on my private errand? "Yes, you have a choice."

"I choose no."

Adam stirred indignantly. "You're talking to a Captain!"

"I know who he be." Eddie's tone was surly.

The middy bristled. "Mind your manners, sailor! This is—"

"Mr. Tenere, leave us." I knew the boy was only trying to do his job. It was a junior officer's responsibility to keep discipline among the ranks.

"Aye aye, sir." With a look of reproach the middy retreated beyond earshot.

"Mr. Boss—" I stopped, tasting bile. Whatever it took, I would do. "Annie is gone, Eddie. She walked out of a hospital. If she's still alive, she's on the streets. We have to find her."

"I don't. You do."

I said softly, "Doesn't she mean anything to you?"

"Annie Wells? The trannie bitch who married some Uppie Cap'n? She don' mean nothin' ta me!"

"Eddie!"

"She don't. You neid—neither."

My knees were unsteady. I sat abruptly. "Eddie, I can't do it without you. Look what happened when I tried." I raised a bandaged hand to the bruises on my face.

His grin was malicious. "I see it, I feel zarky."

I took a deep breath. "Is it . . . Is this about Centraltown? My sending you away?"

"Nah, you think ol' Eddie care 'bout dat? 'Bout bein' put on some big ship, headin' God Hisself know where, away from alla res', away from her?" He waved it away. "With a file says, take this joe outa system, his Cap'n don' like him, so I get to mop frazzin decks alla way home?" He reverted to a parody of his most polished diction. "Think that matters to me, Captain Seafort, sir?" His face was dark.

"Eddie, when I found you with her, I was beside myself." I stared through the window at the baggage carts. "I didn't understand." I forced myself to face him. "But now I do. It wasn't the same, for you. You knew her long before I did. Trannie—transpop culture isn't like mine. Sex is more casual, more for fun. What I saw as betrayal, you saw as—as—"

"It weren't nothin'," he whispered. "Not a damn thing, Cap'n. We be tribe, man. Tribe doin' it allatime! Boys and girls, boys and boys, girls an—it don' matter none, in tribe!"

"Eddie, help me."

His faced hardened. "Nah. I ain' goin' trannie no mo'."

"I'll beg, if I must. Please."

His mouth lit with a cruel smile. "Yeah, I like dat. Beg ol' Eddie, see what he do."

Annie, even this, I love you so. I slipped out of the chair, dropped to my knees, oblivious of the passing throng. My eyes bored into his. "Eddie, I beg you. Help me find—"

He yanked me to my feet. "Don' do dat, Cap'n! Not for no man!" His eyes glistened. "Don' crawl fo' ol' Eddie. Never!"

"Help me," I whispered.

He turned aside, slammed his fist into the bulkhead. It shivered. "God, I wanted ta hate you!" he cried. "Allatime in dat ship, see yo' face, smash it, but allatime it come back, allatime lookin' at me, like when I ask you learn me read. Those eyes, sad, but somethin' else, like you look at Annie, later. God damn, I wanta hate you!" His voice sank. Almost inaudibly, "I couldn'."

"Oh, Eddie."

For a moment his shoulders slumped. Then he straightened, spun around. "Not fo' you! Fo' her, 'cause she tribe! You un-nerstan'?"

My heart leaped. "Whatever you say."

He nodded. "Fo' her." He picked up his duffel, and we started for the corridor. Eddie's fingers closed around my arm. "Fo' her, mos'ly. Jus' a little fo' you."

He couldn't touch the Captain. If the young middy loping our way saw it, he could execute Eddie on the spot. Still, I smiled, gently pressed Eddie's hand. "A little is enough."

Eddie hoisted his bulk out of the heli. I followed to the clinic gate. "She walked out with some visitors, and disappeared."

The sailor squinted at the squatter shacks, but said nothing.

"If we stay here at night, go out each morning—"

Eddie shook his head. "Nah. We don' look here."

"But this is—"

"She be here, she dead." He spoke with authority.

"How can you know?"

"Mira!" His wave encompassed the stadium, the foul streets, the ragged children. "Them be Bronks. Crypsnbloods. Can't you tell? Bronks get her, she gone. Don' bother lookin' no more."

"She's dead?" My tone was bleak.

"I din' say that. Jus', if a Bronk get a Hat . . ."

I shook my head in bewilderment. "Hat?"

"Cap'n, Annie and I be from 'Hattan. Bronks 'n Hats ain' the same. Joeys here, dey eat anythin'. Even their dead, sometime. You think Annie an' me be garbage like Bronks?"

"Of course not," I said with fervor, recalling the urine stains Eddie's transpops had left on my corridor decks, the befouled cabins. "No. The difference is obvious."

He peered at me with suspicion. "Maybe," he conceded, "you Uppies so far up, you can't tell." He spat with contempt at the squatters' hovels. "Dey jus' garbage, man. Come on." He turned away.

Exchanging glances with the astonished middy, I followed. "Where to?"

He spoke as if to a child. "Home, Cap'n. 'Hattan. Annie'd know dem Bronks wanna kill her. So natch she try go home to

Mace. If she alive, dat where she be." Annoyed, he rattled the clinic gate. "Open up, joey! I got a Cap'n wid me."

"Eddie, how could she get back to Manhattan? The transpops tried to kill me on sight. I barely made it a mile."

He grinned sourly. "But you ain't trannie, Cap'n. Annie smart. Stay low, move at night. She a Hat, better 'n any Bronk. Use her head, she get past 'em."

My tone was meek. "Where do we start?"

"Dunno. Fin' Mace tribe, first thing. Might be better I go alone." We crossed the wide expanse of lawn.

"I want to help."

"You don' know tribes. On other han', you be famous joe, on alla news screens. I hear trannies even got special name fo' you. Might help, dey see yo' face. Okay, come along, but get me outa dis billysuit. Can't go onna streets innit."

"What about me?"

He grinned his gap-toothed smile. "You too pretty in whites, Cap'n. Work blues, maybe, like you was goin' out on the hull ta supervise. But 'less you look Navy, dey won' believe it be you." He stopped, scratched his head.

"What should the middy wear?"

"Him? I ain' takin' care a no boy if we wanta fin' Annie." He seemed unaware of Adam's outrage.

"All right." I rang the entrance bell. "Let's hope they have something your size."

"Too small be allri'. Look more trannie."

I made my needs known at the clinic desk. While we waited I asked, "What about all I taught you, Eddie? How to talk, and the rest. It's all gone?"

He favored me with me a long, contemplative look. "My speech is jus'—just fine, Captain, when I use it. I didn't want to be a trannie no more. You say do it. Okay. But you tell me to go trannie, I gotta be trannie inside too."

I reddened. "Sorry I asked, Mr. Boss."

"Don' matter. Sir."

I left him to his thoughts.

From the pilot's seat Midshipman Tenere said, "I'll be there at noon, sir. If you don't show up, noon the day after." He twisted to face me. "Sir, think again. Every sailor going through

New York gets a packet warning that groundside travel is dangerous."

Eddie snorted derisively.

"I'm not worried for myself, sir, I'll get the groundcar through, but—"

"Just be at Thirty-fourth and Broadway." I patted the pocket of my blues, felt the reassuring bulge of the pistol. My other pocket held two recharge packs. A change of clothes, a light and shaving gear were all I'd carry. "Ready, Mr. Boss?"

The seaman nodded. "Dark comin'. Bes' be gettin' on wid it."

Reluctantly, the midshipman started the engines. As we lifted from the Sheraton rooftop, Eddie lifted his lumpy bag. After leaving the clinic we'd stopped at a grocery. Eddie had picked out a couple of dozen cans of meat and vegetables, and a few instameals. At the hotel he stuffed them in a pillowcase. Then, outside on the roof, he'd taken a firm grip on the open end of the sack, and twice smashed it against the cement wall.

"What was that for?"

He grinned his gap-toothed smile. "My cansa be too pretty, dey won' think I be trannie."

Now, as the heli swooped, Eddie turned to the middy. "Bes' yo . . ." He scratched his head, started again. "Mr. Tenere, when you set down, we jump out, you take off real quick. Okay, sir?" The boy nodded. The huge sailor muttered, "Gettin' night now. Never know, Maces and Broads might be dancin'."

Adam came in fast and low. At the last moment he flared, dropped us in the center of the street with a thump. Before I had time to speak Eddie flung open his door, leaped out, hauled me from my seat. He slammed the door. "Outaheah, Navyboy!" Adam lifted instantly.

To my surprise, the streets were deserted. When I'd taken the Gray Line tour, people had been everywhere. Of course that had been midafternoon, and a bit farther uptown.

"Now what do we—"

"Move, man, 'fore some Broad diss ya!" Eddie propelled me toward the crumbling facades. I thrust his hand away, but hurried to keep pace. We moved cautiously down the desolate street. Where I would have pressed against the wall for safety, Eddie stayed close to the curb, staying clear of open doorways. I did likewise.

"Who are we watching for? There's no one here."

He snorted with derision. "It gettin' nighttime, what you expec'? Broads be out plenny inna day. Maybe dance wid us, come dark."

"Broads?"

Eddie favored me with his gap-toothed grin. "Fine time be askin' dat. Broads be trannies live here. Annie 'n me, we Maces. Dis' be Broad turf." We neared the corner.

"How do you know?"

"Don' you listen, Cap'n?" He pointed to the rusting street sign: BROADWAY. "Where else Broads be? Lesgo!" He slung his bag of foodstuffs over his shoulder, sprinted across the street.

We crouched behind the shelter of a gutted electricar. The sign read Thirty . . . it could have been an eight or a nine.

"Next block, lotta buildin's down. Too open. You see anyone, keep quiet, grab my arm." He rose cautiously. My hackles rising, I followed.

"Why didn't we just land at Thirty-fourth?"

"Not so loud." He studied the windows above, finally relaxed. "Ol' Eddie come down outa sky in a heli in middle a Mace turf, anyone gonna listen he say he be trannie? Trannie wuzbe, maybe, but no trannie still."

"I don't under—"

"You wanna find Annie, dey gotta help. No trannie gon' tell nothin' ta no Navyboy come down inna frazzin' heli. Dis way we walk in, natural. Get ready ta run."

He took a breath, sprinted past a lot filled with the rubble of a collapsed building. We came to a storefront with boarded windows. The doorway was sealed with crumpled sheets of siding. Eddie surveyed it, grunted with satisfaction. "Alrigh' here to corner." He straightened. "But better I had somep'n." His gaze fastened on a battered speed sign. He shambled toward it, put down his bag, and took a firm grip on the sign pole. He heaved. The steel post bent only slightly.

"I have a pistol."

"Pistol okay, you wanna diss someone. Scare 'em off, you wan' a pole." He considered the unyielding post. "It's in kinda deep. But maybe—" He grasped the pole, hauled on it until his muscles bulged. It bowed a few degrees. With a grunt of anger Eddie threw himself at the pole, forced it the other way.

I wandered back to the rubble-filled lot. Was there some board, a piece of wood or metal?

"How'm I gonna watch fo' you, jus' walk away?" Eddie had abandoned his battered post.

"I just thought—"

"Never min', let's go. We fin' something." We retreated toward the boarded building. "Two blocks, come to Mace—"

Suddenly we were face-to-face with a gaunt woman and a bearded man, at the boarded door. The man gripped a bat.

I gawked. Eddie thrust me behind him, twirled the sack over his head, lunged forward. The woman screamed. The man took a wild swing with the bat. Eddie dodged the blow. The man shoved the woman back to the door, bared his lips, flexed his bat.

My hand went to my pocket, and the pistol. Eddie snapped, "No, you get us killed." He took a menacing step forward.

The man blurted, "Fadeout be cool."

Eddie hesitated, lowered his sack. "Evenup?"

"You ain' no Broad. Outaheah."

"Outaheah evenup."

The man looked to his woman. She nodded. "Zark." He backed a step to the door.

"Cool," said Eddie. Cautiously, they took a step apart, then another. The bearded man pulled aside the sheeting. He and his woman backed into the doorway and disappeared.

"Run." Eddie's tone was urgent. We dashed across the intersection without checking for hazards. In the middle of the next block Eddie crouched by an abandoned car.

I asked, "Won't he call for help?"

"Nah, he say fadeout cool."

"But what does that—"

Eddie's exasperation showed. "We was ready ta dance. He ask fadeout. Mean we split, no rumb. I made him say evenup too." He searched my face for a sign of understanding. "Evenup, no geteven. Long as we get outa Broad turf, we okay. He won' call tribe."

Eddie peered over the car, decided it was safe to proceed. We hurried on. "Daytime, Maces 'n Broads, even Subs c'n talk, sometimes trayfo. But joey was righ', we on his turf, don' belong." He slowed. "So I din' hurt him none."

I grinned, thinking of the bat the man had wielded.

As if reading my mind Eddie shot me a sidewise look. "You don' know nothin' 'bout ol' Eddie, you think a little bat stop 'im." Still, he looked over his shoulder one more time, for safety.

The litter-strewn avenue stretched into hazy distance. I could see little difference from one tribal block to the next, but nothing recalled the bizarre campfire I'd encountered near the Bronx clinic. Here, no shacks leaned against one another in haphazard lanes of rubble. Tall, neglected buildings brooded above us, but at least they still stood. Maybe someday, money and attention could resurrect the central city.

"C'mon, Cap'n. One mo' block, Mace turf."

"What's a Mace? You keep using that—"

"I showya. Nex' block be Mace."

I glanced around, appalled. "Annie was born here?" A horrid thought.

"Yeah, Annie an' alla resta us." He stomped down the street, muttering under his breath. Then he brightened. "Deke gone on ship, but Sam 'n Boney 'll 'member ol' Eddie. Don' worry none, Cap'n. I talk fo' you." His step lengthened.

"Where to?"

He pointed. "Corna." He straightened, walked proud past the remaining buildings. "I showya where Annie 'n me . . ." He stopped short.

The sack slid from his fingers.

"Eddie?" I gripped his arm; he shook me off as a fly.

He charged into the debris-filled lot. For a moment he stared at nothing. Then he snatched up a rock, hurled it across the rubble. "Maces! WHERE YOU BE?" His agonized cry echoed in the dusk.

I retrieved his sack, picked my way across cement and brick. Eddie hunkered on his knees, scrabbling through crumbled stone.

"What's happened?"

"Mace gone!" His eyes held something akin to madness.

"We must be in the wrong place."

He stabbed at the rubble. "Here, I tolya! We Maces!"

"What's a Mace? I already asked you onc—"

"Tribe! Where we live. Like, Broads live on Broad!"

I stood, turned slowly, searching the empty block. "What was here?"

His finger jabbed at the open space. "I born dis spot. I maybe thirteen, Ma die in rumb wid Broads. Righ' there!" He pointed to the corner. "We a big tribe, hunners of us. I Boss on four flo'."

At last I had a glimmer. "Eddie, this was the old Macy's?"

"I keep tell'n' ya." A tear trickled. "Cap'n, where dey be? What hap'n my Maces?"

"Dey be gone."

We whirled. Four figures, crossing the lot. The leader was male, lean, hard. A ragged jacket. With him were two other men, and a woman.

Eddie leaped to his feet as if galvanized. "Whatchew wan'?"

"Naw, wha *chew* wan'? You on my turf." The leader's tone was sharp.

I swallowed. My hand moved to my side.

The leader barely looked my way. "Prolly fif'y of us Rocks be watchin'. C'n ya take fif'y, sailorboy?"

"Where be Maces?" Eddie took a step forward.

The Rock smiled meanly. "Innifo!"

Eddie opened the sack. "Cansa. Two."

"Prong ya frazzin' cansa." The Rock snickered. "Two minutes, offa Rock turf. Else ya diss." He turned on his heel.

"Rock turf?" Eddie's eyes were wild.

"Eddie—"

"Rock turf?" Eddie's sack lashed out, smashed the leader on the temple. The Rock reeled. Instantly, knives appeared in his mates' hands.

Eddie spat as he advanced, sack whirling. I clawed for my pistol, but the two men were already in retreat. The woman, more intrepid, leaped on Eddie's back. He shrugged her off. She scrambled to her feet; Eddie's fist shot out, caught her alongside the jaw. She dropped.

A retreating figure turned. "You meat, joeyboy! Rocks comin' out now!" He cupped hands to mouth. "Aiyee!"

At the cry Eddie sprang forward. The Rock tribesman turned and ran. Eddie followed a few steps, spun around to see the Rock leader stagger to his feet. Eddie thundered back. His second blow smashed the dazed Rock across the back of the head. The man dropped and lay still. Eddie swung again.

"No, Eddie!" The downed Rock lay inert. I clawed at Eddie's

arm. He raised the sack, clubbed the fallen tribesman yet again. The sack dripped red.

"Stop!" I thrust between him and his victim.

"Mace turf! Was, is, will be! Always!" He stared down at the body, kicked it savagely. After a moment he sagged. His expression lapsed into misery.

"Eddie, get us out of here!"

"Mace gone." He stood dumbly, as if paralyzed.

"Who are those people?"

"Rocks. Useta live uptown in Rockcenta, 'til got pushout."

"We can't stay." I prodded him. "Is there a caller somewhere? We need Adam and the heli."

Eddie looked back at the corpse. "Rocks was never much inna rumb."

"Eddie!"

"All righ'. We go Three Four, eas'."

"Why not back where—"

"Rocks." He pointed across the street. I chilled; men, women, even children, were gathering outside the crumbling buildings. They were ominously quiet.

Eddie seemed to throw off his daze. "Move!" He hurried me along Thirty-fourth Street. Behind us, voices.

"Eddie, the whole tribe is—"

"Who care." Nonetheless, he increased his pace. After a moment he said grudgingly, "Better getcha pistol ready. All Rock places, here." His eyes roamed, lit suddenly. " 'Xcept maybe there." He pointed across the street to a storefront covered with heavy metal plates. "Pedro Chang, useta be. My—a neut." He veered across the street.

The Rocks followed. Unlike the rabble who'd chased me to the precinct house, they kept together, seemed in no hurry to close in. I asked, "Will he help?"

"Dunno." Eddie tried the solid door. His foot thudded into a steel plate.

I said, "Those locks won't help much against a laser."

"No lasers inna street. Recharges too hard ta get, an' Unies dissya onna spot if ya got one." He hammered on the door. "Chang! Openup!" He waited, tried again. The Rock tribesmen were closing in.

Behind the door, a cough. "Close."

"Eddieboss nee' trayfo, man!"

"Eddie be gone three, fo' year. Jerry sen' him outboun'."

A stone thudded into the boarded window. I flinched, drew my pistol, set it to high. Across the street the mob waited. Clubs, spears, children lugging bricks.

"C'mon, Changman, let us in!"

A fit of coughing behind the door. "Innifo?"

"Cansa. Dozen."

I braced myself against the wall, aimed with both hands.

The sound of metal on metal. A lock turned, then another. The door opened a cautious inch. A wizened face peered between heavy chains. Another stone whizzed past.

"Who—Eddie? I din' think—" The door slammed in our faces. I cursed, but almost immediately the door reopened, this time fully. Eddie's brawny hand shot out, hauled me inside. The door swung shut against a hail of stones. The old man scurried to secure his chains.

I blinked. A light mounted on a Valdez permabattery pierced the gloom. The dusty store was filled with boxes, piles, odd assortments of goods. Cans of foodstuffs were stacked on sagging shelves meant to hold lighter stock. Heavy winter clothing was stacked high on chairs. A scent of spices lingered.

"Hola, Pedro."

The old man scowled at Eddie. "You din' say no bringalong."

"Cansa be his." Outside, banging on the door.

"You got. Gimme."

Reluctantly, Eddie handed over the sack.

"Why he widya?"

"I—" Eddie seemed at a loss. "He be my Cap'n."

The old man looked my way, cackled. "Cap'n of what?"

"Navyboy." Eddie drew himself up. "Like me."

"You was sent outboun' when Unies gotcha."

"I be joinup."

"Outaheah, you try swind ol' Chang." The man Eddie had called a neut shook his head decisively. "Trannie joinup? Nevah hearda no—"

Some metal object rapped on the boarded windows. They were braced with iron struts; for the moment we were safe. Chang scuttled to the panels, shouted, "Go way! Don' mess wid Chang!"

A voice from outside. "Give us Maceboy. Wan' venge."

Chang reared back. "I dunno no Rock venge on Mace. You

comeon ol' Chang, he show you venge!" That brought a silence. Chang nodded with satisfaction, said softly, "Dey ain' goin' nowhere."

After a moment he trotted back from the window, looked me over, snorted with derision. "Cap'n, hah!"

"Mr. Boss, who is—"

The sailor scowled. "Dis be Pedro Chang, neut I tolya 'bout. He gone glitch wid old. Usetabe, had mo' chips innis head 'n any six trannies."

Pedro Chang drew himself up to his meager height. "Glitch, he say? Wan' me believe trannie joinup inna Navy an' come back fro' outboun', bringin' Cap'n widim? Who glitch?"

I moved closer to the light. "Look at me. At my uniform."

Chang came close, peered up at my face. "No joeyboy swind Pedro Telamon Chang." He padded slowly around me, grumbling. "Neuts gotta be smarter 'n alla tribe. Rock or Mace or Broad, don' matta. Traytaman gotta be tough." He came close, fingered my tunic. "Navy weave, yeah, but any joe could get. An' Cap'n threads be white. I got holozines."

I didn't move but my voice was as ice. "Take your hands off me." Chang's fingers hesitated, fell back. "A Captain wears what he pleases. I wouldn't wear dress whites in a thrustersuit. Or here."

He clicked his teeth. "Oh, high and mighty, is he. Jus' like Uppie."

"Do you read, old man? Are you smart enough to remember pictures? Do you even have a holovid?"

Chang glared at me, spat.

I hefted my pistol, strode to the door. "Eddie, come along! I'll take my chances out there." I twisted at the locks. "We have at least fifteen charges, maybe—"

"They kill you, Captain Nicholas Seafort." The old man's voice was changed. "You slaughter fifteen, maybe more, if you get to the recharge in ya pocket. Then the rest club you to death."

"You fraud!" I clawed at the chain. "What's happened to that thick dialect, now? I don't need you, I don't want to know you."

Chang ducked under my arm, rebolted a lock. "I don' put nothin' on. I talk trannie 'cause I be one. Jus' 'cause I c'n talk more Uppie if I try, no reason you look down on me." His rheumy blue eyes found mine.

"I don't care what—" I swallowed. "All right."

Chang swiveled to Eddie. "So dat mean you be Navyboy. If Cap'n marry trannie, I guess trannieboy c'n be joinup." His gaze returned to me. "Allatime you on news screens. Course I knew ya, righ' from start. Alla trannies watch screen, high up on tower, but they think stories ain' real. Now, what you doin' inna street?"

"My wife, Annie Wells. She was a Mace. We're looking—"

"Was, is, willbe. Trannie stay trannie inside."

Eddie rumbled, "You don' know, ol' man."

Chang trotted up to Eddie, jabbed his finger in the seaman's brawny chest. "When Maceboy came cryin' dat his Ma be dead, an' wan' venge on the Broad dat done her, was it 'ol' man' you call me, or Mista Chang, hah? When I trayfo Broad's name so you diss the righ' one, even widout you had innifo, was I 'ol' man'?"

Eddie reddened. "All righ', din' mean nothin'."

"Glitched, I be? Maybe I slap yo' face fo' you, Maceboy. I did it when you little, an' raz ol' Chang."

The sailor shuffled his feet. "Din' mean nothin', I said. An' don' go slappin' no one. I ain' joeykit no mo'."

"An' I be Pedro Chang, the one frien' dat Maceboy had." After a moment his expression softened. "Could be still, Maceboy had manners."

Eddie forced his knotted fists to relax. "Don' flare. Frien' what I need, now."

"Ah. Now we talk." The old man scurried to the chairs, transferred clothing onto other piles, bade us sit. "Why you look for Annie?"

I said, "She disappeared from a clinic in the Bronx where she was getting hormone treatments. She's wandering around somewhere, confused and miserable."

"If she be alive."

I forced myself to acknowledge the thought. "If she's alive."

"No good, dem Bronks catch her. Can' trayfo, can' even talk widem. Glitched, alladem."

"Eddie says she'd try to go hom—come here."

"If she could."

Eddie clutched at Chang's bony arm. "Wha happen ta Mace?"

The old man slapped at Eddie's fingers with annoyance. "Don' hol' on, you ain' no babykit." He trotted across the room, rummaged in a bin, emerged with a teapot. He plugged it into the permabattery, poured water from a plastic jug on the floor. "Mace Three Four got tore down two year back. Walls goin' bad, chunks fallin' on street. Jerries come in, by hunners. Bull-dozers. Maces tried ta hold on, got some of themself killed."

From the drawer of a battered desk Chang emerged with teabags. "Less'n a week, dey all onna street."

Voices from outside. "Hey, Changman! You neut or Mace?"

Chang looked disgusted. "Rocks don' know bein' patient." He shuffled to the door, spoke through it. "I talkin' wid Maces. You wait 'n see, like I tolya. Filmatleven!"

"We ain' got all—"

"You ain' got nothin'! Wanna see if ol' Chang still got nitro, jus' waitamin!" Footsteps retreated. Chang grinned through stained teeth.

"Where my Mace go?" Eddie asked.

"The Rocks wouldn' give passby widout innifo. Maces din' have—"

My voice was sharp. "What's innifo? Everyone keeps saying that."

The old man put three cups on the dusty table. "Trannie word. Wha's innifo?"

"I just asked you!"

"An' I tolya." Seeing my puzzlement he repeated slowly, "Wha's innifo *me*? Can' tray widout innifo."

"They wanted—bribes?"

"Course. If Maces wanna cross Rock turf, need innifo. Dat trannie way. But they din' have lotta trayfo lef', pushed outa Macestore. So they fight their way crosstown, past Rocks, past Unies even."

Eddie leaned forward, eyes riveted on the wizened old man. "Did they make it?"

"Dunno, for sure. Rocks din' stop 'em. Heard they got past Unies, heard maybe they push out Easters, but maybe Mace all dead, who know? No one eva came back." He poured scant portions of tea into our cups. After a moment he reconsidered, poured again until they were full.

"Mr. Chang, did Annie come to you?"

"I din' see her."

Eddie growled, "Ya waitin' fa innifo?"

Chang snapped erect. "I givin' you good tea I c'n trayfo cansa or even a holovid. Don' you talk me no innifo!"

"Fadeout. Din' mean nothin'."

" 'Sides, I already got all your innifo." Chang squatted by our sack, lifted out a can. "Real meat, good. Vegs, okay." He sifted through the sack. "You bring good trayfo, boy."

Eddie said dryly, "That was the idea."

"Oh, listen ta sailorboy talk Uppie!"

"Cap'n taught me."

"Sen' you school, hah?"

Eddie averted his gaze, said with care, "The Captain taught me himself. On ship."

"Captains don' do that."

"This Captain does."

Pedro Chang trotted to my chair. He stood over me, arms folded, studying my face. At length he nodded. "Okay, you looked after Eddieboss, I help you some. Not too much, I be a Neut." Before I could ask, he said, "Neut means, don' take sides. What'd you do ta get them fizzed?"

Eddie said, "I dissed a Rock. Maybe two."

Chang sucked air through yellowed teeth. "Can't fix dat, take too much innifo. I gotta give you back."

I said, "Is there another exit?"

"Rocks watchin' all ways out. They not so stupid as Maceboy think." Chang perched on the table, sipped at his tea. "But ol' Chang smart traytaman. Maybe trayfo."

"What is—"

"Trade for," they said simultaneously. Eddie turned back to Chang. "Like you say, we ain' got innifo, 'xcept what we gave ya."

"Them Rocks won' give up venge for cansa. Dunno what ta offa." Chang rubbed his chin. Finally he brightened. "Chang don' offa' nothin'. Askem." He took up a cudgel, crossed to the door, hammered on it. "Rocks! You wan' talk to Chang or no?"

Cautious footsteps. "You got nitro?"

"You need to fin' out, o' we jus' talk?"

"We wan' Maceboy."

"I know dat. One Maceboy, one Rock, talk in Chang house. No rumb."

"Jus' a min."

Time passed. Chang leaned against his door, eyes bright. Finally the voice came again. "Alri', but two Rocks. Jus' talk, no rumb, cool?"

"Chang put his word. Go for Rocks too."

"Zark. Openup."

Chang said softly, "Inna back, both of you, 'til I call."

"C'mon, Cap'n." Eddie was out of his chair. "Cuppa?" He pointed at the tea.

The trader said, "Leave it. Rocks know you here."

Eddie led me to the curtained doorway. The apartment behind was scrupulously clean. In one corner was a carelessly made bed. The wall was lined floor to ceiling with old books printed on real paper. A corridor led back to a heavily barred door.

Straining to hear, I thrust an inch of the curtain aside.

Bolts scraped. Pedro's tone held dignity as an ill-kempt woman entered. "Welcome to Chang house, Tresa."

A tribesman pushed past her. "Nevamin' fancy talk, we wan' Mace!"

"We talk, maybe you get."

He growled, "Talk too much, maybe we take!"

Chang bristled. "You give word, no rumb. How much innifo Rocks' word?"

The woman was indignant. "Rocks' word good! Fadeout, Butchie."

Eddie whispered, "Sheet. Rocks' word don' mean nothin'."

"Okay okay, sit an' drink Chang coffee." The old man busied himself with the pot. "Why you wan' Maceboy?"

Tresa said, "Arno lyin' inna street, head all smash. Wan' Mace fo' evenup!"

"Arno allatime bigmouth. Was askin' ta get diss."

"Nah, he jus' talkin', an Mace whomp him wid sack a rocks."

Eddie hissed, "Not jus' talkin'. He call it Rock turf—"

I jabbed him in the ribs; he lapsed into dark muttering.

Chang poured into metal cups, handed them around. He turned to the woman. "Trayfo evenup?"

"Din' ya hear Butchie tellya venge?"

"Okay okay, Chang be neut, he giveya Maceboy, ya wan-nim."

I stiffened. "You said he was your frien—"

Eddie shook his head, whispered, "Chang ain' givin' me ta Rocks."

"How do you know?"

"He give us tea." It made no sense, but I kept silent.

"What kinda trayfo, afta he diss Arno?" Butchie's laugh was raucous. "Alla Chang store, fo' evenup?"

"Know better'n dat, Butchie. Trayfo wha'?"

"We don' tray Arno's venge fo' no cansa."

Chang didn't hesitate. "Okay, okay, Rocks knows what dey wan'. No trayfo. Finish coffee, outaheah."

Tresa was thoughtful. "Maybe trayfo evenup, one way."

Chang waited.

"I saw Uppie joey hadda laser. Trayfo cansa an' tea an' laser, fo' evenup."

The old man reared back. "Laser pistol, evenup fo' one frazzy Rockboy? Laser be whole Rock tribe, an' a few Unies fo' change."

"You sayin' Rocks ain' worth—"

"I sayin' none a tribes got lasers! Rocks got laser, be bossman onna street!"

Butchie muttered, "C'n rumb wid Broads, we gotta laser. Wid Subs, even."

Exasperated, Tresa snapped, "Keep shut, Butchie! I can' tray wid Chang, you sayin' dat."

Pedro shook his head. "Can' trayfo laser. Uppie still got it."

Tresa nodded as if he hadn't spoken. "Laser, three recharge. An' cansa. Evenup fo' Arno."

Chang folded his arms. "Nah, if Chang get laser he keep it, giveya Maceboy."

"You stayin' Neut?" Butchie's tone was ominous.

"Wid laser in his pocket, Chang be Neut, Rock, anythin' he want!"

Tresa's tone was plaintive. "You say cominheah ta trayfo. Now you won'!"

"I neva tolya no laser. Uppie got laser, maybe won' giveya. Askem, be bes'." Chang trotted to our curtain, yanked it open. Before he turned away, one shrewd eye winked. "C'mon out, talk wid Rocks."

He might have given us warning. Warily, I stepped out of the alcove. Eddie followed.

"You meat, Maceboy!" Butchie.

"Dogs prong ya motha!" Eddie's muscles rippled. "Frazzin' Arno was on Mace turf—"

"Nuffadat!" Chang's growl cut across the rising tension. "Here fo' talk, no rumb. Put word, bothyas did!"

Reluctantly, they subsided. Chang placed his chair between the warring parties, addressed me. "Cap'n, you wanna givem laser, evenup Mace fo' Rock?"

His gaze gave no hint of the expected answer. I thought for a long moment. The laser was our only protection, and Naval Stores wouldn't be pleased at the paperwork involved in its loss. On the other hand, Chang was a skilled negotiator. Should I seem eager, or no? They wanted Eddie's life, and I couldn't allow that. If I guessed wrong, the war would escalate. I glanced at the sullen Rocks. If only Eddie hadn't . . .

I flicked a finger at Eddie. "Give up my weapon, to help that trannie scum?" My voice was cold. "You're glitched, old man. Anyone goes for my laser, I'll fry the lot of you!"

Eddie's fists bunched. "Don' you go callin'—"

"Shut your mouth, joeyboy!"

Chang said, "Gotta put you out, if no. Den dey gonna getcha."

I snapped, "They'll burn first!"

"Rocks wan' Maceboy 'n you, both. Or trayfo—"

"Talk English, you old fool! And forget about trading with trash like those two!"

The Rocks were on their feet.

"Whoa, whoa, whoa." Chang patted the Rocks toward their chairs, pushed at Eddie's unyielding form. "No rumb in Chang house. Uppie thinks like Uppie, whatcha 'xpec'? He won' give laser fo' evenup."

Tresa hawked and spat. "Uppie, you gon fry us Rocks? How many, 'fore resta tribe on ya? An' afta, what, skinya, maybe?"

My smile was nasty. "Try me, bitchgirl."

Chang padded toward me, hands held out in a placating manner. "Okay, okay, Cap'n. Maybe you no unnerstan', lotsa Rock tribe inna street, not jus' two three. If rumb start, don' matter how many it take, dey gonna getya. Bes' you trayfo."

I thrust him away, hoping he wouldn't fall. "We should have cleared the streets years ago! I'll stay here until my bodyguards come looking. There's plenty of food."

Chang bent over the Rock negotiators, spoke in a low tone. "Lemme talk widim. Ol' Chang be traytaman, maybe c'n trayfo."

Tresa's tone was hoarse. "Nevamin' no trayfo, give us Uppie!"

Chang patted her shoulder. "Maybe I talk, he lissen. But gotta talk solo."

Tresa stalked to the door, spat once again. "Bigmouth Uppies think ya own the worl'! One day we get allayas!" She let Chang unlock.

The trader pushed Butchie gently toward the door. "Letcha know. Filmatleven." As soon as the Rocks were gone he re-bolted the locks.

"Mr. Chang, I'm sorry if I—"

"Gottem now!" His eyes danced. "Cap'n oughta be trayta-man, let Chang sail starship!" He trotted across the store, turned the teapot high. "We givem time, hour maybe. Den we deal." He veered around Eddie, who hadn't budged.

"Trannie scum?" The seaman's eyes blazed.

"Mr. Boss, I didn't—"

The old trader poked at Eddie's chest. "Stupid Maceboy, chewin' on Cap'n fo' save yo' life! When crybaby joey teen came knock'n Chang door, din' I teach him smarts? Hah! Chang and Cap'n know, even if Maceboy don'."

"Know what?" Eddie's tone was menacing.

"Yo' Cap'n—" He spoke with dignity. "Your Captain knew Rocks won' tray if they be too mad at Eddie. So he makem mad at hisself. Make all us mad. Now dey forget 'bout you, an' tray."

The sailor glowered. "How I know he din' mean it? How I know 'bout anything he say? My frien', once. Teach me read, talk. Den he sen' me—" Eddie stopped short, muttered, "Dunno."

"He still you' friend, silly young Maceboy."

"How you know?"

" 'Cause he gonna give me laser ta save you." Chang held out his hand. "An' 'cause ol' Chang can' be traytaman, not knowin' insidea joes."

I slipped the laser from my pocket, placed it in his hand. My eyes turned to Eddie.

The sailor shuffled his feet. After a moment he turned away. "Can' figure out nothin, no mo'." His tone couldn't conceal his relief.

When Chang judged the time right, he called back the Rock tribesmen. He dismissed with scorn Tresa's demand for more

booty. She countered by offering safe passage for me alone;
Chang wouldn't hear of it. "Came togetha, leave togetha," was
all he'd say.

Finally they settled on Chang's initial goal: a trade of my
laser and recharge packs for our free passage through Rock ter-
ritory, in the morning.

"An no venge," the old man admonished. "Evenups, botha-
dem."

Grudgingly, they agreed.

"Speakfo?"

"Alla Rocks. I be bitchboss, ya know dat. I say even, is
evenup!" She spat at Eddie's feet. "But nex' time, Maceboy, ya
be meat!"

Eddie growled, but between my fingers digging into his forearm and Chang's warning glare, he said nothing.

When they had gone I asked, "Will they keep the deal after
they get the laser?"

Chang's eyes flashed. "Transpops ain' like Uppies. Word be
good. Dey don' have much else."

I let it be.

Chang puttered about his quarters, disappeared into the cellar,
and reemerged with a handful of cans. Humming to himself, he
began to cook over the hotpad. The aroma of savory chicken
wafted through the store. At length he beckoned us into his
apartment, sat us at a rickety table that reminded me of Father's.
We supped on chicken stew with pop-rolls fresh out of the self-
heating package, and more of Chang's precious tea.

Afterward he showed us the lavatory. To my surprise, it had
running water and was fairly clean. Somehow, I'd expected an
unspeakable midden.

We lay down in Chang's apartment on mattresses he'd had
Eddie haul down from an upper floor. He refused my offer of
help. Apparently the trader's trust wasn't enough to reveal whatever stocks he concealed in the neglected, boarded building.

Exhausted from tension, I dozed, but at first sleep avoided
me. Finally I succumbed.

In the dark a hand shook me awake. I had no idea of the time.
"Why—"

"Shh." The old man led me past Eddie's snores through the
curtain, into the store. I followed, bleary-eyed, to the counter

where the pot steamed, sat where he directed. The tea was dark and rich, a flavor I couldn't identify.

He waited until I sipped through the steam. His voice was soft. "What happen 'tween you an' Eddieboy?"

"Happened? I don't—"

"Nonna this makes sense." The trader perched on the edge of his chair, cup balanced on his lap. "A Captain don't wander streets with a transpop sailor, and sailor don't look at him like he love an' hate him at same time."

I looked away. "It's nothing I care to speak of."

"You owe me innifo, I save his life." He puttered with the pot. "But, okay okay, I talk instead."

He blew across his tea, reflective.

"Chang had wife once, long time go. She good girl. But no babies." He shrugged. "Ain' easy be a Neut in trannietown. Can' show no favors. Like, if you kept laser, I'd a had to give you to Rocks. No choice.

"But if a Maceboy joey come to Chang's door, eyes all red, actin' as much a man as he can, wantin' ta trayfo name of the Broad who diss his mama, a Neut can help little bit. A Neut can maybe see he makes it through first winter, 'til he strong enough be on his own. Maybe even think what a son woulda looked like, he'd had one."

Chang stared into his tea. After a moment, "Okay, okay, Eddie all grown, no baby now. Still, traytaman can think, wonder why Captain whose face be on alla holos wan' dis particular joey ta help him fin' wife."

Silence stretched while I breathed the hot welcome steam. When I spoke, I addressed the wall. "On a ship like *Challenger*, at first you see Eddie as one of a hundred angry transpop faces." I sipped at the tea. "But later, when you're trapped on a derelict vessel knowing no help will reach you, and a joeyboy asks you to make him into something better than he was, you work with him day after day, watching him struggle with the words . . ."

Chang was silent.

"You want so much for him to succeed, you become one with him. He's too old to be a son. A brother, perhaps. You're rescued, and he stays in the Navy and ships out with you again. He's strong and loyal and one of the few people you trust. You're desperate to keep your wife safe. So when civil authority starts to crumble, you have him guard her."

My words came faster. "Then something happens between them, and you rush him off-planet, and because you left her alone she's raped and beaten and her mind is snatched from her. You want to hate the boy but can't, because it's your fault, not his, and the voice you can't silence tells you so, over and over, in the terrible truth of the night."

We drank of our tea.

After a moment Chang said, "He had no one, after his mama. Girls now and then, is all. When jerries took him with the other young ones, I think he was glad." His clouded eyes sought mine. "Ol' Chang traytaman and Uppie Captain, we be his mama."

"I've done him more harm than you can imagine."

"No, you give him someone to respec'. He need that."

I snorted. "Respect? After what I—"

"Revere, maybe. Don' look so surprise I know dat word, you think I got all those books, don' look in 'em?" He waved it away. "Nevamin'. I wan' my innifo."

"I can send you money, whatever—"

His wiry hand gripped my knee with surprising strength. "You keep yo' coin, it don' mean nothin' ta Chang. Want ta pay yo' innifo, gimme Uppie word."

I laughed, a harsh sound. "You said what an Uppie's word is worth."

"That ain' what Navy say. 'An officer's word is his bond.'"

I flushed. "What do you want?"

"Take care of ol' Eddieboss, bes' you can."

"I can't be sure—"

"Bes' you can, I tolya. I don' ask more." He got to his feet, showing his age for the first time. "He be like brother, once? You don' walk away from brother." He took the empty cup from my lap. "Chang din' walk away from Maceboy ask help." He pounded his frail chest. "Eight year, maybe, ol' Chang keep boy like son, in here." His look was iron. "I wan' my innifo. You give or no, as you wan'."

With dignity he padded to the curtain, passed through it. For a long time I sat hunched in the chair in the dim light of the battery lamp. At last, I tiptoed back to bed.

Chapter 15

In the morning Chang tucked the laser pistol in his pocket, unbolted the door, and slipped outside. Half an hour later he returned, a satisfied look on his wrinkled face. "Okay okay, Maceboy. Outaheah, 'fore Rocks say Chang ain' Neut." He scuttled across the store, found our sack of foodstuffs. "Don' go eas' on Three Four, Unies too strong. Rocks take you up one block, you trayfo passby wid Broads."

Eddie frowned. "Wrong way. We need ta—"

"You need ta listena ol' Chang, little Mace. Go back way you came, to Four Two Square. Talk ta Subs, dey let ta walk crosstown unner."

"You glitched fo' sure, Changman. Broads'll ask innifo, we ain' got. An' Subs—"

Chang thrust out the sack. "Cansa be good nuff fo' Broads." He hesitated, fished in the sack, removed two cans of meat. "These be innifo Chang. Broads won' know I took 'em, anyway." He handed Eddie the remainder of his sack. "Jusasec." He disappeared behind the curtain. It was several minutes before he reappeared, a box in his hand. "Uppie Cap'n carry it fo Subs. Dey wan' more 'n cansa."

"What's this?" I asked. It was heavy.

"Batteries. Valdez permas. Subs allatime trayfo permas, nobody know why." He shrugged. "Don' badmouth no Sub, dey rumb fo' dat. With innifo, maybe dey let you through." He opened the door, said, "Outaheah, bothyas."

Eddie looked down, shambled to the door.

My tone was formal. "Mr. Boss, this is an order."

"Huh?" Eddie struggled to change identity. "Yes, sir?"

"Before you go, hug him."

Chang bristled. "Frazzin' Maceboy try touch Chang, I stick him wid —"

"Do it, Mr. Boss." I folded my arms.

Chang backed away. "I'm a Neut, no one touch a—"

Sheepishly, Eddie enfolded the trader in his arms. After a moment, Chang was still.

I picked up my bundle of clothes, opened the door. "Fare thee well, sir. Lord God be with you."

The old man pushed Eddie to the entrance. "Try that again, joeyboy, Chang cut you good! Outaheah! Work to do!" His eyes glistened.

Eddie grinned. "We be gone." He shut the door behind us.

I blinked in the sun. The street was full of people. Some sat with trays of merchandise, others stood around, talking. Down the block, children played. "Lord God!"

"Kinda different." Eddie pointed. "But trash, mosta what they got. Ol' Changman has the only—"

"Lesgo, Maceboy." Three men. One of them was Butchie.

"Okay." Eddie seemed unafraid. "Nor', to Four Two."

"Righ', " They bracketed us, escort or guards, I wasn't sure which.

One of the men fell in alongside us as we walked. To my amazement he chatted sociably with Eddie. Unlike the previous night, streets were crowded with transpops, some with their families.

I said quietly, "Eddie, why didn't we come in the daytime?"

"Tolya. Trannies see us in heli, who gonna help? Even Chang maybe wouldn' let us in."

From block to block we were passed uneasily through the tribal territories until at last we approached an open plaza.

"Where are we, Mr. Boss?"

"Four Two Square."

I looked up. "Isn't that a skytel? We could go in, get a heli—"

Eddie laughed. "In, fro' street? You see door, a window even?"

"A tour bus, or—"

"Likely shoot us soon as talk." Eddie dismissed the idea.

We ventured into the square. In its center the ruins of a tall building clawed skyward. Across the street, crumbling steps disappeared into the ground.

"What's that?"

"Dunno. Sub tribe live there."

"Surely there's a better—"

"Only way we fin' Annie is if she with Maces. How you wanna get crosstown, in heli?"

"You don't even know where your Maces are!"

"Yeah, but we fin' em." Eddie sounded confident. "Maces won' scurry roun' like no mouse. Dey gone eas', tribes'll know." His face darkened. "First, gotta go down."

I hesitated at the gaping cavern. "Couldn't we walk across on Forty—"

"Too far, too many Mids. An' dey don' give passby fo' innifo. C'mon." He took a tentative step downward, then another. "Yo, Sub!" His bellow echoed in the darkness. No answer.

The broken stairwell led to a rubble-strewn landing. Below, another staircase. Well, in for a pence . . . I trotted down, gripping my box. "Anyone here?"

"Easy, Cap'n." The foot of the staircase was a black cavern.

I squinted. "Where are your bloody Subs?"

A voice in my ear. "We here."

"Jesus!" I jumped half a meter, dropped my bundle. "Lord God in—"

A snicker. "Whatchew wan', Uppie?"

"Who are you?"

"I be joey what belong down here. You be joey what don'."

"Ooh, he got a trannie frien'!"

"No rumb," blurted Eddie. "Innifo!"

"Too lay' fa innifo. We gotcha, now." Hands seized my arms, pried loose my box.

Eddie squalled, "You frazzin'—" A thud. He gasped, and his words came painfully. "Tha's righ', whomp on someone can' see ya! Jus like a Sub!" He cried out again, groaned.

"Let him alone!" I tried to pull loose. "We came looking for you!" A fist drove into my stomach. I doubled over, retching. Hands grabbed, hustled us through the darkness.

When I could breathe again, I found myself surrounded by tribesmen in a large tunnel lit by dull overhead bulbs. Eddie lay slumped in an alcove.

My captors were heavily festooned with earrings and chains, their clothing a hodgepodge of lurid colors. Men and women alike had their hair tied with bands at the sides and back. Some sat cross-legged eating from metal plates at a communal pot that simmered over a hotpad; others jabbered among themselves. Ancient broken furniture was strewn about.

"Where are we?"

No one answered. I leaned against the concrete wall, nursing my aching stomach. "Where's my box?" Again, silence. I decided I was already lost, cast caution to the winds. "Animals!"

One youth looked my way. "Uppie talk. Think all trannies be—"

I spat. "I've seen trannies, real ones. Broads and Maces. Mids. You Subs are trash, not trannies!" It brought a few of them to their feet.

Eddie groaned, rolled to his knees. Someone kicked him. He lashed out at the foot, missed.

"Fadeout, Subs!" Across the cavern, a figure waited. "Lettim talk."

My fists bunched. "Who are you?"

"Alwyn be I, Boss Sub, 'til some joey call me out." His eyes roved, as if seeking a challenge. He found none. "An' you?"

"Nicholas Seafort. Captain."

"Jump off yo' tour bus, didja?"

"We came to find you. We brought—"

"Batteries. Nice a yas. C'n always use 'em." Alwyn beckoned to a scrawny girl. "Tell Jossie an' alla res', come mira. Few minutes we gonna diss an Uppie."

"Righ' " The girl scampered off.

"Shouldn'a come down, joey." He came close. Young, muscular, his dress was somehow different from the rest. Fewer colors, more patterns.

"They told us you take innifo, for passby. We—"

"Dey?"

I pushed down my smoldering anger. "A trader. He gave us batteries for you."

"We take innifo when we wan'. No one tell us. You coulda took a heli steada playin' wid trannies. Now you got youself diss."

"We need your help. I'm looking for my wife, a transpop girl. Mace." How could I get through to him?

He swung to the others. "Says his bitch a trannie!" It brought jeers.

Bitch? I surged forward. "She's my wife, damn you!" Someone shoved me back; I slapped the hand away.

Alwyn's voice rose. "Lissenup, Sub!" It brought quiet. "Don' matter why he come. Law be, no one in sub but Subs, less'n we okay firs'!" Murmurs of agreement. "Anyone speak fo' Uppie?" Silence. "Then he—"

"I do!" Eddie struggled to his feet. "Leave 'im 'lone! I brought 'im. Diss me, you wan' blood!" Three Subs tackled him, brought him down amid curses and blows.

"You be nex', joeyboy," Alwyn told him. "Afta Uppie."

The sound of running steps. A dozen more tribesmen crowded near. Lord God, help me. I need time, for Annie.

The Sub leader whipped out a wicked blade, held up a hand for silence. "Uppie, this be why we diss ya. Like you say, we trash." He overrode grumbles of discontent. "But we got lives, jus' like you. We make kidjoes, same way Uppies do. An' Subs die, same as you, jus' fasta!"

He pointed upward. "Onna street, no hosp, no job, no teachin'. Looks like alla 'Hattan goin' like Bronx, nothin' but Crypsnbloods. We can' stop dat. But look 'roun, Uppie! We got food for any Sub who wan', and for frien' if Sub bring down. We got beds, onna track. We got Sub turf, Sub law. I be Sub Boss 'til someone call me out. Here, we say who come in, who don'."

"You kill strangers on sight and call it law?"

"Justice. You Uppies killin' us day by day. I come to yo' sky-tel, ask help, what I get?"

Somehow I had to divert him. I could think of no way. "Alwyn—"

He crouched, gripping the knife. "You be meat, Uppie." He took a step.

I backed into the wall. Despair overcame the last of my sense. My voice rang out. "Alwyn Boss Sub, I call you out! Rumb fo' boss!"

His jaw dropped. "Uppie can'—"

"Gimme blade!" In a fury I lashed out, shoved him across the room. "Law, you say? Rumb wid Cap'n unner Sub law!"

"A Cap'n talk trannie?" Alwyn's gaze held what might even have been respect.

"I be trannie, joey; we all be!" My voice grated. "Ain' no diff when Lor' call us out!" I spat at Alwyn's feet. "C'mon, rumb!"

"You win, an' stay Sub?"

"Long as I wan'. Same as you!"

His mouth twitched in a grudging smile. "Righ', same as. Jossie, give Cap'n shiv!"

The young girl thrust a knife into my hand.

Alwyn feinted. I dodged aside, ran to a steel beam in the center of the tunnel. He followed. Around us a wary circle formed.

We thrust and parried, neither drawing blood. Sarge, what was it you taught us? Crouch, palm upward? I tried.

Across the cavern Eddie struggled to his feet, tribesmen clinging. With a roar he shook them off, jumped onto a table. It shuddered, but held.

"Mira, trannies! He ain' no Uppie Cap'n!" Eddie stomped at grasping hands. "He the one onna joinup sheet!"

What in the name of . . . ? Alwyn, as puzzled as I, raised his hand. I nodded, stepped back.

Eddie's voice dripped contempt. "Subs too glitch to know why news screen allatime talkin' about joinup?"

"Say fish, outdere!" A teen. "Jus' a scare story."

"An' who foun' fish?"

"Some ship—"

"His ship!" Eddie's shout echoed. "He no cap'n, *HE DA FISHERMAN*!"

Into the hush, Eddie spoke more softly. "He's da one what come back in dead ship, save Hope Nation! He da Fisherman Cap'n!"

Alwyn tapped his sheath, slid the knife in for me to see. I nodded. He came close, examined my face. "Swind?" His tone was cautious. "Fisherman be real? Not jus' inna holos?"

I was too enraged to care. "Look at a frazzing poster; it's my face they used! I'm Nick Seafort!"

He shook his head. "Don' need. Same face." His hand darted out, grazed my shoulder, pulled back as if scorched.

"What was that for?"

Alwyn grinned. "How many trannie c'n say touch Fisherman?"

I snarled, "How many trannies c'n say wan' diss Fisherman! You still scum! Puttin' down shiv don' change nothin'!"

He swallowed. "Doin' by law, is all. Evenup?" He held out his hand.

I slapped it away. "You wan' evenup, new law. Else, g'wan, rumb wid me, Subs get new boss."

Alwyn rubbed his stinging hand, spoke with dignity. "New Boss? Subs c'n do dat, anytime dey wan'. I make mistake wantin' ta diss Fisherman, so Subs fin' better boss." He drew his knife, extended it blade first. "G'wan. Alwyn die proud."

"Captain." Eddie jumped down from the table.

"I know." I took the knife, pressed it to Alwyn's breast. He didn't flinch. After a moment I reversed it, held it to my own. "G'wan. Life for life!"

Slowly his hand came up. His fist closed around the hilt. I held my breath as the point pricked my tunic.

His hand fell. "Fisherman Cap'n, be you frien' wid Sub?"

"Frien'." My hand crept out. "An' tribe." In hushed silence, we clasped. Eddie sighed.

"What new law you wan'?"

"Joey come down see Subs, not reason enough ta diss 'im."

"How dey gonna respec—"

"Diss whoever ya wan' if they attack ya. Else, no."

After a moment he turned to the others. "Law?"

Grudging murmurs, then general assent.

"Tribe say okay. Now, whatchew wan' wid Subs, Fisherman?"

My legs were shaky. I moved casually to a bench. "We brought innifo for passby east."

"Talk Uppie, Fisherman. I'll unnastan'. You go eas', den what?"

"Get past the Unies, find my wife."

"Unies bad grodes. Easters too."

"I'll get through. I have to."

"Okay." He raised his voice. "We help Fisherman go eas'. Jossie, Lo, bring innifo Unies. An' fo' Easters."

"How much?"

"All!"

She beckoned another youth. "C'mon!" They disappeared.

Alwyn whispered to a tribesman, who nodded. A few moments later the Sub lugged in my box of batteries. "Yours, Fisherman."

"Innifo for Sub."

"Don' need no innifo fro' tribe."

"Gift, then." I held out the box. He accepted it. I asked, "Why permabatteries?"

Alwyn grinned. "Showyas." He called for lights, led us up a flight of stairs, through a long, dim cavern.

"What is this place?"

"Sub's way, dey called it. Usta ride in, 'fore helis 'n Uppies.

Give it up, 'bout three life back. Track gone, mostly. We tryin' ta fix."

"How many tunnels are yours?"

"Lotsa, in 'Hat. We block off some part. Bad tribes."

"Where we going?"

"Secret place." He stopped, waited for Eddie and a throng of tribesmen to catch up. "Onna street, gotta trayfo passby. Dis better."

As the corridor gave way to a wider tunnel, Alwyn jumped down onto the roadbed, disappeared into the dark. Uneasy, I followed.

He waited just around a bend. "Go eas', you say." He shone his light into the tunnel.

An ancient electricar, of sorts. Its lamps gleamed bright. Alwyn climbed in, held a hand, hoisted me up. "Shuttle, dis be. Four Two Square, Grandcen. Back 'n for'." With hoots and laughter other Subs crowded aboard. I searched, found Eddie chattering with excited tribesmen at the opposite end.

"The subway was abandoned."

"Yeah, long time. But wid 'nough permas . . ." Alwyn opened a compartment door. Inside, he pressed a lever, with care. The car lurched. Slowly, with a screech of rusty wheels, it slid forward.

"We got dis track workin'," he shouted over the racket. "By ourself. Not all trannies be stupe."

"I didn't—"

"Or trash."

"I'm sorry. I was angry."

He shrugged. "You jus' Fisherman, not real trannie."

At last the shuttle ground to a halt, and the Subs piled out. At street level I turned to wave, but Alwyn was gone.

Eddie and I emerged into daylight with an honor guard of Subs. While we waited Jossie bargained passage with the Easter transpops.

She said, "Mace joeys be south, mile. Dey pushout Efdears."

"Who?"

"Efdear Dri'. For groun'car."

"Tolya Maces made it 'cross!" Eddie was jubilant.

I asked, "Anyone hear of a Mace girl who came crosstown, a week ago?"

Jossie jabbered with our guides. "Dunno. Hear maybe six Unies be diss inna night, on Three Four."

"Dat's Annie!" Eddie's eyes glowed. "She see Mace gone, askaroun', someone tell. So she go eas'."

I said, unbelieving, "Annie killed six transpops?"

"If dey in her way. You dunno Annie, Captain. Never did. On ship, in Centraltown, she lost. Here, she home. Ain' no Bronk, no Unie gonna stop 'er."

"Good Lord."

The last mile was like a dream; we strode through sunlit streets with a guard of Subs and Easters.

We crossed a narrow access road, passed ravaged apartment buildings that recalled the devastated Bronx. To our left was the East River, bounded by a crumbling, fenced highway along which occasional groundcars still jounced. A rusted entrance sign proclaimed: F.D.R DRIVE.

As we progressed, our Easter guards grew more alert, kept hands near their weapons. One of them pointed ahead, said, "Two block mo', Easter turf." He hesitated. "'Xcept last block, look out fo' rumb."

"Whyfo?"

"Frazzin' Maces wannit. Rumb ever' week or so, pushem back."

Eddie bristled. I gripped his arm, shook my head. He growled, "Tolya at clinic, can't be sailor 'n trannie same time."

"You're a sailor seconded for special duty, Mr. Boss. I know these were your people, but . . ."

"No 'but', sir. Still my people, was, willbe."

"You started a riot with the Rocks, Mr. Boss. We won't have another." He didn't answer.

The last block of Easter turf was a scene of appalling devastation. The apartments that once graced the riverside were gutted. Those that hadn't been torched were near collapse, stripped bare of even their windows.

"Why do you fight over— that?"

"Weren' dat bad, 'fore Mace. Dey try push us out, we push back."

"Mace live here?" Eddie was scandalized.

"Here, inna river, who know." The Easter spat. "All Maces is glitch."

"Be silent, Mr. Boss!" I was barely in time.

The Easter tribesmen led us cautiously to the disputed block. "We wait. If ya come out, we take ya back."

Eddie and I went on, through sidewalks strewn with rubble. The area seemed deserted.

We reached a corner. A ragamuffin teen leaned against a post under a gutted apartment, fingering a whistle chained around his neck. He jeered, "Whazzis, a Navyboy tribe? Ya pushback Easters?"

Eddie growled, "You Mace?"

"Offa my turf. Move yo' frazzin' ass 'fore it meat!"

Eddie picked him up, slammed him against the pole.

"Leggo me!" The boy snatched his whistle. Eddie twisted it out of his hand, yanked hard, snapped the cord. The boy yelped, rubbing his neck.

Eddie growled, "You be Mace, joeyboy?"

"Go prong—"

Eddie's hand lashed out, slapped him hard.

The boy squealed, "We be Mace!"

"Easy, Mr. Boss."

"Learn him manners!" Eddie thrust the whistle into the youngster's hand. "Call Sam 'n Boney! Call Rafe!"

"Go—" He stopped short at the look in Eddie's eye. He blew three short blasts.

I watched the street, bracing for trouble.

For almost a full minute, no one came. Suddenly three figures leaped from a low window. Two carried knives, one a studded club.

"Back, Cap'n!" Eddie twisted the teen's arm, held him as a shield. "Wanna rumb, Maces? Rumb wi' Eddieboss?" He squinted at a scrawny tribesman barely out of his teens. "Boney, dat you? Ya growed!"

"Outaheah, Easter!" They circled. A club lashed out; I ducked back.

Eddie shoved the boy into the street, snatched the club from the attacker's hand. "Was it some Easter save Boney's ass in rumb with Broads, back when? Mira, joey! I be Eddieboss!" He lowered the club. "I look' allova, fin' Maces! Ya know Eddie!"

The teen yelled, "He whomp on me, no reas'!"

"Hol' it!" Boney held up a hand, peered suspiciously. "Eddie wen' outboun'."

"I come back." Eddie's gap-toothed grin warmed his face. "Home 'gain!"

"Who bringalong?"

"Cap'n, lookin' fo Anniegirl."

The Maces exchanged glances.

I couldn't contain myself. "Where is she?"

"Din' know," Boney said to Eddie, as if in appeal. "Mace bitchgirl come back inna nigh', say she been outboun', see Fish, go nudder place, marry a Cap'n. All glitch fo' sure." He shook his head. "Din' mean nothin', Eddie. Don' wan' no troub."

"What'd you do to her?" My voice was hoarse.

"Din' do nothin, Cap'n!" Boney seemed eager to please. "Din' hurt none, jus' din' help."

Scowling, Eddie took a step toward the tribesmen. They retreated. "Take Cap'n ta Annie rightaway fas'!"

"Sure, Eddie." Boney collared the boy. "Fin' Sam, tell'm Eddieboss back!" He pointed to the alley. "Onna grounflo'. Mos'ly she stay in dere."

I swallowed. "Is it safe, Eddie?"

"G'wan, Cap'n. Dey know we Mace, now."

I ran down the alley, disappeared around the building. A rotted doorway gaped. I peered inside. Broken furniture, trash, an appalling stench.

My wife crouched in the corner, hands over her ears. "G'way, allyas! Don' care 'bout no rumb, no Unies. Don' care!"

"Annie . . ."

She didn't hear. I took a deep breath, said more loudly, "Annie, I've been searching for you."

Slowly, she came around, raised her head. "Whatcha doon here, Nicky?"

"I came to take you home."

"I be Macebitch." She whimpered; the sound tore at my soul.

"You be wife, Anniegirl, fo'ever an' mo'."

For a second, she smiled, then she shook her head. "You be no trannie."

"I be what I haveta be, ta bringya widme."

Her eyes explored mine. "Don' wanna go, Nicky."

"What you want, Annie? This?" My wave took in the filthy room.

"Dunno what I wan'!"

"That's why I came for you." I crossed, squatted at her side. "You're sick from the drugs. Come home."

"We don' got home!"

"I'll take you to Father, then. Away from cities."

"Cities is what I know. I be Mace."

"Not no more, Anniegirl." The voice in the doorway spoke with authority. "You be like me. Nothin' now."

"Eddie!" She scrambled to her feet.

He set down his club. "We ain' trannie, ain' Uppie. If ya home ain' wid him, where?"

Her face twisted. "If I ain' Mace, I do what, Eddieboss? Die?"

He shook his head. "Go wid him. He love you."

"Annie—" My voice was hoarse.

She ignored me. "What kin' lovin', drag me 'notha planet, leave me fo' grodes prong me 'til dey done, drag me back here, throw me in frazzin' hosp?" She slid down the wall, her face in her hands.

Eddie took a slow breath. His words were careful. "None of that was his fault."

"Whose, den? Who sent ya 'way?"

"My faul', prongin' you when I had no righ'."

"We tribe!"

"Not no more." He crossed the room, hauled her to her feet. "Go with Cap'n now. Bes'."

"Wid Nicky?" She twisted around, studied me as a foreign object. "I wan'—wan'—"

With a cry, she spun again, wrapped herself around Eddie, buried her head in his chest.

He stood motionless, arms at his sides. As Annie began to weep, his eyes came up to meet mine.

I nodded.

Slowly, he enveloped her in his broad strong arms, rocked her. "Cap'n the man fo' you, Anniegirl. Hasta be. But I be here, long as he let me. I be here."

In the awful quiet of the room I whispered an impotent echo.

"I be here."

True to Alwyn's word, the Subs provided an escort back to civilization. Twenty Subs and a handful of Mace led us uptown along the river to the new U.N. enclave. Annie clung dazedly to Eddie. She let me take her other hand.

At the U.N. we merged with the lines of tourists passing through the electric fences. Though the government seldom acknowledged transpops as a constituency, under the open access policy even they were allowed in the International Lobby.

I called the Sheraton, told Adam to pick us up. When I asked the Subs how they'd make it home safely, they just laughed. We left them, and waited on the rooftop.

I took Annie to our suite. She was docile, as she'd been since leaving the crumbling apartment.

I helped her bathe away the grime of the streets, spoke gently about my search. It seemed to please her. She told me nothing of her own escapades, and I was afraid to pry.

At the hotel, our dinner was overcooked and tasteless, and made more bothersome by the fact that I was approached for autographs. At the end, I signed for the meal with indifference.

Annie was safe.

I booked the three of us on the morning suborbital for London and went to bed, exhausted. Annie rested her head on my chest, willing to be cuddled. Just before I slept she squeezed my shoulder and murmured, "Maybe time make it different, Nicky."

As Cardiff neared I switched off the autopilot and guided the heli by my own hand. I'd never before flown home, but once I spotted the Bridgend road I followed it through twisting hills until I spotted a pasture and a stone house, set near the foundations of an ancient barn.

Father would consider setting a heli down in his yard a prideful ostentation, so I landed in a meadow across the road. Annie jumped out before Eddie could help her. "This where you from, Nicky?" Her cheeks were flushed.

"Not exactly. The house, over there."

She giggled. "Tha's what I meant." She looked about. "Feels funny, no streets. Kinda like Centraltown."

"Not quite as untamed." I took the duffel Eddie handed down. "Better let me do the talking, when we go in. Father . . ." I hesitated. "He'll treat you well once he knows you, but he's suspicious of city folk." We started up the lane.

"How long we stayin', Nicky?"

I'd already told her, but repeated it patiently. "We'll see how you do. I may go back to Academy and let you recuperate with Father."

"He ain' . . . isn't gonna like me."

How to explain? "If he sounds harsh, remember it's his way. I'm his only son, and he talks to me in the same manner." I wished he'd been home when I tried to call. Though my own welcome was never in doubt, I hoped he wouldn't rebuff Eddie and my wife. If he got on his religious high horse and lectured them I'd have to find some way to intervene.

Annie put her hand through Eddie's arm. "He give me trouble, Eddie take care of him, woncha?" She might have been teasing. Perhaps not.

The sailor gently disengaged his hand from hers, fell back as we strolled to the house. I was grateful.

As the sagging gate creaked I felt a twinge of guilt. Time and again I'd promised Father I'd fix it, and always it was left for last. This time I'd take care of it.

As always, the door was unlocked; Father kept nothing to interest thieves. "Father?" I went in. We'd wait in the kitchen until he got back from shopping.

A teacup and saucer sat unwashed in the sink. He would wash them before taking the daily bus to town; no chore must be left undone. I looked into his bedroom; the bed was neatly made. I checked the lavatory, the storeroom.

"Nicky?" She met me at the door. I brushed past, a growing unease quickening my step.

I found him facedown by the woodpile behind the house. He'd been getting wood for the stove. It had been several days. Dogs and other wild things had worried at him.

I knelt beside him, tried to take his hand. I couldn't force myself to do it; the body was too far gone. I forced down my gorge, sought some prayer that would please him. What came to mind was, *"For in death there is no remembrance of thee: in the grave who shall give thee thanks?"*

It was so grotesquely inappropriate that I bent my head in shame, conjured Father's stern visage from the days when I memorized my boyhood verses. I barely noticed Annie's soft hand squeeze my shoulder.

At last I whispered, *"I have set the Lord always before me: because he is at my right hand, I shall not be moved. Therefore my heart is glad, and my glory rejoiceth: my flesh also shall rest in hope. For thou wilt not leave my soul in hell."* I looked up. "He'd like that verse, if he didn't think it too prideful." I crouched on my knees, oblivious of the damp earth staining my trousers.

"Nicky." She dropped behind me, circled me with her arms.

I pressed her birdlike hands to my chest, those hands that had killed six Unie transpops who stood in her way. With revulsion I thrust away the thought. She was Annie Wells. My wife.

After a while I went to a neighbor, called the coroner. When the van with its flashing lights had carried Father from his house I sat at the rickety table in the bare kitchen, nursing a lukewarm cup of tea.

The old copper teapot needed polishing; I'd have to put it on my list, along with the gate.

"Don't cry, Nicky."

"I'm not." I brushed my sleeve across my eyes. "Where's Eddie?"

"Outside, straightening the wood."

Without a word I rushed out to the woodpile, flung myself at Eddie's crouching form. "Get away from that!"

"Jus' picking up what he drop—"

"I see what you're doing! Leave it alone!" I swept the firewood from his arms, battered at his massive chest.

Eddie regarded me stolidly. "Whompin' ol' Eddie ain' gonna bring him back, Cap'n."

"Don't talk back to me, you trannie—" I checked myself, too late. "Go in the house!"

I busied myself with the wood. Presently I understood I'd been arranging and rearranging the logs, trying to refashion the bundle Father had dropped, exactly as he'd left it. I slumped against the woodpile, hugged myself, rocking back and forth.

In the pasture, birds chirped their discoveries.

After a time I shivered, thrust my hands in my pockets, walked slowly back to the house.

"Sit down with me, please." I pulled out chairs for them. "Mr. Boss, I have no excuse. I'm sorry."

"For callin' me trannie? It's what I am."

"It's not a nice word."

"Nah, we use it alla time." He shifted, and the chair creaked.

"The tribes do, but I have no right."

For a second a wan smile flashed. "Why not? You a Sub now."

Annie giggled. Her hand stroked his arm.

"Pedro Chang made me realize . . ." I trailed off, lost in reverie. "I have no friends left, Eddie. Derek Carr is light-years away, if he lives. Alexi is learning to manage on his own again. Other than them . . ."

"Cap'n—"

"Once, I sent you away. Would you stay with me, now?"

"You don' need no trannie frien'." At first I thought it was sarcasm, but then I saw the anguish in his face.

"Please." It was all I could manage.

We buried Father two days later, at the bleak cemetery on the hill. A cold drizzle saw him to his grave. A few acquaintances, the butcher, the greengrocer, paid their respects while a minister read from the Book.

I stood shivering in my dress whites. Annie leaned on Eddie. When the service was done I trod across the rocky ground to Jason's grave, but could find no tears, even for him. Afterward, chilled, we rode back to the house. I kindled a fire. Annie snuggled at my knees.

"I wish I could stay." I stared into the flames.

The sailor stirred. "Where you gotta go, Captain?"

"They expect me at *Wellington* for the commissioning. We'll have to leave soon."

"You taking Annie to a ship?" He sounded uneasy.

"No, of course not. You'll stay at Academy."

Annie said with force, "I don't wan' go there."

"Why not? They'd take good care—"

"I don' belong!"

For her sake, I tried to suppress my frustration. From her perspective, she was right. Officers and cadets would be scrupulously polite to the Commandant's wife, but she'd have no one to talk to, no one who understood. On the other hand, where else could she—

"Stay here, then." I waved away their surprise. "It's why we came. And the house is mine now."

"I can't stay here alone, I go glitch!" She seized Eddie's arm.

"Not alone, Annie." I looked to Eddie Boss.

"You leavin' me wid her again?" He looked frightened.

"Annie needs someone to—"

"Not widout you!" He scrambled to his feet.

After a moment I understood. "Come outside, Mr. Boss."

We huddled in the lee of the shed. "Cap'n, ain' good idea put me alone wid Annie!"

"Someone has to protect her." From herself, perhaps.

"In Academy, den!" He stomped his foot, turned away. Finally, scarlet, he blurted, "I ain gon' touch her, Cap'n! Swear! Won' touch her never!"

I closed my eyes, remembered her hand seizing his for comfort. "Look after her, Mr. Boss. And if need be . . . " I forced the words. "If need be, touch her. Give peace to my wife."

I hurried back to the house.

PART 3

November, in the year of our Lord 2201

Chapter 16

"The important thing is, you found her." Tolliver's expression was somber. "She'll heal in time."

I couldn't describe Annie squatting in the shack, nor tell him of her dependence on Eddie. "What's come up while I was away?"

"The usual. Two cadets caned, the latest biweekly test scores are on your puter, the new simulator's been delayed again. One other thing. I heard from United Suit and Tank about those serial numbers that didn't check."

"When Branstead was doing inventories?"

"Yes. U.T. and S. says the numbers on our list match the suits they shipped. So I asked them to help identify the numbers on the suiting room manifest." He waited.

"I'm in no mood for games. Spit it out."

"Aye aye, sir. United Suit and Tank says they're old numbers."

"What are you talking about?"

"Sorry, sir. Not old numbers, old suits. Refurbished."

My weary mind tried to grapple. "How can that be?"

"One explanation comes to mind. The new suits were, um, diverted, and old ones substituted." Tolliver waited for a response, leaned forward. "Let me make it clearer. Someone sold the new equipment we paid for, and sent us junk."

"Who?"

"It's the quartermaster's job to check new inventory."

"Sergeant whatzisname? Serenco?"

"Yes, sir."

"What does he say?"

"I wasn't about to tackle that without your presence, sir. Too touchy."

I growled, "That never stopped you before." Childish, but so be it.

Tolliver rose to the challenge. "Very well, I'll deal with him on my own."

"No, let me think on it." I got to my feet. "Anything else?"

"Your friend Mr. Thorne arrived last week. I assigned him a flat." He gathered his notes. "Don't forget you leave for *Wellington* in five days."

"I just got back." I sighed. "I really don't like the idea of bringing cadets to a commissioning. Let's drop that idea."

"After you had me tell them? Forget it."

"I'm Commandant here, not you!"

Tolliver crossed his arms. "You break the news to them, then." I bristled, but he overrode me. "If you'd seen Kevin Arnweil's face, you'd understand. Have you ever seen him smile?"

"He doesn't smile much."

"Now he does."

I sighed again, my ire fading. "They haven't earned special privileges, you know. I really should bring the cadet with the best grades."

"Go ahead. One more won't make a difference."

"Oh, sure. Like a mother duck with—"

"And a middy to take care of them."

"Good Lord." I waved it away. "I'll think about it."

Tolliver stood. "My condolences about your father, Mr. Seafort."

"Thank you. Dismissed."

I sat for a while, brooding about the U.T and S. suits. It was no small thing to accuse a staff sergeant of dishonesty; if I was wrong, our relations would be poisoned. Despite Tolliver's suggestion, the discrepancy in numbers might be accidental.

I could decide later. In the meantime, it would do me good to look up Jeff Thorne. For the first time in ages, my spirits lifted. I left my office. In the anteroom Kevin Arnweil stood hopefully. His glance flickered to my bruised face, and away. Like the others, he dared make no comment.

"I'll be back soon." I tried to ignore Kevin's crestfallen look, stopped at the outer door. "Come along, Mr. Arnweil. I'll introduce you to our new second lieutenant."

"Aye aye, sir." He scurried to my side.

We crossed the quadrangle. "I've known Mr. Thorne ever since I was a cadet."

"Yes, sir."

"He was a middy at the time."

"Yes, sir." He kept pace alongside.

I gave it up. Arnweil could no more imagine me as a cadet than himself as Captain.

Tolliver had bunked Jeff Thorne in Officers' Quarters, but, thankfully, not in the apartment of his predecessor Mr. Sleak. That would have been too much. Despite myself, my heart beat faster as we neared his apartment. Would he take me on another mission, someday? To raid the galley, unbeknownst to all?

I knocked, waited. "Mr. Thorne?"

No answer. "Jeff?"

Nothing. Kevin Arnweil shifted uncomfortably. I sighed. "Another time, I guess. You'll meet him soon enough." I started back to the office, the cadet at my heels.

The depth of my disappointment surprised me. On the spur of the moment I asked, "When you were aloft, did you hear of any middies, ah, leading cadets on unauthorized missions?"

"I . . . " He swallowed. "I guess, I— No, sir."

I stopped short. "Forgive me. That came out badly."

"Aye aye, sir."

"I wasn't asking you to inform."

"Oh, no, sir!" He seemed desperate to please.

"I just meant, I wondered if they still, I mean, I don't know if you'd even be aware—" I clamped my mouth shut. Adam Tenere's babbling held nothing on mine.

"I'm sorry, I always get it wrong." Arnweil smoothed his black locks with a nervous gesture.

"Belay that!" We walked the rest of the way in silence. No point trying to explain; I'd done enough damage.

At the outer door he blurted, "I'm sorry I didn't answer you right, sir."

"It wasn't your fault." I'd already apologized, what else did the young twit want? I crossed to my desk, came to a halt. "Damn it to hell!" I turned back to the anteroom.

"Kevin, come along." I stalked out into the cool afternoon, turned toward the front gate.

The cadet trotted to keep up with my stride. "About what you asked, sir, I could probably think of—"

"I don't want to hear it."

"Sorry, sir."

After a time my pace slowed. I turned from the path, crossed the tree-lined lawn, found a secluded spot. I took off my jacket, loosened my tie while Kevin watched in consternation. I sat back against the tree, patted the ground. "Sit."

I took time to assemble my thoughts. "Kevin, I made a fool of myself, asking you the wrong question. Let me tell you a story. I was a plebe at Farside, probably more scared than you are now. My cadet corporal was down on me, I had almost no friends, I imagined I'd wash out at any moment."

Arnweil contemplated me, saying nothing.

"There was a boy, a middy." I looked into the distance. The words came hard. "He was everything I wasn't. Handsome, likable. He didn't have to bully; he had natural authority. Ever meet someone like that?" I didn't wait for an answer. "Even though I was a mere cadet, he took me aside for talks as if I mattered to him. Late at night he would haul me from barracks on the pretext of hazing, but once we were out of sight we'd round up some others and do crazy things. Spying belowdecks. Raiding the emergency rations in the suiting room. We even reprogrammed the console in Nav class."

I risked a glance. Kevin was engrossed by a blade of grass.

"It ended suddenly when we got caught. I took a caning. But I sometimes realize . . . " I cleared my throat. "If it weren't for him, I couldn't have gotten through. I mean, you can get so lonely." I had to stop, at that.

The boy's tone was urgent. "You don't have to talk about those things, sir."

"Lonely." Annie in Cardiff, her future unsure, only Eddie to guide her. I shook my head. No, this was about the past, wasn't it? "They throw the courses at you, and discipline, and traditions, and sometimes it's too much to take."

She might never come back to me. Even Father's meager comfort was gone. I had no one, not even Lord God. Nothing but my duty, and I was failing at that.

"So, you see, I was just wond—" I tried again. "What that middy did meant so much to me. It's over, as far as my own life, but I needed to know whether it goes on still. If it does . . . "

"Sir, I—"

"It would mean a lot, just to know." Abruptly I got to my feet, faced away. My eyes burned. Damned air, full of pollutants.

After a time I picked up my jacket. "Come, let's go back."

"Aye aye, sir." This time our pace was slower. I walked with hands in pockets, glad of the confession, even if Arnweil hadn't understood a word I'd said. Shy crocuses peeked from carefully tilled flower beds. Someday, I would go home to Cardiff, whether Annie was there, or not. I would till and mend fences, search for elusive peace.

"I wasn't part of it." Kevin was subdued. "Doing things."

"That's all right, lad. I just needed to explain."

"Dustin Edwards . . . we signed up together. We thought —" His voice wavered. "Now that he's gone, there's no one."

"I understand."

"Some of the middies, they're nice. Mr. Keene, Mr. Tenere." His step slowed. "None of them notice me, the way you talked about."

"I'm sorry, I—"

He took a deep breath. "I lied a little, before. There's stories you hear, in barracks. Middies trying to get through the guards, to the gravitrons. I don't know if they bring cadets along."

"Ah." I studied the impatiens. Their colors seemed to brighten.

"Three joes got caught putting jelly in the toes of training suits. I heard it wasn't the first time."

"Terrible."

He saw in my eyes that which didn't match my words. He offered a tentative smile. "Yes, sir."

My tone was gruff. "Thank you." We walked on in silence, paused at the Admin Building door.

"Shall I wait inside for orders, sir?"

"Well . . . " I smiled. I was Commandant, and could do as I liked. "No, take the afternoon off. Get a haircut. Do whatever you wish." Unheard of. A cadet's every moment was regimented, and rightly so.

"Aye aye, sir." He saluted, waited for dismissal.

I opened the door, hesitated. Annie was still in Cardiff, Father was still gone. Lord God's face was still turned from me.

Nothing had changed. Yet somehow my load was lighter.

It was barely a week since I'd last taken my place in the dining hall, but it seemed ages. I ate slowly, thinking about Tolliver's investigation. After Cardiff, Academy problems seemed unreal, and I had to force myself to concentrate. At table, Kevin Arnweil offered me a shy smile, was rewarded with a frown from Sergeant Olvira. I winked.

After dinner Tolliver accompanied me to my office, past Arnweil and Kyle Drew, who'd been assigned late evening duty in the anteroom. They stood, saluted.

I closed the door. "How should I deal with Quartermaster Serenco?"

"Why not just ask him, sir?"

"Oh, come on! 'Good afternoon, Sarge. By the way, have you stolen our training suits?'"

"Something along those lines. 'There's a discrepancy in suit numbers. Can you help us explain it?'"

I bit back an angry reply. It might be the easiest approach after all. "Very well. Have him report in the morning."

"Right. Do you want me present?"

"Yes." Tolliver had the facts at hand, and I didn't. "By the way, Jeff Thorne wasn't at dinner. Know where I can find him?"

Tolliver's tone was cold. "Since when is it my duty to keep track of the Commandant's favorites?"

"Tolliver!"

"We traded shifts. He went to town. Seems he stayed late."

"Why?"

My aide rose to his feet. "Ask Jeff Thorne, not me!" He flung open the door, snapped a wrathful salute, stalked out.

I gaped. For all his foibles, this was unlike Tolliver. Had the two argued? It was important they get along; I intended to send Edgar aloft, so I could spend time groundside. I'd expected Jeff to be his mainstay at Farside.

I brooded at the console. Annie, in Cardiff, pressed heavily on my mind. I had done her so much harm; far better had I left her to proceed to Detour with the others of her tribe. Why was my life filled with misery and death? So much of it could have been avoided, had I been more aware, more competent. Perhaps even Lieutenant Sleak might have been saved.

At least I had Jeff Thorne. He'd help, even if only by offering a sympathetic ear. When would our paths finally cross?

After a time I found myself yawning. I turned off the console. I checked my desk one last time, turned off the light.

"—voice down. He'll hear us!"

I froze with my hand on the knob. Now what were the cadets up to?

"... don't know how you feel? I think about it every day!" A high-pitched voice. Kyle Drew. I leaned my head against the door, the better to hear.

"I never said it was your fault." Arnweil's tone was sullen.

"You don't have to, Kevin."

"Who asked you to bring it up again? He's gone. You can't change that, I can't—" Arnweil's voice caught.

For a moment, silence.

Kyle. "Don't look at me like that! I can't stand it! I'd switch places with him in a second if I could. I dream about it every night."

An anguished whisper. "So do I."

A long time passed. Kevin Arnweil muttered, "Dus and I joined up together. We were close. It was a miracle when they put us in the same dorm."

"You don't know how close." Kyle giggled. "That time he got batonned, you walked like it was you."

"Don't make fun of us, you frazzing little—"

"I wasn't!" The scrape of a chair. "Kevin, I'm so damn jeal—" Silence. "I'm sorry. I just wanted you to know. If there was anything I could do—I'm sorry. I miss him too."

Arnweil sounded weary. "Thanks. You didn't do it on purpose."

Kyle's answer was so low I could barely hear. "What does that matter?"

I leaned against the door. Preoccupied with Nav grades, with laser training and calisthenics, we did nothing for our joeys' aching souls. I thought again of Jeff Thorne, and what he'd meant. He would understand how to help.

I tiptoed back to my desk, groped in the dark for the caller. "Ring Sergeant Kinders for me, please."

Arnweil, his voice all business. "Aye aye, sir."

Kinders answered on the first ring. "Sarge, have Lieutenant Thorne report to my office after breakfast."

"Aye aye, sir."

No, damn it, that wasn't what I wanted. A summons from the Commandant would only emphasize our difference in rank, when I wanted to meet him as an old friend. "Belay that, Sarge." How to—"Mr. Kinders, you're familiar with town?"

"Somewhat, sir. I've lived here for—"

"If an officer were off the grounds, where would you find him? Are there restaurants, pubs?" It occurred to me I'd never left the Academy grounds other than by heli.

"Yes, sir." He hesitated. "Is it Lieutenant Thorne you're . . . ?"

"Yes."

"I saw him in the Athenia Tavern a couple of nights ago."

"Thank you." A few minutes later I was memorizing directions from the guard at the gate. I crossed the commons into the center of town.

The Athenia was on a side street about half a mile distant. I didn't mind the walk; it gave me time to clear my head, compose myself.

Above the entrance was a huge holo projecting a distorted, romanticized view of the Solar System. As best I could tell, the ship that captured that view would be close enough to the Sun to melt its holocamera.

Inside, a jangle of laughter amid stale fumes of drink.

"A table, Captain?" The maître d'.

"I'm looking for—" My eye roved to the booths in the dining room, spotted a Naval uniform. I looked closer, recognized Midshipman Thayer with a civilian. He caught my eye. I grimaced, waved him back to his seat.

"No table, thanks." I turned toward the door. "I thought one of my lieutenants might be . . ." I trailed off. "Never mind."

"There's a young man in the vidroom."

It wouldn't be Thorne. Still, I poked my head in. Someone was in the Arcvid helmet, surrounded by admiring teens. The uniform was unkempt, the body flabby. A drink teetered on the console.

"I've got the bastards!" The young man spun the thrusters savagely, rotating his ship in the enhanced sensory environment of his helmet. A replica on the blue console screen followed his motion. He slapped at the fire control; three of the enemy ships disintegrated. The console flashed a bright green. "Level sixteen! Prepare for attack!"

The teen nudged me. "No one ever gets to sixteen!"

I watched, drawn into the game despite myself. Despite Jason's avid encouragement, I'd always crashed at level four. The player in the helmet spun and fired at his attackers with consummate skill. In moments he was at seventeen. By eighteen, the attackers' speed was simply too great; he went out in a blaze of unreturned fire.

The player slid off his helmet.

"Jeff?" Dismay rose from deep within my throat.

Thorne blinked in the light of the vidroom. "Ah. Our Commandant." He brought himself together in a mockery of an Academy salute. "Lieutenant Jeffrey Thorne reporting, sir."

His shirt was awry; he needed a shave. I stared, at a loss for words.

Thorne chuckled. It was not a pleasant sound. "I'm a bit hungover. Had rather a good time last night." The watching joeys poked each other and grinned.

"Drinking?" Fatuous, but I couldn't help it.

He met my gaze. "Oh, yes. But off base, on my own time. It's never been more than that."

"I wasn't accusing—I just wanted to say hello."

"Hello, then." A silence stretched. At last he said grudgingly, "I have a table."

"It's not—perhaps another time."

"I don't mind." His smile was sour. "Those joeykits want the console. I tie it up for hours." He led me to the dining room.

We sat.

"Sorry, I should have changed clothes. On Callisto Base it didn't seem to matter."

"Here it does." My tone was blunt. "You're supposed to set an example for the cadets."

"I don't hold myself out as an example, Commandant."

"Once, you did."

Silence. He swallowed. "A long time ago."

"What's happened since?"

"I grew up."

A waiter came with menus. I shook my head; Thorne waved his away. "Another gin."

I said, "Mr. Thorne, what's wrong?"

His expression was faintly hostile. "Nothing. In a few months my enlistment runs out and I'll be off."

Enough was enough. I stood. "What you do on your free time is none of my business. But on duty you will conform to Academy standards. And there'll be no more switching watches!"

"Aye aye, sir, fair enough."

"Mr. Tolliver will show you the ropes. Have you any questions?" Hearing no answer, I turned for the door.

"Just one." For a moment he sounded like the Jeff Thorne of old. "What other revenge will you take?"

My fists bunched as I wheeled about. "You're speaking to a superior!"

His voice cut like a knife. "Don't I know! You transferred me to gloat over it!" Conversation hushed; the waiter took a hesitant step our way. Thorne waved him off.

"How could you think such a thing?" My voice was unsteady.

"Why else take someone with my record?" His eyes bored into mine.

"What record?"

"Oh, you've learned deceit, now? As a cadet you were the boy who wouldn't lie!"

"As a middy, you were the boy I revered!" I could have bitten my tongue off, but it was too late. My ears flamed. I managed to meet his eye. "What's on your record, Mr. Thorne?"

"All right, we'll pretend you didn't look. Sit down; I don't mind humiliating myself." He kicked out my chair. Everyone's eyes on me, I sat again.

He said, "I served two years as Academy middy, you remember. Just as you were leaving they posted me to U.N.S. *Targon.* Another year, this time as first middy."

He swirled the liquor around the rim of his glass, drank it all in a gulp. "It wasn't a bad time. Good training, and I made friends." His eyes wandered to the starched tablecloth.

"They rotated me to Lunapolis, to Admiralty. Running petty errands for Captains on leave. It went on month after month. Accommodations detail, they called it. Unambitious middies and bootlicking lieutenants. My requests for transfer were ignored." His mouth twisted. "You know what happened then."

"I don't, Jeff." I felt a chill.

"Lieutenant Tryx was transferred out. It was too much trouble to break in a replacement. They promoted me. Not because I'd earned it, but because it was . . . convenient." He spat the word. "Higbee, in BuPers, told me so himself."

The bastard. "Go on."

"I'd trained as an officer in the U.N.N.S., not as a bloody hotel concierge! Sure, aboard ship, when a Captain asks you to do a favor, no one minds. But this went on for months. Years!" He swilled the dregs of his drink, waved for another.

"What happened?" My voice was soft.

He leaned into my face, said thickly, "I'm no procurer!" He watched my face, as if he expected me to contradict him. His eyes fell to some fold of the cloth. "U.N.S. *Vespa* came in, with Captain Reegis. I made the usual offer, anything I can do to be of service, et cetera. Where the hell is my drink? Waiter!"

"You've had a lot, Mr.—"

"And I'll have more, if I choose." Thorne looked about, subsided when he saw the waiter hurrying with a fresh glass. At length he said, "Reegis wanted a woman, preferably blond, and uninhibited."

"Good Lord."

"Oh, it wasn't the first time I'd been asked, and I always accommodated. This time . . ." He sought refuge in the clear cold liquor. "You see, they wouldn't give me a transfer; I was too good at my job. I felt . . . trapped. So instead of making the usual call to a seedy hotel, I rang Mrs. Duhaney. I knew the Admiral was groundside. I told her Captain Reegis was having a party, and sent her to Reegis' hotel room. Mrs. Duhaney's hair happens to be blond."

"My God, Jeff!"

"I figured they'd cashier me. Well, that was fine if they wouldn't let me in the real Navy." He sipped his drink once more. "Instead, they sent me to Callisto."

"The most remote—"

"You have no idea, Nick." His troubled eyes met mine. "There's . . . nothing at all." He brooded. "Except Arcvid." He flashed a twisted smile. "I took to the Arcworld immediately. It embraced me, whenever I got another lousy rating on my fitness reports. I'm—I was the base champion."

"Jeff, I'm sor—"

"Arcvid's just like life, Nick. You can't win. Sometimes you evade defeat for a long, long time. Once I reached level twenty-three." When he looked up, his expression was bleak. "But Arcvid always gets you, in the end." His eyes lost their focus. He whispered, "Always."

The waiter approached; I waved him back. "He's had enough. Come, Mr. Thorne, I'll take you home."

He stood uncertainly, leaned on the table for support. "Home is where the heart is. Where's that, Captain Seafort?" He laughed.

I threw money on the table, got his arm over my shoulder.

No taxi in sight. I resigned myself to a long walk supporting my half-conscious lieutenant, but the cold night air seemed to brace him. Once, as we neared the commons, he said, "I read all the zines they sent. Saw your pictures."

"Watch where you put your feet."

"Callisto was hell." He stumbled, caught himself. "Knowing you made it much worse."

"How?" I maneuvered him past a tree.

"An example to the cadets, you called it? There I was, consigned to that abyss, and always your holo accusing me, an example of what I could have become. I hated you."

"They wasted you."

"Did you hear what I said? I hated you." I could find no reply. A moment later he dropped to his knees and was sick. After a time, he wiped his mouth, got unsteadily to his feet. "Sorry." He lurched on. "With luck I won't remember any of this in the morning."

I saw him to his apartment. He closed the door without a word. I went to bed, and lay unsleeping until well past dawn.

"Sergeant Serenco reporting, sir." The quartermaster marched in smartly, came to attention in front of my desk. Edgar Tolliver stood at my left, hands clasped behind his back.

"As you were, Sergeant. Please be seated." My tone seemed too formal; I tried to sound more relaxed. "We've been running some equipment checks, Sarge. All routine, but a few gaps need correcting."

"Gaps, sir?" Serenco's guileless blue eyes met mine. "I don't quite understand."

"For example, the training suits." I punched up the figures. "Look, inventory numbers don't match."

"With what, sir? This is the first I've heard of suit numbers." He turned to Tolliver. "Is that why you've been going through my manifests, Lieutenant? Why didn't you come ask me, like any—"

"Because it's—"

"Be silent, Tolliver! Sarge, I told him not to." So much for the tactful inquiry I'd intended. "Purchasing and inventory are a shambles. I wanted an investigation."

Serenco's blue eyes flashed as he got to his feet. "You may have my resignation. I won't have my honesty questioned just because I've done things the way the old Commandant—"

I shouted, "I didn't give you permission to stand!" I slammed my fist against the table. "You'll obey orders like everyone else! Sit!" When he'd complied, I forced my tone to be calm. "No one questions your honesty. I had Mr. Tolliver check on procurement and inventories. A few minor matters have come up and we—"

"Minor? Hauled before the Commandant and his first lieutenant like an errant—"

"Interrupt again and I will by Lord God have your resignation, or worse!" I got to my feet. "I run this place, Serenco. I'll do what I want! Now, how soon can you check on these figures?"

"I have no idea." His fury was barely under restraint. "First, I need a copy of what you found. Then, maybe—" He saw my expression. "Two days, three perhaps. I may have to ask our suppliers."

"You have until I'm back from *Wellington*. By then Mr. Tolliver will have a list of other questions. Dismissed."

When he'd gone, Tolliver crossed to the chair he'd vacated, dropped into it without permission. "Yes, I'm glad I waited. You handled him much more tactfully than—"

"Belay that." I paced, fuming. "I don't give a damn about suit numbers, but his manner . . . interrupting the Commandant! Quarreling! What's happened to discipline?"

"You're shoreside, sir. Shipboard discipline is much more—"

"And he's a Marine sergeant!" I threw myself on the couch. "He's as insolent as you are!"

Tolliver raised an eyebrow. "Bad night, sir?"

"Don't patronize me." Slowly, my anger abated. "I didn't sleep well." I brooded. "The damned impudence."

"Don't complain; you're his role model." He withstood my glare. "Which reminds me: I called BuPers. Higbee is . . . irked."

I sighed. "I would imagine." In obtaining Eddie's transfer I'd been, um, inflammatory.

"What was it you said to him? No, it might give me ideas. Anyway, I arranged an orderly for you."

I sat upright. "I told you when we first took this job I didn't want—"

"Yes, but you changed your mind." He raised a hand to forestall me. "How else would you like to explain Mr. Boss, if someone asks?"

"Lord God." I'd forgotten.

"You had pull enough to yank him groundside at short notice, but if he's to be assigned here permanently, he needs a regular berth."

"Very well." I smiled weakly. "Thank you."

"All part of the job, sir." He stood. "Anything else, before I go?"

"No. Yes, one thing." I sat behind my desk. "Why did you call Jeff Thorne my favorite?"

"I withdraw the remark. I was—"

"Answer!"

Tolliver hesitated. "It's the only explanation that came to mind, considering what I've seen of his attitude."

"Damn it, Edgar, you knew him!"

"Oh, yes. Thorne despised me, though I doubt he even remembers." He shrugged. "Was there something more to him, or did time soften your memories?"

"He had—" No. Tolliver could never understand. "We were friends. Not the way it sounds. I admired him greatly. He had a way about him. I thought he'd inspire the cadets."

"Yes, I'm sure the cadets will appreciate Arcvid lessons instead—"

"DISMISSED!"

This time, he didn't argue.

"Be seated." At every table, chairs scraped. I took my place at lunch. Jeff Thorne sat across, next to Midshipman Sandra Ekrit. His expression was carefully neutral. Whether it concealed a hangover, I couldn't tell. His hair was well brushed, his uniform clean and pressed.

Between bites I studied the florid face, searching for the young Thorne I remembered. Not yet thirty, he bore twenty extra pounds and a manner from which all gaiety had been extinguished.

I was ragged from sleepless hours interspersed with nightmares. Father had been in some of them. The morning's conversation with Sergeant Serenco had left a foul taste. Still, I made an effort to draw Thorne into conversation. At length, defeated, I lapsed into bitter silence, wishing I had never sent for him. Edgar Tolliver watched with barely concealed amusement.

A cadet hurried toward me, out of breath. "Cadet Kyle Drew reporting, sir. Mr. Kinders says, a call, from Cardiff."

I threw down my napkin, strode to the door, willing myself not to break into a gallop. "Annie?"

"It's me, Captain. Eddie Boss." The line whistled and crackled; the voice seemed light-years distant.

"What's wrong?"

"Today's the second day. She won't eat, just lies in bed cryin'." He sounded anxious. "I dunno—don't know if I should let her be or not."

"No, take her—" I paused. Where? To a hospital? Back to the dreaded clinic? "What does she want, Eddie?"

"Lie around all day feelin' sorry for herself, what she want!"

"She's had a rough time, Mr. Boss."

"Yeah, sir, but she not the only one. Time to think 'bout other stuff. Move on." He didn't sound sympathetic.

"Well . . ." I sighed. "Is she taking liquids?"

"Lotsa tea. Thassall she want."

"Wait another day. If she doesn't start eating, call a taxi and bring her to Academy. You know how to use the trains?"

"I ain' no—I'm not glitched, Captain." His voice betrayed injured dignity. "I can find out the schedule."

"Very well. Call if you need—want help." I rang off.

Tolliver raised an eyebrow. I shook my head. Nonetheless, I was worried. If Annie grew malnourished—

"Excuse me, sir."

"What is it, Ms. Ekrit?" My tone held an edge.

"As you ordered, I've been tutoring Cadet Stritz. His biweeklies are up."

"Very well." I tore at a roll.

"I was hoping, uh, that is . . ." She braced herself. "You confined me to base until his grades improved, sir. I thought . . . I mean, would you consider . . ."

"Don't we teach middies how to finish a sentence?" I shook

my head. "Jeff, you had my nose against the bulkhead for an hour when I did that."

Thorne's voice was soft. "Yes, sir, but you weren't speaking to the Commandant at the time."

I scowled at Ms. Ekrit. "Until the cadet's grades improved, I said, and your manners."

"Yes, sir."

"Ask after his next biweeklies." Two weeks on base was nothing. Aboard ship, she might be confined to a tiny wardroom. "If his scores hold I'll let you off."

"Thank you, sir." If she felt any disappointment, she wisely concealed it.

After lunch Jeff Thorne casually pushed back his chair. "May I walk with you?"

"If you wish." We set out across the compound to Officers' Quarters.

He was silent awhile. "About last night, I seem to remember an awkward conversation."

"You hoped you wouldn't."

"If I was rude, I'm sorry."

"You were, but it was the liquor talking." I tried to sound agreeable.

"Let me tell you what wasn't the liquor." Thorne stopped, faced me. "Did BuPers mention that I'm up in five months?"

"Yes, but I knew you'd reenlist."

"I won't." His eyes met mine. "Time for a career change."

My tone was harsh. "Because you blew a chance at advancement?"

"No. Because—" His eyes clouded. "Never mind."

"Belay that!" I startled a passing cadet. "Why, Mr. Thorne?"

His tone was defiant. "'Reenlistment is at the sole decision of an individual officer, and no superior may attempt to force or influence his choice.' Section one hundred two, paragraph—"

"This is me! Nick Seafort!" A gaggle of cadets approached.

His expression soured. "Yes, the hero of—"

I shouted, "Do I look like a bloody hero?" The cadets gawked. I wheeled on them. "What do you joeys—"

Thorne's voice was brisk. "Run along, lads. This is a private conversation and you shouldn't be overhearing!"

"Aye aye, sir!" With hurried salutes they detoured and scurried off.

"I'm a fraud, Thorne! I blundered my way as Captain of *Hibernia*. On *Challenger*, a fish saved us. At Hope Nation I committed treason!" I slammed my fist into my thigh. "I hear enough of that guff in the holos, I won't have it from you!"

"Steady, Commandant." He spoke quietly.

"I won't have it!"

"All right, you're no hero." Seeing no one, he took my arm and led me off the path. "Easy, Mr. Seafort."

His voice was so like the middy I'd worshiped at Farside, I bit back a sob. "Sandra Ekrit, back there. She didn't like dining with cadets, so I grounded her. I have no restraint, Jeff. I need you to do what I cannot!"

He snorted. "She'll manage a couple of weeks confined—"

"You have no idea the bridges I burned to get you! Higbee will never forget. I actually threatened him, and he's my superior!"

"Good, he deserves it."

"You don't understand." I turned away once more.

"I understand you're near a nervous breakdown, sir."

My eyes darted to his, away again. "I'm fine. Never mind that."

"Come to my apartment, Mr. Seafort." It might have been an order. Numb, I let him lead the way.

Inside, he closed the door to his bedroom, but not before I saw the clothes strewn about. He rummaged in a cabinet, emerged with a bottle.

"Don't drink now, Mr. Thorne. Please."

"Not for me. For you." He poured a stiff shot of gin, added ice from the tiny cooler. "Sit." He handed me the glass.

I swirled it, took a sip, grimaced. "I'm all right." I waited for him to take a chair. "All right, I have no legal right to ask why you won't reenlist. But . . ." I brooded. "I need to know."

His wave took in himself, the untidy apartment. "I'm no good as an officer. Those stories we were raised on, of honor, gallantry. They don't describe the real Navy. I don't fit."

I said, "You were the finest officer I've ever known."

"That's goofjuice!"

The drink spilled over my hand as I slammed it on the table. "Do you have any idea what you meant to me?"

"All right, so you looked up to me. Misplaced hero worship. How can you forget the caning I got you?"

"The galley raid? What does that matter?"

He got to his feet, his expression bitter. "I've regretted that idiocy for years! I took you where I couldn't cover for you, betrayed you to—"

"Don't be a fool, Lieutenant." I busied myself blotting the table with a napkin, sipping what was left of my drink.

"Nick, whatever inspiration I offered you is long gone. My foolishness with Mrs. Duhaney proves that. So do my ratings at Callisto."

I nursed my drink, wondering how to reach him. "Outside, with the cadets just now. Why did you interrupt me?"

"You were going to—sorry, it's not my place to say."

"Say it."

"You were about to lash out at them, and they'd done nothing."

"So what? They were just cadets."

"You can't believe that!" He studied my face.

"Neither can you." I swallowed the dregs of my gin. "That's why I want you."

We sat in silence. After a time he stirred. "I wish I'd served with you, sir."

"You might have stopped me from damning myself. No, don't ask, I won't talk about it."

He leaned back, his voice tired. After a time he said, "What happened to our hopes?"

"They're victims of maturity." I stood. "Thanks for the drink. As you can see, I'm at my wit's end. I need you, Jeff."

"It's too late. Even if I wanted, I could never get another decent posting." He saw my eyes, went red. "I'm terribly sorry, I didn't mean it like that. A posting with you is all I could ask for. But I truly thought you called me down to retaliate for that old galley incident. I—it seems I was wrong."

"Please reenlist."

"I'll think about it, sir."

For once I knew to leave well enough alone.

Chapter 17

Restless, I peered out the porthole. At least two other shuttles waited ahead of us for access to *Wellington's* locks. I sighed, dreading the endless conversation I'd face with politicians and brass, all denizens of Admiral Duhaney's "other" Navy.

Behind me the cadets fidgeted. Midshipman Tenere whispered to Johan Stritz and giggled. I fixed them with a laser glance, and they quieted instantly. "If I come to regret I brought you, I'll make you sorry!"

Robert Boland sat up straighter, still pale from his recent bout of nausea. Stritz and Arnweil stared at their laps. Jerence Branstead blushed. After a moment, Adam beckoned, and they slipped out of their seats to wander back to the large porthole.

I took a slow breath, tried to relax. It wasn't the middy's fault we were delayed. I tried to concentrate on my holozine, gave it up.

Why had I brought them to such an important ceremony? Had it really been necessary to give such a munificent reward to Branstead and Boland, our high achievers? A few words of praise, a week's freedom from kitchen and barracks chores, would have sufficed. What would my colleagues think of including untrained children in a state function?

No matter. My accepting the Commandancy had been a mistake. If I could figure how to abandon my post without disgracing the Navy, I'd resign in an instant. All I wanted now was to help Annie heal.

Our shuttle's turn came at last. As we crowded into the mated locks I tugged at my dress whites, straightened my tie. The hatch slid closed behind us.

This was a formal occasion; I cleared my throat, said into the speaker, "Captain Nicholas Seafort and party request permission to come aboard."

"Permission granted, sir. Welcome to U.N.S. *Wellington*." The hatch slid open. "ATTENTION!"

A double row of sailors stiffened at their lieutenant's bellow. Several other officers resplendent in crisp whites came to attention, saluting smartly. Cadet Boland sucked in his breath at the spectacle. Jerence Branstead was less impressed; he'd spent nine months aboard *Victoria* on the way home from Hope Nation. He knew what lieutenants looked like.

"Lieutenant Hollis, sir. Welcome aboard." He gestured to the ladder. "Captain Pritcher will stay on the bridge until the last of the mediamen board. Admiral Duhaney is with Senator Boland and the other guests in the lounge. Where shall I escort you?"

Not to the lounge, and the politicians. "I'll pay my respects to the Captain, if he'll see me."

"I'm sure he will, sir." He eyed Adam Tenere and the unexpected cadets, but his tone remained polite. "And, the rest of your, er, party?"

I couldn't risk sending them to the lounge; Lord God knew how the cadets might embarrass me, or Academy. And if Adam took it in mind to scamper around a corridor bend . . . "They'll come with me."

We trailed the lieutenant along a spotless corridor. The silent machinery, the unblemished decks, the hint of fresh oil in the recycled air all testified to *Wellington's* recent departure from Lunapolis shipyards. She'd completed her deep-space trials only two weeks ago.

While Hollis knocked at the bridge hatch I lined the cadets along the corridor bulkhead, out of the way. "Wait here until I'm through."

"Captain Seafort, sir." Hollis stood aside as I entered.

Captain Pritcher rose, a cold smile flitting across his sallow face. "Dismissed, Lieutenant. Captain Seafort, a pleasure to meet you."

I saluted; he was senior to me by a number of years. "Good afternoon, sir." My eyes greedily roamed the bridge. The huge simulscreen on the fore bulkhead blazed with the lights of a billion stars. The consoles blinked their steady reassurance.

"A rough trip aloft, Mr. Seafort?" He stared at the bruises that marked my encounter with the Crypsnbloods.

I blushed. "No, sir." Best not to say more.

His voice was flinty. "We'll start the speeches in an hour or so; everybody wants to have their say. Deputy Secretary-General Franjee will do the commissioning, but first we'll put the ship through her paces for the civilians."

"I'm sure they'll be impressed," I said.

"They'd better be, for what *Wellington* cost." His smile was bleak. "I have the crew drilling as smartly as can be expected, considering every man aboard is transferred from another ship."

Pritcher must have his hands full. Breaking in new hands was hard enough, but familiarizing an entire crew with the quirks of a new ship was a task I didn't envy him.

I searched for something to say. "Where will they send you, sir?" I already knew.

"We'll join the Home Fleet."

A coveted assignment. Pritcher and his officers would avoid the stultifying tedium of a long Fuse to a distant colony, and they'd never be more than a few days from shore leave.

"She seems a good ship, sir."

"Six banks of midships lasers, the latest model fusion drive. We'll be conducting a tour as part of the ceremonies." His unsmiling eyes met mine. "I suppose I could have someone escort you through the ship now, if you like."

I gave the expected reply. "No, sir, though I appreciate the offer. I'll wait."

"Very well. There are refreshments in the Level 2 lounge." It was a dismissal.

"Thank you, Captain. Good luck, and congratulations." He didn't bother to return my salute.

Now I had no choice but to join the politicians. Trailing a middy and cadets, I made my way down to the Level 2 lounge. Outside the hatch I paused. "Are you recovered, Mr. Boland?"

He blushed scarlet. "Yes, sir. The gravity helps a lot."

"Very well." I frowned at each of them in turn. "You're about to mingle with the top brass, so speak only in answer to a direct question. Don't offer any opinions, don't interrupt, and behave yourselves as gentlemen. Adam, keep them in line." I smoothed my jacket and went in.

"Ah, there you are, Nick." If Admiral Duhaney was put out by my recent escapades it didn't show in his tone. Then again, the drink in his hand may have been a mellowing influence. Though alcohol was contraband aboard a U.N.N.S. vessel, a major ceremony such as commissioning was an exception. After all there were civilians present and, more important, the media.

"Hello, sir."

"Let me introduce you to the Deputy SecGen. He's got a lock on the top spot if De Vala ever retires." He looked over my shoulder. "Cadets, hmm? Peculiar idea, bringing them." He squinted. "Is that Boland's son, by the wall? Now that's smart thinking, Nick!" He clapped me on the shoulder. "His father will be pleased."

My tone was stiff. "The boy earned it. His grades were—"

"Of course." Duhaney smiled. "That's the way." He patted my shoulder again.

A familiar voice, behind me. "Excuse me, sir."

I flared, "Now what?" Adam Tenere should have the sense not to bother me when I was with the Admiral.

The middy took a step back, forcing me to follow. His voice dropped. "Cadet Boland is nauseous again. I can escort him to the head and leave the others, or send him off by himself, or leave with all of them. I didn't know what—"

"Don't annoy me with—" I caught myself; it was a reasonable question. "I don't want you marching out with a flock of cadets, and you can't leave them unattended with the brass. There's a head just off the corridor; point Boland toward it and stay here with the others." I turned back to Admiral Duhaney. "The Boland boy scored first out of—"

"Oh, come along, let's meet Franjee. Over there, with McPhee from *Holoworld,* and the others."

I had no choice but to follow the Admiral to the cluster of civilians at the far bulkhead.

"Mr. Secretary, may I present Captain—"

"Seafort. I'd know you anywhere, even without your famous scar." The short, dark-skinned Deputy SecGen extended his hand. "Thanks to your exploits we should have met long ago, but I understand you're shy of publicity."

"Yes, sir, I—"

"Not that you managed to avoid it; you were plastered across the holos yet again, when you brought *Victoria* home. So, young man, tell me: when are we going to steer you into politics?" Others in his clique smiled. Several gave me appraising glances.

Not during this lifetime. Self-contempt or no, I wouldn't sink so far. I struggled for a polite answer. "My duty is to the Navy, sir."

"Yes, but enlistments end, and life goes on. When you're

ready, talk to me, or Richard here. The Supranationalists could use you."

"I'll keep it in mind." Desperately, I seized on Senator Boland. "Good to see you, sir."

"And you, Commandant." As we moved away his eyes met mine, revealing nothing of his feelings.

I flushed. When last we'd spoken I'd threatened to resign if he so much as called my office. I searched for some appropriate, inane comment.

Richard Boland saved me the trouble. "She's a great ship, isn't she?" His gesture took in the spacious lounge. "I've often thought, if chance hadn't led me along another path, that I'd have wanted to serve in the Navy."

I tried not to show my scorn. Life wasn't a matter of chance, but hard work and perseverance. I'd dedicated myself to a Naval career from the time I was ten, devouring the holozines, studying my math, dreaming and planning with Jason. Had Boland truly wanted a Naval career, he could have done likewise.

I sought a peaceable reply. "At least you'll achieve your ambition through your son, sir."

"His ambition," Boland corrected. He smiled, but his eyes were sharp. "Quite a surprise to see him walk in with you. It would have been nice to know he was coming."

I stiffened. "I'm sure it would have." I'd be happy to notify a cadet's parents when he was assigned to travel. The day hell froze.

Boland's tone was still affable. "By the way, Commandant, that odd personnel matter has been settled."

For a moment I thought he was referring to my problems with Jeff Thorne, but that made no sense. It must be Darwin Sleak, Lord God rest his soul. "He's had decent burial?"

"At Lunapolis." He hesitated. "You handled that well. A mysterious death would have catapulted you onto the front pages, though few in your position would object to that. Calling Duhaney was a smooth way to handle it."

It had been Tolliver's idea. On my own, I'd have blundered into a scandal. "I'm out of my depth in such things."

A new voice intervened. "Ah, Richard, keeping our young hero to yourself?"

"No, Brett, just chatting." Boland moved slightly, made a place for Senator Wyvern.

"They'll want interviews, Captain," Wyvern's chuckle held a hint of malice. "The media can get at Franjee anytime; if they don't call him, he seeks them out. You're fresh meat."

"Not if I can help it."

"Ah, but you can't. That's my point." His manner changed subtly. "On that subject, I have some advice for you. Let's step outside for a moment. Somewhere quiet."

I checked my watch. "They'll be starting in a few minutes."

"And we'll be done by then." He guided me to the hatch. I would have shaken him off, but I'd already made too many enemies for Academy's good.

The corridor seemed inordinately quiet, after the babble of the crowded reception. We wandered toward the corridor bend. I stopped. My cadets were still in the lounge supervised only by Adam, and Lord God knew what he was capable of. I sighed; I never should have brought them. "Advice, you said?"

"Yes." Wyvern's smile faded, and something hard took its place. "You know, the mediamen will press you with questions; you've avoided them too long."

"I'll do my best—"

"They'll ask about your illustrious career, your amazing escapes."

I shook my head. What was his point? "I still don't—"

"They might ask about your lunatic wife slumming in New York—"

"Senator!"

"— and the trannie sailor she prongs while you play the martinet at Academy."

The corridor lurched. My knuckles ached. I stared unseeing, realized that when I'd missed his jaw I'd slammed my fist into the bulkhead. Wyvern waved me away as he backed off. "Don't try that again, Seafort."

"You bastard!" My face was white.

"Better prepare for it, boy. Or maybe they'll ask why you were skulking the streets pretending you're a transpop instead of attending to your duty. Find any nice trannie bitches down there?"

I pinned him against the bulkhead. "Wyvern, I'll kill you!"

"But they'd still ask."

"They don't know about those things!"

"Ah, my boy, I agree. The point is, they will. I can guarantee it."

My rage withered slowly to defeat. I sagged, released his collar. "Why? What do you want of me?"

"Hardly a thing. Just one report, discarded."

"What are you talking about?"

"Your quartermaster, and that fool of a lieutenant who won't let the matter drop. Tell him to forget about it."

I gaped. "Sergeant Serenco? Tolliver? How does that concern you?"

"That's another matter you may forget."

"The man is stealing us blind! Why should I let him get away with—"

"It's a political matter."

"Tell me, damn you!"

His voice came as a hiss. "Because he's my nephew! My niece should never have married him, but now he's family. I'll see to it the loss is covered in next year's appropriation."

"I won't have a thief go unpunished!"

His face turned ugly. "You'd damn well better, or your wife and her lover will be the celebrities of the day!"

My fingers itched to close around his neck. Oh, Annie. For your sake, look what I must do.

No! Get thee behind me, Satan.

"Do your worst, Wyvern!" I turned toward the lounge.

"I will. It will destroy you, and of course her. And Serenco will still get off; I have enough influence to fix that."

I stalked down the corridor, slowed before I reached the bend. Annie, forgive me. I can't let him do it.

"What if I let the matter be?" My voice was unsteady.

"Your word that you'll take no action on my beloved nephew, in return for mine that I won't leak the story. Don't give me that look, Commandant. I'm a politician; if my promise wasn't good, nobody would ever deal."

I could hardly hear myself speak. "All right."

"It's arranged, then?" He knew better than to offer his hand.

"Yes." Soon, Annie. The moment I reached groundside, I would resign. Then Wyvern would have no reason to destroy my wife. I doubted he'd do it out of spite; he was too clever a politician to waste his power. I felt a strange relief, now that my course was decided.

I'd been concerned it would be a slight on the Navy to resign so soon after I'd been appointed Commandant. Now, if I stayed, I'd be nothing but a liability. I'll come home, love. At long last.

Almost light-headed, I headed for the bar seeking refreshment, anything that would remove the taste of our conversation.

"Ladies and gentlemen, distinguished guests, your attention, please." A lieutenant in crisp whites at the hatch, his every word recorded by two mediamen with holocameras. The cabin quieted. "On behalf of Captain Pritcher, we welcome you to U.N.S. *Wellington*. The commissioning will take place on the bridge, but first we invite you to observe several Naval exercises."

He paused. "The first will be a Battle Stations drill. You may observe from the engine room or from Level 1, near the bridge. The crew has not been told the order or timing of these maneuvers."

I corraled my cadets, shepherded them with the other guests to the ladder. Robert Boland's expression was strained. I leaned close, caught the acrid whiff of vomit. "Are you all right, boy?" The last thing we needed was for him to make a spectacle of himself.

He grimaced. "Yes, sir, I think that was the last of it. I'm sorry for the trouble. I'll take the pills next time." He looked away.

I said gruffly, "It's all right, boy. I've been sick too."

He hesitated. "Do I get demerits, sir?"

"One, for even asking." The boy should know better, and if he didn't—

We climbed the ladder, filed along the Level 1 corridor behind the Deputy SecGen. I cleared my throat. "Canceled, Mr. Boland. But mind your manners."

"Aye aye, sir."

Alarms shrieked. "Battle Stations!" Captain Pritcher, on ship's speakers. "All hands to Battle Stations!" I blanched, even knowing it was just the anticipated drill. Mediamen aimed their holocameras at midshipmen sprinting to their assigned posts at gunnery, in the comm room, on the bridge. Scant seconds later the first ratings raced up the ladder to the laser control compartment.

A middy dived through the bridge hatchway seconds before the hatch slammed shut. *Wellington's* bridge was now an impenetrable fortress. Captain Pritcher silenced the alarms, put his caller on shipwide frequency.

"Aft lock reporting secure, sir!"

"Engine room secure, sir! Full power available!"

"Hydroponics secure, sir! Compartment is sealed from ship's air."

Throughout the great warship, emergency hatches slid shut, isolating each section of the vessel for the safety of all. If a sector were penetrated, it alone would decompress.

"Lasers up and ready, sir!" Now, the ship could fight back.

"Comm room fully manned." We could call for help.

One by one the remaining compartments called in: recycling, damage control, galley, sickbay. When the last confirmation came I stole a surreptitious glance at my watch. Not bad, for a new crew. And response times would improve as she settled in to duty, if Pritcher was worth his salt.

"What do you think, Mr. Duhaney?" Deputy SecGen Franjee looked to the Admiral.

"Very smartly done, sir." Duhaney sounded confident. "Twenty seconds faster than last week." Odd; I'd been standing just across from the Admiral and hadn't seen him check the time.

A few moments passed, then Captain Pritcher's dry voice. "All hands stand down, except laser control." He cleared his throat. "Our next demonstration will take place in the laser control compartment on Level 1."

Dutifully, we crowded into the laser room. It bristled with consoles and screens. Two rows of alert ratings, uniforms gleaming, waited at their places. An officer stepped forward. "Good afternoon, Mr. Franjee and other distinguished guests. We're about to conduct a laser firing drill, held regularly on any ship of the line. Today we will fire at real, not simulated, targets. They'll be released by ship's officers from our two launches."

Perhaps the boats would be manned by middies, overjoyed at the rare opportunity to command. Or perhaps, with the brass watching, Captain Pritcher had put more seasoned lieutenants in charge.

The officer keyed his caller. "Laser compartment to bridge. Ready, sir."

"Very well, lasers are activated." A green light flashed at the laser console; the Captain had released the safeties that normally prohibited ship's lasers from firing. "Mr. Johanski, Sanders, begin, please!"

I peered over the tech's shoulder. Live fire drills were a nuisance to set up, and the vessels releasing targets always risked a laser tech misreading them for a target in the heat of competition. On the other hand, a real hit was more satisfying to the gunner than a simulated one, thereby raising his learning curve.

The first target accelerated toward *Wellington.* The tech in front of me dialed up his magnification, graphed the trajectory on his trackball.

With only two launchers releasing targets, the crews knew there would be only two points of origin, and therefore the approximate trajectories. That meant—

"Commence fire!"

All was still except for the sporadic slap of hands on the fire pads. Because of the watching brass the techs were unusually restrained. No muttered curses, cries of satisfaction, calls of encouragement, broke the silence.

From time to time an alarm blared as a missile cleared the ship's defenses. The puter's impersonal voice announced simulated damage. "Penetration amidships, Level 2! Hull damage to hold, port side!"

The incoming salvos became more ragged, degenerating into sporadic individual fire, much harder for *Wellington's* defenders to track. I nodded my approval; Captain Pritcher had made it a fair test. Many Captains would have set up an easy drill with the Admiral and the media watching. But the exercise simulated missile and laser fire, not attacks by the fish that were our most likely enemy.

"Port bow lasers destroyed!" An unlucky hit. The port bow laser console went black as the ship's puter disabled it.

"Two are on me, Charlie, get the son of a bitch!"

The gunnery officer hurried across the aisle to stand behind the anxious young tech. I grinned. This was more like it. Laser fire was a cooperative effort; two consoles working together could get a crossfire on an incoming, and take it out while protecting each other's flanks. It was tense work, and the tech's cry for help was artlessly natural. Had I been his gunnie, though, I'd have stood back. A lieutenant staring over his shoulder would only make the sailor more nervous.

The perspiring tech's fingers danced across his console. The electronic circuitry under his hands was of awesome complexity, yet all boiled down to human, not putronic intelligence.

Puters were intelligent, puters were faster, but only a human could make a good decision on insufficient data while a possibly lethal object streaked across his screen. We could program puters to recognize any known threat, but what about the unknown? What would Darla, *Hibernia's* puter, have made of the fish that emerged from behind the derelict *Telstar*? Would *Hibernia* have survived to make her way home with the news?

Speed wasn't everything.

Judgment was.

Five bells chimed; the lights dimmed momentarily and brightened. The tech I was watching slapped his firing button on a target in the crosshairs, let out his breath in a long sigh of satisfaction.

"All consoles cease fire!" The gunnery lieutenant turned to the politicians and officers crowded in the laser compartment. "In the exercise you just witnessed, the intensity of incoming fire approximated a full fleet engagement. *Wellington* took only eleven hits, while destroying two hundred twelve incoming missiles." A patter of applause interrupted his speech.

As the visitors filed out of the cabin I focused on the silent consoles. Simulated or no, it was the last time I would see a ship under fire.

Secretary Franjee beamed. "What do you think, Commandant? You've seen more action than most."

Caught off guard, I stammered some meaningless words of praise. The Secretary stepped into the corridor. I hesitated at the hatch, stole one more look at the techs and their consoles. True, there'd been over two hundred incoming. But eleven hits would have crippled *Wellington,* perhaps destroyed her.

Though I wouldn't tell the SecGen, our transpop crewmen on *Challenger* had performed better, after our endless simulation drills. Captain Pritcher's dry voice echoed in the speakers. "The final exercise will take place in the engine room." Senator Boland sighed, grinned ruefully at Franjee. Captain Pritcher had the dignitaries trooping about from stern to aft. I beckoned to my waiting cadets.

We followed the others down to Level 2, waited for the civilians to proceed.

Alarms shrieked. "General Quarters! All hands to General Quarters!"

Once again, the thud of running feet. We pressed to the side of the ladder; a rating grinned as he hurtled past, two steps at a time. General Quarters was but one stage of readiness below Battle Stations; emergency hatches remained open and the Captain didn't release the laser safeties, but all crewmen dashed to their duty stations forthwith, and remained there for the duration.

"Just part of the program," Admiral Duhaney told the Deputy SecGen. His tone was reassuring.

"How can you know?" demanded Senator Wyvern. A good question. A General Quarters drill was no different from the real thing. The call must be instantly obeyed; only the Captain knew why he sounded the signal.

"I'll check, if you'd like." Duhaney was eager to pacify his constituents. "If it isn't a drill, I'll have Pritcher announce it on the caller immediately. You gentlemen go on down to Level 3." He trotted back up the ladder like an obliging middy.

He couldn't have reached the bridge before the speaker came to life. "All hands stand down!" Wyvern sighed, muttered under his breath. I grinned maliciously; maybe Pritcher would give the Senator a heart attack. We reached Level 3, trudged past the recycling chambers to the engine room.

"FIRE IN THE RECYCLERS! ALL HANDS TO FIRE STATIONS!" The Captain's tone was taut. "Break out Level 3 hoses!"

I shoved Kyle Drew out of the way as fire crews raced past, their faces grim. Corridor hatches slid shut, isolating the endangered section. A whir and a click indicated the overhead air vents had closed, isolating each section to its own air. Automatically I scanned the bulkheads for canned air storage bins.

Senator Boland nudged me in the ribs. "Isn't Pritcher overdoing it a bit?"

My voice was tense. "If it's a drill." A mediaman shouldered me aside for a better shot of a crewman dragging the bulkhead hose along the corridor. Adam Tenere sucked in his breath, drew back a fist. I managed to snag his arm. "Easy, boy."

"He shoved you, sir!"

I found Adam's outrage reassuring. "He needed to film and I was in his way."

"But you're Captain!"

The hose buckled, sprang to life as *Wellington's* puter opened the valves. I patted Adam's shoulder, smiled. "The contact rules apply to Naval personnel, not groundsiders."

"I know, sir." The middy took a deep breath, forced himself to relax. Then he stepped forward casually, as if to watch the crewmen at work. He planted his back squarely in front of the mediaman's holocamera.

I frowned, but held my peace. In a day or so none of this would matter; I'd be home with Annie.

A middy appeared at the hatch, thumbed the ship's caller. "Recycling chamber to bridge. No sign of fire, sir."

The Captain's voice was dry. "Very well, stand down."

The corridor hatches slid open. Our party of politicians paused to watch the crewmen fold their hoses. One crewman muttered to his mate, "Why don't he just pipe Abandon Ship and get us outa here?" I pretended not to hear.

Ten minutes later we gathered in the outer chamber of the engine room for the last exercise.

The Captain's dry voice came over the speakers. "Ladies and gentlemen, here on the bridge our officers will calculate a Fuse to Vega. We'll copy the data to your engine-room screens. When calculations are confirmed, we will ready *Wellington* for Fusion." He paused. "Those of you with commitments at home will be relieved to know we will not actually complete the Fuse."

The politicians laughed dutifully. A trip to Vega would involve a Fuse of months, with only occasional stops for nav checks.

"Engine Room, prepare to Fuse."

"Aye aye, sir." The Chief Engineer's response was immediate. "Bring Three on-line, reduce all auxiliary output." Engine-room ratings worked their consoles while sailors below watched the drive for signs of trouble.

Secretary Franjee broke off a conversation with a man from Holoworld. "What's happening, Mr. Seafort?"

I pointed to the console. "Right now the Chief is bringing full power on-line to prepare for Fuse. On the bridge they're running nav coordinates."

The mediaman asked, "How do you know what they're doing?"

"For one thing, the calculations show on that screen." I pointed.

"Why can't they run the calculations down here?" the Secretary asked.

"I suppose they could, sir." It would save middies hours of dread under the Captain's stern eye. But calculations were done from the bridge; that was the Navy way. After all, the Pilot's place was on the bridge and he was responsible for the accuracy of the Fuse.

Figures flashed across the screen. Two levels above, a midshipman sweated at his console, no doubt aware of the watching brass.

The puter could run all our calculations faster than any human hand. But the Navy's first rule was: never trust the machinery. All nav calculations, all safety readouts, were confirmed by the officers on watch. Too many lives were at stake to risk the vagaries of malfunctioning circuits. Even massive built-in redundancy couldn't protect a ship against glitches in programming, such as we'd found on *Hibernia*.

"I have coordinates, ma'am." In the speaker, the young middy's voice sounded confident.

Mr. Franjee checked his watch. "Now what, Mr. Seafort?"

"He's passing them to the Pilot. They'll be done in a moment, sir." I tried to sympathize with the Secretary's frustration. All he saw was flashing lights, figures that meant nothing. The Captain would have been wiser to eliminate this drill.

"Pilot?" The Captain's dry tone.

"Confirmed to four decimal places, sir."

"Very well. Harlan?"

The puter. "A match to five decimal places, Captain."

"Very well."

I said, "Now, they'll feed the coor—"

The figures flashed onto our consoles. Captain Pritcher rasped, "All hands, prepare to Fuse!"

"It's just a simulated Fuse, so they won't actually—"

The Chief Engineer roared, "Prepare for Fuse!" He punched in a code on his console. A green light flashed, indicating the Fusion safeties were disabled. He entered Fusion codes.

I pictured the actions on *Wellington's* unseen bridge. The Captain would check the coordinates one final time. His hand would hover over the screen. Then, were we actually to Fuse, his hand would trace a line down his screen to the BEGIN FUSE position.

A bell chimed. "Engine room, Fuse!"

Secretary Franjee looked alarmed. "I thought you said they wouldn't—"

As the Chief slapped the go-pad, machinery hummed and the lights dimmed slightly. "Engine room to bridge. Fusion drive is ignited!"

"It's just a simulation, sir. Though a very realistic one."

N-waves danced on the small screen, next to lines showing expected output. Techs at the nearby consoles struggled to match the two lines exactly. Such simulations were used routinely in training.

"Stations, report!"

"N-wave generation within parameters!"

"Main turbine, no overheat."

"Pumping, normal and no overheat."

Mr. Franjee shifted from foot to foot. "All very well, but how long does it go on?"

"I'm sure they'll stop in a moment."

"Temperature beginning to climb, Chief."

"What's your wave at?"

"Fifty-five percent."

"Get me a match at sixty."

The Secretary looked mystified. I said quietly, "He's matching output to intended coordinates. The simulation's set at sixty percent generation, that is, sixty percent of the N-wave strength necessary to Fuse."

The Chief's eyes never left his console. "That's correct, sir, except that it's not a simulation. We're generating real waves."

I staggered as if struck. "You're what?"

"All today's exercises are real, no simulations. We're holding the wave output down to sixty percent. Don't worry, if we overheat I can shut—"

"Real waves?"

The Secretary cleared his throat. "Captain Seafort, what does—"

I waved him silent. "Chief, disengage your engines, flank! You're caterwauling!"

"Sorry, I have no idea what that means."

"Broadcasting N-waves. You'll attract fish!"

His tone was soothing. "It's only for a few minutes, sir. Ships Fuse all the time, I'm sure it won't—"

"Give me your caller!"

"Begging your pardon, sir, I can't just now. We're engaged."

Senator Wyvern watched with amusement. "Problems, Seafort?"

"Yes, I—" No point in explaining, especially to him.

Pritcher. "Engine Room, go to sixty-five, hold the wave line for ten minutes, then disengage."

The Chief took up his caller. "Aye aye, sir. Sixty-five percent confirmed."

I thrust through the crowd, slapped open the corridor hatch. "Excuse me. Adam, watch the bloody cadets!"

Senator Boland gave me room to pass. "Captain, where are you going?"

"Topside!" I strode down the corridor, increased my pace to a sprint before I reached the bend. I tore up the ladder to Level 2, circled the well.

Abandoned on *Challenger* light-years from home, our cater-wauling had attracted the deadly fish. On Hope Nation's Orbiting Station I'd deliberately set disabled ships to run their drives at low power, to summon all the fish I could to our remote outpost before I blew the Station.

Wellington was doing likewise, in home system.

I pounded up the steps, tore along the corridor to the bridge. The hatch was sealed; I hammered on the tough alumalloy.

The camera swiveled; after a moment the hatch slid open. A young lieutenant sat bent over her console to the right of the Captain's chair, conferring with a middy.

"Captain Seafort reporting. Permission to enter bridge!"

Pritcher swiveled. "Granted."

Admiral Duhaney was perched on the edge of the Captain's console. "What's the matter, Seafort?"

"Shut off the drives before you call the fish!"

Pritcher's face remained expressionless, except for one lifted eyebrow. "I beg your pardon? Was that an order?"

Damn it, the man was senior. "No, sir, of course not." I tried to make my words conciliatory. "Perhaps you don't realize fish can hear your N-waves. If you generate without Fusing—"

"Yes, I know, your report calls it caterwauling. An interesting concept. But even if it's proved, a few minutes test won't call Fish from—"

I wheeled. "Admiral, for God's sake. Have him turn off the engines! You have civilians aboard."

"Seafort, you're overreaching." Duhaney's eyes were cold.

"If you'd been there, seen what they can do—"

"Behave yourself!" The Admiral came to his feet, crossed the few feet between us. His finger jabbed at my chest. "You had your chance for a ship, we almost begged you to take one! *Wellington* is Pritcher's. He's in charge."

"Aye aye, sir. But do you understand that the waves we're throwing are exactly the ones I proposed in the automated bomb to attract fish?"

The Admiral paused. "Exactly?"

"Well, the fish respond even more violently to skewed N-waves than true. But—"

Captain Pritcher snapped, "Our waveline is true. Look at the graph!" With an effort, he made his voice more civil. "Besides, Seafort, we're in home system. Our ships Fuse from here to one colony or another every week, if not every day. One short test won't make a difference. With the Deputy SecGen aboard, I want it to look right."

My shoulders slumped; it was useless. "Yes, sir. As the Admiral said, you're in charge. Sorry I burst in on you."

He sounded only slightly mollified. "Very well."

Duhaney was tentative. "Harry, do you think maybe we should . . ."

"I'll wrap it up shortly, sir. I just wanted them to see how well our techs can hold a line."

"Whatever you say; you have the conn."

His authority confirmed, Pritcher could afford to be magnanimous. "Engine Room, prepare for Defuse." He replaced the caller. "Oh, by the way, Captain Seafort, my lieutenant tells me you've met."

The young woman looked up from her console.

I whispered, "Arlene?"

Her voice was shy. "Lieutenant Sanders reporting, sir." Our eyes met, locked.

Pritcher's dry voice cut into my daze. "Lieutenant, please escort Captain Seafort back to the lounge."

"Aye aye, sir." She rose at once.

Like an automaton, I saluted Pritcher and the Admiral, followed Arlene from the bridge. The hatch slid closed behind us.

Her soft voice seemed hesitant. "Good to meet you again, sir." Automatically, we moved to the ladder, started down to Level 2.

The speaker crackled. "Engine Room, Defuse. Ladies and gentlemen, that concludes our exercise."

"Arlene . . ." I swallowed hard. "How have you been?"

"I've done fine, sir, though for a while I thought I'd never get beyond middy."

I looked to either side; the Level 2 corridor was deserted. Tentatively, I held out a hand. Shyly, she put hers in it.

I had been so young, so hopeful, so innocent.

I moved closer, smelled the fresh clean scent of her hair.

So young.

Sergeant Swopes growled, "Full inspection this afternoon. Word is the Commandant himself may take it. One crease out of place, one speck of dust, and I'll stuff whoever is responsible in the recycler! Is that understood?"

"Yes, sir!" Our chorus was immediate. Despite his warning I wasn't worried. By now we were seasoned second-year cadets, and knew the tricks to passing an inspection. More exciting were the rumors that some hundred cadets had been chosen for promotion. I hoped against hope I would be one of them, but knew how unlikely that was.

Academy had no set graduation date. A cadet remained under the tutelage of his sergeants until he was deemed ready, no matter how long it took. When we took the oath we'd been warned that we could stay cadets for our entire five-year enlistment, and there were rumors it had actually happened, though no one knew of such a case.

After Sarge left, we set about the boring task of getting our dorm ready: mopping, dusting, cleaning ourselves and our environment. Corporal Tolliver strutted about giving unnecessary orders, while making sure not to neglect his own work. He would suffer with the rest of us if our dorm were cited.

As per a long-standing arrangement I did our boots while Arlene made both our beds; I normally made my own, but we relied on her superior skills for the starched creases of an inspection, while I had the knack of turning the toe of a boot into an ebony mirror.

Hours later, I tugged at my jacket one last time, smoothed back my hair yet again. At the hatch, Robbie Rovere called out, "They just left Armstrong, headed this way!"

"Get ready!" Tolliver's warning was unnecessary. We took our places in two lines, waiting to stiffen to attention as the hatch opened.

"Good luck!" Arlene made the crossed fingers sign; I grinned tightly as I replied in kind.

"ATTENTION!" Tolliver's bellow rang through the dorm. We jumped, backs ramrod-straight, eyes front.

Sergeant Swopes entered first, saw us already in place, stepped aside.

I sucked in my breath. It *was* Commandant Kearsey. Lord God help us if anything went wrong.

His inspection was thorough. Running his hand over Donover's locker, he rubbed his fingers as if brushing off dust, but said nothing. The inspection party disappeared into the head, reemerged shortly.

Kearsey nodded to Sarge. "Very well, Mr. Swopes. Passed."

"Thank you, sir."

The Commandant paused at the hatch. "Some of you may have heard scuttlebutt that a promotion list is out. It isn't." A collective, almost inaudible sigh swept the room. "And it won't be, until Free Hour this evening. You'll find it in the corridor." With that, he left.

Silence held for a full half minute. Then the barracks erupted with cheers. Robbie pounded my shoulder, hugged Arlene. "Some of us have to be on it! Maybe me, or you. We'll be out of here!"

"Don't get your hopes—" It was too late. Robbie cartwheeled down the aisle, narrowly missing Tolliver, who aimed a halfhearted kick in his direction.

The day passed in an agony of anticipation. I dreamed through Nav class, earned a sharp rebuke from Mr. Reeves. After that I did my best to concentrate; even if my name was on the list it could easily be removed.

Dinner came and went. If I ate at all, I had no recollection. Milk, perhaps. Or possibly the napkin.

Sergeant Swopes appeared not to notice our odd behavior. It must have taken effort, as Donover dropped a cup of coffee on himself, and Robbie Rovere tripped noisily over his chair.

"Think it's posted yet?" Arlene matched her step to mine.

"Free Hour. Another hour and a half."

"I know when Free Hour is," she said, nettled. She moved on ahead.

"Dumb, Seafort." Tolliver's tone was mocking. "You blew it. Maybe she had the hots for you!"

I whirled, shoved him against the bulkhead. "Watch your mouth! She's a bunkie!"

"Get your hands off—"

Robbie's voice was cold. "I heard that, Tolliver. You're disgusting."

Tolliver's look swiveled from one to the other of us. "Easy, joeys. I didn't mean it." He pushed my hands away. "Watch it, or Sarge'll see you."

I didn't care if I took demerits for disrespect to a corporal. Even by barracks standards, Tolliver had been obscene. Arlene Sanders and I were bunkmates, closer than even brother and sister. The thought of pronging her made my stomach churn. How could I? We shared a dorm, even a shower.

Slowly my anger dissipated. I smiled sourly, sought a reply. "Forget about Sarge. Just hope I don't tell Sanders." Arlene's prowess at hand combat was formidable.

Back at the dorm we spread out our homework, as usual preferring our beds to the study rooms. By unspoken understanding, Sergeant Swopes didn't disturb us during study hour, and we were free to assume whatever relaxed posture we wished. I usually curled up on my side, holo in front of me. Some sat cross-legged on their bunks, others lounged on the deck. Robbie Rovere usually lay on the deck, legs up across his bed.

Though all was quiet, I doubted that much study actually took place. For my own part, I gave up after half an hour, switched off the holo.

I knew I wouldn't be graduated just yet; I hadn't scored well in the last round of tests. But even if I stayed, it meant new bunkmates, perhaps even a new sergeant, as depleted dorms were consolidated and merged.

At last the bell chimed, signaling Free Hour. Two cadets dashed for the hatch. Others stood more nonchalantly, stretched, wandered out to the corridor as if for a walk.

I lay on my bunk, arm over my eyes, depressed. Sooner or later I would pass the postings on the way to class, take a look. There was no hurry.

"Coming, Nicky?"

I uncovered my face. "You go ahead. Maybe later."

She sat on my bunk, slipped on her crisp gray jacket. "I'm scared. Let's look together."

I snorted. "You scared? Right." Arlene Sanders took no guff from any joey in the barracks. Still, once, back in the Training Fuser, she had lost her nerve. Maybe it was possible. "Okay."

I got up, joined her in a stroll to the list posted on the corridor bulkhead. Cadets from several barracks pushed and shoved their way through. Someone whooped.

We shouldered into the crowd. I peered at the two columns, too far away to see anything useful. Someone jostled. I lashed out with my elbow.

"Easy joeys, take your turn!" Midshipman Thorne's voice commanded obedience, and the pushing and shoving lessened. By unspoken agreement we formed ourselves into lines; those in front scanned the list, turned away crestfallen or with unconcealed joy.

Corporal Tolliver was several places ahead of us. He reached the list, ran his finger down the column. He froze, turned slowly. I tried to read his face. He took off his cap, flung it down the corridor against the bulkhead. His grin made him seem almost human. "Yes! I'm out of here, Seafort!"

Arlene's voice was flat. "Congratulations."

Tolliver didn't seem to hear. He ran to the bulkhead, scooped up his cap, flung it again. It sailed past Mr. Thorne's nose, but the middy just smiled. "Careful, Tolliver. You still have Last Night to get through."

"Yes, sir." The prospect of the traditional hazing didn't seem to phase him.

The boy at the head of our line turned. Robbie Rovere. His lip trembled. He made a manful effort, lost his battle. Quickly he wiped a tear with his sleeve. "I didn't make it."

"Oh, Robbie." I sought a consolation. "We'll be together, anyway."

"Yeah." He scuffed the deck. "Maybe next time, huh?" He turned away abruptly, but Arlene's hand darted out, pulled him close. She threw an arm around his shoulder. "You're okay, joey. Kearsey's a blind old fool, everyone knows that."

Lord Jesus. I jabbed Arlene in the ribs. If anyone heard . . .

"You'll make it next time," she said.

"Thanks." Robbie twisted loose, hurried toward the dorm. He almost blundered into Midshipman Jenks, come to watch the comedy. Annoyed, the middy thrust him away.

Only two cadets separated us from our fate; we pushed forward until it was our turn. Arlene's finger ran down the list, reaches the S's. A small sound escaped her.

I said, "You made it!" I threw my arms around her, danced for joy.

She whimpered, turned it into a laugh. "Oh, Nicky, I was so frightened!"

"I'll bet you were the first they picked." I pounded her back, grinning like a fool.

"Move it, you two!" Someone yanked at my arm.

I retreated, but Arlene held me back. "Aren't you even going to look, Nicky?"

"What's the point?" To please her, I searched the list again. "There's no way I—"

My name.

Dumbfounded, I fell back from the list. "I'm—Lord God, I made it!" No, it had to be a mistake. I thrust back into the crowd, looked once more. "Seafort, Nicholas E." I scanned it again, unbelieving. What miracle was this?

"I made middy." It sounded preposterous. I eased my way out of the crowd, passed Jeff Thorne. As I did so Midshipman Jenks stuck out his foot, and I would have gone down if Thorne hadn't caught me.

Back in the dorm I fell onto my bed, raised my hand, inspected the gray wool of my jacket. Now I would trade it for blue. I propped myself up on an arm. "Hey. What was the effective date?"

Sanders grinned. "Go back and look for yourself. I made your bed, what else do you want?"

I sighed, swung my feet off the bed.

"Tomorrow, noon."

"Really?" I hadn't imagined it would be so soon.

Her tone grew wary. "It means tonight is Last Night."

All midshipmen and officers hazed cadets; it was part of the system. But hazing on Last Night could be merciless. I swallowed a foreboding. Whatever they did, by tomorrow it would be over.

Nine in our dorm were to graduate, but the mood was subdued. Friendships would be broken, familiar bunkies exchanged for the unknown. I found myself wishing my name weren't on the list. I felt shame for my cowardice.

They came for us after Lights Out.

Flashlights searched out our faces. Led by Jenks, the middies hauled Reston and Lorca out of bed, ordered them into the corridor. We waited, most of us awake, straining to pierce the silence of the night. Perhaps, in the distance, I heard someone cry out. I couldn't be sure.

An hour passed and I began to doze.

Arlene screamed. I flung myself upright. She thrashed in her bunk, trying to free herself from the drenched sheets. Chunks of ice skittered across the deck. A grinning middy kicked the bucket across the aisle, pulled at Arlene's soaking top.

"You bastards!" I jumped out of bed, shoved the middies aside. "Leave her alone!" I was wearing only my shorts.

Someone caught my arm. I swung and missed; the middy twisted my arm behind my back.

Arlene sobbed in fright and humiliation. I lashed out with my bare foot, caught Jenks in the shin. "You frazzing asshole!"

"What a mouth on that one!" Jenks picked up the empty

bucket, plopped it on my head. I shook it off. "Let's teach him manners." The middy glanced around. "Into the head."

Some brave soul muttered, "Leave him alone!"

Jenks wheeled, his flashlight searching. "Louder, please?" No one answered.

Two middies dragged me kicking into the head. They were bigger and heavier; I couldn't pull loose. Pinned against the sink, I awaited my fate.

Jenks paused at the hatchway. "Corporal Tolliver, join us."

Hazing or no, it was an order and Tolliver had no choice. He appeared in the hatchway, tugged at his shorts. "Yes, sir?"

"Just a moment." Jenks was curt. "Hold on to little Nicky," he told my captors, turning on the sink tap full blast. "Manners, Seafort. You can't be a middy without knowing manners." He held the bar of soap as they forced my head down, pawed at my mouth.

My struggles did me no good. Finally, bruised and humiliated, I held still, tolerated the foul rasp of the soap.

Jenks was thorough in his ministrations. He paused only when two of his henchmen appeared in the hatchway with a hot water bottle. He pointed to Tolliver, whispered to a crony. They seized the cadet corporal, dragged him unceremoniously into a toilet stall. I gagged, tried to spit soap, had my head dunked for my pains.

Behind me there echoed a cry of anguish.

My new uniform seemed strange and out of place, though nothing but the color had changed. They moved us immediately to a new dorm; naturally we middies couldn't bunk with mere cadets. Youngsters who only yesterday were our friends saluted self-consciously; we responded with equal embarrassment.

Few middies were assigned to Academy itself; most of us were to be posted elsewhere. We waited our destiny with trepidation, and as days passed more of us left for coveted ships of the line. Arlene and I were among those who remained.

Jeff Thorne stopped by one day. As a middy posted to

Farside, he bunked in the wardroom, not with us. "You survived Last Night."

"Barely." At times I could still taste the soap.

"I'm sorry. Jenks is an ass, but he's a senior ass."

"It's not your fault, sir."

"Jeff, now."

I grinned shyly. "Yes, si—it's hard to change."

"I remember." He put out his hand. "Tomorrow, I'm off to *Targon.* I came to wish you luck. You too, Sanders."

I shook hands. "Thanks. You—" I hesitated. It didn't matter; Arlene was a bunkie. "You meant a lot to me, Mr. Thorne."

His tone was gruff. "I wish we could have done more. We never got to the gravitrons."

"No one ever does." We smiled.

"As for the rest, I'm sorry." He clapped me on the shoulder, and was gone.

Our orders came two days later. I was to go to *Helsinki,* Arlene to *Freiheit.* We would join our ships at Earthport Station, after four days leave in Lunapolis.

Leave? We stared at each other. For two years we'd been shepherded to meals, to barracks, to exercise, to haircuts. We had barely an hour of our own.

Now we were midshipmen, granted our majority by statute of the General Assembly itself. While civilians of our age were still subject to the dictates of their parents, barred from adult entertainments and pleasures, we were free to drink, go where we desired, even drive electricars if we knew how.

A heady thought.

Five of us took the Farside shuttle to Earthport Station, and thence to Lunapolis. I don't know about the other new middies, but a lump formed in my throat as I peered through the porthole for one last look at the domes of Academy. At the moment, I loved it all, even Sergeant Swopes. Well, perhaps not all. Not Jenks.

Hours later we took our seats on the connecting shuttle for Lunapolis. We all had plans; mine included a tour of the First Warrens and of the Spaceflight Museum. We could have booked rooms in one of the less expensive hotels, but Arlene and I signed into Naval barracks. Though we were now on salary, we had no savings to squander. I'd had to draw against advance pay for my leave.

By the first night I exhausted the tourist sights I thought would last a week. The Museum of Spaceflight consisted mostly of replicas, and I'd seen more vintage craft in my years at Academy than in the exhibits. First Warrens were fascinating, though. I struggled to picture the early settlers living in such primitive conditions.

I spent my second day of leave in a bar, and my second night curled over a toilet, retching until there was nothing more to bring up. I passed my third day battling a monumental headache and an overwhelming sense of shame; by evening I sought out the Reunification Church and prayed forgiveness for my folly.

It was the fourth day, my last, that I summoned the courage to explore the lower warrens.

Like any city, Lunapolis had its good districts. Old Lunapolis wasn't one of them. Dives beyond description offered vices I'd dreamed of in the privacy of my sheets, as well as others I'd hadn't dared to imagine. The health officer's lecture ringing in my ears, I studiously avoided most establishments, ended up alone in a seedy café that my young eyes saw as worldly.

I ordered dinner, boldly agreed to wine. I had no experience with liquors, and let the waiter choose. What I was served bore a strong resemblance to bulkhead cleanser. Nonetheless, I sipped it in manly fashion. Presently, a young woman drifted past my table, stopped to say hello. Shortly after, she was sitting across from me, chatting comfortably. Lynette.

After dinner she took me for a walk. I'd read of a certain type of woman, in histories. I prepared to refuse, indignantly, her demand for money. To my relief, she asked for none. Instead, she put her arm through mine, whispered her desires in my ear. I stared unbelievingly. Did people really do those things?

I had no apartment, and bringing Lynette back to Naval barracks was unthinkable. With little more than a reproachful look she galvanized me into thumbing through my wallet. I tossed bills onto the hotel counter with desperate bravado. The room was as dingy as its location had promised, but Lynette didn't seem to mind. "You and me are the whole world, Nicky. Nothing else is real."

She planted me in a chair, draped herself in my lap, nestled close. I kissed her shyly while she fondled me, whispered of the bliss to come. She put my hands where she wanted them.

At her urging I stripped off my wonderful new uniform, trying to pretend I was back in barracks, that no one but fellow cadets observed my exposed skin. Lynette took off her halter, pressed her hardened nipples against my hairless chest.

A few moments after, I slipped between cold sheets, aflame with fantasies. Lynette pressed close, and I strove to please her. Somehow, her twists and turns were always in the wrong direction. I locked my arms around her, pulled her tight, but to no avail. My lust faded to insignificant proportions. I closed my eyes, willing away the shame.

At first I thought Lynette was trying to excite me anew, and I struggled to cooperate. That seemed to please her, but despite my passionate desire, my tumescence faded to naught. Now her fingers grew cruel, jabbing at my groin, dispelling what little excitement remained.

"Is that how a man acts?" Her voice was cruel.

"I'm—I need—stop that!" I caught her wrist, pulled it away.

"If I knew you were so tiny I wouldn't have bothered. How old are you, joey? Thirteen?"

I twisted away, lay with my back to her, nursing unspeakable hurt. Along with the shame came remorse that I had failed her. "I'm sorry, Lynette. Give me a minute, I'll be all right."

She seemed to calm. Presently she stroked me again. "All right, honey. It's okay. Don't cry." Gratefully I turned back to her arms. For many minutes she was patient, until at last I began to respond. In her eagerness she kissed too hard, bit my lip. I yelped, jerked my face away, tried to concentrate. My hands roamed her body, settled on her breasts. She went inert as a rag doll.

After a moment, I stopped. It was no use; perhaps our chemistry was wrong. I sat up. "I'm sorry. I'll go."

"Running away?" Her voice held disbelief.

"No." I fished for my shorts. "Just going."

She sat up. "Your daddy's in Wales, you said? How would he feel if he knew you were with me?"

About the way I felt, just now. I grabbed my shirt.

"Know something, little boy? The one thing that would disgust him more than you lying here sweating is you not even being man enough to do it!" Her eyes blazed. "There's nothing down there, joey! You're a blank!"

"Why are you doing this?" I jammed my feet into my shoes.

"You'll never be good enough, not for any woman! Try men!"

I slapped at her. She pulled her head out of the way; my fingers barely grazed her cheek.

"Go home, joeyboy! Play with it until you learn how!"

I snatched my jacket and tie, ran to the door. Somehow I got it unbolted, fled down the hall, fumbled at the corridor hatch.

A shrill voice pursued me. "Freak! Do you have a vagina hidden down there?" Her breath came in short rasps as she followed me into the hallway. "You're useless!"

I glanced back, frozen in the agony of my degradation. Her face was contorted with passion, her lips full. She rubbed her hand against her crotch. "Faggot freak!"

I dashed blindly through the dirty corridors as if Satan himself were behind me. Perhaps he was.

Long hours later, I stumbled back to Naval barracks, my feet aching from the unnoticed miles I'd plodded. By now I was past tears, past caring, past life itself. I averted my eyes, certain everyone could read the humiliation in my face, and its cause.

I tapped in my hatch code, slipped into my cabin. I leaned against the hatchway, eyes shut. I tried not to weep, failed. Clawing off my sweat-soaked clothes, I dropped on the bed, jumped off immediately. I wasn't fit for bed. I fled into the head, turned on the shower, stood gratefully under its steaming warmth. Endless minutes passed while I tried to wash away the woman's foul imprecations.

Why had she destroyed me? Could I have deserved

that? The hot spray of water caressed me. Despite myself, my body began to relax. Finally, reluctantly, I took a deep breath, turned off the tap, toweled myself dry.

Celibacy wouldn't be so terrible; someday I might even get used to it. In the meantime there was U.N.S. *Helsinki;* duty would help.

A towel wrapped around my waist, I stepped into the bedroom. Far too miserable to sleep, at least I could pray, and perhaps, before morning, find peace.

Someone pounded at the hatch. I ignored it; in my new life I'd be a hermit. Anything else was unthinkable.

More hammering. If I refused to answer, they'd go away.

"Nicky?"

Damn it, Arlene. Not now. Not even you. I flung myself onto the bed, buried my head in the pillow.

After a time she went away, and I was left alone with Lynette. The vile words echoed. "Freak! Play with it! Try men!" I tossed and turned, sat to retrieve the Bible from my duffel. Sitting on the edge of the bed, I leafed through its familiar pages. Father, forgive me. I was foolish, and I despise myself.

Keep thee from the evil woman, from the flattery of the tongue of a strange woman.

Please, Lord. I repent. Let me forget.

For by means of a whorish woman a man is brought to a piece of bread.

I let the Book fall closed. A lump of bread. For the sake of lust, I have reduced myself to that.

Another knock. "Nicky?"

I sighed. She'd knock again every few minutes, unless I spoke. "Not now, Arlene."

"Just for a minute."

Cursing under my breath I crossed to the hatch, flung it open. "Now what?"

Cadet Sanders—Midshipman Sanders, now—grinned at the towel around my waist. "I like your style. Quite a uniform." Her eyes danced, her breath smelled of sweet wine.

"What do you want?"

She studied my face. "Headache?"

"For God's sake, Arlene! Have your say and let me alone!"

She drew herself up. "Prong yourself! I came to say farewell; wine makes me foolish. Skip it!"

"You stupid bitch!"

Her slap rocked me back on my heels. My hand shot to my stinging face.

"What an ass you are, Nicky! I hate you!" She stalked off.

I paced my room, rubbing my face, cursing a steady stream of obscenities. Passing the chair I gave it a savage kick, spent the next minutes hopping and clutching my throbbing toes. Finally, exasperated, humiliated and in misery, I thrust myself into bed and turned out the light.

For weeks I tossed and turned. At last I gave up, turned on the light, learned that less than an hour had passed.

Damn it, Arlene, why did you have to stir me up? So what if I forgot my manners? I've had the most awful day of my life, and—

No, it wasn't my most awful day. That had been spent kneeling over a blanket on the cold damp grass, in a stadium far, far away.

"Geez, you have a temper, Nicky."

Oh, shut up, Jason, you're dead and gone. I miss you, but don't nag.

"All right." The voice faded.

No, Jase, come back!

Silence. I hunched over my knees, bowed my head, weeping. I'm sorry. I didn't mean it.

The reply was as if a whisper. *"You talking to me or her?"*

You. No, her. Both of you.

Silence.

I reached for my clothes. Moments later, I slipped through the hatch, started down the hall, realized I didn't know her room number. Why was life so bloody complicated? I plodded to the front desk, waited for the rating to look up from his holo.

"Midshipman Sanders; what room?"

His eyebrow raised. "We don't give out rooms."

I spoke with someone else's voice. "You do tonight!"

He stared, found something in my eyes that persuaded him. "Three fifteen."

I climbed the stairs two at a time, hurried to her door. All right, I'd abase myself. She meant that much to me, or had once. For old times' sake, she deserved it.

I knocked. No answer. "Arlene?"

I waited, heard no sound. I swallowed. "I understand, Arlene. Whatever you think of me, you're right. I'm sorry." It was so inadequate, I could say no more. I crept away.

I opened the stairwell door, bumped into someone coming through the other way. "Sorry, I—"

"What are you doing here?"

"I went to your room. Where were you?"

Arlene's voice was small. "At your room, knocking. You wouldn't answer."

"What did you want?"

I held up a hand to forestall her answer. "I came to apologize. I'm a fool, and cursing you was"—I turned away—"despicable." I forced myself to meet her eye.

She said, "I don't know what came over me, telling you off. I just wanted to say good-bye. In barracks I acted tough, but inside, I feel sentimental. Lonely. I—Nicky, don't turn away, let me see! Your eyes, I've never seen you look—why are you crying?"

I mumbled, "It's nothing."

"Oh, Nicky." She drew my head against her shoulder. Grateful beyond words, I succumbed to her caress. After a moment, I straightened, wiped my eyes. "It's been an awful day."

"Tell me."

I couldn't possibly. Still, the urge to confess was almost unbearable. I could talk about some of it, perhaps. Not the worst parts. "Not here." I led her to my room.

Arlene perched on my bed, cross-legged, as time and again she had on Farside. "Tell me."

I began with the casual conversation at my restaurant table. Bit by bit, as if drawn by a magnet, the story tumbled forth. I thought to pass over the details, found I could not. At the end I lay on my side, eyes shut tight, humiliated.

I expected consolation, but her tone was hard as nails. "Can you find her again?"

"Why?"

"I'll kill her."

Awed, I looked up, found her eyes. She meant it. I muttered, "I deserved it."

"Don't be an idiot." She jumped to her feet, paced, stopped to slam the bulkhead with her fist. "The Molesters, they call themselves. A sex cult. The men find young girls, the women boys. They . . . humiliate them. It's how they get their zarks."

I turned on my back. "How do you know?"

She colored. "When the middies had me standing regs, one of them thought it would scare me." She swore fluently. "The worst hazing we ever had wasn't that awful."

"No."

"The bitch wanted to scar you forever."

A whisper. "She did."

Arlene pushed me aside without thinking, sat. "Now you'll think of her every time. Have you ever had sex?"

"Arlene!"

"Just asking. I have. Last year, twice. With joes from a second-year dorm."

"Lord God in heaven."

"Forget I asked. It's no big thing." She patted my forehead. "Jesus, Nick."

A long moment passed. My voice was muffled. "Tonight was the first time." I studied the far bulkhead, my cheeks on fire.

Arlene looked at her watch. "I report in six hours. So little time."

"I know. Get some sleep."

"That's not what I meant." She began to unbutton her tunic.

"What are you doing?"

"Taking off my clothes. It's better that way."

I sat quickly. "Stop it! Not with you, and anyway I couldn't, after tonight."

"Why not with me?"

"You don't do it with bunkies!"

"We're not, anymore. I'm *Freiheit* and you're *Helsinki,* remember?" She slipped out of her slacks.

I cried, "Arlene, I can't! Don't make me try, I'm begging you."

She hesitated, leaned over to brush her cheek against my chest. "If that's what you want. But I'm lonely. Can I stay, just to talk?"

I cast about for a way to refuse without doing her more hurt. I found none. "All right." Somehow, the night would pass.

A while later we nestled in the dark under the covers. "Poor Robbie. He wanted so much to make middy." Her voice was soft.

"They won't keep him long."

"I know." She sighed. "He cried, after Lights Out."

"I heard too."

"Hold me, Nicky."

An hour passed. I dozed in the comfort of her warmth. Then, abruptly, I woke. "Arlene, what are you—"

"Don't talk." She snuggled closer. "You're decent, Nicky. You're kind, under that righteous pose. Anyone can see that." Her soft fingers stroked my flank.

"Oh, Arlene, if only it were true." Still, grateful, I offered a shy kiss.

Her voice held wonder. "I think I love you, Nicky." Her lips met mine. I delved into her mouth, and presently, elsewhere.

Arlene's fingers brushed my Captain's bars. "Who would have thought, sir? So soon."

I closed my eyes, tried to shake away the despair. "It didn't happen like the holo stories. Not remotely."

"I know." As if recalling her surroundings she took a step back, cleared her throat. "I can see it in your eyes."

"I'm all right." My tone was gruff. "Tell me about yourself." We cleared the ladder well, started down to Level 3.

Her laugh was light and brittle. "They bounced me all over the Navy. *Freiheit,* then *Bolivar,* then Admiralty. Now here."

We climbed down to Level 2. "When did you make Lieutenant?"

"Four years ago. A fluke, really; if Captain Voorhees hadn't—"

The alarms shrieked. "BATTLE STATIONS! ALL HANDS TO BATTLE STATIONS!" Pritcher's voice echoed in the speakers.

Arlene Sanders stamped her foot. "What's the matter with the man? We've all had enough!" She started up the ladder.

"He wants to impress the brass. If they—"

The Captain's tone was ragged. "Battle Stations! This is no drill!"

"Oh, Jesus!" Arlene tore up the ladder to Level 2. For a second, I gaped. Then I raced after.

Swiftly as she ran, Arlene was only a step ahead when she charged through the bridge hatch. I dived past just as the Captain slapped the emergency close. The hatch slammed, isolating us from the rest of the ship. The middy of the watch was nowhere to be seen; only the Captain, Admiral Duhaney, Arlene and I.

Arlene dived for her console, flipped to the plotting screen. "Lieutenant Sanders repor—"

"Three of them!" Pritcher's voice quavered. He waved at the simulscreen. "In the training holos the fish didn't seem so . . . so big . . ."

Reports crackled from the speaker. "Comm room manned and ready, sir!"

"Engine room secure, sir! Full power available for thrusters!"

Duhaney clutched the back of the Captain's chair. "Harry, take us out of here!"

Pritcher seemed not to hear. "They can't show up so soon, even if they Fuse faster than we do!"

"Hydroponics secure!"

"Three encroachments confirmed, Captain." Arlene.

"Lasers up and ready, sir!"

"Distances a hundred meters and closing, the second is half a kilometer." She spun up her magnification. "Just a moment on the third."

"Harry—"

"Shut up, I'm thinking!" Pritcher pounded the console.

Admiral Duhaney looked astonished but fell silent.

Icy tentacles gripped my stomach. On the simulscreen, a fish off the port bow seemed close enough to touch. Slowly, it began to form a tentacle.

"Third fish two kilometers, closing fast." Arlene hesitated.

"Captain, we're ready to open fire." She waited. "Sir, may I give the order?"

Duhaney stirred. "Harry, say something!"

I looked over the Captain's shoulder to his console. The laser safeties were still on lock. Pritcher's hands grasped the armrests of his black leather chair.

Casually, I stepped between Pritcher and the simulscreen, bent to see his face. His eyes were glazed.

My tone was soft. "Captain Pritcher, get hold of yourself. Defend your ship!"

No answer.

"Mr. Pritcher, *please!*"

He whispered. "The size of them. They're . . . monstrous."

"Laser control to bridge. Targets acquired."

I cleared my throat, spoke in a normal voice. "Captain, may we clear the safeties?"

"Harry, order a Fuse!" Duhaney.

"Belay that!"

Duhaney whirled at my voice.

"Our coordinates are set for Vega, Admiral. Even if we plot new ones we're too close to Earth to Fuse safely." We risked meltdown, if not worse.

An alarm clanged. Harlan, the puter. "Two encroachments at six kilometers!"

Pritcher whispered; I bent close to hear. " . . . can't be here so soon . . . can't . . ."

The fish alongside twirled its tentacle, ready to throw its acid into our hull.

I swung to Arlene. "Relieve him. I'm not a member of the ship's company; I can't."

Her eyes searched mine, troubled. "They'll hang me, Nick!"

"The Admiral's here! Ask him!"

The tentacle twirled faster.

"Harry, Fuse the ship!" Duhaney was hoarse.

I snapped, "Will you take command, Admiral?"

"What?"

"You heard me. Take the ship!"

"I can't—I mean, I haven't served shipboard for years, not since—"

"Then shut up!" I leaned over Pritcher's shoulder, slapped the laser safeties off, and committed mutiny.

It was a rule so absolute, so ancient, that it needed no restatement. A ship had but one Captain. Rebellion against his authority merited death. And a Captain represented not just civil authority, but the will of Lord God Himself.

There is no power but of God: the powers that be are ordained of God . . . they that resist shall receive to themselves damnation.

So be it. Now I was twice damned.

I thumbed the caller to shipwide frequency. "This is Nicholas Seafort, Captain, U.N.N.S., transmitting the orders of Captain Pritcher." Stating it any other way would only cause confusion.

"Lasers, fire as you bear!" Almost instantly, the lights dimmed, brightened.

"Two squirts, port thrusters. Middy of the watch, get your arse to the bridge! You too, Pilot!" The Pilot was best trained for the tight maneuvering ahead.

The speaker crackled. "We got him!"

I squinted. The fish alongside spewed protoplasm from numerous holes. Its tentacle had stopped twirling. "Go for the nearest first! Fire at will!"

Duhaney said tentatively, "Nick, are you sure you want—"

"Captain Pritcher, Engine room reporting—"

"What is it, Engine room? Pritcher's busy."

"Secretary Franjee wants me to ask who's in charge and will we Fuse to safety."

I snapped, "We've no time for civilians!" I spun the dial. "Comm Room, get off a signal to Fleet Ops. *Wellington* under attack, coordinates . . . you have our position?"

"Yes, sir."

"Laser room reporting, second target Fused to safety!"

A hammering at the hatchway. I swiveled the camera, saw a middy, slapped open the hatch. "Midshipman Rives report—"

"Comm Room, report to Admiralty we have five fish, one dead, the others closing fast."

The puter blared. "Encroachment seventy meters! Another at two hundred fifty meters!"

The frantic middy saluted Captain Pritcher. "Sir, I got caught behind the section six hatch, there were half a dozen locks between — "

Pritcher gave the middy an agreeable nod. "No hurry, Mr.

Rives. Is Mr. Franjee ready for the commissioning?" A fleck of spittle glistened on his chin.

I growled, "Belay that, boy! Comm Room, repeat until they acknowledge, and make that *seven* fish. Ask if there's any help nearby!" There wasn't, I knew. *Wellington* was positioned alone, to emphasize her magnificent splendor. "Laser Control, acquire new targets! Harlan, help plot laser coordinates."

Harlan's voice was cold. "You have no authority aboard *Wellington,* Mr. Seafort. Only Captain Pritcher can—"

"Listen here, puter—"

"Let me, sir." Arlene's tone was urgent. "Harlan, I'm Lieutenant Sanders, officer of the watch. Acknowledge."

"Acknowledged. Of course I know you, that's not the—"

"Acquire targets, puter. Do whatever else—"

"No, Arlene!"

"—Captain Seafort asks."

Too late. She'd be hanged at my side. No time to think of it now. "Arlene, plot a Fuse."

"Where to, sir?" Arlene's face was pale.

It didn't matter; Fusion was a final resort, and might well destroy the ship, if we commenced so close to Earth's mass. "Uh—one point one four AUs should be far enough. Keep us clear of encroachments." If we Defused into space occupied by a planetary body, we'd never know. They'd notice the result on Earth, though, even without a telescope. "Midshipman! Help her calculate."

"Aye aye—I mean, Captain Seafort? What's the matter with Capt—"

"Do what you're told!"

The youngster bent to Arlene's console.

Alarms. Harlan. "Ms. Sanders, eleven new encroachments, one amidships at eighty meters, the others—" I switched off the buzzer. A moment of blessed peace.

"Laser Room, get the midships fish before he throws inside our range!" A warship's guns could depress inward to within a few degrees of its hull, but no farther, else an excited tech might skewer his own ship's sensors.

The aft fish was also ready to throw; he'd Defused with a tentacle already formed. Once the protoplasm separated it would become a much harder target.

"Opening hatch for the Pilot!" Arlene didn't wait for approval.

"Pilot Arnaud reporting." A young man, gaunt. "Who has the conn?"

"Seafort, at the moment." Duhaney.

The Pilot dived for his console, taking in the simulscreen. "Suggest we maneuver to port, that'll give us a few extra sec—"

The tentacle separated from the fish, swirled toward us. I shouted, "Damage Control, stand by for breach! All hands to suits!" Damn my stupidity; that should have been my first order.

"Christ, they're swarming all over!"

"Laser Room, be silent!" How dare they babble on bridge frequency?

The puter. "Two fish closing astern!"

"Where did they come from?" I grabbed the caller. "Laser room, fire on the fish astern!" I whirled to Arlene. "I need a Fusion plot!"

"Working on it, sir." Arlene's fingers flew. "Just another couple of . . . there! We're eighteen minutes from Fusion safety, at flank speed. Mr. Arnaud, confirm!"

"Belay that, Pilot! Stay with the thrusters, keep the fish away from us." I hesitated. "Head us toward Fusion safety if you can."

"Son of a bitch, they're Fusing as we hit them! Sorry, sir, Laser Control here. They Fuse away and reappear, or maybe it's new ones. We keep losing them!"

"Harlan, confirm Fusion plot."

The puter's reply seemed instantaneous. "Plot confirmed to two decimals, divergence at—"

"Close enough. Engine Room, acknowledge coordinates, stand by to Fuse!"

With *Wellington's* mass, Fusing from our current position might well mean death. But if our end seemed inevitable I'd cast *Wellington* to Lord God's mercy, rather than that of the fish.

"Bridge, I need the Captain's personal order to prepare—"

"He's, ah, indisposed, Chief."

"I'm following procedures. I don't care who's—"

I snarled, "Acknowledge *this instant*, or I'll execute you for mutiny in the face of the enemy!"

The speaker was silent for but a moment. "Aye aye, Bridge, standing by."

"Fuse, for God's sake!" Admiral Duhaney jabbed his finger at the simulscreen. "Take the risk. There must be a dozen fish out—"

"Fourteen, at the moment." My hand shot to the simulscreen controls, halted. "Harlan, focus aft!"

Suddenly I was viewing the tapered drive tubes. I recoiled; the fish were so close they seemed within the cabin. The skin of one of them seemed to agitate. Protoplasm spewed from a glowing hole made by one of our lasers. The alien drifted away, propelled by the force of its own death. Meanwhile its companion had begun to grow a tentacle. I looked closer, blanched. The creature's skin swirled in a pattern I remembered all too well.

"Master-at-arms, break out weapons! Prepare to repel boarders astern. Chief, get all civilians topside, flank. The fish is launching outriders."

Duhaney yanked at my arm. "Answer me, Seafort! Why haven't you Fused?"

I shook him off. "Comm Room, did you get off your message?"

"Yes, sir. Fleet Ops says to stand by for instructions. The nearest armed sloop can reach us in two hours."

"No! Tell them not to send the sloop, we'll fight or try to escape!" I swiveled to the Admiral. "If all else fails I'll Fuse, but—"

"The Deputy SecGen's aboard! Once the fish melt our tubes, we're done. Get us out of here!"

"Where to? Do you think—"

"Obey orders, Seafort!"

I couldn't fight the fish and the Admiral as well. I slammed my fist on the console. "You still don't understand! What brought them here?"

His mouth worked in rage.

I shouted, "Months ago I urged you to build a caterwaul bomb, but you did nothing while fish closed in on home system. Do you get it yet, Admiral? *THEY HEAR US FUSE!*" I snatched off my cap, hurled it to the deck. The young middy recoiled, white-faced.

Again the speaker crackled. "Bridge, the fish launched those outrider beasts! They're bypassing the drive shaft, going for our stern lasers!"

I ignored the caller. "We can run, but not far enough to gain any time, and they'll hear and follow. So will every other fish in the Solar System."

"You had coordinates for Vega. Damn it, you still have!"

"*Wellington* isn't stocked for an interstellar cruise. If we aim for a far target and Defuse short, Lord God knows where we'll end up, and we'll be alone. If we stay on course to Vega, we'll be eating each other before we're a month out!"

We eyed each other, both in a rage.

I spun around my chair. "Take over! Fuse wherever in hell you want!" I thumbed the caller. "Engine Room, stand by for orders from the Admiral." I grabbed Duhaney's hand, slapped the caller into it, strode to the hatch. "Fuse! Save yourself the trouble of hanging me." I struck open the hatch.

"Seafort!" The Admiral's voice was unsteady. "I—Jesus, don't leave the bridge."

"Take the conn, or give it to Sanders!"

"Please . . . for God's sake! I told you I'm not seagoing Navy. I don't—it's been too long!"

New alarms shrieked. "STERN PORT LASER DISABLED! HULL DAMAGE, LEVEL 3. DECOMPRESSION IMMINENT!" Arlene reached across, silenced the clamor.

"Nick, please." Duhaney was pale.

Arlene's eyes met mine. More lives were at stake than my own. I swung back to the console. "Captain Pritcher, can you take over?"

The Captain smiled. "Oh, yes, quite." He turned to the middy. "Deactivate lasers. Stand down from Battle Stations." The middy stared. Pritcher reached to Duhaney for the caller.

I didn't hesitate. "Midshipman Rives, escort the Captain to his quarters, by force if necessary."

The boy's eyes were saucers. He gulped. "Aye aye, sir." He leaned over Pritcher, spoke softly in his ear. The Captain shook his head. The boy glanced at me, whispered again.

I pried the caller from the Admiral's limp hand. "Midshipman Tenere, report with your cadets to the Master-at-arms! Harlan, open corridor hatches for them. Master-at-arms, issue my midshipman laser pistols."

I swiveled back to Harlan. "Status report for all stations!"

"Engine room fully operational, Captain. Comm room—"

"Cancel. Status regarding attackers, summary."

"Eleven fish in area. Level 3 portside hull sensors inoperative. Attack assumed in progress by outriders from fish astern. Amidships—"

"What's the stern fish doing now?"

"It's inert, assumed dead. Amidships we have four to six fish, Defusing and Fusing again at irregular intervals. Update, now three fish. New encroachments astern! Total of twelve surrounding ship."

"Pilot, turn us about, our stern lasers are gone!" At my left the middy argued quietly with Captain Pritcher.

The Pilot's bony hands flicked the thrusters. "We're no bloody rowboat, it takes time to—"

"I know." *Wellington's* middy was still urging his Captain. "Mr. Tenere, report to the bridge!"

"HULL BREACH! DECOMPRESSION SECTION THREE! HULL—" I flicked off the alarms.

I pray You, Lord God. Help us.

"Comm Room reporting. Signal from Fleet Ops to Captain Pritcher. From Vice Admiral Llewelin Stykes, officer of the watch. 'Take all necessary evasive action. Seek further instructions from Admiral Duhaney on board your vessel.' End message."

I gazed at Duhaney, said nothing.

The Admiral flushed. "They're playing it safe."

"He must have political ambitions, sir." My courtesy was elaborate.

"Master-at-arms calling bridge! Two outriders burned their way into section three! I have them on camera. I've got four men in there with lasers. Damn, they're fast!"

"Laser Room, fire on the stern fish the moment your midships lasers bear."

"Another few degrees, sir."

A cry from the speaker. "My men are down! It rolled right over them. Christ!"

"Hold the corridor hatches to either side of section three!" If the aliens had the run of the ship . . .

"Aye aye, sir, trying. How do we fight these things?"

"Burn them, full laser charge. Their mothership is dead. If you get the two . . ."

"Right." He rang off.

"Harlan, status!"

"Two more fish disabled, one Fused. Eight attackers, three alongside, remainder closing astern."

The Pilot fired the port thrusters with a savage squirt. "Two can play at that!" Ponderously, *Wellington* turned.

I watched the screen. Three fish within throwing distance. With our aft lasers disabled, we couldn't protect our stern. If I allowed damage to the tubes, we were done. My hand hovered over the Fusion controls.

The fish nearest our stern released a burst of propellant from its blowhole, and drifted closer to the drive shaft. Responding ever faster to her thrusters, *Wellington* turned on her axis, withdrawing her stern from the advancing form.

Harlan's tone was urgent. "Armed party approaching, not ship's company. I've sealed the hatch."

"Arlene, let them in." In the simulscreen, one of the sternside fish had swung into range. As I watched, half a dozen lasers pierced it.

"Aye aye, sir." Sanders got up, slapped open the hatch.

"Midshipman Tenere reporting, with the cadets." Kevin Arnweil, Kyle Drew and the rest crowded onto the bridge. Jerence Branstead was white-faced.

I said, "Captain Pritcher is ill and disrupting the bridge. Take him to his cabin. Now!"

"Aye aye, sir." Adam swallowed, approached the Captain with a resolute face. "Sir, get up, please."

"Midshipman Rives, place yourself under arrest in the wardroom."

"Aye aye, sir. I tried, he just wouldn't let—"

I shouted, "Off the bridge!" Ashen, the boy scurried out of sight.

"Boland, take Mr. Pritcher's arm!" Adam's tone brooked no argument. "Arnweil, help him!"

In a moment, the cadets had hustled *Wellington*'s Captain off his bridge. Arlene stared somberly into her console.

I slipped into the sacred Captain's seat. "Harlan, status update."

"Six fish, two of them astern, one a kilometer off the port bow. The remaining three amidships, starboard side. One is alongside laser bank three, closing fast."

"Pilot?"

He licked his lips, eyes glued to his screen. "The engine room is critical."

"I agree."

"I'll try some spin on the vertical axis . . ." Again he fired our thrusters.

"Master-at-arms calling bridge! The section two hatch is heating. We have our lasers trained on it."

"Fire the instant you see a target."

"Amen. That is, aye aye, sir. I have another armed party at the hatch to four."

"The outriders can just as easily burn through our bulkheads as our hatches."

"Yes, sir, but I can't be everywhere. The camera shows them skittering back and forth in there. If they go for the bulkheads we should get a sensor alarm."

"Where are the civilians? Franjee, the Senators?"

"We moved them to Level 2 mess hall. I have a detail guarding them."

"Very well, keep me posted."

"Laser Room reporting. Two fish amidships destroyed!"

I glanced at the screen. If no more came, we might just make it. My hand eased off the Fusion control.

"Harlan, are any more Defusing?"

He sniffed. "I'd tell you if there were."

I bit back a reply; no point in arguing with a puter.

I snapped off the caller, and paced.

All I had to worry about was decompression in section three, two aliens roaming our corridors, and four fish maneuvering Outside. No cause for alarm. My teeth bared in a travesty of a grin.

I was ready to order the master-at-arms to unseal the section three hatch and attack, when the outriders saved us the trouble. They burned through to section four, where withering fire from the master-at-arm's company turned them to smoking stains on the deck.

"Class A decontamination in effect! Every man to the sickbay for inoculation the moment he's desuited!" I rekeyed the caller. "Continuous fire at remaining fish!"

While we disposed of the last four fish, I tensed for new alarms at any moment.

But the screen was quiet.

Admiral Duhaney sat in the chair I'd vacated. His fingers worked the fabric of his jacket.

After half an hour with no new fish, I began to breathe easier. In an hour, I stood down from Battle Stations. The crew needed a rest; before the skirmish, Captain Pritcher had worked them for hours drilling for the brass.

"Pilot, plot a course for Lunapolis." *Wellington* remained functional, but her damage needed repair.

"Aye aye, sir." His fingers worked the keys. The moment co-ordinates were confirmed I had him fire thrusters at full power, heedless of the waste of propellant.

Chapter 18

I took up the caller. "Attention, passengers and crew. *Wellington* has beaten back an attack by some fifteen fish. We sustained hull damage, decompression of one section, and three dead. We are returning to Earthport Station for repairs. Admiralty has been notified. Lieutenant Hollis, report to the bridge."

My eye fell on Duhaney. I looked away. One more duty, before the ignominious end to my career. I said into the caller, "U.N.S. *Wellington* has proven herself a proud ship of the line. With Secretary Franjee's permission, commissioning will be held on the bridge in two hours." I replaced the caller in its socket.

As my adrenaline ebbed, I became conscious of the electric silence of the bridge. Finally, I stood. "Ms. Sanders, I surrender the ship to lawful authority. Lieutenant Hollis will take the conn. Admiral, what is your wish?"

He barked, "Say what you mean."

"I face court-martial. Shall I report to the brig?"

"I—God!" He hesitated. "Yes. Wait, not until the commissioning. Christ, what a position you've put me in."

I waited.

"You went too far, Seafort. Not just with Pritcher. You refused your orders, in front of the others. It was mutiny." He raised his eyes to mine. "Yes, we'll try you. As quietly as we can, for the Navy's sake."

Good. Better that than Wyvern's way. "Aye aye, sir."

"Just a moment, please." Arlene Sanders's voice was soft, but its edge compelled our attention.

"This doesn't concern you, Lieutenant."

She stood. "Begging your pardon, Admiral, it does. Think twice before court-martialing Nick."

Duhaney's eyes flashed dangerously. "That sounds close to a threat, young lady."

"No, sir, just a fact. Even if you're so morally low as to exe-

335

cute him after he saved you, I'm a witness. They'll interrogate me under drugs, so I can't lie to protect him. But I don't have to."

Duhaney raised an eyebrow, said only, "Go on."

"You dithered after Mr. Pritcher became ill. I was the ship's officer at hand, so Nick asked me to relieve my Captain. I couldn't. I'm a coward, and now I know it."

"Arlene—"

"Shut up, Nick. I mean, Captain, sir." She faced Duhaney, her jaw set. "In desperation Nicky asked you to take the conn, and you also refused. That left him senior officer present, and he took over. True, he wasn't a member of the ship's company, but that's a technicality, and you know it."

"Are you finished, Lieutenant?"

"Nearly, sir. With *Wellington's* Captain in a funk, you pestered Nick to make wrong decisions. That's what I'll testify. At the trial I won't be under drugs. I'll tell the truth, but my manner will say all that's necessary about your behavior, as well as Nick's."

What in God's heaven was Arlene doing? Challenging the Admiral just to save me? I couldn't allow it. I opened my mouth to speak.

No. To save herself. She faced death for concurring in my mutiny. I closed my mouth, held my breath. Lord, help her save herself, at least.

Duhaney shook his head, as if amused. "You dare threaten me, Lieutenant?"

"Not threaten, sir. Warn. Yes, I dare. I don't want to be part of a Navy that destroys Nick Seafort." She turned away quickly, ran her hand across her eyes. My brow wrinkled. Could it be for me, after all? She turned back. "Make your choice, sir. We'll both have to live with it."

I clutched the chair, my knees weak. Perhaps the aftermath of action.

Duhaney seemed more curious than outraged. "What would you have me do?"

"Cover for him. He effectively relieved Pritcher, and you made no objection, therefore you concurred. You're Admiral of the Fleet, and have authority to authorize it."

"So your bargain is, I leave Seafort be, and—"

"No, sir, no bargain. You do as you wish. I'm advising you of my testimony."

Glowering, he wheeled on me. "She's another of your ilk. You trained her?"

"No, sir. *With* her. Ms. Sanders always had the makings of a fine officer." I knew my endorsement was worse than silence, but I couldn't say less.

Lieutenant Hollis knocked at the hatch.

The Admiral growled, "Get out, both of you. I'll think it over."

"Aye aye, sir."

The bridge hatch slid closed behind us. After the frenzied action of our engagement, the corridor seemed strangely still. Arlene strode ahead of me to the ladder.

Thanks to her preposterous defense, I might escape the death I merited. But only because Duhaney was a politician, not a fighting sailor like his predecessor, Admiral Brentley. The Admiral had heard Arlene's threat as an offer to deal, and responded accordingly.

So now I could go back to Academy, saddled with my superior's displeasure, but with no other penalty save that of Lord God. I would concentrate on training my cadets for battles such as we'd just survived.

No. I'd forgotten about Senator Wyvern. My career was still done. For a moment I mourned its loss, then remembered *Wellington's* three crewmen who'd died fighting the aliens. Compared to their sacrifice, mine would be nothing. I closed my eyes, offered prayer for their souls.

At the foot of the ladder I paused, said lamely, "Arlene—Lieutenant—you shouldn't have antagonized him for me. I didn't need—"

"For you?" Her eyes reflected loathing. "For me, Captain Seafort. As penance."

"I don't—look, however you see it, I'm grateful beyond words. Seeing you today meant . . ." Tentatively, I put out my hand.

"Don't touch me! Even as Captain you haven't that right!"

I pulled my fingers back as if burned. Her eyes blazed. "I don't want ever to see you again. What you did to me was unspeakable!"

"What did I—"

"Asking me to relieve my Captain, in front of an Admiral? I'm not the wonderful Nick Seafort; they'd have hanged me without a moment's thought!" She stamped her foot. "You forced me to make the wrong choice between duty and death. We're not all heroes! I can't help my cowardice. You should have known when you put me to the test that I couldn't choose to die!"

"That's not—why would I think that of you?"

"Remember the airlock that malfunctioned in the Training Fuser? That day, I turned to jelly."

"Arlene, please. I never thought—"

"From now on, when I face you, I have to face myself! Get out of my sight, Nick Seafort. Get out of my life!" Without a salute she ran down the ladder, and out of view.

Stunned, I sagged against the bulkhead. I'd meant no harm. Meeting her again had been a ray of hope in the darkness of my soul. And now . . .

After a time I roused myself to join the others in the Level 2 mess hall. As I crossed the hatchway, conversation stopped cold. A barrage of flashes blinded me. Within seconds, half a dozen mediamen surrounded me, holocamera whirring, recorders thrust in my face.

"When did you realize Captain Pritcher lost his mind?"

"How does it feel to—"

"Look this way!"

"—a hero yet again?"

"Are the fish after you personally? Did you—"

"Should Pritcher be court-martialed? Will you testify?"

"—warn Pritcher about the caterwauling?"

"*BELAY THAT!*" My bellow stopped them in their tracks. I swiped at a holocamera. "Get that recorder out of my face!"

For a moment it worked. Senator Boland's eye held a glint of amusement. Then they pressed forward as if I hadn't spoken. "Was Pritcher glitched before the cruise? Did he—"

I turned in disgust, but they danced around me in full frenzy. "Was he crying when—tell us how it felt to—know you were sailing with a coward?"

I spun on my heel. "Captain Pritcher is a fine officer! He reacted to an unexpected fright the way any of you would. He's no coward!"

"Then why take over? Wasn't he disabled?"

I looked to Boland for sympathy, got a shrug, and glared at the nearest mediaman. "Ghouls! Captain Pritcher is ill and miserable. What will your headlines do to him? You're here to cover the commissioning; make your report out of that!"

The holoreporter grimaced. "Hey, joey, this is a bigger story. We can't ignore it."

"You'd destroy Pritcher for a day's story?"

"I'd do *anything* for top of the hour!" The others nodded agreement.

By relieving Pritcher I'd virtually ruined him; if there was any chance to salvage his career I had to divert the vicious publicity. My thoughts whirled. If they had something else to focus on, something of equal interest . . . But what could compare to the spectacle of a Captain cracking under fire?

I tried to contain my revulsion. "What about me?"

"You're the hero as usual, joey, but you've ducked every question we've ever asked. What can we write about you?"

"I'll trade. Me for Pritcher."

The mediaman perked up. "An interview? When?"

"Now, and again after the commissioning, if need be."

One of his colleagues intervened. "Not a five-minute jam. You'd have to open up."

"We'll be hours heading back to Lunapolis; I'll give you as long as you ask. But only if you kill the Pritcher story."

The second reporter looked to the others. "What do you think?"

I saw skepticism, nods of agreement. "It's all or none," I said. "Make up your minds." I poured a cup of hot coffee, turned a chair to face them. It was the least I could do for Pritcher. I, too, was locked in my cabin, sick and afraid.

One by one, they gathered round. The silent cameras spun. A mediaman cleared his throat. "What happened on the bridge today, Captain Seafort?"

"I assisted Captain Pritcher in a skirmish against the fish. We prevailed."

"Tell us your feelings about the fish."

I swallowed bile. A small payment on the punishment due me. "The fish? Well, obviously they're a great menace. What I've found odd about them is . . ."

* * *

The ceremony was an anticlimax, but I found it moving. If there was any doubt the Navy needed battlewagons such as *Wellington,* the attack had dispelled it.

Secretary Franjee spoke earnestly for the cameras; the mediamen dutifully recorded the commissioning. When it was over and the symbolic toasts drunk, I rounded up Adam and the cadets and took them to the lounge.

Walking the Level 2 corridor I marveled anew at the Navy's resourcefulness. Barely three hours after the attack, emergency hull patches were in place, the Level 2 corridor scrubbed and decontaminated, and shipboard life almost back to normal.

Almost, but not quite. Captain Pritcher lay sedated in his bunk, and three young seamen were no longer among the ship's company.

The risk of infection was too great to allow the bodies to remain in sickbay; *Wellington's* dead sailors were jettisoned from the aft airlock with little ceremony, and the lock itself decontaminated. The viral epidemics that had decimated *Portia* and other ships after invasion were taken seriously now; passengers and crew alike had lined up for inoculations.

In the lounge, Jerence Branstead piled his plate with delicacies. I repressed an urge to rebuke him; in perspective, it mattered not a bit. The other cadets clustered eagerly at the buffet.

"A word, sir?"

I turned, found myself face-to-face with Secretary Franjee. "Of course."

"I'm no tactician, Mr. Seafort. They send the fleet here, order it there, and I have no choice but to concur. But I'd like your opinion. Was it wise to gather so much of the top brass several hours from Lunapolis and the fleet's assistance?"

"I'm not part of—"

"Just between us, Captain, to go no further. Tell me."

I hesitated. Admiral Duhaney was no strategist, not a man to direct the fleet's operations. He'd proven that again on *Wellington's* bridge. And Lord God only knew how Pritcher had passed the psych tests; perhaps he too was someone's nephew. Or perhaps the tests couldn't calibrate the horror of a clash with the fish. On *Challenger's* bridge I'd yearned to close my mind to them as Pritcher had done. Now I had the ear of a politician with power to change the policies that had led to today's tragedy.

I took a deep breath. "As I said, sir, I'm not keyed in to fleet tactics; I'm just Academy Commandant. Still, it would seem . . ." Across the room, my eyes caught Duhaney's. He shifted his gaze.

I need have no loyalty to men like Duhaney. Ships might founder, sailors die, due to their fumbling and foolish decisions. I owed it to my compatriots to prevent that. Yet again I hesitated.

I was Navy, Franjee was not. That was all I need remember. "Hindsight is too easily mistaken for wisdom, sir. Naval decisions are made by men such as you and myself. We're fallible, but we do our best. *Wellington* was to take her place in the Home Fleet; it made sense to have the ceremony near her assigned post."

He searched my face. "And the risks?"

"Only three fish have ever been seen in home system. As a society, we've made the decision to combat them, not to cower and hide. There was no reason to think *Wellington* would be in greater danger here than moored at Earthport Station. Except . . ."

"Yes?"

I could have bitten off my tongue, but it was too late. Well, I'd already made my thoughts more than obvious, racing from the engine room to the bridge. "Except for caterwauling. I think that was unwise, and I've always said so. I'm sure fleet policy will be modified, now that we've had a graphic demonstration."

"Is that all you'll say?"

I felt almost at peace. "Yes, sir, it's all I know to say. If the Navy has problems, it also has procedures to correct them." Procedures like the court-martial I so richly deserved. In any event, I wouldn't wash the Navy's linen in the sight of civilians. Whatever foul crimes I'd committed, at least I was above betrayal.

Franjee let it be. After a few words of praise on my handling of *Wellington,* he drifted away. Within moments his place was taken by Richard Boland. The Senator made no pretense at small talk. "Captain, I have a request."

I waited for him to continue, yearning for a drink.

"Since our, ah, conversation a few months ago you'll notice I've done as you asked. I haven't inquired about Robert, either directly or through Admiralty." Yes, I'd noticed, assuming almost daily that his restraint would end, and I'd be forced to resign. I braced myself for another interference.

"Mr. Seafort, please don't interpret this as pressure. But, considering the nightmare we've all been through, and the fact that my son is no more than twenty feet away, would you take it amiss if I spoke to him?"

My hostility vanished. "For as long as you like." My tone was gruff. "He probably needs it more than you do; he's had a rough day."

"I'm grateful." He seemed to mean it.

"He'll relax more if I leave the room." I moved toward the hatch.

"No, if anyone deserves drinks and a peaceful meal, it's you. We'll wander outside, if you'll let him."

"Thank you." I snapped my fingers, beckoned to Adam Tenere, gave orders to let Robert Boland go with his father. I closed my eyes. Would that I could go with mine.

Hours later, we docked at Earthport Station.

I allowed the mediamen one last round of photos—a deal was a deal—and booked a shuttle groundside. Only my letter of resignation awaited.

It was early the next morning when we reached Devon. I saw the exhausted cadets to their dorms, gave Robert Boland an extra clap of assurance. Adam walked me back to Officers' Quarters. For most of the way we were silent.

"Is that how it is on a ship of the line, sir? Mostly quiet, then the alarms?"

He had no business speaking to me, unbidden, but now we were comrades in battle. "Some sailors can't take the boredom of Fusion," I told him. "Other than stand watch, there's nothing to do except what you make for yourself. But it's not a peaceful boredom; you never know when the siren will shriek, or why. Decompression, engine failure, the fish . . . The Navy's not for everyone."

"It's for me." He spoke with certainty. "Sir, the speakers were broadcasting most of the time you were on the bridge. Your orders—we all heard them."

"So?" I reeled with exhaustion.

"I—nothing, sir. I mean . . . someday, if . . . " He pounded his side. "On the bridge. I want to be like that." His voice grew embarrassed. "Like you."

I wheeled. "You may be stupid enough to think that, Mr. Tenere, but don't ever say it again in my presence!"

"But—aye aye, sir!"

"Go to bed!" I stalked off.

In my apartment, I flipped on my console while I undressed. No word from Eddie Boss; presumably that meant Annie was well. I'd call him later, to confirm. I glanced at the other messages, but the screen wavered. I flicked it off, fell into the dark.

Chapter 19

I dressed slowly for my last day in the United Nations Naval Service. Every act, even combing my hair, seemed fraught with significance. I selected a fresh-pressed jacket, resisted the temptation to don dress whites. Before leaving my apartment I thumbed the caller. "Page Mr. Tolliver to my office after breakfast."

I left to take a final walk around the grounds. The sun was barely above the treetops, but squads of ruddy-faced cadets were already concluding their morning exercises. I strode briskly to the gate, paralleled the long fence through the tree-shaded lawn. Not far from here, I'd sat with young Jerence Branstead during changeover. Once, I'd promised his father Harmon that I'd watch over him. After today I could do nothing to keep the pledge. In any event Jerence needed little help. He'd earned the second highest scores on the base.

I followed the track south to the classroom quadrangle. Many years ago, I'd left, thinking I was seeing them for the last time. Now, at last, it was to be so. I'd leave in ignominy, but I'd have time for Annie. Perhaps, in Father's house, I could repair the ruin of our marriage.

I stopped at an empty classroom. On the spur of the moment I stepped in, peered at the hallway pictures. Here, on my visit during Final Cull, I'd encountered two nervous young cadets, and met Sergeant Ibarez. What a hash I'd made of things since.

I checked my watch, and left. Today, it wouldn't do to be late.

I swung open the mess-hall door, and two hundred fresh-scrubbed cadets stood as one. "You may be seated!" I strode to my table.

Adam Tenere and the two lieutenants held their salute until I returned it. I pulled out my chair. "Good morning."

"Morning, sir." Jeff Thorne stared down at his plate.

Sandra Ekrit half ran to the table. "Sorry, Commandant. I was delayed."

"No problem. One demerit."

Tolliver regarded me with curiosity. "I hear there's a special issue of *Holoworld* this afternoon."

"I've no idea what you're talking about."

"Odd, since you're on the cover." He passed me the rolls. "You never stop, it seems. Congratulations on your latest exploit."

"Change the subject." My tone allowed no argument. "What was the Code Two you left on my console last night? I was too tired to decipher."

Tolliver glanced at the middies and the staff sergeants sharing our table. "Yes, I used the cipher. It wasn't for general distribution."

"But I no longer care." I realized I'd spoken the words aloud. Well, no matter. "Go ahead."

"I have a reply from the, ah, sergeant regarding that inventory question. A great deal of verbiage. Everything is as it should be. His reply completely ignores the serial numbers. Meanwhile, I ran some estimates on food purchases based on the figures from five years ago."

"Drop it."

"Aye aye, sir. Sorry, I always seem to be one command behind."

Jeff Thorne bristled. "Mr. Tolliver, would you have me answer you in the manner you speak to Captain Seafort?"

Tolliver rose to the occasion. "Certainly. I should get as I give." Nonetheless, he looked abashed.

Across the table, Sandra Ekrit toyed at her food, her expression sullen. I said with malice, "Perhaps two more demerits would improve your attitude, Ms. Ekrit?"

Her tone was reckless. "Perhaps they would, sir. I have no way to please you."

I gaped at the two lieutenants, astonished at her audacity.

Tolliver said, "I'll handle it. Middy, report to my cabin after the meal!"

"Aye aye—"

"Edgar, I'll need you at my office. Let Jeff instill sense and manners in this—this person. Ms. Ekrit, leave my table! Wait for Mr. Thorne outside his quarters. Regardless of what he gives you, six demerits."

"Aye aye, sir." Her rebellion doused, she fled to her fate.

I wheeled on Tolliver. "That's a result of your insolence. Blame yourself, not her."

"Regardless, she's still a middy talking to a Captain! The nerve—"

Jeff Thorne's voice was as oil poured on troubled waters. "She's having a bad day." His eye held a glint of humor. "We all do, at times."

I subsided, grumbling. Whether or not Thorne chose to cane Midshipman Ekrit, her manner would improve. Jeff had the knack. Once, when I'd been surly, he'd stood me against a bulkhead and . . . I blushed at the memory.

Downing a tasteless breakfast, I brooded on Sandra Ekrit. After a time I shrugged. It was no more than we could expect, demanding adult behavior and judgment from adolescents. Would the Navy be better to enlist its officers at a later age, as once had been the norm?

No, Britannia had ruled the waves for two glorious centuries, and they'd enlisted midshipman younger than ours. And there was the risk of melanoma T that demanded early exposure to N-waves. What was the answer, then?

Musing, I sipped my coffee.

"Midshipman Lea, sit up. One demerit." Billy jerked upright. Furtively, I straightened in my seat, kept my eyes glued to my holovid as if in rapt attention. I hated Law and Regs, but it was part of continuing education, now that I was a middy on *Helsinki*.

Lieutenant Jarewski paced the confines of the comm room, favoring his weak leg. "Brewster, chain of command. Detail."

"Aye aye, sir." Midshipman Tommy Brewster jumped to his feet. "The chain of command runs from the highest ranking line officer to the lowest. It—"

"And if it's broken? By death, for example."

"It automatically relinks, sir. Until the dead officer is replaced, the subordinate reports one link higher."

"That's obvious." Jarewski passed his bleak eye over each of us in turn. "And what if communication is lost?"

"Then the highest—"

"Not you, Mr. Brewster. Seafort, who's dreaming about leave in Earthport with a holo star."

I jumped to my feet, frantically trying to remember the question. "Yes, sir. If, uh, communication is lost the highest available rank takes command."

"Such as a doctor."

"I—" It was heresy to contradict a lieutenant, but I'd learned better than to agree with Mr. Jarewski's false postulates, however casually stated. "Pardon me, no, sir. A doctor isn't a line officer. I should have said, the highest available line officer."

"Such as yourself, Mr. Seafort?"

"A lieutenant at least, sir. I'm a midshipman." Resentful and reckless, I added, "Just vermin."

He'd been about to call on someone else. Now, he just smiled. "And I imagined you were an officer and a gentleman. Do explain your remark."

I wasn't going to get away with it. I did the best I could. "I'm sorry, sir, I was repeating what I'd been told. I assumed a superior officer must be correct." I put on my most innocent expression.

Billy Lea shook his head ruefully, aware that I'd sent myself to the barrel.

The lieutenant's eyes narrowed, but he said only, "An admirable supposition, Midshipman. Yet, what if your superior isn't correct? What if he's dead wrong?"

"I still have to obey him, sir."

"Why? He might get you killed."

"He's my superior officer. I have no choice but to obey."

"Ah." Jarewski limped back to his desk. I waited to sit down, marveling at my good fortune.

Not quite yet. "Always, Cadet Seafort?"

"Yes, sir." I waited for dismissal, realized my trap, blurted just in time, "Unless I'm prepared to relieve him."

His mouth closed, opened again. "On what grounds, Cadet?"

It had become an interrogation. "Mental or physical disability, sir. Those are the only grounds."

"Cite."

I wracked my brain. "Section One hundred and . . ." I was lost. "I can't remember the number, sir, but I can quote it, more or less."

With a smile that sent a chill down my damp back, Jarewski sat on the edge of his desk. "Do so."

"An officer may be relieved of command by his superior for any reason, and by a co-equal or subordinate officer under his command when observed disabled and unfit for duty by reason of mental illness or physical sickness or injury."

"You're referring to Section one twenty-one point four. Are those the only grounds?"

"Yes, sir."

"Well, Mr. Midshipman Vermin. Or rather, Midshipman Seafort." Off the desk now, approaching my chair. "Three demerits. One for insolence, one for being silly enough to provoke me without need, and one for not reading the chapters I assigned. Sit down."

"Aye aye, sir."

He wasn't done with me. "Tomorrow I'll expect you to correct your error."

My encounter had left me with nine demerits. The next one would send me to the barrel; I had to work at least one of them off immediately. I sweated over the exercise bars, knowing I'd been foolish to call Mr. Jarewski's attention. But, nearly seventeen, I'd begun to chafe under the wardroom's unyielding restrictions. I was filling out, my voice deepening, and was reaching for some station, I knew not what.

First Midshipman Arvan Hager found me in the exercise room. He lounged against the bulkhead while I worked. "Who'd you piss off, Nick?"

"Lieutenant Jarewski." I was into sit-ups at the moment, and found it hard to talk.

"How?"

I told him.

"That was notably stupid." His tone modulated the sting his words might otherwise carry. "Even considering the chip on your shoulder."

"I don't have—yes, Mr. Hager." I was in enough trouble as it was.

My sullenness earned a momentary frown. After a moment he said, "What's bothering you, Nicky?"

"Nothing." I finished the series of sit-ups, lay back with a sigh. I was allowed a full minute. His question nagged at me.

Suddenly I battled raging resentment. "Nothing, except people calling me 'Nicky' and treating me like a child."

"You are a child!" His voice had a snap. "You're proving it even now."

"Yes, SIR, Mr. Hager."

He didn't waste time with words; instead he crossed the cabin, hauled me to my feet, and slapped me, hard. I yelped. "Seafort, I like you, but at times you're a total ass!"

To my shame, I found myself crying. I spun to face the bulkhead.

I hoped he would leave, slamming the hatch behind him. But after a moment of quiet, he came to my side. "Sorry, Nick—Midshipman Seafort. Perhaps I overreacted."

"You're first," I mumbled. Any midshipman was subject to the discipline of the senior middy, who ran the wardroom. It had always been thus. I couldn't object, unless I was prepared to offer the traditional challenge. I wasn't ready for that, yet.

"It's just that your sullenness gets under my skin. Have they been riding you?"

I said tightly, "I'm fine, sir."

"No, you're not. Tell me about it."

I wiped at my eyes, trying not to lose control yet again. "There are times I hate this place. I have no freedom, no choices . . ."

"*Helsinki*'s like any ship."

So I'd heard, and was regretting my choice of career.

"Who called you vermin?"

I hesitated, not wanting to carry tales. "Mr. Jenks." Alfred Jenks, nephew of an Admiral, had been promoted from Academy midshipman to lieutenant and posted to *Helsinki*. Mr. Hager was stuck with the situation, as was I. Somehow, that made it all right to tell.

Hager shrugged. "Consider the source," was all he said. I smiled weakly. "Come find me after your shower, Nick. We'll talk."

Later, ashamed of my outburst, I tried my best to be congenial with him. I had few enough friends.

"Are you ready for Law tomorrow?"

"I haven't looked it up yet." If I had to scan the whole manual . . . Well, there was always key word search.

Hager looked about, made sure we weren't overheard. "Try Chapter Six."

"Thanks." I'd skimmed it, and couldn't remember anything about . . . "Oh!"

"You've got it now?"

"Yes, sir. But that just restates one twenty-one point four."

"God, don't tell Jarewski that." It was a mark of Arvan Hager's sense that he left it for me to untangle.

"We'll begin with Mr. Seafort." The Lieutenant rested his bad leg across the other.

"Aye aye, sir." I got to my feet. "Yesterday I forgot about sixty-four point three. I thought it just restated one twenty-one point four. The difference is that to relieve under one twenty-one you have to be in the presence of the commander, and under sixty-four you do not."

He looked surprised. "Very good, Cadet." I blushed, treasuring the unexpected praise. "Right to the heart of it. In fact, under sixty-four, you MAY not be present. It's designed for a different set of circumstances." He waved me to my seat.

Limping back and forth, Jarewski described sixty-four as a relief valve, in case a dreadful error by a distant commander was consigning the fleet to disaster. The penalties for misuse were draconian, but they were also theoretical.

In the history of the Navy, no one had ever sixty-foured a superior.

Arvan Hager found me on the way to dinner. "How was class, Nick?" Not "Nicky." I noticed the change.

"Jarewski wants a paper on when sixty-four might be used," I said, my tone resigned.

"That's easy. Never." His vehemence set me back. "It's an incitement to mutiny. If I'm ever on a sixty-four court-martial board, I'll vote guilty, regardless of the circumstances."

"But—"

"The Navy is about obedience, not rebellion. No one has a right to take over the fleet. Hasn't discipline taught you a thing?"

This time I knew better than to argue.

The next day Mr. Jarewski tore my defense of my paper to shreds. Nonetheless, he graded it an A. Who could figure a lieutenant's mind?

When class was done, I waited until the others had left. "About the other day, sir. I apologize for my attitude."

"Thank you." He eyed me, said not unkindly, "Will you take some advice, Seafort?"

"Yes, sir."

"Be patient," he said. "Adolescence ends."

Breakfast over, I crossed the compound to my office, perhaps for the last time, ignoring a lump in my throat.

I skimmed files until Tolliver arrived. He flipped a salute, headed for his accustomed chair. "Now that we're private, let me show you what I found. Mind if I turn on your console? That thieving son of a bitch took—"

"I told you to drop it."

"When do you want to discuss it, then? Serenco's response is goofjuice; we've got enough to go to the Solicitor Gen—"

"Forget the whole matter. Destroy the records of your inquiry, and mention it to no one."

For a moment he was still. Then he rose, leaned on my desk, studied my face. "By God, they got to you."

"Dismissed, Lieutenant."

He turned to go, made it as far as the door. Still inside, he slammed it shut, stalked back to my desk. "What did they offer you? Flag rank? Or was it the old 'No scandals during wartime'? I thought if anyone would see this through, it was you!"

I came out of my chair. "How dare you!" With an effort I controlled my rage. "Acknowledge your orders!"

"Why? At least in a court-martial the drugs will bring out the truth!" He made a gesture of appeal, cut it short. His expression was bitter. "God, I'm a fool. I keep wanting to trust you."

The caller buzzed. I ignored it. "No need. I'm resigning, as of today."

"All your talk about setting an examp—you're what?"

"I called you to help draft the letter. No discussion, Edgar."

He sank slowly in his chair. "You mean this, sir?"

"Yes."

"Don't." His voice held something I'd never heard before. Entreaty.

"I must, and I won't explain. The stated reason will be that I'm ill from overwork. I want it sent this afternoon."

A knock. Sergeant Kinders, through the door. "Sir, you have a call—"

"No calls, Sarge."

"Aye aye, sir. It's Admiral Duhaney."

"Christ." For a moment I reveled in the blasphemy. "Sorry. Amen."

"Shall I leave, sir?" Tolliver.

"No need." I put the call on the speaker. "Seafort here."

The Admiral's voice was brisk. "Just wanted to tell you the official line. Pritcher was suffering from dehydration and flu, and he's recovering. That's it. He won't keep *Wellington,* of course. Perhaps another ship, later on."

"I hope so. It was his first sight of the fish, and they—"

"Don't tell me my job, Commandant Seafort."

"Aye aye, sir."

"That's all." He hesitated, then rushed on. "No, by God, that's not all. I haven't slept since I got back to Lunapolis. I kept thinking about those monsters, and how you handled them. And about your insolence."

"Sir, I'm sor—"

"Be silent! I tossed half the night realizing what a fool I was, lecturing you. Two Navies, I said, thinking you were an innocent at politics. Ha! You put us pros to shame."

"I don't know what you're talking about!"

Tolliver stood, whispered, "I'd better leave."

"Sit."

"Seafort, I don't care what the Sanders woman said; what you did was mutiny, plain and simple. I may have been mistaken but I was the Admiral; you owed it to me to obey!"

"Sir, I—"

"And you knew it too, so you hurried below to put your face on the cover of every bloody holozine on the racks. The hero of *Wellington,* they're calling you! You know damn well I can't court-martial you now. Well, you got away with it, laddie. For the moment. And what I think of you won't bear repeating."

"Sir, that's not the way it was. I did it for Capt—"

The line went dead.

Ears flaming, I sat with my head in my hands.

Edgar Tolliver said softly, "I don't know what happened, but he's wrong."

"Don't be an idiot. You just said you feel the same way."

"Oh, belay that. You are an innocent. You're the only person I know who cares nothing for self-advancement. You're so undevious you should fall flat on your face, but somehow you don't. You make it hard for even me to hate you."

"Why, thank you, Lieutenant."

"Sorry, it's no time for my—for sarcasm. Why must you resign?"

"I won't discuss it."

"It has to do with *Wellington,* that much is obvious." He studied me. "The Admiral tried to stop you from dealing with Serenco. You should have spit in his eye, but didn't, so he must have something on you. But, what? You have no pride in yourself."

"Tolliver—"

"So instead you resign. What does that solve? Now Serenco will rob the coffers with impunity." He bit his knuckle, frowning. "It all comes down to what they have on you."

He was too close, and his blundering would do untold damage. "Not Duhaney."

"Who, then?"

"I can't tell you. And the reason . . ." I hesitated, threw caution to the winds; we'd been through too much together. "Annie." I started to say more, choked.

"Sir . . ."

After a moment I found my voice. "It doesn't matter. I should have retired long ago, when we brought *Victoria* home." I cleared my throat. "Now, about the letter. I won't allow my resignation to create a scandal; that's the last service I can do the Navy. How do I handle it?"

"Is there any way to change your mind?"

"No."

He brooded. "Be elsewhere when it's released. Where the mediamen can't get to you."

"Hide?"

"I wouldn't call it that. Send the letter from Farside."

I shook my head. No point in going aloft just so that . . . Still, it made sense. I could leave for Lunapolis or Earthport Station whenever I chose. If necessary, I could even lie low at Farside Base until the publicity ebbed. And I'd avoid frenzied mediamen jumping the Academy fence for a picture or a story.

"It'll look strange, my running up to Farside without notice."

"We ship almost a hundred cadets aloft day after tomorrow. What would be more natural than going with them?"

"It would delay my letter two days."

"You send it now, effective Wednesday."

"Very well." I leaned back. "As a courtesy I should address it to Duhaney."

"After the way he spoke to you? Send it to BuPers."

I allowed myself that small satisfaction. "From: Nicholas E. Seafort, Commandant, U.N.N.S. Academy. To: Captain Francis Higbee, BuPers. This is to inform you . . ." It took me no more than a moment. When I was done Tolliver snapped off his holovid, his expression somber.

The caller buzzed. I snatched it. "Now what?"

Sergeant Kinders. "You said to hold your calls, but I thought you'd want me to put Senator Boland through."

I grimaced at Tolliver. "Should I bother?"

"Are you still Commandant?"

"Unfortunately." I thumbed the caller. "Seafort."

Senator Richard Boland's voice echoed in the speaker. "Good morning, Captain. You're recovered from our adventure?"

I snapped, "Is that what you call it?"

"Well, whatever. Congratulations, by the way. They just delivered my *Weekly Holoreview*. You handled them well."

"I'm quite busy, Senator. Is there anything else?"

He sounded jovial. "No, not really, I'll let you go. Oh, one other matter. That topic my colleague brought up with you aboard *Wellington*. It's settled."

"What in hell does that mean?"

Tolliver raised an eyebrow, but I ignored him. It no longer mattered; in hours my resignation would be in Higbee's hands.

Boland's voice sharpened. "I'm trying to tell you to disregard his threats. Go ahead and nail your quartermaster's hide to the wall. I'll handle Wyvern." Too late, I dived for the speaker switch and transferred the call to my handset.

"How did you . . . there are things I can't talk—I mean—" Tolliver watched me sputter, with avid interest.

"Nick, don't worry about that oily son of a bitch. He found your pressure point, but he has a few of his own. As far as you're concerned, he's out of the picture."

"I made a—a bargain," I said quietly.

"Yes, I know. I have his authority to tell you the deal is void, and Mrs. Seafort will be left alone. Go about your business as you would have."

I put down the caller, laid my head on the table. Tolliver . . . the letter . . . Annie . . . My office spun slowly about me.

Tolliver said, "Sir, are you all right?"

I bestirred myself, took up the caller. "Are you sure, Senator?"

"He won't breathe a word, Seafort. Trust me on this."

"Mr. Boland, why are you helping me? Is there a favor—"

"Because I want to." He chuckled and rang off.

"Jesus, Lord Christ." I found myself on my feet, paced, blundered into the end table. "It seems . . . seems . . ."

"That's all right, sir. I'll leave you alone. Ring when you're ready."

"Thank you." It was all I could manage.

"And my holovid must have malfunctioned. That letter is destroyed, whatever it was."

I could only nod.

After he'd left I walked the office, my legs inexplicably shaky. How did the Senator find out, and why had he intervened? I returned to my desk, sat staring out the window.

The caller buzzed once; I ignored it. After a full hour of wracking my brain, I had the answer.

As I reached for the intercom I sighed, hating what I had to do. "Mr. Kinders!" The sergeant came to the doorway. I gave him his orders, paced with growing impatience until a knock came.

The youngster marched in, identified himself, stiffened to attention. His uniform was crisp, as it should be. The shoes gleamed. I'd expected no less. The boy's ears still stuck out, he still had the lankiness of an awkward puppy, but his face held confidence and pride. I'd have to be careful.

I studied him. "The Commandant doesn't involve himself in cadet discipline unless the offense is appalling, as is yours."

"Please, sir, what did I do?"

I slapped him; he yelped. "Don't speak unless you're bidden, or have you forgotten even that?"

"No, sir! Aye aye, sir!"

"Cadet Boland, do you know why you're here?"

"No, sir!"

I forced myself to ignore the tear that trickled down the boy's cheek. "In the Navy, tradition is all. Beyond the regs, some matters are so ingrained as to be universally understood. Wardroom etiquette, shoreside customs, honor, the legacies of those who've gone before. It was Sergeant Ibarez' job to teach you, and he's failed."

I waited, but he didn't dare speak.

I said quietly, "Robert, how did you find out?"

"About what, sir?"

I slapped him again. The boy gave up all pretense of standing at attention; he hugged himself, crying silently.

"Answer!"

"I was sick from the free fall, even after we boarded *Wellington!*" A torrent of words. "Mr. Tenere sent me around the corridor to the head. When I came out, I heard your voice. I intended to excuse myself and go past, but you sounded so angry, I . . ."

"You snooped to listen."

"I thought I'd go back into the head until you were done, but then I heard Senator Wyvern. He's been in Dad's house lots of times." The boy swallowed, wiped his face. "I couldn't help it, I was afraid to open the hatch to go back in, you might hear me. So I just—I listened."

"That's despicable." My mind flashed back to a time, eons past, when I'd skulked in *Hibernia's* corridors to overhear the whispered conversations of my crew. I thrust down the memory. It was my task to make my cadets better than myself.

I perched on the end of my desk, spoke quietly. "Robert, you violated the Navy's honor as well as your own. No, not by listening; though that was bad enough. Your offense was in going to your father."

He whispered, "I only wanted to help. Wyvern was hurting you so."

"You took a Naval affair to outsiders. That's unforgivable, no matter what the circumstances. You've disgraced yourself."

"It was for you." He looked away, eyes streaming.

"That excuses nothing. I handled the matter in a way I found acceptable, and you betrayed me. It's the worst offense I've seen since I became Commandant. I'm prepared to expel you this very afternoon, unless I have your solemn word as a prospective officer that you will never do such a thing again. Naval affairs are for the Navy to handle."

He blanched, and his lower lip quivered. "Sir, I—"

"Take your time, Mr. Boland."

"I promise." His words were barely audible.

"Very well; I'm pleased with your decision. Now, your punishment. Hang your jacket over the chair." I waited. "Bend over my desk. Cross your hands under your chin." I grasped the cane lying against the corner wall, stood behind the anguished cadet. "Mr. Boland, this is for dishonoring the Navy." My cane lashed down on his buttocks with the crack of a shot. His body jerked.

When at last I was finished I sent the sobbing boy back to his barracks. I set down the cane, viewed it with distaste.

Surely there was a better way. What was gained, flogging children for their indiscretions? Had we slipped back into barbarism? Still, the Rebellious Ages had brought such horrors that society had recoiled, determined not to lose more generations to sin, sloth, dissipation.

But why couldn't a child be raised with love rather than pain? Wouldn't I have been the better, had I been so cherished?

Father's visage floated before me. "The Book, Nicholas."

I know, sir. *"Withhold not correction from the child: for if thou beatest him with the rod, he shall not die. Thou shalt beat him with the rod, and shalt deliver his soul from hell."*

I sighed. I was no freethinker, and such matters were beyond me.

Edgar Tolliver and I walked the close-trimmed path as the sun beat down with dazzling brightness. I said, "It's hard to make the transition."

"It must be like a second life." He was still on good behavior.

"Edgar, don't misunderstand. I want to resign, to live quietly with Annie. It's just—"

"You wanted to do it with honor."

"Yes, I— no, not honor, I have none left. There's no vileness to which I haven't stooped. But if I resign, it should be in such a way the Navy isn't besmirched."

"Well, if you wanted to resign, putting yourself on the cover of eleven holozines wasn't a great start." Back to his normal self. I felt better.

"So, now what?"

"Finish what you started with Serenco."

"And then?" Absently, I took a midshipman's salute.

"Carry on. Go aloft to Farside."

"That was so I could resign quietly!"

"Don't forget the Naval Affairs Committee visits soon. You might want to start getting the base ready."

Not only that, but I had the majority of my cadets at Farside, and by tomorrow less than two hundred would be left at Devon. My duty was aloft.

In silence, we neared the mess hall. Regardless of Tolliver's advice, I was free to run Academy as I wished. I'd send Jeff Thorne and Tolliver to Farside, stay here with the remaining cadets. Walk in the spring sunshine, instead of scurrying through cold Lunar warrens. Visit Annie whenever I wanted.

I sighed, as my dream faded. "When do the transports leave?"

As Commandant I'd gone aloft several times, but I'd never organized a shift of plebes from Devon to Farside. Traveling alone, I had only to order a heli to London and fly a shuttle to Earthport Station, where transport would meet me.

Resettling a gaggle of cadets to Farside was organized havoc. Eventually I gave up, and stayed out of the way to let the experienced drill sergeants do their work. They began with rigorous dorm inspections, followed by extra laundry call so the youngsters' duffels would be filled with clean clothes.

In each dorm, a sergeant demonstrated how to pack. After his excited charges had filled their duffels, he opened them one at a time, liberally sprinkling demerits. Then the duffels were repacked to his satisfaction.

Meanwhile, Sergeant Kinders and Ms. Obutu at Farside scheduled the fleet of transport helis that would airlift a hundred cadets to the spaceport.

Letting a throng of boisterous youngsters mingle with civilian passengers at London Shuttleport would be asking for trouble. We had to make prior arrangements with the shuttleport for a private gate.

A hundred cadets and their vigilant sergeants were too great a load for even the largest civilian shuttle; that meant arranging one of U.N.A.F.'s military craft. Here, interservice rivalry raised its head. Glad I could finally make myself useful, I contacted the colonel in charge of U.N.A.F. transport. My name was enough to assure that the shuttle would arrive when needed.

And that was just groundside.

By the time everything was double-checked to my satisfaction my nerves were raw. Late that evening, I sat wearily at my desk with Edgar. "Farside has enough food on hand?"

"For the third time, yes. And oxygen, and toilet pa—"

"Tolliver!"

"Yes, sir, enough food, though it isn't easy putting through indents when your quartermaster is in the brig. I had to—"

"When do they come for him?"

"Tomorrow afternoon. You sent Serenco to formal court-martial, so they'll take him to Portsmouth, where they'll do the polygraph and truth drugs."

"Serves him right." The drugs left one dizzy and nauseous for days, but the truth would emerge. I thrust it out of my mind. "What have I forgotten?"

"Nothing." He stretched. "Ibarez says moving four hundred at a crack is the real fun. Actually, I don't think you'll have much to worry about; they all have their serg—whoops!"

I flinched. "Now what?"

"The special cadets. They're supposed to be your personal charges. Do you want them traveling with the others, or—"

"I'm not a nursemaid!"

"Of course not, you're Commandant of Academy. It's not your job to worry about a few mere cadets, even though you said you'd—"

I sighed. "What do you suggest, First Lieutenant Tolliver?"

"Take them with you, or give up the ridiculous pretense that they're your personal wards."

"It wasn't ridiculous, just the only way I could think to . . . oh, all right. Book seats on our shuttle."

"Aye aye, sir. Do you want Tenere along?"

"No, let Adam help with the main flock. If you and Jeff Thorne aren't enough to tend three runny-nosed cadets, I'll fire the pair of you."

"That might help. Anything else?"

I growled, "Good night."

The next morning we fed the cadets a light breakfast and set on our way. Casual inspection wouldn't reveal any difference between the cadets we took aloft and those we left behind, though test scores and training evaluations would tell a truer story.

After a few last-minute instructions to the Devon staff I boarded the heli with my officers. My eyebrow lifted. "What are you doing here, Mr. Keene? You're supposed to be on a transport with Sergeant Radz."

The boy blushed red to the tips of his ears. "Yes, sir. He told me to, ah, go—come with you."

I strapped down; we lifted immediately. "Were those his words?"

Keene looked unhappy. "No, sir. Not quite."

"Pray continue."

The boy's face fell. "He said to go annoy the Commandant the way I was bothering his cadets." Passively, he awaited the inevitable demerits.

Johan Stritz nudged Kyle Drew; the two exchanged glances in which glee was barely suppressed. I ignored them; it wasn't often cadets got to see a middy squirm.

"I see." Two thousand feet below us the hills drifted past. "Begin annoying me, Mr. Keene."

"Aye aye, sir. I was just trying to be helpful."

"I can imagine." I let him be.

We landed at London just ahead of our first transport, as I'd intended. Sergeant Ibarez seemed almost nonchalant as he directed his charges to the waiting area. Among them I noticed Robert Boland. His gait was stiff from the caning I'd administered. If he saw me, he gave no sign.

I gave in to Tolliver's urging and waited in the Naval Liaison lounge, though I had no idea why my presence might make it harder for cadets to follow instructions. Sometimes Edgar could be quite irrational.

Tolliver, as senior lieutenant, sent Jeff Thorne from time to time to see if embarkation was going according to plan. I was glad of the respite. When I'd asked Thorne if he had come to a decision about reenlistment, his manner had turned surly.

At length Tolliver suggested we board our shuttle.

"The cadets are safely out of my sight?" I didn't feel gracious.

He was at his most bland. "You could have overruled me. I thought a comfortable lounge, a drink—"

I muttered something under my breath.

"What, sir?"

"You should have told me to go bother Sergeant Radz, the way I was annoying you."

Tolliver only smiled, but Midshipman Keene blushed furiously. I clapped the boy on the back. "Let's get out of their hair." We walked across the pad to the waiting shuttle.

Acceleration. Ache. A long wait.

We deboarded at Earthport Station, trudged down the endless service corridor to our transfer shuttle. The cadets would follow on a larger transport. A waste of resources, but I made no objection; travel with a cabinful of excited plebes would lacerate what remained of my nerves.

The U.N.A.F. pilot greeted me indifferently; I pretended not to notice.

The jaunt to Academy Base took over two hours. As setdown neared I watched my three cadets; they seemed at ease. Well, it wasn't their first trip aloft.

I leaned across the aisle to Johan Stritz. "So. How does it feel to be back at Farside?"

"Feel? Fine, sir." He licked his lips.

"The truth."

"Aye aye, sir. I mean, I'm sorry." His eyes flicked to his mates, as if for support. He rubbed the arm of his seat. "I—I don't know how to feel, exactly. Sergeant Radz and I . . . he was kind of . . . I'm sorry."

"Criticizing your betters, Cadet?" My tone was sharp.

"May I have a word with you, sir?" Tolliver, in the seat forward.

"Go ahead."

"Privately." Without waiting, he unbuckled and went to the rear.

I followed. "Now what's the problem?"

"That boy!" His finger stabbed at Johan Stritz. "You hauled him out of his barracks for a special program that didn't exist. You haven't spent—damn it, let me finish!—spent ten minutes alone with him for all the time you had him. You won't let him give you a polite answer about how he feels, but when he admits the truth you chew him out. Go ahead and cane him, if that's what you're after!"

"I spent plenty of time with those cadets! I took them—"

"Did you talk with them? Ever?"

"Of course I did. I had Adam—" I swallowed. "I talked with Kevin, just last week."

"How does Stritz feel about your 'special program'?"

I was silent a long moment. "I don't know."

He said nothing.

"Edgar, what should I do?"

"Do as you please." Suddenly he seemed tired. "I just know I hate bullying."

"You bullied me enough, in the dorms!" What was wrong with me, bringing that up now?

"So you say. Maybe I did. Have we learned nothing over the years?"

"No." Disturbed by what I'd revealed by the one syllable, I blurted, "I've learned I'm worse than ever I imagined." I left him, returned to my seat. "Mr. Stritz . . . Johan—"

The speaker crackled. "We'll be setting down shortly. Those of you who wish to suit as a precaution, do so now." The main transport, half an hour behind us, would be full of suited cadets fogging the inside of their visors with excitement, but our own VIP shuttle would dock directly at the pressured gate.

"Should we suit, sir?"

"Go ahead, just to be safe." I ignored my own suit in the rack above. Let Lord God take me, if that was His wish. I'd evaded His justice long enough.

While Thorne and Tolliver held back in the lock, I stepped forward to take the salutes of Lieutenant Bien and the midshipmen she'd gathered to fill out the welcoming party.

"Welcome aboard, sir."

"Thank you." I forced congeniality into my tone. "Are you ready for an onslaught of plebes?"

"Mr. Radz has them in hand, sir. He's at the main lock. When they're all desuited, shall I assemble them for greeting?"

"I'll see them at dinner. Mr. Keene, settle your middies into the wardroom. Report to Mr. Tolliver for new assignments this evening. I'll see you three cadets in my office now—no, make it an hour." Time to drop my duffel in my cabin, freshen up, walk off some of my restlessness.

A few minutes later I wandered through the barracks area. Everything appeared exactly as it had on my last visit; I didn't know why I'd expected otherwise.

The classroom warrens. I found nothing of interest. Back past the barracks, but there I encountered the first squads of plebes, duffels shouldered, on their way to their new dorms.

To avoid them I ducked into a service corridor, off-limits to cadets. Somewhat disoriented, I struck out toward the Administrative wing.

Around a corner, Lieutenant Jeff Thorne stood, hands in pockets.

He came to attention, saluted casually.

"As you were." My tone was not overfriendly. I made an effort to soften it. "What are you doing here?"

"Thinking about the last time I was in this passage."

"When was that, Jeff?"

He didn't answer directly. "I never thought I'd come back. Did you?"

"After we graduated? No." I leaned against the bulkhead. "It feels . . . odd."

His bitterness welled. "Worse than that. It reminds me of things I'd—rather not recall."

"What are they?"

His eyes swiveled. "Isn't that prying, Commandant?"

I was suddenly tired of reaching out. "Yes. I'll stop. Carry on." I moved toward the hatch.

"Wait." It sounded like an appeal. "It reminds me of—hope, I guess. Or innocence. What I expected from life."

Despite myself, I was moved. "Jeff, it's not too late."

"You think not?" A scornful smile.

"Yes!" I took his arm. "Not for *you,* at any rate! You've betrayed no one but yourself."

He disengaged my hand. "What are you saying, sir?"

"You feel sorry for yourself because you failed to live up to your potential. I've failed Lord God Himself—do you know what I'd give to trade places with you?"

"I apologize."

"Don't be sorry, get hold of yourself!" Was I talking to him, or to myself? "Groundside, when Sandra Ekrit was insolent at table. Did you cane her?"

"Yes and no. We talked. When I was done, I gave her one stroke. I think she might have been happier with more."

"See? You have a natural instinct for handling cadets, and middies too. I've told you that before."

"But I'm lost." He grimaced. "Arcvid, gin, forcing myself out of bed to face another day—"

I wanted to shake him. "Be what you were! What you are!"

He was quiet a long moment. "Do you think I could?"

For a time neither of us spoke. At length I said, "Do you know when I was here last?"

"Farside?"

"No, this corridor."

He shrugged. "Cadets weren't allowed."

"Unless a midshipman took him on a mission . . ."

Bewilderment. Then recognition dawned. "The gravitrons. We never even came close. Old Ridley had the guard."

"And Robbie Rovere stumbled into me, and I went rolling down the ladder. The rest of you disappeared so quick . . ." I smiled. "I've never scrambled up a flight of stairs so fast. All Ridley saw was a blur."

"We deserted you." His face darkened. "As I did later in the mess hall. If you'd been caught . . ."

"But I wasn't." Not that time. "We lived to roam again. Don't forget, when they caught me in the mess hall, you tried to take the blame. I learned something from you, that day."

His eyes shimmered. "What was that, sir?"

Suddenly my voice was strained. "Your courage, in coming forward. Jeff, I've done many things—terrible things, and my soul is forfeit. But I've never betrayed my mates; thanks to your example, at least I've kept that." I had to turn away.

"Easy, sir." His tone was gentle.

"I'm all right." I started slowly for the hatch. "Jeff, get over your regrets. You have a great deal to give the youngsters."

"And give up Arcvid? Sorry, a joke. What I mean is . . . I'll think about it, sir. That's all I can promise." He grimaced. "Maybe here, without the pubs . . . we'll see."

My mood somber, I went directly to my office, found my three charges waiting. I ushered them into my inner sanctum. They wouldn't normally see it unless for extraordinary punishment.

"You may sit."

I laced my fingers, not knowing how to begin. Wasn't it best to avoid the indignity, say nothing, just send them back to barracks?

Father's visage was stern. *"There is no shame to confessing error. Only in committing it."* Yes, Father. Why then did I dread admitting my follies to you, despite the relief it brought?

Kyle Drew squirmed, subsided at my frown.

"I owe you all an apology." My eyes grew heavy with the need to look away. I did not.

Kevin Arnweil ventured, "What for, sir?"

"I've done nothing to help, after bringing you all ground-side." I met his eye. "Kevin, you were in shock after Cadet Edwards died. You weren't coping, and I thought Sarge was making it worse." As if ashamed, he looked to the deck.

"And you, Kyle. How could we make you understand Dustin's death was our fault, not yours? I can imagine the guilt you feel, that it was your helmet that opened his."

Drew stared into his lap, his mouth firmly shut.

"Johan. You got off on the wrong foot. I thought somehow I could help you, and the others. But I didn't."

It was Arnweil who finally spoke, hesitantly. "Sir, are you washing us out?"

"Of course not!" I stood, paced helplessly. "I had to tell you . . . I—I don't know how to help. I intended to give you my time, help you through your troubles. Instead I made you into errand boys, or ignored you. All that's left is to apologize."

The silence stretched.

Kevin Arnweil blurted, "You didn't ignore me, sir."

"Rubbish. The only time I spoke with you was when we tried to find Mr. Thorne."

"Yes, sir. Right after that. We walked, and you told me what it was like for you as a cadet."

"That was nothing."

"For you, perhaps." The boy's expression was almost defiant. "It was good to hear someone else had been through it." His cheeks flamed.

"Oh, I remember how a cadet feels." I gestured. "My second year, Commandant Kearsey put me across that very desk to cane me. In his office I felt the terror you must feel at having to speak to me. But that's why I'm the wrong person for you."

Stritz blurted. "Please don't send us back to Devon." I gaped, but he raced on. "It's our fault too! We keep quiet around you, so as not to make you mad. We don't give you a chance." He looked to the others. "You know it's true."

Kyle Drew studied my face, risked speech. "I guess I was kind of disappointed, waiting around for messages to take the sergeants. I thought you're always learning things at Academy.

Besides the books, I mean. Like, flying helis." He brightened. "But at least I got to see *Wellington.*"

"You deserve more." My tone was gruff.

"Are you sending us back to barracks, sir?"

That's exactly what I'd had in mind, but now it would seem a punishment for being frank. Again, I'd trapped myself. I made the best of it. "Not if you'll give me another chance. I'll try new rules. You're free to ask questions, or to tell me what's on your mind. Sergeant Obutu will get you back on track with assignments."

It wasn't enough; I needed more. "You may do your homework in my cabin before bunking in the dorm." Good Lord. What was I *doing*? "I'll help you with it." I added lamely, "I'll try not to let you down again."

They said nothing. I could imagine what they were thinking. The Commandant had gone quite mad, and they now had to spend their entire day with him.

"That's all." I hesitated. "Unless anyone has anything to add." Heresy. Pure heresy. They were *cadets*!

Chapter 20

That evening I caught Tolliver on the way to the mess hall dome. "I apologized to Stritz and the others."

"Oh, wonderful."

"Now what's the matter?"

He shrugged. "Better than snarling at them, I suppose. Best if you could find a distance and keep it. A Captain doesn't apologize."

"This one does. He needs to." I increased my pace. "I was wrong to give them special treatment in the first place." He made no reply.

Tolliver stood aside for me to enter. Five hundred cadets rose as one.

I took my place. "Where's Lieutenant Bien?"

Tolliver. "She left on the transport, sir."

"Why?"

"I gave you the leave roster last week. You approved it yourself."

After dinner, I again walked the warrens in restless anxiety. Sandra Ekrit and Midshipman Anton Thayer, on some errand, stood aside, salutes held until I'd passed. Hands in pockets, I strode on.

I turned, went through a service corridor. It led . . . where? The laundry? I had no interest in that. I detoured down a ladder halfway through the corridor. It led me deep into the bowels of Farside, on the service level where the technicians and ratings who manned our machinery were housed.

I bypassed the gravitron chamber where a tech stood watch day and night, went instead to the outer fusion control room. A bored tech sat reading a holo. No matter; our power station was fully automated and his watch was excruciating boredom.

He jumped to attention.

"As you were, mister."

"Aye aye, sir. Is there anything I can do for you?"

"No." I pointed at the splotched deck. "What's that, spilled coffee? Have someone clean it up." Perhaps I should run inspections for staff as well as cadets.

"Aye aye, sir."

I climbed the ladder back to the main level, went to my cabin to sleep.

A few evenings later, I sat in my office reviewing memos at my console. A report from Portsmouth: Quartermaster Serenco had confessed to stealing over a hundred thousand unidollars and was remanded for trial. No mention of his relationship with Senator Wyvern; apparently that was part of Boland's deal. I sighed, tried to put it out of my mind.

Memorandum from Admiralty: the caterwauling bomb was being passed to Naval Engineering for preliminary design. At last the wheels were rolling, however slow. Another note. Captain Pritcher was reassigned as Admiralty Chief of Protocol, directly under Admiral Duhaney. Captain Tenere, Adam's father, would take *Wellington*.

I read the message from Eddie twice. Annie was eating again. He had found my old bicycle in the shed, fixed it up, and bought a sturdier one for himself. He and Annie biked into town for supplies each day.

Thank you, Lord. At least that goes well.

Kyle Drew knocked, came shyly into my office. "Am I interrupting, sir?"

"Not if I'm alone, you know that." In the days since our last conversation I'd encouraged my cadets to unbend, and I'd managed not to wither them with a disapproving glare when they did. Awkward, for all of us. I checked my watch. "Isn't it nearly time for bed?"

"Yes, sir." His voice cracked, and he blushed. "I have a few Engineering problems left for tomorrow. May I do them here?"

"Quietly." After a moment I added, "Unless you need help."

"Aye aye, sir."

I thumbed through a few more files while Kyle tapped industriously at his holo. "Why here, rather than the dorm?" I asked.

"I'll go, if you'd like. It's just . . ." He flushed. "It's not very friendly there, sir. Since we were assigned to you."

I should have known. By taking the three under my wing I'd made outcasts of them. Well, it was still better than washing them out, and that had been the alternative.

I freshened my coffee, went back to my files. After a while I noticed the boy crossing and uncrossing his legs, muttering under his breath.

"Need to visit the head, Cadet?" My tone was sharp.

He was startled. "No, sir."

"Stop fussing, then." I dictated a few notes. I'd need to talk to Tolliver about appointing a new quartermaster; if we left it to Higbee at BuPers, Lord God knew whom he'd send.

Kyle Drew sighed.

I glowered. "Get out if you can't keep quiet!"

Immediately he gathered his chips. "I'm sor—"

"Belay that." As Tolliver said, I couldn't find a distance and keep it. "What's wrong, Kyle?"

"I'm sorry, sir. I can't get this stuff." He laid his holovid on my desk. "*Basics of Electrical Engineering*. Ergs and ohms and watts."

"It takes study." I tried to sound sympathetic.

"Why do we have to know this goofjuice? Engine-room gauges tell you if you're in the red." He checked my face, afraid he'd gone too far.

"The Navy wants to make you an educated man, not a gauge reader."

"I know a watt is a measure of power, which we call 'P,' and voltage is a measure of electromagnetic force, and we call it 'E.' But all those formulas . . . I get lost."

I leaned back with a smile. "That's easy, lad. There are just two formulas you need to remember. Say after me: 'Twinkle twinkle, little star; Power equals I squared R.'" Kyle gaped, but repeated the jingle dutifully.

"You know that 'I' is current measured in amps. 'R' is resistance measured in, uh, ohms. Now, voltage—'E'—equals 'I' times 'R.' You can derive the other formulas from that, right? 'I' equals 'E' over 'R'. 'R' equals, um, 'E' over 'I.'" I stopped while I was ahead.

He looked at me with wonder. "How did you learn that, sir?"

I basked in the glow of his admiration. "Don't they still teach the rhymes? Go back to your problems, see if you can get them now."

As a cadet I'd labored for weeks at memorizing the merciless formulas. Two years later, on *Hibernia*, crusty Chief McAndrews had discovered my ignorance when I was assigned engine-room watch. On a practice drill I'd misplotted a Fuse to set us inside the

B'n Auba Zone, so close to the Sun that no vessel, no matter how small, could escape.

Rather than chewing me out and sending me back to the books, he'd taught me the mnemonic, and begun to rectify my ignorance. Thank you, Chief.

For a time Kyle and I worked peaceably at our tasks. The companionable silence mellowed me; I felt almost light-headed.

The gawky youngster stretched. "Thanks a lot, sir, that'll really help my weeklies." He flashed a grin that lit his sallow face.

His relief seemed to affect me; I felt a burden lift. It was as if I were pounds lighter. "I'm glad. Better get back to barracks before Lights Out." I lifted my cup for another sip, and slopped steaming coffee over my shirt. "Damn!"

"Aye aye, sir." Kyle stood. With a startled look he waved his arms as if to catch his balance. "Whoa!"

Alarms shrilled. As I spun to my console the puter came to life. "MALFUNCTION IN THE GRAVITRON CONTROLS! COMMENCING SYSTEM SHUTDOWN! POWER DIVERTED!"

Something was terribly wrong.

I grabbed the caller. "Emergency close all corridor hatches! All hands stand by for suitup! Tolliver, Thorne, to the Commandant's office!"

"SYSTEM DISCONNECT COMPLETE! LUNAR GRAVITY PREVAILS. COMMENCING DIAGNOSTIC RUN!"

"What in hell?" I jumped to my feet, banged my skull on the overhead. I caromed down to my desk, managed to anchor myself. Kyle Drew watched, mouth ajar.

The caller panel lit like a Christmas tree. I rubbed my aching forehead.

Jeffrey Thorne poked his head into my office. Grinning, he entered with the slow-sailing lope characteristic of Lunar gravity. "They did it!" he sounded exultant.

"Did what? Who?"

"The middies finally got to the gravitrons!" His eyes sparkled.

"That's nonsense, they've never . . ." I reached to the console, thumbed the caller. "Gravitron Control Room!" I waited.

A knock. Tolliver, taking careful Lunar steps. Sergeant Kina Obutu was close behind.

"We tried for years, all of us!" Thorne's face was flushed. "They made it at last!"

Kyle Drew's face widened into a grin.

Little pitchers. I frowned. "Cadet, back to barracks."

"Aye aye—"

Tolliver. "He can't, sir. You have all the hatches closed. It took me forever to key in the codes."

"Very we—"

The caller buzzed. "Gravitron Tech Siever reporting, sir. I'm in the power station at the moment. The little bastards recoded my hatch. I can't get in!"

"What happened?"

"A cadet came with a message. The engine-room caller wasn't working, and would I go help—"

"What did he look like?"

"Long blond hair, bushy eyebrows, how should I know? They're all the same!"

Sergeant Obutu muttered, "A wig? None of them have long blond—"

"Sir, even after I figure out how to get in it'll take a good hour to restart—"

I grated, "Have Maintenance burn through your hatch. Get the bloody gravitrons up and running!"

Savagely, I punched a caller button.

"Sergeant Radz here, sir. We've lost pow—"

"I know, damn it!" I spun to Thorne, almost launching myself from my chair. "Find out who did it! Have them thrashed and expelled!"

"Let me use my judgment, sir. I'll handle it." Thorne sounded solemn.

"Not this time, you won't. Send them home! Better yet, send them to court-martial!" I stood to pace, thought better of it.

Ms. Obutu coughed. "It's only a prank, sir."

"Only a—" I stared at the alarms, fuming. Lord knows what harm they'd caused. Thank heaven it had been late in the evening. As it was, they'd caused me to spill hot coffee all over myself, and even now I couldn't get to my feet without risking ballistic flight. The gall of those middies, skulking around off-limits corridors, raising havoc in the night. When I was their age I knew better than to—than . . .

Jeff Thorne stared at me fixedly. When he was sure Kyle's eye was elsewhere, he winked.

After a moment the corners of my mouth twitched. "All right, Thorne, straighten out this mess as you see fit." I hoped he'd have the sense to apply the cane, if nothing else. Long-sought triumph or no, the middies must be taught that all things come at a cost.

I swiveled to Tolliver. "There'll be chaos in the dorms tonight. Pillow fights, or horseplay. Maybe worse. Pass the word to let them be." I shrugged off his surprise. "In the history of Academy, no middy ever reached the gravitrons. Very well, let them celebrate."

Kyle Drew grinned like an idiot. I snapped, "Don't get ideas, joey. It isn't funny."

It really wasn't. But even the Lunar gravity couldn't explain my lightheartedness.

"I really must protest." Ardwell Crossburn wore the stubborn look I'd come to know too well. "The damage they caused. We didn't get the gravitrons back on-line until past—"

"Why not?" I demanded. Crossburn was maintenance officer, and after Lieutenant Sleak's death he'd taken the base's Systems responsibilities as well. All too seriously, it now seemed.

Across the conference table, Jeff Thorne rolled his eyes. Tolliver looked solemn.

"The techs had to burn through the hatch, as you know. Mind you, at the cost of a new hatchplate. Then they had to unscramble the gravitron passwords those criminals had changed. I'm astounded Thorne won't tell me who they are." The man was a fool; he had only to observe which three middies were walking with uncomfortably stiff gait.

Crossburn had gone red. "It's most odd, your letting them off. I must say, most odd indee—"

I came to my feet. "You must say? You dare judge me?"

"Not at all. The comment was in a, ah, private capacity." His tone turned sullen. "I won't speak of it, if you insist. But my advice is to cashier whoever's responsible before the Naval Affairs Committee learns next week—"

I slammed my holovid on the table. The shattered lensplate skittered to the deck. "Mr. Crossburn, pack your gear! I want you off base this very day!"

Crossburn was smug. "Without me you don't have enough officers for five hundred cadets. Mr. Kearsey issued a base regulation on that. Anyway, I'm not needed at Devon and my responsibilities here—"

"Jeff Thorne will take your duties. Don't go to Devon. Report to Captain Higbee at BuPers in Lunapolis."

"And what would you like me to tell him? Everything I know?" Crossburn had thrown caution to the winds.

My tone was glacial. "Tell him you're no longer employed at Naval Academy. Get out! Now, before I call Mr. Tenere to help!" Adam had recent experience in removing uncooperative superiors. I wondered if he'd find a posting anywhere, if I allowed that into his record.

Crossburn threw his notes onto the table. "You'll hear about this, sir. I'm not done—" He saw my expression, and fled.

For a moment all was silent.

"Very instructive, sir. I must remember that technique next time a middy—"

"Edgar, shut up!" He was truly impossible; why did I put up with him?

Jeff Thorne asked in a plaintive tone, "What, exactly, does a systems and maintenance officer do?"

I growled, "There's a manual someplace. Read it."

Tolliver said helpfully, "His main duty is keeping the middies away from the gravitr—"

"EDGAR!"

"Yes, sir. Perhaps we ought to get back to business." He pondered his notes while I stalked the cabin, working off my ire. He said, "Your former associate Crossburn had one good point. The annual Naval Affairs visit next week. They'll expect red-carpet treatment, as usual."

I stopped in midstride. "How?"

"One of Mr. Duhaney's assistants was most helpful on that point. For one thing, we serve them decent food. Steaks, not synthos."

"Take care of it." My mind was still on Crossburn. I should have gotten rid of him months ago. Thank heaven I'd done it now, before he buttonholed some Senator with his ubiquitous black diary.

"I'll order up some fancy fruits and vegetables. Just for the VIP tables, of course."

A bad example for our cadets; in the Navy all ranks were fed alike. It couldn't be helped. Duhaney would have a stroke if I didn't cultivate the Naval Affairs Committee.

"And wine. I can—"

"No." I resumed my pacing.

"Aye aye, sir. These Senators vote our budget. Let them stay thirsty."

I growled, "If they don't like it, let them stay home. No wine."

"Jeff, help me, he's in one of his moods again. Sir, it's only for a week." Tolliver made a note. "I'll bunk with Mr. Thorne for the duration; Ms. Bien can join the middies in the wardroom. That will leave enough cabins empty, if you take two guests in your suite like Commandant Kearsey did."

Only eight Senators. But that didn't count their innumerable aides. We'd have to move some of the techs to provide quarters belowdecks. An inconvenience, but . . .

"This year, only four of them are bringing family. I'll arrange for middies to watch the children. They can—"

"No!"

"Beg your pardon, sir?"

"This isn't the Lunapolis Sheraton! No children!"

"Be reasonable. You can't tell them who to bring and—"

"Who runs this place?" I threw myself into my chair.

"I'm not quite sure, sir." Tolliver regarded me gravely. "Do we get hints?"

Jeff Thorne intervened before I could explode. "I don't mind moving, sir. It's in everyone's interest to please the Committee."

I stared balefully at my shattered holovid. It had been my favorite reader since cadet days. "I'm not turning this place into a shambles for a gaggle of politicians and their families! Cancel the visit!" I picked pieces of lens off the carpet.

Tolliver leaned back, folded his arms. "You really can't do that, you know. Perhaps we should break for lunch?"

"Don't treat me like—damn it!" I sucked blood from my pricked finger. "Get this mess out of—" I took a deep breath. "All right, let them come. But no special food, we'll feed them out of stores."

"Aye aye, sir." Tolliver sounded resigned.

I wrapped my finger in a handkerchief, muttered under my breath. My officers and I would all be dislodged, our schedules disrupted . . .

No. I wouldn't have it. "And you'll stay in your own quarters."

"That'll leave us six places short, sir."

"Eight. I don't take boarders." For a moment I relished his surprise. "Send Krane Barracks to the Training Station a week early. That will free thirty places."

Tolliver gaped. "A dorm? We can't bunk spouses and aides and children in a communal cabin!"

"That's the Navy way. We do it all the time." I opened the hatch.

"But they're not—"

I said sweetly, "Isn't it what they're here to inspect?"

By dinner I had calmed myself, but after reflection, I decided to leave matters where they stood. Political visits to Devon were one thing, unwelcome as they were. Senatorial jaunts to Farside were altogether too disruptive, budget or no. Maybe my actions would discourage them. However, I took the precaution of warning Tolliver not to mention our new arrangements to Admiral Duhaney's office.

During the next week I busied myself with paperwork. I had recommendations to write for graduating cadets, supply indents to approve, a new inventory program to outline so that Mr. Serenco's defalcations would not reoccur. Occasionally, in the evenings, I called down to Cardiff. Annie seemed well, but remote.

The day before the Committee was to arrive, I addressed the cadets about to leave for the Training Station. My goal was to impress on them the need for care without actually threatening dire consequences should they misbehave. I wanted no more deaths on my conscience, and with VIPs looking over our shoulders an accident now would be politically disastrous.

I wasn't sure if they heard me, but at least they stayed awake.

Tolliver and I walked back from the main lock.

"You have someone cleaning the dorm, Edgar?"

"Mr. Diego, with two ratings. Not that they're needed."

I agreed glumly. Sergeant Radz would have made sure the barracks was left spotless.

I was having doubts about my decision to house the VIPs in

Krane Hall. I resolved to think it through again, though a change of orders would make me look indecisive.

In the morning a flurry of outgoing reports occupied my mind. By lunchtime the Senatorial party had arrived in a U.N.A.F. transport, and the die was cast.

I rounded up my officers, greeted our guests effusively at the lock, and let Tolliver show them to their quarters. For the remainder of the afternoon I managed to be too busy to deal with visitors.

Kevin Arnweil fell in beside me on the way to dinner. "Evening, sir. I finished the trig we worked on last night."

"Good."

"Mr. Sties said it was excellent. Should I tell him half the grade is yours?" Well. The youngster had a sense of humor. If I hadn't forced myself to unbend with my special charges, I'd never have known.

"No, thanks. I have no desire to be half a midshipman next year."

Kevin grinned with delight. I felt a twinge of guilt; a kind word from me meant so much to the lonely joeys I'd put under my wing.

"Sir, the word is that you're making Robbie Boland's father sleep in a barracks."

We turned into the main corridor. "Is something wrong with that?"

His answer was quick. "Oh, no, sir. Barracks is—fine."

"Good." As we passed through the mess-hall hatch I called out, "Be seated."

Normally the Krane cadets sat toward the rear of the hall, but I'd had their unused tables moved closer to the front for the VIPs. Tonight and for the rest of the week my officers and I would dine with our visitors; Thorne had braced the middies to be on their best behavior.

I took a deep breath, pasted a welcoming smile on my face as I approached the long table. "Good evening. Sorry I couldn't be with you today."

Hostile expressions, from men and women alike. "Do you know where they took our gear?" Senator Dorothy Wade, of Ontario. "I tried all afternoon to reach you!"

"Is there a mix-up, Senator?" My voice was bland.

"Our rooms. Your idiot lieutenant"—Tolliver, at the opposite end of the table, affected not to hear—"took us to a barracks by mistake." Next to her, an aide listened with smug satisfaction.

Johan Stritz's face went red; he quickly covered his mouth with a napkin. I felt a moment's panic. If he were sick in the company of—then I saw his shoulders shake. Kyle Drew nudged him urgently in the ribs.

I'd gone too far; even my cadets were laughing at me. Best to give the Senators the cabins they deserved, even if it meant ousting my officers on short notice. Blame it on Tolliver; he wouldn't mind. "I'm sorry, I was tied up all afternoon with—"

Senator Myemkin set down his fork. "Really, Mr. Seafort, someone's made an error. They've crowded us into—"

Mrs. Wade said sharply, "There's not even a plug for a full-size holoscreen!"

Myemkin's tone was mild. "Doris, let me handle—"

She overrode him. "And the bathrooms! They're unspeakable!"

I stopped short. "They're not clean?" Someone's head would roll.

"What does that have to do with it? They're stalls, lined up in a row. It's an insult!"

What had I done? I'd have to give them better accommodations, immediately. "Mrs. Wade, please don't take offense. The heads in Krane Hall are like all the cadet dorms. I'll change—"

Her shrill voice echoed through the hall. "They're fit for animals and trannies! We're decent people!"

The mess hall went absolutely still. Slowly, I folded the napkin. "I'm terribly sorry your accommodations don't suit you, ma'am." Tolliver caught my eye, as if in reminder that I'd been warned.

Thanks to the hushed silence, my humiliation would be public. My gaze swept the dining hall. Cadets, oblivious of their sergeants' scowls, sat twisted to face the drama. On their faces were odd expressions. Embarrassment. Shame.

No, anger.

I stood, made sure my voice was just loud enough for all to hear. "I regret Farside doesn't have quarters befitting your station. Obviously you can't stay . . ." Again I looked at the rows of cadets, and stumbled to a halt.

Their outrage was directed at her, not me.

Trannies? Animals? How could I agree with her allegations, in the hearing of these well-scrubbed, starched youngsters? We'd told them over and again that living in close quarters without a shred of privacy was an honor. Ms. Wade's epithets applied to them as well as me.

My tone was firm. "Krane Barracks is the only housing we have available. Our cadets find it an honor to be assigned to them, or any other barracks in Farside. Can you imagine how hard they struggled—" I bit off the rest. What did these folk know of Academy tradition? "However, there's a solution."

Richard Boland cleared his throat. "What can you do for us?"

"I'll make ready your shuttle, Senator. Anyone who finds our accommodations unacceptable may leave tonight for Lunapolis." Tolliver put his head in his hands.

"But the inspec—"

"We'll meet groundside, when it suits my schedule. I understand there are excellent hotels outside the Devon gates." I threw down my napkin. "I find I'm not hungry, and I have urgent work to do. If you will excuse me." I stalked from the hall.

My caller was disconnected, my office hatch closed. I paced the cabin, increasingly distraught. Why hadn't I controlled my temper just this once? At the least, Duhaney would dismiss me as Commandant this very night, as soon as the Senators' furious calls reached him. His contempt for me was already beyond tolerance, thanks to the interviews I'd given on *Wellington*.

The personal cost didn't bother me; now I was free to go home to Cardiff. But my outburst had done incalculable harm to Academy, and to my cadets. I wondered if my successor could ever repair it.

A knock. Sergeant Obutu.

"No calls, no interruptions!"

"Yes, but Mr. Tolliver says—aye aye, sir."

I resumed my pacing, kicked an offending chair out of the way. Animals. Trannies. So what if I'd been provoked? Hadn't I learned to take worse in wardroom hazing?

Another knock. "Sarge, if you so much as come near—oh, it's you." Johan Stritz.

"Sorry, sir. Yesterday you said I should come to do my Nav problems . . ."

"Stay out. I don't have time to—" No, you fool! "Johan, that was uncalled for. Sit and do your work."

"Aye aye, sir." He took a chair, flicked on his holovid. I resumed my pacing.

"You should have seen them after you left, sir. They—"

"Mind your own business." I stalked the office, muttering under my breath. If I took no calls until morning, Duhaney would have to wait until then to let me know I was cashiered. During the night I could creep down to Devon on our remaining shuttle. At least I wouldn't hear the Senators gloat over their revenge.

I could only imagine what had been said about me.

No, I could do more than that. "Tell me."

Eagerly he put down his holovid. "That old grode Wade called—" He saw my expression. "Sorry. Ms. Wade, I meant. You're a muscle-brained adventurer. A sexist Neanderthal who enjoys humiliating his betters. And Senator Myemkin said you were an unprincipled—"

Another knock. I flung open the hatch. "How many times do I—"

Jeff Thorne. "Yes, I know you weren't to be bothered, but this shouldn't wait."

"Tell the whole lot of them to go to hell! I don't care what they want now!"

He stared, then comprehension dawned. "The politicians? No, this is more serious."

"Let the new Commandant handle it." Grudgingly, I stood aside for him to enter. "Make it fast."

"I don't think Stritz should be here."

"Get on with it!"

"Aye aye, sir. You're not going to like this. Olvira found two second-year joeys—" He seemed at a loss for words. "Sorry. They were pronging each other."

"It happens, sometimes." Arlene Sanders had told me as much, long ago in Lunapolis.

"Sir, they're both in his dorm."

Aghast, I said, "Bunkies?"

"Yes, sir. Tanya Guevire and the Chambers boy." He saw my expression, rushed on. "I know, I feel the same way. They're waiting outside my cabin right now, but I thought it deserved a visit to your office."

"Don't bother! Send them home tonight!"

"Sir, that's a bit extreme. They—"

"I want them out!"

His tone was patient. "It's morally repugnant, but—"

"Damn it, how can the middies crowd into a wardroom if everyone's wondering who's pronging whom! Disgusting! Call the Pilot, have him get the shuttle ready. They're both expelled."

"But—"

I snarled, "Can't you obey a simple order?"

"Yes, sir. Aye, aye, sir. I'd like you to listen first."

"Get—" I reached inward, found some last measure of control. "All right."

"Thank you. We both know it's wrong. But that's what we're here to teach them. I'll see to it neither ever dreams again of having sex with a bunkie. You have my promise."

"They're mates, damn it." It wasn't just that the sex was morally repulsive. Our joeys had to learn that the Navy was as one, that we didn't go around pronging our brothers. I thought of Arlene, and felt a hot flush of shame. I glared at Stritz. "What are you looking at?"

He snatched up his holovid. "Nothing, sir."

Thorne waited.

I sighed. "I don't want to see them. Make it a good one, Jeff. See that they can't sit down for a week."

"Aye aye, sir. Thank you for changing your mind." He saluted, left before I could reverse myself.

I'd turned Academy into a madhouse. Cadets were humping in the corridors, a party of outraged Senators roamed Krane barracks, everyone, including me, questioned orders, and I was preparing to empty my desk while a cadet who should long since have been washed out sat where he didn't belong, pretending he was engrossed in his holovid.

Law and order.

I snorted. At least Ardwell Crossburn was gone. His little black book would haved steamed before he was done writing tonight's events.

Another knock. I whirled, looking for something to throw. Kina Obutu. "I know, sir, but it's Senator Boland. Are you sure you . . ."

"All right, put him on." I took the caller.

"He's right here." She stood aside.

"Well?" It was far too late for civility.

"The vote was five to three, Captain. We stay." He glanced at Stritz, turned away unconcerned. He raised an eyebrow. "Your novel hospitality is . . . refreshing."

His dry manner extinguished my temper. At a loss for words, I crossed to my desk, laid my head in my arms. Should I laugh or cry? Perhaps both. "Senator, things . . . got out of hand."

"Really? With you, I'm never quite sure." He sat. "My colleague is somewhat abrasive."

"She set me off, but I accept the blame. My replacement will smooth things over, I'm sure."

"You mean when Duhaney finds out what you've done? That's why I'm here, actually. I've been delegated to make the call, on behalf of all of us."

"Ms. Obutu's caller is on her desk."

Boland locked his fingers behind his neck. "I think the circuit is busy. In fact, I'm sure of it. Tomorrow, I'll have left Duhaney a message. That should hold them for a few days." In a leisurely manner he got to his feet. "Silly old bitch." He paused at the hatch. "Oh, by the way."

I snapped shut my hanging jaw. "Yes?"

"I told you once I'd have liked to serve in the Navy, if I hadn't gone into politics. Is this your way of giving me the chance?"

I fumbled for a reply, but he was gone.

Kyle Drew and Johan Stritz came jauntily into my office, cheeks flushed. Stritz flipped me a casual salute. "May I sit? They're worse than plebes, sir. It took both of us to get Mr. Myemkin suited. Kyle almost had to sit on him."

I smiled wanly. In the two days since I'd made mortal enemies of the VIPs, I'd had the two cadets help shepherd them around the base. Aides and Senators were continually losing themselves in the maze of warrens.

I studied Johan's rosy face. The boy was coming along. The day before, he had made friends with Senator Rudolpho's twin daughters. Audaciously, he'd knocked on the wardroom hatch to ask permission for the twins to look inside, knowing the frustrated middies couldn't blame him for carrying out official duties. Today the twins were presumably out with their parents and the rest of the party, on a daring fifty-yard stroll to the Hull. Thorne and Tolliver would keep them safe.

Still no call from Duhaney. Senator Boland's message must have been pigeonholed, if he'd sent it at all.

Kyle hesitated. "Sir, do you have time to help me with Law tonight? I'd ask Mr. Keene, but he's busy with the Senators."

I patted the empty seat by my desk. "Now would be better, Drew." I sighed. Even in my private office, the boys felt all too at home.

Worse, I was starting to like them.

Chapter 21

I was briefing Ngu Bien on Systems and Maintenance when Sergeant Obutu knocked. "Sir, it's the Admiral."

In the week since the Naval Affairs Committee had left, I'd heard nothing. If Duhaney wanted retribution, surely he wouldn't have waited so long.

"Very well." I warily took the caller.

"Seafort?" His voice was jovial. "Higbee's been complaining again. Some Crossburn fellow. You gave him his walking papers without authorization."

"I do a lot without authorization, sir." He knew it better than I.

"Yes, but you're not supposed to admit it. I put him on headquarters staff for now."

Good God. I'd created a monster.

"Listen, I apologize for my remarks about your being a politician. It seems you're better than even I realized."

"What are you talking about?"

"The Committee, Seafort. You know the impression you made."

I gulped. "Yes, sir, I'm sor—"

"Boland couldn't stop raving. Letting them sit in on classes, that was a masterstroke. And who was it put them through fish simulator firing drill for a whole morning, you?" No, it was Olvira. "Myemkin said he hadn't been so tired in his life, but he understood for the first time why we take our drills so seriously."

I regarded the caller as if it were a snake. "Sir, are you, uh, joking with me? Aren't they—"

"They showed me the preliminary draft. Looks like we'll see our first real budget increase in years. One dissenter, but she was overruled seven to one. They're even giving us funds to upgrade the barracks next year."

"There's nothing wrong with—"

"I have to run, Seafort, another damnfool ceremony at U.N.A.F."

I blurted, "Sir, what about the caterwauling bomb I—"

"It's coming along, Commandant. Good work." He rang off.

I sat dumbfounded.

Everything I tried to do well turned out badly.

It was only fitting that what I tried to do badly turned out well.

I dressed quickly, returned to my office to meet Sergeant Radz. On the caller he'd said it was urgent. Ms. Obutu, whom I'd also summoned, sat in the outer room, yawning.

"What's up, Sarge?" I beckoned to a chair.

"A few minutes ago I heard noises through the bulkhead. It's after midnight; they should all be asleep. I found two cadets in the head going at it full blast."

"Again? Are they all sex-crazed?" One revolting incident was enough. "This time we'll make an example—"

"No, sir, not that. They were trying to pound each other into the deck. A real donnybrook. I flung one of them halfway across the barracks, collared the other. He's in my cabin now."

"Good Lord. What was it about?"

"I don't know. I came here before asking." For the first time Radz showed a trace of anger. "My choice would be to send them both to the barrel, and ask after. But last time you didn't like the way I—"

"Stow that!" I stood, turned aside to pace. Everyone's nerves seemed to be on edge. Mine, the sergeant's, even the cadets'. It was my own fault; the Commandant set the tone. "Send them up. I'll deal with them."

"Aye aye, sir." He saluted, strode to the hatch.

I paced anew. I'd been far too lenient of late. I'd let off the middies, forgiven illicit sex, allowed Stritz and the others all sorts of familiarities. Time to toughen—

A knock.

"Enter!"

The boy limped in, drew himself to attention as best he could. His right eye had begun to swell shut; his lip still oozed blood. "Cadet Jerence Branstead reporting, sir."

"You!"

"Yes, sir."

"What in God's own hell have you been up to?"

He mumbled, "A fight."

"Stand straight! Speak up!"

"Aye aye, sir." He complied, winced from the pain. "We were fighting."

"I know; you're bleeding all over my deck!" He licked at his lip. "Stand easy, if it hurts that much."

"I'm all right, he just kicked me kind of . . ."

"Who? Better yet, why?"

"Cadet Ochard, sir." He hesitated. "Please, sir, I'd rather not talk about it."

"Four demerits, you insolent young—" I strode to the cane. "By Lord God, you'll learn to obey before I'm done with you! Exactly what was this fracas about?"

"I—he said I was your—your . . ." The boy's jaw quivered. He made a manful effort at control.

My anger dissolved. "All right, lad." I led him to the couch, gave him my handkerchief. When I thought he was able, I prodded. "Well?"

"He said I got into the Navy by—by sucking up to you, on *Victoria*. Except, that wasn't how he said it." His breath came in a sob. "I work hard, Captain Seafort. Honest, I do. My coming home with you had nothing to do with my scores. It's true, isn't it?" His eyes flickered to mine. "Didn't I earn them?"

"Of course." My voice was tight.

"Sarge wouldn't give—I mean, if he did, being in the Navy wouldn't mean . . ."

"None of the instructors would dare. Not for me, or anyone."

"Yessir. Some of the joes are always on me about it. Tonight, I had enough."

I shook my head. If it weren't that, they'd have found another pretext. Wolves always sense the vulnerable ones.

My voice hardened. "You expect sympathy, joey? No, what you get is a caning. You sat in a cabin for weeks resisting a vial of goofjuice, and now you fall apart because a boy calls you a toady!"

"Not just a toady, a—" He compressed his lips.

"It's all right, you can say it. My bedmate, I assume. Children's nonsense."

"They're my mates!" An anguished cry.

"All the more reason to hold your temper. How in heaven do you think you'll cope with wardroom hazing if you can't—"

The caller buzzed. "Sir, priority call from Earthport Station." Sergeant Obutu.

"Later, I'm in the middle of—"

"Captain, pick up the caller!" Her voice brooked no argument.

Speechless, I thumbed the caller onto the speakers. "Yes, what—"

"—ERGENCY BROADCAST TO ALL SHIPS, ALL PERSONNEL! REPEAT: LUNAPOLIS BASE HAS BEEN BOMBED, EXTENT OF DAMAGE UN—"

"Lord God!" I stood frozen.

"—ADMIRALTY BASE DOESN'T RESPOND. SHIPYARDS AT EARTHPORT STATION UNDER ATTACK. AT LEAST SEVENTY-FIVE FISH ARE—"

"Captain Tsong on Invincible. *I'm taking—"*

"—OUR LASER BANKS. ANY SHIP WITHIN RANGE, PLEASE ASSIST. WE'RE—"

"Get off this channel; we need it! Until the chain of command is reestablished I'm senior. All vessels moored to Earthport Station, cast off immediately! About a hundred fish have Defused above Earth's atmosphere!"

A hundred? Lord, save us. If—

"Sir, should I—" Jerence was white.

"Shut up!" I bent close to the speaker, strained to hear.

"How the hell would I know, Wellington? *They're not on a social call, that's certain. Take your position and stay off the chan—"*

"Mayday! U.N.S. *Aztec*! We can't beat off attack, they've breached our hull! Mayday! Coordinates—"

I rasped, "Jerence, back to barracks! Move!"

"Aye aye, sir!" He saluted and was gone.

I keyed the caller to general frequency. "Tolliver! Thorne! To my office, flank!"

"Gibraltar to *Invincible*! We killed six, but a dozen more Defused alongside. We're coming up on *Aztec,* will try to help."

The caller buzzed. Sergeant Obutu. "I'm sending Cadet Ochard back to his dorm."

"Who? Yes, of course. Have all cadets report to barracks, flank."

"They're already in bed, sir. It's the middle of the night." The calm of her voice was a warm, gentle wave.

"Very well. Send Tolliver and Thorne in. And you too." I'd want her placid good sense. "Put someone on our landing radar. Wake a tech or one of the sergeants. If anything shows overhead, sound the alarms."

"Aye aye, sir."

"Turn off all outside lights. And no outgoing radio." If by any chance we'd escaped notice of the fish, best to do nothing to attract them.

I turned back to the speaker, as the hatch opened.

"Lieutenant Thorne reporting."

"Listen!"

Tolliver raced in, out of breath. "Hope this is important; I was dreaming of—"

"Quiet, Edgar!" I pulled up another chair. Kina Obutu came in, with cups and a pot of coffee; bless her. I poured a steaming cup, took a sip. "Lunapolis has gone off the air. We have no central command."

Tolliver. "U.N. Headquarters will take over. Or London."

"Groundsiders. We need Fleet Ops."

Sergeant Obutu said, "It may take a while to reorganize. London Admiralty normally relays through Earthport Station, and if the Station's under heavy attack . . ."

Thorne bit at his knuckles. "What's Admiralty supposed to do about it? We can't defend everywhere at once."

"I know that. They have to assign—"

"—OUTSIDE THE HULL! THEY'RE BURNING THROUGH! WE'VE ALL GONE TO SUITS—"

"—*Fusing to safety. We'll reestablish contact when—*"

"—most of the city under several feet of water. The asteroid struck the gulf fifty miles southeast of Galveston. We need helis, medical—"

"Do something!" I set down my coffee to pace.

We huddled at the caller while disaster swept through home system. Five ships were lost outright; thirteen others were damaged but still fighting. Four ships of the line were clear of gravitation and Fused out of the Solar System.

Fish came in droves. According to the scattered reports, almost three hundred aliens roamed home system. Earthport Station fought desperately to survive; if it fell, Earth's vast interstellar commerce would die with it.

Why hadn't the fish struck at Farside? Was it because only an occasional shuttle without fusion drives docked here? Thank Lord God that Radz and his Krane cadets were back from the Training Station.

I muttered, "Maybe we should get everyone suited. If the fish show . . ."

Tolliver. "There's nothing on radar."

"Sooner or later, they'll come for us. They've knocked out Lunapolis and they're swarming around the Station."

Kina Obutu said gently, "Do we really want middies and Sergeants running to help five hundred teens change tanks every couple of hours?"

"Suits without helmets, then." Thorne. "Call a suit drill. Have them practice putting helmets on and off."

Tolliver's eyebrow raised. "In the middle of the night?"

"You'd rather not tell them we're under attack?"

I said, "No one's attacked us yet." Yet I was certain they would, in time. "We'd panic our joeys, Thorne. They're still children."

Tolliver said, "U.N.N.S. cadets can face—"

I waved vaguely at the bulkhead. "They belong at home with their mothers. What right had we to pretend they're adults, take them off-planet to . . ." It seemed too much trouble to continue.

"Farside can't be defended." Tolliver tapped the console. "We have no laser cannon. Even the Trainers are unarmed."

Sergeant Obutu's voice was soft. "Even with weapons, middies and cadets can't hold against an alien armada. What about making a run for groundside?"

"In what, the transport shuttle?" Again I paced. "We only have one, and it's not built for reentry. I doubt the fish would let us transfer at Earthport Station."

She flushed at my sarcasm, but persisted. "We could orbit just above Earth's atmosphere. At least we'd have a chance to maneuver."

"Our transport can't hold more than fifty. Who would we leave behind?" That brought a silence.

"So, we wait?" Thorne.

"Yes. There's nothing else to—"

The speaker blared again. "—narrowly missing Vancouver. Fires are burning out of control in—"

"—FISH OUTRIDERS IN SECTIONS FIVE THROUGH NINE. WE'LL TRY TO HOLD OUT ON THE BRIDGE."

Thorne leaned over my desk, his face inches from mine. "Captain, this may be their last night! Tell them!"

I raised an eyebrow. "Was that an order?"

He blushed. "No. Sorry."

"If it's their last night, would you have them spend it in terror? I'll make an announcement tomorrow, if the fish haven't shown by then."

The voice from the speaker was light-years distant. "Admiral Iskander, speaking from London. We're gathering situation reports, but it's already clear we're under all-out attack."

"Observant of you!" Tolliver's fists bunched.

"Be silent!"

"—til we know enough to develop an overall strategy, every Station, every base, must defend itself independently. Ships in squadrons, follow the orders of your flotilla commander. All vessels within five hours of Earth proceed immediately toward Earth's outer atmosphere where fish are massing. Further orders will fol—"

"—SEVENTY-FIVE OR MORE. NEARLY A HUNDRED STILL SURROUND THE STATION, AND WE LOST OUR TOPSIDE LASERS ABOUT AN HOUR—"

"Mayday! Mayday!"

Tolliver was grim. "It'll be a short war, Captain. They've taken out the Navy."

"Not all of it. We still—"

"—assume Callisto Base is destroyed. That leaves the Naval Station on Deimos as the only—"

"Fiske here, in *Electra.* Am I senior?"

"—Coordinates twelve, two-sixty, fifty-four—"

"—massing over East Asia! For the moment they're ignoring us, but we need help, they're too many for the lasers to take—"

Thorne looked up. "Tolliver's right. We've lost."

"Maybe they'll leave us." On Hope Nation, they'd sometimes withdrawn for no discernible reason. "Once we have time to organize . . ." Wearily, I turned the volume down. If only I'd made my point clearer to Admiralty, we'd have a caterwaul bomb in production.

We sat in silence.

"In a way, it's a relief," Thorne said. My jaw dropped. He added, "We all have to go someday. Now I know it'll be soon."

Oddly, I understood. Whether the fish came tonight or days from now, soon I would face my reckoning with Him. "Even Hell seems preferable to the wait." I didn't realize I'd spoken aloud.

"That's rot, Captain!" Tolliver's contempt was withering. "The renowned Nick Seafort giving up? You've never done that!"

I growled, "What should I do, take command of the Hull?" I waved toward the mockup half buried in the Lunar dust. "We've no ships, no weapons, no place to hide. Sooner or later we'll run out of supplies!"

"Think of something! You always have!" Abruptly he turned away.

Thorne said, "As you pointed out, we're unarmed." When he spoke again his tone was wry. "Now if you don't mind, I'll go to the lounge. I'm of a mood for Arcvid."

Tolliver snarled, "That's what I'd expect of a loser like you!"

I snapped, "Apologize, Edgar. At once." Tolliver murmured something inaudible.

Thorne shrugged. "I don't mind, Captain. He's right. Back when we were cadets and middies, I didn't understand. Mr. Tolliver, I wish you well. Commandant, I think if—if things had worked out differently . . ." For a moment he sounded shy. "I'd have tried to redeem myself for you."

"Thank you." I rubbed my eyes. Hours ago—or minutes—I'd been ready to cane Jerence for brawling. Now our very civilization was crumbling. "Mr. Thorne, go to your Arcvid. Ms. Obutu, you're free to leave. You too, Tolliver."

Jeff Thorne hesitated. "I could stay, if you like."

"I'll call if I need you."

"Do that." He left.

Tolliver waited until we were alone. "Shall I get your suit, sir?"

"No. I won't be needing it."

"If the fish . . ." He grasped my intent, and stopped.

"Aye aye, sir. Will you sleep?"

"I'll wait by the caller." My cabin held nothing. "Leave me be!" Glowering, I watched him go.

I shut the hatch, turned low the lights, sat hunched at the console, scanning channel after channel.

"—onto Lunapolis. We've lost thousands. Admiralty warrens decompressed but there may be survivors. Our puters are offline. If the fish hold off awhile we can—"

"—have a rock! Must be two hundred of them around it. Am tracking—"

"—estimates nearly six hundred fish altogether—"

The fish had scored a complete surprise, and had gained overwhelming strategic superiority. They . . .

Annie! My wife was abandoned in Cardiff, while fish gathered above, shepherding rocks to destroy her.

And I was helpless. I swallowed my impotent rage.

Why did they attack like frenzied sharks? No one knew. I supposed it no longer mattered.

The anguished reports from the speaker faded into distance.

WHY HADN'T I MADE THEM LISTEN?

A distant call. "Be alert for distress call from U.N.A.F. shuttle 382AF or its lifepods. Admiral Georges De Marney, recently returned from Hope Nation, was en route from London Spaceport to assume command—"

A knock. I raised my head.

"Me, sir." Jeff Thorne. For a moment, he hesitated, then his shoulders squared. "I don't know what I was thinking. My place is here."

"In my office?" I waved at the furnishings. "You want the job?"

"No, sir." He smiled at my sally. "You handle it well. My duty is to help."

I looked away, ashamed. His tone recalled a young midshipman I'd once known. "Jeff—"

"Yes, sir." He came to the desk. "Remember when I told you Arcvid's like life? We're at level twenty-three. The ships come too fast. We're about to lose the board." Despite his words, his eyes were animated. "Let's see if we can make another level or two, sir."

"God, Jeff!" My voice was raw. "If only we could!"

"Let's start by closing our decompression hatches; that'll buy time even if a bomb hits."

"The concussion alone would kill us."

"Depends how close it strikes, right?" He gestured toward the barracks. "We want to save as many joeys as we can."

I was silent a moment. Then I stood, offered my hand. "Welcome back, Mr. Thorne."

His fingers clasped mine. "Thank you, sir."

"I wish I'd let them give me a ship. What a mission we could fly, you and I." I smiled, but in truth I was nearly out of my mind with frustration. I needed to do something, anything. Attack a fish with my bare hands. If they came to me I'd . . . My smile faded. Using what, a hand laser?

Anyway, I had no way to attract fish; Farside had no ships to call them.

"Sir, may I close the hatches?"

Static. "—for a broadcast by Secretary General Rafael De Vala."

I bent closer to the speaker.

"Citizens, members of our Armed and Naval Forces. Home system is under intense attack by the aliens known as the fish. Hundreds circle Earth itself. Galveston and nearby towns have been swamped by a tidal wave.

"As we learned at Hope Nation, the fish will use any means to subdue us. They may hit us with a lethal virus. They may try to bomb our cities. They may attack in ways we can't anticipate. There are unconfirmed reports they've already landed on the surface of Earth."

I sat heavily, rested my head in my hands.

"Lunapolis is destroyed, and with it, Fleet Operations Command. We're reorganizing command at Admiralty in London, but meanwhile—" The SecGen's voice wavered, then resumed.

"—though many elements of the fleet remain unharmed, our forces are scattered, our communications disrupted. Fish attack our groundside and satellite lasers in ever-increasing numbers."

Remote-controlled lasers couldn't fight them off. Even the fleet wasn't enough.

"U.N. Armed Forces across the planet are to engage the aliens wherever they try to land. Admiralty sends the following signal to all Naval units: 'All ships withdraw from engagement, and take up position in geosynchronous orbit over North America and Europe. At all costs we will defend our industrial base.'"

He faltered. "Admiralty sends the following message. 'To all ships and forces, everywhere: The United Nations expects every man to do his duty.'"

The speaker went silent.

"He abandoned Asia and Africa!" Thorne was stunned.

"Half the fleet is lost, maybe more! Should we protect African jungle, or the Boeing-McDonnell plants?"

"But . . ."

I sighed. "Go close the hatches, Jeff. There's not much else we can do." If only we had the caterwaul bomb.

"Aye aye, sir." He trod to the console in the outer office, tapped the control keys.

I sat wretchedly, as calls poured over the speaker.

If I took our shuttle, I could get to the fish at Earthport Station.

But the shuttle had no weapons.

Ram the bastards. I'd done it before.

They'd overwhelm me before I had a chance to do much damage. There were myriads of fish, and only one of me.

Time and again I'd refused a ship. Now I was on the far side of the moon, on a training base with no attack weapons.

"Groundside lasers broke it up! Only small pieces left!"

"—N.S. *Targon*. I've got to take the chance and Fuse. They're after our—"

"If anyone can hear me, this is Captain Roman de Ville, in a lifepod drifting inward toward the Sun. Three fish are Outside. One of them is swinging a—"

Please, God. Help us.

Thorne returned.

"Jeff, I want to be alone."

His face fell. "Yes, sir. I'll check the barracks."

"Good." Opening hatches to work his way along the warrens would give me time to ponder my folly.

I'd been the only person who had enough encounters with fish to comprehend their true menace, the one person with influence to persuade Admiral Duhaney to speed manufacture of the caterwaul bomb. I could have made them listen, made them prepare. But rather than annoy the Admiral, I'd worried about my petty career. And doomed the human race.

Lord God, what will I say to You, when the time comes? Do You have someplace worse than Hell to consign me?

"—whatever you can to hold them off. You've GOT to buy us time!"

Buy time for what? The fleet was devastated; we'd need years to rebuild, even if the fish retreated.

"—lost with all hands. U.N.S. Victoria was the fastship brought home some months ago by Captain Nicholas Sea—"

"—need time to evacuate the cities, if nothing else! Attack, I told you! I don't care what odds—"

I became aware of a sharp ache in my hand. I'd scraped my knuckles when I slammed them into the console.

I wrapped my handkerchief across my aching fingers. Had it all come to a hopeless effort to evacuate our vulnerable cities?

In any event, we hadn't enough transports or time to empty cities like New York. And evacuation would start with the influential Uppies; joeys such as Pedro Chang and his tribesmen would be forgotten.

Lord, let me do something. Given time, luck, weapons, I could kill fish. I'd nuked hundreds of them swarming around Orbit Station. I'd fought them in the Ventura Mountains, burned them with *Wellington*'s lasers. I'd even skewered one with *Challenger*'s prow in a desperate effort at revenge.

"—OVER THE MIDWESTERN UNITED STATES! ALL SHIPS, TRY TO BREAK UP THEIR FORMATION! EXPECT A LARGE GROUP WITH A ROCK TO DEFUSE AT ANY—"

I shut off the speaker.

An hour passed, perhaps more. I roused myself, sat staring, opened the desk drawer.

"I'm sorry," Lieutenant Sleak had said to the holocamera, at Devon.

I understood, at last. When he'd uncovered Sergeant Serenco's embezzlement, he blamed his own incompetence as a supervisor. He'd felt it his duty to prevent, or at least discover, Serenco's misdeeds, and the shame had been too great to bear. And so he'd taken his pistol from the drawer.

Oh, yes, I understood.

There's nothing left, you see. I have no way to defend my children, no way to draw the aliens away from Earth. I've no way to destroy them even if I could call them.

I've no way to atone.

I gripped the pistol, thumbed the safety. "I'm sorry."

The empty office made no answer.

I set the pistol to point-blank range, pressed it to my temple. What else could I do? We couldn't repel fish from an unarmed training camp. I had nothing but a base full of cadets, a transport too small to carry more than a handful to safety. And the Training Station, with *Trafalgar* and a few Fusers. All were unarmed. It was hopeless.

Unless . . .

I sat bolt upright. After a time the pistol fell from my hand.

It could be done.

But, Lord, the cost.

PART 4

January, in the year of our Lord 2202

Chapter 22

I rushed to the head, splashed water on my cheeks, stared at the wild face in the mirror.

Back at my console, I opened the decompression hatches throughout the base. I keyed the alarm for General Quarters, thumbed my caller.

"ALL CADETS, ALL STAFF, ALL OFFICERS, ASSEMBLE AT THE MESS HALL, FLANK! TAKE NO MORE THAN ONE MINUTE TO DRESS!"

Ignoring my own orders, I straightened my tie, brushed my hair, smoothed my jacket. Before I left the office, I stooped, picked up the pistol.

During my long, last walk to the mess hall I practiced my calm. No one must suspect.

Edgar Tolliver sprinted down the corridor. "Have they come? What's happened?"

"Not yet." I slid open the mess-hall hatch.

"STAND TO!"

Officers and men, middies and cadets, snapped to attention. I holstered the pistol, strode through the crowd. Boys and girls stood stiffly, cheeks flushed, uniforms awry, hair uncombed. "At ease!"

They complied. For a moment I felt a wistful pride. I would have liked to take them to graduation, and beyond.

For a long time I gazed. Then I began.

"I've decided to take a number of cadets on special mission to the Training Station. You'll be supervised by midshipmen. We leave immediately. Ordinarily I would select candidates based on skills and training, but there are reports that fish have been sighted in home system. Therefore, I will take only volunteers."

Absolute silence. Kina Obutu shook her head sadly. I blushed. As casually as possible I added, "There may be some danger. However, volunteers will receive credit for two months of Nav." Somehow, despite the obscenity of what I'd said, I managed to hold their gaze.

A hand shot in the air, then another.

Tolliver moved to my side, puzzlement battling anger. I said quietly, "Be silent. That's an order."

I looked to the closest raised hand. "Step forward. Name?"

"Rafe Slater, sir." His voice hadn't yet broken.

I forced a reply. "Report to the suiting room."

"Aye aye, sir. Excuse me, should I get my duffel?"

"No." I nodded to the next upraised hand. "Name?"

"Vasily Karnyenkov."

"Very well. Who else?"

A sharp tug at my jacket. Tolliver. "Where do you think you're taking them?"

I thrust him away. "Next?"

"Jacques Theroux, sir."

I frowned. "Your name's familiar. How do I know you?"

"I don't know, sir."

"Report to the lock." I looked around; only a few hands waved.

"You don't even remember!" Tolliver's words came in a hiss.

"I told you to be silent."

"You threw another boy off at Cull, for Theroux."

Did I? That was so long past. A damnation ago.

"Sergeant Ibarez!"

He hurried forward.

"Go to the lock, help the cadets suit up, send them to board the shuttle."

"Aye aye, sir." No questions.

I searched for more volunteers.

"Robert Boland, sir."

"I know." I stared through him. "Very wel—No. refused." The others might be mere names, but I knew too well what the boy meant to his father.

"Sir, please!" His tone was anguished. "You told me I paid for my offense."

"That's not it; it's that I don't want you!" My voice was the harsher for knowing I was unjust.

He whispered, "Please, I'm first in my class in Nav! Let me go!"

I looked around the room. Cadets shifted uneasily from foot to foot, anxious to avoid my glance.

A man chose his own fate. "Very well. So be it."

"Johan Stritz, sir." He stood proudly. Behind him, Kyle Drew and Kevin Arnweil waited their turn.

Why, Lord? They're my special charges. Could you not spare . . .

I made my voice hard. "Very well." One by one, I accepted all three.

"Loren Reitzman, sir." I frowned, then recalled. The boy who'd balked at the oath of enlistment. He'd had a week of misery, then buckled down to the business of being a cadet. We'd had no further trouble. Would he crack again?

"Very well." The cadet trotted off to the suiting room. A tall, gawky girl raised her hand tremulously, gave her name. I nodded; she ran off.

"Jerence Branstead, sir." His bruised features appealed.

I swallowed. I accepted the Boland boy, and all the others. How could I not take him?

No. Lord help me, I could not. I'd sworn to his father to keep him safe, when he'd entrusted the boy to my care on Hope Nation. Even though my word was without value, I would spare at least one child.

I raised my gaze. "No. Refused."

He blurted, "Sir, I know what I'm doing! Please let me come!"

"BE SILENT! I FORBID IT!"

Shamefaced, Jerence crept from my sight.

"Elena Von Siel, sir!"

I nodded heavily. "Very well."

A black-haired dark youngster. "Omar Benghadi." The girl at his side raised her hand tentatively, brought it down. She looked away.

I knew him from somewhere. He fidgeted while I stared through him, racking my brain. Nothing. "Very well. Go with the others."

The girl watched him disappear, her fists clenching. Abruptly her hand shot into the air. "Alicia Johns, sir!"

So young, so vulnerable. I made my voice flat. "Very well." Who were they?

I had it. The young pair I'd met on an idle visit to the Devon classrooms a few days before my appointment; the meeting had led to my chat with Sergeant Ibarez.

I turned to my work.

When the last hand was acknowledged forty-three cadets had volunteered. Were they enough? I could draft just a few, for—

No. That was too great an abomination, even for me.

My voice rang out. "You other cadets! Return to your barracks. Your officers will be along shortly. Dismissed!"

Some sheepish, others relieved, they herded toward the hatch.

I couldn't leave on that note. I called, "Those who didn't volunteer need have no shame. I wish you well." I bit off the rest; it sounded too like farewell.

"Midshipmen, step forward!"

Self-consciously, the seven young officers clustered around. Thomas Keene, Adam Tenere, Sandra Ekrit. Others I hardly knew: Guthrie Smith and Tommy Tsai. Red-haired Anton Thayer. Eduard Diego.

"You're all coming with us. Mr. Keene, have your joeys report to the shuttle immediately." Should I have given them a choice, like the cadets?

No. They were officers.

I was proud that their discipline held. No questions. First Midshipman Keene said only, "Aye aye, sir." He turned to the others. "Let's go."

In a moment no one was left in the hall but the shuttle Pilot, my two lieutenants, the drill sergeants, and a few techs. I beckoned them close.

"Pilot Trayn, you'll take us to the Training Station. Get the shuttle ready. The rest of you, listen carefully. As I told the cadets, there are fish in home system." The Pilot paused at the hatch to listen. "They've done great harm, and it's possible they'll come here. Keep the outside lights off, stay off the radio. Lord God willing, help will arrive." Pilot Trayn nodded, went out to the corridor.

"Lieutenant Thorne is in charge until . . . while I'm gone. You sergeants, follow his orders. If the fish come . . ." Something seemed wrong with my throat. "Get your joeys suited, try to keep them alive as best you can. Perhaps the fish will do their destruction and leave."

"What about you, sir?" Ms. Obutu.

"I'll be at the Training Station." I was careful to say no more; someone might still obstruct me. "That's all. Dismissed."

Sergeant Radz hesitated. "Commandant . . ."

"Yes?"

"Godspeed, sir."

"Thank you."

He snapped a parade-ground salute, turned and strode out. My eyes filled. Kina Obutu lingered for a word; I shook my head.

"Am I relieved?" Tolliver.

"What?"

"You put Thorne in charge. What will you have me do?"

"Go with me."

His tone was bitter. "I thought so. I'm at your orders."

I said gently, "It wasn't an order, First Lieutenant Tolliver."

"What are you up to this time?"

"I can't tell you."

"The last time you said that you nuked a bloody Station!"

"There's none here to nuke."

"I'll go. We started together. It's fitting that we end together. I'll meet you at the shuttle." I wondered how much he'd guessed.

I checked and rechecked my suit. Though earlier I'd been ready to welcome decompression, now I had to stay alive until my task was done.

I tested my helmet clamps one last time, looked to Ibarez. "Is everyone boarded?"

"Yes, sir. Am I to come along?"

He was an experienced hand, but he had a barracks, and his flock mustn't be abandoned. "No. Go back to your joeys."

"Aye aye, sir." He hesitated, gestured to the lock. "Odd mood they were in. Even though they sense something's wrong they were jostling like puppies to go aboard."

"Children think they're immortal."

"Yes." His expression sobered. "That's why we're here. To protect them until they learn otherwise."

I stepped into the lock.

Outside, all was still. I tried to adjust my vision to the pin-points of a billion stars.

I loped across the Lunar dust, waited impatiently while the shuttle lock cycled. Every moment meant lives lost on Earth.

Inside, I brushed past Tolliver and strapped down in the front row. I keyed to suit frequency. "Edgar, tell the Pilot we're ready for liftoff."

"He's not here, sir."

"He's had plenty of time to get ready!" I keyed to base frequency. "Find Mr. Thorne." I fretted while the precious minutes passed.

"Lieutenant Jeffrey Thorne repo—"

"Get my Pilot suited and out here!"

"Isn't he with you, sir? I haven't seen him any—"

"Find him! Move!"

"Aye aye, sir." The line went dead.

Tolliver took a seat across the aisle. "You seem in some haste." His tone was dry.

"None of your lip, Tolliver!"

"No, sir. Of course not. Is there a schedule we have to meet? I only ask as your second in command."

No need to explain; he'd find out all too soon. "We're sitting ducks if the fish come!" I drummed on the seat arm. "Where's the bloody Pilot?"

As if in answer my radio crackled. "Thorne, here. Mr. Trayn is nowhere to be found. We can roust the cadets and search cabin by cabin until—"

"When he shows, brig him! Tolliver, let's go!" I scrambled out of my seat, launched myself toward the cockpit. I took the copilot's seat, waited for Tolliver to buckle in alongside. "Help me lift this bucket."

He said mildly, "We're not rated for—"

"Remember the Venturas shuttle on Hope Nation? Compared to that, this is child's play. You have to *work* to foul up a Lunar launch."

"I see. In that case, would you take the Pilot's seat?"

I ignored him and flicked switches, waited for the puter to self-check. The vessel was fully fueled, as I knew it would be. I pumped a few liters of propellant through the fuel tubes, watched the gauges wiggle.

A dry, mechanical voice. "Beginning preflight checklist. Port thrusters indicate full tanks. Starb—"

I glanced skyward though the porthole. "No time. Cancel the

checklist." A methodical check would consume almost a half hour.

Console lights shifted. "Discontinuing launch at your order."

"No, damn it, prepare to launch!"

"Beginning preflight checklist. Port thrusters indicate —"

I cursed silently. "Puter, prepare for launch without checklist."

"Standing orders require checklist prior to—"

"Cancel standing orders! I'm the Commandant!"

"Only the Pilot may do that. I'm a U.N.A.F. shuttle, not subject to Naval command."

I slammed my gloved fist on the console. "What are you laughing at, Edgar?"

"Nothing, sir."

"Puter, log me on as Pilot."

"U.N.A.F. authorization code?"

"As Base Commandant I relieve the Pilot and appoint myself. Tolliver, is there a manual shutoff to this idiot?"

"I have no idea." He bent to the dash. "Don't see one."

"Power down!" I flicked the switches. One by one the console lights extinguished.

Tolliver said mildly, "It'd take less time to let him run his—"

"We don't need the puter to turn on power." I switched on the engines.

"We need him to plot a course to—"

"Not to lift off." The hell with regs. "All we need is orbital velocity, and the nose pointed away from the ground."

"Right. I'm glad we're doing this by the book."

"By the way, you have the conn." I leaned back. "Oh, don't gape, we both know you have a surer hand." I braced for the mild acceleration.

There was no reason a U.N.A.F. shuttle couldn't launch manually. I recited that, as a mantra, while our engines shuddered and the frustrated pull of the moon thrust me into my seat.

At last Tolliver silenced our motors. I peered out at the Lunar surface far below.

"If you see the Training Station, let me know."

"Don't be silly, it wouldn't be—" I realized he was in one of his moods. Though I'd warned him not to lapse into insolence, I felt oddly relieved. "Turn on the Station beacon by remote." I watched the radar screen, half expecting fish to Defuse at our side.

"Is there a chance the puter would tell us the way?"

"I'd rather walk." Nonetheless, I switched the puter on, waited for its circuit check. "Plot a course to the Naval Training Station."

A pause of at least a second. "Voice ID indicates you are Nicholas Seafort, U.N.N.S. Do you confirm?"

"Yes."

"Who is the Pilot?"

"I am." Another few seconds and I'd do the plot by hand.

"Your name isn't in my Pilot registry."

"All right, have it your way. There's no Pilot aboard."

"A licensed Pilot must be in the cockpit of a U.N.A.F. shuttle prior to launch."

"But we're aloft, and he doesn't seem to be here. Will you plot our course, or does your bloody program call for us to starve until our orbit decays?" Dosmen are all alike. They never program flexibility.

The puter's voice took on a firmer note. "Emergency procedures now in effect. I'm plotting course to Naval Training Station, will initiate automatic course corrections."

"Why, thank you." I knew I ought to recheck the figures by hand, but for once I let it go. My mind was too full.

Figures flashed across the screen. A moment later our side thrusters fired briefly, orienting us toward the Station.

"You're welcome," the puter said. "On return I will file a complaint with U.N.A.F. Transport concerning your violation of regulations, Base Commander Seafort."

By then I wouldn't care. Still, I wasn't about to take any bilge from an animated circuit board. "Puter, on our return I will file a complaint with U.N.A.F. Transport concerning violations of regs by this shuttle."

A puff of propellant; our turn eased. The main engines ignited. "My files show no record of a complaint ever being filed by a human against a puter."

"Then this will be the first. Tolliver, duck back and make sure everyone's all right. Don't be long. I need you to watch for fish."

"Aye aye, sir." He ducked back into the cabin.

Silence, for several billion nanoseconds. A slight hesitation in the mechanical voice. "Query: what would be the consequence if a puter were found in violation of regs?"

Ah. "I'm Navy, not U.N.A.F., so it's not my decision. I would expect complete power-down, and personality dissolve." Heartless, but I was irked. Time and again, on ship or Station, a snotty puter had aggravated me beyond endurance.

Tolliver slipped back into the cockpit. "No one's gravsick, at any rate."

"Good." Perhaps I could let the cadets unclamp their helmets, even walk around. They'd be a long time in suits. But a fish might Defuse alongside without notice, and if it threw, we'd decompress faster than our clumsier youngsters could resuit.

"Commandant Seafort, no violation of regs was intended."

"Be silent, puter. Use your circuits to scan for fish. Alert us for anything within five hundred kilometers."

"Acknowledged, Captain." He subsided.

I flicked on the caller, scanned Naval and emergency channels. To my surprise, the U.N. was broadcasting bad news as well as the occasional good.

In some aspects the situation had worsened. More ships had been lost, more rocks hurled at our cities. On the other hand, we'd reestablished a clear chain of command, and banks of groundside lasers had burst several rocks hurled by the fish into Earth's gravity well.

Though the Admiralty warrens of Lunapolis were devastated, many decompression hatches had slammed shut in time. It appeared most of our brass had survived, though communication was sporadic. Admiral Duhaney, through a multiship relay, had transferred fleet command to London. It was for the best; he was no battle commander.

Until we reached the Station there was little to do but listen. I switched frequencies back and forth.

"U.N.A.F. lasers on the outskirts of Beijing are gone. Nonetheless Beijing command reports—"

"—landed outside Kiev—"

"—locked in the comm room! The hatch is smoking! For God's sake someone help us it's coming—"

"—thirteen settling over Brasilia. Groundside lasers have—"

U.N. military command reported two hundred fifty kills. Yet some six hundred fish continued to Fuse in and out of home system, attacking our fleet, raining destruction on our cities.

Tolliver. "We should report to Admiralty, sir."

"It would serve no purpose." If I told them where I was headed, they'd ask why.

The puter came to life. "Seven encroachments, at outer limit of search zone. Presumed hostile."

My mind snapped back to the shuttle. "Where?"

"Coordinates two five two—"

"Never mind that, just tell me where!" What did I want him to do, point?

"Just short of the Lunar horizon, Captain."

"What's in that direction?" I peered.

"Aliens, as I've said. And Earthport Station. I can contact Station Control and inquire what other objects might be in their zone of—"

"No." I tried to gnaw at my knuckle, bumped my hand against my closed helmet. "How far is the Training Station from Earthport?"

"Calculating. Assuming no orbit corrections by either body, eleven hundred point five one kilometers as of this moment."

Too close for comfort. No one knew what else the fish could sense, in addition to N-waves. If they learned of our presence, how long before they showed up to annihilate us?

I thrust the thought aside. Nothing I could do about it.

"*Bolivar* to London Command! They're Fusing away by the dozen! We're winning!"

"*—lost our tubes, but otherwise we're all right. Only seven of them out there and—*"

"—urge you to let us disengage from over North America. There's so many fish we're not doing a damn bit of good. Earthport needs us, so does—"

I flicked to another frequency.

"Deputy SecGen Franjee has landed in London to establish an alternative command in case U.N. Headquarters is, uh, disabled. UNESCO Director Johanson has issued an advisory warning against any public gatherings during the next month due to the risk of virus . . ."

I muttered something.

"Pardon, sir?" Tolliver

I repeated, "No need to worry about virus. We don't have a month."

"How do you know? They've only hit a few cities, even if the death toll—"

"Didn't you hear? They're Fusing out in large numbers, for more rocks."

"You can't be sure—"

"I know. The bastards have found a weapon that works." I switched back to fleet channel. "I thought that rusty chipboard told us we'd only be an hour!"

The puter spoke with injured dignity. "Forty-seven minutes since I gave you our ETA, Base Commandant."

"We dock in thirteen minutes?"

"In thirteen minutes we begin docking maneuvers. Estimate ten minutes of fuel-conservative maneuvering for close approach, five for mooring and airlock mate."

"No time. Just get us close enough to throw a line; we'll go hand over hand. And don't waste time saving propellant."

"Regulations prohib—"

"Did you hear me, puter?"

Another full second. "Acknowledged, Base Commander." He seemed anxious to avoid further quarrel.

"—masses of fish Defused over Bombay, with an asteroid. A few minutes ago they dropped it on . . . dear Jesus, all we can see is a fireball; there must be hundreds of thousands dead—" The voice broke in a sob.

"You were right, sir."

I made no answer.

Despite the agony of Bombay, Earth had so far been lucky; no other great city had been hit. If New York or London were targeted, deaths would be in the millions.

All I could do was wait. And plan ahead. "Mr. Tenere and Mr. Keene to the cockpit!"

Moments later the two middies appeared, clinging to the bulkhead straps in free fall.

"Check every cadet's helmet clamps, then pump out the ship. Use emergency overrides to open both inner and outer hatches." They listened intently. "You'll find grappling lines in the lock. When we're at rest relative to the Station one of you —Mr. Tenere—take a line across. Secure it and wait with Lieutenant

Tolliver for Mr. Keene to send the cadets over. When the Station lock is full, cycle them inside and come out for more."

"Aye aye, sir."

"Mr. Keene, get the cadets ready."

"Aye aye, sir. What are we doing? Is this a training—"

"Two demerits. Any other questions?"

"No, sir!" He beat a retreat.

Edgar Tolliver studied the gloves of his suit. "Indulge my curiosity. Is there a reason you won't explain what you're up to? What harm in telling them? Or me, for that matter?"

I said hoarsely, "I'll bear the responsibility."

"For what? If anything happens to you . . . "

"Watch for the Station, Edgar."

He sighed.

The puter. "You'll find it about seven degrees to port, distance thirty kilometers."

I peered into the endless night, thought I saw a patch where no stars shone. "Any fish nearby?"

The puter's tone held reproach. "I'd have told you. Your standing orders—"

"Skip it."

"I will approach with my lock facing the Training Station, at a distance of twenty meters."

"Very well, Shuttle. As soon as we've crossed over, withdraw to three hundred meters." I'd need room to dock the Fusers.

A silence. "Usually I have a Pilot. It's not often I take my own conn." His tone was wistful.

My gloved fingers drummed against the instrument panel. "How soon?"

"Approximately five minutes fifteen point three two sec—"

"Tolliver, make sure he doesn't ram the Station." I twisted out of my seat.

"There isn't the slightest danger of contact with—"

"Adam! Mr. Keene! Are you ready? Get your cadets lined up!"

Some of our youngsters had trained on lines strung to the Hull outside Farside, others had not. I had no idea if any of my volunteers had been through their Station training; in my eagerness I hadn't bothered to ask. Well, it didn't matter all that much. They needed only to make their way across to the Station lock; I wouldn't send them clambering Outside after that.

When it was time, Adam gauged his distance to the Station, launched himself with the shuttle's line secured to his waist. Moments later he had it tied to the stanchion just outside the lock. Tolliver crossed next, to help on the Station side.

Under my irascible scrutiny Thomas Keene placed each youngster's hands in the correct position, and eased him out the shuttle lock. Endless minutes later the last of the cadets had crossed to Tolliver's outstretched hand without mishap. Next, the middies. Anton Thayer grinned, swung across the line with agile grace. Sandra Ekrit followed. Then Diego.

Keene and I were last. A moment after I detached the mooring line, the shuttle's side thrusters squirted a cloudy spray of propellant that instantly turned to crystals of ice. The shuttle drifted clear.

Tolliver, Keene and I cycled through the lock, to find middies and cadets milling aimlessly in the corridor. I frowned.

"Adam, run to the control cabin, check the air gauges." The sooner we got our cadets out of suits, the better.

The eleven Fusers were docked in a line extending around the disk. The Station had but two locks. We'd have to bring the Fusers around, a pair at a time. I keyed my radio. "Mr. Tolliver, go Outside and mate the closest Fuser to the forward bay."

Should I send Keene or Adam for the next boat? I knew Tenere could handle the thrusters, but Keene was first middy; if he was incompetent, better to learn it now. "Mr. Keene, dock the second ship at the aft bay." The boy's eyes lit with pleasure; for a few brief moments he'd be in charge of a vessel, however tiny. "Anton, give him a hand."

Tolliver and the two middies cycled through the lock. They would clamber around the rim of the Station disk until they reached the Fusers. Adam and I had done the same on our visit months before.

My suit radio crackled. "Midshipman Tenere reporting, sir. The Station console shows breathable air. I'll start checking cabin gauges."

"Don't bother. Come back."

"But—aye aye, sir."

"You cadets, take off your suits. No, form a single line, first. Midshipmen, you too, over there. We're about to conduct a special exercise." Very special. I spoke as calmly as I could.

"One midshipman and five cadets will man each trainer. I'll

direct, from *Trafalgar.*" Thanks to the legacy of the Screaming Boy, I would be able to call each Fuser, but their single-frequency radios could contact only my command vessel.

I unclamped my helmet.

We had middies enough to launch seven trainers, though I had cadets for eight. I'd assumed the Pilot would take a boat, but he'd heard me mention the attacking fish, and had hidden until we departed.

I myself had to be aboard *Trafalgar,* and I needed Tolliver with me; I couldn't run the Mothership and direct all the trainers by myself.

Even eight Fusers might not be enough. How could I risk it with seven? But how could I put a trainer in the hands of unsupervised cadets?

A bump, barely perceptible, as the lock seals kissed. Tolliver had docked. In other circumstances I'd tease him about the jolt; middies were taught only a perfect mating was acceptable. During my simulation drills on *Hibernia,* I'd writhed in humiliation at my lieutenant's sarcastic mirth.

The outer airlock hatch shut; Tolliver was cycling through. I clawed free from my suit. "Ms. Ekrit, take the first five cadets onto Fuser One. Show them where to sit. They should all be able to read an instrument panel, at least. I want you clear of the lock in five minutes."

"Aye aye, sir. To where?"

"A half kilometer should be enough. Be ready to dodge if another trainer drifts out of control." With middies and cadets at the helm, Lord God knew what havoc we might engender.

"Aye aye, sir. Will we maintain close formation after—"

"Get aboard, Middy!" A sullen look flashed, but she obeyed.

"Ready for orders, sir."

I jumped at the sound. "Where did you come from, Mr. Keene? I told you to—"

"I docked at the aft bay, sir."

I hadn't felt the bump. "Very well," I said, grudging his competence. "You five, go along with Mr. Keene. Slater, into the lock; you can pull off your suit after." I turned to Adam and Tolliver. "As soon as the locks are clear, bring two more Fusers alongside."

Soon the second pair of Fusers were mated to the Station. Fresh-faced Tommy Tsai took Fuser Three. A handful of cadets followed him aboard. As they filed past I put out my arm, blocked Kyle Drew. My hand rested on the lanky cadet's neck, pulled his forehead against my chest. "Godspeed, boy." I had to look away.

His voice was bright. "I'll be all right, sir." He hefted the helmet slung under his arm.

"I know you will."

He stepped into the lock.

Please, Lord. Give me strength to do my duty.

"Fuser Two to Commandant. We're half a kilometer out." Thomas Keene, but how had he reached me? My suit radio wasn't set to Fuser band. After a moment I realized the midshipman had been smart enough to use his own suit radio to contact mine.

"Very well, Mr. Keene. Radio silence until further orders."

Back to work.

Redheaded Anton Thayer, the boy I'd found cavorting on his graduation day, took the fourth Fuser. Johan Stritz strode eagerly into the lock, along with four other cadets whose names I couldn't recollect.

I paced anxiously until boats Three and Four untied and cast off. Tolliver and Adam cycled through the aft lock for two more. Vital time was wasting; Lord God knew what harm the fish had done while I dithered here on the Station.

Several cadets still hadn't finished pulling off their suits. One clumsy lad had his suit half off but still wore his helmet. Plebes; I should never have brought them. No matter. They'd have time to desuit aboard their Fusers.

I was suddenly aware of the silence. I set my suit radio to scan Naval frequencies.

"—above Lunapolis. So far I don't see a rock but if we get too close—"

"We will fight them on the beaches, we will fight them in the cities—"

Guthrie Smith was the next middy in line. Once, he'd been caned for fighting with a cadet in an attempt to enforce discipline. I hoped he'd learned better. "Get ready, boy."

The hatch to Five opened. With Midshipman Smith went Loren Reitzman, the ungainly lad who'd balked at his oath. Four others, whom I barely knew.

A bump. Tolliver, mating the sixth Fuser.

"Edgar, as soon as the locks are clear take Adam out for another two—"

My suit speaker crackled. *"U.N.A.F. Shuttle 20123 to Naval Base Commandant Seafort. Query: do orders given while you were aboard apply after you've departed?"*

"Shuttle, stay off the caller! I have—"

"Very well, I'll assume they do not." The speaker went dead.

"Tolliver, dock yours at the forward—damn it!" I keyed the radio. "What orders, Shuttle?"

"You directed me to alert you of any fish within five hundred kilometers. At that time you were still—"

"How many? Where?"

"Two. Distance seven kilometers, closing slowly. They appeared moments ago, so I assume they arrived by Fusion. They do not respond to—"

"Mr. Diego! Move your cadets into Six, flank!"

"Aye aye, sir!" The middy grabbed the first cadet, thrust the black-haired youth toward the aft lock. Benghadi, I recalled. The next two cadets ran after. A youngster from the back of the line darted forward, inserted herself behind them. "I'll go, sir. Please let me!"

"Who are you—all right, move!"

"Alicia Johns, sir! Thank you!" In mess hall, she'd volunteered the moment he had. Mates.

"Tolliver, how soon can we dock the next two Fusers?"

In my radio, the lieutenant's voice was tight. "Three minutes for mine, but both locks are still engaged."

"Mr. Smith, break away from the fore lock! Now!"

It was an agonizing minute before the response. "Aye aye, sir. Sorry, I was seating the cadets. They don't—"

"Move!"

"I am, sir! Lock is cycled, rocking the seals loose . . . I have breakaway!"

"Clear the lock area, Tolliver's coming round!"

"Aye aye, sir. I'll wait for orders at half a kilometer like you told Ms. Ekrit."

"Good lad, Guthrie. Adam, Edgar, get moving!"

"U.N.A.F. shuttle to Station. Three more fish within the search zone."

"How far?"

"One of them is at three point six kilometers, the other two at fifty meters."

Fifty meters? Lord Christ. I'd told the cadets to desuit. If a fish threw now, and melted our hull—

"Tolliver here." Edgar's breath came fast; clambering over the disk was hard work. "No fish in sight. Ask him, fifty meters from where?"

"Shuttle, did you hear?" A thump, from the aft lock. Midshipman Diego was breaking free without waiting for orders.

"Yes, I monitor all channels used by—"

"Where?"

"Fifty meters from me, of course. All reckoning is assumed egocentric unless—"

"Where the hell are you, Shuttle?"

"Three hundred meters from the Station, as you ordered." The puter's tone was injured.

Still too close. A fish might be upon us before we could launch the next Fusers.

"Guthrie Smith reporting, sir. There are fish near the shutt—"

"Quiet, Middy!" I would give Adam Tenere one of the last two trainers. My plan had been to put unsupervised cadets in the eighth, but now we'd have no time to talk them through breakaway. Could they handle it alone?

"Any of you had Station training?"

A girl stepped forward, said proudly, "I have, sir. Tanya Guevire."

Guevire? Hadn't someone found her in bed with—No time for that.

"I've had training, sir." I caught my breath. Kevin Arnweil, who'd seen his friend Dustin die on the Hull.

Lord, You make it so hard. "Anyone else? Very well. Kevin, you're in charge of Nav. Ms. Guevire will pilot. As soon as—"

"Captain, two fish between us and the shuttle!" Tolliver's calm held, but barely. "I'm on my way with Fuser Seven. Adam just reached Eigh—it's squirting this way! I'm—God, I hate those things!"

"Edgar, take Seven to the forward lock! Adam, thrust to the aft lock. Don't bother trying to mate. Decompress your craft now!" Adam was slower at mating than Tolliver, and if a fish caught his Fuser at the lock the rest of us would die for naught.

I stumbled as I thrust a leg into my suit. "All unsuited cadets to the fore airlock with Arnweil and Guevire! Everyone else to the aft lock. Check your helmet clamps!" They all rushed to comply. The boy who'd never removed his helmet ran to the aft lock, thrust his legs into his suit. He wouldn't have enough time to finish; I propelled him to the fore lock, turned to Guevire.

"Tanya, as soon as your hatch is sealed, run to the console and rock your Fuser loose. Remember how?"

"Portside thrusters. Fore, aft, fore, aft. If the seal doesn't break, both at once for—"

"You've got it." I clamped my helmet tight.

Adam Tenere, his voice taut with tension. "Sir, my mooring line is unhooked; I'll be right there. What should I do if that fish comes at me?"

"Try to evade, or abandon ship at once if it throws at you." I grimaced; I'd wish nobody the death he faced.

"Shuttle!"

"Yes, Base Comm—"

"Turn on your lights! Begin maneuvers. Full spin, X axis. Hold for one minute, then commence spin on Y axis!"

A second's pause. *"That might attract the fish. I am charged with self-preservation unless—"*

"This is an Unless! Do it, or . . ." I groped. "By God, mister, I'll have your circuits up for court-martial!"

I heard Tolliver snort. Well, I couldn't think of anything better.

"Commencing maneuvers." The shuttle.

A bump, not gentle. "I'm docking Fuser Seven, Captain." Tolliver. "I'll have—come on, damn you!"

"Edgar, the second you're mated, come in and help me transfer the suited cadets to Fuser Eight!"

"Will do, but that bloody fish is still nosing around Adam. About sixty meters distant."

I made a final check of my suit. Another bump, from Outside. The lock light flashed; Tolliver had mated. The slim youngster I'd pushed to the forward lock zipped his last suit seal, twisted his helmet clamps just as our inner hatch slid open. "Into the trainer, all of you!"

I herded the six cadets to the lock. In the confusion the boy who'd resuited evaded my arm, dashed instead to the aft lock. Well, he was suited and we'd need him for the last Fuser.

The forward lock shut, cycling the cadets to Seven.

I slapped open the aft hatch. "Everybody in!"

A girl hesitated in the corridor. "Fish are out there!"

"Get in the lock!"

"Not with those things outside!"

I lunged at her; she backed away.

"Come along!" I stepped into the lock, where Tolliver and the remaining eight cadets crowded.

Adam, in my helmet. "Sir, this bloody fish is squirting toward the Station!"

No time to deal with the terrified girl. With the fish approaching we might not have time to launch Fuser Eight.

I slapped the lock shut. "Hang on to the safeties!" I yanked the emergency release. The outer hatch popped open; I felt myself pulled out by the rush of escaping air. One boy lost his grip on the safety bar; I managed to grab his arm while hanging on to the safety with my other hand.

"Adam!" I leaned out into space.

"Right here, sir! Stay clear until I get this thing stopped." Fuser Eight drifted closer, huge from the perspective of a suited figure in its path. I ducked back into the lock.

The middy. "Cabin air is blown, sir. I have my hatch open."

"Base Commandant, four fish are within fifty meters. May I break off maneuver and retreat?"

"All right, Shuttle. See if they follow. If not, reengage."

"That's not the purpose of retreat." The puter's tone was plaintive.

Two quick squirts from Adam's forward thrusters. Fuser Eight came to rest relative to the Station. "Adam, throw a line!" I waited for him to appear in the Fuser's gaping lock.

I cursed. He was taking too long. Someone would have to jump across, help speed things up. Could I launch myself and manage not to miss the Fuser? If I guessed wrong . . . I braced myself against the lock.

Adam clambered into the Fuser lock, a magnetic line draped over his arm. He uncoiled it, swung twice, let go.

The line would miss our lock by at least a meter. If the magnetic disk struck cleanly it would cling to the Station's hull. Otherwise Adam would have to reel it in and try again.

With the maddening slowness of free fall, the line sailed toward the hull. I gripped the safety bar, leaned out as far as I could.

The disk struck the hull a glancing blow and recoiled.

I lunged.

The line caressed my fingers, slipped free. "HOLD ME!" I let go the bar, grabbed at the drifting line. Momentum carried me outside the lock. Adrenaline clutched my stomach. My fingers closed around the line just as a hand grasped my ankle.

"Next time, warn me!" Tolliver grunted with effort as he hauled me back.

I twisted, clamped the disk securely to the hull. "You, cross the line!" I shoved a cadet forward. He placed one hand on the line, then the other. A deep breath, a sob. Eyes screwed shut, he worked his way across. Adam Tenere pulled him into the Fuser.

A young voice, in my ear, surprisingly firm. "Cadet Guevire reporting from Fuser Seven. Am breaking away as per orders."

"Acknowledged, Cadet." I grabbed a boy's arm. "Next!"

"A FISH!" Adam's shriek almost deafened me. The midshipman stabbed wildly with his gloved finger. An alien form drifted just within the horizon of the disk.

"Move, boy!" I put a cadet's hand on the line, thrust him into space.

He grabbed the line with his other hand, kicked as if fighting nonexistent gravity. All that it did was disorient him.

"Hold still! Swing one arm across and—"

The boy tried to comply, missed with his right hand after he'd already let go with his left. The momentum of his lunge propelled him from the line. He snatched at it and missed. Ever so slowly, he drifted away.

He began to scream.

I strained to reach him, but he was too far from the airlock. If I swung onto the line, reached out with my foot —no, the bloody line was too loose. No way to lever myself round.

"I'll get him, sir!" Adam Tenere launched himself across, swinging like a monkey.

"Tighten the line!" I reached for it, forgot I was in free fall, almost propelled myself out of the lock. I grasped Tolliver's shoulder, steadied myself until I got hold of our end of the line. Together, hanging on to the safeties, Tolliver and I hauled the line tighter.

"Easy, sir! We'll pull in the Fuser!"

"Too much mass!" The Fuser was more likely to yank us out of the lock, or pull my arm out of its socket.

"Base Commandant—"

Adam swarmed across the line.

"—do I calculate correctly that your intention is to avoid contact with the fish?"

"Shut up, puter!"

"I could assist."

"Shut—how? Adam, hurry!"

"With thrusters at full, my inertia would be greater than that of the fish."

"So? Cadet, stop that infernal noise, the middy's coming for you!"

"I could"—a millisecond pause—*"muscle the fish aside, as it were."*

I glanced at the fish, saw a tentacle form. Adam neared the frantic cadet. At what would the fish throw? The Fuser? Adam? The Station?

"Shuttle, the acid may melt your hull."

"I'm aware. As long as my thrusters are untouched, hull breach will not affect my operation." The puter sounded quite calm.

"Do it!" I felt a flash of guilt.

"Coming around." The shuttle's bow was blunted, unlike that of a starship. The puter couldn't skewer the fish, but he could ram, unless the fish Fused to safety.

Adam gripped the line, forced his legs up and out to the windmilling cadet.

I peered into the night. Had the shuttle's lights grown closer?

"Got him!" Adam pulled his knees tight as the boy swarmed up his body. The moment the cadet's hand touched the line Adam swung back, straddled the line, closed his legs across it. The cadet lapsed into blessed silence, punctuated by gasps for breath.

The fish let go. The mass of protoplasm sailed across the void.

Toward the Station.

It would miss the lock, miss the Fuser. Adam shoved the hysterical boy toward the trainer's waiting hatch. I thrust another cadet out my lock. "Grab hold!" The youngster did so. I couldn't make out his features. Or hers. "The rest of you, get across before that beast throws again!"

Two cadets dived simultaneously for the line. I hauled one

back, catching a glimpse of blond hair, dampened from the humid suit. Jacques Theroux, the Parisian I'd added at Final Cull. I let go of his arm after his mate had pushed clear.

With the ease of long practice Midshipman Tenere swung himself around the kicking cadets so he was behind them on the line. "How many more, sir? I'll help them over."

Four left. We'd need one on *Trafalgar*. I'd hoped to launch another trainer, but with the fish this close—

I hauled a youngster to the edge of the lock, said to a cadet, "You'll go as soon as those two are clear."

In majestic silence the U.N.A.F. transport sailed across the vacuum. A spray of propellant glittered in its taillights.

The nearby fish had grown another tentacle. Slowly, it began to swing.

"Tolliver, how far around the disk is *Trafalgar*?"

"About halfway. Closer from the west. Shall I go for it?"

"Wait until this Fuser's clear."

The two cadets struggled to Eight's hatch, helped each other aboard.

I shouted, "Go!"

The cadet grabbed the line and launched himself.

Adam made to follow; I held him back for a last word. "Don't bother sealing your lock. I'll unclamp your line the instant you're aboard. Thrust at full power until you're clear of these monsters. I'll send orders from—"

"He's throwing!"

I whirled, or tried to, tangled myself in my own feet. By the time I recovered, the tentacle had broken free.

The acid sailed toward us. For a moment I thought it would splatter against our lock. Then I realized it would not. "CADET! COME BACK!"

The boy looked up. He froze, halfway across the line.

The mass of protoplasm spun lazily.

Behind him the shuttle sailed across the void.

The cadet moaned, flinched.

The twirling mass of protoplasm slapped him from waist to helmet, knocked him off the mooring line. A sizzle. With horror I realized the sound came through the boy's suit radio.

An agonized shriek, a puff of air. Silence. I gagged.

The line to Fuser Eight parted.

The shuttle glided across our horizon. Its prow rammed into the fish. The fish convulsed. Together they floated past the disk.

I was exultant. "Shuttle, come around and go for another!"

No answer.

"Puter?"

The shuttle's tailbeams flickered silently into the galactic night.

"Captain, Midshipman Keene. Permission to Fuse to safety!"

I roused myself. "Is a fish alongside?"

"No, sir. They don't seem to care much about the Fusers. But two more just popped into sight alongside the Station."

I keyed my suit caller to broadcast across a band that encompassed all my fleet. "No one is to Fuse! Stay in the area unless you have a fish within one hundred meters!"

"Aye aye—"

"Shuttle, respond!" No answer. I gave it up. "Fuser Eight! Throw us another line!"

A voice trembling with excitement. "Looking, sir! I'm Theroux. Am I allowed to answer? Mr. Tenere isn't—"

"Yes. Have someone take the conn!"

Tolliver gripped my arm, pointed. A fish drifted slowly toward Fuser Eight.

I shouted, "Belay that line, Eight! Close your lock. Fire portside thrusters, fore and aft together, five seconds! Move away from the fish!" I turned to Tolliver. "We've got to launch *Trafalgar*!"

Adam Tenere gauged the distance to Eight. "Let me jump, sir!" He seemed on the verge of tears.

A squirt of propellant, and the Fuser began to recede. "Too late, Middy." Apparently the cadet helmsman hadn't ignited both thrusters at the same moment; the tiny ship drifted in a lazy circle. I wondered if Tenere mourned the independent command he'd lost.

Adam cried, "There's only four of them! They'll need help!"

I felt a moment's shame. "Everyone out of the lock." I hung on to the safety bar, kicked free, twisted almost double so my boots touched the hull outside the Station lock. I let go with one hand, flicked on my magneboots.

I was clamped to the hull, but I was bent almost backward. Surely someone could design a better way to step out of an airlock. Straining my back and leg muscles, I managed to straighten. Now I stood on the hull at right angles to the lock. I grasped a safety, took a cadet's outstretched arm. For a moment he flailed, but quieted to let me set him on the hull. I reached down and snapped on his boot magnets.

Tolliver hoisted himself out. Below him Adam Tenere guided another cadet out; Tolliver handed her up to me. "Where are the fish?"

"Everywhere." No time to look.

Another moment and we were all on the outer hull. Tolliver pointed. "*Trafalgar*'s there." Beyond the horizon of the disk.

Walking to the horizon on the tiny Training Station wasn't the herculean task it would be on Earthport, or even Hope Nation's Orbit Station. Nonetheless, a Captain often provided his middies a dose of healthy exercise by having them help with tasks on the ship's hull. It was hard work to unclamp each boot at every step. Leading three clumsy cadets made the going even slower.

Someone sobbed. From the pitch of his voice I guessed it was a cadet, but couldn't tell which. I wanted to join him.

The outer edge of the Station disk was relatively free of obstacles. We'd save distance by taking the shorter route across the surface of the disk, but the flat surface bristled with antennas, dishes, and sensing devices; our fastest route was the rounded circumference.

None of us spoke. I grabbed a cadet's arm, flicked off his magneboots, slogged forward as fast as I could. The youngster clutched my wrist in justifiable terror; if I let go of him he'd drift helplessly until caught, or until the fish sensed him.

Tolliver quickly followed my example. After a moment, so did Adam. Painstakingly we made our way across the rim of the disk, each with a cadet in tow.

"Sir, where are you?" Sandra Ekrit.

"On the rim. Shut up!" A step, then another.

"But—aye aye, sir."

"My God. Look!" Tolliver.

The fish to our port side was no more than forty meters distant. While I watched it squirted propellant from its blowhole, floated toward the flat of the disk. Its nose touched. A gentle spray of propellant held the fish against the Station's hull. It wiggled back and forth in a nuzzling motion.

Lights from within, where none had been before. The hull

was breached. I tried to run, almost lost my balance. Without jumpsuits or safety lines, our only means of progress was step after careful step.

"Sir, I can walk, they showed me how."

I ignored the boy. Another step. "Where the hell is *Trafalgar*?"

"Fifty meters or so."

The fish's skin became indistinct, began to swirl. Outriders! I spun ninety degrees to starboard, yanked the cadet after me.

"Adam, over the side!" In three steps I was at the edge of the Station's rim. A shape grew on the fish's swirling skin, began to emerge. I stepped over onto the flat of the disk. Tolliver and Adam scrambled after.

We were now on the opposite side of the disk from the fish. In free fall, up was where you wanted it to be. I oriented myself. Here, toward the disk edge, the surface was less cluttered. Farther toward the center, auxiliary solar panels spread like the wings of mounted butterflies.

Adam screamed.

I jerked with fear, let go my cadet. The youngster convulsed, wrapped himself around my neck.

Adam scrambled back toward the rim. I fought to free myself from the cadet's viselike grip. His wrist rubbed against my helmet clamps.

"Don't go that way, Adam! The fish!" I tugged at the cadet's smothering arm with one hand, reached for Adam with the other.

Tenere screamed again, eyes riveted on something past my shoulder.

I turned.

A cadet, his suit ragged and in places gone, floated idly. After a time I realized I was staring at what had been skin.

"Adam, get hold—"

The middy vomited into his face mask.

He was in trouble. If his air line plugged he'd suffocate inside three minutes; the suit itself held barely enough air for a few breaths, and it would be so foul the boy would try not to breathe it. On top of which, he was blind.

I clawed at the frantic cadet on my back; he paid no mind. In desperation I elbowed him in the stomach. It loosened his grip just enough for me to pry him loose. I wrenched his leg down, flicked on his magneboot, stepped back before he could seize me again.

Adam stood frozen to the hull. His gloved hands scrabbled at his helmet. I slapped them away. Sounds of choking.

"Tolliver, help the others!" I reached down, unclamped Adam's boots, got a grip around his waist. Holding him under my arm like a sack of potatoes, I unclamped my own boot, lunged forward across the flat of the disk. I angled toward the rim. Clamp. Unclamp. Adam flailed.

Beyond the edge of the disk, metal, barely visible in the dark of night. Adam's kicks grew more desperate.

My motion seemed agonizingly slow. "Hang on, we're almost there!" His limbs twisted.

The tail of a ship crept closer. The indistinct metal resolved into fusion tubes. Was it *Trafalgar* or another of the Fusers? Adam's foot lashed out, caught my knee. My breath hissed in pain.

Another step. Christ, why hadn't I brought a jumpsuit? Adam clawed at his helmet.

Two more steps. I clambered past the fusion tubes.

Trafalgar's tubes.

Thank you, Lord. Two more steps. The mooring line was knee high. Rather than try to climb over, I shifted Adam to my other arm, transferred my boot to the ship itself. *Trafalgar*'s hull was laced with footgrips, much easier for an experienced sailor than clamping each boot. But I didn't dare try them; one misstep and we'd lose contact.

Twenty meters to the aft lock. I'd never make it in time; by now Adam barely moved. I bent, flicked off my boots, caught the boy in a scissors grip between my legs, grabbed the nearest footgrip with my free hand.

Like a crab, I scuttled across the surface of the hull. Fifteen meters. Ten.

Frantic with haste, I slapped open the airlock, hurled Adam inside, slammed my hand against the closer. The lock began to pump. I glanced at the gauge; ship air was at one atmosphere. No time to confirm on the bridge console. I straddled the inert middy, hands poised on his helmet clamps.

The light flashed; the inner hatch slid open. I tore the clamps free, yanked off Adam's helmet.

His face was blue.

I rolled him onto his stomach, waited for a breath. If he'd aspirated the vomit —

Tentatively I pressed my palm against his back. A breath. Another. Adam twisted onto his side, gagged until I thought he'd never stop. Finally, another breath. His eyes streamed.

I dragged him into the cabin, dashed back into the lock, slapped it closed. The moment the outer lock slid open I surged out, cannoned into Tolliver. I reeled in pain, marveling that I hadn't cracked my helmet.

"You all right, sir? Take this joey." He thrust a cadet at me, clambered back the way he'd come.

"Where are—" I closed my eyes, willing away the hurt. Robert Boland's voice piped, "The other cadets are on the hull, sir. I'm sorry I hung on to you. I was—"

"Hold on to the safety bar! Don't touch anything!" I was gone.

I risked the footgrips, stumbled my way across the hull. Tolliver had left his two cadets a few meters past the mooring line. With dreamlike slowness I neared them.

From my vantage point on the hull I could look over the Station rim. A motion caught my eye. I squinted through the fog of my overworked suit.

The metal plates of the rim seemed to ripple. My stomach contracted.

I churned my way toward Tolliver, met him near the mooring line.

I grabbed a cadet's arm; Tolliver let go, turned his attention to the second figure.

The tall, gawky cadet twisted loose from my grip. "I can do it, I know how!"

"Hey, come—"

She slipped her boot into a grip, launched forward, caught the next grip, slipped her first boot loose, glided ahead.

I gave up; I'd barely catch her, much less be of help. I reached to Tolliver, snatched the other arm of his cadet. Lifting the youth like a toddler between his parents, we clambered to the lock.

I looked over my shoulder to the Station rim. Deck plates swirled, abruptly dissolved. Something emerged, changed shape to fit the hole. My breath hissed.

We reached the lock.

"Lord Christ!" Tolliver's tone made my hair rise.

Frantically he slapped the hatch control.

Behind us, an alien outrider quivered on the rim of the Station. Specks and odd shapes swirled on its surface. My heart slammed against my ribs. The airlock hatch shut, blocking the view. I couldn't get enough breath. Were my tanks running low? My gauges glowed green.

The inner hatch slid open. Adam lay facedown on the deck. Forgetting we had no gravity, I tried to run to the console. I sailed helplessly across the cabin. I was panicking like a plebe.

I fetched up against the far bulkhead, grabbed a handhold. I flicked on my magneboots, lowered my feet and hobbled across the deck as fast as I could. Sliding into the Pilot's seat, I threw a strap across to hold me and jabbed at power switches with clumsy, gloved fingers.

Tolliver peered out the porthole. "The damn thing's sitting on the rim, quivering. Christ, we're still moored! We—I'll have to go out and—"

I panted, "I'll tear us loose." The console lights glowed; *Trafalgar* had maneuvering power. I fired the port thrusters.

"You'll crumple the lock!" The mooring line was fed through the stanchion just outside the airlock.

"Our stanchion's rated higher than the line." I flicked on the simulscreens. The beast seemed to stare at us, though I could find no eyes. Once more I fired thrusters. The line snapped taut, held.

Tolliver punched open the inner hatch. "I'll go out and untie us."

I slapped the hatch override. "No time!" My ears roared; I couldn't breathe. "My air." It came out a croak. "Something's wrong with my suit!" The cabin swam.

Tolliver flung himself to the console. He thrust my arm aside, peered at my gauges, then at my face. "Your air's fine, you're hyperventilating! Pull your helmet!"

In a fury I tore at the clamps; they came loose and the helmet bounced off the deck. "Watch that demon out there!" If the outrider jumped to our hull we were done for. Again I fired thrusters at full power. The ship lurched, but the line refused to part.

"The outrider's moving! Break us free!"

The alien flowed along the rim toward our mooring line.

I took a deep breath, fired a short squirt from the starboard thrusters. We lurched toward the Station.

Tolliver screamed, "WRONG WAY!"

"I know!" For two more seconds I let us drift closer. Our line slackened. On the Station hull, the alien gathered itself.

I fired port thrusters at full power, added stern thrusters to boot.

The alien leaped across the chasm.

A crack sounded through the bones of the ship. Our broken line recoiled against the Station hull. I jammed down the thruster levers, as if forcing them through the console would add to our speed.

We slipped away from the Station.

The alien drifted closer.

Unbreathing, I willed our thrusters to carry us away. Ever so slowly we gathered speed, but the creature floated within feet of our lock.

Finally, our velocities matched. Then the gap began to widen. The alien receded, until it was but a quivering blot against the uncaring stars.

Chapter 23

"Jesus, Son of God." I let out my breath, released the thrusters.

Tolliver sagged against the porthole. "Amen."

My hands fiddled at the console; in a moment, the gravitrons began to hum. I felt weight settle on my frame. Across the cabin Tolliver hugged himself.

Adam Tenere lay on the deck, lost in a private hell.

"It's all right, lad, pull yourself together." My voice cracked.

A cadet stirred. "Sir, are we—what should we do?" Robert Boland.

It seemed a great effort to think. "Open your helmets."

On the console a comm light blinked. I switched frequencies.

"Mid—Midshipman Thayer reporting, sir! Are you there? Wha–what do we do now?" Close to hysteria.

Stop stammering, for one thing. I made no response.

Robert Boland squinted out a porthole. "I don't see any—"

"Speak when you're spoken to!" Tolliver's voice was thick.

Time to take control. Laboriously, I sat up straighter. My muscles ached as if I'd just run the Academy track.

I keyed the caller to Four. "Mr. Thayer, any fish in your vicinity?"

"I—no, sir. Not right here."

I made my voice casual. "Good. Take a moment to organize your boat. See who's had engine-room training, set two cadets at the Fuser console. Put another at Nav, the last one at radionics." I groped for something familiar. "I'll grade you on the results, so do your best. Report back when you're done."

"Aye aye, sir." Thayer sounded more steady.

Now my own ship. I had Tolliver, Adam, Boland, and . . . who? I was supposed to know these things. "Call off by rank."

"First Lieutenant Edgar Tolliver reporting, sir." His tone had a sharp edge.

Adam Tenere made no response. His eyes were shut.

Tolliver hauled the midshipman to his feet, shook him like a rag doll. "Report to the Captain, or by God I'll—"

"BELAY THAT!"

My throat was raw. Tolliver retreated. The middy stared at the deck plates.

I got to my feet, came close. "Adam, I need you."

"I—can't." A sob caught.

"Of course you can." As my hand came up he flinched, but I only took his chin in my palm and lifted. "Report, Mr. Tenere."

Liquid eyes stared into mine. Then, he shuddered. "Midshipman Adam Tenere reporting, sir."

"Very well." My hand rested on his shoulder, squeezed once.

"I'm sor—" He bit it off. I turned away, feeling a Judas for my encouragement. "Continue."

"Cadet Robert Boland, sir."

"Cadet Rene Salette."

Still facing the bulkhead, the last cadet mumbled something inaudible.

"Speak up!"

He braced his shoulders, took a deep breath, and turned. "Cadet Jerence Branstead reporting, sir."

For a moment my mouth worked. I launched myself across the cabin, slammed him against the bulkhead. "How did you get here?" My slap spun him sideways, gave him no opportunity to answer. "I forbade it! Why, damn you?"

"I—sir, I—" His eyes teared.

Another slap, like a rifle shot. He squealed, "No excuse, sir!"

I raised my hand in fury. It came down hard, on a shoulder that had interposed itself. Tolliver was between us, hands thrust deep in his pockets. I flailed at the youngster I'd sworn to save. Again the shoulder blocked me.

"Tolliver, I told you he wasn't to be allowed—"

Jerence cried, "Sergeant Ibarez left the hall before you turned me down. That's how I knew I could get aboard!"

The mists began to recede. I looked down at my cocked fist, willed it open. My legs seemed shaky. "That will be all, Mr. Tolliver. I'm—myself, now."

He muttered, "How reassuring." He stood aside, unmoved by my laser glare.

The speaker squawked. "Midshipman Tsai, sir. What are our orders?"

I keyed the caller. "Just a moment." I skewered Branstead. "You. I expected better." His face was red, whether from my blows or shame I couldn't know. "You're unfit—" With an effort I stopped myself from saying worse.

"Tolliver, get him out of my sight. Assign all of them stations." I strode back to the console. "All right, Mr. Tsai. Report."

"Very well, all boats stand by for further orders." My uniform was soaked. A precious hour had slipped past, but my Fusers were organized. The hardest to deal with had been the four unnerved cadets in Fuser Eight. None were adequately trained for their mission. I should have chosen experienced cadets instead of calling for volunteers. And I should have . . . No matter. Add it to the multitude of regrets that comprised my life.

With luck, Eight would be able to manage. If necessary, we'd instruct them, switch by switch, how to work the controls.

"Adam. Nav drill."

He roused himself. "Aye aye, sir."

I took my time explaining. It was important that he fully grasped the problem.

The middy's eyes grew wide. "But, sir, that would—I mean, you can't—"

"Mr. Tenere!"

He flinched. "Yes, sir. I mean, I'm— Aye aye, sir!"

"How long will it take to set up coordinates?"

"For all of them? It shouldn't be too—twenty minutes, sir?"

"Very well. I'll be in the comm room." I eased myself out of my chair. Though I could speak to Robert Boland from my console, Adam would work better if I wasn't staring over his shoulder.

"Don't get up, Mr. Boland." I took a place at the comm console, reached for the controls, pulled back my hand. Might as well allow him to help; why else had I brought him? "Merge the incoming Naval comm frequencies."

Perhaps the fish were withdrawing, or at least tempering their attack.

"Aye aye, sir." His hands flitted to the keys. "To earphones?"

He'd learn the truth soon enough, in any event. "No. To the speaker."

A blare of reports permeated the tiny chamber.

"—huge tidal wave rolling across the Sea of Japan—"

"If we don't Fuse now it'll be too late! Sir, let me save my ship!"

"—fish massing over the atmosphere, we're standing back, we have to. There's no way—"

"MAYDAY MAYDAY MAYDAY MAYDAY MAYDAY—"

Reports poured in. Many fish had withdrawn, as the tide from a tsunami. I was certain they would return. When they came . . .

"Acting Fleet Ops to all capital ships. We will retrea—er, regroup the fleet around Deimos. Maneuver to begin in thirty minutes. All ships move at flank speed to positions from which you can Fuse. Prepare Fuse coordinates for—"

"NO!" I snatched the caller, spun the frequency dial. "BELAY THAT! DON'T FUSE!"

Boland's jaw dropped.

"Stay off this channel, whoever you are. Repeat, all ships are to Fuse—"

"Captain Nicholas Seafort in U.N.S. *Trafalgar*. Sir, if you Fuse in a coordinated maneuver you'll lose the fleet!"

A new voice came on the speaker. *"Admiral Richard Seville, acting FleetOpsCinc. Get the hell off my frequency and maintain radio silence!"*

"Aye aye—no, sir, I can't! For God's sake, Admiral, countermand your order." I was beside myself.

Adam Tenere appeared in the doorway. "Sir, I have coordinates—"

I spun to the middy. "Are you sure? Absolutely sure?"

"Yes, sir, I'm sure. But—"

"Send each Fuser its coordinates, to execute at my command. Don't forget our own engine room. And get Tolliver in here." Adam disappeared. A moment later the lieutenant strode in.

"Edgar, walk the cadets on Fuser Eight through the steps. First their engine room, then the console. Tell me when they're ready."

"Aye aye, sir. But Jerence is alone in the engine room. If you're about to move us, I should—"

"Adam will be there to handle it. Move, Edgar!"

I tried again. "Admiral, the fish will return en masse at any moment. If you Fuse to Deimos they'll follow and wipe out the fleet!"

Seville's reply indicated he'd run out of patience. *"How the bloody hell do you know what a fish will do?"*

Captain's intuition, or the grace of Lord God. I couldn't tell him that; I groped for a rationale. "I was at Hope Nation. I saw their tactics."

He snorted. *"Hope Nation survived because those weren't their tactics. The fish never came back en masse. We're under heavy attack, but their numbers are diminishing. We'll try to finish them off with groundside lasers and preserve the remainder of the fleet for—"*

"Emergency bulletin from U.N. Command. They've just told me Melbourne, Australia was struck by a—by a—" The voice caught. "At 11:15 P.M.. Greenwich time a huge meteorite or other object hit the city center. First reports indicate there is nothing left. Of the city. Of the ... people."

I couldn't help myself. I sank to my knees. Lord God, gather those souls into Your arms. Show them Your mercy. I know what You think of me; I ask nothing for myself. Soon, now, I'll go willingly to Your judgment. Please, don't take more innocents.

After a moment I struggled to my feet.

Ignoring Robert Boland's frozen horror, I keyed the caller to all my Fusers' frequencies. "This is Commandant Seafort. We've sent you a set of Fusion coordinates. On my command, bring your fusion drives on-line as you've been taught. Remember, we'll have a substantial radio time lag after you Defuse. Be ready for further orders."

"Aye aye, sir." A voice tremulous with fear.

"Orders received and understood, Capt—"

"Yes, sir. I mean, aye aye, sir."

"Orders received, Commandant Seafort."

When the last boat had acknowledged, I drummed my fingers, waiting for Tolliver to finish instructing Fuser Eight.

"HELP ME!" The anguished cry rattled my speaker.

Befuddled, I stared at the frequency indicator. It wasn't on a Fuser channel.

"THEY'RE COMING! OH, GOD!"

I spun the dial. "Jerence, is that you?"

His voice was husky. "No, sir."

"GOHHHHDD! GET AWAY FROM ME!" Panting.

Cadet Boland. "That's a suit frequency, sir."

But who neglected to desuit, in one of the Fusers?

Lord God, have mercy. The girl who'd run away, at the Station. I didn't even know her name.

I spun my dial. "Cadet, hide behind a—"

A shriek of agony, abruptly cut short.

"Eight is ready, sir." Tolliver. "As ready as they—"

I grabbed the caller. "Execute!" I ran my finger down the line on my screen.

The stars vanished. Seconds later the cutoff alert flashed, and I Defused, flinching unnecessarily. Had the explosion come, I would never have felt it.

"Boland, Tolliver! Encroachments?"

"Yes, sir, one!" Robert had it first; he had faster reaction time.

"Forty thousand kilometers, sir." Tolliver. "She transponds as Fuser Eight."

It was why I'd flinched on Defusing. I'd had Adam send identical coordinates to Eight and our own engine room. Absolutely forbidden by Naval doctrine, though the one percent inherent inaccuracy of Fusion made the risk of collision almost infinitesimal. But doctrine was doctrine, and so I'd flinched, just in case.

"*Trafalgar* to Seven. Respond." I ticked off the seconds. Seven and her cadets were now five million miles outward of *Trafalgar*'s new position. The reply would take almost half a minute.

We'd all started from Lunar orbit; one AU, or some ninety-three million miles from the Sun. Now *Trafalgar* was near the tail of a string of Fusers, spread between one AU and point two five AU. Fuser Eight, with Jacques Theroux and four other unsupervised cadets, was nearest the Training Station. The rest of the Fusers, except for Seven, were inward of us.

"Fuser Seven to *Trafalgar*. Cadet Tanya Guevire, in the comm room."

"Very well. Who's on thruster controls?"

Another maddening minute. "Cadet Arnweil."

"Put him on." Again I waited. If only we were bunched closer.

"Cadet Arnweil reporting, sir."

What I had in mind would take coordination. Five co-equal

cadets probably couldn't achieve it. On the other hand . . .
"Kevin, you've done well. I'm appointing you Cadet Corporal.
Tell the others. You are to commence a fusion drive test at sixty
percent power, random coordinates."

Tolliver's eyes widened.

"Kevin, the test may attract fish. Watch the screens carefully.
Use your thrusters to avoid the fish, but do NOT, repeat — "

"Thank you, sir!" his response seemed bizarre until I remembered the time lag. He was responding to my earlier praise, not
my warning that he'd summon fish.

"—do NOT Fuse if fish begin to arrive. You need to estimate
how long you'll be able to avoid them, and let me know thirty
seconds before that time. You'll say, 'Fuser Seven discontinuing
test.' A half minute after you notify me, stop testing. The fish
should—"

"Won't that attract fish, sir?"

I roared, "Damn it, don't interrupt! Remember the time lag!"

Tolliver glowered. "What infamy have I helped you with?"

I wheeled on him, a threat in my eyes. "Don't speak, Lieutenant."

For a moment he wavered. Then, "Aye aye, sir." He made no
effort to conceal his fury.

Kevin Arnweil, chastened. "Orders acknowledged, sir. I apologize."

My voice was soothing. "It was an error of enthusiasm. Yes,
you might attract fish, but I want—need you to take the risk.
Evade them like . . ." I searched for an example. "Like you
would in Arcvid. You MUST keep testing for thirty seconds
after you give the quit signal. Acknowledge."

An interminable minute. Tolliver's eyes bored into my side.

"Acknowledged, sir. If they get too close to avoid, may we
Fuse?"

"That will only make them follow you. If all else fails, use
your lifepod." I forced the next words through unwilling lips.
"The pod's too small for the fish to see. You'll be safe there
until we come for you." Tolliver stirred. "But I don't want to
lose a Fuser," I added quickly. "Execute."

Tolliver snarled, "Are you *trying* to kill them?"

I made no answer, switched channels to Fuser Six, several
million kilometers inward. "Stand by to test fusion drive at sixty

percent power. Do not begin until I give you the signal to execute. Once you begin—"

Tolliver wouldn't be denied. "Why'd you tell Arnweil he'd be safe in a lifepod?"

"If he thought it would keep him safe, he'd Fuse clear of the fish long before he had to. I want Seven calling fish."

"They're at point nine AU. That's too close to Earth for—"

"We'll pass their fish inward to Six. You're disobeying orders, and I'm short of time." I clicked the caller. "Six, *Trafalgar* resuming orders. Once you begin testing . . ." I repeated what I'd told Seven.

Tolliver. "All right, you send a few fish down the line, and probably lose a Fuser and five cadets in the process. What happens when the fish reach Fuser One, at twenty-five million miles?"

I said, "The fish are organic. Maybe they'll have trouble that close in. It's hot."

He spluttered, "That's the great Seafort plan? Pull them close to the Sun and see what happens? Christ!"

"Don't blaspheme."

"The fish won't follow so close. They must have SOME survival instincts!"

The speaker crackled. "Fish, sir. Two of them!" Cadet Corporal Arnweil, in Seven.

I changed the subject before Tolliver could think it through. "Edgar, get on the horn. Pass the standby orders down the line to Five." I switched back to Arnweil. "Acknowledged, Seven. Take evasive action if they come near. Keep testing." I left Tolliver at the console, strode to the comm room.

"Mr. Boland, listen for a signal from Seven. Do you know the frequencies?"

"Yes, sir." He pointed to the screen, on which he'd posted all the Fuser channels.

I smiled. In a comm-room drill, Sarge would be outraged by the visual aid. "Very well. Listen to Seven, but set your outgoing to Six. If you hear 'Fuser Seven discontinuing test,' then transmit—write it down—'*Trafalgar* to Six: commence test. Execute.'"

Boland tapped himself a note. "Aye aye, sir." A sheen of sweat dampened his forehead.

"Captain! This is Arnweil. We've got half a dozen now. One

was just a few meters off, before I squirted away. May we turn off the drive?"

I took the caller. "Corporal Arnweil, get this straight. Don't stop until your area is swarming with fish. Dozens, not just two or three. You have plenty of propellant and your Fuser has so little mass that the thrusters will flit you around like a top. You can keep clear of them."

I switched to Admiralty frequency.

"—*huge rock, but it's breaking up! Jesus, that must have been a hundred miles across! There are dozens of fish around it, they're—*"

"Captain Seafort to FleetOpsCinc. Urgent." I gripped the caller.

"—U.N.S. *Potemkin* to Admiralty. Do you want us to reengage the fish that brought the rock? We can—"

"Negative, *Potemkin.* Fuse on signal with the rest of the fleet. Countdown is three minutes."

"*Mayflower* to FleetOpsCinc. We got the bloody fish but one tube's melted; I can't join the fleet at Deimos. Is Lunapolis still under attack?"

I pounded the console. "Why won't the bastard answer me?"

Cadet Robert Boland cleared his throat. "Sir, the—"

"Don't interrupt."

"—time lag." He looked guilty. "Aye aye, sir."

I swallowed, loosened my death grip on the caller. "I forgot." The words came hard. "Let that be a lesson to you. When you're on the bridge you'll have to calculate—" I broke off.

"Admiral Seville to Seafort. What now?"

I reddened; his tone said it all. "Sir, I'm trying to draw the fish by caterwauling. Please hold off Fusing the fleet." I waited out the seconds to his reply, hoping against hope.

"You can't help, Seafort. *Trafalgar's* unarmed. That rock we broke up may have been their last try. We'll regroup around Deimos. And if any fish follow, we'll—"

"Sir, don't call the fish to Deimos, I need them here! I'm begging you, give me a chanc—"

"—blow them out of the Solar System. We'll have all the concentrated firepower of—what's that? Christ. *Potemkin,* engage over South Atlantic as fast as you can. There's a squad of fish bringing a rock into —"

"Sir, for Lord God's sake, don't — "

Robert Boland said plaintively, "They won't listen."

"Shut up!" If the fleet Fused, all my efforts would be in vain. I waited, clutching the caller.

"SEAFORT, GET OFF MY CHANNEL! THAT'S AN ORDER!"

I recoiled from his blast.

Then I snapped.

Before I had time to assess my folly I shouted, "Captain Nicholas Seafort on U.N.S. *Trafalgar* to all ships, top priority! On behalf of the Government of the United Nations I hereby relieve Admiral Richard Seville from fleet command!"

Tolliver came thudding into the cabin, aghast.

Now, even if I survived my holocaust, they would have done with me. I raced on, to certain death. "I hereby assume emergency command of the Home Theater of Operations. U.N.N.S. Regs Section—" Lord Christ, what was it? "—sixty-four point two. Uh, three."

"Oh, no!" Tolliver; a cry of dismay.

"All ships, hold your positions, stand and fight! Maneuver by thrusters only! Ignore further orders from groundside, and do not Fuse!"

"You lunatic, you sixty-foured him?" Tolliver. "How could you? You had no grounds! For God's sake, why?"

"—Captain Valdez on *Iberia,* to Seafort. What the hell are you pulling?"

"Admiral Seville to Seafort. You are relieved from—"

"Seafort to *Iberia*. As Theater Commander, I order you to stand and fight, or retreat by thruster. No other option for any ship in Home Theater of Operations. Ignore contrary instructions until the emergency abates!"

As I set down the caller it took an effort to control my voice. "It's come, Tolliver. Armageddon. For us or the fish."

"Christ, you're cracking!"

I laid my hand on the arm of the chair to still it. "No, I'm just—yes, perhaps I am. I don't think it matters."

"Damn it, you always play your cards too close. This time I can't read you! I've got to relieve you, or burn you for mutiny. No other option, as you put it." His hand crept to his holster.

The speaker crackled. Kevin Arnweil in Seven. "Sir, two dozen fish. I can't hold them off much longer! I've got to send you the—oh, God that was close! Maybe another minute—"

I reached for the caller, pulled back my hand. "Do it, Edgar."
I was panting, from exertion or lack of air. Or fear.

Our eyes met.

Slowly Tolliver drew the laser. "I'm sorry, Nicky. Captain. I
have no choi—Ay!" He tumbled to his knees, the pistol slipping
from his fingers.

"Leave my Commandant alone!" The voice was shrill. Jerence Branstead let fall the chair with which he'd clubbed his
lieutenant. He snatched the laser from the deck, scampered
clear. "You let him be, you—you—" His chin quivered.

"Give it back." Tolliver lurched to his feet. "The Captain's
sick. I won't hurt him. I'm going to relieve—"

"No you're not!" Jerence brandished the pistol. "I'm a good
shot; Dad taught me back on Hope Nation. And I read the regs!
Get away!"

"Please, what's a sixty-four?" Robert Boland.

"Jerence, the laser." I held out my hand. "Look it up, Mr.
Boland, you're supposed to know. NOW, Branstead!" Jerence
let go the weapon.

"Aye aye, sir." Boland punched commands into his console,
calling up the U.N.N.S. Regulations and Code of Conduct, revi-
sion of 2087, embedded in every ship's Log.

"Fuser Seven discontinuing test. Oh, God, hurry! So many
fish!"

Boland hesitated, his eyes flitting between me and Tolliver. I
slammed the heel of my hand into the boy's shoulder. "They're
your mates! Help them."

Cadet Boland snatched the caller. "Fuser Six, commence test!
Execute!" I waited out the lag.

Eduard Diego, fear in his voice. "Fuser Six to *Trafalgar,* aye
aye."

Boland turned back to the keyboard, skimmed through the
regs.

"Captain Foss of *Potemkin,* to Seafort. State your grounds for
assuming command. You're junior to us all, aren't you?"

"Section sixty-four." Unthinking, Boland read aloud. I
reached over to his console, flicked on the caller.

"When a commander in the Theater of Operations has data
essential to the preservation of the main body of Naval forces,
and communication with his superiors is restricted through no

act or omission of his own, he may relieve his superior and assume command of all forces in the theater for the duration of the emergency."

Boland stopped.
"Go on."

"In order that authority not be divided or contested, the superior must allow the temporary usurpation of his authority. No challenge may be made to the assumption of command by any other officer under said superior, or any officer not in the theater.

However," —Boland's voice faltered— "upon conclusion of the emergency the relieving officer must show by incontrovertible and conclusive evidence that his usurpation of authority was essential to preserve the main body of Naval forces."

I switched off the caller. "Well, Edgar?"
Robert looked up, his eyes troubled. "Sir, there's more."
"I know. Read it aloud. It may satisfy Mr. Tolliver."
Boland whispered, *"The penalty for wrongful usurpation of authority is death. Any such sentence, once imposed, may not be appealed, commuted, or pardoned."*
Tolliver's eyes were bitter. "You're dead, Nick. Nothing can save you." He sagged. "I'm at your orders, Commander."
He had no choice.

Chapter 24

Fuser Six was close enough to *Trafalgar* for our sensors to detect. It caterwauled for fifteen minutes, attracting thirty-five fish before Midshipman Diego begged for permission to stop, forgetting he had his own authority in my orders. I passed the fish to Midshipman Guthrie Smith, in Five.

Robert Boland huddled with Jerence Branstead at the far console. Rene Salette made herself invisible in the engine room. Tolliver, fielding calls from the fleet, was in a state of barely controlled fury.

Guthrie Smith. "Sir, may—please, may I keep talking with you? I'm—"

I knew the word he was loath to use. "Yes, of course, Guthrie. Just remember the lag."

"Six to *Trafalgar*. They're going, except for—oh, thank Lord God!" Midshipman Diego caught a sob. "There's the last of them. That was horrid!"

"Steady, Mr. Diego." I thrust down words of rebuke. He was an officer, but throughout the fleet older men fought similar terror. Captain Pritcher had crumpled at less.

"Five to *Trafalgar*! Fish! Dozens of them! Jesus!"

"Move about, Guthrie! Use your thrusters!" It would take almost half a minute for my words to reach him.

Smith shouted, "All around me! Taking evasive action. They're—" The voice cut off.

After a moment Robert Boland asked, "May I call them, sir?"

"Yes."

A minute passed, ample time for a response. Any longer and the fish might disperse. Heavily, I picked up the caller. "*Trafalgar* to Two. Execute." Two was far inward of us, fifty million miles closer to the sun. Over eight minutes for a response to my message. Please, Lord. Let the fish follow.

Still no answer from Five. Had Loren Reitzman cried out for his father, for the schoolmates he'd abandoned to take the oath at my urging? Had Guthrie Smith perished with his hand on the thrusters, trying frantically to escape the aliens?

I wrenched my mind from the speculation. For a while more, I needed my sanity.

At last, a response from Two crackled in the speaker. First Midshipman Thomas Keene. "Aye aye, sir. Executing Fusion test."

"London Admiralty to *Trafalgar*. Stand by for relay from Admiral Duhaney in Lunapolis."

The speaker wheezed and crackled. "Nick, are you out of your mind, taking command? The fleet's in chaos!"

"Sorry, sir, it's done. I have to see it through."

The Admiral's voice hardened. "You know perfectly well sixty-four is a dead letter. In two hundred years it's never—"

"It's as dead as the rest of the Regs, sir. Or as alive."

"Don't quibble! And properly speaking, you're not even in the theater of oper—"

"*Lusitania to* Trafalgar. *Permission to Fuse; they're all around and I can't break loose! Three lasers are down!*"

My voice was heavy. "To *Lusitania*. I'm sorry, Captain. The only sound they must hear—"

"*We'll go under, Mr. Seafort!*"

It would be so easy to make an exception, but I owed a debt to Smith, to Reitzman and the others. "*Lusitania*, do NOT Fuse. Take evasive action. Godspeed."

Duhaney's tone quivered with outrage. "Seafort, I never thought of you as a damned sea lawyer. I can't stop you, but I'll bloody well remember at your court-martial. I'll be on the board myself!"

"Admiral, I'm busy and you're distracting me."

Tolliver gasped. Even for me, that was a bit much.

"Seafort! At least tell us what you're doing!"

"Caterwauling. We're distracting the fish from your fleet."

"You're not armed! What can you—"

"But I have my Fusers. Over and out."

Tolliver said through clenched teeth, "What CAN we do, Commandant?"

"You, for one, can obey orders."

"Of course. I'll follow the example you set."

In the resulting frigid silence I checked the computations on my screen one last time. Tolliver busied himself with calls from the harried fleet.

To my surprise, all but a few scattered ships accepted my self-declared authority. Well, it was there in black and white, if one bothered to read the Regs.

It was time.

Fuser Eight had only the four inexperienced cadets. She had to be first. "*Trafalgar* to Eight, respond."

"Cadet Theroux here, sir." The boy's voice held a quaver.

"These are your new Fusion coordinates. Twenty-five, eighteen . . ." I took my time, made sure the cadet had them right. "After you Defuse, I want you to test your fusion drive immediately. Lock your drive into sixty-five percent for fifteen minutes with a random unlock code."

"Aye aye, sir. But, sir, if we lock in the code we can't end the test early if the fish attack."

I made very sure my answer was on Eight's frequency only. "They won't attack you, Cadet. I'm having three boats Fuse at once. That will confuse the enemy's senses. But you MUST lock in your drive. If you stop testing you'll endanger the other trainers."

Tolliver, in a growl. "Poppycock!"

"Aye aye, sir." Theroux. "What do we do after the fifteen minutes?"

"Fuse back to here. Reverse coordinates."

He sounded relieved. "Thank you, sir."

Tolliver stared at the coordinates on my screen.

"Fuser Eight, prepare to—"

"Belay that!" Tolliver snapped off my caller. "Sir, run the calculations again! You're Defusing them inside the B'n Auba Zone!"

I said, "Use the coordinates we have."

"Don't you understand? Eight will be so close to the Sun she'll never be able to Fuse clear!" Tolliver was nearly beside himself.

I said the hardest words I'd ever said in my life. "I know."

Before anyone could move I keyed the caller. "Fuser Eight, execute."

"Aye aye, sir. Executing." The ship disappeared from our screens.

For a moment all was still.

Tolliver leaned so that his head was close to mine. "Oh, you vile bastard."

My voice was ragged. "Tolliver, I—"

He spat full in my face.

I sat as if made of stone. Warm spittle dribbled down my cheek.

I hoped he would do it again.

He busied himself at his console. I didn't dare speak.

"Why, sir?" Robert Boland appealed for understanding. "Why our own mates?"

"There's no other way."

"But—"

"Be silent, Cadet Boland."

Keene's voice in the speakers, his voice four minutes old. "Fuser Two reporting. My God, that's a lot of fish, sir! More than I've ever seen. More than maybe you've seen, even at Hope Nation. They're Fusing in on all sides. I'm trying to get around the main mass . . ."

"*Potemkin to Acting FleetOpsCinc Seafort. We and Hibernia engaged a mass of fish trying to drop a rock over the Atlantic. A whole bunch of them suddenly Fused away. I don't know whether it was our attack that—*"

Keene. "Over a hundred of them now! They see me. They keep trying to—Holy God, what a blast!" The middy's voice trembled with excitement. "Sir, one of them Fused into another! It knocked out visuals right off the screen! If we'd been any closer—get away from me, you son of a bitch!"

Minutes inched past. Boland stared at his screen. Jerence lay slumped in his seat, drained.

"Too many for us! I'm discontinuing— God, it'll be four minutes before you—sir, I can't hold that long! I'm— THEY'RE GOING AWAY! Oh, blessed God!"

Eight had done its work.

"Mr. Boland, try again to reach Fuser Eight." It was a pointless order; even if the fish hadn't destroyed the frail Fuser, her radio had little chance of penetrating the solar haze.

After a moment of static I asked, "Who's aboard her?"

Tolliver found his voice. "Cadet Jacques Theroux. Cadet Vasily Karnyenkov. Cadet Sera Thau. Cadet Kathryn Janes."

I'm sorry, Jacques. And all of you. You'll never know, but you saved Mr. Keene. I need his skills more than yours.

"Pray for them." I cannot. It would be blasphemy.

It was Boland who answered. "Aye aye, sir."

Like an obscene parody of God, I chose who was to live and die.

I had Fuser Seven entice the fish. After a time, I ordered them passed along to Four.

"Captain, I have one question." Tolliver's voice was formal.

I was grateful that he acknowledged my existence. "Yes, of course."

"You're sending cadets to their deaths. How do you know it's working?"

"Working?"

"That the fish are dying."

"They must be." I struggled with the monstrous concept that I'd murdered my cadets for naught.

"You don't know that."

"But—" It had to be so. "Even if fish can survive ten thousand degrees, Fusion follows the laws of physics. The fish are caught just like a ship."

"We don't know that either. They—"

"Captain, permission to discontinue test!" Anton Thayer, in Four, his voice a fearful shout.

"Fuser One, execute!" It would take six minutes for my order to wing inward. I spun the dial. "Mr. Thayer, you must test for six minutes before you shut down. Do your best to evade."

Tolliver persisted. "Before you kill any more of us, how can you be sure the fish follow the last call?"

I thrust away the argument. "We're caterwauling. They *have* to follow. Once they're caught—"

"We have instincts, so must they. How could they survive without knowing not to Fuse near a star?"

"Leave me alone!" He was unfair; how could I know such things? I stalked out, paused at the bridge, turned instead to the rear corridor and the engine room.

"Everything all right, Mr. Tenere?"

Adam looked up from his console. "Yes, sir." Behind him, Cadet Rene Salette anxiously watched her gauges.

I turned to go.

He blurted, "Please, sir—I mean, could you—" He pounded his leg with clenched fist, turned red. A deep breath. "Sir, please, what's happening?"

I raised an eyebrow. "You too, Mr. Tenere?"

"I'm sorry!"

I relented. The usual discipline didn't apply. Perhaps it never does. "We're passing the fish along a great conga line from here to the Sun."

"What happens when they get near the Sun?"

"They die."

The boy's face lit with hope. "It's that easy? We can really beat them?"

I retreated to the hatch. "That easy," I said.

Robert Boland raced out of the comm room. "Sir, Mr. Tolliver's compliments, and would you—"

"Belay that." I didn't care anymore.

"We heard from Ms. Ekrit in One. She says she has fish, they're endangering her ship and she's going to discontinue testing unless you answer."

Cursing, I ran to the comm room. "Tolliver, tell her she'll be hanged if she disobeys in the face of the enemy. She may discontinue in exactly"—I checked my watch—"four minutes. Not before."

Tolliver was grim. "Aye aye, sir." He knew cowardice when he saw it.

Boland stood with me in the corridor, uncertain. I pointed to the comm room. "Back to work." Head down, he brushed past.

Four minutes, before I must pass my next sentence of death. I dropped into my seat, plotted coordinates over and again until I was sure I had them right. Then I picked up the caller.

"*Trafalgar* to Fuser Seven, respond."

It had to be Seven. Kevin Arnweil had twice managed to avoid destruction while his ship caterwauled, but the five unsupervised cadets were still the weakest link in my chain. Their luck couldn't last.

I had to use them before it was too late.

Seven was closer; only twenty-four seconds for my voice to reach them.

"Fuser Seven responding. Cadet Kevin Arnweil reporting,

sir." By the book. The boy had come far from the youngster who wailed over the stiffened body of his friend Dustin.

"Mr. Arnweil, you're to Fuse once more." I swallowed, then continued smoothly. "These coordinates will put you just outside the B'n Auba Zone, near the Sun." A small deceit. My eyes locked on the console, to avoid meeting any others.

"As soon as you Defuse, you're to test again. Set the puter to lock your fusion motors . . ." Painstakingly, I gave him the instructions I'd given the others. "Confirm, please." I checked my watch. "Quickly."

Tolliver watched from the second officer's chair, his eyes boring into my back.

We had but two minutes left, before Sandra Ekrit would stop caterwauling. At last, Kevin's response. "Ready to execute. Please, sir, could another ship call the fish if we can't get away from them?"

I gripped the caller. "Of course, Kevin. One will be standing by. Just let us know."

Tolliver stalked from the cabin.

"Very well, exec—Kevin, you remember Dustin Edwards?" I didn't know why I blurted that.

A long moment, while the last grains of time slipped through the hourglass. "Of course, sir. All the time."

"I do too," I said gently. "Execute."

Five Fusers left, and Lord God knew how many fish. "Mr. Boland, general call on fleet circuits. Each ship in Home Theater of Operations is to report the number of fish in their sector."

The boy made as if to rise. "Aye aye, sir. Shall I tell Mr. Tolliver you asked him to do it?"

"You make the call on our behalf."

His chest swelled with pride. "Aye aye, sir!"

"Fuser One to *Trafalgar*, Midshipman Ekrit reporting. The fish are gone!"

So she'd survived. "Prepare to repeat testing maneuver in approximately eight minutes. We'll send the signal to execute."

It would be a while before she acknowledged.

It was *Trafalgar*'s turn to summon the aliens.

"Carry on, Mr. Boland." I left the comm room, settled myself in the bridge, placed my hands on the thrusters. "Mr. Tenere, we're going to caterwaul at sixty percent. Don't stop before I give the order."

The middy's voice was strained. "Aye aye, sir. Ready at your command." No protest. I felt strangely grateful.

"Commence." I tensed, eyes glued to the screens.

Edgar Tolliver slipped into the second officer's seat. "I would have liked someday to see Vega."

I grunted.

He asked casually, "Do you know how much I hate you, at times?"

"Only at times?"

"Yes, but this is one of them." His stare was defiant.

I wiped imaginary spittle off my cheek. "I know."

He flushed. "You deserved that."

"No, Edgar. Much more."

The speaker blared. "Fuser One to *Trafalgar*." Sandra Ekrit. "Sir, we barely survived the last attack. Whatever you're trying doesn't work. I can't hear what you're telling the other boats but—"

"Obey orders, Midshipman!" I forgot the damned time lag.

"—sending the fish in a circle from one Fuser to another will just get us all killed for nothing!" Her voice rose. "Sir, as chief officer I can't endanger the boat—"

Tolliver's voice cracked like a whip. "Fish, a thousand kilometers!"

"I see them." My back was stiff from tension, but there was nothing we need do. Not at a thousand kilometers.

Alarms clanged. Tolliver grated, "Seven, eight . . . eleven fish! Port, very close, aft, two hundred meters—"

I slammed down the port thrusters. The screen reeled.

"More of them at—"

They were upon us, and I had no Fuser ready to call them away.

I tried to plan while maneuvering. Either seemed too much effort; together it was impossible.

"Look at the bastards!" Tolliver.

I fired thrusters with desperate urgency, trying to maneuver the ungainly vessel like an electricar. If I wasn't careful I could drive the ship into one fish while trying to escape another. If I did, we were finished.

Tolliver's hand tugged at my arm. "Please. Let me!"

I recalled Hope Nation, and a missile leaping toward our heli. "Now!" His hands leaped for the controls.

I grabbed the caller. Eduard Diego was closest, in Six. "*Trafalgar* to Fuser Six! On my command, Fuse to the following coordinates." I punched up Sandra Ekrit's location at twenty-five million miles, outside the B'n Auba Zone. I read off the string of numbers.

"When you Defuse, immediately commence Fusion test at sixty percent, and continue for eight minutes. Acknowledge."

His reply would take nearly a minute. The stars spun crazily under Tolliver's evasive maneuvers.

I switched back to Fuser One's frequency. I had a weak link to repair. "Very well, Ms. Ekrit, you're right. Fuse back to us and wait for further orders." I fed her the coordinates. "Acknowledge and execute." I spun to Tolliver. "I'll need about half a minute's notice to the Diego boy. How many are there now?"

"Look at the frazzing screen!"

A reproach died in my lips. The simulscreen was blotted by dozens of encroachments, many breathtakingly close. Each moment brought more. Tolliver maneuvered to starboard of the main mass, but, as in Arcvid, the enemy could pop onto our screens anywhere without warning.

The delayed response from Six. "Midshipman Diego reporting. Orders acknowledged. Standing by to Fuse. Please, sir, don't make us—" A second's hesitation. "Standing by, sir."

How many fish? Sixty. No, eighty at least. If we—"LORD GOD PRESERVE US!" I flung my arms over my face. A blowhole filled our screen. Tolliver slammed our nose thrusters to full, but our inertia was considerable.

A knock at the hatch. "Sir, Cadet Boland reporting. They—"

"Hang on!"

We glided toward the fish. I braced myself for collision. Damn it, why hadn't we gone to suits? Without them we'd have no—

Meters from our prow, the fish disappeared. I gaped.

Tolliver grinned tightly. "It doesn't like our hydrozine." Our forward thrusters had squirted directly into it.

I took a much-needed breath. "Go on, Cadet."

The words tumbled out of Boland's mouth. "I talked to the warships and they gave me numbers, about eight hundred fish still in the theater but maybe some ships are reporting the same ones, can I go now, please?"

I glanced over my shoulder. The boy's glazed eyes were riveted to the screen.

"Dismissed, Robert."

Tolliver spun us to port. "Sir, you'd better tell Mr. Diego . . ." His voice faltered.

I reached out, shut off hysterical alarms, gazed in awe at the screen.

U.N.S. *Trafalgar* floated within a vast armada of fish. A kilometer from us drifted a sub-planetary body, so huge I would have lost perspective except for the attending aliens, some two hundred of them. A few squirted propellant from their blowholes, and glided toward us.

"Christsir what now?"

As if I had all the time in the world, my hand crept to the caller. "Nothing, Edgar. Don't move us." When I spoke my voice was hushed. *"Trafalgar* to Six. Midshipman Diego, execute. Confirm and execute!" I reached out, slid my finger down the line down the screen, turning off our fusion drive.

Mechanically Adam Tenere, in the Engine Room, said, "Confirm Defuse, aye aye."

"They're still coming." Cautiously, Tolliver fired a gentle squirt. We drifted astern, backing away from a dozen fish.

"In a few seconds they'll hear Mr. Diego." The mass of fish was staggering. Could Fuser Six hold out until I could arrange another boat to call the alien flotilla?

A screen light blinked out. Then another. I held my breath. More pinpoints of light went dark.

The fish were leaving.

A new blip, twenty thousand kilometers distant. More fish arriving, or—my fingers punched the keys, querying our puter. Metal.

A familiar voice. "Fuser One to Trafalgar, Midshipman Ekrit reporting. Sir, I'm sorry if—"

"Belay that, Middy, no time." I ground my knuckle into my forehead, searching for a way. "Ms. Ekrit, Fusers Four and Seven report false readings from their external fusion tube gauges. Our testing may have melted the wires. Who's in your engine room?"

"Two cadets, sir. Bonhomme and Farija."

"Send them Outside—no, I can't rely on them. Do you see any fish at the moment?"

"Only near you, sir. They're forty thousand kilometers from us."

"If I sent you out to do a visual, how fast could you get back in?"

"I'm pretty good on the footholds, sir." Her tone was confident.

"We need to know if the sensors are reliable. Get suited. Put all your cadets at the bridge console except the two in the engine room. I'll stay on Fuser frequency; they can communicate with you via suit channel."

"Aye aye, sir. What am I looking for?"

"Any evidence of bad connections or overheating. You can't Fuse with bad sensors."

"Yes, sir. Give me a minute to finish suiting. Sir, am I in trouble for countermanding your order? I was senior officer present and—"

A Fuser was a boat, not a ship, and she wasn't a Captain. She should have known that. "No, Ms. Ekrit. I didn't realize your problem. Hurry, will you? I need to send you back toward Earthport Station."

"Aye aye, sir. Going to suit frequency."

I closed my eyes, pictured her screwing tight her helmet, checking her suit clamps. Turning toward the lock. Slapping open the inner hatch. Reaching for the pump control.

"Commandant Seafort to Fuser One. Can you hear me? Identify yourself."

In a moment, a nervous voice. "Yes, sir. Cadet Wallace Freid, sir. Cadet Chambers is with me. And Cadet Zorn."

"Where is Ms. Ekrit?"

"The outer hatch just opened, sir. She's Outside."

Damn. I'd waited too long. "Can she hear us?"

"I don't think so, sir. Not unless I press the intercom bar."

"Call the two cadets from the engine room. Hurry."

A muffled instruction. A moment's wait. "The other cadets are here now, sir."

"As your Commandant, I relieve Ms. Ekrit as your superior officer. Do you understand what I said?"

Tolliver whispered, "Watch the time, sir. Diego must be in trouble by now." The screen was nearly empty of fish.

"Relieve? You mean she's not a midshipman anymore?"

"She's no longer in command. You report directly to me, and not to her. Acknowledge."

"I understand, sir."

"All of you!" I waited for the murmurs of assent. "Very well, tell Ms. Ekrit I said she's to come in immediately, never mind the sensor."

"Aye aye, sir." A pause. "She's coming; she told us to ask why." I shook my head. Still questioning orders.

"Look at your console. See the hatch overrides?"

"No, sir."

"Left upper corner, two blue switches."

"Yes, sir. I see them now."

"Turn on the inner hatch override. Acknowledge."

"Aye aye, sir. Done. But she won't be able to—"

"Is she back in the lock?"

"She's just entering now, sir."

"When you hear the pump, flip the outer hatch override."

"But she'll be trapped—"

I screamed, "Obey orders, Cadet Freid!"

"Yessir. The hatch just closed. I can hear a motor, it must be the pump. I turned on the override, sir."

"Very well. Copy the following Fusion coordinates." Grimly, I passed along the lethal figures I'd first given Seven, then Eight. I said to Tolliver, "Deceit. Always more deceit."

"Justified, this time." His voice was a growl. "It was outright mutiny."

"And what I'm about to do?"

His face was grim. "Not justified. Under any circumstances."

I took the caller, once again the Angel of Death. "Fuser One, the instant you Defuse, lock in your fusion drive for fifteen minutes and start testing immediately. Remember how? Good. You'll be all right. I'm having three other ships Fuse at the same moment. The fish won't know what to do." By now the falsehood tripped glibly off my tongue.

"Aye aye, sir." Wallace Freid sounded more excited than afraid. "Ms. Ekrit is pounding on the hatch. What should I say?"

"Nothing. I'll deal with her later. Until then, let her wait in the lock." A lonely death, helpless, disregarded by her shipmates. I flipped a blue switch in my mind, overriding the thought.

"She's very angry."

"Think of it as revenge for the middies' hazing."

His voice was more cheerful. "Aye aye, sir!"

"Mr. Freid, execute."

Fuser One vanished.

We sat in somber silence. I took the caller. "Mr. Boland, check again with the fleet, and have Fuser Six stand by for further orders."

"Aye aye, sir."

"Tolliver, how are the others?"

"Fine, under the circumstances. Jerence Branstead hasn't said much since he came at me."

"He was right, you know. After I sixty-foured the Admiral you were duty-bound to obey."

He shrugged. "I doubt anyone would object if I relieved you."

"Do it!" Let death be on someone else's head.

"No. I've changed sides for the last time. I suppose they'll hang me with you." He smiled, but not with his eyes. "You'll be remembered, sir."

I whispered, *"I was a derision to all my people; and their song all the day."*

"What? Are you all right, sir?"

"Was I ever?" I took up the caller. *"Trafalgar* to Fuser Three. Respond." I waited for Tommy Tsai.

Tolliver's look was grim. "Sir, wait for Boland's report from the fleet. For all we know, the fish follow us until the last call and then go back to attacking Earth."

"They can't. The caterwauling drives them crazy." I spoke without conviction.

"FUSER THREE TO *TRAFALGAR,* CADET KYLE DREW REPORTING. MR. TSAI IS IN THE ENGINE ROOM." The boy's voice was shrill. I turned down the volume.

"Copy the following orders, and inform Mr. Tsai."

Tolliver persisted, "Damn it, you don't know for certain, and you've already killed nineteen cadets!"

Help me, Lord, I know not what to do.

At last I stirred. "Tolliver, call Mr. Tsai and cancel Three's orders."

"They'll be delighted. What now?"

"Plot coordinates for *Trafalgar* to the vicinity of Two." In seconds, we'd be millions of miles inward.

"Aye aye, sir." His fingers were already working. "We mustn't Fuse, remember? We'll attract them."

"That's all right. It won't be for long." We Fused.

I stared impatiently at the blank simulscreen until we Defused. Now I could speak to Midshipman Keene without lag. "Edgar, plot coordinates for Two to nineteen point five million miles."

Gritting his teeth, he bent to the keyboard. I switched frequencies. "*Trafalgar* to Fuser Two. Mr. Keene, turn your heat shields to full, and Fuse to these coordinates, on my order." I read them from Tolliver's screen.

The midshipman's voice came crisp and sure. "Aye aye, sir. What then?"

The contrast to Sandra Ekrit brought a catch to my voice. Well, she was punished.

"The coordinates put you a million miles short of the B'n Auba Zone." I made my tone casual. "For a ship of your mass, the Zone extends to seventeen million miles, so there's plenty of leeway. In a few minutes I'll send your return coordinates." My eyes seemed to blur. I rubbed them. It only helped for a moment.

I rushed on. "After you Defuse, commence a test at sixty-five percent power."

"Aye aye, sir." For all Keene's response, I might have asked him to pick up a holochip from the deck.

A fish appeared, kilometers away. I ignored it, my throat aching. "Mr. Keene, after you begin the test, orient toward the Sun and fire your stern thrusters continuously at full power until you reach seventeen and a half million miles."

I waited for him to object. At length he said, "Aye aye, sir. Let me read back those coordinates, please."

I confirmed them. "Don't stop transmitting to us. Tell us how many fish come to you, and what they do afterward. Watch to see if they Fuse to safety. Remember to transmit constantly."

"Aye aye, sir. Anything else?"

Tolliver swung his chair, his voice low. "Tell him the truth."

"What truth is that, Mr. Tolliver?"

"What you're asking of him!"

"I can't take—take the chance." I found it difficult to speak.

"For decency's sake, you must!"

"If he refuses, how will we know what happens to the fish?"

"Thomas will do what you order!"

I said thinly, "You'd bet the human race on that?"

For a moment Tolliver was silent. Then, "Yes. Otherwise, we're worse than the fish."

I picked up the caller.

"Nick, let him sacrifice himself for you. Don't send him to death with a lie. For the sake of your soul!"

He'd undone me. "Mr. Keene, execute!" I broke from my chair, ran to the comm room console.

I had no soul.

Chapter 25

Robert Boland said, "Sir, no answer from Mr. Diego in Six. I tried three times."

"All right, go help Mr. Tolliver."

I sat alone in the comm room, listening to static on Fuser Two's frequency.

Keene's new position put him sixteen million miles closer to the Sun than *Trafalgar*. Drained of all emotion, I watched the seconds drag across the clock.

"May I come in, sir?" Jerence Branstead, shifting from foot to foot. "Mr. Tenere gave me permission. If it's all right with you."

"What do you want?"

"Just to talk." His eyes appealed.

I shook my head.

"To be with you," he blurted. "Please!"

"Behave yourself. Go back to your post."

"I wouldn't—aye aye, sir." Dejected, he made his retreat.

How dare he. A cadet, pestering his Captain? What were things coming to?

Armageddon.

No wonder Jerence was unnerved.

The speaker came to life. "Fuser Two to Commandant Seafort on *Trafalgar*. Midshipman Thomas Keene reporting." The middy's voice was crisp and formal, as it would be on a drill, with the Captain frowning from the bridge. "We've Fused to new position. Orienting ship."

Silence. If I spoke, how long for him to hear? I was too tired to calculate. A minute and a quarter, more or less.

An age passed. Then, "We're caterwauling at sixty-five percent. No fish yet. Accelerating toward the Sun. Our thrusters combined with gravitational pull will give us a hell of a velocity." For a moment his voice wavered. "Sorry, I didn't mean to be flippant. No fish yet."

I unbuttoned my jacket. The heat would be awesome.

It was necessary. Tolliver was right.

"God, the Sun is huge from here! Our heat shields are on full, and cabin temperature hasn't risen much, but it feels hot. Probably my imagination. No fish."

I'd denied him honor.

"Still no aliens. Aiming directly toward the Sun helps the heat shields, I think. Less hull for the radiation to—whoops! A fish. A big one, close."

I'd denied him truth.

"Its skin is changing, sir. Darkening. It's squirting toward me, I'll try evasives. The side thrusters don't work very well."

Why should one more betrayal matter? I'd hurt everyone I'd ever known. Even poor Jerence, just now. A boy frightened out of his wits, and trying to hide it.

Like Keene.

"Sir, I commend Cadet Elena Von Siel, who managed the Fuse. And Rafe Slater, who's on comm. We're falling faster now. I've adjusted the gravitrons; we're not uncomfortable yet. Another fish, some distance off. Whoa. Two others. No . . . Hey, one Fused away!"

Christ, no.

"I've got a fish close, skin dark red, with an oddly shaped blotch. If it manages to throw, we'll be"—he hesitated—"off the air, I think. Five more fish. Seven. Here they come, sir! Commandant, my cadets are frightened. I've told them it's all right."

I closed my eyes.

"Dozens of fish, now. They orient themselves toward my fusion tubes. The red one is trying to throw, but it can't seem to form a pseudopod. Solar gravity, I guess. Just a minute, sir."

Silence.

My knees trembled. I tried to still them, could not.

"Sorry, sir. Cadet Frow lost control of himself. I left the conn to give him a sedative. I know it was against orders, but the problem was . . . distracting."

Lord, take them gently. Please. Please please please.

My deceit seemed a mercy, now.

"Sir, reports from the fleet!"

I hissed, "Not now, Boland." He crept to the corner, sat waiting.

"The red one just moved closer. It's . . . convulsing? Wow, it's gone. Just Fused away." A long pause. "I don't blame it.

Sorry, please excuse that. A lot more fish now, sir, almost too many to count."

I summoned my voice. "You're doing fine, Mr. Keene. I'll have you up for lieutenant as soon—as soon as you get home."

"THE RED ONE'S BACK!" Keene's voice trembled with excitement. "Sir, they can't stay away. Praise Lord God, we have them!" I stood, hair rising on my neck. "They can't get away! That red fish isn't as close this time, but I see it clearly and it's the same one! I don't—it's all right, Mr. Slater, anytime now he'll give the order to Fuse. A cold shower, after we get home. Sorry, sir."

My hand crept to the caller. I dialed the bridge. "Mr. Branstead to the comm room."

"Sir, we're at eighteen five million miles and accelerating. Comm room says about a hundred sixty fish. The number keeps growing. A while back some were Fusing away, but none anymore. And they aren't throwing at us. Either they're unable or they're confused by the caterwauling." A pause. "And the heat. Our shields may not take much more."

I came to my senses. Perhaps there was time. "Your commendations noted, Mr. Keene. And yourself, especially."

"Cadet Branstead reporting, Cap—" The boy's voice quavered. I beckoned, opened my arms. He plunged into them, buried his head in my chest.

From the speaker, static.

"Commandant, I've sent the cadets to the outer cabin and had them turn off their speaker. My father's name is Raphael Keene, from the Midlands district. You have his address, of course. Please tell him I was thinking of him. Holy God! Hundreds of fish, with a huge rock! It's a miracle they didn't Fuse into us!"

Oh, Thomas.

Keene's voice was fervent. "Sir, they're shriveling! Steam bursts out their blowholes! It's working, sir! That's what you needed to know, and why you sent us."

The transmission was breaking up. He spoke ever faster. "I liked Academy, I really did. Hazing didn't bother . . . much. I'm sorry if I failed you as first middy. My favorite course was Astrophysics . . . must have changed the textbooks since . . . took the course . . . essor Hoskins taught us quite clearly the B'n Auba Zone is a constant . . . twenty point three million miles and doesn't change . . . gardless of the mass of ship."

I shouted into the caller, clutching it with both hands around the tousled bundle buried in my chest. "Forgive me, Mr. Keene! Please! I only meant—I'm sorry! Mr. Keene, I'm so sorry!"

" . . . easily three hundred of them, all shriveling, no one left in the comm room to cou . . . terrible heat . . . breaking up and we . . ."

Static.

"Mr. Keene, I'm sorry!" I was still begging absolution when Jerence tugged the silent caller from my hand.

Chapter 26

"How many of us left?"

Jerence sat very close, his head resting on my arm. "I don't know, sir. Bobby was in charge."

Boland said, "Sir, we have Mr. Thayer in Three, and Mr. Tsai in Four."

"That's all?"

"And us."

"Yes, of course."

I switched frequencies. "*Trafalgar* to Four. Here are your orders." Again I went through the ritual. "Acknowledge."

Fuser Four was ten million miles outward; nearly two minutes until a reply from Midshipman Tsai. I asked, "Mr. Boland, what word from the fleet?"

"Hundreds of aliens, sir. More keep Fusing in. They hit Denver with a rock. Rotterdam's gone too. The tidal wave—Holland's in bad trouble. And fish have landed near Cairo."

Two Fusers and *Trafalgar*. Not nearly enough. Our effort would fail.

"Sir, ships keep asking what to do. What do I tell them?"

It shouldn't come from the boy. I switched to fleet frequency.

"—to Seafort. If you're in charge, answer, or we'll assume you're—!"

"—*last only another couple of minutes and then I'm going to Fuse, I don't care what his bloody orders—* "

"—IN OUR ENGINE ROOM! WE'RE GOING TO LIFE-PODS!"

I keyed the caller. "Nicholas Seafort, Acting FleetOpsCinc, to all ships." I glanced at my watch. "We're calling the fish away from Earth and the fleet. You should already be seeing results. No vessel is to Fuse for two hours. Unless I issue further orders, command will then revert to Admiralty London and you may Fuse at will. For now, *Trafalgar* remains in command. I now initiate radio silence for two hours."

For eternity. I switched off the caller.

I should have told them how the fish were being destroyed; it would have given them heart. But I couldn't bear to admit what I'd done. After we were gone, they'd figure it out. Or perhaps they would not.

Jerence searched my face. Ignoring him, I hurried down to the engine room.

Midshipman Tenere's eyes were troubled.

"Adam, you and Selette be ready to test at sixty-five percent, then Fuse, and test again. We may repeat that several times."

"Aye aye, sir." He hesitated. "Sir, what's happening to the Fusers?"

A lie sprang to my lips, died unuttered. Face-to-face, I couldn't manage it. "We're losing them. One by one they're calling fish."

"To where?"

"The Sun." Seeing his face I couldn't leave it at that. "They're magnificent, Adam. They're heroes."

The maturity of his answer came as a shock. "Does it matter, now they're dead?"

"Be ready for Fuse," I said curtly. "Whatever you do, don't let our tubes overheat."

I turned, and had almost reached the safety of the corridor when his voice pierced me. "Sir, forgive me, I know it's not my place . . . sir, you're doing the right thing."

"How dare you!"

His tone held resolve. "You were right, sir. We have to stop them. I just wanted—you to know that."

I managed not to strike him, slapped the hatch shut, stalked back to the comm room in a blazing fury, in time to hear Midshipman Thayer's distant reply.

"Fuser Four to *Trafalgar,* orders acknowledged."

A good lad, Anton Thayer. "Execute."

In a few moments, Four began to caterwaul.

"Tolliver!"

He ducked around the bulkhead and appeared in the comm room hatchway. "Yes, sir?"

"Once we start caterwauling we'll get a lot of fish. Be ready to Fuse a short way out of the main mass."

"You know better than that. Minimum Fuse is seven hundred thousand—"

"Run it like a nav drill!" We routinely taught middies to plot two Fuses, out and back, to reach a point closer than the minimum Fuse. The maneuver, though a good teaching tool, was rarely used because the margin of error made results erratic.

There was little I could do until Tolliver finished his calculations, except prepare Tommy Tsai. "*Trafalga*r to Three. Respond." I waited out the lag.

"Captain?" Jerence was subdued. "Was it true, what Robbie said? Are they going to hang you?"

I said gruffly, "No. They won't."

"You'll be acquitted? You had cause?"

"No."

After a long moment my meaning reached him. He clutched my arm, forgetting all he'd been taught. "After the last Fuser it's—it's—"

Cruelly, I waited him out.

"—our turn." He licked his lips. I nodded.

"Fuser Three to *Trafalgar*. Cadet Kyle Drew reporting."

"Enter the following Fusion coordinates, Mr. Drew." I read them off. "After you Defuse . . ." I went through the ghastly instructions. "Acknowledge and wait for my order to execute."

Another lag. I turned back to Jerence. "I ordered you not to go. I wanted to save you." Ashamed, I had to look away. Lord God had rebuked me for playing favorites.

"I thought you were mad at me, that I wasn't good enough."

"None of you knew what I was asking, or you'd have known better than—"

"I understood!" He added, "Don't you remember? You were about to give me a licking when the reports came in. I knew about the fish!"

I said, unbelieving, "And you came? Even if you had to sneak aboard?"

"I wanted to be with you." His bruised face wrinkled. "You protected me, always. And if you were going into danger—" He spun away, his voice muffled. "I wanted to help . . . for you."

"Oh, Jerence." I let my hand stray to his shoulder.

A new voice on the caller. Johan Stritz. "Fuser Four to *Trafalgar,* too many fish! Over a hundred, and they—oh, God, Commandant! Please! Help us now!"

"Engine Room, sixty percent Fusion!" I changed frequency. "Fuser Four, discontinue test!"

We would gather fish as long as we could, then send them to Three. That would doom young Tommy Tsai. And Kyle Drew. He'd bear no more guilt for shattering Dustin Edwards's helmet.

"Tolliver, hurry with those coordinates. Stand by to maneuver!"

I sat brooding until Tolliver's voice crackled in the speaker. "Coordinates are ready. I think you want to stand by to help."

I stood. "Jerence, I'm sorry."

"I don't want us to die."

I tried to grasp his sentiment. Only the assurance of death, of Lord God's most awful hell, sustained me.

For the last time, I took the bridge of a U.N.N.S. starship. Tolliver's eyes met mine. Sensing something of the formality of the moment, he rose to salute me.

"Carry on, Mr. Tolliver."

"Seven fish, so far." He pointed at the screen. None were near.

Alarms clanged; *Trafalgar* lurched.

"Close. God, sir, if we only had a laser." The screen was filling with encroachments.

I asked, "How many now?"

"That's your bloody job!"

Chastened, I made a rough estimate. No more than sixty.

"JESUS!" A fish loomed. Tolliver rammed down a starboard thruster. A snap, as the lever broke in half.

"God damned half-arsed Naval consoles—" His hands danced from thruster to thruster.

He pushed up the jagged stub, quieting the thruster. "The lever still works."

"A hundred ten fish!" Was there no end to them? Within the mass, a small asteroid, a hundred meters in diameter. "Edgar, we'll have to Fuse in a—"

Lights flashed from one end of the screen to the other, each indicating a fish. He shouted, "NOW!"

I jabbed my finger down the control. The stars blanked. Two seconds later I slapped the Defuse. I called up our return coordinates. Again I Fused.

No encroachments within throwing range but the screen was white with fish—

An immense explosion. The air inside our ship slammed

against the hull, popping my ears with the sudden change in pressure. The simulscreen went black.

"WHAT HAPPENED?" I could barely hear.

"A fish must have Fused inside another."

"No, the explosion was too big—" Then I had it. "Rocks! They must have Fused one into —"

"I can't see with the screen out!"

I punched in the alternate circuit. It restored most of the screen, but our starboard fore sensor was gone. *Trafalgar* was half blind. Tolliver swiveled on our linear axis so our port sensor faced the fish. Over half of the accumulated mass had been obliterated when their rocks met.

As I watched, other fish Defused to take their place.

"Tolliver, you'll have to handle them alone."

"Where do you think you're going?"

"Outside. We have spare sensors in the rack in the—"

"You idiot, what if I have to Fuse?"

"Then you'll lose me. And a cadet." I keyed the caller. "Rene Salette, get your suit on, flank!" When we'd raced to board the Mothership, it was she who'd skittered expertly along the hull footholds.

I ran to the lock, grabbed my suit off the rack, fumbled into the legs. Rene was already sealing her helmet. I cursed as my foot caught in the webbing. No time to be clumsy now. I thrust one arm inside, struggled with the other.

"Here, sir." Jerence Branstead helped me insert my arm. While I grappled with my helmet, he dived into his own suit, faster than I'd have thought possible.

"You're staying here." I snapped the clamps.

He thrust in his arms, reached for his helmet. "Please, sir, don't make me disobey again. I'm still a cadet."

I swallowed, nodded reluctant assent. The three of us entered the lock. I slapped shut the hatch, opened the lock's supply rack. I'd only need one spare; no other sensors had faced the blast. Still, best to bring two, in case we inadvertently let one loose and it floated off. "Hold this!" I dumped the first replacement in Rene's arms. I clutched the tools and spare sensor.

The airlock pump took forever. Too late, I remembered to check my suit air. Enough. If I didn't slow down and follow procedures, I'd get someone killed. I snorted at the irony.

"Captain, hurry! We're picking up fish like fleas on—"

"Hold your water, Tolliver." I slapped open the outer hatch.

Jerence gasped. A dozen fish, plainly visible.

"Move!" We clambered onto the hull. "Don't miss any footholds."

The girl pointed aft. "Which one is it? There?"

"No, forward." Agile, she swung around, slipped her foot into a hold, drifted forward along the line of footholds in dreamlike slow motion. I did my best to follow.

Urgency sped our steps. In a minute we'd reached the sensor mount. My breath rasped in my helmet, clouding the faceplate as fast as the suit could clear it.

"Captain, move! One of them is only seventy meters—"

As I watched, the fish drifted closer.

My wrench fumbled at the mount. Jerence said quietly, "Sir, if you let me, it'll go faster."

Astounded, I looked up, saw calm confidence. I handed him the wrench. Still in the same foothold, he knelt, turned the bolts easily. He slipped it into his suit pouch. After a moment, another bolt. He grinned, ignoring the looming fish. "These are like the motor mounts on my electrobike. I used to tear it apart all the time. Dad hated—" His face clouded. "Dad." Harmon Branstead had stayed on undefended Hope Nation.

Tolliver fired our port thrusters. The fish receded slowly.

As soon as Jerence pulled the last bolt Rene Salette changed footholds, carefully dropped to her knees, extended the spare sensor. "Here."

Jerence fitted it into place. I stooped, unclamped the line, fastened it to the new sensor while Jerence turned the nuts.

"SEAFORT, LOOK OUT!" Tolliver, his voice ragged.

I looked up, froze. A fish, no more than seven meters away, bow on to us, drifting ever closer.

"I CAN'T THRUST TO STARBOARD, ANOTHER ONE'S TOO NEAR! GET THE HELL INSIDE—"

"Leave it!" I pulled Jerence to his feet. The fish's skin swirled.

Rene scampered along the hull. Jerence stared, mesmerized. I thrust him past me toward the sanctuary of the lock.

"GET IN! GET IN!" Tolliver was hoarse with frustration.

The fish's skin went indistinct. Abruptly a outrider was pulsing on its surface.

Rene clambered toward the lock. As she groped for a

foothold the alien flung itself across the gap. It wrapped itself around her faceplate. Her foot came loose from the hold. She shrieked. Together, they floated off the hull.

"Please oh God please not like this help me—"

Branstead tugged on my arm until he finally penetrated my funk. "Come on, sir! The lock!"

Beyond us, the girl's shape seemed to waver. A yelp, and the radio went silent.

I took another step, still clutching the tools and spare sensor.

Jerence tugged at my arm. "Hurry, it's coming!"

The fish had drifted almost close enough to touch. Its nose came within a meter of where I stood.

"Captain, we have to Fuse NOW! Get in the lock!"

The fish had no eyes, no mouth, no discernible features. The skin at its prow began to swirl. In seconds another outrider would emerge.

Jerence tried again to pull me to safety. I shrugged free, all the rage in the cosmos exploding within me. I set my boot in the foothold, inches from the fish. "BE GONE, THING OF SATAN!"

The alien's translucent skin parted. The form of an outrider began to appear.

"ENOUGH!" My voice broke. "LUCIFER! IN THE NAME OF LORD GOD ALMIGHTY, I BANISH THEE!" In a frenzy I swung the sensor over my head, plunged it into the widening, swirling surface. My foot twisted. I slipped to my knees.

The fish convulsed. Almost instantly a blowhole tore open. A swirl of propellant streamed over my head, shot past the curved hull of the Mothership.

The fish receded, its colors a violent swirl.

Jerence tugged. I lost my balance, and my foothold. I floated helplessly while he hauled me toward the waiting lock. He steered me in, pushed me to the inner bulkhead. I made no effort to grasp it. Jerence swung himself in, slapped the hatch closed.

His hands scrabbled at the caller. "Sir, we're inside!"

The stars blinked out.

Unresisting, I let Jerence Branstead strip off my suit. When he was done I stood for a moment, walked with toddler's steps to the bridge. I found my seat.

"Sir—" Tolliver's eyes searched my face. "You—I've never—" He said nothing more.

I gazed at the screen. Could there be so many fish in the universe? Hundreds upon hundreds. Their blips punctuated the screen like . . . I knew not what.

Jerence crept into the cabin, took a seat, stared at me as if in awe. I studied the screen. Lights began blinking out, reappearing closer, searching for our drive tubes.

I found it hard to form words. "Time, now. Fuser Three."

Tolliver said, softly, "Captain . . ."

"Time to kill Tommy and Kyle." I reached for the caller, couldn't close my hand around it.

Tolliver was far away, "He's in shock. Get the medkit!"

I brought the caller to my lips. "Captain Seafort to Fuser Three." What was it I had to tell them? Something about fish.

"Christ, Captain, hang on. I've got to—" Tolliver's hands slammed the thruster controls.

Jerence skidded back onto the bridge.

Tommy Tsai, Tommy Keene. It was my task to kill Tommys. I smiled.

"Fuser Three here. Midshipman Tsai reporting."

Jerence held my right arm. Tolliver abandoned his controls, brought the medgun toward me. My left hand lashed out, snatched it away, smashed it on the edge of the console. "Not yet, Mr. Tolliver." My eyes made him recoil. "It still has to be done, you see. And the guilt has to be mine."

"Sir, you're—"

"Insane. Yes, I know. It doesn't matter."

Jerence sobbed. I took up the caller.

With a curse Tolliver worked the thrusters, spun us away from a looming fish. The lurching screen made me dizzy.

"Tommy . . . Mr. Midshipman Tsai. It's your time." I smiled at Tolliver, spewed my villainy to Fuser Three. "Execute."

"Aye aye, executing. Sir, will the fish attack us?"

It would take a long time for my reply to find him. "Not if you lock in your fusion motors. Mr. Keene is testing, and Mr. Diego. Together you'll confuse them."

Eternity passed.

One by one the lights of the fish began to blink out.

"We sent Tommy a lot of them." My tone was conversational. No one replied. Jerence wiped his eyes.

I took the caller. "Fuser Four, respond."

I hummed. We had a few minutes, until Fuser Three's work was done. "Edgar, this time we'll have to caterwaul a good while. Better set up more coordinates."

Tolliver reached for the medkit. "Sir, you're not well. Let me give—"

"No, thank you. Tend to your duties."

He stared into my eyes. At length he nodded, subdued.

"Fuser Four. Midshipman Anton Thayer responding."

"Jerence, don't cry. It distracts me."

The boy jumped. "Aye aye, sir." To my surprise, he stopped.

"Mr. Thayer, stand by to Fuse and test again." I gave Jerence a reassuring pat. "It will be the last time."

I waited out the lag, nodding satisfaction.

Midshipman Thayer's voice was troubled. *"Commandant, what are we doing? How does this help?"*

"We're confusing fish so they'll Fuse home." I began to tremble. After a time, it ceased. "Take care if fish come close, and don't forget to lock in your drive for the test." My head ached. I wasn't sure if it had just begun, or had been aching all my life.

Waiting out the lag, I said, "What's wrong, Jerence?"

"Nothing, sir." The boy swallowed. "You're doing fine."

It wasn't his place to tell me that.

"We'll lock in the motors, sir. Standing by to execute on your order."

I marveled at how well Thayer had managed the transition from cadet to middy. Foolish, to think of disciplining him over a mere pillow fight.

The last Fuser, before our own turn. I let relief wash over me. "Mr. Tolliver, begin testing at sixty-five percent." That was the loudest we could call without risking the tubes.

"Aye aye, sir." Tolliver passed the order. "Captain, I want to Fuse sooner this time, before they surround us."

"No, we're summoning them. They need a point to aim at."

"Let me Fuse out and back. We'll last longer."

My thoughts were fuzzy. "Very well. You're in charge of evasives."

Fish popped onto the screen.

I leaned back as if viewing a holodrama. Encroachment lights flashed, a few at first, then by the dozen. Tolliver Fused; we were alone in the deep. Immediately he Fused back. We emerged nearly a million kilometers from our start. A bad roll of the dice from Fusion's margin of error.

After a time, the fish found us.

Some two hundred, now. Rocks were scattered among them. Lord God knew from whence we summoned the aliens. In the last hours, we'd caterwauled longer and louder than had ever been done.

Hundreds of lights. Explosions. We Fused.

I contemplated our silent, dreamlike dance through the cosmos. Perhaps it was His cosmic joke, to fight the evil of the fish through the evil in me. It satisfied me to be His instrument, even in this.

"Captain. Captain!"

I struggled back. "What, Mr. Tolliver?"

"Look at them! We can't avoid all—" He cursed, sent us spinning, Fused again. "We've called at least five hundred of them, maybe more. If we don't survive we can't pass them on to Four!"

I leaned back. Our time was not yet. Fish still swam.

We Fused clear. The relief of blank screens. Back.

"Lord Jesus!" Again, we'd Defused into a vast mass of fish. Tolliver slammed his hand against the console screen; the stars vanished once again.

His hands trembled. "I can't take any more! Enough!"

"TAKE US BACK BEFORE THEY DISPERSE!" I pounded the console, catching my palm on the broken lever. Cursing, I sucked at blood, punched in new coordinates. Our return Fuse put us near the edge of the huge flickering mass.

"You'll get us killed for nothing! Give the order to Thayer!"

"Not yet." I watched the ever-increasing lights.

"It has to be now! We're almost out of propellant!"

I checked; he was telling the truth.

Reluctantly, I gave the order. "Mr. Thayer. *Trafalgar* to Fuser Four. Fuse and commence test! Acknowledge."

Three fish squirted toward us. Tolliver looked up, cursed, used the last of his prepared coordinates.

I asked, "How far are we?"

"From the fish? About two million miles."

"Go back. I want to see."

"Wait until the order gets to Thayer."

"That's less than a minute. Go back."

Tolliver sighed. "Aye aye, sir." He took his time preparing coordinates, but I knew it was useless to complain. He'd only use the interruption to delay further. At last, he was ready, and we Fused.

Fish swarmed.

"Thayer didn't caterwaul!"

"Be patient," I said.

"We Fused here. They'll have heard that."

As if to prove his point, a fish Defused alongside. Tolliver reacted instinctively, slamming the starboard thrusters to full. We veered away. The fish followed. Two others appeared, one directly astern.

"Captain, you waited too—"

The fish disappeared.

Thank you, Anton.

A few lights blinked out. Then dozens.

The middy and cadets in Four would be engulfed by fish trapped by the vast Solar gravity, wilting in the unbearable heat.

Try to understand, Anton. I had to do it.

I waited. At last the screen was empty of fish. I calculated the coordinates we'd need.

"Tolliver."

"Yes, sir." Still shaken, he stared at the console.

"Go below to the engine room. Mr. Tenere may recognize the final coordinates."

"He'll obey."

"Go below. Just in case."

"Aye aye, sir." Obediently, he left his chair. At the hatch, he hesitated. "Sir, what I said before, about hating you—"

I was unconcerned. Nothing Tolliver said could harm me now.

"I want you to know, I don't hate you. What you've done . . . sir, it's beyond love or hate. You're saving the—"

"GET OUT!!" I'd been mistaken. He could hurt me.

I picked up the caller. Suddenly the speaker crackled to life. Freak radio waves, pierced the veil of Solar radiation, cluttered with static.

Anton Thayer, on Four. A sob.

"Sir, they're all around us! You said we'd be safe!"

I swallowed.

"Captain Seafort . . ." The middy's voice was sick with hurt and wonder. *"YOU LIED!"*

The speaker crackled static.

I sat still for a terribly long time, blood from my palm dripping on the console. At last, I picked up the caller. "Engine Room, sixty percent Fusion power."

Midshipman Adam Tenere, his tone firm. "Sixty percent, aye aye." The line on the screen began to pulse.

I waited. Thayer's voice echoed in the silent cabin.

I readied our final coordinates: eighteen million miles. As soon as fish responded to our call, I'd go immediately to perdition. I couldn't risk freeing them if they attacked our tubes.

Come to me, spawn of Lucifer.

I stared at the screen until my eyes watered.

Nothing. On the console, the Fusion line wavered.

"Mr. Tenere, check your gauges!"

"Aye aye, sir. Sixty percent."

I cursed. "Increase to sixty-five!"

"Sixty-five, aye aye."

I waited, forcing a semblance of calm. No fish.

Our drive was malfunctioning. Yet it had just Fused us ten times or more. "Adam, what in God's hell is wrong down there?"

It was Tolliver who answered. "Nothing, sir. We're caterwauling."

"No we're not! There isn't a single—"

"Come check for yourself. We're heating. I know there's power going out!"

"Comm room to bridge, Cadet Boland reporting. Sir, I've—"

I switched off the speaker. Come to me, you bastards.

No fish.

I snatched the caller. "Seventy percent!"

Adam. "Sir, we'll melt—"

I yelled, "Seventy percent, you mutineer!"

"Aye aye, sir. Seventy percent." The line on my console leaped. We couldn't maintain seventy for long, I knew.

Nothing.

"God damn you, come to me!" My outburst startled Jerence; he drew back.

Robert Boland burst into the hatchway. "Sir, the fleet!

They're calling from all over home system. No one sees any fish. They're gone!"

I shrieked, "OUT!" He recoiled.

"They'll come!" I spun to Jerence, my eyes wild. "They have to!"

He backed away.

I shouted into the caller, "Come to me when I call you! *I'M THE FISHERMAN!*"

Jerence turned and ran.

"Captain, we'll melt the tubes!"

"Throttle down to sixty-five, but no less!"

The cursed screen remained blank.

I cried, "Damn you, God! DON'T DO THIS TO ME!"

Nothing.

The Lord's revenge; He would even deny me oblivion.

Father's visage swam. Grim lessons, across the kitchen table: *"Nicholas, Satan's deceit knows no bounds."*

You almost had me there, Lucifer. But I know we're calling from the wrong place.

I rechecked coordinates. "Engine Room, Fuse and resume caterwauling!" I ran my finger down the screen.

The stars refused to blink.

"Fuse, damn you!" I hammered my fist on the console, caught the jagged edge of the broken throttle. Blood sprayed. Welcome agony flowed up my arm.

Faces appeared in the hatch. I appealed, "Can't you see? We have to Fuse!"

The screens remained dark.

I pounded the broken lever over and again until my palm was ragged.

"Fuse! I'm begging you! Don't make me live."

They came closer.

"Fuse!"

A gentle hand fell on my shoulder.

"Fuse!" My voice broke.

Chapter 27

I woke in an unfamiliar cabin. I ran a numb hand across my eyes; a bandage scratched my face.

Tolliver looked up.

"Where am I?"

"*Prince of Wales,* sir. The first lieutenant's cabin."

"How did . . ."

"They met us, yesterday. You were still sedated."

My mind veered away from the bridge, and my failure.

"The fish?"

"None anywhere. That last great caterwaul of ours, before we pitched them to Fuser Three . . ."

"Where are we headed?"

He said simply, "Home."

"Court-martial." Then, surcease. I could wait, if I must.

"Yes." A knock; the hatch opened. A starched midshipman with a tray. He saluted, and left.

"How soon?"

"We dock tomorrow. Earthport has only two undamaged bays for the entire fleet, but they want you groundside."

"Thanks be to God."

He hitched his chair closer. "What do you mean, sir?"

"They'll help me end."

"You're that anxious to die, Nick?"

"Not anxious. Desperate."

"The guilt you spoke of."

"Edgar, it's unbearable."

"I understand." His look was one of pity. "But you can't confess. Not all."

"Don't be silly. I want—"

"Think, sir." He crossed to the hatch, made sure it was sealed. His voice dropped. "What do you intend to tell them?"

"That I stole command of the fleet. That I tricked cadets into volunteering, betrayed them with lies, sent them to—"

472

"Captain!"

His tone brought me to a halt.

"Imagine you're the father of a fifteen-year-old. Kyle Drew, let's say. Proudly, you sent him to Academy. Now you get a fax. Your son was roasted in a Fuser spinning toward the Sun. He didn't sacrifice himself bravely; his Commandant tricked him into it. All you have left is that memory."

"It's truth."

"Truth is too cruel!" He leaned forward until his head almost touched mine. "Our cadets were heroes. Do you understand? Heroes!"

"I can't live with betrayal! Confession is—"

"They volunteered for a suicide mission, every last one of them!" He grasped my lapels. "You have no choice. Demented or no, you can't be so vicious as to deny their families that consolation."

"But you know, and Robert. Jerence. Adam Tenere. It will come out."

"I've already explained to them. They won't be charged, Captain; command was yours. So no P and D for them." He eyed me. "Confess what you must, but not what you did to the cadets. That's obscene."

I shook my head. "The truth, before I die. Just once."

Tolliver's eyes glistened. "Nick, you'd do that to Thomas Keene?"

I cried, "In Keene's case it was so! He went knowing!"

"What about the others? You'll tell their parents they died fools, not heroes?"

My voice was hoarse. "Don't do this to me! I don't have the strength."

"You know the truth. I know. That's enough."

I whispered, "Edgar, I beseech you. It's the only consolation I'll ever know."

With the finality of a judge, he shook his head.

I let them clothe me in my dress whites, lead me silently through crowded corridors to the forward lock. Every man in *Prince of Wales* had found excuse to be present, to see the notorious Nicholas Seafort one last time.

Stone-faced, I showed them nothing.

We cycled through to Earthport Station, strode along patched

corridors to the waiting shuttle. I took my seat, fumbled use-
lessly at the belts with my injured hand, allowed them to strap
me in.

They lodged me at Portsmouth, where I'd sent Sergeant
Serenco for trial. The next day Admiral Duhaney, lips pursed,
himself handed me the indictment. The formality of his salute
startled me, but I returned it crisply.

I saw no one else except Captain Jason Tenere, appointed my
counsel. He told me of the crowds massed in the streets outside,
hoping for a glimpse of me.

Captain Tenere ignored my instructions to plead guilty. Over
my outraged protest, he entered a plea of innocence. I tried to
dismiss him, demanded to speak for myself, but the Court refused. I would have to undergo trial. Because of my attempted
plea, I was spared the misery of the drugs.

The trial lasted two weeks.

Entering and leaving the courtroom I endured the bright lights
of the holocameras and the forest of mikes thrust in my face.

I refused to speak on my own behalf.

Cadet Boland was one of many called. Young, proud, he
stood before the bar in crisp grays, a splendid specimen of the
Navy to come. If it weren't for the obscenity of his testimony,
even I would have been moved. He spoke earnestly of my intent
to join my victims in immolation, and of the vast hordes of fish
we had summoned and passed down the line.

One by one, Captains in the Home Fleet waited their turn to
attest to the hopelessness of their situation, before we'd begun
to caterwaul.

Even Admiral Duhaney made his appearance, acknowledging
that I'd submitted a caterwaul bomb proposal and begged him to
speed its development.

By the time an aide to Admiral Seville came forth, to testify
regarding the welter of unconfirmed reports and pleas for help
that had inundated London Admiralty, I suspected the worst.
The Navy was gathering around one of its own.

When it came to pass, my acquittal didn't shock me. Holding
my nausea in check, I stood at stolid attention while the Presi-
dent of the Court extolled my resourcefulness and heroism, and
cited the incontrovertible and conclusive evidence that it was
necessary for me to relieve Admiral Seville to preserve the fleet.

After, they sent me back to Admiralty House.

Lord God wasn't done toying with me.

A week later, they summoned me to Duhaney's London office. I went, my resignation typed and ready in my pocket.

The Admiral's aide showed me in. Senator Richard Boland was present; I hadn't expected him. Well, no matter. I saluted, held attention until released.

I listened to what the Senator proposed, refused at once.

"Good heavens, man, you're a natural," Senator Boland said. "You saved the world. As a candidate you're unstoppable!"

"You're mistaken." I peered down from the window to the pedestrians scurrying in the warm afternoon sun.

"No, I'm not. You don't know politics, Seafort. You'll be—"

"I'm stoppable. In fact, I'm stopped."

The Senator crossed glances with Duhaney. "What do you mean?"

"I resign the Commandancy of Naval Academy. And I resign from the Naval Service of the United Nations." I unfolded my formal paper, laid it on the desk.

Duhaney gaped. "Resign? Don't be ridiculous, Seafort. If you won't help us in the legislature, the Navy needs you. Your image is invaluable, and we have a fleet to rebuild, the aliens' home planet to find—"

"No."

"Let me remind you," he said with asperity, "you have no choice. Captain or Midshipman, you serve where you're assigned."

"True. I'll admit freely at court-martial that I refuse your orders."

"Court-martial?" His tone was unbelieving.

"Yes. Let me go, or try me all over again."

"Is it because of how I spoke to you on *Trafalgar*? You were right, we were confus—"

"You misunderstand. I'm done, for my own reasons."

Duhaney said, "All right, perhaps we shouldn't push you into politics, no matter how much it would benefit the Navy. But you can't resign; you have your duty. Your honor must rise to that."

I walked toward his desk, spread my hands on its gleaming surface, leaned close. My voice made even my own hackles rise. "Duhaney, if you again use the word honor in connection with my name, I'll kill you with my bare hands." I held his gaze until he could not.

The Senator studied me with interest. "What will you do, Seafort, without the Navy, without politics?"

"Do? It's none of your concern. We've nothing further to say to each other." I crossed to the door.

"Mr. Seafort, thank you for saving my son."

I'd tried to kill his son. I strode to the door, and to purgatory.

Epilogue

That wasn't the last of it, but in the end they had to let me go.

I rode the ancient electric railway to Cardiff, but with Father gone, nothing was the same. Eddie and Annie met me at the cottage door. Their anxious pretense at welcome set my nerves on edge. After a time Annie noticed my discomfort when her hand strayed to Eddie's for a reassuring touch. On the few occasions she ventured to stroke my shoulder I responded with rigid indifference.

We endured the mutual misery for three days. I brooded, and visited Jason's grave. Then I left.

I took a flat in Devon near Academy, but word of my presence soon spread, and I had no peace.

I wandered Britain, looking for I knew not what. When recognized, I fled.

One bleak day my path led me to the Neo-Benedictine order at Lancaster. My interview with Abbot Ryson was difficult; he seemed to take a visceral dislike to me. Nonetheless, something in my recital moved him to admit me as a novice. Three weeks later I took vows of chastity and obedience, and moved into the cloister bringing only the clothes I wore.

Father Ryson had warned that monastery life would be hard. I didn't mind. Testing my vow of obedience, he obliged me to weeks of absolute silence, a requirement normally reserved for punishment or as a mark of disfavor.

The silence eased my way. Each morning I rose, filed with the brothers to matins, prayed on my knees on the cold stone floor. After, I toiled in the bakery where I learned how to knead the dough for three risings, preparing the sweet hot rolls that graced our meals.

At night, I went to my bed in the tiny room called a cell, but which wasn't such. I said rote prayers while making ready for sleep. The ritual words gave a certain remembered comfort, but I couldn't feel the presence of God.

At least they helped me not to think.

Kneading dough helped me not to think.

Cleaning latrines helped me not to think, a duty from which Father Ryson eventually relieved me, over my bitter protest.

A parishioner recognized me at services, and for a time public services were unusually well attended. I focused my gaze on the stone floor, managing not to see the pointing fingers, not to hear the murmurs. Once a congregant brought a holocamera to services, but, thank You, Lord God, was bustled out by two burly monks before he could torment me further.

Not thinking is difficult, when you've spent your life training to be a more precise thinker. Failing at it only makes me try harder. I've opted for confession, now a voluntary rite. Weekly I confide my sins to Abbot Ryson, whom I elected my confessor.

Among my sins is the self-absorption that requires me to think of who I am and what I've done.

Perhaps as penance, Father Ryson has required me to set down the history of my life in such detail as it takes for me to adjudge it complete.

And so, these many months, I've sat in my tiny, scrubbed cell after the day's baking, and scratched with an old-fashioned pen onto real paper these recollections of my life. Written ostensibly to Abbot Ryson, they are actually addressed to You, Lord God, as if You could not read that which is inscribed in blood in my heart.

With the detached observation that has always been my burden, I've described my self-ordained slide down the greased chute to hell. It started, perhaps, with the undeserved pride that made me offer myself to the Navy, and the foolish complacency that allowed me to stake my soul on the certainty that I could fulfill my oath.

I slid further by lying to myself on the occasion I saved Vax Holser from the penalties of his disobedience, when he refused to abandon me on *Telstar*. At the time I pretended it was an act of mercy, but now, I know better. It was dereliction of duty.

I slid faster, until I could skirt my oath of obedience merely to save Midshipman Philip Tyre a caning. Gliding ever onward, I found myself able to refuse an order from my superior Admiral Tremaine to take on the passengers he had disembarked.

Could I ever have stopped, saved myself? Truly, I don't know.

By then it had become so easy, You see. I confess: duty had replaced You as my beacon. To protect my ship, my people, I knowingly swore Elena Bartel no harm, then shot her through the heart, exploding beyond pretense the myth that my oath, my covenant with You, was a thing I valued.

What matter, after such folly, that I lied glibly to my superiors about Vax Holser's conduct at Orbit Station? By now I was sliding with breathless speed, the breeze against my face ever warmer.

And so we come to my ultimate folly, wherein I tricked obedient boys and rosy budding girls into casting away their lives to save my planet from the alien fish.

Would they have given themselves willingly?

I don't know. I never gave them the chance.

Was what I did necessary?

In a sense, yes. Because I had no faith that You would save Your people, Your Church, Your creation. In my arrogance I believed that my acts alone could draw away the fish.

But at night, when I compose myself for sleep and lie tossing until the early hours of the morn, I commune with Kevin Arnweil and Kyle Drew and Jacques Theroux, and so many others. At times, Midshipman Thomas Keene sits charred at my bedside, to vanish when I wake.

I see them, please forgive me, at matins when my mind should be on the prayers I chant, and when I should not, of all times, be forced to *think*.

I see them now, when I prepare to lay down my pen and attend to vespers.

I am damned. That is as it should be, for what I have done is damnable.

But yet . . .

In the silence of the night I sit at the side of my bed, robe thrown over my bare shoulders, and I wonder . . .

How is it that I know that You are a God of mercy, a God of love, yet, nonetheless, I know equally well You must not forgive me?

You see, if You could forgive the frightful evil I've done, then, Lord God, I'm sorry, I could not believe in You. For the sake of the children, if naught else, You must mete justice, and I, of all men, have earned punishment.

But after I return to bed, and lie sleepless through the waning night, sometimes a still, small voice wonders, Oh, Lord God, surely You knew what You were doing, when You fitted my cog into the complex interwoven gears of Your creation?

You made me what I was, and You provided the circumstances by which I threw myself from Grace. It was You who made it appear that my world and its people could not be saved unless I led those bright trusting children to their doom.

And then, I ask:

Lord God?

Lord, why hast Thou forsaken me?

Afterword

So ends the as yet unpublished autobiography of my friend and mentor Captain Nicholas Ewing Seafort, U.N.N.S. These painfully frank pages are the only record he has made of his accomplishments.

Though his story ends here, history's judgment of Mr. Seafort is less harsh than his own. As we all know, ten years after he completed these writings, he emerged from seclusion and plunged himself into the world of politics, drawn by a plea for help from an old friend.

Allying himself with the Boland organization, Seafort was elected to the U.N. Senate with virtually no opposition. From the start he demonstrated the unswerving, selfless honesty that was ever after his trademark. His divorce from Annie Wells Seafort, later Annie Boss, had left him alone and desolate, a condition he endured for several years until his marriage to Arlene Sanders in the rotunda of the U.N.

Most biographers have underestimated the effect of Abbot Ryson's harsh mercy on the tormented ex-Captain in his care.

Drawing on Seafort's unbroken relationship with Lord God, Ryson evoked from him the depths of his anguish, and its cause. The means by which Nick Seafort unburdened his tortured soul and became reconciled to his past is unknown. But ever after, he would brook no evasion, no dishonesty, not the most insignificant white lie.

This characteristic made his company uncomfortable for some, but wiser men, and I, found it reassuring.

During his term as SecGen, Mr. Seafort staunchly supported the Navy while it rebuilt from its debacle with the fish. Yet, at the same time, he moved firmly and decisively to quell the Navy's chronic nepotism. Today's Naval meritocracy is a direct result of his efforts.

Nicky Seafort was utterly inept at traditional political skills. He tolerated no diplomatic lies or convenient subterfuge. In the Port of London scandals, it was his unflinching honesty and refusal to disavow blame that led to the fall of his government and his personal disgrace. Had he been less blunt about his failure to oversee Senator Wade's misdealings, his administration might well have survived the March 2224 vote of confidence.

Over time, the public and the Senate have come to appreciate Seafort's refusal to exculpate himself. His admissions are now admired as a mark of integrity and honor, and there are those who have called for him to cast aside his premature retirement and enter again the public arena. His urgent need for privacy, his troubled nature, and his distrust of power make that event unlikely.

It is hard, in times of relative tranquillity, to recall the turmoil and uncertainty of those perilous days when fish roamed unchecked and the colonies struggled to recast their relationship with the home world.

Today, unmanned Caterwaul Stations in permanent Solar orbit safeguard the security of mankind. It would seem the threat from the fish has ended, but the Stations remain sentinels of our vigilance, serviced by Nick Seafort's beloved Navy.

I met Captain Seafort again on several occasions when business brought me to Earth or politics took him to Hope Nation. When together, we often reminisced about living friends and long-departed comrades, and those young days when our destinies lay ahead.

Despite the honors and achievements of later years, Captain Seafort once remarked that never in his life did he feel as fulfilled as when first we'd met, while he served as senior midshipman on U.N.S. *Hibernia,* on our first hopeful voyage to the stars.

> Derek, Lord Carr
> First Staadholder
> Commonweal of Hope Nation
> October, in the year of our Lord 2225

<u>MEMORY SEED</u>

Stephen Palmer

There is one city left. And soon that will be gone, for the streets of Kray are crumbling beneath a wave of exotic and lethal vegetation as it creeps south, threatening to wipe out the last traces of humanity. In the desperate struggle for survival, most Krayans live from day to day, awaiting salvation from their goddesses or the government. Only a few believe that the future might lie in their own hands.

'Palmer's style is purposeful and fluent, and engages from an early stage. This attractive voice, coupled with a complex and fascinating plot, makes *Memory Seed* a notable debut novel. Stephen Palmer is obviously a writer to watch out for'
SFX

'Palmer's imagination is fecund'
Interzone

'Palmer is a find'
Time Out

Set on a world both deadly and fascinating, *Memory Seed* is a compelling first novel which heralds a powerful new voice in science fiction.

BRIGHTNESS REEF

David Brin

'Exuberant . . . suspense-filled . . . delightful . . . I couldn't
put it down'
Interzone

On the distant planet of Jijo, six exiled races live side by
side. Only ancient relics from their home planets, fragments
of half-forgotten stories and the crumbling ruins of the
mysterious and god-like Buyur remind the dispossessed of a
more noble past, when they were full citizens of the Five
Galaxies. The races of Jijo, it seems, have been forgotten,
along with whatever crimes they committed. But for
how long?

It is at the time of the Gathering, the council of the sages,
when the spacecraft is first spotted. For some, it offers a new
hope. For others, it heralds a time of reckoning.

Brightness Reef is the story of a world threatened by its past
and fighting for its future. With a gallery of extraordinary
characters, and a wealth of thought-provoking ideas, it is a
novel fuelled by the spirit of adventure and discovery.
Brightness Reef is David Brin at his very best.

Also available from Orbit:

The first Uplift trilogy
SUNDIVER
STARTIDE RISING
THE UPLIFT WAR

Little, Brown and Co Order Form

Little, Brown and Company, PO Box 50, Harlow, Essex CM17 0DZ
Tel: 01279 438150   Fax: 01279 439376

Please send me

_____ copies of	Midshipman's Hope	David Feintuch	£5.99
_____ copies of	Challenger's Hope	David Feintuch	£5.99
_____ copies of	Prisoner's Hope	David Feintuch	£5.99
_____ copies of	Memory Seed	Stephen Palmer	£5.99
_____ copies of	Brightness Reef	David Brin	£6.99
_____ copies of	Sundiver	David Brin	£5.99
_____ copies of	Startide Rising	David Brin	£5.99
_____ copies of	The Uplift War	David Brin	£6.99

Payments can be made as follows: cheque, postal order (payable to Little, Brown and Company) or by credit cards, Visa/Access/Amex. Do not send cash or currency. UK customers and BFPO please allow £1.00 for postage and packing for the first book, plus 50p for the second book, plus 30p for each additional book up to a maximum charge of £3.00 (7 books plus). Overseas customers including Ireland, please allow £2.00 for the first book plus £1.00 for the second book, plus 50p for each additional book.

Name _____

Address _____

_____

_____

☐ I enclose a cheque/postal order made payable to
Little, Brown and Company for £ _____
or
☐ I wish to pay by Access/Visa/Amex* Card
(*delete as appropriate)

Number ☐☐☐☐☐☐☐☐☐☐☐☐☐☐☐☐

Card Expiry Date_____ Signature _____